The Rescue of Charles de Simpson

The Rescue of Charles de Simpson

Book One in the Dorchester Chronicles

J.S. Witte

Elm Hill

A Division of
HarperCollins Christian Publishing

www.elmhillbooks.com

The Rescue of Charles de Simpson
Book One in the Dorchester Chronicles

Published in Nashville, Tennessee, by Elm Hill, an imprint of Thomas Nelson. Elm Hill and Thomas Nelson are registered trademarks of HarperCollins Christian Publishing, Inc.

Elm Hill titles may be purchased in bulk for educational, business, fund-raising, or sales promotional use. For information, please e-mail SpecialMarkets@ThomasNelson.com.

Publisher's Note: This novel is a work of fiction. Names, characters, places, and incidents are either products of the author's imagination or used fictitiously. All characters are fictional, and any similarity to people living or dead is purely coincidental.

Library of Congress Cataloging-in-Publication Data

Library of Congress Control Number: 2018946225

ISBN 978-1-595557353
ISBN 978-1-595557377 (eBook)

DEDICATION

To August, who set out on his own adventure as a young teenager.
To Todd Hollins for reminding me a goal has a completion date.
To Lindsey for setting and accomplishing her own incredible goals.
And to my amazing, super model wife, Wendy. I love you to life.

J. S. Witte

Acknowledgments

There have been many men and women who have influenced my life and personal growth over the years. Some spoke so directly to me their "voices" are heard in the following pages. It is to them I wish to give a sincere thank you.

John Maxwell; when the student is ready the teacher appears. From your books I have read to the leadership conference my wife Wendy and I attend each spring where you are one of the key speakers, I am truly grateful for your words of wisdom. Many of the concepts you teach are conveyed within this adventure and I thank you for the inspiration. Your Rule of 5 is at work in the completion of this novel.

Pastor Paul Tsika; a godly man if ever there was one. Your approaches to life, living, adversity, perseverance and forgiveness became corner-stone teachings for me to build on.

Mrs. Folsom; my high school creative writing English teacher who encouraged me to pursue the dream of writing a novel. I don't know if she ever realized just how impactful her words were to a nerdy, geeky sixteen year old.

To all my mentors within World Wide Dream Builders, especially Scott, Mike and Bob. Men, husbands, business owners and role models.

Thank you all so very much for continuing to believe in me even when I didn't believe in myself, until I believed in myself more.

To a true cowboy, musician and preacher, David Hinton. In 2004 at a St. Louis meeting for Christian businessmen you stopped in the middle of your guitar picking and preaching to ask a simple question. "Why does the secular world have *Harry Potter*™ and the phenomenal success of the books and films while the followers of the Creator of the universe can only best come up with a vegetable show for kids?" He meant no insult to a very wholesome children's TV show, but the comment struck a chord and continues to resonate within me to this day.

Last, yet first and foremost, my Lord and Savior Jesus Christ. I was as "lost as a hoot owl," to quote a friend, but did not realize it until you showed up. Your hand is on this entire work and I thank You and glorify you for it.

For a moment, William watched his teacher walk down the road to Salisbury and he murmured to himself. "Dream bigger and greater dreams than you even thought possible, William, dreams so big God has to help, but never forget to live today." He was glad no one else was on the road with them. He felt a little foolish speaking out loud to himself.

Chapter Three

They spent that first night a short walk from the edge of the old Roman road. On the southern side a well-drained heath of various shrubs and tall grasses marched off into the distance. Gone was the bright spring green grass of his home. They found shelter beneath a rather large group of whortleberry. Nearby stood a small grove of rowan trees whose branches, with their early spring leaves, added even more protection from the gentle rain which had begun just before sundown.

Robert led the way and crawled into a tightly packed group of berry bushes. William followed and inside they found a large, hollowed space, canopied over by the densely packed branches. The ground beneath was dry and slightly sandy and just comfortable enough. They set no fire that night, eating their meal cold, as they pulled their cloaks closer about them. Spring had come early but that evening a touch of chill was in the air, as if winter wasn't quite ready to give up its grip on the land.

"Did you know your father and uncle used to make this same trip each spring?" Robert had taken his pack off his shoulders before he scrambled into the bush and, after setting out their meal of oatcakes and apples, was busy creating a makeshift bed for himself.

Chapter Four

William had never seen Salisbury Cathedral before. As they followed the old Roman road into the late morning, it left the ridgeline and began a more or less straight course for the River Avon. Just before noon, as they crested a small hill, he was taken aback to see a tall spire rising off in the distance. It flashed a nearly brilliant white in the late morning sun.

"Is that Salisbury Cathedral? How tall is it, do you suppose?" William wondered aloud.

"I once met the great grandson of Nicholas of Ely, the original mason for the cathedral. He told me the tower is over four hundred feet tall." William shook his head in disbelief. The keep at Crandor Castle stood just over forty feet. It took a moment for him to do the math in his head before he realized that ten of his keeps could be stacked one on top of the other to reach as high as that spire. His eyes widened in wonder.

After traveling for the better part of a day and a half without meeting another traveler on the road, things changed dramatically as they drew closer to the river, its bridge, the town, and cathedral beyond. For the better part of an hour they walked amid a flock of sheep while Robert kept up a steady stream of conversation with the shepherds.

"I do not ever remember seeing a breed of sheep where the ram and ewe both had horns, Thomas." He had used the shepherd's first name, which caught William off guard. They had introduced themselves when they first encountered each other on the road, but he had promptly forgotten their names.

"That you will not," answered Thomas, shaking his head at the same time. "Outside of Whiltshire you will be hard pressed to see another."

Robert rubbed his hand down the straight back of the closest ewe. An odd look crossed his face and he ran his hand over the back one more time. "Thomas, I have never felt a fleece like this. What kind of sheep is this?"

Thomas laughed out loud. "No fleece to speak of on this marvelous breed and that is a fact. Just that fine mix of hair which it sheds on its own or we brush out and save." William caught a bright sparkle in the shepherd's eye and noticed he certainly was smiling a lot.

"Are all of these sheep from the same flock?"

"No sir that they are not. There is a better part of four flocks mixed in here. I am taking them over to the other side of the road for some better grazing and then we will come back to our village later in the day. These sheep are marvelous sir, marvelous. As soon as we get close to home they start splitting up and heading to each of their own pens." Thomas' fellow shepherds nodded in agreement.

"Well, that is a sight I will have to see some day, but not today. We have business in town." At this Robert nodded his head toward the spire, which continued to get larger, the closer they came to Salisbury.

"This is where we part ways then," Thomas responded, as they came upon a small dirt track, which ran off from the north side of the road. "God bless you and God speed you on your way, sir."

"God grant you rain and sun and the right amounts at the right time, Thomas."

A few moments later William turned to his old tutor. "I did not realize you had such an interest in sheep." Before Robert had a chance to answer they found themselves in the midst of a large group of men and women. The group was on the way to Canterbury, via Salisbury, in a pilgrimage and had overtaken them when the two had stopped to say farewell to the shepherds and their flocks.

They had obviously come in the middle of a heated discussion between two of the pilgrims and it ended with raised voices. "Before you forget why you are on this road, is there anything I might do to help?" Robert offered.

"Not unless you have judged a storytelling contest," said the first and larger of the two men.

Robert shook his head, "that I have not." Then added, "but I have had the privilege of listening to some of the best in England, even once at Windsor itself." The offhand mention of the castle long associated with the English kings had an immediate effect. Not only did the two men end their argument, but also most of the other pilgrims stopped their chatter.

One of the two who had been arguing, the smaller one, removed his flat cap and turned to Robert, "would you consider having a listen and giving us your impression, sir? I have a dinner wager riding on this."

"As do I," added the first man.

"Fine sirs, I do appreciate your situation, however, you must also consider mine. I and my young companion are on a most urgent quest, one in which time is of a critical nature. We do not have the luxury to stop and listen but must continue to press on to Salisbury and then south to the sea."

"Then your quest will take you across the channel?" asked the larger pilgrim.

"Across the channel and out of English held lands I am afraid."

Now Robert and William had all of the pilgrim's attention. "It seems to me, friend, your own story may be far better than either of our homespun tales," interjected the first man, while the second nodded. A murmur of agreement spread throughout the group.

Robert looked about for a moment, as if trying to make up his mind about something. "The only problem sirs, and ladies," he added, nodding towards the three women who accompanied the group, "is you catch us at the beginning of our tale. Or, rather, you catch us in the middle of a much larger tale, in which we are playing a small part."

"But an interesting tale nonetheless," added one of the ladies.

"Perhaps even worth a dinner itself," suggested yet another.

"Can you give us an idea what your tale involves?" asked the second man.

William was about to speak up at this point, but at a signal from Robert he remained silent. "It involves love and pain, suffering and joy, quiet peace and blasts of war, victory and honor, defeat and imprisonment. But, as I said my gentle pilgrims how will it all end? Who can say…?"

For the next several minutes they continued walking in silence, the spire continuing to grow on the horizon. And then the first man volunteered, "I cannot say for all of us sir, but for myself, I would be willing to give my share of the dinner prize to hear your story and the part it plays in the bigger story, even if the end is not in sight." He smiled and Robert nodded gravely while "hear, hear" came from the rest of the pilgrims, even the second man.

Then might I suggest the following arrangement?" Robert replied.

"It was our plan to make it to Salisbury by sunset and find a modest inn to spend the evening. In the morning we were to set out on the road south. I will begin my story even now. Once we reach Salisbury, I will complete it at an inn of your choosing (based on the talents of the speaker and the quality of the story, he added as an aside). If you find enjoyment in the telling, then I will leave the reward up to yourselves."

The entire group agreed and so Robert began.

•••

"To truly understand our story, you must take yourself back to the time of King William and the establishment of his reign here in England." He immediately had every one's attention, including his young student. Here was a part of his family story William was little familiar with. If he thought long on it, he would have realized how little he actually did know about his family. But that thought was fleeting as he quickly found himself caught up in the tale his teacher told. "Those first few years after Hastings were troublesome for the new king. Small areas of heavy Saxon influence still caused problems. The king and his lords and knights spent much of their time, those first few years, building castles in order to hold their lands. Some were modest and nothing more than wooden keeps surrounded by a fence with a moat and bailey. Others were more elaborate and permanent. It seemed that the greater structures were given based on loyalty, title or relationship.

"On the Dorset downs, just outside of Dorchester they built a castle. Not as large as some, and really more of an elaborate manor house with tower keep surrounded by a stone wall, it was made up in part with the native limestone of the area. Because this "castle" sat close to the Roman road we find ourselves walking upon, and commanded a view of the rich pastoral lands of the west, William entrusted it to his own cousin, Thomas Simpson, making him the first Earl of Dorchester. Despite his Norman heritage, Thomas became known far and wide as fair in his dealings with remaining Saxon landowners and thanes. While rebellion and fighting continued for years after Hastings, Thomas' shire remained peaceful. His family crest contained a crane or stork, the symbol of vigilance, beside a closed door, as if guarding it or patiently waiting for the master's return. Either way, the people took to the symbol and used it to name the castle. Eventually it was shortened to what we now call it: Crandor Castle.

"Before old age and dotage overcame Thomas he was killed while on a hunt in the New Forest. Dark and evil it is to name those woods at Crandor, even to this day. Many of the kings' own family, as well as a king himself, spent their final hours on earth beneath its boughs." Robert paused a moment, his head bowed. Finally he took in a deep breath and continued.

"Thomas left behind a young son, several daughters, and a wife of iron clad will. Much of the Simpson strength and resolve in the face of adversity can be traced back to Adelia of Anjou. When the king heard of the death of his cousin he sent his sympathy and his replacement for the lost earl. Adelia had no intention of simply stepping to the side and told the envoy of the king the same. Then, in the bravest of actions, she placed her family in the care of one of the former Saxon lords and rode to London and the king. There are no scribes who recorded the encounter, however, she won her case and returned as the Lady Adelia, dowager Duchess of Dorchester. The Domesday Book records the same to this very day.

On her return, Lady Adelia honored the Saxon lord with the title of Seneschal of her household. His family has held that title ever since."

Here Robert paused as William's eyes widened in understanding. His tutor wasn't just a tutor, he was a direct descendant of the man who protected his own ancestor all those long years ago.

"Whenever king and country called, a Simpson was there. They fought beside Henry in Ireland. They crusaded with Richard, all the way to Jerusalem and were alongside him on that fateful day in Chalus, remaining at his bedside through that long, terrible night. Another Henry became king but his was not a good government and for the first and only time, the family broke troth and sided with the barons in their war on the crown.

Three times they fought with Edward the Longshanks, once in Wales and twice in Scotland. They were called and fought with his son at the battle of Boroughbridge and now they have continued to fight with the third king Edward.

With the defeat of the Scot's at Neville's Cross, Lord Charles de Simpson was awarded the Order of the Garter. But on that same fateful day, when the highest of honors were bestowed upon him, the hardest of blows came. His younger brother was killed even as he struck down Lord Robert Keith, the great Marischal of Scotland. David, King of the Scots was captured soon after.

Lord Simpson returned to Crandor with a heavy heart, despite the honors awarded him on the field of victory. Word of the loss of his brother fell heavily upon his sister in law. Feeling a strong sense of responsibility, the Earl of Dorchester took in his nephew, William, as his own and named him heir, having lost his own son many years before during a famine which struck southwest England. William's mother mourned the loss of her husband, and despite the assurances of her brother in law that her son would be taken care of and raised as the next

Lord Simpson, she fell slowly into a dark despair. Her life ended a few months later.

Shortly after defeating the Scots, Lord Charles found himself called once again by king and country. This time he would sail across the channel. I still remember how he proudly wore the garter as he boarded ship at Southampton last year. Fair was the weather the day they set sail, the pride of England with Henry Lancaster to help end the siege of Calais.

News travels slowly in times of war and, although we learned of the fall of Calais and the English victory, we did not learn of the fate of our lord until three days prior when a French courier came to Crandor Castle to tell us the news and deliver a message. Lord Charles de Simpson, Earl of Dorchester was captured at the battle of St. Omer. A ransom has been demanded but other ideas we have…

Now you know our story and we find ourselves in Salisbury." William had been so caught up in the tale he didn't even realize they had crossed the bridge over the Avon and stood on its eastern bank, the cathedral rising majestically before them. The quickly setting sun blazed a reddish purple, it's colors seemed reflected or even absorbed by the gray-white stones of the church.

The group of pilgrims stood for a moment, lost in their own, individual thoughts. "That was well worth the time and what a tale," one of the ladies said, her voice slightly cracking, filled with emotion. Within moments the entire group was huddled around Robert, shaking his hand and thumping his back amid many a "well done."

William stood off to the side, lost in his own thoughts. He hadn't had much time to learn of his family history before his father went to fight alongside the king and failed to return. Robert, at the request of his uncle, had been steadily covering more and more, even as he taught him his primers. It seemed, in his ears, he could hear far off battles. The scream of horses, shouts of men, crash of arms. He blinked rapidly to hide some of his own emotions. He wanted nothing more than to have some time alone, but that wasn't going to be the case this evening.

A moment later he realized that the taller of the two men, who had been arguing a short time ago, stood before Robert, saying, "...well worth the effort. Well done indeed. I think we are all in agreement, sir. Your tale is worth dinner. There is an inn not far from the cathedral. There we will make good on our promise."

As the group moved towards the city, Robert made his way next to William. "I am sorry I have not had the proper time to teach you all you need to know about your family. There is more, much more, but I did not feel all of it should be shared with this group. My guess is they will spread the tale to all who will listen as they continue their pilgrimage."

"Has your family served our family all those years?" Robert answered with a curt nod. "And before King William conquered England?"

"My ancestors were hundred Eolders in Dorset and they were privileged to be invited to sit on the Witan, when it was called together at times of great need." He paused and looked with quiet, calm eyes at his young student, then added, "But that was a long time ago. Now, I teach and watch and protect."

William stood with his head bowed. The events surrounding him and what he was attempting to do were crashing down on him. He could feel their weight on his shoulders and they sagged beneath the burden. He suddenly remembered the last time he saw his mother alive. There was tightness in his throat and his eyes burned. It felt as if the joy in his life was slowly draining out of him. Why was all of this happening to him? Why did his parents have to die? Why did his uncle have to follow the king to France? In that very moment he felt really small and knew he wasn't ready to do what needed to be done to free his uncle.

Robert saw this and placed his hand gently but firmly on the young boy's shoulder. He needed to offer a distraction to his young ward; something that would take his mind off of the overwhelming nature of what had to be accomplished. William took a deep breath, wiping his eyes on his sleeve and looked up into the sparkling grey eyes before him. "I apologize for not answering your question earlier," Robert said solemnly. "I am actually not very interested in sheep. But then again, those shepherds were."

He turned and followed the group of pilgrims as they led the way to the inn. William stood for a moment wondering what he meant. Robert had called the shepherds by their names and spent the entire conversation talking about their sheep. What was the significance of that? While he watched the last of the sun's rays touch the cathedral's spire and the sky turn a deeper purple, a single star jumped out in the sky. Like a flash of enlightenment, William clapped his hands and ran to catch up with the group.

"I supposed when you use a man's name, and remember his name in a conversation, it is a sign of your respect for him. To find out what he is most interested in and being willing to show an interest in that subject will help earn his respect for you." He had caught up to his mentor and was excited to share his revelation.

Robert nodded gravely and then smiled. "Never forget, William. No matter how big or small the man is, he will always feel better at having met you if you remember his name and take an interest in what he does. His name is honey to his ears and his interest is the sweetest subject." A moment later they entered the inn, just a few steps behind the others.

Chapter Five

It was warmer and more comfortable than William had expected. He had only stayed in one other and it had been so run down and dirty he didn't even sleep on the bed in the room. Instead, he had curled up in a blanket he had brought with him and slept on the floor. That had been several years ago, when both his parents were still alive. The inn had been in Dorchester, and had been neglected for decades, so he really didn't have much of a reference.

The White Hart Inn was a timber framed two-story building with a steeply sloped roof, shingled with newly cut planks. It was primarily used as a coach house, but if a guest arrived by foot or carriage, they were more than willing to put them up for the evening. From the large entryway William could hear a good size crowd already creating quite a stir in the common room off to the right, through a set of double doors. These swung open and closed several times during the brief moment it took them to get their rooms and William could just see within through a light haze of smoke from the deep-set fireplace near the bar. Although it was early spring, they still kept a lively fire crackling over the chatter. The crowd inside was certainly a loquacious bunch. A wide set, thick beamed staircase on the right led to the upper bedrooms, while a smaller door, opposite the entry, led to a footpath, a well-tended garden, and the river just beyond.

A moment later he and Robert were settling into their room when there was knocking at their door. It was the landlord. He wasn't a tall man, but he made up for it in his girth. His face was flushed and he was slightly out of breath.

"Begging your pardon, sir, but I have been told you have the gift of storytelling." He was addressing Robert and paid William little attention. "Would you consider joining the crowd in the common room this evening? They would be much appreciative of a good tale." Robert nodded his acceptance, "thank you sir," the landlord added, as he turned and hurried back out of the room.

For a moment they both stood quietly in the room until William spoke up. "I am not even sure the landlord knew there was anyone else in the room beside you." Later on, he had to admit to himself he sounded more like a hurt child than a young man with a grievance.

"Oh? I am not sure I noticed."

"Well, I did." William brushed past his tutor and followed the landlord out the door, not quite slamming it in the process. He turned left and quickly walked down the hall. Taking the stairs two at a time he paused at the bottom for only a moment. Seeing the rear door he'd noticed when they arrived, he crossed the stone floor and found himself in a small garden with a well-tended footpath leading away from the inn. Without really thinking about where it would take him, he struck out.

An internal argument had started before he even left his room and it continued as he followed the crushed rock path. The white stone made it easier to see in the darkening night. "You are acting like an arrogant fool, William," it had started out.

"Not a fool, no. I am to be Earl of Dorchester someday."

"Someday, yes, but not this day."

"Still, I am heir to my uncle, not Robert. He is my teacher, my family's servant..."

"And he is a good friend."

"Friend... would a friend not even notice when I have been offended? He should have said something to the landlord."

"What offence, William? We are not traveling as the heir of Lord Charles de Simpson and his servant, are we?"

"...No."

"No, we are not. In order to keep our identities hidden we are traveling without title. It has to be this way, especially as we draw closer to French territory." The path led out of the garden and down a close cut lawn just alongside the River Avon. A smaller path split off to the left and ran directly to the river. He continued straight for some time.

"We are in Wiltshire still. What could possibly happen?" This last part he happened to mutter out loud and was startled when another voice spoke from out of the gloom ahead of him.

"Wiltshire has been known to be a dangerous place, if one does not keep his wits about him." William didn't recognize the voice and realized he'd left the room in a hurry and didn't even have his hunting knife with him. A quick glance back made him realize he had come quite far. The large wings and tall roof of the inn were nearly hidden in the gloom. He saw the white stone path leading straight back towards the inn but the grass on the riverside was already hidden by a thickening fog.

He squinted into the gloom ahead and thought he might be able to make out a dark figure several paces before him. One of Robert's earliest lessons suddenly came to mind. "When you come upon a stranger remain on your guard even if your only weapons are your fists. Never strike first, but be prepared to defend yourself." Without even realizing it, he had already balled up his fists. He also found himself wishing he hadn't rushed out of the room the way he had, acting the part of a spoiled child.

"I will do my best to do so." William tried to keep his voice from cracking. He mostly succeeded. "I thank you, sir, for your advice. Good evening." Without turning his back on the dark figure in front, he slowly started walking backwards on the path. He really wished there had been a brighter moon. As it was, this late in March 1348, it was nearly a new moon and the small sliver which remained cast only a dim light and distorted shadows. The fog from the river continued making its way across the lawn and the path.

William kept his fists balled but the only sound he heard was that of his own steps on the crushed rocks as he backed farther away from the voice ahead of him. Crunch, crunch, crunch and then he stopped. It wasn't a sound he heard which made him do so. It was what he felt, the sharp point of a blade in his lower back. Either the speaker who had been before him had somehow, in the mist and darkness, slipped behind him, or there was a second involved. Whatever the case, this suddenly was more dangerous than just an evening conversation.

"You find yourself between a rock and a sharp place, sir." This was definitely a different voice. It was raspy and dark and it alone sent a shiver up William's spine. The holder of the blade sensed this and chuckled.

To William's right there was the expanse of lawn and dark bushes he could just barely make out. If they really were bushes, they were at least 20 feet away. If he got to them they certainly would know where to look. To his left he couldn't make out the dark bank and even darker river beyond but he knew they were there. The mist had rolled in even thicker, turning quickly into fog, as the night air dropped rapidly in temperature over the warmer water of the river. Just a few yards from the gravel trail

Robert, his legs barely supporting his own weight. Someone was wrapping something around his left arm. Just before he lost consciousness, he had the strength to mutter, "Past the garden… off the path… s'one there." His head dropped and he remembered no more.

•••

An astringent, pine-like aroma tickled William's nose. He could smell smoke and sat up alarmed. He wished he hadn't. His head swam and black spots leaped up in his vision. His left arm throbbed as he slowly lowered himself back down. It was only then he realized he was lying in a bed. The heavy curtains were drawn closed over the windows so he had no idea what time it was. There was definitely smoke in the room. It wasn't the smoke from a fire. This smelled more like burning herbs.

"It is past noon. You have been abed since we brought you in late last night." He hadn't noticed Robert sitting at his bedside watching him as he furrowed his brow and rubbed his nose. "That is rosemary and thyme. The doctor has been here today. He prescribed burning them both to keep the humors in balance. It seems to me it has only made the room stuffy. Even my head is spinning."

William tried to speak and found his voice weak and cracking. "Did you…?" he hoarsely whispered. "Did they find…?"

"The landlord's servants found a mostly unconscious man just off the main path, outside the garden. Right where you told us he would be." Robert stood and crossed the room, throwing back the curtains and opening the shuttered window. Sunlight and a cool spring breeze entered the room, instantly refreshing both of them. Once back by the bed, the tutor took a little red wine and mixed it with some water and gave it to William to drink. It was tart but cool and soothed his throat.

"What will become of him?"

"I think you know the penalty for attempted robbery. The King's Law is quite specific and strict in this case."

"Will he be tried?"

"The evidence will be presented to the Justice of the Peace at the Magistrates Court, who will be responsible for determining the course of action." He paused and sat quietly for a moment, as if studying his own student. "It is a difficult thing, William, to know, after the blood has cooled and the fight is over, that a man may still die because of last nights' actions."

"If the fog had been thinner and his aim better, I might never have gotten back to the inn." William gingerly fingered the rough bandage wrapped around his left upper arm. He tried not to move it because each time he did a spark of pain shot down to his wrist.

"As to that, William, what was it that bothered you last night?" He watched through half lidded eyes as his young student squirmed a little before he answered.

"It seemed serious at the time… now I see it for the petty injury it was." Robert turned to look him directly in the eye.

"Consider the answer carefully before you give it William. Do you honestly believe the landlord was intending to insult you or belittle you in any way?"

William's eyes wandered from the fire to the windows to the curtains and to the door. He didn't want to meet his mentors own. He didn't want to admit the truth too quickly. A little of the resentment from last night welled back up in him again. He swallowed it back and shook his head to clear his thoughts. He had already had this discussion with himself last night, before his adventure.

"No. I do not honestly believe he was intentionally trying to belittle or dishonor me."

Robert nodded his head slowly, and then smiled. "Always remember, William, it is easier for us to judge people on their actions, while we expect to be judged on our intentions." He stood up and headed out the door. Just as he was about to shut it behind him, he paused and turned back. "Remember, if God will not judge us until we come before Him in heaven after our life is over, why would we think we can attempt to judge others now?" He left William alone to ponder this before drifting back into and uneasy sleep.

Chapter Six

William woke once that evening, to relieve himself, and then restlessly drifted off to sleep again. Something Robert had said, as he left the room, continued to bother him and made sleeping difficult. Not to mention every time he tried to roll over he awoke to shots of pain down his left arm. Did he have the right to judge the men who attacked him? He didn't even know why they had done it. Was it for money; or something even worse? His uncle suddenly entered his mind and he realized if there was to be a trial, he would have to be a witness. How soon would it happen? As Robert told the pilgrims, they didn't have the luxury of time. They needed to leave Salisbury as soon as possible.

The next morning was overcast. The gray sky held rain and the threatening soon turned violent with thick sheets coming down, along with the occasional burst of lightning. The mild start to spring had snapped and a chill was in the air. Robert was sitting at his bedside when he awoke.

"Salisbury's Magistrate will hear the case today. God-willing we will see the end of it and be on our way."

"And the accused?"

"If he is found guilty, he will pay the price for his actions." After a moments pause, he added, as if understanding what William had been wrestling with overnight. "Understand this, William. We all must pay the price for our actions, no matter if they are honorable or not. Every action leads to and causes another.

"Even God has told us that we reap what we sow. If you want good results in your life, then you must be willing to sow good things no matter the cost. Even if all around you are sowing evil, you must be willing to stand up and do what is right. To accept this and to do what is right may even cost you your life. A man's true character is shown at times like these."

He paused a moment, staring into the fireplace, and then added, quietly, almost to himself, "When men sow evil, they should not be surprised when evil shows up at their door. This man intended evil. Perhaps, if given the chance, he may have even killed you."

"What about turning the other cheek?"

"We are also to honor and obey those in authority, William. The king and the courts say this is how we are to live in England so we will obey."

"What if they are wrong?"

Robert paused before answering. "You are young enough to, perhaps, not understand what you have just suggested." And here, Robert moved closer to the bedside and leaned over, barely whispering. "What you suggest, William, is treason. Have a care what you say and around whom you say it. There may come a day when a careless word spoken around the wrong ears makes its way to the Kings' Court and you could be called to defend yourself."

William's breath caught in his throat and he nervously glanced about the room, thankful there were no other ears to overhear their conversation. A moment later he let out a deep sigh and closed his eyes. "I am honor bound, as my father before me, to serve the king and uphold his laws. *Vivo servire.* I just wished a man did not have to die because of this oath."

Robert leaned back in his chair and continued to study the fire. A moment later he took in a deep breath and turned to his young student and smiled. "It is that very thought William, which, if always remembered, will see you one day to be the finest of the king's men."

•••

A short time later there was a knock at the door. Robert crossed the room and opened it, letting in a young page. His surcoat displayed the Salisbury city crest, two double-headed eagles supporting a purple and gold shield with the Latin inscription above reading, *Civitas Novar Sarum*, or the New City of Salisbury. William translated it quickly enough and then wondered what happened to the old city.

"Your pardons sir, but your presence is requested by the Justice of the Peace of Salisbury, at the trial of the accused highwayman. It is to begin on the hour, by the tolling of the bell tower of the cathedral." He spoke quickly and, William felt, with a strange accent, not anything like the locals of Wiltshire he had met so far.

"Robert nodded gravely, "we will be ready to attend after a few moments preparation."

The young page bowed and added, as he backed out of the room, "I will be ready to escort you there, at your convenience."

With his teachers help, William dressed and then slipped his left arm in the sling Robert had made for him. He could feel the linen bandage wrapped around his arm occasionally tugging at the wound and he winced when it happened. "Breathe through your nose and out through your mouth. It will help you steady yourself." William took his advice and in a moment found himself in the hall, following the young page down the stairs and out the front door.

The cool damp air stung his eyes and they watered slightly. He used his right hand to pull the hood of his cloak over his head to help protect him from the chilly breeze, which blew from the north. At least the heavy rain and lightning had ended.

The page continued at a brisk pace, the edges of his surcoat flapping in the wind. In order to forget how miserable he felt, William instead chose to spend his time focusing on the young boy in front of him. The surcoat was clean, but showed signs of being repaired several times. The use of it, in itself, said something to William. This was an article of clothing which had fallen out of favor over fifty years ago, replaced by linen shirts with a fitted cotte, either laced up or closed with buttons.

Beneath, William could see a hauberk of mail occasionally exposed as the wind continued to tug at its cover. It seemed to be a small shirt with no sleeves and extended just below the hips. The mail looked to have been well cared for and the infrequent ray of sun sparkled on its surface. The young boy wore cross-gartered hose and leather shoes, which appeared either new or very well maintained. Despite some of the outdated attire, all other appearances suggested the Justice of Salisbury was a well-funded position.

The distraction helped. Before he realized it, William was following the page into a large timber framed building, opposite the front entrance to the Cathedral of Salisbury. It took a moment for his eyes to adjust to the torchlight inside. Fortunately the overcast skies made it easier.

The doors opened to a small antechamber. Robert helped William remove his cloak and hung it on a peg next to his own. A loud bell sounded outside and the page immediately opened the doors, ushering both into a long, well-lit hall. A dozen or so people stood on either side of the rectangular room, creating a nave, which the page proceeded to walk down. As they approached the far end of the hall they found two men seated. Two pike carrying soldiers flanked one of them and the other sat in a large chair on a single stepped dais.

The page stopped ten feet from the raised platform and bowed. "My Lord, may I present William Edwardson of Dorchester." The boy made no mention of Robert, who William noticed stood a few paces behind him and to his right. When he looked back at the Justice of the Peace of Salisbury, he realized he was being studied. William took a quick mental inventory of what he wore, from the mud covered boots up to his bandaged arm in a sling and decided there wouldn't be anything among his attire which should give him away.

"My Lord," William said as he bowed slightly from his waist, his right hand at his side. His left remained in the sling. Robert had coached him on the proper way to address men in the service of the king, based on whether they were peer or commoner, and he hoped he had gotten it correct. This bow was deserving of a peer of the realm, whereas a bow of the head and the title of "your honor" would be more appropriate for a common born officer. A quick glance to his right revealed Robert offering him a brief smile and a short nod of approval.

"Are you still in much pain?" Without preamble, the Justice spoke. His voice was deep and slightly melodious. It reminded him, just a little, of his father. In fact, it was similar enough that a swell of emotion tried to overcome him before he could answer.

"The wound is not deep but will take time to heal, my Lord."

"If your attackers aim had been better…"

"The new moon and the deep fog were to my advantage two nights ago."

"If you are up to it, would you tell of the events of the evening before last, leading up to the attack and what followed?"

William bowed again and began with his leaving the inn through the back door. He told the Justice he wanted to clear his head and didn't feel up to joining others in the common room. A few moments later he ended with his collapsing in the arms of his friend at the back door of the White Hart.

The Justice of Salisbury sat silently for several moments, his hands folded in his lap, and his eyes fixed on a spot on the floor half way between himself and William. Finally he asked, "Then you never actually saw your attacker?"

"No my Lord…"

"So there is little chance you could even identify this man," and here he pointed to the man seated between the pike armed soldiers, "which was found lying in the grass, just outside the garden of the White Hart?"

William turned and studied the man. He was taller than average with dark curly hair that was nearly shoulder length. He wore a simple linen shirt, a woolen vest, and trousers, which were stitched to the top of his ankle high leather boots. His eyes were filled with a strange madness, as if he was trying to look right through his accuser. Even as William watched, he could see the stranger trying to get out of his bonds. It appeared his wrists and ankles were bound securely with leather thongs.

"Although I have never seen this man before, I would feel confident, my Lord, that I will remember both of those voices I heard last night, until the end of my days." William said this with such conviction the Justice of the Peace and those nearby were startled to attention.

"What was it, precisely, they said to you?" Now the justice was leaning forward, his hands resting on his knees.

"The first voice came from in front of me. I could almost see a shadow of the figure, but no features at all. He said, 'Wiltshire has been known to be a dangerous place, if one does not keep his wits about him.' A moment later, with a sharp blade sticking me in my back, a deep, dark, raspy voice said, 'you find yourself between a rock and a sharp place.' A moment later, he called the one who had been standing before me Davey. I never did take the time to turn and address either properly." A loud guffaw and a few chuckles echoed through the hall. The Justice held up his hand and the noise died off immediately.

He turned and nodded to the guards and they helped the bound man stand to his feet. "My guess is Davey Martin has long since fled the county. What say you to this, Samuel?" The wild-eyed man shrugged his shoulders but his eyes betrayed him. He was looking for any means of escape. "Well, just to make sure we have the right man, Samuel, repeat after me, you find yourself between a rock and a sharp place."

Samuel dropped his head and murmured the same, just loud enough for those around him to hear. A shiver shot through William and he closed his eyes, bowing his own head. A small part of him had hoped they hadn't found the right man.

"This is the same voice, is it not William?"

"Yes my Lord." His voice cracked as he answered.

"Samuel Thompson, in the name of Edward, King of England and the power he has vested in me, I pronounce you guilty of assault and attempted highway robbery." The Justice nodded and the two soldiers each grabbed an arm of the wild-eyed, raspy voiced Samuel and dragged him out of the hall, through a side door, which William hadn't noticed before. Robert had already told him earlier the sentence would be carried out swiftly; he just hadn't realized how quickly it would all take place.

"It is a difficult thing, William, being an instrument of the king's peace," the Justice commented. The young nephew of the Earl of Dorchester nodded, but kept his head bowed as he struggled with his emotions. He was realizing that it was one thing to hear stories of battles and war and victory and defeat and quite another to be the person responsible for another's death. He felt sure he would never forget the look on Samuel's face as they dragged him out of the hall. He swallowed thickly, taking in a deep breath and relaxing his shoulders. Up to that moment he didn't realize how tense he had been.

William finally looked up only to find the Justice watching him closely. He was leaning forward, elbows on both knees and hands beneath his chin. "Samuel's punishment is not your fault, William. He never understood how his daily actions had daily results, or how those daily results added up over time. But there is something even more important he missed, or more likely, never even knew." At this point he stood and stepped down off the dais and crossed the ten feet to stand before the young boy, resting a hand on his right shoulder.

"The simple will see a personal fault and try to correct the fault by trying to change what they do. This will not fix anything. The Apostle Paul understood this and explained it in one of his great letters. You are what you think about, William." He paused just long enough to make sure he had the boy's attention, and then gently tapped the side of William's head with his index finger.

"What you think about will lead to what you speak. What you speak will lead to what you do. What you do, over and over again will become your habit. And finally, William, your habits will determine your character." Another pause and this revelation began to sink in. "Samuel did what he did because of his true character. This came from his habits, which arose from his actions, which came from the words he spoke, which came from the thoughts he had. If he had only learned to discipline his thoughts, perhaps the results of his life would have been much different."

He turned back to his seat, speaking over his shoulder as he walked away, "it is times like these I remind myself to guard my own thoughts."

He waved his hand in dismissal. A moment later, William and Robert were back outside the hall, and the Cathedral's bell was ringing again. They had been inside one hour. The wind and rain had passed and the sun was breaking through the thinning clouds.

William let Robert take the lead, as they made their way back to the inn to collect their packs before leaving town. There was still one thought he kept coming back to and finally was able to put it into words for his mentor. "Do you think Samuel got what he deserved?"

For a moment Robert didn't answer. The only sound, besides the birds in the trees along the road, was their footsteps on the crushed rock and chalk. They were half way to the White Hart Inn when he quietly responded. "Even if he did, William, do not show or gain pleasure from it. Never allow yourself to be happy when someone gets what you think they deserve. Instead, pray for them. In the end, I think this is what God wants us to do."

William nodded and began praying for the man, who had only last night tried to kill him. By the time they got back to their room, he was feeling better. His arm still hurt, but his mind was clear and he was ready to leave Salisbury.

Chapter Seven

A short time after returning to the White Hart, William and Robert found themselves on the road, which led back across the Avon and then turned south to the channel. Already it was late afternoon and there was little chance they would be able to make it before nightfall as over 25 miles still stood between them and the port of Southampton.

A large portion of the land between Salisbury and Southampton makes its way through the New Forest, and neither one had any intention of making that part of the trip during nightfall. Nor did they have any intention of simply sleeping off the side of the road, in the forest or on its eaves, as they did the first evening out of Dorchester.

After having learned more about his family history, William would have preferred not to go in the New Forest at all, however, Robert convinced him they would stay to the main road and move through during the early part of the next day. If they took the longer way around to the east, it would easily add an extra day or two to their trip and William was anxious to get aboard ship. For some reason in his mind he didn't feel as if the trip had begun until they were finally at sea.

"I know you are anxious to get across the channel, William," his teacher stated, interrupting those very thoughts, "but you have had a nasty go since you were attacked two nights ago. We are going to have to take a rest before we reach the Forest. The best place to do that will be in Downton. We can overnight there and then start early and make our way through the Forest during the brightest part of the day." They were already several miles out of Salisbury with only a few more to go before they arrived in the village, which straddled the Avon River. Dark clouds were starting to billow up from the west and William scowled then caught himself.

"Those clouds coming our way," he nodded off to the west. "I am having a hard time imagining myself being in a good mood when they find us still outside of Downton and we enter the village soaked to the bone." A chill ran through him, even as he thought about it. The wound on his left arm was really starting to bother him and his mood darkened even as did the sky to the west.

For several moments they walked in silence, side by side. The only noise was their footfalls and the occasional song from the thrushes and finches still wintering in the dry grasses on either side of the road. "The most difficult thing about being happy, William, is the decision to be happy," Robert, stated. "No matter what life throws at you, once you make the decision, then just be happy. It sounds simple, but it is such a difficult option that most people never even try. Watch their faces. See how they walk. Is their head up? Do they shuffle along like the world has already beaten them down and they are just waiting for the end or do they walk deliberately? This has nothing to do with their station in life. You can make that decision as a peasant in the field or a lord in his manor."

"The Justice of Peace was trying to say something similar, was he not?" The conversation was turning into a great distraction from the pain in his shoulder.

"In a way... yes. He said that all of your thoughts will ultimately determine who you are; your character."

"I am not sure I understand what that means. What is my character?"

"All that you say and all that you do will spell out who you are. That is your character. Another way to look at it, William, is to ask yourself, what are the things I do not have to do, which I am willing to do anyway, when no one is paying any attention? Just as this makes up your character, so does the choice to do those things only when no one else is looking." He could see that last comment puzzled his pupil and he followed it up with an explanation. "Why were you attacked in the dark of night and not during the day when we walked into town? The choices we make, right or wrong, will determine our character."

Several minutes passed and the ground began to slowly, slightly drop away. Ahead of them, in the distance they could see a slim shimmer of sunlight on the water of the Avon River as it looped from their left. As the sun was beginning to set, clouds rolled in from the west darkening most of the sky, nearly hiding it as it reached the horizon. The sound of thunder followed the clouds. William took in a deep breath and could smell the rain. It was only a matter of time. He pulled his cloak closer and his hood down farther, trying and mostly failing, to keep from rubbing the thick cotton material of his bandage against the fresh wound of his arm.

"Well then... if someone had something about their character they wanted to correct..." Robert waited as William processed the answer to his own question. "Instead of working on fixing the flaw, they should look to their thoughts first?"

Robert smiled and nodded his head in agreement. "Precisely, William, which is why, even knowing that we will probably get drenched with rain before we ever reach Downton, I can still remain happy, because what I think is not under the control of my surroundings."

"I sometimes wonder if I will ever learn all I need to know," William muttered his head hung low.

This time Robert leaned his head back and laughed a huge, loud, joyful laugh. "Oh, William," he said, after wiping a tear from his eyes. "You will never stop learning." He must have seen his young students' expression, because he quickly added, "to live life is to be constantly learning. As soon as you stop learning you are going backwards. It is like picking an apple from the tree. Once you pick it, it stops growing. Once you pick it, it starts rotting."

This last comment caused William to pause a moment and the two stood on the side of the deeply rutted road, letting an ox pulled cart slowly pass them. "If I am supposed to be learning and growing each day, how will I know what the lesson is?"

"That is one of the biggest hurdles for most people. They are stubborn and prideful. They think they can figure it all out on their own. In the end, you know what happens after too much pride, yes?"

"A fall." Lightning lit up the western sky and a moment later a loud clap of thunder shook the air.

"Yes, William. Pride certainly does come before a fall."

"Then how does not being prideful help me to learn what I am supposed to have learned that day?" They began walking again, making sure to avoid the occasional pile left behind by the ox.

"Because men who are humble are willing to ask for help."

"Well, I am constantly asking you for help," William looked up and smiled at his tutor. Robert didn't meet his gaze at first but looked to the south, towards Downton. A brief moment later he smiled as well.

"You will always be able to ask me for help, William. I am here to serve." Then Robert turned serious. "There will come a day, preferably later, but always the chance of sooner, when I will no longer be here for you. When that day comes there is one other, with even greater understanding than I, who you can always turn to for help and guidance and wisdom too." They walked along for a minute or two, both in their own thoughts, and then Robert added, "Seek and you shall find. Knock and the door will be opened. Ask and it will be given to you."

"I can ask God to help me understand what I should have learned today? Is he not too busy to worry about me?"

"His word says He has counted the hairs on your head. He knew you, even before you were formed in your mother's womb. If He is willing to care for the smallest of these thrushes and those finches, imagine what He is willing to do for you." For a brief moment, William saw the world in a completely different light. God was intimately involved in the life of each and every creature, including himself. He was suddenly even more embarrassed over his thoughts and actions when he stormed out of their room the other night.

"I acted like a fool and He was there, watching. How can I go to Him and ask for His help now?"

"You always can, William. Just remember, when you do, to tell Him you are sorry. And if you say it to Him, you had better mean it too. Ask Him to forgive you, and He will. He always has and He always will, as long as your heart is in the right place and you really mean it. That too is being humble. Believe me; you will feel better when you do this. Then, you will be able to ask Him for His help."

"And He will show me what I should have learned that day?"

"With God there is a season for planting and season for sowing. You may not get your answer immediately and other times you could.

Although you never know when you may get an answer, you can be assured He will answer you… eventually."

The first, large, wet drops of rain began falling. William lowered his head and spoke with a little crack in his voice. "I am sorry for behaving the way I did the other night and I could really use some help in understanding what I should be learning from this."

Robert rested his hand on William's shoulder for a moment as the rain began to come down in earnest. Before he withdrew it, in order to cover up with his cloak, he murmured, "amen." A moment later they crested a small rise. Before and below them, in the river valley stood the village of Downton.

Chapter Eight

Although Downton wasn't very large when William compared it to Dorchester, what it lacked in homes and farms, it more than made up for in mills. William counted seven all together, alongside the river. At least one resembled a grain mill, similar to those he had seen close to his home. The others were unusual in shape and size. Despite the steady rain, these buildings were still large enough to recognize, even from their vantage point on the hill overlooking the town.

Robert told him they were woolen and linen mills. It was here the fullers cleaned and then pounded out the wool in order to make cloth. Some would stay for use in England, but most of the processed wool would be bundled into large sacks which would be sold across the channel to Flanders and even as far away as Florence, Italy. In Southampton, it was most likely they would find passage aboard a ship transporting this same wool as most of the shearing had just recently been completed for the year.

"Have you been here before?" William asked.

"Several times, however it has been a few years since the last I crossed the bridge from the Borough into the village proper. The mills here are some of the oldest in England and they use the river to help full and felt the wool as well as crush corn. There used to be a market on the west side of the river each Thursday. I remember it being rather lively." Robert paused a moment, and if William had been willing to turn back into the wind and the rain, he would have seen his tutor smiling over some long past memory. "Despite Salisbury being so close, the town has done well for itself.

"There is an estate, Downton Manor, on the west side of the river. It is perhaps as large as 100 head of cattle or 100 hides as it may be called. Most of its farming tenants live on that side of the river. The Bishop of Winchester lives in Downton as well. If the rain breaks you will see the church before we cross the bridge. Nearby there used to be several inns. We will find a dry place to stay in one of those." He pulled his cloak closer and shivered. The temperature had dropped even as the sun slid below the horizon. They were now only a quarter mile outside the Borough and William was picking up the pace. He too, wished to find a dry place to get out of the rain.

The rain was already turning the well-rutted road into a sloppy mess when they crested another small hill. Before them stood a scattering of homes, Downton Manor, the bridges, the mills, and Downton Village just beyond. The sun had completely set and the rain clouds hid what little sliver of moon would have been visible. The chilled air was already causing a mist to form over the river. The landmarks which did stand out seemed muted and blurred from the wind and rain.

William shivered as he remembered his attackers using the mist and darkness to their advantage and hoped they would get across one of the two bridges and into the village before it thickened into fog. He didn't like the idea of stumbling about a strange town, looking for lodging, not being able to see more than a few feet in front of himself. At least this time he had Robert beside him. That one thought lent him more courage than he would have imagined.

"We should be able to cross the river before the fog really sets in." It was as if Robert had read Williams' mind. "Once we cross over the river, a few blocks away is a large open square. On one side is the church. You can still just see the steeple, despite the rain. Opposite it is where there used to be several inns. With God's blessing, in a short while we will find a room where we will be able to change out of these wet clothes and into dry ones then warm ourselves beside a fire. As sore as my bones are today, I am not much up for the crowds of a common room. What about you, William?"

For a moment his young student plodded along the muddy track. The sound of his boots sucking against the mire each time he took a step was occasionally matched by a deep grunt. He hung his head lower, barely focusing on his own feet. His left arm throbbed in time with the blood coursing through his sore head. He was weak and tired and felt as if he could just curl up on the side of the road. He didn't even care if it was raining. He couldn't be sure, but he felt that his wound had reopened. It was as if his body moved and his legs took their steps without his control or authority. He had had hard days of work (his father and uncle had made sure he knew what it meant to get his hands dirty) and had been tired and sick before, but this was like all of those combined, along with the worry that maybe all this was really happening as a way of punishment.

"Having… a hard time… thinking…" He mumbled his answer, almost to himself.

"I understand, William," his mentor empathized. Despite his age and his own struggles on the muddy road, he still held his head high and seemed to be able to fight the urge to just want to lie down on the side of the road like William. "The best thing to do when you feel this way is to thank God for the trial."

"You want me to thank God for punishing me?" Williams' voice cracked.

Robert shook his head. "No, William. That is not what I said. Thank Him for the trial, not that He caused it, but because He will turn it around for good and, in the end, this trial will strengthen you and your faith. As you grow and really begin to believe you can see your way through tough times, even harder trials will come. As a matter of fact William, they will always come. You only need to be worried if you find yourself not going through a trial, coming out of a trial or going into a new trial. To be anything else suggests you are no longer a threat to God's enemies.

Each successive trial you go through, and each victory you obtain, grows you and your faith; while each struggle and success grows your patience. You will find yourself believing what Paul wrote: I can do all things through Christ who strengthens me. So, smile and thank God. There is a reason for this trial. Be patient and He will help you see it through."

This was the last thing William wanted to hear. He wanted Robert to tell him it was going to be fine. His arm would heal, his strength would return. He wouldn't feel sore and weak and tired. They would find the inn and sleep warm and dry soon enough. That was what he wanted to hear, but it wasn't what he needed to hear. He had been around Robert long enough to know he taught, not on feelings, but on purpose. It may not always be the easy thing to hear, but it was the right thing. He took a deep breath and let it out slowly.

"Thank You, God for seeing me through this trial. When the time is right, please reveal to me what its purpose is." He murmured this to himself and then added, "Amen." For the next several moments his mind wandered from thought to thought, always returning to why he was going through this. What purpose would it serve? Why did it have to be so hard?

Suddenly he found himself no longer slogging through a mud-rutted road but walking on flagstones. He blinked and wiped the rain out of his eyes. Looking up, William realized he was on the bridge over the River Avon and would soon be in the Village of Downton. Somehow that last quarter mile had passed much quicker than he expected. Despite the cold rain and wind he felt a warm glow spread through him and he smiled. He still didn't understand why each day seemed harder than the last, but he was beginning, slowly, to understand where he could go for help.

Chapter Nine

At the other end of the bridge they found a wooden gate blocking their way. Actually, it was a thick log set on legs at either end and was long enough to completely block their path. William was just about to hurdle it when a voice called out from a small hut just beyond the end of the bridge. As dark and rainy as it was, neither William nor Robert had noticed the little shack and the voice startled them both.

"The village is closed at sunset to any but respectable folk. State your business in Downton and be quick about it." A shadowy figure had emerged from the doorway of the hut and shambled over to the barricade. He held a small, shielded oil lamp before him, which did nothing except cast his features into an even deeper darkness.

The rain continued to beat down on each of them as William tried to answer the best way he knew how. Just before doing so he felt Robert's hand on his shoulder and heard a faint whisper, "let me."

"Tis a miserable night for sure, sir. We do not wish to put you out any more than need be. We are simply traveling from Salisbury to Southampton. Our cousin runs a brewery there and he sent us a letter asking for our help. Seems things go well for our lads across the Channel and they are a thirsty lot." William immediately noticed a change in Robert's voice. The accent was different. He didn't sound at all like his tutor who could read and write at least four languages. He sounded uneducated.

"You should have started earlier in the day. You would have made it to town and maybe even through the Forest depending on your pace."

"Right ye are sir, right ye are. We were held behind in Salisbury. Seems the Justice o' the Peace needed my young prentices word in a trial this mornin'." William suddenly found the lantern shining him squarely in the face. He squinted from the bright light.

"Is that so… what did the Justice need with you lad?" His voice was calm, but under it there was a note of sincere interest.

"I was a witness in an assault and highway robbery case." William stood his ground and tried, in vain, to glimpse the face of the gatekeeper.

"You do not say…"

"When the Lord Justice tells ye to come, ye come. No matter how long of a road lies before ye. The lad told his part and justice was laid down swift." Robert gave William's shoulder a gently squeeze. He wanted to do the rest of the talking.

"We have had our share of troubles here. Two men have been such a plague on the village as well as those passing through these parts we had to put up this barrier. It'll be a brighter day, no matter the weather, when their lot is handled. You said justice was done?"

Robert nodded and smiled, despite the rain, which now seemed to be coming straight down and from the side. "That it was. I expect Samuel Thompson's feet have stopped kickin' by this time. His partner, Davey Martin got away though."

At this the gatekeeper let out a loud whoop and nearly dropped his lantern. "Now that sight I would have liked to have seen meself. Both those boys have been causing the worst kind of trouble up and down the road. Some say they were even causing mischief in the forest. But we had to deal with what we could here." He hurriedly returned to the hut and set the lantern down in the doorway and then returned to help Robert move the barricade.

"You are both welcome in Downton. If you will help me put the gate back in place, I will show you to a fine inn, just a few blocks away. They will set you right there."

"Thank ye for lettin' us in. It has been a rough trip so far and we still have the forest to deal with."

The gatekeeper smiled and touched the wide brim of his hat. "It is this town what will be thankful, once they hear of what has happened to that black heart Thompson. Unless I am much mistaken, I think you will find yourselves very welcome this evening."

As they followed the limping guard down the main street, which led away from the bridge, William caught Robert's eye. The latter simply smiled and winked, obviously pleased with himself.

•••

The gatekeeper, whose name was Richard, was correct in his impression of nearly the entire town's reception. He led them straight away from the bridge and they crossed two other streets before entering a small square. Just to their left stood a timber framed two story inn. William couldn't be sure because of the rain and darkness, but it looked like a boar was carved on the hanging sign above the door.

The downstairs windows were shuttered but behind several of them the bright yellow light of candles or the darker red of a well settled bed of coals in the fireplace grate of a room shone through the cracks. As soon as the front door was opened a bright, cheerful, warm light from a well-tended fire in the hearth opposite the entrance flooded the step. William had to blink repeatedly and nearly stumbled over the stone doorsill as his eyes adjusted from the darkness outside and a weariness clung to his limbs.

Robert followed him into the inn and a moment later Richard had introduced them both to Baldwin, the landlord. Although William couldn't remember the name of the keeper of the White Hart, he was sure these two men had to be related. The stocky frames, bushy eyebrows (which, by the way, shot up at the right moments during Richards relating of their story), flushed cheeks and general sense of intense need to hurry off to the next task at hand, were identical in both men.

"Well, I for one am glad to hear this told." He wrung his hands and wiped them on his dingy apron repeatedly as he spoke. "It is no lie that those devils on the road have hurt our business this last year. If what Richard says is true, the Bear and Boar will soon see better days and busier evenings and for that, I am very grateful. I dare say all the local folk who have gathered in the common room this evening will be equally pleased."

He glanced about, as if looking for something or someone, then found it when a young girl came through two double doors carrying an empty tray. She looked to be about William's age and, despite wearing a homespun long wool tunic, gathered at the waist with a belt and a simple ribbon tied in her auburn hair to keep it out of her face, she immediately caught his attention. Her bright green eyes flashed and she smiled as she came across the room and William felt himself stand up just a little straighter. He suddenly wished he didn't look like he had just walked a quarter mile through the pouring rain along a muddy road.

"Ah, there you are Agnes. I need a room arranged for these two travelers. They have not asked but I am much mistaken if they would not mind a hot bath and then a chance to dry out." He turned from the girl, who nodded and spun about, briskly heading out another set of doors, opposite the ones she came from. "My daughter will set things right, sirs. I know you have the cold and chill to shed, but, if either of you are up for it, the other guests in the common room would surely enjoy hearing you tell your own story. A few are just passing through and it may make them feel that much safer, knowing the roads hereabout may not be quite so dangerous for a while." He spoke in such a hurry it seemed his thoughts came out in one long sentence.

"I cannot say yea or nay for the lad, but for myself, after the bath and dry clothes I will simply call it a night." As Robert was answering, William looked to his mentor and tried to read a suggestion in his eyes or expression. Either there wasn't one, or he was too tired to notice. Of course that thought alone should have been his answer.

"If telling the tale of the last few days will help you and your business, sir, I will do my best to come to the common room and oblige your other guests. I imagine, after the bath, dry clothes and a bit of warm food, I will find myself nearly set right."

Baldwin nodded and smiled, "it would do wonders, young master, wonders." A moment later Agnes returned through the double doors and her father ushered them out of the foyer. They followed her down a long hall, at the end of which they turned left and found themselves in a wing of the inn, which turned back from the street. A short distance down she opened a door on their left.

The room was set up as a suite. The front room already had a crackling and snapping fire roused in the grate and it was driving the chill out of the air. Several large, thick tallow candles were lit about the room, throwing more light into the corners. It was a simple, but cheery room with a few chairs and a small table. The shutters and thick curtains were closed but William was pretty sure he could hear the rain hitting on glazed windows.

"This door leads to your bedroom." Agnes said as she pointed to a door just to the left of the fireplace. "I have set a fire in the grate there as well. It is a smaller room so it should warm up quickly."

"Thank you for your kindness," Robert stated as he bowed his head slightly. William noticed he had dispensed with the uneducated accent. "You and your father run a very fine house."

The young girl blushed slightly and did the two of them a small courtesy. As she stood up, William caught her eye and saw an emerald green flash in the candle and firelight. He smiled back. "I will show you where the baths are for this wing of the inn. It will take a little longer for the rocks to heat up, but when they do, I will bring them straight away."

She led them back out of their room, further down the hall to a large double door. Inside sat several copper lined wooden tubs, two of which had already been filled with water. The fire had recently been roused and several split logs were spitting and snapping as they sizzled and flamed. The windowless room was tiled with large flagstones and had several drying racks around the room. Chairs were strategically placed beside each of the tubs, as were thick towels for drying and a soft lump of soap, which smelled faintly of thyme and rosemary. They seemed to have thought of everything.

As soon as the door closed, William and Robert took off their packs and began removing their soaked, wet or slightly damp clothes, depending on the layer. "I am grateful you suggested I wear my boots today. They may not be the most comfortable, but my mostly dry feet thank you." His tutor smiled and nodded but didn't answer. A few moments later their cloaks, hoods, tunics, leggings, stockings and other items were hanging on the racks to dry and they were each wrapped up in a large thick blanket, awaiting the rocks.

Even though William had never been to a public bath before, he had heard of them and knew that the rocks were heated in a fire until red-hot. They were then dropped into the bath water to heat it and produce a tremendous amount of steam. He was looking forward to the hot water and to clean away the dirt and grime of the last several days.

"Are you all right?" While they waited, William had been watching Robert and noticed him slowly lowering himself onto a chair beside his tub. He groaned a bit as he did so.

"Aye, William, I am. Thank you for asking. The cold and wet have entered my bones and I feel stiff like an old gate in winter that is all; nothing a hot bath will not fix." He smiled to reassure his young student, but his eyes betrayed him.

"How long have you served our family?" William wanted to ask him how old he was, but didn't think that was an appropriate question.

"I was your age ten years before your father was the same. It was at that time I came to work with my father at Crandor Castle. He had tutored your grandfather and his father as well. As you heard me tell the group of pilgrims, my family has served yours for a very long time."

"Do you ever wonder what life would have been like if things had been different?"

Robert paused before answering. He turned his head staring into the fire for a long moment then took in and let out a deep breath. "Do you mean, do I ever think about the life which could have been, had my family still held the lands and titles they had before they were conquered by William of Normandy?" Robert had turned to face William as he answered and the young boy found he had a hard time meeting Robert's eyes, but he slowly did and then quickly nodded.

"There was a time, when I was younger, when it filled my thoughts. I struggled with anger and regret and frustration. My father saw all these and he was wise enough to guess at their source. He had felt the same way at one time, as I came to realize later. Eventually he took me aside and confirmed his suspicions. It was then he taught me one of the most important lessons I have ever learned in my entire life. To this day, I have not forgotten what he told me." Robert leaned forward, his elbows on his knees, his head slightly bowed.

William pulled his chair around to the other side of his tub, in order to be closer to his tutor and sat down leaning forward; nearly mimicking the position Robert had taken. "Will you share with me what your father taught you?"

Robert nodded and when he answered his voice was deeper and fuller. William guessed this was what his tutor's father had sounded like or at least what the memory of his voice was like. "Rob, my lad, you must learn to live a life of no regrets. You must not let anger and frustration rule your day. Men have wasted their entire lives, losing any joy they may have had along the way, wishing and hoping for what might have been. Be willing to thank God for what you have been given and be humble enough to say to Him, 'Your will be done Lord, nothing more, nothing less, nothing else, at any cost.' It was the hardest thing for me to hear, but it was the right thing for him to say." He paused a moment, then added, "It took time for me to accept it and an even longer time to learn how to live by it."

"And since that lesson?"

"I have no regrets, William. I have been blessed to share in the lives of a wonderful family, teaching and learning from two generations of good men. I have also had the opportunity to travel and study and to see things, which I may never have had the chance to see, if my life had been different. No, I have no regrets, and anger and frustration are no longer a part of my character."

"When you decided to accept his advice, did you try not to be frustrated and angry, or did you start at the beginning and work on changing the way you thought?"

Now Robert leaned back in his chair, folding his arms across his chest and smiled a great, big, toothsome smile. "Well now, someone is paying attention." He paused and chuckled and his eyes sparkled in appreciation. "Well done, William. Well done. And no, I did not work on changing the way I thought. I had not read and studied enough at that time in my life to have learned that particular lesson. You have now been taught it years before I came across it."

A knock at the door interrupted their conversation. In an effort to get to the door quickly, William nearly knocked over his chair. Agnes was there, wearing thick woolen gloves and holding a large black iron pot with a heavy lid. A pair of tongs was stuck in her belt. He quickly backpedaled, allowing her room to cross to the fireplace and hang the pot on a swinging arm, which William hadn't noticed until then. Slowly she removed the lid and set it on the hearthstones. Inside, William could see the red glow of extremely hot rocks. Each was about the size of his two fists together. Over the course of the next few minutes she carefully transferred the rocks from the pot to the two tubs until the room was filled with steam and the water in each felt just right. After resetting the lid, she swung the pot over the fire. All this she did without speaking, while William and Robert were content to watch her work.

"If there is nothing else, sirs, I will be… oh dear Lord, your arm!" She had crossed back to the door and was just about to leave when she noticed the bloody bandage on Williams left arm. Without even thinking, William reached over and touched it, then winced in pain. "That bandage should be removed and cleaned." She paused a moment in thought, then added, "We have something in our pantry that will help the healing. I will return with it in a little while. Until then, please, both of you enjoy the bath. And you sir," and here she turned directly to William, "pay close attention to washing that wound." She dipped her head to both and in a swirl of cloth, spun and left the room. William stood motionless, lost in thought for a moment, until he heard Robert lower himself into his tub with a huge sigh of utter contentment. A moment later, his bandage removed, he too entered the steaming water of his own bath.

•••

Blissful moments drifted along with the steam in the room. The fire continued to blaze and the warmth of the water and the room finally began to seep deep into their bones. Several times William heard Robert heave a deep, self-satisfied sigh as they both set about scrubbing themselves with the soap. The only other sound was the occasional drip of water falling from their hanging, slightly steamy clothes, as it hit and sizzled on the flagstones near the fire where they had moved the racks in order to dry the garments more quickly.

William's earlier impression of the soap was correct. Not only was it scented, but it contained pieces of the herbs as well, which yielded just the right amount of abrasion for scrubbing away the grit and grime of their first four days on the road. As he washed and rinsed and soaked and sighed, William began to wonder how often he would have a chance like this before he found and freed his uncle. Perhaps because of his age, it hadn't even occurred to him, not even in the darkest regions of his thoughts, he might not be able to find, let alone figure out a way to release him.

Chapter Ten

Eventually, it was time to get out and dry off. William's palms were wrinkling and the heat of the water, combined with the steam in the room, made him extremely thirsty. He looked forward to the common room, where he hoped they had decent ale he could enjoy. Just the thought of it had him licking his lips in anticipation as he vigorously rubbed himself down with the thick towel he had been provided.

He was just lacing up the hose he had pulled out of his pack when there was a knock at the door. He looked up and Robert nodded his approval. He too had slipped into his spare breeches. It would still take most of the night for their clothes to dry completely. William was pleased to find Agnes at the door with a large earthenware jar in her hands.

"My mother made this to use when we have any cuts in the kitchen. When I saw your arm, I just..." she stopped short when she looked up and her gaze met William's.

"I hope I was... um... able to clean it well enough." William stammered. For some reason, when he looked at Agnes, and her sparkling emerald eyes, he had a hard time keeping track of his thoughts. He just wanted to say 'thank you' and take a little of the mixture and be done with it. But between his heart pounding in his chest, the blood rushing in his ears, and his tongue stuck to the roof of his mouth, he found himself unhinged. Fortunately Robert came to his rescue.

"That is very kind of you miss. How much should he use?"

Agnes blinked several times and then turned slowly to face the older of the two guests. "Just two fingers worth," she explained as she took off the lid and dipped her fingers into the contents. Although the color of what came out was in no way appealing, it had a pleasant, clean fragrance. Setting the jar gently down on the floor by the door, she approached William, taking his arm in her left hand, while applying the ointment with her right. William noticed both of her hands trembled slightly. He also noticed, now that she was quite close to him, her hair smelled of ripe apples and another, altogether exotic scent he wasn't familiar with. She had to be able to hear his heart beat now, as close as she was. It was nearly deafening to him.

She finished applying the mixture and then took a small linen strip she had tucked into her belt and wrapped it around his arm, loosely covering the wound. She was gentle and tender and made sure to tie the knot just strong enough to keep it from slipping but not so tight as to hurt. Once more she looked up into his eyes and his heart skipped a beat.

Without thinking about what he was doing, William reached for her right hand, brought it up to his lips. He brushed it gently then let her hand drop down at her side. She stared at him wide eyed as he murmured, "thank you for the kindness. I will not forget it." Almost as if retreating, she stepped back away from him, collected the jar from the floor and left the room without a word.

A moment passed and then Robert spoke. "It was a chivalrous deed you did, William. She will likely never forget it."

As if coming out of a spell, William blinked rapidly and took in a deep breath. "I have to admit, for a second my thoughts were in no way tied to chivalry. I have not felt that way before. It was as if I had no control over my actions. My thoughts are still spinning. My God, my chest feels like my heart is going to burst from it."

"The presence of a beautiful woman, no matter what station in life she holds, can have that effect on a man, William. Consider it part of a rite of passage from youth to manhood." He placed his hand on William's shoulder, as he had done hundreds of times before during his lessons, just to make sure he had his young students' attention.

"Always remember, William. Every woman you meet is someone's daughter or sister or niece or even mother. If you would not want someone to think those thoughts about your daughter (If God blesses you with one) or your mother (God rest her soul) or your wife (all in due time), then you had best not think those thoughts of the woman you are with or even one you meet by chance. At least not until you are sure to be married." With this last statement he added a smile and a twinkle in his eye and then turned to finish getting dressed.

It took William longer than usual because, at first he had a hard time keeping his hands from shaking. Finally, in disgust, he shook his hands hard, wiped them on his trousers and muttered to himself, "Get hold of yourself, William. She is only a girl with green eyes." That actually seemed to help.

A few minutes later they were back in their rooms. The logs in the grates were crackling and blazing and they moved their still slightly damp clothes onto a rack, which had been set up before the fire in the fore room. The bedroom, as a smaller room off to the side, was warm and inviting.

Robert sighed. "If you insist on going to the common room this evening, William, have a care. I find myself needing nothing more than a long, uninterrupted sleep." At this he turned to face his pupil, his hands on his hips, his brows brought down and together in the closest he could come to a serious scowl. "Remember your lessons. We are not traveling as ourselves, but that does not mean we should not be true to our character." His face softened and he smiled. "Enjoy a pint; tell a tale to cheer the crowd, and then find your way back here." He turned and entered the bedroom, shutting the door behind him.

William stood alone for a few moments, lost in his own thoughts. Did he really need to have an ale? Was it just because he might see Agnes again or was there another reason? He had told the landlord he would do his best to come and tell the story of his attack and the justice done on Samuel Thompson. It seemed the right thing to do to help where he could. And, of course, there was the chance he would see Agnes again.

With his mind made up, he made sure his clothes were straightened and ran his fingers through his hair. In order to pack lightly, he had been forced to leave most of his personal "non-essentials" as Robert called them, at home, including his comb. He ran his hand over his face and realized he also hadn't shaved in several days. Although it was patchy, there was still some stubble there. Shrugging his shoulders, William stepped out into the hallway, shutting the door behind him and headed to the still busy common room.

It was a strange sensation he felt as he walked down the hall. First, he noticed that his palms were sweating. He wiped them on his breeches only to realize, a moment later, they were damp again. It was then he felt his heart beating in his chest. He was having a hard time not trotting or even running down the hall. Finally he paused and stood still, his arms akimbo, shaking his head and muttering to himself. "For heaven sake, William, all this over a girl? You do not know anything about her. She is just a pretty face." He had to admit to himself that it was true. He didn't know anything about her but he was pretty sure she was interested in him as well.

"Remember what Robert told you just moments ago. She is someone's daughter and possibly a sister or niece as well. What are your intentions? Are they honorable?" Deep down, in the darkest reaches of his thoughts, there was a small voice which answered, "No."

It shocked him. Robert had said if he did nothing else to be true to his character. Was that thought part of his character or just a stray idea planted there? Before he realized what he was doing, he bowed his head and whispered, "God. Help..." He couldn't even put into words what he really wanted to say, so he added, "I am sorry God. Please help."

He started walking again. This time his heart didn't seem like it was going to burst from his chest. He walked at his normal pace and smiled, no longer feeling the desire to run. She was just a girl, after all. William was crossing the foyer and entering through the double doors of the still busy, crowded common room before he realized his hands were no longer sweating.

•••

A few moments later he found himself with an earthenware mug in hand and the first sip of a top-notch ale making its way down his throat. He had to admit it was better than he had imagined. He wasn't an expert on the product, but he did know what he liked; neither too bitter nor too sweet. Balanced was the word he was looking for and this had it. He smiled and sipped again, enjoying the warming sensation.

"I am so glad you made it, sir." It was the landlord, Baldwin, and he was just as red and still out of breath but he seemed genuinely happy to see William. Agnes was nowhere to be found. "I have to admit, I have mentioned your tale to one or two of the guests, but was not sure if you would feel up to entertaining us with the deed. It really will calm some nerves in these parts to hear what you have to tell."

"I am happy to be able to do a service for you but I have to admit myself, I have never stood before a crowd and told a tale. I am not sure exactly what to do."

"Oh, there you have nothing to fear, lad; nothing to fear. I will make an introduction and those who want to listen will and those who do not will not." He smiled reassuringly but William didn't feel reassured. "A good story is even better when told by one who experienced it. Tell them what happened in your own words and if I might make a suggestion..."

"Please do."

"Do not just state the facts. Add something of what you felt and what you were thinking. These things always make a story that much better." He smiled one more time then turned while speaking over his shoulder, "follow me."

A moment later William was standing before a large group of, mostly, interested faces. He looked at them and realized some seemed anxious; others even eager and there were some who seemed rather dark and brooding. There were two or three like this and they sat huddled together and muttered to one another as he spoke which, at first, was very distracting.

He cleared his throat, took another long gulp of his ale and plunged into his story. He had decided to tell virtually the same version he had told the Justice of the Peace, with more personal details, per the recommendation of the landlord.

"Speak up a bit, lad," shouted one of the more interested faces in the back of the room. William smiled and nodded and started again. "Two evenings back, my uncle and I found ourselves in Salisbury as guests of the White Hart Inn." He paused because there were suddenly a few guests booing and one or two who were politely clapping. Apparently some inns had reputations and followings.

"It is a fine inn, but I have found the hospitality of the Bear and Boar much more to my liking." Suddenly there were cheers and shouts. Mugs were thumping on the tables and several people stood and called out for three cheers for Baldwin. William waited patiently for the noise to die down and then he continued.

He started, hesitantly at first, but then warmed up to the task and within a few minutes had the attention of the whole room, even those few who sat huddled together, muttering and frowning. When he got to the point where the two voices spoke to him from the gloom and fog, he did his best to imitate them. He must have done well, for when he spoke Samuel's words, many of the people in the crowd shuddered. A few of them even made the sign of the cross. The rest simply shook their heads, leaning forward so as not to miss any of William's tale.

He finally wrapped up with his encounter with the Justice of the Peace of Salisbury and how hard it was to know that what he said that afternoon had sent a man to his death. "I do hope you will find the road through your town and even in the forest will be safer after all this. As for me, I find myself thinking more and more about what the Justice told me after the trial. My thoughts will determine my actions and ultimately who I become. I need to be more careful of what I think and what I say."

It took a moment for the crowd to realize he was finished, but once they did, nearly every one of them cheered and called for more ale. Several came up to William and shook his hand, introducing themselves and thanking him for his bravery. This way he met the town baker, a mason, a fuller at one of the woolen mills and a footman from Downton Manor who had the evening off and had crossed over the bridge just before the gate went up and was looking forward to crossing freely, no matter the time of day.

His mug never emptied that evening and he eventually lost count of how many he had. Someone took up a fiddle and began playing a bright, festive tune. William found himself laughing and clapping along with most of the others, especially when several of the guests started a tumbling routine to the music. The evening passed quickly but he eventually realized he needed to return to his room to rest. His arm was starting to bother him again. It was stiff and sore and itched a little.

He was passing through the crowd towards the doors, which lead to the foyer when two men came alongside him. He recognized one of them who had been muttering and frowning at the beginning of his story. "We wondered if we might have a word with you," the one on his right muttered.

"I am sorry, but I really must head back to my room. Perhaps in the morning…"

"I think we will talk this evening," said the other and William felt something sharp pressed against his lower back. His arms were grabbed in such a way if anyone happened to glance at the three of them it would appear that a few friends were helping William out of the room.

What could he do? If he called for help he would find whatever was held close pressed deep inside. They walked through the double doors and the noise inside the common room was cut off as the doors shut behind them. William's ears were ringing and he could feel his heart beating strongly in his chest. "We will just take a short walk outside and talk about our friend Samuel."

Suddenly William realized what was happening. Here were two of the recently executed highwayman's accomplices. For all he knew, one of them might even be Davey Martin. Now William's throat constricted and his hands started sweating. A few more strides and they would have him outside and all to themselves. Once again he found himself out of his room without his hunting knife. Whatever happened, he decided he wasn't going to go without a fight and balled up his fists. Just then a voice called off to his right.

"William, there you are. I have been looking all over for you." It was Agnes and she was smiling. The two men paused for just a moment and turned to the girl. William could still feel the blade at the base of his back. "Your uncle had asked me to come find you and help you back to your room. He was concerned the evening might have been too much for you." She walked right up to the three of them and then addressed the other men.

"Thank you, sirs, for helping, but his room is this way." Agnes grabbed William by the right arm and gently but firmly pulled him out of the grip of the other men. In perfect timing the doors to the common room opened and several men and a few women came into the foyer, laughing and talking loudly. Both men stood staring darkly as they were suddenly surrounded and then caught up by the tide of the boisterous group. Agnes led William off to the right of the foyer and through a set of doors.

As soon as the doors were shut behind them, William stammered, "Miss, you have no idea how grateful I am. Those men were…"

"I know who they were and I can guess what they had in mind. For now though, hush and follow me quickly." She led them up the corridor, past a half dozen doors and then turned into one on their right, shutting it behind them. The room was dark but William could hear her throw the latch, locking them in.

"I was in the common room and watched them as they came up to you as you were leaving," Agnes whispered. Although he could barely make out her silhouette, William could hear in her voice she was as scared as he was. Her voice was trembling, almost as much as his hands. He crossed his arms to keep them from shaking. "I could see in your face something was wrong and as you walked out, the glint of metal caught the light. I did not like the look of them when they came into the inn earlier today. Father felt the same way, but he has a lot on his mind all the time and things like that which are urgent are replaced by the immediate later on." Agnes had turned towards him after locking the door and stood close in order to continue speaking softly.

"I am in your debt. There is no doubt in my mind, if you had not come when you did, I would have been found in the morning, dead outside the inn. I think one of those men may have even been Davey Martin." Agnes inhaled sharply and William shuddered as a chill marched up and down his spine. "I should have stayed in the room tonight. Every thief between here and Southampton will know of us now and probably do all they can to slow or stop us from getting there." His legs felt suddenly weak and his head was spinning from more than just the ale he had drunk, although that didn't help at the moment. He reached out to where he thought Agnes was standing and gently grabbed her arm, steadying himself.

"I am sorry but I find myself a little unbalanced."

"You can lean on me for a moment or two more and then I will help you back to your own room." His eyes had finally adjusted to the darkness of the room. A crack around the door let in just enough light for him to make out the shadow of the young girl in front of him.

"Thank you," he whispered and took a small step forward. He was close enough to feel the material of her long shirt brush against him. Once again his heart thundered in his chest and pounded in his ears as she moved just a little closer. "I am in your debt. Somehow, some day I will find a way to repay it." He put as much sincerity as he could in what he said and he meant every word of it. "That was a very brave thing you just did…"

"You were very kind to me earlier," she murmured, her voice now a little louder but still unsteady. He heard the latch on the door and then a second later the knob turned and light flooded into the room. Agnes looked up and down the hall before motioning for William to follow. She took him back to the foyer through the doors, which led down another corridor, and eventually to the door of his room.

As she turned to leave him at his room, he grabbed her hand and she turned back to face him with a look of expectation on her face. "Thank you again. I will not forget this." William smiled and for just a brief second he thought he saw a slight hurt on Agnes' face but then she smiled too and did him a courtesy. As she stood back up he brought her hand to his lips and kissed it just as he had done earlier in the bathroom. Her palms were rough from the work she did for her father, but the back of her hand was soft. He held it to his lips for a moment and then let her hand drop to her side. "Good night, Agnes." William turned and entered his room, shutting and latching the door behind him. She briefly stood in the hall and then smiled when she realized he had called her by her first name. She quickly headed back to the common room to help her father begin cleaning up.

William stood for a moment in the room. The fire had died down and was now only dark red coals and ashes in the grate. His heart was pounding and he had to take several deep breaths, letting them out slowly to regain control of his emotions. He had gone from being kidnapped, nearly murdered and then saved by a very pretty young girl all within a matter of moments and the realization was beginning to hit him.

"Why not kiss her?" the voice in his head asked. *"You know you wanted to and she wanted you to also."*

"You are probably right but that does not make it right. In the end, I have to be true to my character."

"You do not even know what that is."

"Maybe not all of it, but this one thing I do know; whatever I do to the least of these, that I do unto Him. I will not take advantage of the emotions of the moment in order to have my way with someone. That is definitely not part of my character."

When the voice didn't answer, William smiled and then added, "thank You, God for giving me strength I needed just now to do what was right and not what I wanted to do and the wisdom to know the difference." A moment later he had slipped under the covers of his bed and quickly fell asleep, the last sound he heard was the gentle rumbling of Roberts' snoring.

Chapter Eleven

As far as William was concerned, morning came too early. Robert shook his shoulder a second time. "William, wake up. We need to leave soon if we are to make it through the forest today." His eyelids felt leaden and his eyes seemed filled with gravel. His legs were having a difficult time finding their way out of the covers and he didn't want to think about what might have died in his mouth to make it taste the way it did.

"Mm… up," he mumbled as he swung his feet onto the floor and unsteadily stood up. "I do not believe going to the common room was the best idea last night." He found his way over to a basin of water and spluttered and huffed as he splashed water in his face. It was cold and really helped get him one step closer to fully awake.

"Why would you say that?" Robert asked, and then added, "Besides the obvious physical effects." He had already changed back into the previously rain-soaked clothes, which seemed to have had enough time to dry, and had his pack slung over his shoulders. A mischievous grin brightened his face.

"I am willing to accept the results of one too many ales, but what I was not counting on was Davey Martin and one of his accomplices being in the room last night." Roberts grin dropped away. "Needless to say, they were very interested in taking me for a walk afterwards."

"How did you manage...?"

"Agnes rescued me; she was brilliant," he added quickly when he saw the reaction on Roberts' face. "She saw the two of them grab me, in a not too friendly way, as I was trying to leave the common room. One of them had a knife in my back, which she also noticed. In the bustle of most of the others leaving at the same time, she was able to pull me away from them."

"I hope you thanked her for her bravery." Robert shook his head. There was more than just a look of amazement on his face. "I do not know if she realizes the danger she has put herself into."

"She is quite smart. When she saw the men approach me, she recognized them from having come in earlier in the day. Even then she and her father had decided they had an air about them which neither liked. As soon as they approached me and asked to go for a walk, she decided on her own they must have known or worked with Samuel Thompson. When she came up to them she said she was on an errand from you to bring me back to our room. I do not believe they will suspect her."

Robert nodded and let out a deep breath. "Thank God," he said with a very slight smile and then he turned serious again. "Even though we are still in England, our road has now become even more dangerous."

William had retrieved his own dried clothes, finished putting them on, and was just about done folding and filling his pack, when Robert made this statement. "How could it get even more dangerous than it already has been?" After all he had nearly been assaulted twice and both times had a knife in his back. He thought he was lucky to still be alive.

"Davey Martin and his friends will not stop after last night. My guess is they will be waiting for us somewhere along the road through the forest. Word will travel fast in such a small village and I would imagine most people already know we head to Southampton. Our path leads through the Forest, there is no other way."

William set his pack down and lowered his head. "Now I really wish I had stayed in the room last night." He wasn't sure if the churning of his stomach was from the pints of ale or from the realization he had put both their lives in even more jeopardy, just because, deep down, he had hoped to see a girl again.

Robert crossed the sitting room and put his hand on William's shoulder. "There is a bright side to this, William. There always is."

"If there is, I do not see it."

"You are not looking hard enough. Whatever is meant for harm, God can always turn around for good. I have no doubt of that." His grip tightened and William met his eyes. He was standing close enough to see they weren't completely blue but had flecks of brown and green in them as well. "Think hard. What possible benefit would it be to us, knowing that Davey Martin knows who we are and which direction we are traveling?"

William stared into his tutor's eyes and was lost in thought for a moment. He took a deep breath and then it hit him. Smiling slightly he answered, "Since we know he knows who we are, we can be more cautious on the road. It will mean going slower but we can stay in the heaths and near the bogs and away from the dense patches of trees."

Robert smiled back and thumped him hard between the shoulder blades. "Excellent, William, now you are using that head of yours for something besides a cap rack." He chuckled at his own joke then turned more serious. "It had been my intention to take the quickest, most direct route to Southampton and travel as fast as we were able. Now I see we will need to make some adjustments." He paused, scratching his chin in thought, and then added, "It is always easier to avoid a trap when you know it is there before hand, agreed?" He smiled again and led them out of the room, down the hall to the foyer, and out into the early dawn light.

Although the sun was still just below the horizon, it looked to be the perfect spring day. The chill and slight dampness in the air was invigorating and helped clear William's still foggy head. He took in a deep breath and let it out slowly, watching as the steam from his breath was caught by the slight breeze and carried away from him.

Crossing back over the bridge was much easier than the night before. The gate was already pushed to the side and there was no sign of Richard the gatekeeper. Although much of the village was still asleep a few men were making their way down to the mills. Those they passed hardly acknowledged them except for an occasional nod of the head or grunt.

To the south of the town, spread out before William and Robert, was the New Forest. Here in the spring time stretched heath and moor, blazing gold from the extent of gorse and furze. Nowhere in England could rival the lichen draped oak-woods and the groves of beech trees, the branches of both so woven together they created an intricate pattern of light and shade on the forest floor of red and brown leaves. This was forested land, protected for the King himself. None had leave to hunt within its territory without Edward's consent. Sections were set aside for grazing of livestock but the majority was as wild as it had been since time out of memory.

The farther from Downton and the closer they got to the New Forest, the more William thought about his great grandfather's great grandfather, Thomas Simpson. He had gone hunting with some of the King's own family and never returned home. Did he have any idea what might happen to him that day? For that matter, did his father know he would die that day at Neville's Cross, or Robert Keith? So deep was he in thought, William hadn't noticed they had left the main road and struck off on a slightly narrower track to the left.

Soon they found themselves in rolling hills covered in golden colored gorse. The ground rose and fell in gentle waves and at the trough of each there were stretches of standing brown water where the heath became more like a bog. The stench of rotting moss and plants was almost overpowering in these little valleys. William was glad they were traveling in early spring and not later in the summer when the heat would probably make the stench even stronger. It was no wonder few people lived in this area.

As they approached the top of the next hill a sound came to them in the breeze, which caused them to slow and then stop all together. It was the sound of several voices. They couldn't make out what was being said but, there was at least one woman shouting, several children crying, and the rough laughter of more than one man.

Robert motioned to keep silent and drop to the ground. Without hesitating William was on his chest in the rough furze just to the left of the path. The short, dense shrubs had sharp needles, which scratched his hands and arms but he bit back a curse as the shrieks, cries and laughter grew louder. He mimicked Robert, who was on the opposite side of the path, as he shrugged off his pack and crawled from bush to bush moving toward the top of the hill.

The effort to remain concealed while getting to a proper vantage point paid off after an interminable minute of crawling and pausing. What he saw caught William's breath and he had to swallow back a rush of bile, which burned its way up his throat.

About twenty feet below the crest of the hill, just to the right of the road, was a small handcart, turned on its side. Its contents, which seemed to include nothing more than some clothes and dried turnips, carrots and cabbages was scattered around it. Huddled together were two small girls, the youngest of which was crying the loudest. Another girl, just a year or two younger than William, was being held to the ground by a skinny, dark haired man. From the look on his face he had other thoughts than just keeping her quiet. One hand covered her mouth while the other frantically worked on loosening his trousers. The girl was trying desperately to kick and beat him off but she was no match for his size.

William immediately recognized him as being one of the two men who tried to escort him out of the Bear and Boar the night before. He felt fear paralyze him. He grabbed the bush in front of him; completely ignoring the bloody cuts the needles made in his palms. A few seconds later he found the skinny man's partner, or at least who he thought might be his partner. A pair of legs, with pants down around the ankles was just visible on the other side of the cart. It was from here the shrieks and laughter were the loudest.

"Shut your mouth, or your children will never see their mother alive again," shouted the voice from behind the cart. The shrieks instantly turned to sobbing.

"Oh God… help! Help us!" was the woman's hoarse plea.

"Shout to God all you want, He cares less and He will not come to help." The voice and laugh that followed turned something over in William's mind. His heart was hammering in his chest and thundering in his ears but he hardly noticed. All he could think about was stopping this from happening. He stood up and ran over the top and down the side of the hill. He found himself several paces behind his teacher.

Robert had wasted no time in watching what was taking place. One quick glance told him all he needed to know. He began crawling, keeping himself hidden in the bushes as best he could until he was only a half dozen feet from the cart. Even as William realized he had to do something, Robert rose up, taking a few leaping strides towards the skinny man and the young girl. William could see in his hand the glint of the early morning sun off the blade of the hunting knife he always carried.

The man had his back to Robert and never saw him coming. The last thing the attacker felt was a tug on the hair at the back of his head and a sharp point on the side of his throat. William got to him just as he slumped forward and dragged him off the girl, letting him lie face down in the gorse on the side of the road. His body twitched a few times amid the sound of gurgling and then ceased moving all together.

The young girl sat up, staring at William. She hardly realized what had happened but was panting and had a wild look in her eyes. A second later the two younger girls ran over and threw their arms around her neck. Tears welled up in their older sister's eyes and she broke down sobbing.

William slowly stepped toward her, then knelt down at her side, patting her on the shoulder, "it will be all right, we are here to help," he hoarsely whispered then turned and hurried around the side of the cart to find the other man having met the same fate as his partner. Robert had dragged him off the side of the road as well. It was such a strange sight as he lay there face down, his pants still down around his ankles.

"Are you all right? Did he hurt you?" William asked the young mother. One cheek was puffy and already turning a deep shade of purple and her lower lip was split and bloodied. Her blond hair was a mess of tangles and furze needles and her skirt was still pushed half way up her thighs. She was staring at him with a wild look in her eyes and her hands were shaking uncontrollably so that she couldn't grab the hem to pull it down.

"The children are not injured," Robert told her, taking a knee beside her. William noticed his hands were blood stained and shaking too. "Steady yourself. You are safe now. Those men will not try to hurt you or your family ever again." His voice was softer than usual but it had a strong, calming and reassuring quality to it. Without taking his eyes from hers, he gently grasped the hem of her skirt, straightening and smoothing it out.

What happened suddenly occurred to William. He had just watched his tutor, the man who had been his teacher for over a year, single-handedly take the life of two men. These were the same two men who had threatened him the night before, and quite possibly, one of the two who tried to assault him in Salisbury. He took his eyes off the mother for a moment to look closely at Robert.

"Where did you learn to do that?" Robert acted like he didn't hear the question.

The battered and bruised woman put her hands up to her face and began sobbing. A moment later the girls came around the cart and tears of joy replaced those of fear as the four of them sat huddled together, arms interlocked, rocking back and forth. The mother looked up, eyes closed with a slightly bloodied smile and murmured, "thank You God for sending us these angels."

"William, help me get the cart set back up and loaded," Robert whispered. The two of them withdrew and a few minutes later had the cart righted and all the contents put back in place.

"Why are there men in this world who believe what happened here is all right?" William asked as they were picking up the clothes and a few blankets. "I cannot imagine even thinking about doing what they did. Does God even care that this woman and the girl could have been violated or even killed?"

"Of course He cares, William. He did not send these men to do what they tried to do, no more than He sent Samuel and Davey to harm you. We live in a world stuck in the middle William, with heaven above and hell below." Robert had gathered an armful of beets and carrots and was depositing them into the cart next to a pile of cabbages William had placed there.

"I do not understand..."

"God has named it a fallen world in which we live, William." Robert paused in packing the cart, his head bowed and eyes closed. "Evil surrounds us and tries to affect our decisions and distract us every day."

"Distract us from what?"

"From our walk with God; from a personal relationship with our creator." Robert raised his head and looked directly into William's eyes. There was a seriousness, which his young pupil had only seen on a few occasions. "Understand this, William, the enemy of God comes to lie, kill and destroy lives, but when he comes, it is quietly, smoothly. He comes into your thoughts, planting seeds of doubt, despair, anger, jealousy, envy, self-centeredness, rudeness, and evil. Remember what the Justice of the Peace told you about Samuel and his thoughts?"

William nervously looked about then cast his eyes down at his feet, "I do not know if I can stay vigilant all the time. I do not know if I can keep a check on all of my thoughts all the time." He sighed and shook his head, "sometimes it feels like God expects the impossible from us."

"He will never expect more from you than you can handle, William." Robert grabbed his young pupil by the shoulder, his grip just hard enough to get his undivided attention. William stared at the dried blood-stained hand. "Remember, He knew you even before you were formed in your mother's womb. He knows how much you can take." Robert paused and took a deep breath, letting it out slowly. "The biggest challenge, for all of us, is trusting God to know how much we can handle and remaining humble enough to always ask Him for His help in dealing with our problems. As soon as you think you can handle it on your own, that is when serious trouble steps in."

"Do you think God knew this was going to happen today?"

"I do not believe God is ever surprised, William."

"Then how could He let it happen?"

It was a long moment before Robert answered. "There is love in this world because God gave us the free will to choose to love. It is this very same free will, which allows some men to do evil things. Evil men exist and bad things happen because God wanted us to be able to choose to love Him and each other. He wanted each one of us to be able to decide this, to make it our choice, to seek Him out on our own. Without this freedom to choose, there would be no evil but there would also be no love. Did you ever consider, William, that this took place, here, now, because God knew we were coming down this road?"

William looked back up to the top of the small hill, which just moments before they had both peered over. "It is more than God just wanting us to save them, is it not?" There was a thought, which was just touching the edge of Williams mind, but he was having a hard time grasping hold of it.

Robert paused a moment and shut his eyes. "A mile back we came to a fork in the road and I took the left. We should have taken the right. It was the shorter distance to Southampton. There was no reason for us to use the left, but I felt, inside, that we had to. William, we were meant to come this way at this very moment, to do what needed to be done."

William looked over at the mother and daughters, several yards away, still holding each other, still sobbing and still thanking God. "We were not just meant to save them," he began speaking his thought out loud. A small light began to flicker in his mind and he grabbed hold of it. "There is something more we need to do. Do you think we should take them with us, or should we go with them, to see them safe to their destination?"

Robert paused a moment to consider the suggestion then shook his head, "that decision will not be up to us, William. We will honor God with our offer to help, but these women will need to decide if they want our company."

"Surely they will see the need…"

"William, you do not understand what they just went through. It may be a very long time before they trust another man, especially a stranger."

"But if we had not come when we did…"

"We were meant to be here, William, that is true and I have no doubt about it. God meant for us to be here to stop this from happening. I have asked Him to forgive me for the way I handled it though. I do not think that was what He had in mind."

"Can He forgive even this?"

"There is no sin, William, which is so big that God is not willing to forgive it, if and only if, you seriously ask for His forgiveness and you are honestly sorry for what you have done. I think you understand, William, after the results of the trial yesterday, you would do all you could to change its results. I feel the same way but I do not know how I could have acted differently. Now it is done and I have committed murder to save the lives of at least two innocents. Until I stand before Him, I will not know if there would have been a different choice to make. For now, I must live with my decision and find some peace in knowing that God will not hold this against me after asking for His forgiveness."

"What about my father and uncle and others who have gone to war and killed?" He hadn't thought of this until now. Before his father was killed in the battle of Neville's Cross, William had often dreamed of riding off to war. After his mother died of grief he didn't often think of going to battle, even after his uncle left for France. Did his father ask God to forgive him for what he did, before he was killed? He didn't want to think that his father wasn't in heaven waiting for him.

"Always remember this, William. A king or a lord or a leader of an army may order or ask any man to do something like we did today, but it is that man's responsibility to care for his own soul. If you are ever presented with an order or request, which you feel violates God's teachings, remember what I have said here today. You will not be able to try to explain to God that you did what you did because someone told you to. Your soul is your own responsibility, just as your actions are your own decision."

For a moment they stood, side by side, each in their own thoughts. William's mind continued to swirl around the idea he was God's instrument in this world. He didn't feel worthy. Finally, Robert spoke up, "we should move the bodies farther away from the road. We can bury them in that small grove of trees." He nodded to a tightly packed group of beech trees fifty or so feet to their right. As an afterthought he added, "And I need to wash my hands."

A few minutes later they had dragged both of the men into the trees. After some searching they had found a couple dozen small and medium sized stones and did their best to pile them up over the bodies. "Why should we take the time to do this for these men?" William asked. This didn't make any sense. They threatened him last night. One might have threatened him in Salisbury. They had tried to have their way with a woman and her daughter. These men weren't just bad they were evil.

"As hard as this is to understand, William, it is not right to bless and thank God for all He has done and is going to do in your life and then turn around and curse somebody else, who was also created in the image of God. These men died un-repented sinners, but they are still children of God and deserve this." Robert set the last stone down, bowed his head and his lips moved silently for a moment. William couldn't think of anything he could say which wasn't spiteful. The best he could come up with was, "God forgive them." Robert walked over to a small creek, of fresh looking water, in order to wash and scrape the dried gore off his hands and from under his fingernails.

As William stopped to consider what his tutor had just said and did, a horse whinnied nearby. A second later it sounded like another may have answered. Both came from farther inside the grove of trees.

Robert heard them as well. He motioned William to keep silent as he made his way back to his side. Once together, the two of them slowly began picking their way through the underbrush. Each step crushed dried red and brown leaves beneath their boots and the sound seemed amplified in their ears. William's heart was beating so hard he could feel his chest throbbing. The trees were growing so closely together they couldn't see more than a few feet in front of them, and they were far enough inside the interlocking canopy of branches overhead shaded all sunlight. It felt to William as though he was making his way deeper and deeper into a dark tomb.

They had been cautiously moving forward for a few minutes when they suddenly heard the stamping of hooves on the soft ground and a horse's snort. Both froze in mid step as seconds crept by. William was sure there were dozens of pairs of eyes trained on him; hidden eyes, concealed in the dense set of trees and thick underbrush. Robert motioned with his head and they took another half dozen steps forward.

Suddenly William found himself looking at a wide-open space within the center of the grove. Two horses had been hobbled here; however one had broken his lines and was grazing on the far side of the circle. A small ring of stones in the center of the clearing contained a smoldering fire, which gave off only the slightest amount of smoke. The mare closest to them looked up, while still munching the grass in her mouth. William guessed her to be a small rouncey, probably used as a packhorse. She was shaggy with her winter coat, but appeared to be fairly well taken care of, with trimmed hooves and a brushed out mane and tail. The mare snorted at them then turned her attention back to the grass around her. Close beside her sat an odd assortment of sacks, tack, and a beautiful, well-oiled saddle.

The horse on the other side of the clearing was completely different from the little mare before them. Although more than twenty feet away, William could clearly see it stood much taller, with longer, more muscular legs. It tossed its head upon an arched neck and whinnied when it saw them. A few seconds later the stallion trotted up to them, then stopped short, as if sensing they weren't whom he expected.

He was jet-black and gleaming. His winter coat had been brushed out and his mane trimmed short. His nostrils flared and he stamped at the ground before them with an iron-shod hoof, his ears only slightly set back. Despite his height and power, he wasn't a heavy warhorse, but one of the lighter coursers. He was strong enough to carry a man, lightly armed, into battle, or conditioned to travel twenty or more miles in a day if less encumbered.

William could sense the stallion's hesitation, but it was Robert who made the first move. Slowly reaching forward, with his hands extended, palms up, his tutor began murmuring soothing sounds without any real meaning. He took a step forward and paused, only moving again when he was sure the powerful beast was willing to accept his advance. A few more steps and he had hold of the rope halter and gently stroked the beautifully arched neck while gazing deep into the dark brown eyes.

"William, hold the halter while I untie the hobbles."

"I do not think we should linger here very long. We have already left the women alone for quite some time," William responded even as he did what Robert asked. He didn't like to think of the two of them getting caught in this camp either.

"I agree. We will get them both untied and then saddle this one and load the packs on the other and lead them back to the wagon."

A few minutes later both horses were released from their hobbles and the black stallion was saddled and bridled. William had cinched the pack on the mare, which stood placidly waiting to be loaded down. The first two bags contained some bread, a smelly chunk of cheese and a several sets of cloaks and clothes. The next one, however, was much heavier.

"Dear God, will you look at this?" William had opened the sack when he tried to lift it, only to realize it was much heavier than the others. Inside were rings, coins, bracelets, and brooches. He had never seen so much silver and gold in one place. The sack must have contained the spoils of several years' worth of preying upon those who passed too close to Davey Martin, Samuel Thompson, and their skinny friend.

"When you are hasty to be rich at any cost you shall not go unpunished," Robert murmured looking over Williams shoulder.

"This was Davey and Samuel's plunder was it not?"

"That would be my guess, William."

"Do you think there is enough here to free my uncle?" The gold and silver sparkled in the early morning light and William found himself mesmerized by it all.

"I think there is more than enough there… if that is what we are to do with this," Robert cautiously answered.

"What else would you suggest we do with it? We should not just leave it here." After speaking in hushed tones for the last several minutes, William's voice rose a little louder and it had an anxious tone to it.

"I am not suggesting we leave it William, however, there may be other uses for this and other reasons we came across it."

William paused for a moment to consider. A little thought had entered his head and he began rolling it around. Without even realizing it, he spoke his thought out loud; his voice sounded a little strained and tensely pitched. "After all I have been through the last few days; maybe this is a reward from God… I think I should keep it."

"Knowing we had this with us would make our task much easier, William, of that I have no doubt…"

William picked up on his tutor's hesitation. "You do not think I should keep this, do you? What do you suggest we do with it then?"

"There may be others whose needs are greater still…"

"After all I have been through the last three days, not to mention what my uncle is going through right now, you are suggesting we give this away?" William's voice rose up another notch and the mare shied to the left, picking up on the intensity of his words.

"I believe there is blood on this, William. We should be absolutely certain we are doing the right thing with it and using it for good. To do otherwise could encourage evil to join us."

"This is gold and silver, nothing more," William muttered, but his eyes betrayed him. Already it was playing on his mind. Already he was trying to calculate how many florins were in the sack, and if there would be any left over for himself after he set aside what he needed for his uncle.

"William," his tutor began firmly, "set the sack down for a moment."

His young pupil looked up at him accusingly and for a long moment they stood there, face to face, the younger glaring, the older with soft care in his eyes and peace on his face. A battle raged behind William's eyes. His mind was racing with conflicting thoughts. Suddenly, into the mix, a quiet voice entered. It sounded a little like the Justice of the Peace at Salisbury. "Samuel's life followed his thoughts. Be careful to guard your own."

It was like lightning arcing across his vision. He immediately dropped the sack and stepped away from it, shaking his head to clear it. When he looked up, Robert was watching him closely, a concerned look on his face. Seconds later it softened and he smiled. "Well done, William, well done."

"My thoughts were so dark…and they came so suddenly." He wiped his face and rubbed his eyes.

"You were serving your own desires, William."

"Yes… yes I was." He nodded, his eyes downcast. How could those thoughts have attached themselves to him so quickly? "I found myself arguing over why I should keep it and how much I would still have left after getting my uncle free." He shook his head again, but the thoughts hadn't returned. "I cannot believe how fast that happened."

"You cannot serve two masters, William. You will either love one and hate the other or stand by one and despise the other. You cannot serve God and the desires of deceitful riches."

"But I could use this to set my uncle free." His voice was quiet now and there was just a touch of a plea in it.

"Yes, William, you could but you should not be anxious towards that end. Trust God and rid your thoughts of all worry. When has worry or being anxious ever added a moment to anyone's life?" Robert paused a moment and looked around the open space and the tightly packed trees lining it. "Look at these birds, William." He pointed to the larks and warblers who were all singing in the early morning sun. "They do not sow nor do they reap nor do they gather into barns, yet God keeps feeding them. Are you not worth more than they?"

William dropped his eyes and murmured, "I wished I knew what to do with this."

"Do not worry, William, instead, aim and strive after God and His way of doing and being right and then all things will be given to you."

"But what about Uncle Charles?"

"We must not worry about that for now, William, it is a problem for tomorrow and tomorrow will come with its own concerns. Today we have been given an answer to today's troubles. Do you see this?"

"The sack… and the mother and her children?" William answered hesitantly at first and then the idea seemed to blossom in his mind. He could do something great with this. "We can change lives with this," he added out loud, while smiling and realizing inside how this suddenly felt like the right answer.

"First and foremost," Robert quickly added, "let us get packed and find our way out of this clearing. If either of those men had any more accomplices, we do not want to be here when they return."

William found his hands shaking as he tried to tie the sack to the harness of the mare. He closed his eyes for a brief moment and slowly exhaled a deep breath. "God, we can do some great and good things with this. Give me the wisdom to do what is right as well." It was a simple thought, coming in a flash. When he opened his eyes, William's hands were no longer shaking.

As soon as he finished tying the last strap to the harness, the mare began walking away. Even as William reached for the halter, she quickened her pace to a trot until she turned towards the tree line on her left. He was just able to get a hand on the rope as she picked her way between several trees and then struck a path. "You sure are a smart girl," William smiled and shook his head, patting the neck and scratching behind her ears. The mare blew a deep breath through her lips, as if saying "what did you expect?" William turned to see Robert several feet behind him, leading the black stallion along the same path. It seemed both horses knew their way out of the clearing.

A few minutes later found them back out in the early morning sunshine. After having been inside the densely packed grove of trees, William immediately noticed how refreshing the breeze was. As he inhaled deeply he also noticed just a hint of the sea in the air. As soon as the stallion was out of the tree line his nostrils flared and he neighed so loud William wondered if Robert's ears were ringing like his own. The little mare answered with a high whinny of her own.

From around the side of the handcart, just ahead of them, several heads and pairs of eyes appeared. "Look at the horses, mother," one of the youngest of the girls squealed with delight. Her oldest sister had a tight grip on her arm to keep her from running up to them. As it was, William and Robert were soon alongside them.

The mother stood with her oldest daughter next to her. The two younger girls had been scooped up and were each in a set of arms. The mother looked scared, the oldest looked worried but the two youngest were squirming and begging to be let down so they could pet the horses. "Hush lambs, hush," the mother admonished them. The bruise on her cheek had darkened a little more and it looked as if she had rinsed most of the blood off her split lip.

"Those men will no longer harm you or your family," Robert repeated what he had last told her.

"I have no way of repaying you for what you did," she began and tears started to well up in her eyes. "For me or for my daughter…" William could see her hands were still shaking and emotion choked her voice.

"We did what we felt had to be done at the moment," Robert stated, and then added, "Does your husband await you at the end of your journey?"

She shook her head and all four pairs of eyes looked down. "He was killed in France at St. Omer. We found out earlier in the winter, but were waiting for better weather before we set out. I have family in Dorchester…"

"St. Omer? That is where…"

"William…" Robert stopped him from completing the sentence and placed his hand on his young pupils shoulder. "What will you do when you find your family in Dorchester?"

"My aunt lives there. She works for the household of the Earl of Dorchester, as a housekeeper. I was going to apply to his lordship to work, in exchange for a small room for the four of us."

"I am going to work too," the oldest daughter stated. Her chin was held high and a look of defiance, as if she dared either of them to suggest she could or would do otherwise, was set on her face. For the first time, William noticed her bright blue eyes, which sparkled in the early morning sun. She was nearly as tall as he and yet seemed, in some way older or at least more mature. There was no doubt in his mind that she would and could work very hard and yet there was still a young girl's tenderness there. Part of him wanted to encourage her and yet part of him felt intimidated. Here was soon to be a very strong woman and yet, she was still like a flower, just before spring, not yet ready to fully bloom.

William and Robert looked at each other and nodded knowingly. Despite the oldest daughters impact on William or better yet, because of it, he knew what needed to be done. God really did mean for them to be here, on this road, at this time. What they had to do was clear and it was right and it was a good and great thing too.

"Take what you need off the cart and lash it to the harness of this mare," William began, handing the rope halter to the mother.

"Her masters no longer need her service," Robert added as the mother started to silently protest, shaking her head.

"When you get to Downton, go to the Bear and Boar Inn," William continued. "The landlord's daughter, Agnes, will take good care of you. You will be able to bathe and change clothes and share a good meal. Make sure you tell Agnes that William sent you to her. If you are up to it, you may share what happened with her and her father, but I would steer clear of the common room," he added.

"I have nothing to pay… no way of…" she completely choked up now and both William and Robert could see disbelief growing in her eyes.

"The wealth of a sinner will eventually find its way into the hands of the righteous for whom it was set aside," Robert quoted as William loosed one of the sacks and pulled out a gold coin, setting it in her hand. The mother and her oldest daughter's eyes grew huge. The two little ones were still too interested in getting down and petting the horse to pay any attention to what their mother was holding.

"There is more in here," Robert continued. "It is yours to use as you choose, but remember where it came from. Men and women who were not as fortunate as you once owned some of these treasures. It would be best not to show it to any others but keep it close to yourself. Use what you need to help you on your way to Dorchester. Once there, find your aunt and tell her what happened. She will know what to do."

"How…? What can I…? I do not even know who you are." She stammered through tears of shock and disbelief.

"We are Robert and William, of Dorchester. That is all we can say for now. Perhaps, if God wills it, we will see each other again. But for now, we must part here, for our road lies to the south." While Robert told her this, William had taken the few sacks out of the cart and tied them to the mares pack harness. She shook her mane and snorted, but otherwise showed no sign of the slightly increased burden she bore. A moment later he returned from the top of the hill with their own packs, which they had left on the side of the road only a short while before.

"You will travel faster without the cart and the little mare can easily carry your two youngest," Robert explained. He reminded her of the Bear and Boar and of Agnes and to let no one know of the treasure they carried with them. "Go quickly and quietly and may God grant you safe travel to Dorchester."

Tears continued to stream down the mother's face as she looked up to the young and older man before her. William could see in her eyes and her face the desire to do and say more than she had, but there was something still buried deep down inside. After today, it would be a very long time before she would completely open herself up to a man. Such as it was, she reached out with a trembling hand and gently touched each on the cheek, "God bless you both and may His face shine upon you and be gracious."

Robert bowed his head and murmured, "Amen," then turned and mounted the stallion. He reached down and offered an arm to William who pulled himself up behind his tutor. A moment later they were up and over the next rise, the abandoned cart, the mare, and the family lost from sight. The last William heard was one of the little girls asking her mother where they were going.

It was several minutes before either said anything, until Robert spoke up. By then they had trotted and cantered up and down several more hills until the land started to slowly rise up before them. "I am very proud of your decision, William. It was good and great and the right thing to do."

Robert slowed the stallion from a canter to a walk before William answered. "Thank you. I hope, in the end, we will find them safe at Crandor."

"We may yet, William. We may yet."

Chapter Twelve

The next hour they spent alternating between walking and trotting and quickly found themselves deeply surrounded by the New Forest. It was hard for William to imagine all the land before and behind him was held for the personal use of the king. They had passed beyond the rolling hills, and after a long steady rise, found themselves facing a forest of oaks, spreading as far as they could see to their right and left. If it hadn't been for their encounter earlier that morning, William would have shuddered with dread having to enter into the deep shadows of the lichen draped oak canopy. As it was, he surprised himself by almost smiling as they crossed out of the sunlight and into the quickly deepening gloom.

One of the first things William noticed on entering the woods was the dampened sound of the hoof falls of their horse. Their courser seemed to notice the difference too and tossed his head after taking in a deep breath and snorting. The path didn't run straight through the trees, but instead tended to switch back on itself, winding its way around extremely large boles or dipping into small ravines, which seemed to open up before them, with steep, sometimes slippery sides and small creeks at the bottom.

In these valleys the air took on a dense closeness and all the other sounds of the forest seemed to become even more muted.

Each time they rode back up one of these steep sided ravines William breathed easier. After the fourth one in quick succession, he asked his tutor, "how far will we need… to travel through this wood?" He tried his best to control the emotion in his voice but surprised himself when it broke in mid-sentence.

"From Downton to the walls of Southampton would have been a long day walk for us, William. Even with the delay, being able to ride will quicken our pace but we still may not get there before nightfall. As far as this wood," Robert looked around and shrugged his shoulders, "it is the first time I have been through it."

"I wonder if the air ever moves in here."

Robert nodded, "it does feel close. I doubt if much has changed in this wood since William's army took the hill at Hastings."

"Was any of my family there?" The mere mention of that fateful battle sparked an interest in William. He often was told he was named after that distant, victorious, and long passed relative.

"Most surely Thomas Simpson was there, as he was a cousin of the Duke of Normandy. He would have been in the cavalry which charged the shield wall on that hill…"

William paused a moment, unsure if he should ask the next question, then curiosity got the better of him. "Were any of your family there?"

From his vantage point behind his tutor, William couldn't see his facial expression, but he could tell Robert stiffened at this question. It was a long moment before he answered. "My family was called to the Witan when Edward died. We spoke in favor of Harold Godwinson, over the claim some made, including William of Normandy. One fell against Harald Hardraga and his army of Norsemen at Stamford Bridge.

Others of my family fell alongside their new king at Hastings, even as many in the army fled into the forest behind. In the end, one survived and it was he to whom, several years later, your great grandmother's great grandmother gave the title of Seneschal of Crandor."

"Was William's army better than Harold's? My father told me it was the heavy horse of Norman knights who took the field that day."

"It is true that Harold had no cavalry, but there was one other factor in play that day, which led to William's victory."

When Robert didn't quickly finish his thought, William asked, "What was it?" Robert held up his hand, even as he slowed their mount from the trot it had been doing for the last several minutes to a walk. Something had caught his attention but William couldn't tell if it was a sound or a movement. He suddenly wished he wasn't sitting behind his tutor like a piece of luggage. He rephrased his last question, whispering "what is it?"

"Listen."

William looked about and strained to pick up something out of the ordinary but only found he could hear the slow steps of the courser as its hooves crushed the dried and decaying leaves on the path and the sudden drumming of his heart in his ears. "I do not hear anything," he whispered in return.

Robert nodded in agreement. "Exactly, William; what happened to the bird song and squirrel chatter?"

"Did we cause them to stop?"

"No, William, our intrusion on their world had not disturbed them, they just now suddenly stopped."

"What should we do?"

Robert tugged on the reins, bringing the courser to a halt. "We will wait and we will watch." They had just come up over a small rise and the path led mostly straight ahead. It was clear and didn't appear as if anyone had traveled on it in a while. When William looked over his shoulder he didn't see anything on the path behind but he could definitely tell where they had come from. The leaves had been churned up enough to show a dark contrast to the undisturbed dried leaves around them. He could feel Robert settle down in the saddle, dropping his heels and noticed him take a slightly tighter grip of the reins.

William was wondering how long they would need to sit and watch when the baying of a great hound broke out to the far right of the path. Its deep basso howl rose and fell, both in volume and scale. Their courser laid its ears back and became skittish but Robert was ready. Seconds later there was a crashing in the underbrush and a large boar burst through and across the path. Dark brown bristles stood up along the ridge of its spine and its yellow-white tusks curved up and out of its open jaw. Their horse reared, striking at the air with its front hooves and William tumbled off, landing flat on his back. The air rushed out of his lungs and he gasped for breath as he struggled to sit up. Stars sparkled across his view and he shook his head to clear his sight.

Even as the boar disappeared to the left of the path, the first of several hounds came bounding out of the undergrowth. He was black, his coat was slick and he was huge. To William it looked like he was smiling with mouth open, tongue swollen and hanging out the side. He paused for a brief second, bent over to smell the path and then lifted his head and howled. William clapped his hands over his ears and watched as the hound bounded off in pursuit of the boar. His ears were still ringing as three more hounds followed the first.

Seconds later the sound of horses crashing through the brush was quickly followed by the shouts of men. William sat up straight as the first of a half dozen men appeared out of the dense woods and brush. The first four never broke stride as they kept their mounts in fast pursuit, but the fifth slowed just as he cleared the brush and entered the path. The rider was middle aged, with black hair streaked with silver. His beard was trimmed sharply and from his fine leather boots to his linen shirt covered with a richly embroidered sleeveless vest, he had the air and confidence of wealth and rank. William was immediately reminded of his father as he turned to face them, staring with slightly open mouth and piercing blue eyes.

The rider reined in his horse, even as another rider crashed through the underbrush checking his courser, "why pause now, Sir Robert? We have the beast on the run. The hounds will have him at bay soon enough."

Sir Robert held up his hand and then pointed at their courser. "Do you not recognize this horse and its tack, Thomas?"

The younger of the two turned to look, as if noticing William and Robert for the first time. It appeared to William that his expression changed several times in quick succession. There was recognition, then perhaps fear, followed very quickly by steely anger. "Rogues, robbers, murderers, highwaymen! The gall you have to ride in the open as if you have not a care in the world."

William quickly stood up and tried to brush the dirt and leaves off his clothes and out of his hair while wondering what offense they had given to these men. He glanced up at Robert and could see he was trying to work out the puzzle as well; even as Thomas raised a horn to his lips and blew three short blasts. Fire! Fear! Foes! It was answered a few seconds later by a long, low bass note, which called off the dogs and signaled the return of the other riders.

Sir Robert drew his sword and advanced on the two, pausing with the tip of his blade just a few feet from the old tutors' chest. William could see the older knight's hand tremble slightly. "In the name of Edward, King of England, as the appointed high sheriff of Hale Purlieu and New

Forest, I charge you with the murder of John de Brent, Lord of Charing Manor… and my brother." William stood open mouthed, unable to fully understand, let alone respond to the accusation. Sir Robert didn't seem to pay him any attention either way.

Seconds later the four riders who had continued to follow the hounds returned to the path, the dogs following a moment later, the fire of excitement extinguished out of their eyes. "What is afoot, Sir Robert?" asked the older of the two. His steel gray eyes quickly darted from the knight to the shabbily dressed older man on the horse and Sir Robert's drawn sword. To William, it seemed in the sweep of a moment his piercing eyes took in more than others may have seen. His own observation noted the wealth of his attire, from hand tooled calfskin boots and richly embroidered waistcoat and linen shirt, but most of all the medallion on his chest, which hung from a thick gold chain about his neck. His horse tossed its head and snorted in frustration after the abrupt ending of the chase and he leaned forward to stroke it gently and scratch behind its ear.

"My Lord High Admiral, I have arrested this man for the murder of my brother, John, whose body was found only two days ago on the edge of Netley Marsh." William's eyes widened, not because of the revelation regarding the loss of Sir Robert de Brent's brother but because of who was sitting upon the horse before him.

"Did you see him do this deed, Sir Robert, or you Lord Denebaud?" When neither answered quickly, he added, "Then with what proof have you drawn sword and used our king's name to charge this man?" His voice was deep, deeper than William had encountered before. It was almost as if it resonated out of his chest like a drum.

"He rides upon Sir John's own courser, even the tack was his," Thomas answered in a rather thin, high voice, then hastily added, "my Lord."

The Lord Admiral sat back in his saddle and crossed his arms over his chest but his eyes never left Robert. William continued to study him, as this was the closest he had ever come to one of the oldest of King Edward's friends. "I must admit there is more to this chance meeting than first glance would suggest." For the first time his eyes fell on William and he found himself being measured from head to foot in the glance. He stood up straight, no longer trying to brush himself off and raised his chin a notch. The old knight raised his eyebrows briefly then turned back to Robert.

"What say you to this accusation? Will you identify yourself and state how you came by this horse?"

Robert raised himself up and slowly swung his leg over the saddle, stepping down to the ground. He handed William the reins and then, as gracefully as he could, despite the stiffness of being on horseback for the first time in a very long while, bowed deeply at the waist. "I will gladly do so, my Lord, but I would like to say that it is indeed a sincere honor today's chance meeting, not only brought me into the presence of Sir Robert de Brent of Cossington and his brother in law Lord Thomas Denebaud but you as well and especially, my Lord de Clinton, 1st Earl of Huntingdon and Lord High Admiral, friend and trusted advisor to our king."

A long moment of silence followed as everyone stared at Robert, mouths agape; everyone except William and the Lord High Admiral. "Your murdering highwayman certainly knows his peerage and his manners, Sir Robert." Lord de Clinton smiled at his own jest but his eyes never left Robert or William.

"Even a beautiful flower can have a serpent coiled beneath it, my Lord." Lord Thomas wheezed.

"Indeed it can, Lord Thomas, indeed it can." The jest was gone from his eyes and it seemed to William that something else, some other question or concern lingered there in its place.

"My Lord de Clinton, I am in possession of certain knowledge which will immediately clear this matter and put to rest any suggestion that I or my young traveling companion are highwaymen or robbers." The courser tossed his head several times and neighed loudly, forcing William to take a closer grip on its reins while avoiding the occasional impatient stamping of its iron shod hooves.

"It is a bluff and a waste of our time, my Lord." Thomas protested, then turned and added, "Robert, this man rides your brothers' horse!" His nasal squeak rose to a near shriek.

"Be at peace, Lord Thomas," the Lord de Clinton advised, then added, "and you, Sir Robert, lower your blade for the moment, but keep it handy, just in case." Sir Robert complied without question but it seemed to William that Lord Thomas was overly irritated with the delay. "Continue, goodman."

"On July nineteenth in the year of our Lord 1347, you sat as a juror of a court of honor and fixed your seal to the charter recording the decision."

For the briefest moment William could see complete surprise cross the Lord de Clintons face. This was not at all what he had expected. He regained his composure quickly and asked, "And if I did, how are you aware of it and what bearing does it have on the accusation before you?"

"William, I will need two of the letters you carry with you. You know which two."

William handed the reins back to his tutor and removed his pack, setting it on the ground before him. His hands were trembling as he untied it and gently removed a large leather pouch. Inside were several pages and folded letters including one in French. He gently removed the last letter he had received from his uncle, as well as the couriered message he had received only days before. He carefully folded and tied the leather pouch, placed it back in the pack and slung it over his shoulder. Then, without hesitation, instead of handing them to his tutor, he approached the horse of the Lord High Admiral of England, bowed at the waist and handed them to him, while trying his best to choke back his emotion. As it was he could only get out, "*vivo servire*," before his voice cracked.

At this the Lord de Clinton froze, his hand poised in midair. He slowly took the letters but waited for William to stand again in order to stare even closer at him. His steel gray eyes seemed to be trying to penetrate and read William's mind. The only thing the young man could think of doing was smile back and nod reassuringly.

The Lord High Admiral opened the first letter and William recognized it as the last note he had received from his uncle. It told of the fall of Calais and the coming war to expand Edward's claim in France. It also asked about his studies and reminded him to trust the judgment of Robert, as he had been his tutor as well and was one of the wisest men he had met, next to… suddenly Williams face brightened. He remembered what that last letter had mentioned and why Robert had wanted him to give it along with the couriered message.

The Lord High Admiral refolded the letter and stared at it for a long moment. His horse was restless and stomped on the dried and dead leaves. William realized the birds and squirrels had resumed their chirping and chatter. The couriered letter he held close and examined the seal even closer. His eyebrows shot up in recognition and he then unfolded it to read its contents. A minute later he refolded it as well and murmured, "The Earl of Warwick never should have been put in charge of that raid."

"My Lord?" one of the young men who had accompanied them in the hunting party asked. The Lord High Admiral waved it off.

"Put your sword away, Sir Robert. These are not the murderers of your brother."

"But my Lord, how can you be so certain. Any highwayman can steal a pack as well as a horse…"

"Lord Thomas, these are not the men you are looking for. I will not reveal what they wish to keep hidden, but I will speak with them in private." The Lord High Admiral said this with such certainty and finality that Lord Thomas' mouth audibly snapped shut. Sir Robert sheathed his sword and turned his horse up the path trotting fifty or so feet away. Reluctantly, Lord Thomas followed, as did the others.

Once they were well out of hearing, Lord de Clinton leaned over and handed William the letters, holding onto them just long enough to make William look up into his eyes. For a moment they remained like that until the Lord High Admiral let go. "Keep those letters safe, William."

"Yes, my Lord," he answered, bowing again at the waist.

"What are you and your wards plans?" he asked, turning his attention fully on Robert.

"We intended to quietly leave England, cross the channel and make our way to Chateau de Coucy. Once there…" Robert shrugged, holding his hands palms up.

William de Clinton, First Earl of Huntingdon and Lord High Admiral chewed the inside of his cheek for a moment. "I do not believe I see a better way. It certainly will not be easy…"

William snorted and then caught himself. "Please forgive me, my Lord."

"You reminded me of your uncle when you did that just now." The

Lord High Admiral turned the memory over in his head and then added, "My guess is you have already found leaving England, difficult."

"Yes, my Lord."

"Then tell me of the horse…"

Within a few minutes, Robert had summarized the day's events from finding the family, dealing with the attackers, their burial (at which point he raised an eyebrow) and the finding of the courser and a packhorse, which they sent with the mother and her daughters to aid in their journey. He didn't mention anything of the plunder.

"If Sir Robert wishes to have the horse back, we will gladly return it to him. It is not ours, after all and we will only have to sell it once we get to Southampton as it will not likely cross the channel with us." At this suggestion from William, Lord de Clinton smiled but assured them it wouldn't be necessary.

"I will take care of Sir Robert…"

"And Lord Thomas," William started and then caught himself.

"What of Lord Thomas, William?"

"Nothing, my Lord; forgive me. For a moment I would have spoken my mind but now I think it is better if I keep it to myself. After all, having just been accused of something I had no part in without any evidence to back it up, I will not, in turn, do the same to another."

The Lord de Clinton paused to consider this. "You do your uncle credit, young man."

William lowered his head slightly, "thank you, my Lord. I have had two very good teachers."

"Humility too; well, when I find the time, I must make my way to Dorchester. If more young men would be brought up this way, the future of our country would be blessed, indeed." He paused and turned to look back at the rest of the hunting party. Several sat quietly and complacently on their horses but one appeared agitated and nervous. "As to Lord Thomas, not to worry, William," and the Lord High Admiral of England turned back, leaning over the withers of his horse, placing his hand on the boy's shoulder and looked him right in the eye. "I never have trusted a man who will not look me straight in the eye." He smiled a great big smile and William couldn't help but return it.

"I will not forget that, my Lord."

A moment later the Lord High Admiral of England and one of the closest confidantes of Edward III spun his horse about and trotted back to the group. Although they couldn't hear what was said, William could tell when the Lord High Admiral spoke and when someone else replied or questioned. It seemed Lord Thomas with his distinctive voice did most of the latter. A moment later the group left the path and turned to the north, toward Hale Purlieu.

"You know William, God can turn even the worst possible situation around, if you trust Him." They had set out again, this time on foot, leading the horse.

"Do you think God set it up so the Lord High Admiral was here today?"

Robert chewed on the inside of his cheek a moment before answering. "I do not think anything ever surprises God. He knew our paths would cross with Sir Robert. If our thoughts and actions had not been in line with what He wants of us though, we might have had a very different outcome today." He paused and let his young student think that over, then asked, "What was it you wanted to say about Lord Thomas, William?"

They walked side by side for a long minute before William carefully answered his tutor's question. "Have you ever had a really strong feeling about someone; something that you just could not shake?" Robert nodded, so William continued. "I just had the strongest feeling about Lord Thomas. I happened to be looking right at him when he turned and saw us. It looked to me like his very first reaction, after recognizing Sir John's horse, was one of fear. At least that is what the look on his face was, but he masked it quickly with anger."

"Why do you think he would have been afraid to see his brother-in law's horse, William?"

"I did not realize Lord Thomas and Sir John were related."

Robert nodded. "It is always wise to do the best you can when studying the list of peerage along with marriage alliances." William made a mental note to find his uncle's book of lists when they returned to Dorchester and Crandor Castle. "Lord Thomas' sister, Elizabeth Denebaud, is married to Sir Robert and Sir Robert's and John's sister, Joan, is married to Lord Thomas. Lord Denebaud is the third son and therefore has little of his own inheritance; but the de Brent's control large land holdings and are quite powerful on their own." As if realizing what he just said, Robert stopped in the middle of the path, his eyes, looking off in the distance but not focused on anything.

"If Lord Thomas had something to do with Sir John's death…"

"I think you hit the nail on the head, William. But of course we have no proof. Lord Thomas would have wanted us arrested and quickly executed if we had any knowledge of where the horse came from. The last thing he could afford would be a trial and evidence."

"Do you think he paid Davey Martin or Samuel Thompson to do it? If they just found the body two days ago, they may have done the deed before they moved north to Salisbury."

"One or both, it is hard to say. But for us, William, I think it is time we mounted and moved with all haste to reach the gates and get inside Southampton this very evening. The Lord High Admiral will certainly keep a very close eye on Lord Thomas; he sensed something as well. But there is still a chance Lord Thomas might have someone try and meet up with us before we reach the gates. Once we are there, we will have to wait for the tide to board ship and cross the channel, but I will feel better with a large thick stone wall between us and this forest."

They mounted the courser and, several minutes later at a nearly non -stop canter, William noticed the trees beginning to thin out and then, almost suddenly, he found himself back in the open sky. The sensation of fresh air on his face was even more of a shock as it was filled with a strong scent of the sea. Not far ahead, William could see gulls circling, a ribbon of late afternoon sun shimmering on moving water on his right, a large stone bridge ahead, and a walled city just beyond.

"You asked me a while back what made the difference in the battle of Hastings; it was pride, William. The pride of Harold Godwinson was his undoing." The comment took William off guard and he had to think back to the conversation they were having before running into the Lord de Clinton and his hunting party.

"He was so proud he lost the battle at Hastings?"

"Harold was so proud of the fact that he and his men had marched from Dover to the northern edges of England, fought and defeated the invading Norsemen, then turned and marched immediately to meet William at Hastings; he did not feel he needed to wait a day or two for the stragglers to catch up, or for a reinforcing army to join him, or simply to give his men a much needed day of rest. If he had not been so proud, nor felt so invincible, the results of that battle may have been very different. Always remember what comes after pride, William."

"Pride goes before destruction," William murmured to himself, then added, "Remember what the Lord High Admiral told you; humility is a trait even he admires." He wasn't sure if he knew exactly how.

Robert noticed the concerned look on his young student's face and added, "Just try and remember it is not all about you, William. The surest way to remain humble, throughout your entire life, is to not worry who gets the credit for what is accomplished. If the deed is done and the goal is met, does it matter if the accolades fall upon you or another? When you are ready to honestly answer that question, knowing that it does not matter, you have found true humility. It is then God will find a great use for you."

The trail they followed led out of the forest and quickly joined other small tracks to form a larger rutted dirt road, which eventually became paved with closely set stones, as they approached Southampton and the sea.

Chapter Thirteen

"I had no idea how big Southampton was." William murmured to himself.

"It will be the largest city you have seen so far, but not the largest ever. It is one of the great sea ports, but even it had to learn its own lesson in pride."

"What do you mean? What does pride have to do with Southampton?"

Robert pointed to the large wall surrounding the city, which they could clearly see encircling the landward portions of the city, farthest from the sea. It was also the first time William noticed that the wall wasn't complete. There were definitely several sections still under construction, and some sections which seemed to be in the process of being added onto and strengthened with large towers. "That wall is being extended and strengthened because of the pride of the Englishmen of Southampton. The city had grown as a great sea-trading center and English ships frequently traveled back and forth across the channel. Because of their city's size and commerce they felt they had little to fear. Ten years ago, a fleet of French and Genoese ships sailed right into the harbor and sacked the town, slaughtering any who did not flee inland. A year later King Edward ordered an expansion and strengthening of the wall to completely close in the city, including the seafront. It is a little late to shut the barn door after the horses are out, but still it is better late than never."

As the road rose to meet the bridge which crossed the River Test, just prior to the opening of its mouth and the quays of Southampton to the south, William had a chance to marvel, not only at the immensity of the city before him, but also at the arched stone bridge spanning the tidal waters flowing silently out to the channel. The sun was still a short time from setting, and its deep red and purple glow shimmered on the water before them and the walls further ahead. He suddenly felt a weariness pass over him. It had been a long day already and they still had some to go.

As the hooves of the stallion clattered on the stone pavement, Robert checked him to a walk while leaning forward and to the side, looking over the low wall of the bridge and the water below. He shook his head and muttered to himself.

"What is wrong?"

"We are crossing the River Test and soon we will be in Redbridge. It is a small ship building community, just outside the walls of Southampton. This river is tidal this close to the channel; its level will rise and fall with the tide. Look to the banks and tell me what you see."

William leaned around his tutor and looked to the far bank. At first he wasn't sure what he should be looking for. He saw the bank with patches of densely packed reeds. Low buildings stood beyond these and further downstream were several quays and possibly storage houses beside them. The quays were empty, the thick, dark stained beams exposed in the late evening sun. William shook his head. Robert had said the river was tidal and would rise and fall. Then a flash of insight hit him.

"The river is low. I can see several feet of the beams of the quay exposed, where they would normally be covered in water."

"Exactly, William; one other thing, which you would not know unless you have spent time around rivers of this kind and tides in general, is the nature of this particular tide." Robert looked back over his shoulder and motioned with a quick nod. "The moon is nearly quartered now, William. Sailors call this the neap tide, when there is little difference between high and low. Neither of us wishes to be here longer than we have to, but we will not find any ship leaving Southampton for a day or maybe even two. Least ways, not until the neap tide is past."

William considered this for a moment, then asked, "What makes the tides rise and fall?"

Robert laughed loudly, startling a few people crossing the bridge beside them. "Oh, William, if I could answer that for sure, I would be wise and wealthy indeed. Although men do not know why, they do know the tides follow the stages of the moon. But what her smiling, changing face has to do with them, no one I am aware of has yet figured out."

A moment later they crested the bridge and began the gentle descent into the small town of Redbridge with the wall and gates of Southampton beyond.

•••

They passed through the narrow, twisting streets just outside the wall before William spoke over the steady plodding of their stallion. "Do you think Lord Thomas can reach us here, in Southampton, if we have to be here more than a day?"

Robert cut him off short, "If you are anxious, William, it would be best if you do not focus on those worries. Fear, doubt, and indecision are welcomed bedfellows. When you have one, you get the other two for free. Always remember, what you think about most and what occupies your thoughts the most will eventually become real in your life."

"Then I can think my way into getting my uncle out of the French castle he is being held in?"

"Yes and no, William." When he saw the question in his student's eyes, he added an explanation. "All these things you see around you, created by other men, were originally just an idea. At the same time, they did not just imagine them into existence. Our faith and belief also takes works; in James's letter he tells us that our faith is dead if we do not follow it up with works. So we cannot just believe it to happen, but we need to start with a belief that it can happen. All ideas begin as a thought, the seed of an idea. Even all those oak trees we just found ourselves riding through today began as simple acorns. The birds of the air began in an egg and the walls before us began as an idea of one or more men. When we take that idea and add emotion and action to it we will surely see it come to pass. You cannot just wish for it William. You have to put actions behind your dreams. That is, after all, what faith truly is, yes?"

"I am not sure my faith is big enough for this..."

"You can always grow your faith, William."

"I can grow my faith? How is that possible?"

"Everyone is given a measure of faith. In Paul's letter to the Romans he tells us that faith grows by hearing the Word of God. The more you hear His Word the more real it becomes in your life and the easier it is to believe His promises." His tutor paused a moment as the courser continued to clop across the cobblestones. "Picture in your mind what you truly want, William; see it so clearly you can imagine every little detail. With your eyes closed you can see and feel and smell what it will be like. Do this every day while speaking out loud what you are seeing. It will take time, but eventually you will completely believe it and then, it will become truth. But have a care, William. If you do this with the wrong thing, an evil thing, it would make it come to pass as well."

"So, in order to free my uncle I should see us freeing him; feel his embrace and the joy of knowing he is free? We are already putting in the action to make it happen so as long as I keep focusing on this one desire, it will come to pass and he will be free? Is that all? It seems far too simple."

"It is simple. The most powerful things in the world are the most simple. Men tend to complicate them, but that is not how God designed things. You can use this to build your faith in anything, William. When you concentrate of your desires, as long as they are in God's will, you will find the ideas and solutions you are searching for. The problem with most people is they find themselves focusing and seeing the negative in their lives and the doubts and fears and they wind up building their faith in those things. Faith and fear cannot exist in you at the same time, William. They are exactly opposite of each other."

"What really is faith then?"

"I remember my father telling me that faith is the coin of heaven, it opens doors which no man can shut and pleases God when you have it. But, to answer your question best, I once heard it described as the belief in the good and wholesome things we cannot see. Fear is the opposite. The Norsemen tell a story in which each person has two wolves living inside them. A wolf called faith and a wolf called fear. They constantly fight each other for control over our actions. Everyone feels the tension between these two powers. The one which governs your life and determines how you act is the one you feed."

"So, I build my faith by feeding it the good I want in my life and starving it of the evil?"

Robert halted the horse, just before a large open gate in the tall wall before them and turned, as best he could, in his saddle to face William. There was a broad smile on his face. His steel grey eyes sparkled in the setting sun and it seemed he squinted and blinked for reasons other than just the bright light. "William, if you truly understand what you just said, and you embrace that truth and live your life by it, you will accomplish anything you set out to do. Doors will open, men and mountains will move and the very windows of heaven will pour blessings upon your life." Robert paused a moment to study his young student's expression. He saw the beginning of belief and realization dawning and knew that, although neither wanted this quest, it could quite possibly be the very best thing for his young student to endure. "This is what is meant to live a life of faith, William." Robert turned back and clucked to their mount, nudging it in the ribs with his heels. It quickened to a trot and they found themselves passing by large oaken doors, under a raised portcullis, through the thick wall, and into the bustling seaport of Southampton.

•••

It wasn't difficult for Robert and William to locate the portion of the city where horses were stabled, bought, and sold. If nothing else, they could probably have done so just through their sense of smell. As they approached the warren of stables and stalls, some of which were built right up against the newest section of the wall, they dismounted and while picking their own steps carefully, began surveying the vendors who seemed to sense their purpose and joined them in the road. Although the wall now stood between them and the setting sun, there was still plenty of light to pick their way down the narrow alley.

"That is indeed a fine beast, sir, would you consider selling it?"

said one tall, well-dressed merchant. He flashed a smile at William and added, "I will give you a fair price, lad." His eyes sparkled in the dim light of dusk.

"King Edward and the Black Prince will need mounts such as it for the war," chimed in another. Something in this voice caught William's attention and he turned to see who spoke. Two stalls down stood a shorter hunch back. An old, ill tended scar trailed down the side of his head where his left ear should have been. His gnarled and swollen knuckled hands were held in front of his waist and he smiled a slightly, gap toothed smile.

William's attention turned back to the nicer looking of the two merchants and began to lead their stallion in his direction when it suddenly, obstinately, stood its ground. "C'mon, lad," William encouraged but it was no use. The stallion had been compliant all day until this very moment but now it wasn't going to follow.

"He will do as you say, lad. Just give him a little of the incentive." The merchant held a small switch in his hands and bent it gently, while continuing to smile.

Glancing back at the stallion's face, William noticed something. His ears were lying back, his nostrils were flared, and he could have sworn, if the horse could speak it would have told him not to have anything to do with that man, despite his dress and manners. He took a step closer and gently ran his hand down the courser's thick, arched neck. "Easy there, boy; it is all right…" William was shocked to feel the beast trembling. Something about the well-dressed, well-mannered merchant was frightening the stallion. He blew hot breath out of his nostrils and stamped the cobblestones with his iron-shod hoof. When William looked closer it was as if he could see fear in his eyes. Without glancing to his side, he grabbed the reins tighter and continued following Robert down to the second stall and the stunted merchant. The stallion eagerly followed.

"Fairest price in the city is here…" the first merchant's voice trailed off and then was lost in the commotion of dozens of voices.

William found Robert in mid conversation with the disfigured merchant. "It was at Neville's Cross, where I got that, sir." He was pointing to the long, jagged scar, which began near the crown of his head and ended below the collar of his dirty homespun shirt.

At the mention of that battle, William was taken back and then hurriedly interjected, "it was at Neville's Cross where…"

"David, King of the Scots was captured." Robert cut him off. A stern glance passed from the old tutor to William. But here was someone who had been there, that last day. He bit his lip and swallowed heavily.

If the merchant noticed the unspoken signal, he didn't let on. "Aye, sir that he was; I was there, not far from the very spot, with a group of other Welsh long bowmen and men of Northumberland." He smiled and held up his hand in front of him, turning them so they could see both sides. "You may not believe it sir, but these hands can draw a yew bow and strike a target at center over 700 paces away." As if to emphasize the fact, he stood as straight as he was able and mimicked pulling a bowstring to his right ear.

"Did the long bow help carry the day, as it did at Crecy?" William asked with obvious interest. This was the first person he had met, beside his uncle, who had been in the very battle where his father had fallen. For obvious reasons, his uncle had always been reluctant to share with William what had happened that day. The most he could get from him was that his father had 'done his duty to his country and family.'

"We surely did our part, but once all your arrows are spent, a knife or hammer is all you have to defend yourself, and against the Scots, that is not bloody much." He paused, seeming to recall something, and his face darkened as his voice dropped to a hoarse whisper. "They fell upon our position as soon as they realized we were spent. The Marischal himself led the assault on our flank." He shook his head and closed his eyes a moment. "Half of them had their faces painted and their bloody screaming was terrifying. Those who still had shafts let 'em fly and then they were in among us; it was kill or be killed, hand against hand. Robert Keith himself gave me this with the end of his lance," pointing once again to the long jagged scar.

"How did you survive?" William asked.

"Two knights, Lords they were, or so I was told later, pulled a small group of Dorchester men out of the reserves and they fell upon the Scots. For as long as I live, I will never forget the emblem of those men. It is a sight I will take with me to the grave and never has an Englishman been more grateful than I. Their shields bore a white crane beside a red door on a black field."

"Dear, God…" Tears welled up in William's eyes and he choked back a year's worth of emotions. He could see the horse merchant staring at him but could hear nothing over a loud hammering in his ears. Later he realized it was the sound of his thundering heart.

Robert stepped around the horse and said something to the stunted dealer. The hammering grew louder in his ears and William suddenly felt light headed. Before he knew it, he was being half led, half carried through the door of a shed, beyond the first room and into another.

A moment later William found himself sitting on a stool, his head in his hands and hot tears streaking his face; his throat was still tight and he swallowed heavily while wiping his face and nose on his sleeve. He looked up to see Robert with a serious look of concern on his face and the merchant on one knee before him.

The heavily scarred horse dealer was wringing his swollen knuckled hands and leaned closer, staring intently at William's face. "Is it true lad? Or should I say," and he leaned closer and whispered, "my Lord?" Apparently Robert had at least enough time to describe part of their situation.

William shook his head and swallowed again. "No, not a Lord, not yet anyway," He smiled weakly while his voice cracked. "The arms you describe are those of my house. The men you saw were my father and uncle. My father," his voice broke again and he paused a moment before continuing. "My father brought Lord Keith to bay and brought him down, but fell soon after, never seeing the capture of King David by the squire, John Copeland, or my uncle receiving the Order of the Garter from King Edward himself."

"John Copeland..." Gilbert added more to himself than to William, "A cousin he is, and true hearted; he stood beside me when the Scots came. A stout man at arms he is, or was the last I saw of him when all of our fates changed that day. And now you find yourself...?"

"Secretly crossing the channel and making our way into French territory to rescue my uncle from imprisonment after his capture at St. Omer."

The merchant sucked air between his gapped teeth whistling in the process. "You are wise to hide who you are sir, even while still in England. Not everyone you will meet loves the crown, even here on English soil." He paused a moment and scratched at his straggly beard and then shook his head, smiling slightly. Despite his outward appearances, there was a strange fire in the disfigured horse trader's eyes. It was compelling. William could feel it. This was a man he could trust with his life.

"God moves in strange ways that is for sure. There is no doubt in my mind you were meant to come to me today because just this morning I was approached by a courier from Calais. King Edward and the Black Prince are in desperate need of horses for their campaign. That courser of yours will purchase your trip across the channel as well as see you outfitted for your trip inland."

"We will need a safe place to stay in Southampton until the neap tide passes," Robert interjected.

The merchant paused a moment to think, crossing his arms, tapping the side of his nose and nodding slightly, while staring at his nearly crushed hands, turning them over slowly. William could see strange half-moon shaped scars on the back. "After I collapsed they were stomped on by one of the Scot's horses," Gilbert told him, noticing the way William stared at them. "Strange that I now find myself working with the very beast which took away the one skill I did so well."

There was a moment's pause as William's thoughts swirled around his father and uncle and their charge into the Scottish ranks. It had been a long time since he had thought of his father and it took a moment for him to bring a clear picture in his head. He was brought out of his thoughts by a question from the merchant.

"Lad, if I may ask, what is your name?"

William looked up to Robert, who nodded his approval. "I am William Simpson, nephew and heir to Lord Charles de Simpson, Earl of Dorchester. And you sir, may I have the honor as well?"

A startled look came over the merchant's scarred face. Slowly he stood, as straight as his curved back would allow and placed his gnarled right hand on his left breast and bowed deeply, "Gilbert Copeland at yours and your families' service, sir."

William stood up and offered him his hand. Wide-eyed Gilbert took it and found himself shaking the hand of the future Earl of Dorchester. "Thank you, Gilbert, not only for your service to England but for relating to me my father's last day. You have no idea how grateful I am to know he did his duty well and saved lives in the process. It is a memory I will keep with me forever." He watched as tears began welling up in the eyes of the deformed and scarred merchant, spilling down his cheeks, creating tracks amid the dust and dirt. For most of his life he was invisible to people; they looked right through him, ignoring him and his deformity. Now, standing before him was the son of the man who helped save his life and he was grateful to him! William could feel his own tears threatening to spill down his cheeks even as his throat tightened.

As tears continued to fall down Gilbert's face, he smiled the largest gapped toothed smile William had ever seen. His eyes shone and it was obvious he had struck upon an idea.

"God is truly shining upon our chance meeting. The same courier who brought the message travels back to France at the first turn of the tide. I know where he stays and on which ship he sails. I can take you to him. As I said, your courser and its tack will more than pay for your passage and help speed you on your way once you are across the channel."

"No one must know who we are, or what our goal is, Gilbert." Robert interjected. "We travel in secrecy as two simple yeomen in hopes it will call less attention to ourselves."

"Then, again, it was best you came to me and not another of the horsemen on this street."

His comment triggered a memory of William's and he quickly asked, before it flittered away, "Two stalls down there was a tall, well dressed merchant. My first impression was to talk with him, but our stallion would have nothing to do with it…"

Gilbert nodded and turned very grave. "I have found, as I have been working closely with these good beasts, they have a sense to them which more men could use." He suddenly realized what he had said and then quickly added, "Not that I am suggesting you do not have any sense, sir.

It is just that they can feel what is right and wrong, just as they can feel if you are frightened of them or not."

"And what is wrong with the merchant I was speaking to?"

"Well, first, not many of the horses he purchases ever make it past the slaughterhouse…" Gilbert paused and it seemed he was carefully considering what he said next. "There are some noblemen who have stayed behind, rather than fight with their king. Some do so because they have to or because they have been commanded to. Others do it because it presents opportunities of the basest kind. Rumors spread through the merchant section of town like wild fires. A Lord was recently killed, his body found less than a day's ride from here. The rumors suggest his brother in law was involved. If that is true, then Benedict, the broker you spoke with, was elbow deep in the deed."

William looked to Robert at this revelation. His tutor posed the question they both came up with. "Is it possible the nobleman you speak of is Sir John Brent?"

"Aye, sir that it is," Gilbert paused a moment and considered the question closer while lighting a thick tallow candle on the small table at their side. It sputtered and smoked and lit up the room brightly. It was only then William realized the sun had finally set. "You know more to this tale than the rumors I have come across?"

William nodded and Robert quickly described what took place that day, from their encounter with the mother and daughters on the road, the finding of the horses, and finishing with Sir Robert Brent, Lord Thomas, and the Lord High Admiral. When he was finished, Gilbert sat on the stool opposite William and blew a shrill whistle through his teeth, shaking his head in disbelief.

"So, the courser you have to sell is…"

"Sir John Brent's," Robert completed. "So it would seem."

"Once again, God is smiling on our meeting today, William. If you had completed business with Benedict, he would have given you a fair price and even suggested a place to stay the night, but as soon as you turned your back he would have let his sources know exactly where you were." He paused, considering what he just said. "I have heard it suggested he kept highwaymen in his employment. They kept whatever treasure and trinkets they would find on the person and they gave the horses to Benedict for sale and a profit."

"We need to move from here as soon as possible," Robert stated. "If he recognized the horse as Sir John's, he may have already sent word to men in his employ as well as Lord Thomas. I have little doubt, once he finds where we are, that he will send men to deal with us. Hale Purlieu is only a short cross country gallop after all."

"If Benedict and Lord Thomas converse and put two things together, they may realize we are the cause of both their irritations."

Gilbert's gaze seemed to lose focus for a moment then he stood, his gnarled hands on his hips and his feet set wide apart. "I made a vow as I recovered after the battle; if ever I had an opportunity to repay those men whose actions on the battlefield saved my life, I would do all in my power to aid them and theirs." He paused and his eyes misted over and he blinked repeatedly to clear them.

"William, I owe your father and uncle my very life." He stopped to clear his throat. "I cannot think of a better way to repay that debt than to see you safely out of Southampton, and on board a ship for Calais. I have been in this city long enough now to know a trick or two to get you down to the Shipwright's Inn near the largest quays. I will introduce you to the courier and they will stable your horse there." He started toward the door they came in and then paused.

"If you both leave through that other door," and he nodded to a small door on the opposite side of the room, "you will be in a short hallway. Go straight to the end and out the door into the alley. Wait for me there. I will be around in a moment with your horse."

William and Robert followed his direction and even though they had to feel their way down the hall and out the door, once in the alley, the moon gave just enough light for them to make out the shapes of other sheds, buildings and doorways across the alley and down on either side.

"William, before Gilbert returns, I wanted to tell you how proud I am of your actions this evening. Your father and uncle also would have been very proud." As he stood basking in the glow of his tutor's affirmation a chill ran down William's neck and he shivered. The breeze was coming in from the sea and though it took a while to find its way this far into the city it still held a cool, damp touch. Without realizing it, both William and Robert opened their packs and pulled out their cloaks.

"Gilbert would not have been my first or possibly even second choice of merchants today," William admitted as much to himself as to his tutor.

"Do not always trust your eyes, William. They can deceive you."

"How is that so?"

"Too many people are not willing to believe something until they see it, and yet God tells us to trust the opposite. Once we truly believe something, then we will see it come to pass."

"It is much easier for me to believe in something if I have seen it already."

"As it is for most everyone, William, but our Lord said, if you truly believe, you can tell a mountain to cast itself into the sea and it will do so. If you have faith and believe, it will come to pass. Thomas did not believe it was the Lord returned from the dead until he placed his fingers in his side and his hands. Jesus told him how much more blessed were those who would come after who would believe without seeing or feeling."

"There have been times when I cannot seem to see a solution to a problem and I feel like I might not have enough faith to believe there is a way out."

"First of all William, if you will be positive and continue to believe, your faith will increase. Of that I have no doubt. Secondly" and here Robert turned and set his hand on his young student's shoulder, looking him directly in the eye, making sure he had his full attention, "have you ever seen the wind, William?"

"Of course I have. I have seen it blow across the fields, bending the grass and moving through the trees."

"What you have seen is the effect of the wind, but have you ever actually seen the wind?" William considered what he was asked, and then shook his head. "So, even though you have never seen the wind you believe it exists. The same is true of God and His ability to bless you. Believe He can do so, because He has done it before for all those people you have heard about in the Bible and it will come to pass for you too. There are blessing blockers in life though; doubt, fear and indecision are the biggest. Anger, jealousy, envy, unkindness, rudeness, and evil thoughts are some of the others. If God is going to bless you with what you believe Him to do, you have to remove these from your life."

"It seems that it all comes back to approaching every day and every situation positively." William smiled beneath his hood and added, "I seem to remember you mentioning something about that that first morning beside the old Roman road in Dorchester."

"You are right William and the reason you are right is because it is up to you to be positive. God is always positive."

William rolled these thoughts around in his head and was about to ask another question when he heard the slow clopping of iron-shod hooves approaching. A moment later Gilbert appeared out of the dim gloom leading their courser and he paused just long enough to make sure he was addressing the right people as what little light there was cast both Robert and William's faces, in deep shadow.

"He really is quite a beauty." Gilbert paused, stroking the arched, well-muscled neck and scratching behind its ears. "'Tis a shame you need to part with him, but I can see how he would certainly call unwanted attention to yourselves." The stallion seemed to agree as he snorted loudly and tossed his head. "Normally it would only take me a few minutes to get down to the inn where the courier told me he was staying, but I think we should be cautious. I will take some turns and double backs just to make sure we have no one following us."

For the next several minutes no one spoke as Gilbert led the way, the courser plodding along beside him. William and Robert followed a few paces behind, while their eyes, hidden in the darkness of their hoods, searched side streets, alleys and thoroughfares, which crossed their path. Gilbert would occasionally pause at certain intersections and turn his head from side to side. William wasn't sure if he was looking or listening or both.

Sometimes they would continue straight, other times they would turn to the right or left. Either way, their path began to gently slope down and they soon found themselves coming across more and more people. Now the benefit of having Gilbert as a guide became even more apparent. Here was an invisible man in most people's eyes. They would see the hump, the halting, limping gate and badly scarred head and neck and turn their eyes, many times even crossing to the other side of the street. No one even attempted a hospitable, "good evening." A lump began forming in William's throat as he realized how lonely his life must be. As hooded figures following their invisible guide, they themselves became invisible.

An idea was beginning to form in William's mind and he decided to pose it to Robert. Even though he spoke in hushed tones, the fact he had his hood pulled down low seemed to amplify his voice alarmingly. "Gilbert's life seems like it would be sad and lonely. Even the people he passes on the street go out of their way to avoid him."

"I have noticed the same, William." They had dropped back a few more steps behind the stallion, to make sure they were out of Gilbert's hearing.

"Dorchester was once renowned for the horses sired on its green rolling hills." William paused and then continued when Robert didn't respond. "Perhaps it is time we found someone to reintroduce that tradition. The stables at Crandor can certainly accommodate many more brood mares along with a few stallions."

When Robert still didn't respond, William turned just as his tutor grabbed his arm while holding a finger up to his own lips. Several paces ahead, standing beside the courser, they could just make out Gilbert's silhouette and he was talking to someone directly in front of him. Although they couldn't hear everything, nor even see whom Gilbert spoke to, the conversation didn't seem a pleasant one from the posture and gestures of the merchant.

Robert gently pushed William into a darkened alley just to their side. From its shadows they could still see the heated exchange; but at least the two of them were no longer standing in the middle of the street. Even as they watched, William noticed another figure enter the road from an alley opposite their own. This person also had a hooded cloak, pulled down low, covering their entire face in shadow. The individual slowly approached the stallion, making his way carefully around the near side, coming within just a few feet of where they stood. William held his breath and tried not to make any movement, which would draw attention to them.

Although the dark night and deep shadows hid most of the figure's features, William could tell it was a man and as he saw a glimpse of the stranger's expression, his breath caught in his throat and the sound nearly gave them away. As it happened, at that exact same moment the stallion neighed loudly, tossing his head and snorting. The hooded stranger took another couple of steps and then paused alongside the flank of the courser, oblivious to Robert and William hiding in the alley just a few feet away.

There was absolutely no mistaking the figure's intent, especially when William suddenly realized he carried a long baselard in his right hand, its blade glinting in what little moonlight there was. Was it possible Benedict had already sent word to Lord Thomas and these were men dispatched to deal with him? Or were these just thieves, bent on waylaying the deformed merchant in order to relieve him of the horse. Either way, William realized he had to do something but his legs felt like lead and his heart was beating so hard he thought it would burst his chest.

Robert made the first move, stooping down to pick something up. It took a second for William to realize it was a large stone, which he was then handed. William stared in incomprehension until Robert mimicked knocking himself on the head with his closed fist and then pointed at the person standing just a few feet behind Gilbert. His tutor wanted him to use the stone to knock him out. He swallowed audibly, his tongue suddenly stuck to the roof of his mouth and then nodded.

Without hesitation, his teacher moved out of the shadows of the alley and crept slowly around the other side of the stallion. William found it interesting how he suddenly seemed to see and feel so much more detail than a moment ago. He watched as Robert's right hand gently touched the courser on the rump, letting the horse know he was there, as he crossed behind him. The feel of the hard, lump of rock in his hand, as well as the uneven surface of the road through the soles of his boots, made him acutely aware that he had followed his tutor out of the alley and was slowly approaching the back of the cloaked assailant. William raised his hand over his shoulder. His arm, like the rest of his body, felt as lead. Risking a glance to his right, he saw Robert nod and mouth the word, "Now!"

Without stopping to think, William swung and felt, as much as he heard, the grizzly crunch as the stone struck the hooded figure in the back of the head. He collapsed instantly, dropping the long baselard in the process. It gave off a loud clang as it struck the stone road and bounced twice before lying perfectly still. William thought it was strange that he watched this as if time itself had slowed around him.

Gilbert turned, a look of shock and surprise on his disfigured face. It was then William recognized, not only the face to whom the merchant had been speaking, but also saw him raise a baselard of his own. Before William could shout, let alone move, two separate things took place. Someone stood up behind Gilbert's assailant and snaked an arm around his neck, pulling him backwards while grappling with the hand, which held the long dagger. The small sliver of moon slid out from behind a bank of clouds to reveal Robert wrestling with Benedict.

That same, small amount of moonlight was just enough for Gilbert to see what no one had expected. The hunchbacked merchant shouted to William and moved with such speed he wouldn't have believed it possible if he hadn't been standing there. As it was, William found himself shoved to the side of the narrow road, hitting the timber framed building, nearly knocking the wind out of him. Stars sprung up in his vision as he spun around to see Gilbert grappling with yet another cloaked assailant.

A second assailant had quietly waited in the shadows of the opposite alley and crept out after seeing Robert pass around the rump of the stallion. He was going to follow the tutor until he saw William leave the alley with a large stone in his hand. He couldn't stop the young boy from knocking his brother unconscious but he could take care of the whelp in his own way.

He had taught his brother how to use the baselard and the long dagger had become their favorite hand weapon. It wasn't much for throwing but in a tight spot it was much handier than even a short sword. As it was, he rounded the back of the stallion only to see William tossed to the side like a sack of apples by the hunchbacked merchant they had been paid to "persuade" to tell who had sold him the courser. He was just as shocked as William at Gilbert's speed, and was surprised when he realized the merchant had launched himself in his direction.

The collision with the hardened, hunchbacked merchant knocked him off his feet and he landed hard, his head snapping back and hitting the pavement. His arms became flaccid and his mouth dropped open while Gilbert sat up, swaying slightly, struggling to get to his hands and knees, his breath coming in ragged gasps.

William shook his head to clear his vision, took a deep breath, and went over to help the merchant to his feet. Even as Gilbert sat up, they both looked down at the long, H-shaped hilt and blade sticking out of the hunchback's shoulder.

"Dear, God…please no… HELP!" William didn't care who would hear. He didn't even care if there were more men waiting in the shadows to come for him. All he cared about was the dark shadow of a stain slowly soaking and spreading across the corner of Gilbert's dirty homespun shirt. Seconds later Robert was there and he helped lay Gilbert back on the cold stone pavement. He winced and shut his eyes tightly, biting his lower lip until it bled.

Hot tears began streaming down Williams face and he wiped his nose on his sleeve. "Gilbert, please do not die. You cannot… please…"

On hearing his name, the merchant opened his eyes and he smiled a rather large smile considering the situation. His pale lips trembled slightly and his dry, hoarse voice croaked as he reached up and grabbed the front of Williams' tunic, "partially repaid… William…"

William couldn't help but smile himself. "Does it hurt badly?" he asked, sniffling loudly.

Without missing a beat, Gilbert answered, "Ever heard of being hurt well?" He took in a deep, ragged breath and then slowly exhaled. "The blade is wedged in my shoulder joint; I can feel it against the bones." He turned his head towards Robert and added, "We have not much time before all lower Southampton turns out for this… pull the blade and staunch the wound with some cloth." Robert nodded and took a firm grip on the hilt. William knelt beside Gilbert and took his right hand, holding it in his own.

A quick jerk and the blade slid free, only slightly grating on Gilbert's humerus in the process. He inhaled sharply and squeezed William's hand with surprising strength. Blood welled up out of the hole but Robert was ready with a strip of muslin he had taken out of the saddlebags. He pressed it down firmly and took Gilbert's hand out of Williams and placed his arm across his chest and his hand onto his own shoulder. "Press down here," he advised. "It will help staunch the bleeding. William, Gilbert is right; we cannot stay here any longer. Can you walk?"

"I can bloody well walk out of here." It took both William and Robert's help to get him to his feet and he stood on very wobbly legs.

"William, help me get Gilbert up on the horse. You can ride these as well as sell them, yes?"

Gilbert nodded but didn't answer. At that moment he was trying hard to focus on standing while all the rest of the world seemed to be spinning and tilting at the same time. Dried and caked on blood was staining his fingers, but it didn't seem like the wound was continuing to bleed. He didn't appreciate it at the moment, but Gilbert knew in the back of his mind it was a good thing.

It took more than one attempt but they were finally successful in getting him on the courser. William stepped around and under the neck of the horse in order to grab the reins and lead him. Robert went back and retrieved the baselard, wiping it on the trousers of the man Gilbert tackled and then stuck it under his own belt, beside his skinning knife. While his tutor did this, William looked around realizing for the first time, Benedict was also lying crumpled up on the stone pavement just a few feet ahead of the stallion, who seemed to sense something was wrong and was nervously striking the road with his forefeet. Without giving it a second thought, William picked up the long dagger lying on the pavement and tucked it beside his own skinning knife.

"Gilbert, you told us the courier was staying at the Shipwright's Inn. We need to get there as quickly as we can without worrying about who might still be following us."

"Should we just leave those men here?" William asked. "Will they not still come looking for us?"

"I do not think we have much to worry about with them, William." Gilbert advised. His voice was shaky but still had strength behind it. "Men like these look for easy prey and do not like ones which bite back." He drew himself more upright and took another deep breath. "Turn right here and go straight until you come to a large, wide, well-paved cross road. Take it left and keep straight on until you come to the inn. It is clearly marked with one of the king's signs.

William led on and the courser was more than happy to leave the huddled, still unconscious figures far behind. Robert walked just ahead his young student, keeping a sharp eye on the road before them, while occasionally turning back to make sure there was no one following.

As it was, in a short time they found the crossroad and began the sometimes gentle, sometimes more aggressive, slope down as if the wide road was a mountain stream, making its way to the sea. As the stallion plodded along William made sure to keep an eye on Gilbert. He noticed him sway a few times and wince in pain when the courser stumbled over the rough pavement but he continued to use his right hand to keep pressure on his left shoulder while his left arm simply hung down at his side.

The road widened as it continued to gently follow the slope down to the quays. As the buildings receded, William could take in even more of the city before him. Although the thin quarter moon gave them little light, there was enough for him to make out large shapes of ships at waterfront, the quays and warehouses, several steeples, and the dark line of the wall as it stretched down along his right to the very edge of the water and then turned to follow the coast out of sight. Such a city he had never seen, but it was the smell which he would recall later; a mixture of sea spray, old fish, human waste and wood smoke. Needless to say it wasn't entirely pleasant and he wondered why people chose to live here. Not for the last time did William wish he were back in Dorchester where the air was fresh and clean and smelled of grass, hay and sheep.

A moment later Robert stopped and pointed and William smiled. Just ahead was the inn.

Chapter Fourteen

The Shipwright's Inn was similar in most ways to the Bear and Boar, although larger and more elaborate. A large, double hung front door let out just enough warmth, light and noise to suggest the common room was very full. William made a promise to himself that neither he nor Robert would venture there this evening. The inn faced the street they had descended and had two large wings, which turned and ran a considerable distance back from the road. William hadn't ever seen a building this large which wasn't a church.

After helping Gilbert down off the stallion, Robert placed his shoulder under the merchant's right arm and led the hunchback up the steps and into the foyer. He signaled William to stay with the horse, as he needed Gilbert to make contact with the courier.

As William stood in front of the large inn, he couldn't help but recall the day they'd had. The rescuing of the mother and her two daughters flashed across his mind. He paused a moment to recall their faces and realized that, although he and Robert had introduced themselves, he had never learned the mother's, her eldest daughter or the two little one's names. There was no doubt her aunt was Sara Pendelton, his uncle's housekeeper. She had never mentioned her family and he was embarrassed to realize he had never taken the time to get to know her, or any of the staff, in more than a cursory way. "When I get back to Crandor, I will do a better job of getting to know them; to learn more about them and their families." He spoke to himself. Whether he realized it or not, the life lessons Robert had already begun teaching him were starting to, albeit slowly, sink in.

His hand gently stroked the arched neck of the courser as he leaned his head against the dark, warm cheek and inhaled deeply. Horse musk, sweat and saddle leather filled his head. The night had already begun to cool rapidly and a fine wisp of steam rose off the stallion's back. William could feel the tension in his shoulders and neck release and he exhaled slowly. Despite the dim light of the moon, he looked up to see the large mottled brown iris and dark pupil of the horse staring at him. The stallion's nostrils flared and he blew warm air in William's face. He smiled and closed his eyes again, picturing their encounter with the Lord High Admiral, Sir Robert, Lord Thomas, and their small hunting party. Once again a chance encounter had led to more trouble.

As William considered each event over the last few days, another thought began to dawn on him. In each instance, there was always someone put in his path to keep things from getting worse, first the Magistrate, then Agnes, the Lord High Admiral, and now Gilbert. "God, are you trying to tell me something?" He asked honestly and sincerely and in a flash a thought occurred to him. God was watching out for him and would continue to do so. A chill crept up his spine as he remembered some of the thoughts, which had gone through his head in the last few days. If He was watching William that closely, then He also knew what he had been thinking. He silently asked God to forgive him of those as well.

The more he considered it, the more he realized how blessed his trip actually had been so far. Even with the hunchbacked, deformed and scarred merchant. As he had admitted to Robert, Gilbert would not have been his first or second or even third choice. He didn't like admitting it, but he felt he needed to be true to himself. He had allowed Gilbert's personal appearance to cloud his judgment. If he had followed that impulse he wouldn't have had the chance to meet someone who had been there on his father's last day, someone who had fought alongside his father and uncle, and who owed his very life to them. It was like looking at a great, intricately drawn circle, with lines of others' lives intersecting and crossing over each other. Here was his life and lives of those people who had come in contact with him so far in his short time living.

God had orchestrated their meeting with Gilbert, knowing his personal history and how much it would mean to William to know someone who had been at Neville's Cross. There was a lesson there as well and it teased at the corners of William's mind. He had been ready to judge Gilbert based on his appearance. Without knowing anything about either Benedict or Gilbert, William would have initially chosen based solely on looks. He had judged. Then a thought hit him and a quote came to mind, "judge not lest ye be judged." Robert had told him several months ago that life serves back in the coin you pay. Here was a lesson he would not soon forget. He was alive because of Gilbert, his last choice.

Since God had obviously orchestrated their meeting, it was God who knew what would happen on the road to the inn. He wanted Gilbert there in order to protect William. Another chill ran up William's spine. Who was he that God should be so mindful of him? "God, I am just William Simpson. I am an orphan trying to find his uncle and bring him home. What could you possibly want from me? What have I done or what could I do to have earned this?"

A thought, a very small, quiet voice spoke to him in a flash. "You cannot earn what I have given William and you have already done my work since you set out from your home. In Salisbury, Downton, the New Forest, and now in Southampton, evil has been replaced with good. What was meant for harm you have helped turn around for good. Stay humble William and I will continue to use you…"

Tears welled up in his eyes and spilled down his cheeks. Did he just imagine this or did God really just speak to him? Was there now some even greater purpose God had in store for him? A second, more frightening thought crossed his mind. If God has already used him to do His purposes and he has already gone through all these trials, how much more was he still going to have to go through? Another chill raced through him as he imagined each day getting harder and harder. He didn't think the trip would be easy, but he never envisioned this either. He wished Robert would come back quickly while these thoughts came to mind, so he could ask for his advice. He was afraid, if he waited too long he may not remember the voice and what it suggested.

"God, grant me the strength I need to do the work you have set before me because I do not feel very strong right now." As if in a way of reminder, his left arm began throbbing where it had been cut during his assault in Salisbury. Up to that point, William had just felt lucky the knife which had been thrown at him had not done more harm. Now a new thought flashed through his mind. Perhaps it wasn't luck. Maybe that was God too, keeping him from further harm? After all, a few inches to the right and the knife would have landed in his back. If God was willing to intervene on his behalf, he hoped he wouldn't do anything, which would stop that hand of protection in his life.

"If sin rules in your life William, my power in your life will be killed. If you let me rule in your life, sin will be killed. Sin is the greatest blessing blocker in everyone's life."

"God, give me the strength and wisdom and understanding to know what might be a sin and to avoid it at all costs." William dropped his head and said, out loud, "Amen."

Seconds later the doors to the inn opened up and a group of five loud, seemingly happy men came out and down the steps and onto the street. As they passed William and the stallion, he could smell the strong aroma of ale as it trailed behind them, and at the same time he realized one of them was actually a young woman. He just caught a glimpse of her bright copper colored hair as it glinted in the pale moonlight. She stood almost a half head taller than the men around her and was nearly eye-to-eye with William. He wouldn't have thought anything else about it if he hadn't caught a glimpse of the faces of two of the men as they brushed beside him. There was something about the intention in their eyes. He was beginning to better understand that look and the motives behind it. A worried thought crossed his mind.

He had no idea who the young woman was, but he didn't believe she realized the danger in which she had placed herself. Whatever they had told her or promise they had made to get her to follow them out of the inn, the group continued to walk down the street, laughing and making their way closer to the warehouses and quays and ships at anchor. Just as William was wishing Robert and Gilbert would come out, the group turned the corner and disappeared down a side street; seconds later a shriek and a scream for help split the night. Somewhere nearby a dog barked and the stallion tossed his head, snorting and stamping his front hooves on the stone roadway.

The scream came again and then was suddenly muffled. The dog continued to bark and another took up howling. The stallion now began straining against his reins and William grabbed his bridle at the cavesson, placing his hand on the horse's nose to soothe him. As he did so he looked into the coursers' eye and what he saw shocked him. It wasn't fear, as he thought. Instead he saw something else. Something deep down which was finding its way to the surface. The stallion didn't want to run away from the screaming. It had been trained as a light warhorse, to carry an armed man into combat and the screams awakened inside it the training it had received.

Without second guessing himself, William put his left foot in the stirrup and, pulling himself up by the pommel, threw his right leg over the cantle. Before he even had a chance to get his right foot in place the stallion began trotting and then cantering down the street. William had just enough presence of mind to find his seat and make sure he had a good grasp of the reins. A few seconds later he was able to get his right foot in the iron stirrup only to look up and realize they were near the side street the group had turned down.

What little light there was on the street had come from the occasional street lantern or torch beside a doorway. As it happened, the men had picked a side street without a lantern at its corner, and William found himself turning into a darkened alley with his heart thundering in his ears. Although the darkness made it difficult to see clearly, his other senses were sharpened in the moment; the feel of the well-oiled and smooth reins in his hands, the salty, slightly fetid breeze in his face, the breathing of the stallion and the feel of the saddle beneath him. He gripped the courser with his knees even tighter as he swung him into the alley and kicked his heals once to speed him on.

His mount needed no such encouragement and neighed loudly. The barking and howling dogs were still at it. And there, just a short distance down the side street he could see a tight group of men in the middle of a struggle. Muffled cries came from the group as well. The stallion inhaled deeply and neighed so loud even the dogs were forced to stop. William wasn't sure what would happen next or what he was going to do, but the courser had no such hesitation. Seconds later two of the men looked up to find a jet black, steaming charger bearing down on them. They froze at the sight and then just as quickly panicked when they realized the horse wasn't going to slow down.

William watched as these two fled farther down the darkened street, leaving only two others. One of the attackers was holding the girl, an arm wrapped around her neck and the other hand clamped firmly over her mouth. A bruise was already visible on the side of her face. The other was struggling with her arms as he tried to tear open her loose blouse. He held in one trembling hand a small blade and sheer terror was marked in the wide brilliantly blue eyes of the young woman as she tried to kick herself free.

Even as William and the stallion got to them, the one with the knife looked up in time to see the horse racing down on him. He screamed a curse and flung his hands up over his head, dropping the knife in the process. Neither helped as the horse simply ran him down, striking at him with its front hooves even as its momentum knocked him aside. He crumpled into a heap and lay quite still, face down with one of his arms twisted at an odd angle beneath him.

William swung the stallion around to the right, only to find the girl slumped on the ground and her last attacker standing defiantly over her body. She seemed to have fainted but William could see she was still breathing. Her light blue cotte had been torn open, exposing very pale, freckled skin of her neck and shoulders and a linen kirtle beneath. The lone attacker's grin was hideous with its broken, darkened teeth and in his hand he now held a baselard. "She is not yours boy. I was sent for her. Now take your horse and ride on home."

Something about the way he spoke of the girl lit a fire inside of William. Without realizing exactly what he was doing, he reached for the long dagger he had taken from Benedict. Its iron hilt felt cold in his hand and he willed himself not to shake as he pointed the blade at the attacker. "You do not know what you do or to whom you speak. If you leave now, no harm will come to you."

"Brave words, boy," he spat and then lunged forward, around the neck of the black stallion trying to drive his blade deep into Williams exposed thigh. The movement caught William off guard and he hardly had time to react as he swiftly brought his own blade down to parry the thrust.

The horse wasn't as surprised. It danced to the right, pulling William out of the way of the attack, and then half spun to the left while turning his head almost back on himself. In doing so he was able to grab the man at the base of the neck, catching mostly just the shirt and sleeveless cotte. A painful shriek from the man suggested to William the stallion may have grabbed more than just clothing with his teeth. The courser lifted him off the ground and shook once and the dagger clattered to the ground. He shook him again and then with a toss of his head sent him sailing across the narrow street and into the wall of the building opposite them. He hit headfirst and fell to the ground where he lay motionless.

William tucked the baselard in his belt and jumped down off the stallion. As he came upon the girl, her eyes were just starting to flutter open and as she saw him approach she raised one hand in defense while the other clutched at her torn cotte, attempting to cover up her exposed linen undergarment. "I am not here to harm you," William explained as he held out a hand to help her on her feet. "We should not stay here though," he looked around at the two unconscious men. "We need to get back to the Inn. Can you ride?" He motioned with his head to the stallion, which stood proudly beside William, stamping at the stone pavement and tossing his head slightly, as if to say… "We need to go, now."

The girl mutely nodded and took William's offered hand while trying her best to hold the remains of her cotte together. He helped her stand, only to have to reach out and grasp her arm as she tottered and swayed in place. A moment later and more assistance on his part they were astride the courser and trotting back out of the alley and up the hill to the inn. "What is your name?" William asked over her shoulder. The girl sat before him, and leaned back against him for support. "Helen… Helen de Tuddyr." She had a strange, lilting accent. He had never heard it before.

"Where are you from Helen, and why did you follow those men?"

"I am from York and I was under the impression those men would help me get back. They told me a ship would be setting sail for the eastern coast on the morrow and I went with them to gain passage." Her voice cracked and was as unsteady as herself, but there was something in the way she responded. It was more than just the accent.

Before he could respond, they found themselves in front of the inn, with Robert and Gilbert waiting outside. Neither one looked at all pleased but their expression changed as soon as they realized he was not alone. William dismounted, and then reached up to help Helen down from the saddle. It was difficult because she had to keep one hand firmly on her cotte to keep it closed. Gilbert had already grabbed the stallion's bridle and was stroking its muzzle and scratching it under the chin.

"You have both been in a fight, eh, William?" Gilbert had noticed something in the stallion's eye.

William nodded and then quickly recounted what he had watched happen as the noisy group of men came out of the inn and the realization that a young woman was with them. When he heard the scream he didn't think but simply reacted. "If not for the brilliance of this horse, I am not sure the outcome would have been the same. Whoever trained him, did it right." This was the first Helen had heard what had happened after she collapsed trying to fight off the four men and her azure eyes lit with admiration for her rescuer and his horse.

"You are luckier than you realize lad," Gilbert advised. "If the horse is that well trained, one word, spoken by you or anyone else, and he would have thrown you to the ground." William considered what he said and was about to ask for the word, when he realized courtesy required introductions.

"May I introduce Helen de Tuddyr of York. She was under the impression the men she accompanied would be able to take her to a ship which was to set sail for the eastern coast." William introduced Robert and Gilbert to her and when she turned her attention on the hunchback, she caught her breath in her throat.

Gilbert smiled a sad, understanding smile. "It is all right, lass. You may not like the looks, but my heart is in the right place and the two of us find ourselves with a debt to pay to the same young man and his family. As for the ship you are seeking, there are none setting sail for the eastern coast this time of year."

Robert turned and looked back at the inn and thought a moment. "William, we have a room and Gilbert has made contact with the courier. Let us get inside where it is warm and we will eat and decide what is best to do next. It may be another day before any ships will set sail."

"And what of the stallion?"

"I will take care of him," Gilbert answered despite William's protests over his shoulder injury. He waved it off, and despite being still a little unsteady on his feet he led the horse a little farther up the hill and through an archway on the front of the inn. Robert led the way into the inn and William removed his cloak, placing it around Helen's shoulders.

"Pull it closed," William suggested, as they took the steps back into the inn. "If those men had friends, they will have less chance to notice you have returned." He pulled the hood up and over her bright copper hair, hoping it would help. She suddenly seemed unsteady on her feet and William offered her an arm as they entered into the Shipwright's Inn together. He could feel her shaking beneath the thick woolen material and he gripped her arm tightly. "It will be all right. No harm will come to you my lady, I promise."

•••

It only took a moment for Robert to lead them down a long hallway and into a room, very much like the one they shared at the Bear and Boar, with a warm fire crackling in a well-furnished sitting room and a door to the side leading, presumably, to a bedroom. Helen hadn't spoken since she had introduced herself to William outside the inn and as soon as they entered the room she began shaking uncontrollably. Robert saw this and led her to one of the chairs closest to the fire. "You have had a terrible fright, lass. Sit, breathe deeply and thank God you are still whole and unharmed."

Helen nodded and then her lips began trembling. Seconds later tears started spilling down her cheeks and she lowered her head into her hands, sobbing deeply. Robert turned to William, grabbing his arm and leading him away from the fire and closer to the door they just entered. "Now I wish we had Agnes here," he whispered. "We need a woman's touch. The last she needs after what she has been through is more men around her trying to help."

"The best we have to offer is some warm food, wine and a dry bed. I have no problems sleeping on the floor by the fire. We should try and find a way to replace or repair her cotte though. It was torn open by those men. I do not think the kirtle beneath was damaged though." William tried his best to wipe from his thoughts the memory of her pale, freckled skin, reflected in the dim moonlight.

Robert nodded his agreement. "The food and drink should be here soon," then in an afterthought he added, "Do you know anything else about her?"

William shook his head. "No more than I told you and Gilbert. But there is something else. Something different about her…"

Robert turned and looked again at the young woman. Her sobs had quieted and as she leaned over, her bright red hair fell out of the hood of William's cloak, surrounding her pale, freckled face. The old tutor chewed on his inside cheek a moment and murmured, "Besides the obvious beauty?"

Just then there was a knock at the door and Helen inhaled sharply, standing and backing away towards the fire, her eyes wide with fear, nearly knocking over the chair in the process. She clutched at the cloak, drawing it closer about her as if she meant to use it to disappear. William took a step closer to her, and then turned his back in order to face the door. Robert drew the lock then opened it enough to see Gilbert standing in the hall with a tray laden with roasted beef, cabbages and carrots and a small pitcher of what was probably wine. He ushered him in and then set the lock after. The savory aromas rushed into the room before him, setting all their senses tingling. It had been hours since either of them had eaten.

"I asked the landlord for a little extra as well as a mug for each of us." He quickly set the tray on the table and then turned to Helen, bowing dramatically while flourishing his hands in the process. William wasn't certain if he was being overly dramatic or comical. It seemed like a little of both. "My lady, will you do me the honor of dining with the likes of myself and these two good men?" He smiled in such a way you couldn't help but want to say yes. At least William found himself thinking that.

Helen blinked thick tears from her eyes and then wiped her face on the edge of William's cloak. She took a deep breath and stood up straight, dropping the hood back in the process. In the fire and lamp light her hair appeared the color of darkened coals which only made the flawless, almost milk white color of her skin seem even brighter. She swallowed and nodded, smiling a shy but still brilliant white smile, doing all three a deep courtesy, her head just slightly bowed. "I thank you for your kindness; each of you." And here she turned her attention to William.

His breath caught in his throat when her vivid blue eyes met his. As Robert said, she was beautiful, despite the fact that her eyes were red rimmed from the tears and the darkening bruise on her left cheek. Agnes' warmth had attracted William. The strength of the oldest daughter he and Robert had helped rescue that morning intrigued him. And yet here, standing before him, was a woman who he was sure knew her way around a court. He couldn't be completely sure but if he guessed he would have thought she was also a few years older than him.

Her bearing and carriage suggested a certain maturity and teaching. This wasn't some simple peasant girl as he first thought. He was sure, like Robert and himself, she was hiding something. William smiled and bowed, purposely bending at the waist instead of a simple nod. "William Edward's son of Dorchester, at your service, my lady."

Robert and Gilbert introduced themselves and then offered her the first chair. She accepted and glided into it, quickly clasping her hands before her, with her head bowed in prayer. William, Robert and Gilbert followed suit. With that strange, lilting accent, she spoke quietly, yet fervently. "God bless my rescuers and see them safely on their way, wherever they fare. Watch over them, guide them and let your hand be upon them. Bless this food that it strengthens me in the task You have set before me. I ask this all in Jesus' holy name. Amen." The three men in the room echoed the same, "Amen," and then took their seats.

For quite a while no one spoke. Neither William, nor Robert had eaten since they entered the New Forest and the smell of the roasted beef and vegetables had their mouths watering. One thing William noticed when he finally did take a moment to pause and look up from the meal: He, Robert and Helen only used their first three fingers while they ate and yet Gilbert used all five. Although it wasn't common throughout all the land, most wellborn learned to eat this way, while peasants simply used all the tools God gave them. The thought quickly faded though, as he was consumed with how the food was deliciously prepared and the wine was outstanding. When William mentioned this to Robert, it was Gilbert who clarified things.

"William, in Southampton, we ship English cotton and wool for French wine." He paused a moment to suck the marrow out of one of the bones on the platter. Once he was confident he had worked it clean, he continued, "It is what has made this city rich. This close to the quays and their warehouses is where you will find some of the best wine. Many times it never leaves the city." Several minutes later, William found himself comfortably stuffed and just a little heady from the wine. His ears felt warm and he was smiling a lot.

He had pushed back from the table and folded his hands in his lap, closing his eyes and nearly resting his chin on his chest. He felt so completely comfortable and at peace, he murmured to himself, "thank You God for your protection and guidance today. Continue to watch over us and bless us in the days to come." It wasn't until Robert muttered back, "Amen," did he realize he had spoken out loud.

William looked up to find Helen staring at him again. It seemed there was a question in her eyes, but she didn't voice it. Instead she rose from the table, "I have no way of repaying you for your gallantry this evening, at least not at this moment." Despite the torn cotte and William's weather stained cloak draped over her shoulders, she held herself with regal bearing.

Before she could continue, Robert held up a hand. "Lady Helen, you will find through that door, a small bedroom with a well-tended fire. It will not exactly fit, but I laid out an extra short sleeved cotte of ours to replace the torn one you wear. The door can be locked from the inside so you will be safe and I dare say the rest will do you good. We will make ourselves comfortable here. Be assured, no one else will try to harm to you or bother your sleep this evening."

Helen stood in thought for a quick moment and then made up her mind. She nodded and smiled at all three of them. "Until the morrow then; good night, gentles all." She did a courtesy and crossed to the bedroom.

"*Tan y bore. Chysgu'n dda,*" Robert added.

With her hand on the latch, Helen turned her head to smile a flashing smile. "*Chysgu'n dda,*" she replied, and then the smile dropped from her face. A flush of red rose to her cheeks and she looked angry, her brow furrowing. She stood a moment in uncertainty and then quickly slipped into the bedroom, latching the door locked behind her with a loud snap. He couldn't make out what she said, but he could hear her let out a loud exclamation.

For several moments, William found himself lost in thought as he continued to stare at the door to the bedroom. There was something about Helen which tugged at his mind. An elusive thought he just couldn't grasp hold of. It was replaced by a question, "What was it you said to her and why did it anger her do you think?"

Robert pushed his chair back from the table and stretched his legs towards the small fire. The night wasn't chilly enough to require it, but it certainly made one feel more at ease. "Your uncle's holdings require him to deal with many different nations, including Wales. I learned a little of the Welsh language to make sure the merchants and the Lords of the Marches we dealt with were not trying to use it as some secret during any negotiations." He stared at the fire for a moment, his thoughts seemingly lost in the mesmerizing dance of the flames. "Her accent gave her away. She is not who she claims to be, much as we are not simply William and Robert of Dorchester. I wanted to test her to see if she was from where I believed."

"What did you say to her?" Gilbert asked smiling and enjoying the clever trick Robert had made to uncover a little of the truth about the beautiful young woman in the adjoining bedroom.

"I simply told her to sleep well." He then drew his legs up and turned back towards William while taking in a deep breath and exhaling slowly. "William, there is something about this young woman I do not understand. How did she find her way to Southampton in the first place? What was she doing in the common room of this inn tonight? It is obvious from her manners at the table, as well as her poise, she is not what she appears."

"I feel the same way. She has been raised in privilege or very closely around it."

"I think she has only ever been around it," Gilbert added.

"What makes you say that?" Robert asked.

"She has the manners but she lacks a little of the common sense. It is either that or she has a tremendous amount of self-confidence.

Whichever the case, she is a beautiful woman, apparently traveling alone. After what happened earlier, why would she agree to come to a room with three strange men unless she grew up trusting everyone around her or believing, without a doubt she could handle the situation?"

"Do you think she will be willing to tell us more about herself in the morning?" If he closed his eyes, William could see Helen standing beside the bedroom door, smiling at him. He shook his head in an effort to clear his thoughts. It didn't really help much. Maybe it was the red hair. He hadn't met very many people, let alone women, graced with such color as hers.

"She may be willing to tell the two of you, but as for myself" and here Gilbert stood up from the table, wincing slightly, "I do not plan to still be here when she awakes." William started to protest but the merchant simply held up his right hand. "I have introduced Robert to the courier and he has agreed to take the stallion. Your passage across the channel will be aboard the same ship. All expenses and then some are already covered by the good beasts' worth."

"What will you do? Benedict is not dead. He could come after you…"

"I have done well for myself this last year or so, William, just as I learned to do before the battle. I will continue to do so. For now though, I will tend to this wound and recover my strength as it heals."

"What if there was another way forward?"

Gilbert paused and his brow furrowed. "What do you mean?"

Now it was William's turn to pause and consider. He turned to Robert who held both hands out; palms' up, signaling this was going to be William's decision alone. As the future earl of Dorchester, he would have to make these. Robert had told William a long time ago, one of the most difficult and important tasks he would ever have was surrounding himself with the right men. "A wise man has many counselors, William,"

Robert had told him that day. "Just be careful you choose those closest to you wisely for their counsel will help determine your future." Did he consider Gilbert the right kind of man? So far by all his actions he thought so.

"The ancestral home of my family, Crandor Castle, sits on the rolling hills outside of Dorchester. Those hills and the green turf covering them were once renowned for the horses raised there. It could be that way again. Would you consider coming to Dorset County and creating just such a thing? The stables would be yours to do with as you see fit. Lord knows there is plenty of room after uncle took the last of them with him to France."

William watched Gilbert closely. It looked as if the merchant was going to be angry and then he realized it was taking all his effort to keep his emotions in check. They spilled over slightly as a single tear dropped from his eyes. To keep his lips from trembling, the hunchback bit the lower of them. Dropping his head slightly, he shook it, slowly, from side to side. "I already owe your family so much… Why would you offer this?"

"Because my father never came back from Neville's Cross and you did." On hearing this, the hunchback looked up, locking eyes with William, "and you would honor his memory and the sacrifice he was willing to make by taking this position." They continued to stare at each other. For William's part he wasn't sure if Gilbert would agree but he knew he was offering this for the right reasons. In his own mind he could see this simple, disfigured merchant, because of his way with horses, creating something great in Dorchester.

"I would like the night to consider and sleep on this decision."

"I would expect nothing less." Gilbert nodded to Robert and then turned once again to William. It looked like he might say something more, and then simply turned away, excusing himself and wishing them both a blessed evening.

As soon as the door shut and the steps in the hallway faded, Robert turned to his young student, staring intently and then grasped him on the shoulder, as he always did when making an important point. "Do you realize you have accomplished more for the good in these last few days than most men accomplish in their entire lives?"

William smiled broadly. He couldn't remember the last time he had such a compliment.

Robert cut in on his moment of glory. "Never forget, though, William, what follows pride." His young student closed his eyes a moment and nodded his head. It was a repeated reminder and one he gladly accepted.

"I do not feel like have done anything myself. I have just been in a certain place at a certain time and these things have happened."

"Do not fool yourself, William. God will put you in a position or a situation and give you the choice to do good or not. That is what He always is looking for; those men and women who are willing to do good, no matter what, in whatever the situation."

"It sounds like the oath my uncle told me a knight takes after he earns his spurs."

Robert nodded. "To be without fear before all your enemies; to be bold and upright that God may love you; to speak the truth, no matter the cost, even if it means losing all you hold dear, and to safeguard the innocent, protecting those who are too weak to defend themselves." Robert's voice had deepened and as he spoke William could feel the small hairs on the back of his neck prickle. "That is a knight's oath and the entire oath is his way of life, not just one part or another. What God cares about most is here," and Robert pointed to William's head, "and here," and then his heart. "When both of these say you are doing what is right, then it is the right thing to do. And you do not have to have the spurs to live your life this way."

"My heart and my mind say that what I have offered to Gilbert is the right thing and it is for the right reasons and great things could come of it."

"And mine agree, William. Now it will be up to Gilbert to decide. We give him the free will to choose, just as God gives us the free will to trust and walk with Him, or not."

William nodded and then added as an afterthought, "and what of Helen?" He turned and looked once again at the door of the bedchamber.

Robert stood and stretched and began unpacking a blanket, spreading it out on the floor in front of the small grate and its glowing embers. "That will be for the morning to show us William. We will also give her free will to tell us what she feels is the right thing to say. Whether it is the whole or even partial truth will be up to her. As for me, and after this long day, I am ready for sleep and quiet dreams." Even before William arose from his chair, Robert curled up in his blanket, rolled over and quickly drifted to sleep as evidenced by his deep sonorous breathing. All this took less than a minute.

William sat watching his tutor for a while, his mind drifting from one thought to another, not lingering for long on any until it caught on an idea and stuck with it. He smiled and closed his eyes, imagining life at Crandor after the return of his uncle, this time adding Gilbert to the image. Robert had told him of the power of a vision. "God gave each of us the ability to dream for a reason," his tutor had told him. As long as he continued to keep it vivid and real in his mind it would come to pass.

All great and wonderful things began as someone's dream. William's was such a vivid vision he could almost believe it was a memory and not a pleasant thought for the future. Either way he soon found himself nodding off where he sat and decided a blanket on the floor seemed a better idea. A moment later with Roberts slow, steady breathing only a few feet away, and the deep crimson glow of the coals visible even through his closed eyes, William drifted into a sound sleep. He was too tired to notice the bedroom door had been opened slightly during their discussion and now closed silently with the lock resetting. After all, it had been a very full day for them both.

Chapter Fifteen

A knock at the door roused William from a deep sleep. The coals in the grate had completely burned down to a pile of dark ash. His body didn't agree with the sleeping arrangements and all he felt was stiff and sore. The wood planking of the floor was roughly sawn and the boards were full of knots. Several must have been right where William chose to sleep and had pressed on his lower back. He had been so tired the night before did not notice them before he fell asleep.

Robert must have felt much the same because he was moving just as slowly. As William sat up, rubbing the sleep from his eyes, and stretching the kinks out of his back, the knock came again. He and Robert were on their unsteady feet at about the same time and crossed the short distance to the door together. Robert quietly drew back the lock and opened it just enough to reveal a well-dressed young man. William noticed a small crest sewn onto the left chest of his short-sleeved woolen cotte; it was quartered with opposite corners containing the three gold lions on a red field of England, and the other two sections with the gold fleurs-de-lis of France, on a blue background. He recognized the sigil at once. Standing before him was a courier of King Edward III!

For over 150 years the three golden, walking lions, stared out of the

Royal Arms of England from their red background. Since 1198 and the time of the first king Richard they had come to stand for England. With the passing of Charles IV of France in 1340, and no male heir, Edward laid claim to the French crown through his mother, Isabella, Charles' sister. Although French law asserted that no female could inherit the crown, Edward suggested it did not disallow a male heir through the female line. His mother was the only surviving sibling of Charles and therefore he had the closest claim to the throne. He asserted this by quartering the royal arms of England with the arms of France and thereby claiming France as his own. Obviously the French king Philip, cousin of Isabella, took a dislike to this arrangement. Eight years had passed and the war between these two kings continued.

Robert instantly recognized the young man's face and smiled broadly while opening the door completely. "Sir Geoffrey, come in." Robert stepped back to allow the young man to enter and then turned to William, adding, "may I introduce my travel companion, William of Dorchester."

William nodded deeply and muttered sleepily, "at your service, Sir Geoffrey." He failed in his attempt to stifle a yawn, despite the fact he was in the presence of the king's own representative. When this young man spoke, he spoke, not only with the authority of the king, but as the king himself.

"Forgive my early morning intrusion, but I have just been notified by the captain of our ship, the tide has shifted enough that we will get ready to set sail. He expects to be underway no later than 3 bells." Something about his manners caught Robert's attention.

"If I may be so bold as to ask, Sir Geoffrey, is everything all right?"

The young, knighted, royal courier shook his head and a worried expression crossed his face. William then noticed he looked as though he had even less sleep than the two of them. "I had other duties to attend to while in Southampton and one of those charges has not happened the way it was expected. Now I find myself in a position in which I will have to explain to the highest authorities why I was not able to do all I was assigned." He dropped his eyes a moment and shook his head, muttering, what William thought was, "silly girl."

"Although we just arrived in Southampton yesterday evening, we have made acquaintances and could make inquiries if they could help your situation. What is it you find yourself unable to accomplish?" Robert asked.

The young courier's eyes brightened and he smiled just as there was another knock at the door. This time, William answered and let Gilbert into the room. Having done business several times in the past few months, the merchant and courier exchanged little in the way of greeting beside a quick smile and a nod of acknowledgement. "Sir Geoffrey just let us know the tide is changing and they will set sail this morning. Is the stallion ready for the trip?"

Gilbert nodded to Robert and then turned, bowing slightly to the royal courier, "he is ready, Sir Geoffrey and can be sent to the ship in a moment's notice." The royal courier nodded his approval.

"Gilbert, perhaps you can help us in another task," Robert continued. "Sir Geoffrey was just going to tell us of a difficulty he has to overcome before our ship sets sail this afternoon."

"If I can help, Sir Geoffrey, you have my assurance I will do all I can to assist."

"It is a very delicate matter and one which will require the utmost discretion." And here, the young knight paused, considering what he had just said. "Please, I mean no offense, however, although I know guild man Gilbert and have had opportunity to work with him these last several months, I do not know either of you and therefore, as much as I would appreciate the help you may offer, I must decline."

Before either Robert or William could respond, Gilbert spoke up. "If I may be so bold, Sir Geoffrey, I can personally vouchsafe for both of these men. Although they travel without revealing their identities, for personal reasons, I can assure you, I hold William's family in the highest regard and even owe my life to his father and uncle. Since their arrival in Southampton last evening, I have again found myself in his debt and have even been offered a position in his household." On hearing this, the courier's eyebrows shot up and he turned to take a closer look at the young man still rubbing the sleep out of his eyes. Up to that point he had assumed William was just another apprentice, traveling with his master on business. "I asked to sleep on the decision and made my way here this morning to give them my answer."

"And what have you decided?" Sir Geoffrey asked, taking a quick interest, which was peaked in him by just enough information given by the hunchbacked merchant.

Gilbert smiled and bowed deeply at the waist towards William. Upon rising he had a large, gap-toothed smile spread across his face. "If he will have me as I am, even with this shoulder, which will take time to heal, I offer to give him my best."

William smiled in returned and extended his hand to the merchant. Gilbert stared at it a moment, hesitating. He looked up into William's eyes with a tear, threatening to spill over and down his cheek. "As I said last night, Gilbert, it would be my honor to have you with us in Dorchester." Gilbert took the offered hand and William drew him a little closer, his hand on his good shoulder and whispered in his ear, "an honor." When he released him and drew back, Gilbert kept his head down for a moment, hiding the emotions, which threatened to overwhelm him.

Sir Geoffrey watched with fascination and again turned his attention to the young man he had just met. What was it about that town in Dorset County? What significance did it have and why would Gilbert bow to this young man as a peer of the realm? Before he could follow the thought to its conclusion, Robert interrupted.

"Although, as Gilbert has said, we are not in a position to reveal ourselves completely, if you will find the confidence given by guild man Gilbert, we will do all we can to assist you and in that way do all we can to serve him whom you represent and serve."

Sir Geoffrey chewed on the corner of his thin moustache, nodding to himself for a moment. Finally he came to a decision, "very well, I accept your offer." He took a deep breath and continued, "Yesterday evening it was arranged for me to meet someone here and find her safe escort to the Marches. To safeguard her identity, even from myself, I was told little about her other than a few personal features and her name. The reason I was in the common room last evening was to meet my charge and see her safely on her way. Needless to say, that never happened."

William and Robert exchanged knowing glances. The Marches were the independent borderlands between England and Wales. The Lords of the March were powerful men, and as recently as 20 years before, several of them had helped overthrow King Edward's father. It was even claimed, that King Edward's mother, the Queen Consort, Isabella of France, took Roger de Mortimer, First Earl of March, as a lover after leaving Edward. Edward II was little loved by most of the people of England and even less so by his own wife. Isabella and Roger eventually raised a small army in France and returned to England, captured the king, and placed Isabella's son Edward III in his father's place. For three years she and the Lord de Mortimer became rulers of England in all but name, only to be forced aside by Edward III when he came of age. Isabella was allowed to live, although out of favor and not at court, however, the new king had her lover hung without trial.

"I know she arrived in Southampton because the ship which carried her from Calais arrived the day before last. Previous arrangements had placed last night and this inn as our time and place of rendezvous. The last person I have found to see her was the Captain of her ship." The young knight paused at this point after noticing the glances passing between Robert and William. "It would seem you may have information I need."

William nodded and Robert answered, "Yes, we do Sir Geoffrey. William met someone yesterday evening. I will let him tell the tale, but to make sure she is the same, what were you told by way of description and name?"

Sir Geoffrey paused and looked back at Gilbert. The hunchbacked merchant nodded, smiling, doing his best to assure the courier all would be well. He took a deep breath, holding it for a short moment, then added, "she is tall, fair skinned with bright red hair, crystal blue eyes and she would be traveling under the name of…"

"Helen de Tuddyr of York," no one had heard the door open to the adjacent bedroom. Helen stood with her arms across her chest, wearing the short-sleeved cotte offered to her by Robert and a dark look on her face. "Well met, but late, Sir Geoffrey."

The young knight and royal courier bowed his head slightly, never taking his eyes off the beautiful young woman before him. "My apologies for not finding you last night…"

Helen waved off the apology and stepped out of the doorway, crossing the room and doing the young knight a courtesy. When she arose there was a slight flush on her cheeks. "I find myself in an embarrassing situation, Sir Geoffrey and feel I should explain how you come to find your charge in the room of strangers." The courier blinked several times and shook his head slightly, in an effort to clear his thoughts.

"The situation does present questions… and concerns."

"If I may, Sir Geoffrey, I believe the whole situation is our fault to begin with," suggested Robert. This took William and the others by surprise, including Helen.

"How so?" Sir Geoffrey asked.

"When Gilbert and I arrived at the inn last night, in search of you, the young lady was searching for you at the same time. When she was unable to locate you quickly, after all, she had been in Southampton since yesterday and was anxious to continue her journey, several men struck up a conversation with her and assured her they would help her obtain her destination. You were not present to meet her because you were meeting with us at that very moment."

William took up the tale from there, describing what he saw as he waited outside, and what transpired after in the alley, and the offer to keep her safe for the evening.

Sir Geoffrey's eyes widened, as did Helen's, as the tale unfolded, especially when William described taking on the four men on his own. "A very brave thing to do, young man," the knight commented. Helen nodded an agreement. "If you are or were noble born, there may be a pair of spurs for you when this is all said and done."

William smiled briefly, and then shook his head, "I had little time to think or contemplate the risks… or rewards," he added as an afterthought. "What spoke inside of me said that this was not right and I could not stand by and let it happen." He did his best not to meet Helen's gaze. Her clear blue eyes were fixed on him with a look of deep admiration. He was afraid, if she did catch his eye, he would find it nearly impossible to retrieve.

Robert may have noticed this because he quickly cut in, "now we find ourselves at the end of the tale and the beginning of the decision. How can we safely see this young woman to the Marches? I trust she knows who she is supposed to meet once there?" Robert turned to Helen with the question.

"War has come again to France, the more so in the north, and it looks as though it may be there for a long while, or at least, that was the concern of those who were my caretakers. It was their suggestion I should leave France and return to my father's homeland." She turned her attention to Robert and added as an aside, "you rightly guessed this Welsh heritage sir, although how you did it is beyond my understanding." Turning back to the others, she drew herself up to her full height and straightened her shoulders, seeming to draw an aura of royalty about her as she continued. "I am traveling to Wigmore Castle, where the Earl of March is to be my protector."

At the mention of Roger de Mortimer, 2nd Earl of March, all eyebrows were raised. After what his grandfather and Queen Isabella had accomplished there was little to no telling where or how far this family's ambition would take them.

"I am sure Lord de Mortimer will gladly receive you," Robert offered after clearing his throat, "but the question still begs an answer, how do we see you safely there?"

"There may be one other question we should consider," William posed. When he had their full attention, he asked, "begging your pardon, my lady, but should we even consider sending you to them?"

"They are my family!" Helen suddenly sounded wounded and imperious at the same time. She shook her head, crossing her arms even tighter than before. On her face was a harsh scowl. "You know not what you speak of. You cannot…" She paused a moment then threw up her arms in disgust. "Why should I even try to reason or explain to you…" She did not have to say more. William understood. He would have made the same judgement just a few days ago.

It was Gilbert who came to his defense. "My lady de Tuddyr, it is you who do not know what you speak of. If you only knew…"

William stopped him in mid-sentence when he reached out and grabbed his good shoulder. "I travel as I am for a very good reason, Gilbert. You know this and you know why we must keep it this way…"

"I agree, William," Robert added. "The course of action I suggested when we left Dorchester has not changed. The less who know the truth the better off we will be."

Helen and Geoffrey continued staring at William, as if trying to read him better, and then she slowly added, "You may be more than you suggest, William. There is something… But that still does not explain why I should not go to the offered protection of Lord de Mortimer."

William shook his head slowly, then finally raised his eyes to meet her own. Even in the darkened room they were such a crystal clear blue. It was like looking into the sky on a spring day after a fresh rain. A slight splash of freckles across the bridge of her nose and upper cheeks added just a touch of color to her pale skin. Wrinkles around the corner of her eyes suggested she was more likely to be found laughing than not. "I do not believe I can say why this is so, only that the same voice, the same feeling I had last night outside the inn, when you passed with those men, speaks to me now. As soon as you mentioned Lord de Mortimer I felt it… or knew it." He paused, clearly trying to put to words what he felt. "I believe he is an honorable man and the king believes as well, otherwise he would not have returned the title and lands stripped from his grandfather. But I cannot shake the feeling that you are not to go there."

Robert saw the looks, which passed, between his young student and the beautiful woman he rescued the night before and wondered if there was something else at play. "Try talking it out William. What concern could there possibly be in returning Helen to her family?"

William closed his eyes and asked God for wisdom. Robert had told him that if he honestly desired it, he should ask for it and God would grant him the wisdom and understanding he would need. "God, help me put into words the concern I feel inside," he thought to himself. In a flash another thought hit him and before he realized it, he had spoken it out loud, "because of her real name, not the one she travels by."

Now it was Sir Geoffrey who interrupted, "come now, William, how can you possibly know…"

Helen cut him off when she raised her hand and lowered her eyes. "Because you saved my life, I feel I owe you this." She took a deep breath and closed her eyes a moment. William and Robert could both tell what she was about to reveal was as close to her as their own secret. "My real name is Helen d'Abbeville; I was born and spent most of my life there. I have known little outside the walls of that house and its surrounding grounds. My father was killed before my third birthday and my mother," her voice broke and tears began spilling down her cheeks, "my mother is…"

"Dear Lord," Robert interrupted. "Say no more my lady." He bowed at the waist and signaled to William to do the same. Gilbert followed suit, while Sir Geoffrey stood looking confused and puzzled. When Robert stood back up he turned straight to Helen and, with his hand on his heart added, "I have the privilege, my lady, of introducing you to William de Simpson, nephew and heir of Lord Charles de Simpson, Earl of Dorchester, master of Crandor Castle and Knight of the Garter." Sir Geoffrey's mouth opened and he stared as understanding slowly came to him. Turning to William, Robert continued, "William, may I introduce

Helen d'Abbeville. Beyond that, no one should speak." Turning his attention to the royal courier, he asked, "Sir Geoffrey, when do we need to be aboard ship?"

The young knight was taken aback by the question, his mouth audibly snapped shut and he thought for a moment before answering. "Three… three bells is when the captain thought he would be ready to cast off. The stallion will need to be aboard as well. I do not understand…"

"Very well," Robert purposely cut off his question. "Gilbert, will you escort the courser to the quays and make sure it is aboard the correct ship? Sir Geoffrey, if you will accompany him to ensure all is as it should be. William and I will ready ourselves for the trip across the channel."

"And what of my charge with Lady de Abbeville, or rather de Tuddyr?"

"You were to safely see her on her way north, yes? We will discuss those arrangements when you return." William added. He spoke it in such a simple, confident manner the young knight found himself nodding his approval. If the heir of the Earl of Dorchester suggested it…

As soon as the two others left the room, Robert crossed to the door and listened as the echo of their steps in the hall slowly faded, then turned to his young student. "William, your intuition serves you well." Turning to Helen, he continued, "I have to agree with William, my lady. Now that I know who you are, I too feel that those closest to you will use you and your birthright…"

"I have no birthright… I am a ba…"

"You are the daughter of Roger de Mortimer, first Lord of March and the Queen Consort, Isabella, daughter of Philip IV of France. Do you not see the significance? You are the half-sister of our own King Edward and your mother is cousin to Philip of France." Now it was William's turn to stare, mouth opened. She herself couldn't lay claim to any title, but through her, men could wield power in England and in France. Another thought began to dawn on him, one more sinister and dark.

"I am the product of a love affair which should never have happened. She was still married to the king, her husband..."

"And yet, here you are. We may not always understand God's plan in our life, but be assured my lady; He does have a plan for you." Helen dropped her eyes and a single tear fell down her already streaked cheek. Robert reached out and gently took her hand. When she looked up, startled, he added, "The first thing you need to do is believe, without a doubt, you were created for a great purpose. Never doubt that. God knew all about you, even before your mother birthed you. He even knows the count of all those red hairs on your head." This got a smile from the young woman and she wiped the tears with her free hand.

"I... I thank you for your discretion. This secret has been such a burden, ever since I was told the truth last year."

"You never knew who your parents were until a year ago?" William asked in shock. The idea caused him to momentarily lose the train of thought he had been following. He couldn't imagine going through most of his young life not knowing his parents, or at least who they were. Then he realized how much he had learned about his father in the last few days. It seemed he didn't really know much about his own family, even though he grew up with them. "I am sorry," he added, "that must have been very difficult for you."

Helen nodded. "I was raised by a wonderful family with an estate just outside Abbeville. I know now they were devoted members of my mother's household and agreed to care for me when she and my father returned to England with their army. For the longest time I simply called them aunt and uncle. It was their position in her household which kept the property safe from the French, and my relation to Lord Mortimer which kept us safe after the battle of Crecy." She shuddered as she remembered the horrible sounds of the battle, which was fought less than a day's ride from where she grew up. "While still an infant I was to join my parents in England when the news came of my father's death…" Her voice cracked and she looked on the verge of tears once again.

This time it was William who offered his support. "My father was killed at the battle of Neville's Cross, fighting the Scot's. He and my uncle helped save the life of Gilbert and a group of Welsh bowmen during the battle. When news reached us, my mother shut herself in her room. She died a few weeks later. My uncle agreed to take me in, as his only son had died in a famine several years earlier. He named me his heir in his place." William paused, suddenly feeling emotions tighten his throat, making it difficult to speak. He did so, heavily and took a deep breath, "just over a week ago I received a couriered letter from France saying my uncle had been captured after an ill-prepared skirmish at St. Omer and was being held for ransom by Count Jean Libourne at Chateau de Coucy."

"I know this name," Helen muttered. "I have heard my aunt… my guardians speak of him. He is a fierce knight… and an honorable man." She paused in thought, "what do you intend to do?" The way she posed the question, it was almost as if she already knew the answer.

"We travel in secret as two freemen. Our intention was not to call attention to ourselves, but we have had difficulty with this since we arrived in Salisbury." Robert quickly retold the last few days' activity, including their meeting the Lord High Admiral and their concern with Lord Thomas. Helen's eyes widened as their adventures in England culminated in their attack in the street on the way to the inn, followed by her own rescue.

"You did more yesterday then I did in all my years," she muttered in astonishment, then added quickly when a thought hit her. "I can help you!" Her eyes lit up and a wide smile spread across her face. "My guardians have their family estate just outside Abbeville. The Somme is nearby. Once you get to the estate, they can help you cross into French-held territory with enough supplies to make the trip to Chateau de Coucy and back." She turned to William and the look on her face was so intense it caught him by surprise. He found himself staring into the sparkling blue depths. Her brows were arched and they perfectly framed the smile on her face. He was close enough to see the detail of each and every freckle across her nose and on her cheekbones. Her lips were turned up in a soft smile and white teeth showed beneath.

"Our intention was to land in Calais…" William muttered, still lost in her features.

"On foot it will only take you a few days from the port to the estate outside of Abbeville," Helen continued. She turned to Robert, and William blinked as if newly wakened. "From there, if you use the river, it will take just a few more days to reach Chateau de Coucy."

"We still have not answered my concern," William pointed out, his clouded thoughts sluggishly clarifying. "I do not believe you should go to Lord Mortimer. Something just does not feel right." William stopped a moment and considered what he said, then added, "In the end, it will be up to you Lady Helen. I just wished I knew what the alternatives were."

A knock at the door interrupted all their thoughts. Robert crossed the short distance and let Gilbert in. The hunchback bowed and bobbed his head to Lady Helen and then turned to William. There was a worried expression on his flushed, sweaty face. "William, there is trouble at the quays."

"What kind of trouble, Gilbert?"

He turned to Helen and bobbed again, "beg pardon, m' lady," then turned back to William and Robert, "but Sir Geoffrey is dead."

"Dead?" William asked, incredulously.

"Dear Lord in heaven," Helen murmured while making the sign of the cross and bowing her head. She took a few steps toward the table and sat heavily on one of the chairs. Misfortune seemed to surround her every move since she had left France.

"What exactly happened, Gilbert?" Robert inquired.

The hunchbacked merchant closed his eyes a moment, and then began. "We made our way from the inn to the lower levels of the city with no incident. As befitting a knight, I allowed him to ride the courser, while I followed behind. I did not believe this was a good idea, after what happened last night with Benedict and his men, but Sir Geoffrey would have none of it. 'I am a knight and will ride as one, not walk like a commoner,' he said.

Robert closed his eyes and shook his head slowly, a sad look upon his face. William read his thoughts, reminding himself, once again, what comes after pride. Gilbert paused a moment, then continued, "Since Sir Geoffrey knew which ship you are taking, he headed straight for it. The crowd is thick down near the quays, especially after a neap tide and today was especially true. At one of the closer ships, he dismounted and led the stallion to the ships master and exchanged a few words with him. The stallion was a bit skittish at this point and I was there to help but it took a moment to quiet him down. When I turned back, Sir Geoffrey had finished speaking to the master and captain and I noticed someone step out of the crowd and approach him. I never did get to look on his full face, as he had his back to me.

"I could see Sir Geoffrey's expression and it became quite animated. He shook his head several times. As it happened I was able to push my way back through the crowd and get close enough to hear some of the conversation. The person he spoke to had a very distinctive, high-pitched voice; it was more near a soft screech than a man's normal voice."

At this both William and Robert started. "Gilbert, was this man short, stocky and of fair hair?" Robert asked.

"No, he was not. In fact, I would describe him in the opposite. He was taller than Sir Geoffrey and seemed thinner. Although he wore a cloak, his hood was pushed back. His hair was black as a raven." The description fit Lord Thomas completely. William shook his head in disbelief. They were leaving for France, why would he continue to hound their steps?

"What happened next, Gilbert?" Robert asked.

"I could hear the sound of their voices, but not all the words, except for something Sir Geoffrey exclaimed. 'On my life, Sir, I will not say to your question, regarding the stallion or the woman you speak of…' The stranger muttered something in response, which might have been, 'as you wish.' Just at that same moment the crowd surged around me and I found myself pushed to the side, nearly losing my balance in the process. When I regained my footing and turned around, Sir Geoffrey was nowhere to be seen.

"A woman's scream followed seconds later and I struggled to make my way through the press of people. The good knight lay in a pool of his own blood, a short blade, much like the ones we saw last night, still stuck from his lower chest. Despite his condition, he was trying to speak."

"Dear, Lord. After all that, he could still talk?" Helen muttered her hands were tightly clasped before her, in her lap, to keep them from shaking.

"He only uttered a part of a word, and then he passed on. There is little doubt in my mind he sits with the angels now, after defending you both with his life."

Robert must have seen the look on William's face and read the thoughts behind it, when he added, "it is not your fault William. Sir Geoffrey understood his oath greater than most men: to safeguard the innocent, no matter the cost. These were not just idle words to him. He lived by them… and yes, he was willing to die by them as well." Robert bowed his head and murmured, "no one has greater love than to lay down his life for his friends." He paused a moment further, his lips moving silently in prayer, then turned back to Gilbert and asked, "What did he say?"

"Nothing understandable; not even a word, just, 'Deneh…'"

The room was instantly quiet. Even the soft sobs from Helen were muted in that moment. Then William spoke, "there is no doubt in my mind," he murmured. "Lord Thomas Denebaud is no longer interested in trusting others to deal with us." He turned to Helen and added, "And for some reason he also has interest in you, my lady." The train of thought he was following earlier slowly started coming back.

"He is a desperate man, now, William. He is even willing to kill a courier of the King. Nothing will be beyond him." Robert paused a moment and then continued, "We need to get aboard ship, Gilbert, but we have to be able to do it without attracting the attention of the man you saw. Is there any way to get to the quays and avoid the crowds?" Robert asked.

"I am not staying in this room or this inn on my own," Helen had stood and dried her tears. There was fierce resolution on her face and her hands were clenched in fists. "Sir Geoffrey's mission was to escort me safely out of Southampton and see me on my way to the north. That is not going to happen now, but I will not simply sit here and wait for fate to deal me its hand."

"You must not stay here, my lady," William added, as his thoughts continued to coalesce.

"Gilbert, did Lord Denebaud see you?" Robert asked. He stood with his arms crossed, chewing on the edge of his right thumbnail. William had seen this look before.

"I am a disfigured hunchback," Gilbert answered with only a moderate amount of sarcasm. "No one notices me or looks at me or thinks twice about me."

"It is for that very reason you are the best man for this job."

"What job is that?"

"After getting us to that ship, you will escort Lady Helen out of Southampton as far as Salisbury. There is an inn there; The White Hart, that has frequent visits from coaches. One of these will surely be making its way to the Marches. Once in Salisbury, Lady Helen will need to decide for herself if she will follow the path further north or take another. From Salisbury you will only be two days from Crandor Castle. Since no one notices you, no one will notice her."

Gilbert turned and looked at the young Lady. "It would be an honor… but I frighten her and if we are to walk this path together she will need to trust me. Will you be able to trust me, milady?"

Helen smiled weakly but spoke firmly, "what I do not trust will help me to stay alert. It will help me to watch out for you as well."

Gilbert smiled a broad, gap-toothed grin and chuckled deeply. "Milady honors me with her suggestion I am worth guarding." His smile faded "as for our next move…" In a moment Gilbert set out his plan to get them to the quays. They didn't have much time; two bells had already sounded.

Soon after William found himself walking out of the inn with Robert, Gilbert and Helen. His instinct told him to keep his head up; his eyes wide open, scanning the crowd of people streaming down the hill toward the quays. But Gilbert's plan called for something different. He lowered his eyes and his head and did his best to not walk and act like the heir to the Earl of Dorchester.

The quays of Southampton were packed with a milling mob of people. Several different languages were being shouted out, including English, French, Italian and something, which included a lot of sk's and dvuhs and was certainly nothing William had ever heard Robert mention.

It was a sea of brown with only an occasional spot of color. These immediately attracted attention. A group of very blond men walked past speaking a harsh language, which William thought was Germanic. Robert had mentioned it to him several times and had spoken examples of it during his lessons. They seemed so long ago now.

A moment later William noticed several men and a few women with bright red hair; this was the workingman's section of the quays. There were no gowns here and most dressed the same, in their drab colored clothes, so it was their height or their hair color, which made people stand out.

Now William understood why Gilbert had him walk and act the way he was. His pack was stuffed under his cloak, giving him an odd shaped lumpy hump over one shoulder. With his head cocked to one side and his shuffling gate, he found most people purposely avoiding him as they passed by. None ventured to look at him for long.

The soot and ash from their fireplace, mixed with just enough water, made a dark, nasty smelling paste, which they had rubbed into Helen's hair, hiding the naturally bright, and eye catching color. A few streaks on her face and a smear across her brow and bright red became raven. As the crush of people nearing the quays forced them closer together, Gilbert led the way. The smell of the smoke from the blackened ash and soot in her hair was nearly overpowering to William, who was standing closest to Helen. He could only imagine what the smell must be like for her. When he glanced to the side he noticed she was sweating; black streaks were beginning to show on her temples.

"I told you she has bright red hair; you cannot miss her. Those other two are no longer a concern of yours; I will deal with them myself…"

William recognized the voice, as did Robert. It was Lord Thomas and he was just behind them. Somehow they had passed him without realizing it, or he had moved quickly through the crowd. Either way, it was obvious he was keeping a close eye on their ship. William pulled his right shoulder up at a steeper angle, just as Gilbert had showed him, and hung his head lower. He couldn't risk calling out to Gilbert since his voice might be recognized. As it was, Robert nudged Helen closer to William and fell in behind them, putting himself between the two of them and Lord Denebaud.

"We are nearly there my lady," William whispered. "Just a few more paces…"

"You there, hunchback, stand fast!" William's heart leapt into his throat while at the same time, hammered in his chest. It was Lord Thomas again. William could see the ship; they were nearly to the gangplank.

Gilbert turned while signaling William and Helen to keep moving. The merchant stood his ground as they passed him and he spoke just loud enough for them to hear over the noisy crowd around them, "keep moving, no matter what you hear or see happen." William glanced to the side as they passed him and was surprised by the look on the merchant's face. It changed from fierce resolve to blank stupidity with a lopsided grin. He was bobbing his head and appeared to be drooling.

William grabbed Helen's arm and began using his other elbow to push his way through what little crowd remained between them both and the ship. Several people turned in irritation, but upon seeing the misshapen hump on his back immediately retreated out of his way. A dozen steps later and they were on the gangplank when they heard a loud commotion behind them. Shouts were followed by screams, which were followed by bells tolling. Three sets of bells tolled from the tower at the far end of the city.

William and Helen reached the deck of the ship and turned to see Robert only a few steps behind them. Gilbert was not with him. A moment later the sailors pulled up the heavy plank and stowed it alongside the rail. Ropes were cast off by barefooted men who quickly moved about the rigging amidst orders shouted by the captain, who stood on the forecastle watching the progress as the ship was pushed from the quay by dockhands using long, thick poles.

The three of them rushed to the rail and began searching the crowd for any sign of Gilbert, even as the ship slowly entered the current and the single main sail was unfurled filling with the sea borne breeze. They could see a knot of people, not far from the point where they had just cast off, but couldn't make out what was happening until one man stepped out of the crowd and ran to the edge of the quay. It was Lord Thomas but he was too late. The strong breeze in the sail continued to widen the distance between them. They could see him scream but the words were lost over the shouted orders of the captain and the sound of the waves on the hull of the ship. He stood on the quay shaking his fists but slowly shrank in sight as they were propelled farther from the city.

"Did you see what happened to the good merchant?" Helen asked Robert. Genuine concern was mixed with fear on her face.

His tutor turned to the rail, lowering his gaze and shaking his head. "I glanced back just as the shouting started. The last I saw of our friend he was standing with his back to us, his arms were crossed, and Lord Thomas was screaming at him. I think I recognized one of the men in the crowd nearby as Benedict, but I cannot be sure. I only had time for a glance."

"The poor man…" Helen muttered and lowered her gaze. She clasped her hands together and brought them up under her chin, whispering, "God watch over him. Bless and protect him. Keep him safe and far from harm…"

"Amen," William responded. Beneath the deck, the stallion and a few other horses gave a mixed chorus at the same moment, as if echoing the request. In any other time, William would have been relieved to finally be aboard ship, making its way to the channel and eventually France, but now he found he was worrying for the misshapen merchant who had quickly become a part of their close knit group.

Chapter Sixteen

"Tell me your names and be quick about it. If you are not who you should be, you will soon find yourself swimming back to shore." The ship's captain stood before them, arms akimbo and feet planted far enough apart to keep his balance as the ship rocked heavily amidst the quickly rolling waves. He wasn't a tall man, but he made up for it in his girth. His belt was so long it looked like it could be used to hang a man. A bristling black beard covered nearly all his face, hiding his mouth. What stood out the most were the piercing sea green eyes beneath his bushy, dark eyebrows. William felt his stomach lift, then fall with the ship and decided he better keep swallowing to remind it which direction things should travel. They weren't even out in the channel and yet he was sure he wasn't ready to know what it would feel like then.

Robert turned to the captain and gave him a quick nod. "Captain, my name is Robert Buckley and this is my nephew William. We are both from Dorchester and our transport was paid for by Sir Geoffrey and the black stallion you have in your hold." He turned to Helen and blinked a few times, trying to come up with a good explanation for her.

The young woman turned to the captain and stood up straight; drawing to her all the regal bearing she could muster. It was almost palpable.

Even William felt like bending a knee in her presence. "I am Helen d'Abbeville. I am returning home and find myself in the debt of these men who realized my life was threatened in Southampton. They aided me in my safe departure. One of their companions stayed behind to ensure it. I pray he has not paid too high a price to see me away safely."

The captain scratched at his thick beard and William thought he saw a flea leap out. "Who was that screaming on the dock?" His voice was deep and held a strength which would come in handy when shouting orders over the crash of the waves.

William turned to Robert with a questioning look. How much should they tell him? Robert nodded his understanding and muttered, "Speak the truth always, William, no matter the cost."

He turned back to the captain, "that was Lord Thomas Denebaud, the brother in law of Sir Robert Brent of Cossington. We met both men in the New Forest yesterday morning. It was not a pleasant meeting and Lord Thomas accused us of a crime we did not commit. If not for the intervention of another, on our behalf, we would not be speaking to you now."

A slightly worried expression crossed the captain's face. William could almost see the questions crossing the captain's mind. Who were these passengers? If they weren't the simple travelers they appeared why were they hiding their identity? There was no way to allay those fears without giving away more information than he knew he should, so he held his tongue. The captain scratched again at his beard as he thought over William's statement.

"Sir Geoffrey covered your crossing, however, he did not cover the woman's. This is a transport, built to hold and move cargo, not ship ladies across the seas…"

"We have coin, if it is a matter of payment," Robert interjected.

"The lady may have whatever space you had set aside for me. I will sleep on deck if I have to," William added.

"If the weather turns, you will wish you never made that offer, lad. But I will honor it, and accept the payment once we reach Calais. As far as a place for the lady, the only space we have on this ship is the open room beneath the forecastle. It is not much but I can have a curtain put up to give her some privacy."

Helen did the captain a courtesy and lowered her gaze slightly. "I am in your debt, captain. Whom do I have the honor of addressing?" As she took the captains gaze in her own, he stared a moment, open mouthed, and then stumbled over his answer. "David… David Stockton, my lady." Helen smiled a flashing smile and the captain returned the same, his eyes seeming to light up in the process. "It is a privilege to have you aboard my ship…"

"I appreciate your willingness, Captain Stockton…" Helen and the captain continued their pleasantries as William turned to look out over the rail on the larboard side. He crossed the short distance and stood holding onto the twisted rope rigging which helped secure the mast to the rail. They were following the coast, making their way towards Portsmouth and from there the open waters of the channel. "How long will it take us to get there?" He asked, not really expecting an answer.

The captain chuckled, turning from his conversation with Helen and answered anyway. "We will follow the coast over to Dover, lad. It is an easier run this time of year if you stick close. The winds tend to be more favorable as well. From there we will make the short trip to Calais. God willing, the weather holding, and the wind at our backs, we should be in the French port in just under two days."

"Will we stop in Dover, Captain?" Robert asked.

"The hold is full and our ballast is set. We have no need to stop." As an afterthought he added, "And it will cost you more if we do."

William and Robert turned to Helen and, echoing each other, said, "We are sorry."

Helen turned back toward the English shore and stared at the quickly receding city of Southampton. "Perhaps this is for the best. I do not know…"

"At least, if we do not have to stop in Dover there is no way Lord Thomas could possibly make an attempt on your life, my lady. For now the dark waters of the channel are your best protection." William offered.

"Do you believe he was looking to take my life?" The thought staggered Helen, literally, and she had to steady herself on the arm of the captain who she quickly thanked and let him move away to the stern to continue focusing on the task of running his ship.

Finally William spoke the thought, which had begun forming back in their room. "I believe there are men, both in England and in France who would find two different uses for you, my lady." A small voice said there was a third, but William shook that thought off. "They will want to keep you very close, even to the point of making you their wife, and therefore through you, gain access to the birthright of either of your parents…"

"Or the other?" Helen asked shakily, somehow guessing what it might be.

"Remove you so as to prevent a rival from using you to move against them." William watched her close as he said this. Her eyelids fluttered a moment and he was afraid she would collapse. But she took a deep breath, steadied herself and stood up straight, throwing back her shoulders and meeting his concerned gaze.

"They will find it exceedingly difficult to do either. I will not be a pawn to men who believe I will cower, whimper and do as they command."

"Then we will do our best, my lady," Robert added having joined them at the rail, "to guard your person for as long as we are able."

William considered what Robert had just said. Safeguarding the innocent; it was the oath of a knight again. Sir Geoffrey had paid the ultimate price, laying down his life to protect Helen's and their own in the process. He wondered if he would be willing to do the same if the time came for him to decide. He thought it strange to consider an act of love to be willing to die for someone else and decided to ask Robert.

"William," he answered, smiling and gripping his shoulder, the way he always did when trying to make an important point, "what exactly do you think our Lord did for each one of us?" He let his young student roll that around for a moment.

"He allowed Himself to be taken, beaten and hung on a cross."

"Yes William; even Paul said, 'this one thing I know and count on, Jesus' death and resurrection is why I am forgiven.' He loved each of us, even those who were not born yet. He loved us so much He was willing to go to the cross for each one of us. He was willing to lay down His life for you and me, William."

William had heard this before and thought he understood the importance, but until Sir Geoffrey's death he hadn't seen anyone follow the example. The knight wasn't some religious fanatic; he was simply a man who was willing to pay the price to see them safe. "So, did that mean Sir Geoffrey loved us?"

"I would say he loved us even more than some husbands love their wives. Or rather, he loved us with a greater love."

William rolled this thought around as well. He noticed, out of the corner of his eye, Helen seemed to be thinking about the same things. The thought, which seemed to return over and over again, was the idea of a greater love.

"If it was a greater love, then there are different types of love?"

Robert shook his head slowly. "Not different types, no, but I would say, rather, different levels of love. Think of it like steps of a ladder. Many people who simply do not understand what it truly means toss around the word love. Most times, they are confusing love with other base emotions, especially lust. Love is a decision, William. It is not an emotion. Emotions are fickle and change like the direction of the wind. But true love stays the course, no matter what. Every step of the knight's oath is another description of a type of love, or rather, another rung on the ladder."

"To be without fear in the face of your enemies is the first part of the oath," William added, thinking out loud. Robert held back his comment to let his young student sound out his thoughts. "Is that a form of love too?" How could facing your fears be a form of love he wondered?

Then another thought crossed his mind. When the time came, and he was certain it would come to him, would he be able face it without fear? Something Robert had told him a very long time ago suddenly returned to mind. 'Courage is not the absence of fear, William, it is doing what you know is right and what needs to be done, even when you are afraid.' Then the answer sprang to his thoughts and he spoke out loud before even realizing it.

"When the time comes, and I have a choice to do what is right or do what is easy concerning those close to me, and I choose to do what is right, despite my fears, I am showing my love for them."

Even though he posed it almost as a question, Robert still smiled and nodded his agreement. "Now you have it William." He thumped him on the shoulder with his fist, hitting home the point. "Never forget, William. Love is a decision. It is the greatest decision we can make. Paul said that love is patient, kind, never envious or jealous, not boastful nor conceited, does not insist on its own rights or its own way, it is not self-seeking, it does not rejoice at injustice but rejoices when right and truth prevail. Love allows us to bear all things, believe all things, hope in all things, and endure all things. Love never fails, William."

As William considered this he watched the dozen or so sailors as they climbed the braided rope rigging, making the single square sail secure, trimming it when called upon by the captain, or checking on the cargo below the main deck. He turned back to the rail, watching as the shore slowly slipped by, his thoughts buzzing in his head like a hive of honeybees. "Can someone fall out of love then?"

His tutor shook his head slowly. "If any decision you make is based on how you feel, William, then it can change, just as your feelings change. Always remember, love is a decision. Once you make that decision, just as the knights' oath, no matter the consequence, you will see it through."

"I remember you telling me, the day the courier came," it was hard to believe it was only just a week ago, "that the price would have to be paid early, often and more than I expected. The decision to love is the same, then, is it not?"

Robert stood and stared at his young student. A broad smile slowly crossed his face as he nodded. "William, I have never thought of it in that way, but you are right. This decision you made, to seek out your uncle, no matter the cost, is a wonderful example of love in action."

William breathed in deeply, closing his eyes and listening. He could hear the sound of the ship in the water, the creak of planks beneath his feet, the stretching of the rope rigging, the wind in the sail, and the orders of the captain. It all felt right, even Helen's presence. He was here, doing the right thing for the right reason. "Love never fails, William," he said to himself and then smiled. After all, he was certain he loved his uncle.

The day passed with little incident, and as the sun fell behind them, it looked to William as though it was dropping into the sea. As he watched he thought he saw a moment when the red, orange and slightly purple reflection of colors flashed brilliantly across the water and then the sun sank out of sight. He was startled out of his thoughts when Helen spoke at his side, "I wonder where it goes?" He hadn't heard her join him at the rail of the stern. Even as he considered her question, it appeared as though the moon was thrust into the night sky and just as suddenly the stars began sparkling on the waves.

"My father once told me it leaves us and night comes to remind us that, just as there are day and night, winter and summer, there will be seasons of change in our lives. Sometimes they will be good and sometimes they will be bad." He paused a moment, fighting back some emotions which threatened to come to the surface as he remembered the conversation. William cleared his throat and then continued. "Robert told me it is a sign you are growing up when you are able to take the good with the bad and be able to count it all joy."

"Your tutor seems to be a wise man." Then, almost as an afterthought she added, "Did you know your father well?"

"What child really knows his parent?" William asked, then paused a moment before adding, "I am sorry, that was not a very kind answer. Forgive me." From the corner of his eye he saw her bite her lower lip and then close her eyes and nod. This was a young woman with strong feelings, he reminded himself, not his tutor. He forced himself to temper his response. "In the last few days I have learned more about my father and the type of man he was than I would have imagined." He watched the wake of the ship trail out behind them, and then added softly, "I am sorry your father was killed when you were so young." William wanted to say more, but wasn't sure how to put it in words. Robert had told him of a proverb from Solomon, the wisest of the ancient kings, who said, even a fool will appear wise if he keeps silent. He decided to appear wise.

Helen smiled a little over his concern. "When I was younger I used to imagine stories about why they were not able to come and get me." The ship rolled up and over a wave and Helen reached out, grabbing the stern rail to steady herself. "The truth was not nearly as romantic or pleasant."

As dusk deepened to night, more and more stars appeared on the waves. The moon, even as it continued to wax, added a little more light. In the twilight William noticed Helen's pale skin seemed to glow with a light of its own. He forced his eyes closed; focusing his thoughts on what it must have been like to grow up not knowing who your parents were or why they did not come for you. How would he have felt? A flash of revelation, like the setting sun on the waves, struck him. He would have felt abandoned, unloved, maybe even deformed in some way he couldn't see, otherwise, why would they have not come? The very thought rocked him. Her childhood must have been so much harder than his.

"We have a fair wind," William began, stumbling over the words. He wasn't sure if he should say more or not. "We should see the coast of Dover by tomorrow afternoon." He turned to walk away and then paused, adding, "Robert was right, my lady. God thought about you long before you ever thought about Him. He created you with intention. He spoke through Jeremiah the words, 'before I formed you in the womb I knew you, before you were born I set you apart.'" He nodded to himself and then turned from the rail. He said what he said as much for her as for himself. Now he really wanted to speak to his tutor. With his back turned, he didn't see the single tear fall down Helen's cheek, nor hear her whisper, "thank you."

He found his teacher on the forecastle speaking to the captain about the draw of the ship, how much cargo it could hold, and how it handled the open sea. William stood to the side and waited several moments for a break in the conversation. In the process he discovered that their ship ran best with the wind at its back and contrary winds could force them to stop at any point along the coast. The most difficult task would be to find themselves in rough seas in the channel, no matter how short the distance to Calais. "If the waves top eight feet you had better hope you are a good swimmer." The captain said this with a bitter smile and then turned back to scanning the horizon.

Robert paused a moment in thought and then turned to William. Something he saw in his young students' expression got his full attention. "You look troubled, William. Does the captain's revelation worry you?"

"Not his… Helen's."

His tutor paused and a concerned look crossed his face. "What did she reveal that worries you?"

"It is not what she said but a thought which crossed my mind. I did not know how to express it to her, or if I should. I wanted your advice."

Robert nodded his head slowly. He was wondering if this conversation was going to take place. After all, they were two young people, confined together on a small ship for the next few days. She already owed him her life after all. "Clear your thoughts, William. Take your time and then ask your question."

His young student smiled, despite the situation. He had heard this directive so many times before in all manner of lessons. Even that day just over a week ago as they studied outside the walls of Crandor, his tutor had told him the same. William closed his eyes and took a deep breath, letting it out slowly. "Her childhood was much harder than she suggests." William's statement surprised his tutor and his face reflected it. "Were you expecting something else?"

"I have to admit I was. What is it that makes you think of her childhood?"

"She asked me about my father, and as I sought to put words to some of my thoughts, I was struck with a realization." Now he had his tutor's full attention as he turned to face William. "I realized if I had spent my childhood as she did, I would have grown up thinking there had to be something wrong with me. Otherwise, why would they not come for me? I would have felt abandoned and even unloved." His voice trailed off even as his thoughts.

"Your insight does you credit William." Robert turned to look aft but Helen was no longer standing at the stern railing. "I believe you are right. I am sure her guardians took good care of her, but there had to have been unanswered questions." As he had done so many times before, Robert crossed his arms and absentmindedly chewed on the corner of his right thumb. "She has spent many long years listening to herself instead of speaking to herself. What has taken a long time to build will take almost as long to replace."

"Is it possible?"

"After what you learned in Salisbury? Whatever a man sows, that alone is what he will reap. Think about it William; what will she have to do to repair the damage done over all those years?"

Now it was the student's turn to assume the same pose. He did it without even thinking about it. "She will have to change the way she thinks about herself."

"Yes, but there is more to it than just that," William furrowed his brow, deep in thought. "She will have to want to change the way she thinks. She will have to change the picture she has of herself in her mind. It is not an easy thing to change all those years of doubt. My father told me once that it takes almost three good things to think about in order to cancel out one evil thought; three positive seeds against one negative."

"She could pray for wisdom…"

"Absolutely, William; first and foremost she should do that. Paul also told the Ephesians to be constantly renewed in the spirit of their mind. This will be an ongoing process for her, but when we put our faith and trust in Jesus we are assured of a sound mind."

"So, it will be very difficult and take a lot of time, but there is still a concern." William moved to the bow rail and leaned against it, watching the waves break across the prow. He was almost getting accustomed to the rise and fall of the ship. Almost.

"The vision she has of herself will continue to affect her actions. Is that your concern?" His student nodded while continuing to stare out at the water before them. "I think, whether she realized it or not, the way she sees herself has already affected the decisions she has made on this trip." Robert stepped over to the railing. "I do not think she would have accepted the help of those men last night, if she had not felt the way she did. There is a good chance she travels with us for the very same reason."

"She acts so confident at times though…"

"I think she uses that to hide how much she hurts." Robert paused a moment, then added, "And she will do all she can to keep people at arm's length."

"Why would she do that?"

"Because, if she let someone get too close they might see the flaw in her and then they would leave her just as her parents." His tutor sighed, a sad look crossing his face. "She is a beautiful, yet very complicated young woman, William."

Despite the serious discussion, William laughed. "My father told me once, just a few years ago, that all women are complicated. 'They are a study in contradiction, William.' He also said marriage does not make life with them any easier, it simply exposes more of their complications."

"It is always wise to listen to someone who has been married when seeking advice on the subject."

William realized he didn't even know if his tutor had been married. Did he have any children? He wasn't sure what, if anything he should ask, or if there ever would be a right time to do so. It was beginning to dawn on William how little he actually knew about his teacher. He should have made the effort to learn more about him but it hadn't occurred to him before this trip. Here was a lesson he had learned on their second day out of Dorchester. To be interested in those around you shows them how much you care for them. Even as he considered how to bridge the subject, the concern over Helen forced its way back to the surface. "Should we keep a close watch over her, just in case?"

"I do not think she will make any decisions which will hurt her while she is on this ship. But once we are in France," Robert shrugged, "who can say." The sky above them was clear. Not a single cloud obstructed their view of the stars or moon. He wished the conversation with his student had been lighter. It would have been easier to enjoy the rare gem of an evening. "I will think clearer after a good night's sleep. Rest well, William. I will see you in the morning."

He listened as his tutor's steps receded from the forecastle. Sometime soon he would find a way to learn more about his teacher, but for now, William could feel sleep pulling at him as well. After retrieving his pack, he spread out his wool cloak, using the hood as a pillow. A moment later he found himself stretched out on the forecastle deck, the rise and fall of the ship rocking him to sleep, as the stars and moon wheeled overhead.

Chapter Seventeen

A sudden jolt rocked William from his sleep. For a brief moment he couldn't remember where he was and then it all flooded back to him. The ship slipped over on its side, as it rolled down a rather large wave. Dawn was still a little ways away but the eastern horizon was already a blend of red and purple.

After rubbing the sleep from his eyes, William stood on unsteady legs only to notice the wind had shifted to the north. Because of this they were now cutting almost perpendicular to the wind and, although the sea didn't appear any rougher, the ship wasn't designed for it. He remembered the captain mentioning something about it yesterday. As he tried to recall the conversation, Robert came and stood by his side.

"The captain said a red sky in the morning could mean a rough day ahead of us."

William smiled weakly as he reached out to steady himself on the rail of the bow. "Good morning to you as well." When his tutor offered him a piece of stale bread and a little cheese he had to think twice before accepting it. Although the breeze off the water was refreshing, it was mixed with the slowly increasing pungency from the horses in the hold below the main deck. Couple that with the stiffness he was still trying to stretch out of his muscles and it made for a grumpy and less than hungry attitude.

"The change in the wind will slow us down, will it not?"

"It already has a little." Robert turned and looked aft. "It is taking two men to hold the rudder and keep us on course now as well, but we should still be able to reach Dover sometime this afternoon."

"I would give almost anything for a warm bath and a change of clothes," William muttered to himself.

"I understand what you mean, William, but be careful what you wish for. Esau gave up his birthright to his brother Jacob for a warm bowl of lentil stew." He watched as his young pupil chewed on the inside of his cheek as he rolled the thought around in his head.

"I am sorry. I just woke up, and not very well at that. I am not sure if I am ready for a lecture or lesson right now."

"Fair enough, William, but let me ask you one question." He continued after he got a nod of approval. "If you wanted to attack someone when would you do it? When they were rested and ready or when they were just waking, sleepy and not thinking clearly?"

Robert's reasoning was sound and there was no room for William to argue, so he let him know it. "Guard your thoughts and words all the time, William. There is no such thing as an insignificant reply."

William closed his eyes and lowered his head. He knew his teacher was right but his brain was still sluggish after a restless night's sleep on the foredeck. Even as he thought about it, the ship rolled over another tall wave and he had to grab hold of the bow rail even tighter to help keep his feet. "I know you are right, but what you are suggesting…"

Robert reached over and grabbed William's left shoulder, making sure he had his full attention. It had only been five days since his attack in Salisbury and although his arm had begun to heal quickly, the extra pressure from his teachers grasp helped to waken his senses. "William, look to the aft of this ship and the two men on the rudder." When he was sure he saw them, he added, "Your tongue, William, is like that rudder. In a letter from James, our Lords brother, he says the same thing. Something as small as that plank of wood can turn even a ship of this size. No matter how this wind has changed, they are able to use something that small to steer by."

"I know I should guard my thoughts, but to guard everything I say as well…"

"In the same letter James says that although we have gone out and tamed every beast and bird on land and sea, our tongue is the most difficult to control. He says it is restless, evil and full of deadly poison. With the same tongue we bless the Lord and then curse men who were made in God's likeness."

"Then what can I possibly do?"

"Stay humble and be willing to constantly ask God for His help."

"I am pretty sure I can do that. Is there anything else?"

"Choose your words carefully, William, no matter how you feel. My father told me once, when I was just a little older than yourself, that words are like feathers on a breeze. They are easy to release but nearly impossible to retrieve."

William shook his head, paused, and then sighed deeply. "I will try my best, but right now, I feel like what you suggest is impossible."

"If you try to do this on your own, William, it will be impossible. Just remember, you can do all things through Christ who strengthens you. God is with you, He is helping you and He is guiding you. If God is for you, William, who can be against?" Robert paused, smiled at a memory from his past, and then added as an afterthought, "My father also told me there is no try. Either you will do it or you will not."

As William considered this he realized the sky had lightened in color to include a blend of oranges and pinks mixed with the red and purple and they were all beginning to reflect off the caps of the waves before them. Sunrise would come soon enough. So much had happened in the last several days. So many lessons taught and some learned. He hoped he would be able to remember them all and maybe, one day, God willing, he would be able to pass them on to his son. Suddenly a question from the night before entered his thoughts and he asked it aloud just as quickly.

"When I have sons and they are to be taught, will your sons teach them?"

A painful expression crossed Robert's face and he wiped his face with the back of his hand while trying to act as though the sea had sprayed its mist in his eyes.

"I am sorry, I should not have asked the question. Forgive me…"

"There is nothing to forgive, William. As your uncle's heir, you have a right to know about the disposition of your household." The way his tutor answered made it feel, to William, like someone grabbed his chest and slowly, relentlessly began squeezing it. He found it difficult to breath. Tears filled his eyes and he tried his best to blink them away.

"I am sorry…" his voice broke and he dropped his head, letting the emotion flow through him. It felt like everything he had been through in the last few days suddenly overwhelmed him like a wave on the sea. He almost choked as if physically drowning.

A moment later he felt his tutor's arm around his shoulders as he mumbled a few comforting words to his young student then did his best, while fighting his own emotions, to answer Williams' question. "It happened before you were born, so you never knew. My wife died while in childbirth. Our son should have been the first of many, instead neither survived. I was left alone, hurt and angry. I questioned everything I had been taught by my father and never remarried."

William took in a deep breath of the salty sea air. It cleared his senses and he stood up straighter and his eyes searched the horizon and the waves for a response. Finally, he was able to say, "Thank you for the confidence." There was still something he wanted to know though. "How were you able to get over it?" The pain of the loss of both his parents, although lessened a little with the passing of the last year would still, occasionally, come to the fore and nearly overwhelm him.

"Eventually I renewed my faith in God, asked His forgiveness for the doubts and blame I had laid at His feet. It took some time, but I was finally able to thank Him for the time I had with my wife. As soon as I honestly came to that point, He responded by giving me a renewed purpose in life."

William turned to look at his tutor, who had returned to the rail while avoiding the gaze of his student, and asked, "What was the purpose God gave you?"

Robert didn't answer right away but stood with his head slightly bowed. A moment later he turned to look right into William's eyes and without blinking said, "To teach your cousin, and now you, all I know and all I have learned and all I can remember, so you will be ready when the time comes. I have no son of my own to pass this on…" He turned and left the forecastle, slowly descending the narrow steps to the main deck, as the ship rolled over another steep wave.

When William turned back to the eastern horizon, the bright orange sun was up, and it warmed his face. Despite everything else, William smiled and closing he eyes, said a quick, silent prayer of thanks to God for putting Robert in his life.

His head was still bowed and eyes closed when Helen spoke at his side. "It is a beautiful sunrise, is it not?"

William nodded as he sniffed loudly and blinked several times to clear his vision. "God has given us another wonderful day," he said, doing his best to not let his voice break with the emotion, which still felt as if it was squeezing his throat and slowly crushing his chest.

"I wanted to thank you for what you said last night." When William didn't respond immediately, she continued. "How long have you been without your parents, William?" It was the one question he wasn't prepared for. Tears spilled down his cheeks and he turned toward the sunrise as he tried to dry his face on the shoulder of his shirt.

"My father…" his voice cracked and he cleared his throat. "My father was killed at Neville's Cross, just over two years ago. When my uncle returned with the news, my mother followed him a month later. The priest said she had a brain fever, but I do not think that was what it was. My uncle eventually took me in and claimed me as his heir, since my cousin, his only son, had died during a famine when I was quite young."

A moment passed as William looked out towards the sunrise. He thought it was interesting he could look directly at the sun, as it came up over the horizon but now that it was just a little higher in the sky he could not. "What do you think caused it?" Helen asked.

"My uncle Charles is the eldest and so his marriage was arranged for the benefit of the family. My aunt was from France not far from where, in the distant past, my family came from. Robert told me once that the marriage helped solidify our family's ties near the Somme. I do not remember much of her, other than she was very beautiful but sad." A strange looked passed across Helen's face, but William didn't notice it, as he was staring out over the water as he spoke.

"My father, as the younger brother, was able to choose more to his liking and interest. Mother was…" William paused again, closing his eyes a moment, while taking a deep breath and slowly exhaling. For the second time in moments he found himself struggling with the emotions surrounding his parents and wondered if the pain would ever leave him. *"God grant me Your peace,"* He prayed. The warm sun on his face caused him to smile and it was as if the grip on his throat and chest relaxed. The pain was still there but he could handle it now. *"Thank You, God."* He smiled again and continued.

"She was wonderful and at times patient, but there were moments when she would lose her calm. It was then I did my best to get out of her way. Father was good at calming her during those storms. He had a way of looking at her, smiling and gently touching her shoulder. When he did that, she would stop."

"Did they meet and marry for love?" Helen's voice held, what William thought to be hope. "I have never heard of families of peerage doing such a thing."

"Well, they were introduced by their parents. With the title and lands going to my uncle, father did not have much to bring to the marriage other than the spurs he won at a young age at Halidon Hill where he fought on foot in Edward's vanguard. Mother was a niece of Lord Henry Beaumont, on his father's side, and, before she married, my mother was the handmaid to Lord Henry's daughter, Isabel, before she herself was married to Henry the Earl of Leicester and Lancaster."

"I have heard of Lord Beaumont. My guardians told me of his exploits in the wars with the Scots. As she was on his father's side, then your mother also would be descended from John of Brienne."

William looked back to the horizon, a little embarrassed to admit, "My father did not spend much time teaching me the history of my family." Then realizing what he just said, added quickly, "He was more often in the field, serving the King than at home. I have learned a lot more about my family since I left Dorchester just over a week ago."

"Then we have something in common," Helen smiled, her eyes sparkling in the early morning sun. A moment later she turned and crossed the forecastle, making her way down the ladder, and returning to the room the Captain had set aside for her. William watched her go and then returned to gazing at the horizon. It didn't occur to him at the time, but Helen had managed to find a way to wash all the blackened ash out of her hair and off her face. William knew it was important to learn of the relationships of his relatives, but he found more comfort in looking forward rather than back.

Robert returned sometime later with a couple dried apples and oatcakes, which had been hard enough to chew on the day they left Dorchester, but now were nearly rocks. William broke off a piece, with a lot of difficulty, and held it in his mouth to soften. "Who was John of Brienne?" He muttered around the dried clump.

Robert paused in mid chew. "Now there is an interesting relative of yours. Your mother would have been his granddaughter's daughter I believe. If ever there was a true knight errant, it was King John."

"King John? King of what?"

"First he was King of Jerusalem. Eventually he made his way to Constantinople and was asked to sit on the Imperial throne for a time. He died with little to show for it, but nonetheless he led a very interesting life. Why the sudden interest, William?"

He shrugged and finally chewed the large piece into pieces small enough to swallow. "Just a comment from Lady Helen a short while ago. It made me realize how little I know about some of my family."

"To know where you come from is very important William, but never lose sight of where you are going. Men have wasted their lives digging through the past, searching out long lost relations, all the while forgetting to live today; forgetting about where they are and what they are doing." He paused a moment as he took a large bite of dried apple. "Do you remember one of the first lessons I taught you on the Roman road outside of Dorchester?"

William thought for a moment and then nodded. "You told me to never forget to live today. Yesterday is over with no chance of us returning to correct or change it. Tomorrow is a promise with no guarantee we will even be there to see it happen. Today is all we have; right here, right now. Be mindful of the future and be willing to learn from the past, but do neither at the expense of the present."

"Exactly, William. Every day is a gift from God. Too many people think that eternity is some far distant future. It is out there. I will always have tomorrow or next week or next year to make the decision to follow the Lord, they think to themselves. What they do not realize is the border to the hereafter runs alongside them every day. It only takes one small step and you cross over.

"It is your daily habits which will determine where you will be in the next few years, William. And this is a process, which never ends until your life does." Robert held up another dried apple. "As soon as this apple was picked from its tree, it began to rot." He slowly turned it over in his hand. "Your life is the same way, William. Stop learning; stop growing; stop discovering and creating new habits and you begin to rot, just like this apple."

His tutor turned to him and grabbed his shoulder. William had come to realize that this meant one of his teachers' most important lessons was coming. "This one thing, William, affects all other things. This one habit will determine if you ever develop any of the other habits we have talked about. From this one decision, the rest of your life is affected." He paused as the ship rolled over a slightly larger wave and he had to steady himself on the railing before them. A large, mostly white cloud crossed in front of the sun and the glare off the waves decreased immensely.

"The rest of your life is affected by your daily habits. Those decisions will seem so simple you might even consider them of no consequence. There is no such decision. Can you think of a simple decision you can manage every day which would fall into this?"

It didn't take William long to come up with an answer. He had thought about it each day and had tried his best to manage the decision since. "On our first morning, and again, on the road outside of Downton, you told me being happy was a decision I needed to make, no matter what the situation. That is a simple habit; just decide to be happy. Although I have found it to be more difficult than it first seemed."

Robert nodded and smiled. "Well done, William, and I agree with you. It is one of the more simple decisions and not in any way complicated. However, it is also one of the most difficult to manage every day. If you do this, you will not notice a difference in a week or a month or even perhaps a year. But there is no doubt over time your life will absolutely be better off. If there is any doubt, consider the opposite decision and imagine your life."

William looked out over the waves and horizon. Not far ahead he could make out another set of sails. Between themselves and the coast a ship passed in the opposite direction. An idea was buzzing around in his head and he was trying to find words to it. "Deciding to be happy is just another way of controlling my thoughts, is it not? I mean, the Justice of the Peace in Salisbury certainly made a good point as to why that was important."

Robert nodded, smiling as he, once again, thumped William on the shoulder a few times for emphasis, stinging the wound on his upper arm each time. "Now that is very well done indeed, William. It is one thing to recall an idea or a single lesson, but quite another to combine two and understand how they work together." His teacher paused a moment, then added, "I think you might actually, really, understand this."

William's smile in response to the praise of his teacher was broad and toothsome. It felt good to know Robert was pleased with his progress. In the back of his mind, a small voice, like an outside observer, spoke to his thoughts, "beware of pride, William." In response, he immediately changed his focus. *"God, thank You for the wisdom and understanding you have given me."* It was just the reminder he needed. He knew God was the source of the understanding he had been gaining these last few days. After all, he had been asking Him for it since that rainy day outside of Downton.

"What else did you and Lady Helen speak of?"

"I asked him if his parents had married for love." Her voice startled William out of the train of thought he had been following. There was still a question he wanted to ask his teacher, but now he found it pushed aside and he couldn't recall it immediately. Neither had heard Helen approach from the ladder, and William wondered how long she might have been standing and listening in. Both bowed and at the same time, speaking almost as a chorus, "My lady."

"Did you sleep well?" Robert asked.

"Better than some recent days. But still…"

"You find your thoughts troubled?"

Helen turned from Robert's question and looked out over the bow of the ship. The early morning sun shone in her hair and made it look as if it were brightly polished copper. The wind from the north added to the effect. Her pale, freckled face glowed brightly, then a cloud crossed the sun, the light was dimmed and she looked diminished somehow. "I do not need to seek sleep to find my thoughts troubled."

"If there is any aid I can give, *vivo servire*." Robert placed his hand over his heart and bowed fully from the waist. William watched Helen's reaction closely. It was as if she expected that response. But there was something else. Although he could only see her profile, there was a look she held. It was as if…

"You do not need our service, my lady; what you need and what you want is to know we speak the truth." William blurted it out before he even had time to consider what he said or debate over the appropriateness of the response.

"You overstep yourself." Her eyes flashed as she spun to face him, her hands clenched at her sides. "How dare you suggest you understand… that you could possibly know… that?" Her face was flushed and there was a wild look in her eyes. Clouds covered the sun again and it was if its veiling only accentuated the frustration and anger, which filled her face. William was sure he had said what she needed to hear, although it certainly wasn't what she wanted. She collected herself, closed her eyes for a moment and let out a deep breath. "Do not presume you understand… anything, William." She nodded to Robert and with a twirl spun away from them, quickly descending the ladder disappearing beneath them into her room.

William's tutor watched her with a note of amusement in his eyes. "I think your insight continues to serve you well. Just remember though, when someone has been hurt and is still hurting, they tend to be easily offended and more often than not, respond by lashing out and hurting those around them."

"That is a comforting thought." When his tutor looked back at him, William added, with a twinkle in his eyes and a smile on his lips, "We still have another long day or more aboard this small ship with her."

Chapter Eighteen

As the morning progressed a few more clouds rolled in from the north and the smell from the horses in the hold became more noticeable. They were still making pretty good progress despite the shift in the wind and William found himself standing on the larboard rail, watching the coast of England slowly drift by. They had already passed Brighthelmstone, and Captain Stockton pointed it out to William in passing. Most of the local fishing ships were already at sea but a few remained, pulled up on the sandy shore.

"We will pass Hastings within the hour, if the wind does not shift."

"Can we see where the battle took place?"

"Not from this vantage point. Duke William and his lads landed not far from here. You see how long and sandy these beaches are? Just a little farther up the coast we will come upon a small bay: Pevensey Bay. That is where he landed and there was not a single man there to bar their way. The battle took place a few miles north of the town."

William nodded and spoke mostly to himself. "All the men were up north at Stamford Bridge fighting Hardraga and his Norsemen."

The captain turned to him with a slightly startled look on his face. "You know about that, do yah lad? William nodded but didn't meet his gaze. He could see, out of the corner of his eye, he was being studied but he did his best to keep a neutral face. "Well, our Harold, the last elected King, found himself in tight spot; Normans from the south and Norsemen to the north. You will see Pevensey Castle as we come near the bay. Harold spent the summer there with his army, expecting the Duke of Normandy to land first. When they did not come, the Norsemen did and Harold took the counsel of those closest to him and set off north."

"Why did the Normans not come then?"

"Well, they were ready, that is for sure. My family have been sailing these waters for time out of memory and I was told, long ago, that the wind stood in Duke William's face and so he had to sit and wait. His whole army of men and knights and their horses as well sat on the shore just across the channel but could not move because of the wind. Of course, if the wind had been different, Hastings may never have happened. Harold would have been here waiting for them."

"I wonder who it was counseled King Harold to move his men north." The captain didn't answer but muttered something into his beard, which William thought was something like "different lives." Robert was standing on the forecastle and he thought he would ask him. After excusing himself, he made his way to the ladder, only to nearly run into Helen as she came from behind the curtain of her room. She didn't say anything but scowled at him and then stomped off to the hatch and ladder, which led to the horses and cargo in the hold. As the captain said the day before, this wasn't a ship for transporting ladies. The only private place she had to relieve herself was below deck.

The look she gave him distracted William. He slowly climbed the ladder to the forecastle as his recently focused thoughts and the questions he wanted to ask his tutor were suddenly clouded. How could she irritate him so easily? She hadn't even said a word. Why was she so upset with him anyway? What he told her was the truth. That part of the knight's oath came to mind: to speak the truth always, no matter the cost.

As he rolled these thoughts and questions around in his mind, he crossed to the railing and stood just a few feet from his tutor. He took a deep breath of the early afternoon breeze and shook his head in an effort to clear his thoughts.

"Does her attitude affect you that much?"

William nodded without answering at first. Here was an opportunity to control his thoughts before they took control of him. Here was an opportunity to demonstrate his ability to remain happy, despite the irritation he felt. After all it was Helen's decision to become upset with him after what he said. Especially since he didn't intend to upset her. There really was no reason for him to be irritated. And yet, he was.

Robert's next question broke into his thoughts, "William, what are your feelings for Lady Helen?" This caught him by surprise and he turned to see his tutor's slate grey eyes staring at him, as if to pierce through to the truth.

"Right now I feel as though she is under my skin, like an itch I cannot scratch." As if in demonstration, he scratched at the back of his head. Secretly he hoped he hadn't gotten the fleas the captain carried. "I cannot imagine having gone through the life she did, and yet I do not understand why she is upset at me and still remains so." He closed his eyes again and took another deep breath. "I know it is my decision to remain happy, no matter the circumstance but right now, I am having a hard time."

"It appears as though you care for her quite a lot."

William found himself cautiously forming a response. "I wish her well. I am sorry she has had the truth of her parents kept from her all these years but I do not know if there is anything I could do to help. I also do not know where she will go or what she will do once we reach France."

"William," and once again he grabbed his student by the shoulder, "you are focusing on your worries. It is a good thing you are concerned for her future. I find myself concerned as well, however, we have our own challenge to consider. For the time being Helen is joining us on our path. God will decide how long that will continue."

His tutor paused a moment, then added, "being able to put yourself in someone else's position and understand, even to a small part, what they are going through and perhaps even understanding their feelings is a tremendous trait, William; never lose that. If you are willing to put others first, in the end, you will find yourself finishing in that position.

"Should I not consider my own desires in the matter?"

"I am not asking you to be like the reeds thrown on the floor of a banquet hall; there to be walked on by all the guests. Our Lord is described as the Lamb of God, but He is also known as the Lion of Judah. Put yourself in their position but not at the expense of your own convictions."

"If I did put myself in Lady Helen's position," William considered, almost as if thinking out loud, "I would think she would be very angry at the lie told to her all those years." Robert nodded his agreement. "I would also be sad to know the truth of my parents." William paused to consider his next thought. As he did so, Hastings Castle slowly slid past them as they sailed by Pevensie Bay and continued eastward along the coast. "After mother died, I felt as though God had messed up and there was no real reason for me to be alive. It did not make any sense leaving me alone. I was even angry at God." William lowered his gaze as he admitted this. "I even thought about taking my own life."

This was something William had admitted to no one up until now.

He found his throat tightening and tears welling up in his eyes. Rather than hold them back and try to choke them down, he let them spill over. Spasms shook his shoulders as the tears continued to fall soundlessly down his face. Robert stood there, quietly, gently resting his hand on his young student's shoulder. Finally, after a minute or two, he spoke. "What made you change your mind, William?"

His young student sniffed loudly, cleared his throat and wiped his face on his sleeve. He cleared his throat one more time and tried his best to smile, despite the fact his nose was still running, "I asked God to help. I remember my father telling me, once, long ago, that if I ever needed to, I should call on the name of the Lord.

I was standing at mother's gravesite, on that small hill just to the south of Dorchester. We used to take our meals there, when the weather was beautiful and she wanted to be outside. It was late summer and the sun was still warm and the breeze was up from the sea. All I could think about was how sad and alone I felt. Even the sound of the gulls, which had made their way far inland that day, seemed to echo the sadness I felt. Then that memory of my father came to me. I remember being so overwhelmed I fell on my knees and it felt as though I cried hot tears. 'God I know you sent Your Son Jesus to live and die for me and my sins so that I could come before you wiped clean and trust You to give me what I ask for. Show me Your strength, God. Help me to find some peace and show me the reason I am still here.'

"As I knelt there it felt as though someone put their arms around my shoulders. I cannot describe what happened or how it happened but it was like getting filled inside from the toes to my head with warmth like the embrace my mother used to give me as she would take me in her arms and place me on her lap. And yet it was more than that." He shook his head, "I do not know how else to describe it and I am not even sure if I am making sense."

"Paul called it the peace which surpasses all understanding."

William nodded. "That is what I felt. A deep wonder-filled sense of peace. It made no sense, considering nothing had really changed in my situation."

"So, on that grassy hill, despite everything happening to you, you decided to give your life to God and accepted His Son, Jesus Christ, as Lord?"

"I would not have said it in those words, but I am pretty sure that is what I did."

"Then what you felt William was God giving you the chance to be reborn."

Now his young student turned to him with a confused look on his face. "I was born a second time? How is that possible?"

"Jesus told us that we all have a birth from our mothers; our first birth. We then have a birth of our spirit, when we call out to God, with our own free will, to accept His Son and therefore accept Him as Lord of our life. On that grassy hill, on that late summer day, William, you became brand new through Christ."

"It was that same afternoon," William added, the revelation of what had really happened that day slowly crystallizing in his mind, "you found me returning from her grave and told me uncle Charles had called for me."

Robert smiled a broad smile. It was the kind of smile, which lit up his eyes and his face shone brightly in the afternoon sun. "It was no coincidence, William. Until that very morning, your uncle still had not made up his mind on whether he would ask you to return to Crandor. Nor had he decided to make you his heir until we returned together. He told me later, he saw something in your eyes and your face, when you arrived, which moved him to give you the birthright of his long past son."

"I wonder if anyone ever told Lady Helen what my father had told me. If she called on the Lord…"

After a pause, Robert finished the thought, "There is no limit to God's ability to forgive. His word says He will remove your sin from you as far as the east is from the west. She too could ask for God's peace. Right now, though, I fear she lives on the battlefield in her mind."

"The battlefield? What battle is in her mind?"

"The enemy hasn't changed what he does since the very beginning. He has always attacked us in our thoughts and he will continue to do so. If he takes the time to change what he does, he may miss helping tear someone away from God. Look at what he did in the garden. He came and challenged Adam and Eve in their thoughts. He wasn't frightening and he certainly did not scare them, he simply came to them and suggested they misunderstood what God had told them. He planted doubt in their minds and sat back and watched them make a decision, which still affects us to this very day.

"When you questioned God's purpose in your life and even considered ending it, no matter how briefly" which he added when he saw a look of regret and embarrassment cross William's face, "the enemy planted that thought there. I am afraid Lady Helen has been facing that battle for a very long time. After a while it becomes easier to believe the lies than it is the truth."

"Is it easier to believe a lie?"

"If you listen to something often enough, William, even if it is a lie, you will begin to believe it. It is similar to what the Justice of the Peace in Salisbury told you."

"He told me I needed to guard my thoughts because they will ultimately determine the situations I find myself in."

"Exactly, William. Now, tell me how this pertains to our Lady below."

William stared out over the bow of the ship while he considered the question. After passing Hastings Castle several ships had left the small, shallow, unsheltered harbor and began following their course along the coast. One of the ships split away from the others and seemed to angle towards them. William watched it draw nearer as he sounded out his answer. "Any lie she has listened to long enough will seem to be a truth to her." Robert nodded while he waited, hoping his pupil would be able to tie the thoughts together. "That thought, even though it is a lie, would eventually determine the situation she finds herself in."

Robert smiled. "Well done, William. Always remember, any thought, even if it is a lie, if dwelt on long enough, will affect your words, which will determine your actions which will become your habits, character and ultimately your circumstances."

"Is there anything we can do to help her?"

"Pray, William. Pray and trust God to give us the opportunity to speak the truth over her and back into her. Also pray that God will open her ears and her heart to what we have to say."

"We may only have another day or so with her and right now she is doing all she can to avoid me. I do not see how this is going to be possible."

"Well, William, always remember, with man it may not be, but with God, all things are possible." Robert paused as he noticed the ship William had seen earlier continue to draw closer. "This is the same God, after all, who raised Jesus from the dead. In the end, it has to be her choice. We cannot force this on her. To try to do so would only cause her to push us and the truth aside."

William nodded in understanding. His thoughts on how he might try striking up a conversation with Lady Helen were interrupted when the Captain shouted to them from the main deck. "We have a problem brewing!" Then added, "Milady I need you out on deck as well."

"What trouble, Captain Stockton?" Helen had come out from behind the curtains to her room, as soon as she was called. Robert and William crossed the forecastle deck and descended the ladder as the Captain answered her.

"Begging your pardon milady but we are now on the coast line of the Cinque Ports. They do not tolerate trade outside the ports unless you are willing to pay their fee."

"Are you sure it is a port ship?" Robert asked. William noticed Helen move away, in order to have the Captain stand between herself and the two of them, as she avoided his gaze.

"Aye. No doubt about that. In fact, it is flying the colors of the Lord Warden. You can see the three gold lions joined with three gold ships on red and blue." The quickly approaching ship had the advantage of the wind at its back as it left the port and was making good time. William could easily see the flag now. "If they fly those colors then the Lord Warden and Admiral of the Ports is aboard that ship." The Captain scratched at his beard as he realized what it meant. Silently he wondered if these problems were because of the woman he took on board. He shook his head, a sad look crossing his face and then let out a deep breath.

"To be safe, I need all three of you below deck in the hold with the horses. You will be able to hear what happens but you will also be out of sight just in case it turns to mischief."

"Do you think it could lead to that?" Robert asked.

Captain Stockton continued scratching at his beard while shaking his head. "It is hard to tell, but I would rather be safe now than sorry later. Besides, these Cinque Port types are not known for their manners." Turning to Helen, he added, "I would rather they not know you were aboard, milady."

A moment later, William found himself in the hold, with the horses, his tutor, Helen and a much stronger, nearly eye watering reek. He never realized how much waste a few horses could produce in such a short time. In no time at all, his eyes were watering and the back of his throat started to burn. All he wanted was fresh air and the breeze in his face. Suddenly it dawned on him that Helen had been using this same area for privacy when she needed to relieve herself. "I am sorry you have to come down here." He murmured, while holding his hand over his mouth and nose. "I had no idea it was like this." He had to keep blinking as tears threatened to spill down his face.

Helen seemed to be less alarmed at the situation. "You get used to it after a while," she answered then turned away and walked over to the stall where the black stallion was kept. As soon as it saw her, it whinnied and stuck his head over the low stall door so he could nuzzle her hand. She stroked his arched neck and William was pretty sure she was smiling. Overhead they all heard stomping and loud voices.

Although there didn't seem to be any air moving in the hold, the stench of urine and manure did swirl around, building up at times and then dissipating a moment later. During one of the waves, when the smell became almost overpowering, William felt himself beginning to gag. Robert saw and leaned over, keeping his voice low, "breathe through your mouth, William. You will not smell as much."

He closed his eyes and nodded and took several deep breaths through his mouth, while willing himself not to throw up. His stomach had other thoughts and although the advice from his tutor helped, it was too late.

Bits and pieces of dried apples and oatcakes made their way up and out along with a lot more liquid than he thought his stomach could hold.

William felt more embarrassed than anything. Neither his teacher nor Helen had gotten ill from the smell. With no water to rinse his mouth, all William could do was spit out what remained and had to use his sleeve to wipe his mouth. When he looked up, Robert had politely turned away, but Helen was staring at him. He thought, for a brief moment, he saw sympathy in her expression, then she rolled her eyes and shook her head. His eyes were watering and his throat burned and she had to look at him that way? Why; because the smell had overwhelmed him?

He quickly went from embarrassment to anger. After all they had done to help her. After all *he* had done. God knows where she would be right now if it hadn't been for him and Robert, Gilbert and even Sir Geoffrey. At that moment, William realized he hadn't even thought about Gilbert since they made it safely out of Southampton.

He had been so concerned about Helen and what she had been going through, the man who risked everything to see them safely aboard this ship had simply slipped from his mind. As the ship rolled over a larger wave, William turned from anger to sadness. He didn't know what had happened to Gilbert on the docks. Had he met the same fate as Sir Geoffrey? Did he pay the ultimate price to see them safe? A sudden conviction came over him and he bowed his head, his hands clasped in front of his chest. "God, let Your hand be on our friend Gilbert. Protect him and keep him safe. I am sorry he slipped from my mind…" William made a commitment right then to pray for their friend, even as he prayed for his uncle each morning.

Tears and an intense sorrow choked at William as he turned to clear his nose. Even as he used his sleeve to wipe his eyes, the voices on the deck became easier to understand. They seemed to have moved closer to the hatch and the stairs, which led down to the hold. When William looked up, he could see shadows crossing the narrow gaps in the planks above his head. A voice was raised and he was sure it was the captain. Although he couldn't be certain what was said he could tell the old sailor wasn't happy.

Robert motioned to William to move away from the stairway and they both backed further into the shadows of the hold. William glanced up to see Helen open the stall door of their black stallion and then drop down after closing it behind her. There was nowhere else for her to hide.

Despite the fact they hadn't done anything wrong, William found his heart beginning to beat quickly and his palms were sweating. His tutor looked concerned, but didn't seem anxious. He tried to take comfort in this, but it mostly didn't help.

Within seconds, the hatch opened and sunlight streamed into the hold. Several of the horses, including the stallion, responded to the light and entrance of fresh air with whinnies and neighing. The stomping of several horses hooves echoed through the entire hold even as someone began descending the steps. Robert thrust a large fork into William's hands and nodded to the sodden mess in front of the nearest stall then jerked his head over to a small barrow. He turned and dug his own fork into a pile in front of him. It took a few seconds then William realized what his tutor was suggesting: make it look like you are working. He needed no other encouragement but turned his back to the steps and used the fork to transfer some of the muck onto the small handcart.

William forced himself to keep his head down and not turn to look at who was approaching. A strange voice, with an odd accent cursed behind him and muttered, "I will never get used to this awful smell." After tossing another fork full onto the hand truck, William risked a glance over his shoulder. To his surprise he was staring at a weather worn and wrinkled old man with timber sized forearms and muscular, slightly bowed legs. They stood like that for a moment, while the bow-legged old man just scowled, his gray eyes slowly moving back and forth between William and Robert. William tried to smile but managed more of a smirk. While pinching his nose, the weathered old man asked, "Anyone else down in this wretched place beside the two of you?"

William remembered how Robert had changed the way he answered, based on the person he was speaking to, and decided it best if he acted the part of a stable hand. He gave a lopsided grin and nodded to his tutor then shrugged his shoulders as if unable to answer. Those gray eyes continued to stare at him, as if through force of will he could make William to give up the truth. Another moment passed and a voice called out from the deck, "What are you doing down there, Walter? The Lord Warden is anxious to continue his journey to France while the weather holds."

"You," and here Walter poked William directly in the chest, "and your companion get on deck with the rest of the crew." William smiled and shrugged and did his best to act the part of a slow-witted stable hand. Robert bobbed his head but didn't smile as he passed by. Out of the corner of his eye he could see his tutor limping along, a few feet behind him, as if one leg wasn't working quite well. Between the two of them, they certainly came across as the type of crew who would be willing to spend their days below deck with the animals and the stench.

As William started up the stairs, the stallion, looking out of his stall towards him, neighed loudly, making their ears ring in the confined space. He tossed his great head and looked as though he would do anything to get out of the stall and follow William up onto the deck and fresh air. As it was, he stomped several times; the last time caused a loud exclamation to erupt out of his stall.

"For the love of Jesus' mother Mary…" William and Robert froze on the stairs. In a flash, Walter was at the stall, but was too short and couldn't look over the top of the door. Without thinking, he raised the latch and started to swing the gate. This was all the stallion needed and in a blink, he pushed his way out of the stall, past the startled Walter, who found himself knocked down and rolled into the filth covered deck.

The stallion made his way to the same stairs William and Robert were on and they realized they had no choice but to get run over, run down or run ahead of him out onto the deck. They both chose the latter. Seconds later they found themselves surrounded by both armed and unarmed men, Captain Stockton and most of the crew.

The stallion followed them, leaping up the last few steps and out onto the deck. William turned and could see the confusion and fear in the courser's eyes. His ears were laid back on his head and his nostrils were flared. Without even thinking, he reached up and grabbed the halter and placed his hand on the trembling muzzle, putting himself directly in front of the beast. "Easy there, lad, easy there." Despite the confusion and the racing of his heart, William was able to force himself to sound calm and soothing. It worked.

"Dear Lord, William, is that you?" A deep, melodious voice, with an obvious hint of disbelief added to it, spoke from somewhere in the group of armed men. The guards parted, and as William turned to see who had addressed him, he found himself standing face to face with the Lord High Admiral, William de Clinton.

"My Lord?" For a second William forgot himself, then shook his head, stood up straight and bowed deeply at waist. "My Lord de Clinton."

The Lord Admiral smiled broadly. "I would recognize that magnificent stallion anywhere. Is it here to secure your passage to France?"

"Yes my Lord." A questioning look crossed his face and the Lord Admiral picked up on it immediately.

Turning to face the men who accompanied him, he drew himself up straight, pulled his shoulders back and tucked in his chin. William thought, at that very moment, not only did he remind him of his father and uncle, but also he believed he would be willing to follow the Lord Admiral anywhere he led. "As Warden and High Admiral of the Cinque Ports I, William de Clinton, name this vessel, its crew, cargo and passengers as privileged within and among our ports." He then turned to a young man beside him and added, "return to our ship and record this so I may attach my seal to it."

Even as the young man scrambled over the larboard rail and down into one of the boats they had used to come aboard, a scream broke out from the open door of the hold. "You will take your hands off of me, you dirty little man." Every eye on the deck turned to see Helen being half pushed, half pulled up the steps. Her bright red hair was caught by the strong breeze, just as the sun came out of cloudbank. To William it looked as though she was on fire. Her expression suggested exactly the same.

"I found her hiding in the stalls, my Lord," Walter stated as he tried to present Helen to Lord de Clinton.

Helen drew herself up, still struggling to release the vise like grip of the short, horse muck covered sailor. "I was not hiding," she sneered. "I was simply doing my best to avoid notice." In any other circumstance, William would have burst out laughing, but he realized this was not the appropriate response.

For some reason, the Lord Admiral had turned a shade paler and his mouth slowly dropped open and he was shaking his head slowly. William would have sworn he heard him mutter, "It cannot be…"

"My Lord de Clinton, may I introduce Lady Helen d'Abbeville. Lady Helen, it is my honor to introduce William de Clinton the Lord High

Admiral and Warden of the Cinque Ports." Robert took the initiative and made the introduction.

"It is my pleasure, my lady." Lord de Clinton bowed and smiled but William could see the troubled look stayed on his face. Something was definitely bothering him. "Although we have not met Lady Helen, your name proceeds you. Although, how anyone in the realm would not have heard of your beauty before, is beyond comprehension."

"My name, my Lord? How so?" William could see Helen had been caught up in the flattery of the comment but there was something about Lord de Clinton's admission which bothered him. He glanced at Robert, only to see him carry the same worried expression.

"Not three days past, a fellow guest of Sir Robert Brent's received an urgent message. I was not privy to the details of the note, however I distinctly remember your name as well as a meeting at the Shipwright's Inn, two evenings past."

"My Lord Admiral," William interrupted, "may I be so bold as to suggest the name of the person who received the note?"

"You may, William, although how you could even guess is a mystery to me."

"My Lord," Robert interrupted. "I suggest we move to Lady Helen's quarters before recounting the details of the last two days. The information we need to share is important." Robert then lowered his voice to just above a whisper. If the wind had been any stronger, and the waves any louder, the Lord High Admiral wouldn't have been able to hear him, as it was, he could lean forward just enough to hear Robert tell him it wasn't for other ears to share. William nodded as he looked to Lord de Clinton.

A moment later, the stallion was handed back to a sailor who slipped a large, folded cloth over his still, slightly wild eyes. Almost instantly the courser calmed down, his head dropping forward, followed by a deep breath, which he slowly released. Without complaint, he was led back down the stairs he had recently ascended and quietly returned to his stall.

The Lord Admiral sent most of his men back to their ship, telling those who remained to await the return of the notice of Right of Passage and that he would sign and seal it as soon as their meeting ended. A moment later William, his tutor, Helen, and the Lord High Admiral made their way into Helen's small, semi-private space under the forecastle of the ship, drawing the curtain screen closed behind them.

"I wish we had met under better circumstance, my Lord de Clinton. You find me out of sorts and certainly not at my best today." Helen had turned as soon as she entered the room and did the Lord Admiral a courtesy as she addressed him. She stood and looked up smiling one of her warm heart felt smiles, which William had seen turned on him once or twice. Even though she was focused on the Lord High Admiral, William could see her expression from where he stood in the small space. He found himself smiling as well.

"Now, William, what is this guess you have made regarding the recipient of the note I described?" The Lord de Clinton had seated Lady Helen at the only stool in the room, while he and the others remained standing. It was no surprise to William that the Lord High Admiral easily kept his balance despite the ships occasional rolling over larger waves. His title, after all, was not an honorary one.

Instead of simply answering the question, both William and Robert recounted the last two day's events, from the moment they left the hunting party to their narrow escape from Southampton. The only thing they did not reveal was the secret entrusted to them by Lady Helen. Her true identity would remain her own choice to share. Robert concluded by adding, "We believe the group which assaulted us in the streets, as well as the men who attempted to abduct Lady Helen, were both coordinated by Lord Thomas. We have no proof, other than his actions yesterday morning on the quays of Southampton as well as the last words of Sir Geoffrey."

William de Clinton was unable to stand still during the description of the attack on themselves, as well as the attempted abduction of Lady Helen. He paced back and forth in the small chamber, his movements making the curtain flutter. "By God, the balls of the man!" Quickly realizing what he had said and in whose presence, he begged forgiveness of Lady Helen.

"If it was his knife which killed Sir Geoffrey, he now finds himself a traitor to the crown. What would drive a man to do such a thing? To even think of raising your hand to a courier of the king is to raise your hand to the King himself…" Lord de Clinton stopped in mid-sentence and turned to Lady Helen. The pale, shaken look William had seen just a few moments before returned to the Lord High Admiral. He had hit the nail on the head and looked as though the answer he guessed at wasn't at all pleasant.

"Lady Helen, I find myself wishing to ask you certain, uh, how can I put it… indelicate questions." Robert and William exchanged knowing glances. Somehow, the Lord High Admiral either knew or guessed at something of Lady Helen's true story. For some reason, William found himself suddenly apprehensive. He didn't know why, but he didn't think it would be best if Lord de Clinton knew what Robert and himself knew of her parentage.

Helen lowered her gaze and dropped her voice to just above a whisper. "I am your servant, my Lord."

The Lord High Admiral cleared his throat. From where William stood, it seemed his features covered both worry and fear. Why would he be afraid of Lady Helen? What about her background would worry him? Before he could answer his own question, the Lord Admiral began. "I am familiar with some of your family and have been to The Marches this past year. How I could possibly have missed you while there, I can only attribute to my complete lack of observation." He smiled gently, but his eyes betrayed his thoughts. William could see it. There was something definitely troubling the Lord High Admiral.

"Ah, but there you are mistaken, my Lord. My family is from York, and it was there I was returning after spending several seasons with relations near Abbeville."

"But your accent…"

"My handmaid for these last few years was from The Marches that is true. I did not realize my speech had been so affected." William was impressed, not only in how she carried herself but her ability to think quickly. "I must admit, my Lord, the last few days have left me quite shaken." As if on cue, she clasped her hands together, in her lap, to keep them still.

Lord de Clinton's expression softened a little more. Concern crept over his features. "Do you have any idea why Lord Thomas would take such an interest in you?" He didn't have to ask why he would have killed to get to her. Despite the worry and fear, which William could just barely see on his face, the Lord de Clinton kept his civility. After all, this was a woman and a Lady he was addressing.

"Until I met William and Robert I had never heard mention of his name or title, my Lord." She kept her eyes down, focusing on her hands in her lap. Even her voice seemed to flutter with emotion. At some point, since coming up out of the hold, William realized she had pulled her hair back and knotted it upon itself. From where he stood, he could clearly see her pale throat. What surprised him was the rapid pace of her pulse.

Her heart must have been pounding. Did she also sense the Lord High Admiral's concerns?

"What do you plan to do once you return to France, my lady?" It was a simple question, but William felt something behind the question. There was definitely something troubling Lord de Clinton. William glanced at Robert and it seemed his tutor noticed it as well. He looked as though he was simply listening to the conversation, but William could tell he was tense as bowstring. What was it that he had missed?

"Because of the gallantry they showed me, and the personal risk William took to safeguard my person, I offered to help in their quest, my Lord. I thought I could do that best by giving them supplies and a small boat they can use to travel up the Somme. The estate of my family is just outside of Abbeville and we would have everything they need there."

The Lord High Admiral nodded slowly, eventually turning to William. "The quickest way to reach Chateau de Coucy will be on the Somme. There is no doubt of that. If the riverboat Lady Helen provides has a small sail, you could make very good time against the current. The river is rather broad at Abbeville, but have a care; the French hold most of the land as you travel south." He paused a moment then turned to William, "I would assume Lady Helen knows your true identity?"

"She does, my Lord. It was revealed to her the morning after her attempted abduction."

He nodded and then, almost to himself, muttered, "Good, good… it is best not to hide who you really are for too long, William. You may, eventually, find yourself unable to believe the truth." William nodded his agreement. He was afraid, if he spoke at that moment, his voice would crack. Fortunately, a throat cleared itself on the other side of the curtain.

"Yes, what is it, Simon?"

"I beg pardon, my Lord, but the Right of Passage you requested has arrived."

The Lord High Admiral nodded but didn't move. It seemed as though he was on the verge of saying or asking something, then, in an instant thought better of it. Instead, he turned to William and smiled at him, gripping him at the shoulder. Fortunately it was his right, otherwise he would have found himself wincing from the pain, which still persisted in his left.

"Continue safeguarding the innocent and putting the cares and concerns of others before your own, William and you will certainly earn your spurs." William smiled a great big, toothsome smile.

"Yes, my Lord. I will do my best." He lowered his eyes just a little and could feel the heat rising up in his face and ears. It was amazing how just a little comment could create such a current of emotions in him.

The Lord High Admiral turned, bowing to Lady Helen. Although his eyes still betrayed his feelings, he smiled, "it was a pleasure to make your acquaintance, Lady Helen." He gave a curt nod to Robert and then thrust aside the curtain.

On the main deck the Lord High Admiral signed and sealed the Right of Passage document and handed it to Captain Stockton. "Guard your cargo well, Captain," then added, very quietly, to himself, "Unless I am mistaken it is much more valuable than you realize." No one heard this over the crash of the waves and the wind snapping at the sail and the rigging. A moment later, he and the last of his men had descended a rope ladder to their small boat and set to the oars.

William and Robert had followed the Lord de Clinton out onto the deck and watched as the boat was slowly rowed away from their ship, making its way back to its own, with some difficulty as the waves were cresting still higher. Once the rowboat was over half way back, William let out a deep breath, dropping his head and closing his eyes in the process. "Thank You, God for watching over us."

"Amen, William." Robert had joined him at the rail and the concerned look was still there on his face.

"What was it about the Lord High Admiral? He noticed something or there was something which concerned him about Lady Helen."

Robert stood quietly for a moment, lost in some thought. Finally, lowering his voice just a little, he answered and William was shocked to hear it tremble slightly. "Lord de Clinton grew up as a boyhood friend of our King Edward. It was he, the young king and several of the king's companions who secretly entered Nottingham Castle and captured Isabella and her lover, Roger de Mortimer. Lord Mortimer's execution followed quickly after a very short trial."

"Dear Lord!" William had to grip the rail tighter. He found his head spinning at the thought that the man he admired, who was standing on the deck of this ship just moments before, was the same man who helped imprison and execute Helen's father. "Do you think he somehow recognized Lady Helen? If he suspected she was the king's half-sister…"

"She would have the king himself, as well as Lord Thomas to worry about. She also would prove inconvenient for the Queen Mother, despite her exile from court."

"The Queen Mother? How… how could Helen be an inconvenience to her own mother?" He understood the potential threat to the king, but to her mother?

"When Lord Mortimer was tried for treason, they portrayed Isabella as an innocent victim of his schemes. There was never a mention, in public, of his relationship with her. Helen's very existence would prove otherwise." Robert bowed his head and it shocked William to see the depth of emotion his tutor was fighting to control. "It is as if the whole world is aligned against the poor girl. Everywhere she turns she will find herself facing enemies." He paused a moment in thought, then added, "I suddenly wonder why her guardians decided to move her now? Is there something else at play? Is it possible they found personal gain in encouraging Helen to leave her home?"

"You make it sound like a game."

Robert nodded, "a horrible game, William. To lose this game will mean Helen's death, of that I am sure. The problem is I still do not know who we are playing against."

"Do you think there are others besides Lord Thomas?"

Robert took some time to answer and when he did, William was shocked at what he heard. "Lord Thomas wants power, pure and simple. I could sense it in the forest and knew it for certain from his actions at the quays of Southampton. By having Sir John Brent killed, only his brother, Sir Robert stands in Lord Thomas' way of controlling a large portion of Southwest England. With that accomplished and Helen at his side, he could make a play even for the throne itself."

"Helen would never agree to it."

"Of course she would not, but you are assuming, William, that she will be asked. As for others involved…" Robert shook his head slowly, his brow drawn down, a look of intense concentration and worry combined in his expression. "I really do not know, William. Perhaps, once we get to Abbeville, some answers will be revealed."

William looked back out over the waves, which separated them from the Lord High Admiral's ship. The rowboat was already tied to the side and there was no sign of Lord de Clinton on the deck. He tried to collect his thoughts and eventually came to the only conclusion, which at the time made the most sense. "I have offered to protect Lady Helen for as long as she is with us and I will stand by that promise, no matter who or what may threaten her. I will honor my commitment to safeguard the innocent, no matter the cost."

For a long moment, they stood, tutor and pupil, side by side at the rail, neither saying anything. So much had happened in the last several days since they left Dorchester and the relative safety of Crandor Castle. William felt Roberts arm come across his shoulders as his teacher gave him a sideways embrace. "The path and choices we are to make are set before us William. Do we choose right or left? The less difficult and easier paths may only appear so on the surface or at the outset. This path is usually well worn since most people choose that way. The other road may look as though overgrown with brambles and weeds. Less people have chosen this path and yet it could lead us safer to our goal. We have to embrace these choices, William, no matter their appearance and know that our lives and those around us will be affected by which path we choose.

"Since we set out from Dorset County we have relied on the strength of One greater than ourselves, William. Do we turn from Him now and attempt this with our own abilities? I for one, will not. We must continue to lean on and rely on His grace and strength. Our hands will do what they can and we will trust His ability to empower us while keeping the eyes of the great and the dangerous elsewhere. The path you are about to choose will make all the difference."

William watched as the Admiral's ship adjusted its sails and pulled away from them. His ship was riding higher than William's and obviously was not burdened with a full hold. "God grant me the strength I need to see this through and the wisdom needed to choose the right path even if it appears to be the more difficult."

"And I as well, Lord," Robert added. As if on cue, they both added, "Amen."

William shut his eyes and dropped his head, taking a deep breath and slowly exhaling. "God, grant me Your peace. Bless me indeed in the decisions I need to make." He spoke these words, silently to himself. As he stood at the rail, next to his tutor, he could feel the comfort and peace settle over him. Despite the great difficulties he knew were still ahead, William smiled. After all, if God is for him, who can be against?

Chapter Nineteen

While William still felt the warmth of both spiritual and physical embraces, he decided to find Helen. Several conversations were swirling around in his thoughts as he approached the curtain to her room. He would have to tread cautiously. He couldn't afford to let her get to him, become irritated, and then let an ill-timed comment destroy any chance he had of clearing the air between them. He was certain her safety depended on Robert and his help. He just hoped she saw it the same way.

"Lady Helen, may I speak with you?"

There was a long pause with no answer. William self-consciously straightened his cotte. He found himself wanting to itch the healing wound on his arm, while at the same time, wishing he had a comb to straighten his hair. "You may come in, William."

Her voice sounded strained and he understood why when he pulled back the curtain and stepped into the small room. She obviously had been crying. Her face was streaked, her eyes bright red and her breathing rattled. She was sitting on the edge of her small frame bed, her hands still clasped in her lap. She made no attempt to rise or wipe the tears from her eyes. Williams's propriety told him to leave the cloth pulled back a little. After all, she was a young, beautiful woman and he didn't want any rumors flying through the crew.

In that instant, William felt as though a great fist reached out and began squeezing his chest. His breath caught in his throat. Without even realizing it, tears of his own threatened to overwhelm him. None of that really mattered though, because he hated seeing Helen look like this. In the darkness of the room, she seemed dimmed and diminished somehow. Even her shoulders were sagged, her posture nearly folded in half.

As if not under his own control, he found himself walking over to her and dropping to one knee. His hands were trembling, but he still managed to reach out and take hers in his own. She looked up, slightly startled. There was so much William wanted to say, but all he could manage was, "I am sorry for my comments this morning. Please forgive me. I really had no idea…" He couldn't finish his sentence before his voice broke with emotion. The tears, which had only threatened, now spilled over. He lowered his head and repeated, "I am sorry."

"Oh, William…" she pulled one hand away from his and reached out, lifting his chin so she could look into his face. What he saw made him smile because it wasn't pity there. The tears and intense sadness were, but there was also just a hint of a smile. "I am sorry I acted so childishly. None of that seems important now, not after…" her voice trailed off and more tears spilled down her cheeks.

"You know who the Lord Admiral de Clinton is, yes?" Helen closed her eyes and nodded. "Do you think he recognized you? Because if he did…"

"I know… I will have both Lord Thomas and my brother Edward as my enemies." She pulled her hands away, burying her face in them. "Oh God, I do not want to die, William." She sobbed and her shoulders shook. As he watched, it was as if a wall Helen had built over the years suddenly crumbled before his eyes. Her sobs racked her body as she rocked on the edge of the bed.

He felt foolish just kneeling there, watching her. Part of him understood how she felt. It was as if God had turned His back on her, allowing so many things wrong and some evil to overtake her. William knew this wasn't true, but he also realized Helen was in the middle of losing the battle of thoughts and ideas planted in her head. He had felt the same way after his mother died.

William reached out and grabbed Helen's hands by the wrist, gently pulling them from her face and folding them at her knees. He tried his best not to focus on the strong, rapid pulse he felt. "I do understand something of what you are going through. I felt the same way when my father was killed and my mother simply faded away. I questioned God, His actions, and what He was allowing to happen to me. Why would He leave me here, alone? Why would He take away my parents? Was it something I had done wrong?" He paused a moment to collect his thoughts.

"How did you get past it… or did you? I am so scared of what might happen to me, William and yet, at the same time, I am angry too. If He is so good, how could He possibly let this happen?"

Kneeling there, in front of Helen, William bowed his head. He really did understand what she was going through. Those exact same thoughts had gone through his mind as well. For a brief moment, he could almost sense someone or something trying to poke a hole in his mind, as if trying to replant those thoughts and those questions. He shook his head to clear it. He had been taught enough over the last few days to understand how important it was to guard his thoughts. He had seen, firsthand, what could happen to someone who wasn't careful and constantly on guard. He decided he wasn't going to be easily led down that path again.

"First things first," he started. His voice cracked with his own emotions and he cleared his throat. "The first thing is to find a way not to focus on what might come to pass…" William paused, trying to find a way to phrase it. In a flash he remembered what Robert had told him on more than one occasion since they left Dorchester. "Yesterday is past, there is no going back and doing it again. Tomorrow is a promise, but not a guarantee. We do not know what might happen or where life might take us. We do not even know for sure if we will be here to see tomorrow. All we have, Lady Helen, is today. This moment. Right here and now.

"Close your eyes and listen to the sounds around you. What do you hear?" William paused and waited until she did what he asked. As he watched, it seemed the lines of worry slowly faded from her face.

"I hear the wind in the rigging, the waves against the ship, wooden planks of the deck creaking, men moving about, orders given and one of the horses whinnying. I hear you breathing as well."

William swallowed hard. For some reason that last comment affected him more than he imagined. "When you live in the moment it is hard to worry about what may or may not happen in the future. My father told me once that no man ever added even a day to his life worrying about tomorrow. Even God tells us we should not worry about tomorrow because today has enough problems of its own."

Helen smiled and even laughed just a little. "Well, William, I do feel a little better."

"I have dealt with some of those same feelings in the last two years, and even a few times since we left Dorchester. I cannot speak for anyone else, but I will tell you, there is only one reason I still know for certain I will make it through this and see my uncle returned safely home."

"How can you possibly know that, William? How can you really be so sure?"

"Because, with God on my side, nothing can stand in my way. Even though I may find myself walking through the very valley of death, I will fear no evil for my God is with me. His very words say He will prepare a table for me in the presence of my enemies; my head will be anointed and my cup will overflow. Goodness and mercy will follow me all the days of my life."

As William spoke these words, God's own words, from a song of King David, he felt a renewed sense of well-being. It was as if a surge of power began to well up inside of him. His skin seemed to tingle and as he knelt there, holding Helen's hand, he asked God to fill her with His power, the same way He had filled himself. As if in response, a small voice inside said it was up to him to lead her.

"I know those words, William. I have heard them before myself, but I still do not understand how God could let all this happen. Does He not care?"

"Helen, He cares so much about you that He sent His own Son, Jesus, to live as we live, to eventually be beaten and ridiculed and even killed by the very people He came to save. He did this so that His Sons' sacrifice would, once and for all, allow us to come before God, on our own, to His very throne of grace and gaze on His loving face, realizing He had created a special space, a hole in each of us, shaped just like Him. We can stand there in His presence and ask for His peace, which surpasses all understanding. And we can know, without any doubt He is God and we are not. And when that time comes, we can surrender to Him and His will in our life. And that very moment we surrender it is like allowing yourself to empty of anger, bitterness, and resentment; and He comes with His Spirit and fills the hole. Once you do this, your life will never be the same."

Helen turned away from William and looked out past the open screen to the mast and the stern and the sea beyond and asked, "How can you possibly know that for certain, William?" Her eyes held more than just the question. He thought for sure he saw just a glimmer of hope as well.

William smiled a sad smile and blinked a tear out of his eye. "Because, one sunny day last summer, standing near the grave of my mother, feeling as though the whole world was crashing down around me, and my life was no longer worth living, I cried out to God, turned all my problems and fears over to Him and asked for His help. Robert told me on that day I was born a new person. I am not sure about that, but I do know for certain what I felt afterwards." He paused and broke into a smile that could light up a room. Even his eyes were smiling and Helen thought they looked as if they were shining. She caught a small gasp and stared. "It was as if my mother was there, holding me in her arms, comforting me, and yet it was more than that." He shook his head, lowering his eyes, "I am not sure if that makes any sense, but that is what happened to me."

Helen wanted William to look up at her again with his eyes the way they were. She had never seen anything like that before. She had been taught about God all her life. She had been taken to church every Sunday, since she could remember. She had been told she was baptized, but it had happened when she was still a baby and so she didn't remember it. For most of her life, she believed God existed, but she felt He didn't have any reason to concern Himself with her and her troubles. After all she was just one girl.

Once she found out her true parentage, and the trouble which quickly followed, a gnawing thought had crept into her mind. It had started small, but eventually turned into a nagging doubt as to even God's existence. *'If He was God and He really cared, He would not have let all this happen, would he?'* That was the thought which had been growing in her mind for such a long time that she didn't even really remember how or when it began.

Now this young man, helped by his teacher, a hunchback, and a knight who lost his life to defend her, saves her and yet all the while she still seemed to doubt God's existence. Where was He when these men were the ones sacrificing so much for her? Then William looked at her with those eyes. Were they really shining with light? She shook her head. It had to have been her imagination, nothing more than that.

"I believe you, William, but it is just…" She couldn't seem to put her thoughts into words. It was as if her tongue was suddenly stuck to the roof of her mouth while her mind went blank at the same time.

William thought he understood what was holding her back and took a chance, "one thing I have to keep reminding myself is that God is God and I am not. Robert told me once that James wrote in a letter that all the great and good in our lives comes from God because He is great and good. There is no evil in God, so it is not God's doing if we find ourselves facing evil in our lives. In fact it is impossible for it to be God's fault."

"Then where has He been in all this?"

William stood. He had just enough wisdom at that very moment to realize, no matter what he said or how many times he said it, Helen just wasn't ready to hear. Her eyes were lowered and her head tilted forward so that her bright red hair covered her face. He wished there was a way he could get her to understand the way he did. As he turned to leave, a thought hit him and he stood for a second, torn between leaving well enough alone and adding one more comment. He chose the latter.

"Perhaps, Lady Helen, it was God who sent us to you." William turned and walked around the half closed curtain and back out onto the main deck.

It was already late afternoon and William noticed a bank of dark clouds rolling in from the west. The wind had shifted as well, and as he stood near the mast watching the sun seemingly get swallowed by the gray cover, he saw a flash in the distance. It was still far enough away that he didn't immediately hear the rumble but he was certain it was lightning. A storm was rolling up behind them, and at the same time, driving them forward with even greater speed.

To be in the middle of a rolling field in Dorchester, with the sheep lying about and dark clouds rolling in with thunder and lightning, is one thing William was very familiar with. This storm, out over the sea, with only a few planks of wood between him and the frigid waters of the channel was completely different. Even the faint echoing boom of the rolling thunder from such a distance seemed magnified, as if the waves themselves tossed the sound about, just as they tossed the ship. Another flash illuminated the western sky, as a half dozen streaks of lightning arched through it, racing towards the water at the same time.

The sail above his head was completely filled and the rigging was already being stretched to the point of protest. Just at that moment the captain was making his way from the forecastle to the stern. As he passed William he paused briefly and quietly murmured, "We are making best time now, lad, but the question will be whether or not we can make the turn to Calais and still stay out in front of that beast." He squinted toward the western horizon and shook his head, "it is a beast, all right. A big, bloody, dark beast." He continued onto the stern and William could still hear him muttering to himself as he walked away.

"What does the captain think, William?" He hadn't heard Robert approach so he jumped a little at the words spoken over his shoulder. "He says we are making the best possible speed now because of the wind driving us before this storm. What he is not sure about is making it from Dover to Calais without finding ourselves in the middle of that," and he nodded to the brewing mess to the west.

"Well, this is the only way to get from England to France that I am aware of, so we will have to rely on God to get us there safely. After all, Jesus told the Sea of Galilee to be calm, and a storm which threatened to flood the boat they were in, suddenly stopped, and they were able to make it to the other side. God does not change nor do His abilities, William." His tutor smiled and turned back towards the storm, nodding to himself a few times.

William watched as Robert stood there, on the rolling deck of the ship, his arms crossed, a smile on his lips, and he seemed completely at ease, almost as if he didn't have a care in the world. William himself certainly didn't feel quite that confident. Between everything happening to Lady Helen, and now this storm, his faith was taking a serious beating. Somewhere deep in the back of his mind, in a far, out of the way corner, a little thought was planted and he didn't even realize it. *'What if this storm overtook them? Could this ship handle it?'* Even as those thoughts crept in, William stood and watched his tutor continue to smile.

"How can you be so happy right now? Do you see how large that storm is? If it overtakes us, I do not know if this ship could handle it."

"William, are you telling me that storm is bigger than God? Is there any such storm?" Robert shook his head and then turned to face his young student, a more serious look on his face. "I am smiling and at ease William because I am not standing here telling God how big this storm is. He knows how large and dangerous it is. I am smiling and at ease because I am telling that storm how big our God is. How He can handle and calm any storm. He is my refuge and strong tower and it is Him I turn to in times of trouble. When you know, without a doubt how truly amazing God is, William, you will find yourself at ease and confident even in the face of a storm like this."

Robert said all of these things calmly and in a matter of fact manner, but William could see the earnestness in his eyes. This was a lesson he needed to learn and learn quickly. As he stood there on the main deck thinking, the ship rolled down over a much larger wave and the next crest crashed in over the bow, just clearing the forecastle, spraying them both with cold, salty water.

It was like a brisk, wet, chilly slap in the face. The spray actually stung, like little icy needles. William blinked the mist from his eyes and wiped his face on his sleeve. The temperature of the air had certainly dropped and he was glad he still had the hooded cloak in his pack. It took nearly a minute of half walking, half sliding across the deck to retrieve it and his pack but felt immensely better when the warm, heavy wool was wrapped around his shoulders and the cowl pulled down low. He noticed Robert had retrieved his own pack and had it slung over his shoulders.

As William stood there, trying to keep his balance on the rolling deck, Robert turned and pointed to his left, "Look, William, Dover." There, just off the larboard rail, were the white cliffs he had heard both his father and uncle speak about. Here was the last chance the captain would have to turn to shore and find shelter or turn to sea and make a run for France; left or right; larboard or starboard; run to safety or run before the storm? As if in answer, William heard a shout from the stern.

"Hard to starboard! Coming about!" Even as the ship heeled to its side as it turned out to sea, the boom of the main sail swung about. William had just enough presence of mind to duck before the large oak beam would have swatted him into the sea. As it was, the sailors laid out the rigging to allow the sail to swivel along with the change in course and the boom missed him and his tutor as they both squatted on the deck for a moment.

The sail strained even harder under the force of the wind, which was now coming from their rear starboard quarter. William was pretty sure he could see the top of the mast bending with the strong winds. The sea didn't want to be left out of the tempest either. At the crest of each wave, William could almost feel the ship leap up and out of the water, only to come crashing down onto the next wave, or sometimes into the trough between. When this happened, icy salt water sprayed across the deck again. He was not sure his stomach could handle several more hours of this.

Lightning flashed behind them and several loud thunderclaps echoed out over the sea. William and his father used to sit under a lean-to shelter during storms such as these, which occasionally rolled across Dorchester. But here, out in the channel, it was different. Even as far away as the front of the storm looked, he could feel in his chest the thrumming vibration as it rolled over the waves. The flashes and the rumblings which followed were mesmerizing. He wasn't sure how long he stood there, simply watching and feeling the growing maelstrom advance on them.

At some point Helen joined them near the mast. William noticed she had pulled back her hair back into a braid and was wearing her own heavy wool cloak. She held it close to her throat with her hands, which seemed paler than usual and shaking. "If I stay in that room any longer I will lose all sense of top and bottom, as will my stomach." William smiled and Robert nodded, but Helen looked grim. "Will it overtake us before Calais do you think?"

Robert waited for a series of thunderclaps to finish echoing across the waves before answering. "Normally it would take this ship six or seven hours to make the crossing to France from Dover, however, it is making best time now. We may see the coast in as little as three hours." He paused a moment, and William realized he hadn't actually answered Helen's question. "We are in God's hands, my lady, and I have no doubt He will see us through." He spoke this with such conviction it surprised

William. "My only concern will be our need to find shelter when the rains come in. As much as you dislike your room at the moment Lady Helen, we may need to impose on you and set ourselves in there."

"It would be nice to have the company..." A tremendous flash and explosion rocked the air around them and William was startled to see the boiling black, gray, and brown mess of clouds change its course. Now it looked to be bearing straight down on them. As if in answer, the wind picked up even more, the mast creaked even louder, bending even further against the pressure, as the sail strained against the rigging. He couldn't believe it was possible but William was pretty sure the ship was moving even faster now. The rhythm and pace of the rise and fall of the ship over the waves had definitely picked up.

As if in response he could feel his heart thunder in his chest. The distant rumblings were not as far away as they had been just moments ago. Even as the storm advanced on them, the ship responded with increasing speed. There was only one problem and that was how long it could hold itself together against the punishment it was receiving?

William looked to the stern where the captain stood with one of his crew, bracing the rudder with their weight to keep the ship on course. Even though the storm hadn't fully overtaken them, a thick bank of dark clouds now stretched from horizon to horizon. How the captain had any sense of where they were going was beyond him. He had no idea whether they sailed north, south, east or west or whether they were simply running in circles. Robert had told him Calais was southeast of Dover, and on a clear day you can see the white cliffs from the French coast. But here, as they approached what they guessed was the middle of the channel, with the storm clouds rolling in and the waves cresting at chest height, he couldn't see much beyond the bow of the ship. As he tried to maintain his balance while keeping his cloak wrapped tightly about him, William's chest ached from the constant drumming of his heart. He wasn't sure why, but his throat hurt and his neck and shoulder muscles were bunched up and straining, as if to will the wind to stay back.

He could barely feel Robert when he reached out and grabbed his arm, while leaning over to shout into his ear. "Try to relax your shoulders, William! You will exhaust yourself if you do not!" He knew his tutor was screaming at him but he could hardly hear it over the wind and the crash of the waves. Still, he tried his best to relax. He closed his eyes and asked for the peace which surpasses all understanding to come upon him. He rolled his shoulders and twisted his neck, feeling the knots release and the tension decrease a little and gave a silent thought of "thanks." The wind and waves continued unabated.

As he stood a moment with his eyes closed, enjoying the drop in tension, he heard, and then felt, the rain begin. At first it was thick, heavy drops, few and far between. They landed large and wet and simply mixed with the sea spray. Eventually it started coming down harder and then in sheets. The distant roll of thunder was no longer distant, but the rain seemed to dampen the sound around him, and he was unable to judge how far the strikes were from the ship. As if on cue, all three of them began slipping and scrambling their way into Helen's partitioned quarters. Although the curtain did little to keep the wind and rain from whipping into the room, they were at least under shelter.

William lost track of time as they stood on the deck, after turning from Dover. His mind seemed to be slowly struggling forward, stumbling over little thoughts. The ship continued to roll up, over and down the choppy waves; the wind and rain continued as well, as did the thunder and ever approaching lightning, and yet he stood there, in the middle of that small room, as if disconnected from it all. His heart had slowed a little and his shoulders didn't feel as though they were knotted anymore and yet there was something unreal about how he felt. He sat down on one corner of the small frame bed in the room, just a few feet from Helen and Robert and yet his thoughts were miles away.

A rare gem, that was what Robert had called that morning just over a week ago. When he closed his eyes, William could see the green grass moving in the breeze and hear the lolling of the sheep as they grazed on the hills around Crandor. The sky was a deep blue with only a few high clouds. In spite of the present situation, he smiled to himself. The doubt, which had crept into his thoughts, was suddenly revealed as he reflected on that beautiful spring day.

He shook his head a little and took in a deep breath as he realized he couldn't let that doubt take control of his thoughts. If he didn't control those ideas, they would certainly take control of him. Even as he wrestled with these thoughts, the sky flashed a brilliant, intense white light, briefly detailing the pattern of the cloth used as the screen, and seconds later, a sharp crackle and deep explosion followed. Helen jumped to her feet, clutching even tighter at the cloak around her shoulders. Her knuckles were white from the grip and her expression and the look in her eyes was one of stark terror. In the seconds following, the horses below deck voiced their fear as well. Then the rains returned even harder than before and drowned out their protests.

Robert was on his feet first, and grabbed Lady Helen at the shoulders. William could tell it was a hard, attention-grabbing grip. Her eyes shifted from terror to anger, which was exactly what he had hoped for. "We will make it to France, my lady." He was so confident, and emphasized the word "will" so strongly, it even caught William by surprise.

"How can you be so sure…?" Her expression softened in the face of his conviction and her eyes dropped to the planks at her feet where seawater and rain splashed together. As if an afterthought, she added, "I do not want to die."

Robert lowered his voice and it soften gently as he asked, "If this is your last hour on earth, my lady, do you know where you will go after?" It seemed an innocent enough question, but William could see the earnestness in his tutor's face. There he stood, with the sea and the storm raging around him, and he wanted to make sure Lady Helen's soul would find its way to God.

"I have never missed mass and I learned all of the prayers in Latin."

"That is not what will save you, my lady. Jesus Himself said so." Outside another bright flash lit the sky. This time, the explosion was so quick to follow William thought he actually felt the hair on the back of his neck stand on end.

Helen hesitated for a second, her hands trembling as she bit her lower lip, then asked, "What must I do?"

"Believe that Jesus is Who He said He is, the Son of God. That He lived among us that He died for our sins and He rose from the dead. Repent of every sin you have committed, turn your back on them once and for all, and ask Jesus into your life right now, to lead and guide you as your Lord."

Helen bowed her head, letting go of the cloak in order to clasp her hands together. She squeezed her eyes shut and repeated Robert's words in a loud, clear voice. When she finished she opened and lifted her eyes. Tears streamed down her cheeks and there was a smile on her face. "How…?"

"Your soul is at peace with God. No matter what happens, from now on, God is with you, helping you and guiding you."

William had felt like a spectator through all this. Physically he was there, in that small room, being tossed about on the sea by the storm but his memories were miles away. It was summertime in Dorchester and he was standing again at his mother's grave. "God, I do not want to ever forget that day or that decision." The sky was clear blue and large white clouds drifted overhead.

Even as he sat on the edge of that bed, recalling that memory, he felt the hair on the back of his neck stand on end. He froze. Robert reacted faster, pushing Helen down to the deck and covering her with his body. William had just enough presence of mind to throw his hands up in front of his face. The light, the explosion, the scream of horses and men, the smell of charred wood, and a metallic taste in his mouth all happened at the same time. The curtain wall was shredded before William's eyes. He felt several objects fly past him, felt several hit him and heard more shattering of wood on the deck.

His hands were shaking and when he looked down at them he realized they were bleeding. Several large and a few small needle sized splinters of wood were sticking out of both of them. His right hand had a particularly large one, which ran clear through to his palm. Blood was already dripping out of the smaller holes and streaming from the large one. He raised them up to his face, as if looking at someone else's body and then his vision blurred. His eyes burned and he tried using his finger to wipe them clear. They came back red. Several more splinters were imbedded in his forehead and eyebrows. He pulled the first one out and stared at it. It was jagged and almost as long as his forefinger.

It was probably only seconds that he sat on the edge of the bed, staring at his hands, but it felt so much longer. He no longer noticed any sounds around him. He could see through the tattered curtain, thick sheets of rain continued to fall on the deck and even noticed a few men scrambling about. He couldn't be certain, but it looked like two others were crumpled up on the wood planks, like a couple mounds of dirty rags.

His heart was pounding in his ears so loudly he didn't even notice Robert talking to him until his tutor gripped him at the shoulder. He slowly turned his head and looked up into his teacher's eyes. They looked like the stormy sea, which surrounded them and continued to threaten them.

"I asked if you are alright." He finally heard the words but it still took a moment for his mind to process their meaning.

"I am pierced like a pin cushion." William tried his best to smile. Slowly his brain started moving again, "how is Lady Helen?"

"God be praised, neither of us were injured." Helen had stepped over and knelt next to William. She tenderly took his hands in hers and looked up at Robert. "What are we to do?"

Robert took a deep breath and paused, with his eyes closed a brief second. "First we are to thank God we are all still alive. Second, let us make sure we stay that way." He too knelt in front of his student and took his hands in his own. William noticed both of their hands were shaking. He wasn't sure if his shook more than the others.

"I need to remove as many of these as possible, William." That was all the warning he was given. There was no time to consider options. One moment he was looking into those storm grey eyes and the next he felt his tutor begin pulling splinters from his face, forehead and hands. It actually went very quickly. Finally the last one left was the largest, which had completely pierced his right hand. Robert stared at it a moment. "I am going to have to push this through and then pull it out from the other side, William. It will be easier that way."

William swallowed down the warm acid he felt trying to make its way up and out of his stomach. He nodded in understanding. *"Yeah… easier. For who?"* he thought, then closed his eyes and asked God for the ability to endure just a part of what Christ himself might have felt. Robert took his hand and in two quick movements pushed the splinter farther in and then pulled it out from the other side.

Tears welled up as a burning sensation spread from his hand, up his entire arm. Drumming pain pounded through his hand, timed with his hammering heartbeat. He hadn't even had a chance to cry out in pain. He could feel warmth run down his fingers, dripping off of them and onto the deck.

Opening his eyes, William made sure not to look at his hands. What he saw instead make him feel any better. Robert still knelt before him, staring at the thick, jagged splinter, which was nearly as long as the width of his palm and almost as thick as his little finger. Blood dripped from it and he could see what had to be part of the skin and muscles of his hand stuck to its edges. He felt lightheaded and was glad to be sitting on a bed. Helen's arm wrapped around his shoulders and she helped him lie back. "Keep his hand up. I need to tear some linen to bind the wound," he heard his tutor state and then darkness swirled around the edge of his vision.

It felt as if the ship itself was spinning. How appropriate, he thought. First the storm destroys us then the sea swallows us. He closed his eyes and tried to breathe deeply. For the first time in a long moment he actually noticed the sound of the rain on the deck, the shouts of men outside the room and the scream of horses. Was it his imagination or could he actually make out the voice of the black courser over all the cacophony? "Stay with him a moment, Lady Helen. I need to see what has happened to the ship." Lying there with his eyes closed, thinking about the horse, he hadn't even realized his tutor had bandaged up his hand. It still pulsed and he couldn't move his fingers without feeling shooting pain run up his forearm, but Helen's touch was warm and comforting, despite her trembling fingers. She laid her hand on his forehead, lightly brushing his hair from his eyes, all the while being careful not to touch the places where Robert had pulled splinters.

Lightning flashed again but this time it was a little farther away. The strange sensation he had felt on the back of his neck didn't repeat itself this time. The peal of thunder was delayed a few seconds and William let out a short sigh. Perhaps the worst of the storm had passed them by.

William wasn't sure how long he lay there. The ship had stopped spinning but now it seemed to heave and crash over the waves even higher and harder than before. Every time it came down over a crest and crashed into the trough at the bottom or into the wave following his whole body was jarred and his hand was jolted. Sharp, shooting, stabs of pain lanced up his arm and he found himself biting his lower lip until he tasted the metallic warm saltiness of blood.

Robert's voice forced him to try and sit up. "We do not have much time. The ship is sinking."

"Dear Lord," Helen muttered, squeezing William's good hand in the process. His eyes fluttered open and he blinked a few times to bring his tutor into focus.

"What has happened?"

"The lightning struck the ship at the top of the mast and then smashed through the deck. There is a hole the size of a large stone just a few feet from this room. It struck one of the horses dead and then blew through the side of the ship. Every time we roll to starboard we take on water in the hold. They plugged it with some canvas but that will not keep us afloat for long. The horses are panicking and the captain is going to let them onto the deck. He thinks some of them may be able to swim to shore."

"How close are we then?" Helen asked before William had a chance. He was trying to sit up without his head spinning and his vision going dark.

"Not that close. Even in calm water a horse can only swim a few miles." Robert paused a second, then added, "But God will make a way." Neither Helen nor William responded, so he added, "we should saddle the stallion as soon as he is brought up. If he goes over the rail, we would have a better chance making it to shore with him if we have something to hang onto."

William finally managed to sit up, although he kept his eyes closed and had to swallow a few times to keep from throwing up. "How far do you think we have come since we turned from Dover?"

"The captain has kept bells on the hour, matching the marked candle in his room, which miraculously has stayed lit during this storm." The sky flashed and seconds later another echoing explosion followed. Maybe it was his imagination, but William thought the rain was letting up just a little. At least, through the torn and tattered curtain it didn't seem to be coming down in thick sheets.

"We are just past four bells since we turned from Dover" Robert continued. "Normally it would have taken us five or more to reach the shore but the captain knows we have been making much faster time ahead of the storm. Through the rain though there is no way to tell just how close we really are." William nodded his understanding. If they made a straight run for Calais they could very well be only a few hundred yards from shore. Then again, once in the storm, they really have no idea where they were actually heading.

The sky lit up again and to William it looked like everything on the deck froze for a brief second. He saw sailors in mid stride, as they crossed the deck towards the stairs to the hold. Even the rain seemed frozen in time, then the great crashing, as if sheets of iron were being ripped apart, followed and William felt a pressure on his chest. "That was pretty…"

He never had a chance to finish the sentence. A second flash followed the first and once again, the hair on the back of Williams's neck stood on end. This time he had more presence of mind and dropped back onto the bed, rolling to his side while throwing his arm over Helen, who he suddenly found lying next to him. They were both face down so they didn't see what followed but they heard and felt it.

In the split second between the brilliant flash, which, even with his eyes closed, caused lights to dance before his vision for a few minutes afterwards, and the explosion, Robert threw himself away from the open doorway to the deck, even as an eerie, greenish spark slashed through the sky and struck the deck at the base of the mast. The explosion followed almost immediately, which in turn was followed by the sound of shattering wood and snapping ropes.

The mast was severed at its base and collapsed down through the main deck while falling over onto the starboard rail. More shattering wood followed and the ship listed to starboard as the sail and rigging fell into the sea, dragging the ship with it like an anchor not low enough to catch ground.

"We must get off this ship, William," Robert scrambled to his feet, even as the ship rolled farther to starboard. "Lady Helen, can you stand? If we do not leave quickly we may never get another chance." He pulled on both of them and they all three managed to shuffle and crawl out of the room.

The deck was chaotic disaster. The mast lay on its side with rigging and canvas on the deck as well as in the water. The rain continued, as did the wind and thunder. The ends of torn ropes whipped about, snapping in the air like vipers. The only man William saw on the deck was the captain. He stood at the stern, trying his best to control the rudder. William could hear him shouting over the waves and rain and scream of horses, but he had no idea what he was saying. In the brief moment they stood on the deck, taking all the wreckage in, a large wave burst over the starboard side. As it pulled back, it dragged even more of the mast, sail and rigging with it. The ship followed and listed even harder to the side.

"William, look after Lady Helen, I am going below to see to the horses." Without waiting for a response, Robert turned and scrambled across and over and around the shattered mess. Seconds later he disappeared into the hold. William could still hear the screams of the horses over the rain, wind and waves.

As he stood there he realized he had been given a charge and moved closer to Helen, wrapping his left arm around her shoulders. He turned to her ear so he didn't have to shout. "We will make it through this, I promise." If his teeth weren't chattering and his body shaking, he might have actually sounded convincing. As it was, she smiled weakly and nodded. Her eyes gave her away. She was as terrified as he was.

William could feel his heart thundering in his chest. The ship lurched farther to starboard and they found themselves half sitting, half crouching on the deck to keep their footing. Waves continued to crash over the starboard rail, which was now only a few feet above water. Even as William stared out over the rail, watching the waves rush in, another flash of lightning lit up the sky. For the briefest moment he could see what was ahead of them, and despite the circumstances he smiled, then opened his mouth and laughed.

"Helen, I saw it, I saw the shore just now!"

"Where?"

With his bandaged right hand, William pointed in the general direction he had seen sand dunes and rolling hills rising up from the sea. "If the tide was out I think we would be beached already." As if in answer to his observation, the ship jarred to a stop, as if hitting and sticking on something. The bow stuck fast, but the stern was still loose and the crash of the waves left the planks of the hull screaming.

As the ship continued to roll onto its starboard side, Robert appeared up out of the hold. Several horses followed and surrounded him and then they passed him by, running a few steps across the deck and leaping over the low rail and into the waiting waves. William watched as their heads bobbed back up out of the water and they began swimming in the direction of the shore.

"I have seen the shore!" He yelled to Robert, who was trying to control the courser and keep him from jumping as well. "The horses are heading in the right direction and it is not far at all!"

His tutor nodded his understanding. "I am going to let him go. When I do, we will all need to follow. As soon as you come back up, get as close as you can and grab some of his mane or even his tail and hang on. He is a strong lad, he will do the rest." William nodded and then looked at Helen. She was still scared, but a desperate resolution steeled her face.

"I am ready," she told him. Together they moved across the wreckage and shattered boards until they were only a few feet from Robert.

"On three, then. One, two…" He didn't get the next word out before a tremendous wave, larger than any they had encountered yet, crested up and over the entire deck, washing them all up, off and out. William lost his grip on Helen as he also lost his orientation. He had no idea which way was up. The wave rolled him and spun him about and then slammed him into sand. His heavy wool cloak, now completely water logged, wrapped around him like a constrictor. Desperately he tore at the clasp beneath his chin with his clumsy left hand until he felt it release and the cloak opened up and began sliding off his shoulders.

The impact had knocked the wind out of his lungs, which were now burning for air. Even as he wriggled to shed the sodden wool cloak, he reached out with his left hand and felt the sand. By instinct alone, he planted his feet and launched himself up with his legs. The cloak held him back a moment and he nearly panicked. Desperately he kicked, thrashing his legs, with what little energy he still had. Slowly he worked himself loose. Seconds later he broke the surface like a whale spouting foam and gasping for breath. He had never thought of how sweet air could be until that very moment.

Lightning flashed again and he saw the sandy beach one more time. It was only a couple dozen feet ahead of him now. Despite the fact he was shaking from the cold water and his right hand screamed with pain, he flailed his arms and kicked his feet and slowly he made his way forward. A large wave would propel him forward, launching him so close to his goal only to find himself getting pulled back as the wave receded.

He wasn't sure how long he could keep this up and part of him began to worry he was being pulled further from the shore and making no progress. His shoulder and arms were burning with fatigue and he was nearly ready to simply stop and let the water have him when his hand struck sand. A sharp, stabbing pain lanced up his right arm and he screamed out loud. Slowly he reached out his left hand while lowering his feet. And there it was, solid sand and waist deep water. He took a few tentative steps and then forced himself to move forward. His whole body shook. He shook with exhaustion, with pain, with hunger (he hadn't realized how hungry he was until that moment) and with joy.

A few more steps and he was up out of the surf and crawling across the beach. His feet and legs felt as if they were made of stone and too heavy to move. He was trying to make for a low, level berm, rising just ahead. It looked like it might be the highest point nearby. He scrambled on all fours, unable to stand, up the few feet of incline and made it to the top. There he collapsed, completely spent. He couldn't move another step. His brain felt as water-logged as his clothing. He thought there was something he should try to do, but he just couldn't remember what it was. For now, all he wanted to do was lie down and sleep.

Even as he curled up, pulling his knees up to his chest to keep warm in the cool wind and light rain, a single thought flashed through his mind. "Thank You, God, for getting me through the storm." Darkness swirled around and overtook him and he remembered nothing else.

Part Two

Chapter Twenty

William awoke to the sharp scent of rosemary, thyme and spring poppy flowers and for a brief moment thought he was back in the White Hart Inn, the morning after being attacked. His entire body felt sore just like it had that morning. He found himself in a soft bed, covered in a light homespun blanket, his head resting on a down filled pillow. Despite his weary and aching limbs, he smiled and opened his crusty eyes. Above him was a low ceiling of rough-hewn timbers. Just past the foot of the bed was an open window, whose wooden shutters were thrust back. A warm breeze blew across his face carrying with it the scent of the sea, the cry of gulls, and a sweet, warbling whistle of songbirds just outside his room. Mixed into this refreshing air was just a hint of mustiness, as if the room had been closed for quite some time.

Like a flood the memories returned. He suddenly recalled the unending string of challenges and attacks, the kindness and sacrifices, the storm and the shipwreck. Warm tears spilled down his cheeks. Tears of joy and relief overwhelmed him as he realized he had made it to France. "I wonder where I am." Then added, as more tears spilled down his face, "God, I hope Robert and Helen made it safely to shore."

A voice from a corner of the room spoke in answer. "You are in the coastal house of Lady Helen's family, near the mouth of the Somme. As for the rest…" William turned his head, and there, leaning back in a large chair, sat his tutor with a broad smile on his face. He laughed a deep, rumbling laugh, which filled the room and caught William up in the same. William spilled a few more tears of joy and for a moment he thought Robert would do the same. The laughter made the day seem even brighter outside and William felt a growing sense of thankfulness sweep over him.

As he raised his hand to wipe the tears from his face, he found himself staring at the sealed hole in his right palm. The edges were still pink and slightly swollen but it was healing. He made a fist, which stung tremendously but didn't shoot pain up his arm. It would be a while before he could grip a knife with any strength. "How… how long have we been here?" He suddenly realized just how dry his throat was, as his voice cracked and sounded like rustling leaves on the floor of the New Forest.

"Lady Helen and I were able to stay with the courser, and though he struggled tremendously, he brought us safely to shore near a small fishing village." Robert must have realized his condition because he stood as he spoke and poured William a cup of water from an earthenware pitcher near his bed. "The villagers seemed little surprised when we stumbled in, completely water logged, barely able to stand, with a half exhausted horse in tow. Apparently shipwrecks are rather common on these shores. They took us in, and fed and clothed us, and we were able to explain how we were separated from you." After filling the cup and handing it to William he crossed back to the window and stared out, his hands clasped at his back.

"At first they did not think it was necessary to look; they were certain the sea would have claimed you, but Lady Helen was adamant. Once she set her mind to it, they did not have a choice." Robert smiled at the memory, and William could picture her standing there, exhausted and yet alive, her red hair dark from the sea and the rain but her blue eyes flashing an inner light, while convincing the village he was alive as well.

"They found you the next morning. By the time we brought you back to the village you were deathly cold and shivering uncontrollably. When I saw your color the joy of finding you alive was stolen from me. Again it was Lady Helen who came to the rescue. Rather than immerse you immediately in hot water she suggested warm water, which we gradually heated until it was steaming. Your color returned, and with it your breathing gradually deepened. Eventually you stopped shivering. That was just over two days ago. Yesterday we hired a cart and brought you here, to her family's cottage near Le Crotoy."

"Three days," William muttered. "No wonder my stomach feels like an empty sack." As if to emphasize its condition, his stomach protested loudly. Just then there was knock at the door. Robert opened it and a savory aroma of broth and bread swept into the room. Every salivary gland in William's mouth opened at the same time, as Helen came in carrying a tray laden with steaming soup, a lump of butter, and what looked like a half of a loaf of farmhouse bread. He was torn between his primal desire to fill his stomach or stare at Helen. He had only seen her in traveling clothes, and days without bathing at that. She set the tray down on the small table beside his bed. He could have sworn he smelled lavender over the broth and bread.

"It does me good to see you awake, William." She smiled and it seemed to him the song birds outside his window broke into chorus at the exact moment. He found himself suddenly unable to do anything except smile and stare. Her hair had been washed and braided in a strange three-part fashion, falling down to her middle back. Her skin was a pale pink, as if it had been scrubbed several times over to remove all the vestiges of the last several days. Her freckles shined like flecks of copper, and her blue eyes, in the sunlit room, seemed to darken just a little. She wore a simple linen dress, with half sleeves, belted at her waist. But over top of it she wore something William had never seen before. It looked a little like a man's vest but was laced up the front and was very tight fitting. Not since he saw her walk out of the Shipwright's Inn did he realize just how truly beautiful she was.

William blushed at his thoughts and was finally able to stammer, "I thank you for your concern, my lady." Once again, his stomach protested its emptiness and he was able to use the meal as an excuse to focus on something other than Helen.

The broth included tender pieces of roasted chicken, flour dumplings, carrots and onions, along with several savory herbs William had never seen before. It was delicious. The bread and butter were equally spectacular. As he ate, he tried to think back to the last real meal he had. It had been the dinner they had shared in their room with Helen and Gilbert. He paused a moment his full spoon, suspended in midair as he, once again, realized he hadn't thought of Gilbert in days. He closed his eyes briefly and asked God to watch over their friend. He finished his meal as he prayed for Gilbert, and the mother and daughters who they had saved outside the New Forest and Agnes.

As William ate, Robert had offered Helen a seat beside the open window. The window faced south, and despite the spring day, the sunlight warmed the room. She sat, with her eyes closed and a smile on her face, enjoying the peace of the moment. The breeze continued, occasionally stirring the rosemary bush which stood just outside, as did the warbling of the songbirds. To William, it was almost as if the last several days hadn't really happened. That is until he tried to spread some butter on a piece of bread and couldn't grab the knife with his right hand. He awkwardly used his left. That would be one reminder of this trip. He had completely forgotten about the cut he had received on his left shoulder almost eight days before.

Finally, he had eaten all he felt he should. There was still quite a bit of bread and a little soup left, but his stomach wasn't able to hold as much as it used to. Nevertheless he was content and full and accepted the glass of slightly watered down wine Robert offered him. "Thank you… thank you both," William said and smiled broadly. "I did not foresee this as the journey I would have to take to find my uncle but I could not have asked for better travel companions."

William paused a moment as a thought came to him. "I suppose, Lady Helen, your debt to me is paid in full, now that we have rescued each other." She smiled but he could see there was some concern in her thoughts. "Now that you have safely returned to France there is little reason to continue into harm's way with the two of us."

Helen nodded but didn't respond at first. William looked to Robert who wore a blank mask. He couldn't see any emotion or suggestion of help. Surely they had talked about this over the last two days. Finally, Helen spoke. "Although it is against your teacher's wishes, I will accompany you both to the estate where I was raised, just outside Abbeville. There are some questions I would like answered." Now William understood. Robert was against this. He wanted Helen to stay here, near the coast, out of harm's way.

"Is there a concern with Lady Helen returning to her guardians' estate?"

"Yes, William, there is; Lord Thomas Denebaud."

"What would Lord Thomas…" at first William didn't understand, and then a revelation struck him. His eyes widened and he looked to his tutor, who simply nodded in agreement. "Lady Helen, I believe Robert is correct. I do not wish you to return to the estate."

"You too, William? What possible harm can come of it? Robert has insisted, but has given little in the way of convincing evidence. Besides, I want to know why they sent me away when they did. Did they ever truly care for me…?" Her voice broke and she turned in her chair to the window. Even though he could only stare at the back of her head and shoulders, William could see the emotions she was struggling to contain.

"Lady Helen, I believe it was because they cared for you so much they sent you away." Robert spoke slowly and carefully, and William was surprised at how much emotion he carried in his voice.

"How is that possible?" William thought she wanted to sound defiant but he could tell there was hope in her voice.

"As soon as you landed in Southampton there were men there, agents of Lord Thomas, who knew your false identity as well as the ship you had sailed on and the inn where you were to meet Sir Geoffrey. They knew all of this because someone had told them all this." Robert paused, waiting to make sure he had Helen's full attention. "Either your caretakers had completely betrayed you, or he forced it from them. Or Lord Thomas has agents here in France who had discovered your identity and passed the information along to him."

"I do not believe they would have done so…" Helen murmured, almost to herself, her head lowered and hands clasped at her waist.

"From what you told us of them, I do not believe they did. But I do think they understood the danger imposed on you if you stayed in France. If you stayed in their home, Lord Thomas would find you an easy target. The harder thing for them was to send you away, under a false identity, in the hopes you would slip past his net and find your way to your father's family in the Marches."

"If they did this for me…" her voice broke and she swallowed heavily, sniffling in the process. "Why would there be a concern with returning to their home?"

"It is possible Lord Thomas is still watching the estate." William finished the thought for his tutor. He now was beginning to understand just how dangerous Lord Thomas had become. He was a man capable of anything, especially now that William had stood in his path at least twice. "There is even the possibility he knows of this home and already has word been sent to him advising of your return."

Helen took in a deep breath, and exhaling slowly, nodded to herself. "I understand more now, thank you… both. I do not believe Lord Thomas would know of this home. It has been a long time since we have used it, and even then it was infrequent. The last several years my guardians had found reasons to stay very close to the estate." As soon as Helen said this she paused, as if realizing the implications.

"Is it possible Lord Thomas made his intentions known long before this?" She had stood and now began pacing the floor. William could see the concern in her face. There was a question there as well. Then she stopped and suddenly turned to face Robert. "Nearly three years ago we had a gentleman call at the estate. I never actually saw him, but I know his presence upset the household and my guardians. It was immediately after that we stopped coming here…"

"I believe you are right, Lady Helen." Robert agreed. He crossed the room and looked out the window and across the beach to the bay. "It was either Lord Thomas himself or one of his agents who made that visit. Either way, somehow your guardians were told or guessed at what he was capable of and responded in the only they way they knew how at the time; they walled you and themselves up in the estate." He stood a moment longer, his hands clasped behind his back, rocking up and back on the balls of his feet. William recognized this immediately. His tutor was in the process of very carefully trying to work something out. A moment later he stopped rocking, nodded to himself, and then turned back to into the room. "There must have been some drastic change recently which would have forced them to set you on this path. Can you think of anything recently?"

Helen shook her head slowly. "Ever since they told me of my family in the Marches and their desire to see me returned to them, I have asked myself the same question. I know they had a good reason and I believe they thought they were doing the best thing for me, but for the life of me, I cannot say what it may have been."

William used his elbows to prop himself up in his bed and then waited for the swirling spots and lightheadedness to recede. "It seems to me," he said, swallowing and taking in a deep breath, letting it out slowly through his nose, "this storm and the shipwreck may have been the best thing for you, my lady."

Helen turned to William with a startled look on her face. "How is that possible, William? So much was lost, we landed far from Calais, and you were nearly drowned."

"This is all true, my lady, however, God pulled us through. What was meant to harm us has actually helped us. We find ourselves in a safe place to recover, the ship we very publicly departed Southampton on is wrecked, and there is little chance anyone of consequence has found out you returned to France. We actually have a better chance now than we may have if we landed in Calais."

"Then there should be no problem with me returning to Abbeville. No one here will still be looking for me."

"Unless there is still someone there, on the estate or watching it very closely."

"Which is why both myself and Robert do not wish to see you return there. It is very likely even the roads will be watched."

"Then it is best we do not take the roads."

Robert paused a moment. "What are suggesting Lady Helen?"

"I grew up here. I know these waters and these lands. I could nearly walk from here to Abbeville with my eyes closed." Helen smiled as she said this. It wasn't boasting or bragging. This was the truth and she knew it. "But I also know that, during high tide, the River Somme swells and widens, and it is then we can make our way to Abbeville. The tide is slacking right now. I saw the level even now as I looked out this window. The small boat we used to take out on the river is still tied just below. When the water rises, it will only be a few feet from the edge. Tonight we will have a high tide, and with luck, we will have some clouds to cover the waxing moon. We can leave then under the cover of darkness. The local villagers will take no notice of us departing nor of the boat being gone in the morning." Her eyes were shining as she said this and even Robert noticed her excitement.

William stared at Lady Helen. He never would have guessed she knew anything about the tide and its levels or the terms she so easily used. He wasn't even that familiar, but the way she spoke stirred up a confidence in him. He wanted her to go with them. Something inside, some little voice said she needed to come along. Perhaps there was something else she was supposed to do, something besides what she had done these last two days.

Robert was about to speak again, when William interjected. "Lady Helen, would you give us a moment alone?"

Lady Helen paused just a moment, then smiled and did both he and Robert a courtesy. Seconds later the door was shut behind her and

William was alone with his teacher and the warbling birds just outside his window. "What is it, William?"

William was so thankful for the warm soup and the bread. He felt satisfied, warm and comfortable. He looked one more time at his right hand and the pink, puckered scar and the quick healing which was taking place and smiled. "The more Lady Helen spoke, the more I felt as though we should bring her with us." As Robert started to protest, William held up his injured hand and his tutor stopped. "I know what it looks like to the eye. It would appear as though she would be safer here, rather than walking right back into the lion's den, but there is something inside which is telling me she still has a part to play in this. Not just in clearing up the questions she has, but in what we have set out to accomplish. I am sorry I am not able to put it into words better…"

"But you feel this strongly, William?" His young pupil nodded and Robert watched him closely. Was there any other reason he would want Lady Helen to come along? Could he have other feelings developing, which she may have no inclination for? He could be hurt deeply if that was the case. But looking at William, he saw none of this. He genuinely felt that she needed to be with them. Robert took a deep breath and sighed, then nodded his agreement. "Very well… I agree. We will ask Lady Helen to show us the river path to Abbeville and her estate." Robert left the room, and despite just waking up after almost 3 days, William found no trouble falling asleep that afternoon.

Dinner that evening was eaten in excited silence. Most of what was kept at the summerhouse was dried fruits and a block of very hard cheese, which Helen assured them was quite good once you scraped off the blue-green discoloration. There was still a large piece of bread left from Williams's earlier meal, which between the three of them they managed to completely finish. All in all, despite the lack of diversity, each one of them filled themselves to satisfaction.

As the continued to eat it became quite obvious to everyone, including William, that his hand would keep him from accomplishing even the simplest tasks. At one point Robert passed the butter, and without thinking, William reached out to grab the small plate and immediately dropped it on the table. His eyes watered from the shocking pain which shot up his arm, and he remembered the same feeling when his hand struck the sandy shore. "Are you all right, William?" Helen asked as she reached out to keep the plate from spilling onto the floor. William could only stare at his hand while slowly trying to make a fist. It was stiff and very sore and it was only with great difficulty that he actually could close his hand completely.

Robert noticed this and added, "As your hand heals it will become more difficult to close. You must take every chance you have to keep the fingers moving, making a fist over and over again. If you do not…" he spread his hands out before him and shrugged his shoulders. William had seen this hundreds of times before. He was going to have to finish the thought himself. Fortunately he already had realized the same.

He turned his hand palm side up, stared at it and muttered, "I will not be much use if I have to defend either of you… or myself with a weapon."

"Never mind a weapon, William," Helen interjected, "you will not be any help with the boat this evening that is for sure." William looked up to see her smiling and knew she was doing her best to help him feel better about the situation. He smiled back hoping she didn't realize it wasn't.

"William, there was one other thing I had planned on telling you, once we landed in France…" Robert began, then smiled and laughed to himself. "It seems ridiculous to say after all you have been through since we left Crandor." He shook his head then shrugged and continued.

"Now that we have landed in France, we must remain watchful and vigilant. Many here have little love of the English, and even more still remember the pillaging, including the burning of this village, by King Edward before the victory of Crecy."

"Which, by the way, those same Frenchmen would call an inglorious defeat and the shame of all France," Helen quickly added.

"As you say, Lady Helen, as you say," Robert agreed. "In any case, we must be watchful." He spread his hands out and shrugged, smiling. "As I said, William. It seems rather late to remind either of us to be careful."

William was about to respond when a bell sounded from somewhere in the town. It wasn't marking the time because it was the first William had heard it. Before he had a chance to question its source, Helen spoke up, "the tide is changing. The bell announces it because it happens very quickly. My guardians used to warn me about crossing the sand and mud flats between here and Saint Valery. When the tide is out you can walk from town to town, but people have been swept off their feet by the waters' quick return, as well as its equally quick departure.

Almost on cue, the sun started to settle behind the western shore and shadows lengthened into the room. William took a deep breath and a large yawn, stretching his arms and legs in the process. "I may not feel completely myself yet, but the meals and the company have certainly helped." He smiled, more to himself than anyone. "How soon before we should leave for Abbeville?"

"Not long now. Once dusk passes and the sun has fully set I think we will be safe in setting out. It should only take us an hour to reach the estate. The western edge of it comes right down to the river when the tide is high. We will want to get there before it begins falling again. If not, it will be a little more difficult working against the falling water."

Robert stood and smiled. "If Lady Helen will excuse me, I will see to our packs and our provisions." He bowed at the waist and left the two of them alone in the room. William noticed he did not close the door behind him.

Helen stood as well and turned to leave, but William reached out and caught her hand. "Thank you, my lady." She turned back and a warm smile crossed her face. The fading sunlight in the room made her hair turn dark amber. "Thank you for not giving up on me."

She paused a moment and her smile faded just a little. Her eyes wandered across the bed, over to the window, and finally made their way back to William. She started to say something, paused and shook her head slightly. Finally, her face brightened a bit as did her smile. "You came for me in Southampton. It was a debt I needed to repay." She squeezed his hand and, dropping it, she turned back to the door. "I will lend Robert my assistance. We should be able to leave within the hour." She left in a swirl of linen and William was alone with his thoughts for the first time since he awoke.

"Thank You, God for seeing us safely ashore." He closed his eyes and folded his hand, as best he could with the sharp pain still present. "This was not what I had in mind on how we would get here, but Your way seems to have worked out to be the safest. Watch over Gilbert, the mother and her daughters, and Agnes. I pray the Lord High Admiral is safe as well. Amen." He remembered Robert describing life and death like roads, which ran alongside each other. At any moment you could take a short step and find yourself out of the middle lands of the living and into the realms either above or below. He silently hoped if any of the people who he and Robert had helped, or who had helped them were no longer living they had found their way to God's presence.

William sat there, propped up in the bed, his head bowed and eyes closed for several minutes. The birds were silent outside and he realized that, above the sound of the surf, he now heard the typical night sounds of insects chirping and screeching on the other side of the open window. Occasionally some waterfowl honked and a dog barked somewhere in the village. Despite the pain in his hand, and overall soreness, he felt at peace.

Chapter Twenty One

He wasn't sure how long he rested with his eyes closed and his ears filled with the night sounds outside. Eventually Robert came back into the room. "It is time, William." Helen had not exaggerated when she mentioned how far the tide would come up to the cottage. There was a short path of only a few feet, which led from the side door off the kitchen. Its white crushed rocks glowed slightly in the pale moonlight. It was a mostly clear night, but an occasional cloud would cross the sky and it was at one of these moments they made their way onto the boat.

It took William a few tentative steps to finally make his way into the craft. Not having his right hand to use to steady himself was much more of a handicap than he would have thought. As it was, since he couldn't use the oars or help with the small rudder or simple rigging, he took his seat at the bow. Helen and Robert found their places, he at the oars and she at the stern. It took longer than William expected, but eventually all three were settled in the small, flat-bottomed boat with their packs at their feet, leaving little room to move around.

Before the nearly half moons' face revealed itself again, they had pushed off from the shore and were several hundred paces upstream. William turned after a moment to see his teacher slowly drawing long steady strokes while Helen comfortably leaned back against the stern with the rudder tucked under her arm. She smiled and the moonlight caught the flash of white from her teeth. William smiled back and then turned forward to watch the shore slide quietly by.

"It was right here, that your name sake and distant relation assembled his army of knights and foot soldiers before sailing across the channel." Robert spoke over his shoulder and William turned around again to look towards the southern shore. The village on that side of the river seemed to be made up of mostly small stone cottages. These looked north and seemed cheerless in the moonlit sky.

"And it was here, William, that King Edward sacked and burned Le Crotoy." Helen pointed with her left hand to the opposite shore, where they had just set off. "By a miracle of God, our beach home was saved from Edward's looting. William looked to the north, as they slowly moved upstream and could tell many of the buildings and houses looked newly built, most of which faced the water. The river ran from east to west at its mouth and the best homes were along the northern bank, facing the water. The small home they left was near the end of the beach, not far from the channel.

It didn't take long for the small craft to make its way into surrounding farmland. The river now curved to the south and was still very wide at this point with many of the trees, which lined both of its shores, draping their long branches over the swollen banks. Some even touched the water, as if they were stretching their fingers out to see how pleasant it was. William dipped his own fingers in at one point and found the water cold to the touch. The tidal flow brought with it cold water from the Channel.

"Why did Edward pillage and burn the village?"

For a moment, no one answered. Robert continued to row, while

Helen turned to stare back at the homes she remembered once standing along the eastern bank. "Near the end of July, just two years ago, Edward had captured the city of Caen one day and then set out along the western shore of the Seine River the next, looking for a point to cross." Robert paused to catch his breath as he lifted the oars out of the water a moment. The momentum and the direction of the incoming tide continued to carry them upstream.

"The French army retreated before him but left nothing in field or fodder for the English. Without food, Edward's campaign would quickly end. By luck, they found an unguarded ford at Poissy and crossed the river after building a temporary floating bridge. Now Edward threatened the heart of France and Paris itself, but Philip felt he had his enemy right where he wanted him; trapped between the impassable Seine and Somme Rivers; spring rains had swollen both over their banks in many places. The French king made sure all the bridges and fords were heavily guarded, leaving Paris and moving to Amiens. Eventually he, with his much larger French army, entered the lands between the rivers to hunt down Edward. The English army continued to follow the Somme, looking for a weak spot to cross, while Philip crossed over to Abbeville thinking Edward might try to attack the bridge there."

"I remember those few days," Helen interrupted. "With our estate so close to the river we could see the whole army as it crossed the bridge and entered the town. I had never seen so many knights and men at arms. I even remember the banners of the Genoese, who my guardians told me were there as mercenaries." She shook her head and her expression turned sad so quickly, William thought she might cry. "I do not like to think about what happened to most of those who marched north a few days later." Her voice cracked with emotion as she turned away in order to wipe her eyes on her sleeve.

"Philip must not have realized how close Edward and his army really was that day. He was camped at Acheux."

"Dear Lord," Helen murmured, turning back to start at William's teacher as he took up rowing again. "I have walked there and back on beautiful days."

"A fully laden army is a ponderous thing, Lady Helen," Robert pointed out between strokes, then added, "though I have no doubt you have made that walk in the past."

"How did Edward get across if all the bridges and fords were guarded?" William asked.

"The letters your uncle received never explained how he came by the information, but somehow King Edward found out about a lightly guarded ford near the village of Saigneville. The ford was named for the white stones which line this river near there." Robert took up his oars again for another momentary pause and turned to look left and right. "If you look to both shores, William you will see those same stones in the shallows. We find ourselves at the ford of Blanchetaque."

William's eyes grew wide as he looked both east and west. "It was right here that the Earl of Northampton forced his way across the river and up onto the bank?" William stared at the eastern edge, which they closely followed. There was little light from the moon, which had slid behind a large group of clouds, but he could still see the pale reflection of the stony shore and the sloping bank.

"It was right here, William, but when Edward arrived he had to wait. The tide, just as it is tonight, was at its crest and it would be several hours before he could make the crossing. This gave the French plenty of time to make their defense." The rowing continued once again.

"I remember that night," Helen admitted. As the night turned colder she had pulled her cloak high about her shoulders and pulled its cowl over her head. Her face was now in the shadows of the hood so William could only hear her voice and not see her expression. She sounded grim and sad. "It was just two days before the battle at Crecy. King Philip's men were in high spirits. They knew Edward's army was tired and hungry and had no food and little supplies. They also felt the Somme was secure and there was no chance the English could cross it. I heard several of the knights' boast of how they had left nothing standing between the Seine and Somme in order to starve the English. They were so confident the English were stuck they did not bother about the eastern side of the river." While she spoke, Robert paused again and he sat, listening and nodding.

"Their boasting stuck in their throats when the first of the fleeing defenders made their way to Abbeville pursued, almost to the city gates by English cavalry," Helen continued. "King Philip wasted no time in rousing his men in order to challenge the English at the ford, but it was too late. The whole of Edward's army was across the river before noon and marched north, finding the countryside rich with food and spoils. It was during this feeding frenzy of his half-starved men, that Edward either lost control or simply chose to turn a blind eye and they burned the towns of Noyelles-sur-Mer and Le Crotoy."

"How could the king lose control of his men?" William wondered out loud.

"Any army has to have discipline as its secure base, William. Never forget that. As you move from the lower to upper ranks, each rung of that ladder looks to the one above for reassurance and control. When the leadership at the top turns a blind eye, it quickly runs through to the lowest man. Noyelles-sur-Mer was burned first. Afterwards I believe, and it is only my opinion, Edward realized if he did not gain control of his army it would turn into a mindless mob. By the time he was able to put a stop to it, most of Le Crotoy was burned as well."

"Most of the fishing families are still there. They told me when they saw the English they knew what was coming. They put their families in their boats and cast off from the shore. Sitting there, they watched as everything they knew was stolen or destroyed. A few lucky ones had a home to return to."

"I still do not understand," William began. There was a thought rolling around in his head and he was having a hard time expressing it. "Our king has claimed the throne of France, through his mother. He believes he is the rightful heir to the French throne."

"Is there a question there, William?" His tutor asked. He had paused once more from rowing and was rolling his shoulders, stretching their muscles.

"If he is to rule France, why would he allow his men to loot or burn any of it? Would it not be better to treat the people well and thereby earn their respect and loyalty?"

William still couldn't see beneath Helen's hood but he noticed she sat very still, hardly seeming to breathe. Finally, Robert broke the silence as he took up the oars and began rowing again. "William, it was that very sentiment which earned Thomas Simpson the respect, admiration, and even love of the Saxons which surrounded him in Dorset. If you believe what you have said, then you find yourself in rare company, and show yourself to be a true descendant of one of King William's best nobles and cousins."

Despite the darkened sky, William was sure Helen could see him blush deeply. He remembered Robert's story, told to the pilgrims on the road to Salisbury. Was it something about his family or being a Simpson, which made him think this way? Or was it simply his ancestor also believed the rule passed down by Jesus was the best to live by. "Treat others as you would want to be treated." He hadn't realized he spoke out loud until his tutor answered him.

"It is such a simple idea, is it not William?" He asked in mid stroke. "To look at each and every person you meet as a child of God, made in His image, just as you are. People may mess up and do bad things, but God does not. He cannot."

"You told me about the simple decisions we make each day and how they affect us over our lifetime. This is another simple decision, yes? It is easy to do, just as it is easy not to do." William turned around to look up river. The bank was steadily sliding by. The white stones of Blanchetaque were far behind them now and yet the shore and the river appeared the same. It was wide and slow moving. Tranquil. That was the word for it. It seemed odd that this place could seem so peaceful and yet such violence had occurred here and still much was occurring in the surrounding countryside.

"You are right, William. It is another easy decision. Too many people go through life missing out on the significance of these simple decisions. They think that there will always be a chance to make up for it tomorrow. Or even worse, they do not even realize they have made the decision, which over time will take them down the wrong path."

"Too many people do not guard their thoughts. If they did, they would see what this one decision would do," the young heir to the Earl of Dorchester reflected.

William couldn't see the smile on his tutors face, but he could hear it in his voice when he answered. "Stay humble, William, no matter what, because, if you continue learning and applying these lessons, you will find yourself blessed beyond measure."

"Thank you." William wanted to say more, but he found his voice suddenly chocked off and was only able to add, "I wonder if my father or uncle realized how lucky they were to have you as their teacher?" Robert didn't answer but continued his slow, steady stroke of the oars.

For the next several minutes the only sound was the light splash of the oars in the water, the water dripping off of them as they came back out, a pause, which had lengthened the farther they went, and then another splash. Darkened trees, most still bare from the winter and a few with buds for the spring, seemed to hang wearily over the water's edge. Reeds cropped up more frequently as they traveled farther inland. The moon had traveled across a portion of the sky, and William was going to ask how far they had come, when Helen suddenly spoke. "Abbeville… my home. There it is."

They had come around a bend in the river, one of many they had passed on the way in. Unlike most of the rivers William had seen in his time, or even some of the small streams of Dorchester, this river seemed to have fingers spreading out into all parts of the surrounding land. If it hadn't been for Helen's guidance they could have easily found themselves traveling up a small branch only to come to a dead end and have to turn around. It was obvious to William she had certainly spent time on the water. He was glad Robert had changed his mind and allowed her to come with them.

The City of Abbeville spread out on the eastern bank of the Somme. On the west bank there appeared to be open stretches of farmland and a wide, white stone bridge connected the two sides. Although even darker with the waxing moon behind the clouds, William thought, from what he could see, the town was a little smaller than Salisbury. He also noticed there was no cathedral towering overhead. "Should we worry about the French seeing us approaching?" William asked.

"The French do not control Abbeville, William," Helen answered. "The Counts of Ponthieu used to hold this county of France, but for almost 70 years the English have claimed these lands as their own. They use Abbeville as the capital of the region."

"If this is the English capital of the region then how did Philip come to stay here before the battle of Crecy?"

"What England has claimed her own and what she has ruled have not always been the same thing," Robert commented.

"That certainly has been the case here," Helen added.

This information didn't make William feel any more comfortable. In fact, after all he had been through while still in England, he was hoping he had finally arrived in French controlled territory. It seemed safer to him. To take his mind off of these thoughts, he focused his attention on studying the estate where Helen had grown up.

From the river, he could see a low pale stonewall, perhaps made of rough cut limestone blocks or stones, coming down to the very edge of the water. On the far side of the wall it looked as though a small quay of thick timbers was set, half in the water and half on land. As it was high tide, the majority of the quay and bank behind had water around it. One boat, not much bigger than their own was already tied up to the quay.

The ground gently sloped up and away, eventually leveling out in a large, well cleared field. It was here the estate was built. Between the bank and the home it looked like there were gardens and an orchard. Several smaller stone houses were spread out from the main house. Having grown up around Crandor Castle most of his life, William guessed these were ground and gamekeeper's huts and possibly even a tenant farmer who worked the land or kept the orchards.

The grounds were dark, as were the huts and the main house. As they pulled up to the quay, William was listening as intently as he could but didn't hear anything other than the croaking of some frogs in the nearby reeds, the chirping of crickets, and the soft splash of water as Robert finished his final stroke, propelling their boat right up to the quay. Despite his injured hand, William was able to move quicker out of his seat, than he did getting in, and up onto the wooden dock. It took a moment of concentration but he was eventually able to take the rope handed to him by his tutor and tie it off on the small metal cleat.

He offered his good hand to Helen and she took it, carefully stepping from the rocking boat onto the steady quay. William then turned to help Robert as well. "What do you suggest we do, Lady Helen?" William's tutor asked as he shrugged his pack onto his shoulders.

"We should seek out our old gamekeeper, Chrestien. If anything has happened here since I left just a few weeks ago, he will know. Still… there is something odd."

"It seems quiet," William observed.

"Too quiet for sure," Helen responded. "That is what is odd. Chrestien keeps two dogs on the grounds. They should have announced our arrival or at least come up to greet me by now."

"Which of the huts is the gamekeeper's?" Robert asked. He had moved to the end of the quay and was staring intently across the grounds towards the darkened estate.

"If we follow this stone wall there is a small house nearly half way to the main house. There is a well-worn path here we can follow." Helen stepped forward, and as she did so, the moon slid out from behind the clouds and illuminated the fields, gardens and orchards. "Dear Lord, what has happened here?" It looked to William like hundreds of feet and dozens of hands had done their worst.

What had looked like well-tended gardens and orchards were now revealed to be a complete disaster. Hedges were trampled over by what may have been men on horseback. The flower and herb plantings were crushed or scattered across the lawn, and the stone wall, which at first had looked completely intact, seemed to have been knocked down in several places.

"It looks like a battle took place here," William muttered. His heart was suddenly hammering in his chest and he quickly looked from left to right, expecting to see mounted soldiers riding down on them any moment.

A cry of grief croaked from Helen, "Dear God, please let my aunt and uncle be safe." Without waiting she quickly moved down the quay and was nearly past Robert when he reached out and grabbed her arm. As she spun about there was a look of alarm and anger on her face.

"Forgive me, my lady, but we cannot simply run down the path to the house. Whoever did this may still be near or even watching now. It is best if we do what we can to stay in the shadows. The closer to this wall the better. The moon is low enough now you can see the darkness stretching from the stones. We may even get to Chrestien's house from here without leaving the safety of the darkness. Once we are there, perhaps we can find out more of what has happened."

Helen took a deep breath and shut her eyes. Seconds later she opened them and nodded. "As you wish." To William, although her expression appeared calm, her voice sounded like steel.

"Please let William and I lead the way, my lady. Whether you believe it or not, your safety is our greatest concern." Without waiting for an answer, the old tutor set out and William hurried along the quay in order to catch up. As he passed Helen he heard her mutter to herself.

"Why would he care?" she whispered.

"He cares because God cares," William answered. They kept their voices barely above a whisper, both to protect themselves and to keep Robert from hearing. "We are all children of God," he continued explaining, "which makes you his sister; granted a much younger sister. In his eyes though, Robert will care for you as if you truly were his own."

"I have never met anyone like him." She paused a moment as they continued creeping through the shadows, keeping the stone wall on their left. “How long has he served your family?”

“Most of his life I think. He came to serve when he was a boy and learned from his father, as he had from his. His family has served the Lords of Crandor since the time of King William. Before that they were lords themselves.”

“Saxon lords?”

“Yes, but they called themselves something different; Thanes is the word I believe. Still, they were respected enough to sit on their council of lords- the Witan, during times of important decisions.” Before Helen could ask the question, William filled in the answer. “The Witan was entrusted with, among other things, the decision on who to support as king.”

“Their kings did not inherit the throne?”

“The first born son was always a contender but there was no guarantee. At least that is the way I understand it used to work. King William placed his claim to the throne before the Witan, along with several others. They decided not to choose the Norman.”

“How did he come to serve your family if he was a lord of the Saxons? From what I was told, they continued to fight against King William and his lords for years after the battle of Hastings.”

“There was rebellion around most of England for decades, except in Dorchester. Robert told me my long past relative, King William’s cousin Thomas Simpson, earned the respect and admiration of the people of the county, including Robert’s family. When Thomas was killed during a hunt in the New Forest, my great grandmother’s great grandmother, denied the kings offer to step aside and allow another to take her place. She even traveled to London to confront the king, placing the care and safe keeping of her children in the hands of a Saxon lord.” William paused a moment while Robert stopped. He had come to a gap in the wall and seemed to be looking and listening. A moment later he set out again.

"King William gave in to her demands and she became the Lady Adelia, dowager duchess of Dorchester. When she returned to Crandor she honored Robert's ancestor by naming him seneschal of her household. His family has held the title since."

"All these years and his family is still serving your own?" William didn't answer because Robert, who was several strides ahead of them, had now made it to the stone hut and held up his hand, signaling them to stop. He then, slowly, made his way around to the front step.

William held his breath. He could hear his heart pounding in his ears and feel his pulse thrumming up his neck. He was sure Helen could hear it as well, as close as she crouched next to him. As Robert rounded the corner of the hut, Helen reached out and grabbed William by the arm, and he could hear her catch her breath. It was as if she was clinging onto him hoping to stay afloat in a rough sea. It was his left arm she was holding onto, and, despite the slight protest from his mostly healed knife wound, he didn't mind at all.

If he was trying for complete secrecy, the door gave Robert away. As he swung it on its pegs, it screeched in protest. William felt his heart leap into his throat as Helen's grip on his arm increased dramatically. Despite his racing heartbeat and the growing pain in his arm, William didn't notice anything else. Nothing stirred across what was left of the gardens and yard.

A long moment later Robert returned from the hut, shaking his head. As soon as he got close, he whispered to both, "It is empty. No sign of a struggle, but whoever has been here took everything they could eat or carry." He looked once more up towards the main house, then continued, "Let us keep to the wall, just in case, but I think we will find the other huts and perhaps even the main house in the same condition. I do not believe the grounds are being watched, but we should still remain on guard."

"Who would have done such a thing?" Helen asked once again, then added, "What do you think has happened to my guardians?"

Robert shook his head again. "I do not know either of those answers yet my lady, nor do I wish to hazard a guess until we know more." Turning to William, he added, "Hush now, no more tales. The night is far too quiet and your voice carries." If it had been lighter he would have seen his student blushing as if caught trying to sneak food from the pantry after dinner.

"As you wish," William answered, dropping his eyes in embarrassment.

The next several moments passed uneventfully. They kept to the shadows along the wall, pausing as before when they came to any gaps. Helen kept shaking her head and muttering to herself but William couldn't make out exactly what she said. Eventually they passed trampled flowerbeds and herb gardens and then came to a crushed stone path, which led to a darkened doorway. Robert stopped and signaled the two to come along side. "William, I want you to stay with Lady Helen. I will go in first." Before his student could even start to protest, he quickly added, "No argument now. Safeguard Lady Helen. Remember your oath."

William nodded but felt trapped. He wanted to be there, to watch his teachers back, and to be another pair of eyes. With his right hand bandaged and sore, he didn't feel much like a protector. As Robert set out towards the path and the back door, Helen asked. "What oath have you taken, William?"

"There are two actually."

When he didn't add any more details, Helen asked, "And they are…?"

"Our family motto is v*ivo servire*; I live to serve. It means more than just service to our king and to our country. Robert has taught me what it really means to lead." He paused as he watched his tutor follow the last several feet of the stone path and pause at the opened doorway. At least this time they wouldn't have to worry about the noise.

"And what is it he believes it means?" Helen asked. Although her voice was trembling slightly, as she watched Robert disappear inside her home, she was genuinely interested in what William was sharing with her.

"The greatest of them all is the servant of many. To lead is to serve. It is not the other way around as too many men and women believe."

"I do not believe any men or women I grew up around or have known think any other way than to be served. He learned this from his father? Where did he learn it from?"

William turned and looked directly in her eyes. In the partial moonlight it was difficult to see just how vividly blue they were. He smiled as he looked. She was close enough he could feel her breath on his cheek. "Christ taught him."

The answer floored her. She was not expecting this at all. She had imagined some dusty book of ancient lore handed down through his family and now he was teaching it to William. How could he have learned this from Jesus? "How is that possible?"

William nodded towards the darkened house. "He has taught me that I need to look no farther than Jesus to see the perfect example of a leader. Our Lord told his apostles, when they were arguing amongst themselves as to who was the greatest, that to become the greatest they had to learn to be the most humble servant. To serve is to lead. That is the oath I swore when my uncle took me into his house and named me his heir."

Helen thought about this for quite a while. Robert had been in the house now for several moments, but her mind was no longer paying attention to the time. Instead, she was busy trying to process what she had just been told. She had learned about Jesus growing up, and had heard the stories of His miracles and His sacrifice, but she was never told about His serving. As she rolled this thought around, she realized something. "You said there were two oaths you have taken, William. What was the second?"

Before he had a chance to answer, Robert stepped out of the shadows of the doorway and signaled them to come forward. By his gestures William guessed that the house was clear. A moment later they were beside the older teacher and they noticed, even in the dim moonlight, his face looked grave. "What did you find? Are my guardians gone?" Helen would have rushed into the house if Robert had not been still standing near enough to block the way.

"Lady Helen, is there anywhere else your guardians would have gone besides the house in Le Crotoy?"

"So, they are not inside? You were not gone long, did you look through all the rooms?" Helen was clearly agitated and anxious to get a closer look inside. Something about his teacher's appearance caught William's attention.

"What is wrong inside?" He asked.

"It is best you do not go in there, Lady Helen," Robert stated. His expression changed to one of deep sadness and sympathy.

Helen tried to look over his shoulders, as if she could see into the dark depths of the shadow behind him. "What is it you are sheltering me from? What happened inside?"

"If I would have to guess, my lady, the old gamekeeper held up in the house while all this," and he waved his hand out over the fields and garden, "was going on. He never left."

"Chrestien… Oh dear Lord, who would have done such a thing?" It was the third time she asked and this time she didn't expect an answer.

Instead she buried her face in her hands and began weeping. Robert stepped forward and folded his arms around her, gently patting her back while rocking back and forth.

William watched this while anger and frustration started to build up inside. That man would stop at nothing. He had proved it again. What could they possibly do to stop him? William looked down at his right hand and tried to make a fist. He could almost bend his fingers so their tips touched his palm before the pain brought tears to his eyes. They spilled down his cheeks as he fought back the feeling of being overwhelmed. "Please God, help. I cannot do this on my own." He thought desperately.

"There now, my lady." Robert continued to rock gently while holding Helen tenderly. William dried his eyes, wiped his face and thought his tutor looked as though he could be Helen's father in the way he cared for her. This is what he could do; care for the one who needs it most. Safeguard the innocent.

"I do not know for sure who did this or why. I do have my suspicions though and the passing of a day or two have not changed that opinion. From the look of things, this happened several days ago, if not a week. Perhaps it happened soon after you left for Calais. If I had to make a guess, I would think you left just in time. If he had caught you here, you would now be his possession." The way Robert said this last statement caught William by surprise.

"He would look at Lady Helen as just such a thing?" His tutor looked up and nodded in response to William's question.

"There are others who would do what they would to keep you from ever finding an ally in England, Lady Helen, but Lord Thomas is not one of them. I believe he looks for you to use you to his own ends."

"What must I do? Where can I go…?" She began to sob again, her shoulders shaking and her head bowed forward onto Robert's chest. Gone was the defiance she had shown a few days before when confronted with this same realization. But now, the stark reality of what this man was capable of struck home.

"You must find your strength in the Lord, Lady Helen. It is when we feel weakest, He shows us His strength." Robert paused and waited for her to catch her breath. "And you must think, my lady. Where could your guardians have gone? Was there any other place they could have fled to?" His voice was quiet, but it held iron strength behind it as he repeated the question asked just moments before. Even William felt compelled to answer.

Helen shook her head, while drying her eyes on the back of her hands. She sniffled loudly and then stepped back, blinking rapidly to clear her eyes. "There may be a place… it has been several years since I have seen it, but there is a home along the main canal in Amiens, nearly opposite the cathedral. It is possible they may have gone there."

"It was always our plan to make for Amiens next," William pointed out.

Robert nodded his agreement, but added, "There is one thing you and I will need to do, William, before we leave." He turned back to Helen. "My lady, I do not think it will be best for you see this, but William and I should do our duty and give the gamekeeper a proper burial. It is not right for us to leave him where he lies."

"What can I do? I should do something to help…" She sniffled loudly and cleared her throat. "I want to help see him put to rest properly. He was always very kind to me."

"When I looked in his house I noticed he kept many tools… picks and spades are there for tending and working in the garden. We will need both." Helen nodded and made her way back to the small, one room hut they had passed several moments before. She returned with an iron pick and a spade.

While she was gone, William and his teacher entered the back door of the main house. The first thing which hit him was the smell. He had prepared himself, keeping his mouth open and trying not to breathe through his nose, but the stench of decay and death was overwhelming.

William staggered as they entered a long, wide hallway immediately after crossing the threshold. Robert reached out and steadied him, propping him up under his own shoulder. "It is not as strong once you get through the hall," he pointed out. William nodded but was doing all he could to keep from throwing up. Once, when he was quite a bit younger, he had come across a sheep which had been attacked and killed. His father thought it may have been a wolf. What was left was rotten and maggot filled and even out in the wide open, the stench had made him sick. Now, stuck in this closed house, with no way for it to leave, the rotting simply intensified. It didn't occur to him then how lucky he was that it wasn't summer yet.

He took two or three steps down the hallway and felt himself gag. Robert had already passed him and had made it out of the narrow passage and was in the shadows beyond. William closed his eyes and forced his feet to move. "Dear God, give me the strength to get this done," he silently prayed and took a couple more steps.

A moment later he found himself through the hallway and into what looked like the pantry. There was a window just to the left and Robert was at it, throwing back the shutters, letting in a fresh breeze. The cool, slightly damp, night air smelled amazingly sweet and William rushed to the sill, taking a deep breath, trying to replace the stench inside his lungs. It helped immensely, although, at that moment he couldn't imagine ever forgetting that odor. “Stay here, near the window, William. I will find a blanket we can wrap him in and use it as a sling.”

William nodded and stood at the window. He listened as Robert’s steps receded down one of the halls and then turned to look for the gamekeeper. He was not hard to find. His body was slumped over the table in the center of the room. William had been so focused on making it over to the open window he had rushed right by without noticing.

The room was filled with shadows and yet he could still make out some details. What he saw turned his stomach even more than the stench. The old man hadn’t just been killed. He had either been tortured first or beaten after. Either way, William knew he couldn’t let Helen see this. As he stood there, staring at the corpse, for some reason Gilbert entered his thoughts. He hoped he had survived his encounter with Lord Thomas and was safely finding his way to Dorchester. He also thought of the mother and daughters they had rescued on the edge of the New Forest. He said a silent prayer for all of them.

As he stood in the window, with his head bowed, thinking and praying, Robert returned with a thick blanket, which smelled musty, and slightly of horses. It took the two of them just a short moment to wrap the remains, despite William’s injured hand. As they did so, Robert pointed out to his pupil “it has been several days since this happened.”

“How can you tell?” William asked, while trying to only breathe through his mouth. The open window helped, but moving the body didn’t.

“Within a few hours of death a body will become very stiff. Eventually, after a few days, this will go away. If this happened recently he would be very difficult to move.”

“What happens to someone, once they die? Do they go right to heaven… or the other?”

“Paul said that to be absent from the body is to be present with the

Lord. I believe, if you have made the decision, which you have William, as soon as you pass you would find yourself in God's presence." They had shifted him off the table and were now using the blanket as a sling and carrying him down the hall. William followed his teacher, carrying his end with his left hand. He just couldn't hold anything with his right.

Between the open door and window, the stench had decreased dramatically in the last few minutes. Still, William was worried he would never be rid of the smell from his hands or his clothes. He didn't like the idea of having death being stuck on him, like a terrible overcoat.

"What do you think it is like there?" He often thought about heaven after his mother died. Was she there with his father? Did she think about him? Did she miss him as much as he missed her?

"We live in the land in the middle, William," Robert reminded him of any earlier conversation about the same subject. "We are neither in heaven nor in hell, but the battle lands in between. In heaven there is no pain or fear or worry or sickness or anger nor any kind of evil. Hell is the opposite of heaven but it is worse than that because there is absolutely no sense or presence of God there. Even our worst day here still would not compare to how awful it would be there."

As William thought about what that must be like, they stepped out of the back door and found Helen standing a few paces away, holding a spade and pick. She looked determined to help until her eyes dropped down to the blanket. Tears began to spill down her cheeks and her lips trembled.

"Is there a place you think he would have liked to be put to rest, my lady?" Robert asked as soon as they crossed out of the shadows and into the clear moonlight. She sniffled loudly and nodded, blinking to clear her eyes.

"He was very fond of roses. There is one bush in particular; He told me once it was older even than he. It is there," she pointed a dozen or so paces from the back door, in the center of the yard. Robert nodded and then signaled to William to keep walking while making for the large bush just ahead of them.

Out in the open air, William noticed less and less the stench from the house and more and more a slightly sweet, spicy aroma. He had never smelled anything like it before. As they approached the bush Helen had pointed out the scent grew a little stronger. In the moonlight William could see the bush already had tiny bulbs beginning to open and it was these, which were already giving off the heady aroma.

His uncle had a small flower garden just outside Crandor's keep and it included a white rose bush, but William hadn't spent much time there. In the year he had been living with his uncle he hadn't found much time for sitting and smelling flowers. It was one thing to be named his uncle's heir, it was quite another to become prepared to accept the title when the time came.

They set the gamekeeper down just in time. William's left arm was burning and his hand shaking as they approached the bush. The light breeze stirred up the sweet aroma and it completely drove the remaining smell of the house from William's memory. Later on he could recall the smell of that bush, and gratefully, had a hard time remembering the inside of the house.

Robert handed William the spade and took the pick himself. In a few short moments of hard swings he had softened up a large hole just in front of the bush. The ground had been well tended and fertilized over the years and gave way quite easily. As he stepped back, wiping the sweat from his brow with his sleeve he nodded to William. "Do you think you can manage with your hand?" He asked. William nodded.

It was actually harder than he had imagined. He steadied the spade with his left hand while stepping on it with his right foot. It easily sunk into the softened earth. Getting it back out was the tricky part. After a few attempts he finally managed to figure out how to use the fingers on his right hand without actually grasping the handle. It was slow going but he eventually shifted all the dirt his tutor had managed to break up.

Robert stepped down into the hole and took to the pick again. William watched as sweat dripped down and off his nose. He could feel it running down his own back, despite the cool breeze. Several deep breaths later and he could feel his shoulders begin to relax. A moment after that he had taken Roberts place and finally moved all the loose dirt up and out of the grave.

Robert helped him out and they both stood, out of breath with their hands on their knees. During this whole time Helen had stood off to the side on her own, her arms crossed tightly in front of her chest. She looked cold, but William understood. He had felt the same way when they buried his mother on that hill in Dorchester not far from Crandor Castle.

"My lady, would you like me to say a few words?" Robert asked, after they lowered the old gamekeeper into the grave. She nodded and tried a brave smile.

"God fashioned Adam from the dirt and breathed life into him. Chrestien no longer has the breath of life in him and so we return him to the soil. Life is a vapor, a wisp of smoke. So quickly we can step from the road of the living and onto the road of the departed, but to be absent from this life is to be present with our Lord. God, take this hard worker into your loving embrace and give him rest. Amen."

"Amen," William and Helen answered. She moved to the side of the grave and pulled a couple buds from the rose bush, setting them down on the blanket, then stepped back a pace. "Thank you for your kindness."

She knelt in the grass, her face in her hands, and wept. Robert took the spade from William and began filling in the hole. A moment later it was finished.

Robert stood up, stretching his back in the process and moaned slightly. "I am sorry my lady, but I will not be much use on the oars until I have a little rest." She looked up from her place beside the grave and William could see the tears streaking her cheeks. She nodded and pulled a kerchief from a pocket on the front of her vest, dabbing her eyes and wiping her nose.

"Just a short distance up the river is a small village. There is a manor house, very near the water's edge, with several smaller homes around it. The tide will still be in our favor for another hour or two, which should give us enough time to get there. If we can get that far tonight, I will find you a safe, warm bed to rest and recuperate."

"How well do you know the keepers of that house? Is it possible your guardians made their way there?" William asked as he offered his assistance to Helen. She gladly took his hand to stand. Robert stood off to the side, his breath coming in deep gulps, his hands still on his knees. He didn't appear to be listening to their hushed conversation.

"I do not believe they would have made their way there. It is too near. I was close with the grandson of the brothers who keep the house. He never returned from Crecy.

"They will not wish to keep two Englishmen beneath their roof, will they?" William asked.

"No, they will not. But they will allow my valet and his young apprentice stay in one of the smaller houses in the yard." She smiled and her eyes sparkled in the moonlight.

Chapter Twenty Two

A few moments later and they were once again in the small boat, making their way up stream. The tide was still near its crest and it didn't look like it had begun to fall. Despite this, Helen was suddenly anxious to get moving. She used one of the oars to push the craft away from the dock and then stowed it, setting the small sail and adjusting it to catch the breeze, which still blew in from the sea. They were far enough inland that setting the sail didn't seem as if it would send up a signal to anyone watching for them. The river had been empty up to this point, but they had seen several other boats of similar design pulled up along the banks since they had departed Le Crotoy.

The wind filled the cloth and slowly began carrying their boat against the lazy current. It wasn't as fast as Robert's rowing, but, as he said, he was spent. He didn't even make any small talk as they glided along but instead was slumped forward with his arms resting on his knees. He looked to William as if he would fall asleep any moment.

As he sat in the bow of the boat, he wondered just how old his tutor was. If Robert had been William's age when he became his father's apprentice and then began tutoring his uncle and father soon afterwards, he would be 55 or 60 years old. It was difficult for William to imagine being that old; and yet he didn't really consider his tutor to be old. "Why is it some people seem to get so much older earlier than other people?" He wondered aloud.

Helen shrugged, probably realizing William's question was more of an audible thought, but Robert decided to answer it. "That is a great question, William. What do you think would age someone faster than another?"

"Hard work?"

"Not if they have joy in their heart. Paul wrote that we should count it all joy and do our work as if we were doing it for God." He took in a deep breath and sat up straight, rolling his head while stretching his neck and shoulders. "So, if it is not hard work alone that would do it, what do you think it may be?"

His young student had seen that expression before. Even in the dim moonlight he could see the look. This was no longer just an idle conversation. There was an important lesson buried here, somewhere. Realizing this, William paused and tried to reason it out. He had discovered some time before this that if he sounded his thoughts out loud it helped. "Hard work can age someone early if they are not joyful while they are working. So, if they are not joyful…" he paused to think. "If they are not joyful it is because they are unhappy for some reason. Does being unhappy make someone get old earlier?"

"I think it does, but there is still one thing more; one more important thing to consider, besides just being unhappy. Actually, it would cause unhappiness, just as it causes someone to get old quicker. What do you think that would be, William?"

Sometimes it was like this with his tutor. He felt like it was some sort of a game where they tossed questions back and forth between each other, gradually getting closer to the answer. Now it was his turn. He scratched the back of his head in thought. "There must be something which causes unhappiness and steals your joy and makes you get older faster. Something, which would be the root cause of these…" His brows furrowed in deep thought and he slowly shook his head.

Suddenly he sat up, his expression one of excitement and he clapped his hands in emphasis. "Worry would be the root of all their problems, would it not?"

Robert nodded and grinned back at his pupil. "Do you remember what the Justice of the Peace of Salisbury told you, William?" He nodded and tapped the side of his head. "Exactly. You must guard your thoughts at all times. Not only can they lead you to your circumstances, but they also will affect your whole outlook on life, and even change your appearance."

"So, if I want to remain young looking longer, I should try to control the worry in my life?" Helen chimed in.

"William, how would you answer that?" Robert asked.

His pupil paused for a moment, collecting his thoughts. "If I were you and you asked me that same question, I would say that there is no try. There is only to do or not to do. I would tell you that worry and fear share each other's company and you get both for the price of one. I would tell you that if you truly have faith in God you cannot have worry because worrying is the opposite of faith. Worrying is the belief in the negative you cannot see, while faith is the belief in the positive. They cannot exist at the same time. If you find yourself worrying then stop and ask God for help in the building up of your faith."

"Very good, William, very good indeed." He turned slightly to look over his shoulder. "Did he answer your question, Lady Helen?" She nodded while deep in thought.

For the next several moments no one spoke as the boat quietly glided up stream, while patches of farmland, orchards and the occasional house slowly drifted by. The river before them twisted on itself, like a great fresh water leviathan, snaking across the countryside. Several times it completely doubled back so they couldn't see what lay ahead until they turned the corner.

As they came around one of these sharp turns, Helen was adjusting the sail with the change in wind direction and she saw ahead of them the small enclave of buildings they were looking for. The river straightened before them and on the gently sloping eastern bank there was cluster of small houses, surrounding a much larger home. It looked to William as though it was larger than the home Helen had grown up in, but what it gained in size, it lacked in gardens and surrounding landscape. There was a small yard of turf surrounding the home, and then just outside this, an almost complete circle of buildings.

There was something curious about that house which puzzled William and he asked Helen and his tutor about it. If Robert knew the answer, he let their navigator answer.

"What looks strange about the house William, is that it was designed and built much like a castle's keep. Do you see the crenellations along the roofline? You can climb up to the top and stand on the roof, looking out over the surrounding farmland. It does not have a moat, nor wall, but the houses surrounding it act as part of its defense. I have stood upon the roof many times, looking up and down the river and over the rolling hills beyond. When I was quite young I thought it a very impressive site. That is until I visited the Fortress de Ham. After seeing a true castle I returned here sometime later and thought it looked very small in comparison."

William wondered what she would think if she ever saw Crandor Castle. Probably rather provincial he decided. Despite that, he suddenly missed the green grass, rolling hills, flocks of sheep and farmers. Even the sometimes drafty house seemed warm and inviting now that he was far from home with little chance of finding a decent bed to sleep in.

A sudden twinge in his right hand shook him from his thoughts of hearth and home. He massaged around the edge of the wound as he clenched and unclenched his fist. The muscles were tight and sore and he noticed that it had started itching. He hadn't realized he had already been scratching at it since they left Abbeville.

As they approached the village William noticed several boats, similar to their own, pulled up onto the bank. Helen was obviously making her way towards them but their progress had slowed considerably. "Have you rested enough?" Helen asked his tutor. "The tide is starting to go out. We are already making little headway; soon we will find ourselves pulled back downstream."

Robert took a deep breath and nodded, picking up the oars and setting them in their rowlocks. It took him about a dozen strokes to propel the boat right up to the bank. William jumped out into the knee deep water and, using his left hand, helped pull their boat up onto the bank. His tutor helped Helen stand and move to the bow, where William lent her a hand as she climbed over the rail and onto the sand. Robert followed and as William helped his tutor over the edge, he muttered, "I am ready for a good night sleep, William." He tried to hide it, but his student could see the exhaustion in his eyes.

"Lady Helen, what do you suggest next?" William asked.

"First, I suggest you do not speak, William." He started to protest, but she added quickly, "Remember, English voices and the men who carry them are most unwelcome here." Her own voice was just above a whisper, now they were only a short distance from the nearest house. William nodded his understanding. He looked to his teacher and he could see it in his eyes. They were in Helen's hands.

It seemed strange to William that they had just been talking about worry, faith, and trust in God. It was almost as if the conversation was the reminder he needed right now as they followed Helen between the two nearest houses and into the open yard between them and the central keep. The grass was cropped short and William wondered if there were sheep kept nearby. For the second time that evening he thought of Dorchester and its rolling hills. He missed his home.

It was well past midnight and still several hours before dawn as they crossed the open space. Somewhere on the other side of the village a dog began barking and it was picked up by one or two more. The waxing moon slid out from behind a large bank of clouds and dimly lit the yard and buildings around them. All three stopped in their tracks. Standing before them were several pike carrying men at arms. Their iron blades glinted in the moonlight and were pointed straight at the three of them.

"*Avant de faire un pas de plus, dites-nous qui vous êtes*!" A fourth soldier stepped away from the others and addressed all three of them. He didn't carry a pike and looked to be perhaps a sergeant by the feather in his cap and the small sword at his hip. Even in William's limited time spent learning French, he knew they should stand where they were.

"*S'il vous plait, pardonnez-moi. Je m'appelle Helen d'Abbeville. Il y avait une époque où ma présence était bien connue ici et où j'étais la bienvenue.*" Upon hearing his native tongue, the sergeant visibly relaxed and motioned with his hand to the armed guards. They reluctantly lowered their pikes. William understood enough and his teacher even more of Helen's answer.

"*Merci sergent. Les anglais ont envahi notre domaine à Abbeville. Mes compagnons et moi les fuyons. Cette maison fut le premier endroit auquel j'ai pensé pour être en sécurité. J'ai passé plusieurs étés heureux ici dans ma jeunesse.*" Now William began to understand her game. If her story is checked they will find the estate abandoned and the grounds overrun. Although they couldn't say for sure it was the English, the sentiment of the town would certainly lean that way.

Before the sergeant could answer, William noticed Robert raise his hand to his face and wipe his brow and then take a step to his left, leaning upon William's shoulder. "*Puisse Dieu m'aider*," his teacher muttered and then his knees buckled and he collapsed upon William, who was just able to grab him about the chest and sink with him to the ground. As he lay him down on the grass, in the pale moonlight his face looked ashen and William wasn't sure if he was breathing.

"*Nous venons d'enterrer notre ancien garde-chasse. J'ai l'impression que la besogne lui était trop difficile. S'il vous plaît, apportez-lui du Cognac.*" Helen knelt down beside William and took Roberts hand in her own and caressed his brow with her other.

The Sergeant hesitated for a brief moment and then turning to one of the pike carrying guardsmen he muttered, "*Réveilles le majordome et apportes-moi de l'eau de vie, Geoffrey*," as he jerked his head towards the keep. It was difficult for William to remember he was supposed to be a servant. He wanted to look up and stare into the eyes of the men who still faced them with their weapons, but his full attention was drawn to his tutor.

As he looked upon his face, William was suddenly reminded of his mother. She had that same look when he found her that morning, still lying in her bed; she had been the same color as well. He lay his teacher's gray head down upon the short cut grass and stared at him. That same feeling of loss and helplessness, which tore at his heart all those mornings ago, boiled back inside of him. Other than his uncle, his tutor was the only family he now had left. He didn't want to imagine what it would be like to lose him and his companionship. He wasn't a servant to William, he was his friend, his confidant, and his teacher.

Gently laying his injured right hand on Roberts's chest, William bowed his head and prayed the strongest, most heartfelt prayer he could manage. *"Dear God, You are the same today as you were when Jesus walked in Palestine. Your abilities and desire to do good are the exact same. Jesus called out for Lazarus and his friend answered his call, defying death in order to glorify You, Lord. I call on that same power and I call for my friend."* In his best French, he called out in a strong voice, "*Robert, réveilles-toi… Au nom de Dieu… lèves-toi*!"

As if commanded, Robert's chest expanded with a large, deep breath, which was followed by another and still another. Seconds later his eyes fluttered and the ashen color of his face slowly washed away with very pale pink. William could feel his teacher's heart beating strongly beneath his hand. He lowered his head and muttered, "*Merci Dieu*."

Helen echoed him with "Amen," which was followed by a chorus of "Amen's." William looked up startled to see the guards, including the Sergeant, on their knees. Several had their heads bowed as they made the sign of the cross. No longer were they eyeing them with caution. Instead their expressions were a mixture of fear and awe; one or two even had tears. William noticed the sergeant was staring at his crippled right hand and the wound made by the large splinter, which had completely penetrated it.

The older soldier made the sign of the cross again and muttered, "*Par le sang du Christ*." William looked again at his hand and suddenly realized what they were thinking. Robert began sitting up and William shifted positions so he could whisper in his ear.

"Are you all right?" he asked his teacher. The way he had looked just a moment ago, William would have sworn he was dead or dying. Now to see him sitting up, giving him a weak smile and a nod, he felt himself overcome.

Tears spilled William's cheeks and his body shook as he knelt in the grass beside his tutor. It wasn't grief which overwhelmed him; instead it was relief and thankfulness. He was relieved to know he wouldn't be alone, at least not for a while still. He was also relieved to know his tutor would be all right. Mixed in with the relief was a heartfelt, deep sense of thankfulness. He couldn't imagine how to thank God for bringing Robert back to life, for there was no doubt in William's mind that his old teacher had died.

"You called for me, and I am here, William," Robert whispered back and wrapped his arms around his young pupil, pulling him close in a warm embrace. He was light headed and his arms and legs felt like stones but, as he sat in the grass, the embrace of his young student comforted him. Seconds later he felt Helen wrap her arms around both of them and they sat for a moment, the three together, on the grass, in the open space between the houses and the keep.

They sat together until William heard the soldiers muttering and heavy footsteps moving away from them. He wiped his face on his sleeve and looked up. The Sergeant was still kneeling in the grass, watching all three of them, but his sword was no longer drawn. Only one pike man remained, the expression on his face a mix of fear and excitement. William wasn't sure what had happened to the rest of the soldiers.

"*Qui êtes-vous?*" he asked.

It took a few seconds for William to process the question in his head. Once he realized he was being asked who he was, he knew the story they had come up with earlier simply made no sense. Like a flash he remembered Robert teaching the knight's oath, and the importance of telling the truth, even if it leads to pain, suffering or death. Turning to Helen, William asked her, "Will you translate for me? It would take too long for me to say it in French." She nodded, wide eyed.

William stood up slowly, making sure Robert was supported by Helen, and turning to the Sergeant, nodded his head and cleared his throat. "My name is William de Simpson," he began. Helen echoed his remarks. "I am the nephew and heir of Lord Charles de Simpson, Earl of Dorchester. May I present Lady Helen, who has been raised in Abbeville since her birth, and this is Robert Buckley, my tutor and close counselor to my family." As Helen translated, William watched the Sergeant's changing facial expression. He expected anger, hatred, perhaps even fear but what he didn't expect was shock.

"*La famille Simpson de Ponthieu*?" William didn't need to wait for Helen's translation.

He nodded gravely, answering, "Yes, my family originally came from Ponthieu. They joined with their cousin, William of Normandy, when he sailed for England many, many years ago."

The Sergeant turned to the remaining pike man, not even waiting for Helen to finish translating, and muttered something to him. When the foot soldier responded curtly, the Sergeant raised his voice enough for William to hear his response. "*Réveilles-les. Ils voudront savoir qui est arrivé.*" Helen whispered the translation.

"William," Robert muttered. When he looked down, his tutor was gesturing him to come closer. He knelt beside his old teacher once more. "I have done my best to teach you this last year, but there has been much I have had to set aside, in the hopes of coming to it later."

"What is it I should know? Something about this village?"

"The last time a Simpson traveled to this part of France, your grandfather was still alive. He sent your uncle and father across the channel as young boys. While they were here, they stopped and visited their close relations who still lived in the water tower." William mouthed the words, "water tower," and then looked up at the keep before him. A light dawned on his thoughts.

"Eaucourt… the water tower? These are the relatives my father and uncle have spoken of?" Helen gasped slightly and stared even closer at William, as if for the very first time.

Robert nodded. "They are, and there is more but…" Just at that moment the doors to the keep were thrust open and several lantern carrying people marched across the courtyard. One was the pike man, who had been sent at the Sergeant's command. The other two both looked like they had been roused from a deep sleep and were still in the process of waking. In their hurry, they hadn't even had a chance to tuck in their nightshirts or properly lace up their hose.

They quickly covered the short distance between them, and then the two newcomers came directly up to William and the others. Helen's bright copper hair caught the lantern light and seemed to turn to flame. The younger of the two men, and young was a relative term since they appeared to be even older than Robert, bowed at the waist upon recognizing the young lady. "Welcome back to Eaucourt sur Somme, Lady Helen. We have seen dark times since you last graced our home, but we have seen nothing of your beautiful face." Despite his age and the weight it carried in his words there was something about his voice which seemed almost familiar.

"Yes, welcome back Lady Helen," the older of the two remarked. His voice was dry and raspy like old leaves rustling on the New Forest floor. "And who do we have here?" His watery gaze turned to William and they stood a moment, nearly eye to eye. He must have been tall and powerful in his youth, William thought, since they now stood face to face, despite his slightly curved back.

In that brief moment Helen cleared her throat, and doing the two older men a courtesy, answered, "My Lords, may I present to you William de Simpson, nephew and heir of Lord Charles de Simpson, Earl of Dorchester. William, the Lords of Eaucourt, Matthew and David de

Simpson." William suddenly found himself staring into two separate lanterns and he had to squint his eyes to keep them from watering.

"Charles is Earl then is he? Well, well… time has certainly sped along, hasn't it brother?" The older of the two asked in his dry cracking voice. He spoke English well, but with a very thick French accent. His brother nodded but they both kept a very close eye on William. It was as if they were studying him, perhaps even gauging him and his response.

William bowed at the waist and addressed the two as he stood up, "my Lords. It is a pleasure to meet you both; All the more so because we were not seeking this reunion, but rather only searching for a safe place to spend the night, and avoid prying eyes before traveling on to Amiens tomorrow."

At this admission, the younger of the two's expression changed slightly to one of interest. The older did not change at all except to perhaps look with even deeper scrutiny. "Whose eyes are you avoiding, William?" The younger brother asked. Despite the innocence of the question, William could see by his expression he was extremely interested in the answer.

"Nearly seven days past we encountered an English Lord while traveling through the New Forest. He took a strong dislike to us," at this Matthew snorted, "and has pursued us since. As God would have it, we have come to find out he also has designs on Lady Helen, who we have taken into our safekeeping in the hopes of returning her safely to her relations."

"And who is this Lord of England which pursues you and why would you not stop in Abbeville?" asked David. Matthew, in the meantime, moved his lantern towards Helen, who had knelt once again, beside Robert.

"Dear Lord, is this a Buckley? Are they still Seneschals of your house?" The older lord had bent over, as best he was able, and was studying Robert very closely. William's teacher's breathing was stronger and the color had returned to his face, but he still hadn't managed to stand.

"My apologies, my Lord." Robert's voice cracked and he cleared his throat. "I find myself unable to stand and bow at the moment," Robert stated. At this the Sergeant stepped up from the shadows and whispered in Matthew's ear while pointing, first at Robert then William, then back again to Robert. Lord Matthew's eyes widened and he muttered something to himself in French.

"Brother, we have left guests out in the cold in the middle of the night. Where are our manners?" Matthew asked. "Will you be able to stand… with help?" he questioned Robert. William's teacher closed his eyes a moment and taking in a deep breath, nodded.

Without hesitation, William knelt beside his tutor and taking Robert's arm around his shoulders, slowly stood up, lifting him up in the process. They stood that way, albeit wobbly and Robert muttered, "thank you, William."

"*Vivo servire*," William answered and then looked up to see both Lords of Eaucourt staring at him. Their expressions were nearly identical, a mixture of surprise and perhaps even admiration. Robert shifted his weight, standing a little more on his own and William smiled at the two brothers before him.

It took several moments of shuffling and pausing, but William was able to help Robert move almost as quickly as the old lords who led the way. David had motioned to Helen to walk beside him as they returned to the keep. And he kept up a steady stream of questions and conversation in French as they went. William was too focused on keeping his feet under him to have the energy to catch the snatches of sentences and translate them in his head.

Finally they came to the large oaken doors, which were still standing open. Warm firelight streamed out and William could hear the spit and pop of green wood burning in an open-hearth somewhere inside. Lord Matthew turned on the threshold and bowing stiffly said, "Welcome, cousin and guests to Eaucourt sur Somme." He turned and led the procession inside.

"Any last moment lessons I need to know before we follow?" William asked his teacher. He was smiling, but beneath the façade he was nervous. Something about the way Robert had told him there was more about Eaucourt than just a place with long distance relations had stuck with him. Under it all he found himself nervous.

Robert shook his head. "I am sorry, there is not enough time right now, but" he took in a deep breath and straightened up, standing on his own feet, holding his own weight, "we will enter without fear. We will be bold and upright, for God loves us and sets a table for us, even in the presence of our enemies." His tutor took a few tentative steps on his own and then made his way across the threshold and into the warm invitation of the firelight. William paused just a moment longer to reflect on what he had just been told.

"I wonder if that means I am entering the presence of my enemies." He murmured to himself and then followed the others inside.

•••

Eaucourt was designed like any other keep. Once inside the central hall, a circling staircase ran along the outside wall, with a landing at each floor above. Although it was visually nearly a perfect cylinder from the outside, once in the entryway, William could see it had several chambers inside, which were built into the base of the tower. The others had entered one of these just to the left of the entrance and William followed them as he continued to study the interior. Reeds were thrown on the floor and they crunched as he walked across them.

A large round table stood in the center of the entry hall. Lying on it was a heavily damaged shield, still containing the shafts of arrows, which had pierced it in several places. Next to it lay a notched and broken sword. For some reason William felt very sad looking at those, as if they were set in place as a memorial. "William, come and join us by the fire," Lord David called from the side chamber and a moment later he was seated in front of a crackling and popping hearth with a cup of red wine in his hand and a plate of fresh bread and cheese on a small table before him. The wine was delicious and it quickly found its way to his head. As he sat there, relaxing for the first in a very long while, he could feel sleep pulling at him. He tried to fight his eyes as they closed on their own in ever longer blinks.

Helen was seated to his left, with both brothers in chairs close to her own. They had kept up a steady stream of conversation in French since they had made their way toward the keep. The dry, rasp of Matthew and deep sonorous rumble of David, intermingled with the high lilt of Helen. It was almost like singing and acted like a lullaby to William. He turned to his right and saw Robert already slumped in his chair, his head dropped forward onto his chest while his hands were folded in his lap. He was breathing deep and steady and William was pretty sure he was snoring.

He tried a small piece of the cheese on the cutting board and took another sip of his wine. The combination of flavors was amazing. If he hadn't been so completely exhausted, he would have been overwhelmed by what he tasted. As it was, he simply smiled, took another sip and set down his glass. For a moment he stared into the flames, mesmerized by their dancing and the occasional snapping spark leaping from the logs.

His mind rushed through the last two weeks as he stared at the gold and red colors. If he hadn't experienced it himself he never would have thought it possible someone could go through as much in such a short time. His right hand itched and he shifted his gaze. In the dimly lit room, with the flames dancing before him, the wound appeared dark and almost sinister. He would have a large scar for the rest of his life. He tried to make a fist and could nearly get his fingertips to his palm. It made him smile to think he might actually be able to use his hand again someday.

He wasn't sure how long he sat there, shifting his gaze from the fire, to his teacher, to his hand. Eventually Helen came into view carrying two, thick blankets. She placed one about Robert's shoulders. It was long enough to wrap completely around him and he looked like a caterpillar that was stuck partially out of its cocoon. When she came to William and started wrapping him the same way, he grabbed her wrist and she jerked in alarm. "I am sorry, William, I thought you were asleep. Lord's Matthew and David have returned to their chambers."

William looked up and smiled. "Thank you for the kindness of the blanket but I would rather not sleep in the chair. My neck and back would not appreciate it tomorrow. I will just curl up in front of the fire, near the hearth." He took the blanket from her, but she was suddenly reluctant to give it up. There was a strange, sad and serious expression on her face. "What is it? What is wrong?"

Helen shook her head and smiled but William could see she was hiding something. "Nothing important. At least nothing important which cannot wait until morning." She released the thick cover and stepped back. "Sleep well, William. The dawn will come early." With that cryptic remark she turned and walked out of the chamber. His eyes followed her as she ascended the stairs and he listened as her steps slowly faded in the night.

Standing, William carried the blanket with him until he was near enough to the hearth to feel the warmth, but safely enough away to be sure no sparks would land on him. He set another split log on the fire and turned the coals until the fire flared up again and the wood began to crackle. A moment later William was wrapped up in the blanket, his arm cradled under his head like a pillow and he drifted off to sleep.

•••

He woke to a deep-throated rumble next to his ear. At some point in the night one of the dogs had made its way to the hearth and lay stretched out next to him. William found his arm thrown across the rib cage of the wiry-haired beast and the contented rumble of the canine's snoring had been his wake up call.

The fire had died down to leave a pile of gray ashes mixed with dark red coals. A chill had entered the room with the lowering of the flames and he could feel it trying to make its way into his bones. The blanket and the dog both helped to keep it at bay. Patting the latter, William rolled over and slowly sat up, stretching the aches away. The rumbling at his side shifted in frequency as his companion noticed he was no longer touching him. A thick, hairy tail thumped the ground several times, but otherwise, the dog didn't move. For some reason William thought a slightly animated rug would have been a great description for the hound and then smiled at his own sense of humor.

As he sat there he realized two things; one, Robert was not in his chair, and two, he needed to quickly find a place to relieve himself. Fortunately both were answered within seconds as his teacher walked from behind a large tapestry. He must have seen the look on William's face and answered his unasked question. "Behind the tapestry is a door to a small garderobe."

William stood and stretched and thanked his teacher as he passed him on the way to the room of relief. He found it cramped and rather odiferous and was thankful it wasn't the middle of the summer and extremely hot outside.

When he returned he found Robert staring at the coat of arms, which hung over the rough stone hearth. He had just stirred up the coals and put another split log on the fire. The lively flames lit up the room, while at the same time, casting eerie shadows around and above the hearth. William hadn't looked closely at the family crest the night before and took his place next to his tutor before the newly roused fire. "Do you see anything wrong with these, William?" He asked.

Ever since his uncle had taken him in as his ward and heir, William had found himself drawn to the coat of arms which hung over a similar hearth in Crandor Castle. He had stared at it for so long and so often it was clearly etched into his memory. And yet now, as he stood there in the keep of Eaucourt, he knew there was a difference but it eluded him. The stork was there, as was the door. The red field and… "It is the door," he suddenly realized. "Why is it a different color? Who would have done that?" The white door on the crest of his family in England had been made black here in France.

"I believe I know the answer from something Lady Helen told us yesterday, as well as the shield and sword in the entry hall." If Robert had looked pale, ill and troubled yesterday, today he just looked sad.

"You told me yesterday, God would set a table before us, even in the presence of my enemies. I had wondered if these, my distant cousins, would have been those enemies, but I do not feel that." William paused, trying to find the right words. "It is not a feeling really. It is more like someone gently pushing me. I do not feel that here."

"You are being prompted by the Holy Spirit, William. Trust it when it is leading you. It will not guide you astray."

"The Holy Spirit? But, I thought it came on the day of Pentecost, like tongues of fire and those in the upper room were filled with it. What does it have to do with me?"

Robert chuckled and gently shook his head. "William, it has everything to do with you. Jesus told His followers that, once He was gone, He would send a helper, a comforter, a guide, the voice of wisdom and understanding, to help each one of them."

"I remember reading about that. But, again, what does it have to do with me now?"

"Do you think God has changed at all since Jesus lived, died, and rose from the grave?" William shook his head. "Good, that is right. God has never changed and He never will change. He is the same yesterday, today and tomorrow. Now, tell me what these ideas have to do with each other." Robert took that pose William had seen so many times. His arms were crossed and his right thumb was gently tapping on his front teeth. His gaze was directed straight at William and he was not blinking. If he hadn't been used to it, this might have unnerved William, instead, he actually found it comforting. It reminded him of his time studying in Dorchester.

William, without even thinking about it, crossed his arms as well and turned his gaze to the glowing embers. "God sent His Holy Spirit on the early church, just as Jesus told them He would do; and God never changes. So… if He never changes then…" His brow furrowed for a moment, then relaxed and he smiled. "His promise is still the same today as it was then?"

Robert mirrored his smile. "Exactly, William. Just as we can ask God for His wisdom, we can also ask Him for the indwelling of the Holy Spirit and a greater sense of its prompting in our lives."

"Why would God want to do so much for me? I am not at all that important…"

"Do not ever think that William," Robert admonished. "Remember how important your words are. You know that. You have seen how your thoughts and your words lead to your circumstances. Remember Samuel Thompson and the Justice of the Peace in Salisbury?" It was the most stern he had heard his tutor since they had left Dorchester and it caught him by surprise, but he knew he was right. His eyes dropped to the fire again.

"I am sorry," He paused to quietly ask God to forgive him of doubting his importance and then realized what had prompted the whole discussion. "If the Holy Spirit is prompting me that there is nothing to be concerned about here, what was it that concerned you last night? And what do Lady Helen and those things on the table have to do with each other?"

Robert turned sad again and, once more, turned his eyes up to the coat of arms. "Helen told us she used to come here often and that she and one of the boys had become close friends; possibly even more than that. Then came the battle at Crecy, from which he never returned." William nodded his understanding. He remembered her mentioning it when they arrived earlier that morning.

"What Lady Helen did not realize at the time was the significance of that boy's death. He was not the only one to fall at Crecy. His father fell as well."

The realization hit William like a thunderbolt. "Then that would mean Lords David and Matthew…"

"Are all that are left of your family line in France? I am afraid it is so, William. If there had been more time I would have prepared you better for these realizations. As it is, I am not sure you truly realize the significance." His teacher sounded somber and yet earnest at the same time.

William tried to think of a reason why and finally decided to keep sounding out his thoughts. "Lords Matthew and David are the last of the living de Simpson's in France to bear these arms," he thought out loud. "With no living heir their family future seems black and so they painted the door the same?" It wasn't an answer really. It was more like William had posed a question. Then he continued the thought further, "nothing good would come through that door as far as they were concerned."

"That is right William. They see the end of their line and the end of their family. There is no heir to carry on the name of de Simpson of Eaucourt sur Somme.

"Would you have been concerned if there had still been an heir alive? Would they have tried to do something to me?"

"I do not know for certain William. What I do know is what I had been told by my father, and I believe your grandfather shared it with him. 'Beware the Simpson's of the Water Tower. They share our name and common ancestor but little else.'"

"That is not very helpful, is it?" William asked rhetorically. As he thought about it he realized morning had fully broken and yet there seemed little astir in the keep. "Have you seen Lady Helen yet this morning?" He wondered aloud.

"I am right here." Her sudden appearance made the two of them jump. William felt as if his heart leapt into his throat and it hammered in his chest for a long moment.

"Lady Helen," Robert smiled and bowed. "Good morning to you. I hope you slept well."

"Well enough, although it looks like there is little staff here. It certainly is not the way I remember."

William looked back up at the coat of arms and asked, "Was the door always painted black or did this happen recently?"

Helen paused as she entered the room and considered the heraldry above the mantle. Slowly she shook her head and sadness came over her expression. "It was not. The last I was here, Henri and Geoffrey were still…" her voice cracked and she choked back a tear. Robert immediately crossed the room, took her by the arm, and led her to the chair he had recently slept in. There was still a little wine left in the decanter on the sideboard and he poured her a small glass. She took it with a slight smile and murmured her thanks. Despite the darkened room (the windows were still shuttered from the winter) William could see her eyes were reddened and puffy, as if she had been crying. She sniffled loudly and continued, "Lord Matthew's son and grandson were still alive the last time I was here. Geoffrey and I spent many afternoons walking the grounds, talking about our lives, and where we would like to live, and what we would want to see of the world. We both thought traveling would be exciting."

She paused a moment and stared into the glowing embers and then spoke, almost to herself. "I remember the last day I saw Geoffrey. King Philip had camped in Abbeville, and as soon as he heard Edward had crossed the Somme and was near Crecy-en-Ponthieu, he ordered the army to move. They needed little encouragement. I could hardly believe my eyes when I looked upon the thousands of men; even crossbowmen from Genoa seemed eager to meet the English in the field. The sky was beginning to darken and it looked like a storm was approaching, but for a brief moment the sun was still out and the glare off the shields and armor was dazzling."

She dropped her gaze again and William could see the glint of the firelight off the tears as they ran down her face. She was leaning forward, her arms folded across her chest and she was rocking back and forth. She uttered no sound at all. He knew that look and understood what she was feeling. He had felt the same way when he heard about his father and again with his mother. It was the same feeling he had for a long time when he thought of them after their passing. It was then the realization hit him. Helen had been in love with Geoffrey and perhaps even more than that.

William tugged at Roberts sleeve and motioned him to come out into the entry hall. As soon as they were out of Helen's hearing, he turned to his tutor and asked, "Is it possible Lady Helen was betrothed to Geoffrey?"

"I did guess that might have been the case from what she said last night."

William nodded, his brow furrowed in thought. Something his teacher had mentioned just a few moments ago came back to him and he asked, "What other significance could I not realize about the death of my cousin and his father?" Robert was about the answer when a voice, coming from the stairs overhead took away his chance.

"The significance, William, is my grandson's agreed upon betrothal to Lady Helen." It was Lord Matthew. He had washed, shaved and changed into a fine pair of cross-gartered hose. His linen shirt and vest were richly embroidered and William could see at least one gold ring on his fingers. He certainly appeared dressed for more than just an average day at Eaucourt. Before he was half way down the last flight of stairs, his brother emerged from the landing and stairs above. He too, was dressed as if receiving a special guest.

William bowed at the waist and addressed the both. "My Lords. Good morning. I trust you slept well?"

"I slept like an infant," David began and his brother rolled his eyes in mocked disdain. "Waking every third hour to cry." He smiled a broad smile and it seemed, to William his eyes flashed. William smiled back and decided he would try to remember that answer, in order to use it when humor was called for.

"Enough, brother," Lord Matthew scolded. "We have important matters to discuss with our cousin. Come, William," he spoke over his shoulder as he strode past them and into the adjacent room. "You may attend upon him, Buckley," Lord David added cheerfully as he passed his older brother and made his way to the shutters. Releasing their clasps, he threw them back letting bright sunlight flood the room. William turned and glanced back at his tutor but his expression was completely blank. He had only seen that once before when a guest at Crandor Castle had insulted him and did not ask for his forgiveness. After all, he was just a servant to the eyes of most people. William smiled weakly and turned back to the brothers.

Lord Matthew had stepped over to Helen and set a calloused hand upon her still bowed head. "I am sorry this has been so difficult for you, dear, but I am afraid it is not going to get much easier."

Helen nodded, sniffled loudly and cleared her throat. "I understand." For William, it felt like he was the only one in the room who didn't. It was like he was in a strange play whose plot still didn't make sense.

The old lord paused a moment in thought. For the last time, he stopped to debate with himself over the course of action he and his brother had agreed to last night. He also wondered if she truly understood. Either way, she would find out soon enough.

He turned from Helen and approached the fireplace, clearing his throat in the process. To hide his nervousness, he turned his back to the hearth and clasped his hands behind his back. "As you have already discovered, William, my son and grandson," and here his voice cracked and he had to pause and clear his throat again. When he continued, his voice was smaller and carried less confidence than before.

"My son and grandson fell at the Battle of Crecy…"

"The inglorious defeat of Crecy," David added, then snapped his mouth closed when he saw the glare in his brother's eyes directed at him. To avoid the gaze he turned his attention away from the room and out the open windows.

"It was a dark day for all of France, as well as for our family. My brother and his long since passed wife, God rest her soul, had only one child, a daughter, and yet we thought the line secure with two male heirs. No one foresaw what would happen on that muddy field. I still remember the arrival of the herald the next morning. The memory shall forever be carved in my mind's eye. As my whole world and the future of our family collapsed around me I can still hear his apology and need to hurry on to the next estate. Nearly every family in France lost a son or husband or brother or grandchild that day. Later that night I darkened the door of our family crest."

"I am sorry for your loss," William stated, and then added quickly, "None of our English family was upon the field that day."

"I am well aware of that, cousin," Lord Matthew snapped, then took a deep breath and slowly let it out. "I am sorry, William. The pain is still great."

"There is no apology needed, my Lord. My own grief is for the loss of my parents, later that same year. I cannot imagine what it must feel like to lose a child and grandchild on the same day."

Lord Matthew nodded, his eyes wandering across the intricate pattern of the hearthrug he stood upon. "News travels slowly in time of war, but even we eventually heard of the battle with the Scots, the death of your father, and the elevation of your uncle. He sits now in higher circles." William wasn't sure how to respond to the last comment and then he remembered Robert teaching him from the book of Proverbs that even a fool will appear wise if he keeps his tongue. He decided not to say anything except to nod and look thoughtful.

"As you can imagine, cousin, it was months before I could face the task of dealing with their personal belongings. It was during this time I came across a letter, whose contents will make clear what I am to propose." At this, he withdrew from his coat pocket the letter. Helen immediately sat up, her eyes wide and William thought, looking just a little fearful. "The letter is from Lady Helen to my grandson, Geoffrey."

"That is a personal letter and I do not see why you would wish to expose…"

"Hush child, let him speak," Robert had stood beside Helen since entering the room, and when she rose with agitation over the recognition of the letter he immediately stepped up beside her. She turned to him, her face flushed, but seconds later she dropped her gaze, bowed her head and sat back in the chair. "You may continue, my Lord de Simpson," he stated as he bowed at the waist.

"As Lady Helen has already mentioned, it is a personal letter and therefore will be kept private, except for one statement made near the end." He unfolded the heavy yellow parchment and cleared his throat. His younger brother, who had been sitting, got up and went back to the window. He crossed his arms over his chest and stared out into the morning. "In answer to your repeated question," he began, his voice sounding even dryer than the night before. "I have received confirmation from my guardians of my eligibility and therefore answer yes to your proposal and offer. I will wear your gloves to church this Sunday." He stopped and stood staring at the note.

"I do not understand the importance of all this, my Lord," William stated, shaking his head. He certainly didn't understand the comment about the gloves.

"My grandson proposed to Lady Helen. In this letter she accepted his offer and sealed her commitment by wearing his gloves to church."

Matthew turned to Helen and addressed her directly. "Do you agree with this?" She lowered her eyes to the carpet and nodded. For some reason, to William, it felt as though she was on trial. He was surprised how much it bothered him and wanted to object, but was cut short as his elderly cousin continued.

"My grandson was the only heir of our family in France. With him was the future hope of our line. With his death and the death of my son, that future was darkened." Now he paused, took a deep breath and turned from Helen to William. "That is, until you arrived last night."

"I, my Lord? What can I do for you and your family?"

"It is no longer just my family you can help, William. It is your own. My brother's daughter, my niece, was married to a very distant relation in England. She bore only one child, a son, and shortly after passed away. Her son followed her several years after and his father, in an act of kindness and mercy, took in his newly orphaned nephew as heir."

The hair on the back of Williams's neck and arms stood up on end and he rubbed at the nape reflexively. "If I understand correctly, my Lord, my aunt was…"

Lord David turned from the window, tears streaking his cheeks and his voice broke as he spoke. "My only child and the blessing of my eyes." His breathing was rattled and he continued to keep his arms folded across his chest.

"Your inheritance as heir to your uncle and future Earl of Dorchester, William, will include the dowry we sent with Marie… a good portion of our holdings in the Somme valley. Lady Helen's acceptance of our grandson's proposal gives her rights to the rest, as he was the sole remaining heir of our own estate. But as an unmarried woman it will pass up to her father's family. Now the de Simpson's have lost all they were once entrusted to care for, and will soon lose the rest when we are both gone."

Now William began to understand. Or at least he told himself he understood. Then Lord Matthew spoke again and he found himself completely dumbfounded.

"The French courts will look upon the letter and Lady Helen's acceptance as a betrothal. There is no doubt in this as it has precedence. What we propose however does not." He stopped and looked once more at his brother. Lord David had wiped the tears from his cheeks and dried his eyes but they were still red and puffy. He sniffled loudly and nodded to his older brother. "You said it yourself, William, *vivo servire.* As a de Simpson, we all live to serve. This is how you can serve us."

A long moment later William couldn't believe what he had been asked to do. And he wasn't the only one in the room who felt that way. Helen had almost immediately stood, shouting her protests over Lord Matthew's plan. William looked to his teacher for guidance but Robert was as shocked as his student and gave no indication on how he should respond. For the first time since they had left Dorchester, William felt alone and without counsel.

"God, give me the wisdom I need and the understanding in order to make the right decision." He closed his eyes as he prayed this simple prayer and then took a deep breath and as he let it out, he thanked God for His presence.

Helen's protests were just as loud, and Lord Matthews's dry voice was still answering each of her concerns with long, well thought out responses. And yet William was able to stand there, totally at peace. He knew there was only one way he could be this calm; God was at his side. His word said He would never leave William nor forsake him and here He was. He was a comforter, a voice of wisdom and strength just when he needed each.

"I believe there may be another way." He didn't say it loud, but there was a conviction in his voice, which turned all heads to him. "I believe there is another way, but first I must have permission from Lady Helen to reveal a secret she entrusted to me." He turned to Helen and stared into her dark blue eyes. Their color this morning reminded him of the water in the Channel during the storm. Her face was flushed and she was taking rapid breaths, as if she had just been running. He tried his best to tell her to trust him, without saying a word.

They stood there, staring at each other for a long moment. Finally Helen nodded and murmured, "You have my permission, William."

He smiled, trying to reassure her and took a deep breath to reassure himself. "If you did not name an heir, to whom would your lands and title go?"

"All of these lands were given as part of the dowry of Princess Isabella when she was married," David answered gruffly. William nodded. He had remembered Robert telling something similar just a few days before, while crossing the channel. "Through her they will become English at her passing." This also did not surprise William.

"And if there was a way for Lady Helen to inherit these lands without marriage and not forfeit it to her father's family?"

"What you suggest is impossible, William," Lord Matthew began. His dry voice was raised slightly in his agitation. "The only way she could possibly do this is if she was the daughter of…" His watery eyes widened as the thought sprung to him. For the very first time, since she had been visiting his home all those years, Lord Matthew turned and looked on Lady Helen and perceived the truth. "Highness," he muttered, bowing as deeply at his waist as he could at his age. His brother stood struck dumb, shaking his head with his mouth slightly open.

"Not Highness my Lord. No title for me. Just Helen d'Abbeville." She had moved towards him as he realized the truth and she saw he wasn't repulsed by the thought. She sincerely had believed people would label her or worse, shun her when they found out. He reached out and took her hand and covered it with his own. Despite the fact they were rough and dry, Helen smiled at the old Lord who had always been so kind to her.

"No not Highness, nor princess. No matter your parentage, you have always had a place in our home. Now our home and that place are both secure."

Tears began to freely spill down Helen's cheeks. She really didn't believe she would have been accepted like this. As soon as she found out her parentage, she was convinced any joy in life had ended. Now she found acceptance in this home. It was almost too much to bear. She smiled through the tears, thanking Lord Matthew for the continued kindness.

"There is only one problem which I see, my Lord," Robert suggested. He instantly had everyone's attention. "The Queen Mother has never acknowledged Helen's existence and therefore Helen has been given no inheritance or title, as you pointed out Lady Helen." He added the last thought and bowed to Helen in the process.

"This is true," began Lord David. He had finally recovered from the initial shock and was beginning to work out the problem in his mind. Although Lord Matthew held the title and lands, it was his younger brother who had come up with the idea in the first place. "But where there is a will, there is a way." He smiled a gap-toothed smile and William found himself doing the same, although he did not know why.

"There is something you know that I do not, my Lord," William responded, still smiling. His tutor had told him, what seemed like ages ago but was really just over ten days, that the simple act of smiling would make any problem seem easier, any load lighter. He was, once again, correct.

"There is indeed, William. There is indeed." He continued to smile while tapping the side of his nose. William wasn't sure what that meant but as he stared intently at his distant, elderly relative, an idea began to dawn on him. Without realizing it, he spoke it out loud.

"The Queen Mother is in France." William stated it as fact and as soon as he saw the expression change on Lord David's face, he knew it was. One moment the old Lord was smiling and even slightly smug and the next moment he looked as shocked as he had moments ago when he learned of Helen's heritage.

"Lady Helen! Help!" William turned to see Lord Matthew reaching out to catch Helen as she collapsed onto the floor, her eyes rolled back in her head. He and his tutor got to her at the same time and they caught her at the shoulders and waist and gently laid her down on the hearthrug.

William could see she was still breathing but her color looked even more pale than usual. He grabbed one of the blankets Helen had brought down for them the night before and quickly rolled it up and propped up her head.

"David, pour a small glass of the Brandy we were given by Lord Henri in Burgundy last year," Lord Matthew suggested.

"Brandy, my Lord?" William asked.

"Never fear lad, it will do the task and restore the fire." The old lord rubbed her hands gently and murmured to himself, "she is as cold as ice, but just a sip will warm her to flush."

David returned with a small glass holding a deep amber liquid. William caught just a hint of the aroma, as it was handed to Lord Matthew and he immediately thought of wine, but more than just wine. There was sharpness, pungency and a clarity he had never seen in a wine before. "*Aqua Vitae*, William," his tutor explained. "That is what the Romans called it. Water of life; the spirit separated from wine. Very strong and aged for years and meant to be sipped and savored."

Helen's eyes fluttered and then opened. It took her a moment to focus on their faces, collect her thoughts, and realize she was lying on the floor with all four men in the room hovering over her. "I must have gotten a little light headed," she muttered and then her eyes betrayed her thoughts as she remembered what had troubled her in the first place.

"Try just a sip of this Lady Helen," Lord Matthew suggested and offered her the glass. Helen took one sniff, smiled and took, what appeared to William, a very large gulp. She closed her eyes and the smile stayed on her lips as a bright flush rose up her cheeks.

"Thank you my Lord. I feel much better now." She took a deep breath of the fresh breeze blowing in through the window and sighed. "I knew there would come a day when I would find my mother. I had dreamed of it often as a small child. Now that I find myself confronted with the very opportunity and I am not sure I am ready."

"Any time we are confronted with unanswered questions and unresolved doubts and concerns about our family it can affect all of our decisions greater than we expect, my lady," Robert advised. "Look no farther than the Christ's parable about the wayward son and his eventual return home."

"I have often thought of that story," Helen admitted. Her color was returning to normal after the flush of the brandy and her breathing was steady. "I imagined I was like the son who was gone, only it was not my decision to go. I had been sent away. None the less, would my return home be met with the same joy and celebration as his?"

"God gave each one of us free will, my lady," Robert answered. William noticed how closely both his elder relatives were following the conversation. "Without free will, there would be no love in the world."

"God wanted us to choose Him; to make it our own decision," William added. Without realizing it he was repeating some of the same conversation he and his tutor had in the New Forest. "The only problem is free will allows each one of us the choice to do evil, just as easily as good. You cannot eliminate one without taking the other with it."

"The Queen Mother has this same choice when she sees you, Lady Helen," Robert continued. "Although there is no doubt in my mind how she will respond, it will still come down to her free will and her decision." He paused briefly, then added, "Always remember your decision in the channel. God will never leave you nor forsake you and He will be with you even when you meet your mother for the very first time. If you find yourself feeling weak and unsure, call on Him and He will come to aid you."

"I do not want her to turn away from me again," Helen muttered quietly to herself. They had helped her up from the floor and she was seated in the chair Robert had slept in. Her hands were folded in her lap and her head was bowed. "After all these years I am worried she will not acknowledge me…"

"Do not center on your anxieties, Lady Helen," Robert gently corrected her. He moved slowly, knelt on one knee before her, and took both her hands in his own. She looked into his slate grey eyes as he spoke to her. "You must learn to guard your thoughts and think and speak what you want, not what you do not want. The words you speak come from your thoughts and will determine your circumstances. Too many people look to their lives and try to change them without changing the thoughts which led them there."

"So I could think my way out of this problem?" She asked.

"Yes and no," Robert answered. "In James' letter, the Lord's brother tells us when we find ourselves going through trial or troubles, they were not sent by God. God does not test us. Those troubles are in our lives because of our sinful nature. Because we failed to guard and take captive all our thoughts, we find ourselves going through these things. The first step then is to change the way you think and what you think about, but there is more than just that. You also need to pray to God and ask Him to forgive you of any sins in your life, and, at the same time, ask Him for His wisdom. Then you need to act on what He is leading and guiding you to do. In the end the outcome is according to His will- nothing more, nothing less, and nothing else."

"I do not see how I could guard every single thought that goes through me," she murmured, shaking her head slowly.

"God will not expect of you any more than He knows you are capable of handling," Robert answered. There was such a conviction and sincerity in his voice that even William sat up and noticed. It was as if he was hearing this again for the first time. "Paul says we can do this by renewing our minds every day."

"How do I do that?" Helen asked.

"By reading and studying His word, Lady Helen." Robert's answer was made in such a way no one doubted his sincerity. "You will not learn to do this by only going to mass on Sunday and listening to the priest once a week. In order to change how you think, and win the battle of the voices of doubt, fear and indecision you hear, you need to read and apply what you are reading. You have to put an effort behind it. It is not wise to simply sit and wish and hope and dream. You need to get up and be a doer. Doers are blessed. Without doing something to back it up, what you believe in and what you have faith in will die."

William stood for a long moment in the silence which followed. He'd had several discussions with his tutor over similar subjects, both before and after leaving Dorchester, but none of those came across as straightforward. "It seems so simple when you put it that way," he found himself saying out loud.

"God's plan for our lives *is* simple, William. We are the ones who complicate it."

"How can I know what He wants from me and my life?" Helen asked cautiously. Her voice sounded hurt and hopeful simultaneously.

"Take time in the morning to speak to God," Robert suggested.

"I would not know what to say," Helen muttered.

"Just talk to him as you would a parent or someone who deeply cares for you, because He is both. We were created for this relationship. You can look all the way to the beginning in the garden. God created us in His likeness, not to serve Him, but to build a relationship with Him. Once you start, you will find yourself looking forward to those moments of quiet connection you have with God. Ask Him for the wisdom to know which direction to take. In the letter from James we are told, if we need wisdom we should ask for it and God will give it to us." William nodded in agreement.

"Lady Helen, I was taught the same thing, days after leaving Dorchester," William added. "If you will ask me, I will tell you it was the best advice I received so far. Without that connection and His willingness to give us wisdom when we ask for it, I could not imagine where we would be."

Helen took a deep breath and nodded. Just the barest part of a smile crossed her lips and her eyes lit up just a little. "Thank you for the advice and the counsel," she said to Robert and then turned to their hosts. "And thank you both for the kindness and hospitality you have shown myself and my traveling companions. Their journey will take them to Amiens next. But I am not sure where I should go, or if, perhaps, I should remain here for a time."

Neither brother spoke but they caught each other's eye and held the other's gaze for a moment. Finally David nodded and Matthew cleared his throat. "If I may give some advice, Lady Helen, I would continue traveling with our cousin and his tutor."

"It was our plan to continue on to Amiens, hopefully to find my guardians at their home on the canal. Now I am not sure I should continue there, or if I should instead seek out my mother and her blessing." Helen paused a moment and considered what she said. Suddenly a thought struck her. "Do you know where my mother stays?"

"Not precisely… no," David began. He cleared his throat and tried again. "It is mostly rumors and thoughts spoken out loud and overheard."

He halted and paused. His brother finished his thought. "These would all suggest she is with England's peace envoy."

"She *is* King Philip's cousin." A thought struck her like lightning. "And he is the King of France…" The reality of the thought was still very slow to sink in. She shook her head, her mouth open slightly and her eyes stared, unfocused, into the fireplace.

"And your brother is King of England," William added.

"Which makes you, at the same time, very powerful and in great danger," Robert advised. "There are forces at work who either wish to use you for their own ends or remove you from their plans. Whichever step you take, whichever direction you proceed, will be filled with difficulties and dangers."

"What would you suggest I do? Stay here in hiding for the rest of my life?"

"No my lady," Robert answered, shaking his head. "We must be doers. We must move forward but we must do so, knowing danger lies there."

"The best way to avoid a trap is to know of its existence." Lord David muttered, as if giving counsel to himself, not realizing it was the same advice given by Robert to William just a few days before.

"As you say, my Lord," Robert agreed, bowing slightly and then turned back to Helen. "I do not counsel rushing into harm's way with no thought to your safety. What I suggest is to realize there are dangers ahead, perhaps even more so than what lies behind, but moving forward, know there is no weapon formed against you which shall prosper. God even prepares a table for you in the presence of your enemies. These are His words and His promises."

"I can do all things through Christ my Lord, who strengthens me…" Helen quietly stated, then stood up straight and took in deep breath. "This still does not explain why I should continue to Amiens if it is my mother who I seek, unless… The peace envoy is in Amiens, is it not?" Helen felt her heart skip even as she spoke.

"Those are the rumors, my lady," Lord Matthew bowed, deeply, at the waist and when he stood he looked graver than they had seen him. "I would caution you on this quest, Lady Helen. I do not pretend to understand what manner of men would want to use you or remove you, but I do see danger ahead, even as it lies behind. I fear for your safety and…" His voice trailed off without completing the sentence.

"The future hope of the de Simpson family in France stands before you, my Lord," William stated. "I have already taken one oath to do all I can to protect Lady Helen, and here, in your presence I repeat that oath. I will not back down nor shy away from danger but will do all in my power to keep Lady Helen safe."

"As will I," His tutor added. "I will also do all in my power to keep William safe, as heir of the Earl of Dorchester and inheritor of Lady Marie's dowry."

"I would expect nothing less of a de Simpson, nor his household," Lord Matthew stated, and then paused, as if realizing what he had said. His expression became somber and sad as he turned to the hearth and stared at the slowly dying embers. "It occurs to me just now, how little we have done to maintain our side of the family estates these last two years." When William tried to interrupt, the old Lord waved him off.

"We will not deny it and I will not hear excuses for it. My own eyes failed to see what hope the future bore for our family. Now, the two of you return hope to our home."

"The hope you speak of was always here, my Lord," Lady Helen advised. Her voice carried a tremendous amount of emotion and it startled William into turning to face her. All eyes followed William's to see her no longer head bowed or downcast. She stood with shoulders back and head held high and there was a brilliant clarity and sparkle in her eyes, which seemed to catch the sunlight coming in through the open windows.

"What hope have we missed, Lady Helen?" Lord Matthew asked.

"The same as I, my Lord. The hope and the promise of God's own words, which tell us He is near the broken hearted. He will never leave us nor forsake us and we are capable of all things, including living beyond our grief, because Christ is our strength. It was these two men and their genuine walk of faith which restored my own and called to mind God's grace, which He had freely given and I simply needed to freely receive."

"When did this happen Lady Helen?" Lord David asked.

"While aboard ship in the channel. When the fear of shipwreck and death at sea seemed so utterly real I could not imagine any escape. I accepted God's grace, accepted His salvation and was immediately given a peace, which I cannot describe. Even as the storm continued to rage, I no longer was worried. I finally understood what Paul meant when he wrote, 'and my God shall supply all of my needs through His glory and riches in Christ Jesus.' This was not a sermon from the pulpit, this was real life."

"I have not had the sleep of peace since they left to join Philip in

Abbeville," Lord Matthew admitted. His younger brother nodded his agreement.

"Do you want that peace, my Lord?" Helen asked. A wonderful smile broke across her face and not only did her eyes shimmer, it seemed her entire complexion glowed. William couldn't help but feel a chill march up his spine and the hairs on the back of his neck stand on end.

"I would give all I have for it," Lord Matthew answered.

"And I as well," his brother added.

William watched as this young woman, who he had only met a few days before, helped lead these two noble gentlemen into a personal relationship with God. All their life they had believed in God, and attended mass, and followed the sacraments, but for the first time they truly put their trust in Him. The transformation was immediate. To William it looked as if a great weight they each carried was lifted. They stood taller and smiled, just as Helen did. He would never forget those smiles. Suddenly, William was on that hill in Dorchester, beside his mother's grave that morning he made his own decision. The joy and peace he saw in their faces reflected the same in his.

"For too long we have mourned the passing of those who have gone to God before us. I see now we have not honored their memory with our actions."

"But we will still honor those who have fallen," Lord David stated and his older brother nodded, but no longer looked grave.

"Honor them in memory and now in deed, brother." Lord Matthew smiled and rubbed his thin, wrinkled hands together, turning to face his younger sibling. "It is time we get to work. Much has been neglected." He started to walk away; Lord David close behind and then paused, as if realizing he still had guests standing in his parlor. "The tide has receded again and it will be several hours before it rises and swells the Somme.

Rest now. Break your fast. I will make sure there is food set out within the hour. Walk about the village if you wish. Our house and our grounds are at your disposal… you are family, after all." He smiled again and this time a bit of mischievousness twinkled in his pale blue eyes, as if saying he would have offered the same before but wouldn't have meant the same by it. "Soon after sunset," he continued, "the tide will begin to return and you may depart for Amiens. If all goes well, you should see the cathedral's fleche at dawn tomorrow."

He turned once more and they both quickly strode from the room. It appeared to William as though several years had fallen from the elderly lords in the last few moments. Lord Matthew's shoulders were back, his head held high and his stride had purpose. His voice, as he called out for the staff, seemed to come from a younger man and no longer carried with it a sense of death and decay.

Lord David turned just as quickly to the front doorway and they could hear him calling to the several members of the household outside. William smiled and when he turned to his tutor he was happy to see his approval. Robert smiled then turning to Helen, he bowed as the waist, stating, "It is a very brave and noble thing you did, my lady."

Helen smiled and quietly answered, "Brave or not, it is something I had to do. It was something I knew I could tell them because it was real to me."

Robert nodded and smiled again. "Heaven has gained two more souls because of your obedience. Because His word says so, I believe your faith pleases God Himself." Turning to William but addressing both, he continued, "Can there be any doubt in either of your minds that God's presence in anyone's life will bring with it a peace which surpasses all understanding?" They both shook their heads while smiling similar smiles. "Then remember this day. God's word tells us to create memorial stones, to write these down so we will never forget what He has accomplished in us and through us. Also," and now he grabbed William by the shoulder and took Helen gently by the hand. His young student knew exactly what this meant. Here was a lesson he must commit to memory, to be ready to pass along to the next generation. "Never forget it is Christ's death and resurrection, which makes all this possible. Without His sacrifice, death, and rebirth, we would never find ourselves capable of entering into God's presence. It is Christ and He alone, not our works or our good deeds or our effort. That is the ultimate sacrifice and the ultimate free gift."

William closed his eyes, nodding his understanding and said a silent prayer of thanksgiving to God and Jesus for all they have done for him and all they continue to do for him. He also prayed for his uncle, for the mother and her daughters who they rescued in the New Forest and for Gilbert. *"Father God, watch over them all. Keep them safe. Let no weapon formed against them prosper. Amen."* When he opened his eyes he noticed Helen and his teacher both looked as if they had also just finished their own silent prayers.

Seconds later one of the kitchen staff brought in a tray filled with some crusty bread, cheeses, a few dried apples and ham. Three glasses and an earthenware pitcher filled with what looked like ruby claret rounded out the assortment. Robert rubbed his hand together, smiling toothsomely, "anyone else hungry?"

Chapter Twenty Three

They broke their fast in blissful silence. Each one lost in his or her own thoughts while completely enjoying the simple yet wonderful food they were provided. They had left the window open and the late morning sunshine carried with it the sound of songbirds on the breeze. The heavy curtains, as well as the large tapestry beside the hearth, moved gently in the air.

William hadn't noticed the scene depicted in the detailed stitching until just then. It was a boy, perhaps a squire, standing over a fallen knight. The tapestry must have been very old, for the arms and armor worn by both were in common use several hundred years before. The youth held a sword and shield, protecting the stricken chevalier. The knight's destrier stood next to the youngster. Together they looked as if they would take on all comers. Snowy peaks stood stark in the background as the two found themselves in a high mountain pass.

"Do you know why your family motto is *vivo servire*?" Robert asked. He had noticed William studying the tapestry. His young student shook his head. "Do you recognize the history of the tapestry?" Again he shook his head. His teacher took a deep breath and sighed heavily. "This may take some time, but it involves a story of your family, long before William of Normandy set sail for England."

Now William sat up alert. He was always interested in his family history, especially when it surrounded events whose recording would require the commissioning of a tapestry such as this. He didn't notice, as his attention was fixed on his tutor, but Helen's own interest was piqued and she remained seated around the small table, slowly picking at the remaining crumbs of cheese and bread before her.

"After the fall of Rome, a darkness fell over its once mighty empire. All things good and bright seemed to vanish overnight and for several hundred years petty kings, no more than local lords, fought amongst themselves and the remains of Rome's once mighty colonies; Francia, Germania and Hispania. Out of these, one stood higher than the others and eventually created a line of kings, named after himself, Charles Martel."

"I have heard of him," William stated. His love of history was bubbling to the surface and he leaned forward, nearly across the table, taking in everything his teacher mentioned. "He was king of the Francs, was he not?"

"King in all the power but not in name, William." Robert corrected. "Charles was named Mayor of the Palace of the Merovingian kings, giving him all the powers of the government. The kings were called rois fainéants, the do-nothing kings, because of the decline of their power. His son, Pepin, succeeded Charles, but it is Pepin's son who you will more quickly recognize. Carolus Magnus, or Charlemagne."

"Your family is related to Charlemagne?" Lady Helen blurted out. There was shock and surprise in her voice. Robert quickly corrected her.

"I have not yet revealed the identity of the youth in the tapestry, nor the circumstances surrounding it, nor even the origin of the family motto. And I certainly have not yet suggested the de Simpson family is somehow related to one of the great kings in this country's history."

"No, of course not," Helen's eyes looked down and for a brief moment William thought he might have seen even a little disappointment. "I am sorry I interrupted, please continue."

Robert smiled, "As you wish, my lady. Charlemagne was a great leader and mighty warlord and fought campaigns in France, Italy, Saxony and Spain. It was while leaving Spain, we find the subject of the tapestry. If you look close enough you see the Great Pyrenees Mountains in the background. The young lad and the warhorse stand over the fallen knight in a mountain pass. It was not a great battle which took place that ill-fated day, but rather an ambush and small skirmish."

"A small battle would hardly seem worthy of the time and effort to make this tapestry, would it not?" William asked.

"It would, if this had been any other day. But on that particular day, as fate would have it, some of the best and bravest of Charlemagne's knights fell."

"What was the name of the pass?" Helen asked quietly. Her mouth had dropped open and her eyes were passing back and forth from William to the tapestry.

"I think you know already, my lady. It was Roncevaux Pass."

"Roncevaux…" she muttered. "The very pass where Roland fell?"

"The very same, my lady," Robert answered. "And not just Roland. Falling beside him were some of the kings most trusted and exalted knights, including the Mayor of the Palace and the Count Palatine."

"How did this happen?" William asked.

"The king's campaign in Spain did not go as well as he had hoped and so he turned back to France. All which stood between him and home were the Pyrenees. What he did not realize was the people who lived among the rocks and crevices, the Vascones, had set up an ambush for him. As soon as the majority of the army passed over, they set upon the rearguard."

"Is there any way the king could have known ahead of time about the ambush?" William asked his tutor. Robert shook his head.

"I know what you ask William, and you are right. The best way to avoid a trap is to first know of its existence. King Charlemagne had subdued the Vascones in an earlier battle and felt secure in their defeat. What he failed to realize, or may have never known, was this people's ability to stubbornly remain free. Even during Roman occupation and its conquest of Gaul, these people paid no tribute to the Emperor. The Pyrenees and the Vascones are best left to themselves; that is the advice given today. The King did not know this, or ignored it. Either way he paid for it with the loss of his best men."

"And the boy in the tapestry?" Helen asked.

"When the Vascones attacked the rearguard, they created such confusion in the army they were able to completely sack the baggage train. Nothing was left. They took all the plunder, gold and silver they could carry and then set out to defile the bodies of the fallen warriors. When they came upon the Lord of the Breton March, they found, standing over him, a young boy and his warhorse. As the tapestry shows, the lad had taken up the lord's sword and shield, even though he was not familiar with their use."

"Was he a squire to the Lord Roland?" William asked.

His tutor shook his head. "No, William, he was not. He was a simple peasant, a lad from the baggage train who did not flee or get killed with the rest, but was willing to stand his ground and defend the King's best man, despite the impossible situation." William's eyes dropped and he lowered his head slightly. This was the first time he had heard the de Simpsons had not always been noble.

Robert noticed his students' slight change in posture, "Never worry of your family's origin, William. All noble families have a humble beginning. The problem is, most of them forget and lose their humility. Remember what comes after pride?" William nodded his understanding. He knew a fall would always come when pride took precedence but he still felt some disappointment.

"When the Vascones turned their attention on the fallen knights, as I said, they found the boy and the destrier guarding the bodies," Robert continued. "The hill people laughed and mocked the lad. When he continued to stand his ground, they asked him why he would die to protect one who had already passed over. His answer was simple; *vivo servire*; I live to serve, even if those I serve no longer live."

"He does not sound like a peasant," William muttered. Despite his disappointment in discovering his family origin, he sat in awe at what his ancestor must have felt as he stood facing such a force. "He had to know there was no hope…"

"Perhaps he did, William. In either case, although the Vascones closest to him laughed and taunted him, their leader, Lop the Duke of Vasconia, silenced them. 'Why do you stand and protect those who have already fallen?' he asked the boy, repeating what his men had already asked.

"These knights deserve a Christian burial and even though they are your fallen enemy they should still command your respect. I am a servant of the king and will continue to serve until my Lord releases me… or death takes me." He spoke with such authority the Duke was shocked into silence. For a long moment he stood, leaning upon his short spear, carefully studying the boy before him. Finally, he called for his troops to withdraw and they melted into the night, as if they had never been. The Duke saluted the boy and turned, leaving him alone, even as King Charlemagne arrived with the vanguard.

"The King was beside himself with grief when he saw the field; the baggage train destroyed and the loss of so many of his most trusted knights and Lords. Within your family it is told he quoted Leviticus when he said, 'Five of you shall chase one hundred and one hundred of you shall put ten thousand to flight and your enemy shall fall before you by the sword.' He fell to his knees and wept for the loss of life, and ordered all memory or tales of the Spanish campaign cast aside, save one. He never forgot the boy, standing beside Lord Roland's horse, the only defense given to his fallen comrade's body; defying even Duke Lop himself. He honored that memory, and the bravery it exemplified, by knighting the boy on the field of battle and giving his family some small amount of land near the mouth of the Somme. He knelt at the king's feet, still holding Lord Roland's sword and shield and took the oath. He arose as Sir Bernard, Simeon's son."

William and Helen sat quietly for some time, each lost in their own thoughts. It was Helen who spoke first. "Was Eaucourt a part of that inheritance?"

Robert shook his head. "No, my lady. The sons of Simeon have always done well through marriage and have steadily added to their French holdings since the time of Charlemagne. They acquired Eaucourt many years later." He turned to his student and studied his face for a moment, trying to read his thoughts. "What troubles you, William?" he asked.

He tried his best to put it into words. "I guess I thought we had always been a noble family."

"Many noble families started with simple beginnings. And many of those, if they chose to look back far enough would find their entrance into nobility under much less noble circumstances." He paused to see if his student really understood what he had just said. He noticed Helens demeanor change slightly and he was pretty sure she knew where her family line could be traced. To make a point and settle both of them, he added, "You do realize, our own Duke of Normandy, your namesake and the first Norman king of England had his own inglorious beginnings."

His young pupil nodded his understanding. He had learned long before of King William's parentage; his mother was a member of his father's household, not noble born, unmarried to the father of her child. "It just feels different, knowing it is my own family line. Somehow, it feels less like we were meant to be the Lords of Eaucourt and Earls of Dorchester and more like it was mere chance…"

"It was not chance which placed your distant relative as part of the baggage train, in that pass, to witness the ambush. Nor was it chance which prompted him to stand and not run. There is a reason for everything under heaven, William. Never forget that. Even those things we see as evil, God can and will turn around for good."

"I know He does not cause the evil of the world," William stated.

"You are right, William. He does not. There is evil in the world because, as the bible tells us, this is a fallen world. For a time, the lord of the earth is the fallen angel and his followers. They will do all they can to stand in the way of God and His followers. If it was their plan to cause the ambush in the hopes of killing the king's most trusted knights, what they did not plan was one young boy standing up for the right, despite the desperate situation. That alone should give you great joy and hope, for that would mean he was meant to be there; he was placed there by God and given the opportunity to show God he could be trusted."

"What was he trusted with?" Helen asked curiously.

"We are all given, sometimes daily, opportunities to show God we can be trusted with the task set before us. Sir Bernard was given the opportunity to stand for what was right, despite the overwhelming odds against him. God gave him the choice to stand or to run and he chose to stand. As we grow in our walk in His way and He sees He can trust us in small ways, He will slowly increase the size of the opportunities to match our abilities. Never forget this, William, or you Lady Helen; God will not give you a challenge greater than you are capable of handling. Follow Paul's advice and count it all joy, thanking God for adversity and for abundance. When you can gladly do both, without fear or reservations, you are on the right path."

"If he was meant to be there, then are we meant to be here?" Lady Helen asked.

"There is no doubt in my mind, my lady. Consider what you just did and where you led the Lords of Eaucourt; could there be any doubt in your mind God wanted you here?" Robert paused a moment to let them both consider what he had just explained. Finally, he asked one further question. "Perhaps it is best if you both think on what it means to be noble. Only when you truly understand its meaning will you be ready for its responsibility." He pushed back from the table and stood while looking at the two young people before him. "I will take our host's offer and walk about the grounds of the village. I feel the need for fresh air and to stretch my legs." He bowed at the waist, "I will return for the evening meal." With that he turned and left the room. A moment later they heard the front door of the hall open and then close.

William found himself alone with Helen and it made him a little uncomfortable. He had a lot to think about and wanted some time alone. When he glanced at Helen it seemed to him she felt the same way. "If I follow the stairwell up, will it lead to the parapet?" He had remembered her telling him the day before of her walking it with Geoffrey.

She nodded, being careful not to meet his gaze. "Follow the stairs to the last landing. There you will find a ladder, which will lead you to the summit." Helen paused a moment and added sadly, "it is a wonderful view."

"Thank you, my lady. If you care to join me…"

"I think not," Helen snapped, then added more gently, "thank you, William, for the offer. I would like some time alone to think."

"As you wish," He replied as he rose and bowed, then turned and left her to her own thoughts.

•••

There were four flights of stairs William ascended before reaching the ladder and the roof beyond. By the time he made it, he was out of breath. He hadn't realized how fast he was taking the steps, having become lost in his own thoughts as soon as he reached the first landing. A debate had arisen within him, and before he realized it, he had become entangled in it.

Why had Helen reacted so strongly when Lord Matthew and David proposed she should marry him in order to keep the land in their family? Was the thought of being with him that abhorrent? Deep down, a part of him wanted to believe she desired to be with him, but the way she spoke this morning pushed that far to the side. Now that she knew the origin of his family she certainly wouldn't want anything to do with him. *"Of course she would not,"* he thought.

Even as he worked his way up the staircase, he remembered he was supposed to be thinking about what it means to be noble. Another thought entered his head. If he really were noble, wouldn't Helen want to be with him? Wouldn't his true nobility show through, such that she would have no doubt of its authenticity? *"If you really were noble you would know what it means to be such,"* he thought. *"You would not have to waste time standing on the top of a pitiful water tower hoping to somehow discover the truth. You would just know."*

William felt an anger growing inside as he reached the final landing and came to the ladder. Why did he need to know what it meant to be noble? What was the point of this ridiculous exercise? He was the heir to the Earl of Dorchester. It had already been decided and decreed by his uncle. Whether old age or injury takes him, after his uncle's death, he would be the next.

The last landing was very dark. No torches were set in the sconces but William didn't mind. A dark space matched his dark thoughts. Just as quickly as he had taken the stairs he mounted the ladder and began climbing. He reached the top and threw back the hatch. Sunlight flooded the opening and he squinted in the bright light. Pulling himself up onto the open summit, William lay a moment on his back, catching his breath and allowing the sun to warm his face.

The brilliance brought a tear to his eyes and he wiped it away with his sleeve. A thought hit him. He wasn't sure if it was something he had read or heard, but it resonated with him, *"I am the light of the world; my light will shine before men."* This was his role in life. No matter how he felt or what others might think, this was his task.

Suddenly he realized what had just happened. He had failed to guard his thoughts. The disappointment was still there and some of the anger, but it was quickly fading as he realized the truth. No matter what the circumstances or even the results; he was created to be a light towards others. This was what it meant to be noble. This was why his family motto was so much more important than most. To live to serve and not to be served were Jesus' own words. His desire was to have His followers follow His own example. His family had a responsibility to lead and at the same time they were meant to serve.

Could he do both? Could he be a servant and a leader? He had never heard anyone talk of this before. How could you lead and be a servant?

Didn't being a leader mean that others served you? Did the king serve anyone? Once more his thoughts turned to Jesus and His example. All of His good works were examples of serving, from washing His disciples' feet to feeding 5,000 hungry people. People followed Him because His words and His actions matched. He didn't come to set down a whole new set of rules and laws, He came to fulfill them all and set an example of how one man could change the world.

The sun continued to shine on William as he lay on the wooden roof of the tower. Tears, which first came from the brilliant light, now flowed freely. He no longer tried to wipe them from his face but allowed them to fall. Where moments ago there had been darkness and anger, now was joy. He smiled and then laughed out loud. "Count it all joy, William," he reminded himself aloud.

Whatever the outcome with Helen, he knew he would continue to find joy in his life. This is what God wanted from him. This was God's gift to Him. His gift back to God was what he decided to do with it. Lying in the sun on the top of the tower of Eaucourt, William decided he would live to serve. These were no longer just hollow words it was a lifelong commitment. "God, I will always serve You and those around me, no matter the outcome or consequence. I choose to serve; I choose this freely."

Another thought struck him as he lay there. This was the same commitment as the knights' oath. To do what was right, no matter the cost. To be a knight was to be noble and to be noble was to be a servant and a leader, so a knight must be a servant leader as well. This was why Charlemagne knighted his ancestor and gave him land. The king was simply giving title to what Bernard had already proven himself capable. As a young servant he understood how to care for others before himself;

and by standing up for what was right, no matter the cost, he showed he was willing to make the sacrifice all nobles may be called to make.

"God, grant me the strength to care for those around me, to do what is right, no matter the cost, and to follow You and Your example all my life. When I am weak, You are strong in me, Lord. God, I ask for Your continued wisdom, knowledge and understanding to guide me, all my days. Thank You, God for my nobility, passed on to me through my family. I pray You aid me as I strive to live up to that gift. Amen."

The sun slowly wheeled across the sky as he continued to lie there thanking and praising God. He lost track of time and fell asleep at least twice. Each time he awoke, William started out by thanking God for the life he had, the family he came from, and the guidance He was giving him. He made sure to add Gilbert, the mother and her daughters, Agnes, Robert, Helen, and his uncle in his prayers. Anyone who would have come out onto the roof would have found him, lying on his back, his head cradled in his right arm, eyes closed and smiling.

A ringing bell woke him from another stretch of slumber. The sun had passed low enough to create a notched shadow, mimicking the crenellations of the parapet. William was half lying in the shadow and he realized, once out of the sunlight he felt chilled. He wasn't sure if it was the loss of warmth from the setting sun or the shadow which woke him, either way he was happy to be so, and sat up, stretching. A moment later he made his way back down the ladder, onto the landing and down the stairs to the first floor.

When he arrived in the entry hall, he found Helen and his tutor already seated around the small table near the fireplace. The room still held a chill and a fire had been built up and was crackling in the open hearth. Most of the smoke found its way up the flue. Lords Matthew and

David were nowhere to be seen but the evening meal was already set. William made his apologies for being tardy and took his seat.

He didn't realize how hungry he was until the savory aroma from the roasted chicken, vegetables, and fresh bread caused his mouth to water and his stomach to growl audibly. He smiled and apologized for the second time. Robert bowed his head and blessed the food, passing the platter to Helen first. They ate in silence, relishing the deliciously prepared meal. Small pitchers of wine and water had been left for them and William found the blending of the two was best to lighten the intensity of the dark ruby, slightly tart vintage. The bread had a thick, crunchy crust with a warm, soft interior. Fresh butter was on the table but William didn't feel the bread needed it. Instead he moistened it by soaking up the juices from the chicken on his plate.

After quite a while with no more noise than the sound of eating and drinking, Robert pushed back from the table and let out a sigh of contentment. "Perhaps, when we return to Crandor, we can find a way to teach the cooks how to make such a meal." William smiled at the thought. Not just of eating such a meal at home but his eventual return. There was still so much to do and it seemed the closer they got to his uncle the more obstacles they had to overcome.

A comment his teacher made on the day he received the letter concerning his uncle's capture and ransom came back to mind. This dream or hope of his return to Dorchester, to a long life surrounded by those he cared for, would require more than he expected, more frequently given, and ultimately could cost more than he was willing to give. The sun on his face and the warmth of the rooftop was replaced by a colder reality. He still had a long way to go.

"What troubles you, William?" His tutor asked. He was watching his young student closely and could see the expression on his face change.

"I was remembering the conversation we had, outside Crandor on the day the courier arrived. You told me the cost of my vision of a peaceful future together at home would come at a cost and that cost would come sooner than I expected, would require repeated payments and may, eventually, cost more than I was willing to pay."

Robert nodded but his face was a mask. If William had happened to look into his eyes he would have seen trouble and even worry working their way inside. "Well remembered, William," he answered quietly. "Now, tell me what is troubling you."

"There have certainly been payments made already as we have worked toward our goal. Some of those were much more than I expected," he looked at his right hand and the pink, puckered, nearly sealed hole through it. "I know there is still a long way to go and I wonder what else I will have to pay before it is finished."

"Your return to Dorchester will not be the end, William, just the beginning of a new chapter. But that day is still far away. Paul tells us to not focus on tomorrow and its concerns, for today has troubles enough of its own. He is not suggesting we do not make plans, he simply points out the danger of such worrying. Men have sat still as stones, William, stuck because they were so worried about one decision over another and what may or may not happen. We are not to know all ends and all outcomes. Plan for the best and prepare for the worst and then go out and do something. Blessed are the doers. Never forget that."

William nodded his understanding. He had heard this now for the second time in two days and realized how important of a lesson it was.

Robert shifted his chair to face the fire and stretched out his legs. It also gave him a chance to turn away from his pupil's gaze. He hadn't shaved in several days and he scratched at the stubble, which grew in patches over his cheeks and neck. "I am curious what you discovered this afternoon, besides some time in the sun." William was pretty sure his tutor was smiling broadly. His face did feel a little warm and he was sure he would notice it more in the morning. "What do you think it means to be noble?"

He found himself staring at the tapestry for a moment. It seemed like the thoughts he had earlier had slipped his mind. He felt like he was trying to catch smoke in his hands. Finally he closed his eyes and remembered the warm sun on his face as he lay on the roof of the tower keep. His thoughts returned like a flood. "Any person can be noble in their thoughts, their words and their actions. When you put the care of others before your own, when you look for ways to serve them, with no thought to what they can do for you, you are expressing your nobility. A title may give a person certain benefits but it is what they do with the title which shows how much they want to benefit others."

"And why do you think King Charlemagne gave Bernard a title?"

"I think the king understood this, and realized my distant ancestor was so willing to live it out, even to the point of disregarding his own personal safety that he was already noble in thought and actions. He gave him a title, not because he deserved it, but because he already held it."

"Well done, William. If you can truly live this out, to serve others and think of their needs before your own, you will find yourself in a very small group. This is perhaps one of the hardest lessons to follow because it is our nature to think of ourselves first. The greatest heroes in the Bible are those who were able to live this way, although some of them for only short periods in their lives. None were perfect, save one, our Lord and Savior, Jesus Christ. Some came close though. Can you think of one example, William?"

For some reason, William immediately thought of the men and women he read about in the first five books of the Old Testament.

"Abraham," he answered. "Abraham followed God and trusted in His promises, even when everything around him suggested they were impossible. His thoughts were on God, not himself. He was even willing to sacrifice his only son, despite God's promise to make him a father of many nations. In the end, God saw how strong his faith was and rewarded him for it."

"There are very few people described as the friend of God. Abraham was one of those, William. He focused on what God wanted, which is one of the hardest types of nobility. To know and understand the will of God is difficult enough. To be able to disregard what everyone else around tells you, and to trust in God's still small voice is one of life's greatest tests and greatest rewards."

"How do you know if the voice you hear inside is God's?" Helen asked.

"The enemy likes to plant thoughts, lies, in your mind, this is true. He hasn't changed since the garden. So, how do you tell when it is God and not the enemy?" Robert restated. Helen had sat quietly throughout dinner, politely answering any questions posed to her, but seemingly in deep thought. Now she was focused on Robert and what he said. She nodded quickly, leaning forward, her hands clasped in her lap. "When you are still and quiet, ask God if the thought is from Him. He rarely answers audibly, but you will know. As a sheep to its shepherd, you will know His voice. His peace will come with the answer. It may not be what you want or what you expected, but, when it is His will, even if it is a challenge, He will give you the strength to overcome." His own eyes drifted back to the flames and he sat, quietly staring for some time.

Helen dropped her eyes and head and sat staring at her hands for a moment. "I know you asked us to think about what it means to be noble, but I am sorry, I spent the entire afternoon deciding what direction I should go from here." Normally her voice was strong and decisive but now it sounded small and timid. "Should I continue on to Amiens? Should I seek out my mother once I arrive? What if she will not acknowledge me? Is there another way than what my Lord de Simpson suggests?" She asked these questions in such quick succession she nearly ran out of breath by the last one and had to pause to inhale.

Before she could continue, William's tutor reached out and placed a hand on hers. Startled, she looked up into his slate grey eyes. "Be at peace child. Take a deep breath and let it out slowly." When she had done this, he continued. "God's peace is here for each of us. He even tells us, we have the peace which surpasses all understanding. No matter the situation, we know He will never leave us nor forsake us. You have that assurance, my lady."

"I am frightened and I do not know what to do next." For the first time she sounded like the wall she had put up around her had been taken down and she sat before them as a frightened young woman; nothing more. The emotion in her voice stirred something in William. Without thinking, he moved from his chair and knelt beside Helen's, placing his hands on his teachers and her own.

"We are here beside you, my lady. No matter what may happen, no matter the outcome, we are here." He smiled that smile she had seen on board the ship as they crossed the channel. It was a smile, which could light rooms and chase away dark thoughts. Despite the tears, Helen smiled too.

"Thank you, William. Thank you both." Now the tears flowed freely and her shoulders shook gently. "No one… no one could ask for better companions."

Robert leaned forward, placing his hand on William's shoulder and whispered in his ear, "and that, my young friend is true nobility."

Chapter Twenty Four

The braided leather thongs they used to bind Williams hands behind his back were tearing into his wrists. When he first awoke, his initial struggle seemed to only make them bite harder. Since then he lay still, slowing his breathing and quieting himself in order to focus on what he remembered. His heart was pounding in his chest and he could hear it thrumming in his ears. He closed his eyes, but wherever he was, it was so dark, he could not tell the difference. He took a ragged, deep breath and slowly let it out. God had helped him through so much since leaving Dorchester. He would see him through this as well. With that thought in mind, he took another deep breath and did his best to remember the teaching he had just received on the use of his senses to help observe his surroundings. As he lay on the hard ground, William tried to piece together what had happened, and where he was.

•••

They had sat together like that, each holding the others hand, heads bowed, nearly touching, for a long moment. Lord David's sudden entrance into the room startled them. He was out of breath and his face was flushed. "You must hurry, please. Grab your packs and come quickly." When they sat, each staring at him, unmoving in their chairs, he added breathlessly, "the English are here!" As if to add extra emphasis, a bell began ringing somewhere in the village.

Helen sat frozen, her eyes wide with fear. William and Robert leaped to their feet, scooping up their packs in the process. "How many are there? Where have they come from? Do they know we are here?" Roberts' questions were shot off in rapid succession and Lord David did his best to answer, despite being out of breath.

"I do not know how many. A guard on the tower saw them coming up the road from Amiens. There are a dozen or more riders on horseback, coming with all haste. Please you must hurry or they will know you are here for sure!" With that, Helen shot out of her chair.

"I left a pack in the chamber upstairs…"

"I have it, my lady. Now, please, we must hurry before…" The bell rang faster and then a dull thud echoed through the tower. There was shouting outside in the courtyard. William thought he heard clash of arms as well. They were in the central chamber standing near the table at the base of the stairs. The sword and shield sat in the same place they had since the Battle of Crecy took their owners. William eyed both. Part of him wanted to take them and rush out the doors, despite his hand and its inability to hold the broken blade, while another part of him wanted to run and hide.

His tutor must have noticed his hesitation. "There is a time to stand and fight, William, and a time to ensure the safety of those you have sworn to protect. We must get Lady Helen to safety. Is there a postern door, Lord David?"

"Not for a tower such as this, but there is the servants' tunnel. Follow me quickly," he said over his shoulder as he led them past the staircase to a paneled portion of the wall. "This will take you to the kitchen and from there you can get back to your boat." He pushed on one section of the carved wooden trim and a door swung in on silent hinges.

"Watch your step, the hall is short and at the end there are stairs leading down to the tunnel. Follow it to the other stairs, which will lead back up to the kitchen and pantry of the keep. It is one of the outlying buildings. My brother and I will keep them occupied for as long as we are able."

"Thank you, my Lord," Helen and William spoke at the same time. Lord David smiled briefly then turned back to the door when the banging increased in frequency and intensity.

"Fly, now," he said over his shoulder as he stood up straight and pulled back his shoulders. He glanced back one last time but they didn't see him. They had already entered the short hall and closed the door behind them with a snap of its latch. It took a moment for their eyes to adjust to the dim light from the outline of the doorway.

"Stay close, Lady Helen. If you hold my pack I will lead the way. William, help her if she should stumble." His tutor set off slowly and within a few strides came to the top of the stairs. Candlelight flickered from below; otherwise he may have missed the top step. At the bottom of the stairs was a well-laid, straight, stone walled tunnel. A tallow candle sputtered in a niche in the wall. The air was cool and dry with just a faint mustiness. A dull thud echoed around them and they set off quickly down the long, straight passageway.

There were no turns and the walls were smooth, as was the well-worn floor. Despite moving as quickly and as quietly as they could, the sound of their breathing and three pairs of footfalls seemed to echo loudly in their ears. William kept glancing over his shoulder, but no one was following them. As the light from the first candle dimmed behind them, another before them took its place. It too sat in a niche at the bottom of a staircase. Robert paused and then began climbing, taking the steps slowly, judging each one to make sure it was solid. The second from the top creaked loudly when he placed his weight on it and he paused, in mid step, while each of them held their breath.

William counted heartbeats. When he got to fifty Robert shifted his weight to the step above. Helen and William each took a longer stride, skipping the tread when they came to it. At the top was another short hall, which ended with a door. Robert pushed on it, expecting it to swing open as in the keep, but it wouldn't budge. In the dim light he groped around until he found a cold, iron ring and the latch above. He was able to slowly pull back the bolt with little noise and then leaned forward, putting his ear to the door.

Another fifty heartbeats; they were still quicker than normal but his breathing was slow and steady. His tutor nodded and then slowly turned the ring. The door opened towards them and the bright light of lamps streamed in through the widening crack. For a brief moment William panicked. After traveling in the darkened tunnel it took time for his eyes to adjust. He squinted and blinked and finally was able to see into the room beyond his teacher.

They were looking in on the kitchen for the household of the Lords of Eaucourt. The hearth fire was bright and appeared as though wood had only recently been added. Sparks sputtered and popped, and above it a large kettle hanging from a hook was swung over the open flame. Various roots and vegetables were in different stages of chopping or peeling and sat on the cutting board, next to a pair of skinned hares.

Robert grabbed a small sack and quickly stuffed in it several carrots, a turnip, some beets, a half dozen dried apples, a wedge of cheese and a broken loaf of bread. He handed it to William and then headed to the door. "Lord David said we would be able to move from here to the landing, where our boat still sits. The sun is sinking fast and will cast shadows in which we can move. Dusk is the most difficult time for men to see. It plays tricks on their eyes. If we are quick and we are quiet we stand a chance of escape."

"Surely they will be watching the boat." Helen stated. Her voice was strained. "Will they not see us on the water?"

"There is a good chance, if these men do know you are here, they do not know how you arrived. We will have to trust God to watch over us, to be our shield and strength. When Lot and his family needed to escape from Sodom, God was able to blind the men who tried to harm and hinder them. He can do the same for us." With that he turned and made his way through the cluttered kitchen to the far door, which led out to the courtyard.

William's tutor paused and pressed his ear to the wood, his fingertips just touching its surface. It was as if he was straining all his senses towards whatever may be on the other side. He stood like that for a very long minute. Finally he let out a long, slow breath and nodded to himself. "The horses are in the courtyard but I do not hear any voices." He turned and looked at both William and Helen. "Remember; quick and quiet."

As his teacher turned the ring and pulled open the door, William wished he had a taken the sword which sat upon the table in the entry of the keep. Since he had not, he made a fist, remembering the same lesson he had recalled on that night in Salisbury. The fist only reminded him his right hand would be of little use. For a moment he had almost forgotten its injury. It seemed such a long time since they had set out from Crandor Castle. Now they were in France, nearly to Amiens, with a dozen English soldiers looking for the woman he had sworn to protect, probably standing right outside the door he was about to walk through. This certainly wasn't the path he expected to take in order to release his uncle.

The door opened noiselessly and Robert paused to peer into the fading sunlight beyond. Already long shadows were being cast across the courtyard and soon it would be covered in darkness. He could see the horses tethered across the yard near the tower, and stood silently for a long moment, allowing his eyes to adjust. His father had taught him long ago the key to seeing in the half dark; ignore details, and instead focus on movement. When the shadows play tricks, the mind's eye will still see movements within them. Long practice allowed him to look quickly about the courtyard and realize there was none beside the stamping, steaming horses.

William held his breath as his tutor stood in the doorway. Finally he turned and signaled both of them to follow. William could feel his heart pounding in his chest as he did his best to control his breathing. If he looked down he would have seen his hands shaking. Instead he made sure Helen and he kept to the shadows as they moved from building to building.

At least twice William was sure he heard footsteps behind them and he froze and turned to look over his shoulder. Both times there was no one there. Slowly they made their way toward a dark gap between two stone houses. The empty space held the way to the water's edge and their boat. It was the same gap they had entered through when they came up into the village the night before. William thought it was ironic that armed men had barred their way both into and out of Eaucourt.

Robert had been right. The only sound in the courtyard came from the horses, which were tethered near the keep. As they moved from shadow to shadow one or two of the horses would nip at another, which would set them neighing and tossing their heads. Nothing more than a horse normally would do when forced to stand still after a hard ride.

The moon slid out from behind a large cloudbank and bathed the courtyard in silvery light. All three froze. There was now only one house separating them from the opening to the river. Robert and Helen had moved ahead and were crouched in the doorway of the last home. Her hair looked nearly black and her face ghostly pale as she knelt next to his teacher in the shadows. She looked frightened as she tried to press herself as far as she could into the doorway.

William found himself stuck between the two buildings. The space from his corner to the doorway where Robert and Helen crouched was bathed in moonlight. If he tried to move, anyone would be able to see him. He took a deep breath and let it out slowly. From where he knelt he could tell his tutor and Helen still had shadows to move in and could make it the last several paces to the gap and river beyond. "*They should go now,*" he heard a strong voice say.

From where he knelt he waved his hand to get his teacher's attention. It took a few seconds but he finally conveyed the idea and was understood. He thought his tutor looked grim as he nodded and then whispered in Helen's ear. She shook her head but had to follow when he stood and began moving along the last portion of the wall and the gap beyond. As they slowly moved in the shadows, William looked up into the sky. The clouds had completely parted. There wouldn't be any shadow for him to move in for a very long time.

Robert paused at the corner of the house and turned back to his student. William mouthed the words, "go," and for emphasis moved his hands like he was brushing crumbs off a table. He nodded his understanding and slowly stood up, pulling Helen with him. Before they turned the last corner and disappeared, William watched as his teacher bowed at the waist. A second later they were around the end of the house and making their way down the path to the river's edge. "*God, watch over them and keep them safe.*"

He knelt there, between the two buildings for several long minutes. He counted 100 heartbeats five times and then decided it was safe to move. He couldn't go back through the tunnel, and he didn't want to draw attention to the river, so he decided he would make his way to the gate. He could see it standing open, almost directly across the courtyard. The only things separating them were a dozen horses, a wide yard and the tower.

There were no more shadows for him to hide in, so his choice was simple. If he wanted to get to the gate as quickly as possible, he would have to cross the open yard. He smiled as he knelt there, imagining himself simply walking through the open doors while the men searching for them were still inside the keep. With that picture in his head, he stood and strode out into the open.

The night was cool and there was a touch of breeze in the yard, but his heart was racing and his hands were sweating. He wiped them nervously on his hose and winced a little as the rough material scratched at the still tender wound on his right hand. There was enough early spring growth of the grass in the yard to make it soft and to muffle his steps but he still found himself nervously glancing from side to side.

It could have been pitch black and he would have known he was getting closer to horses. After having spent even a short time in the hold of the ship, he knew he would never forget that smell, or the look on Helen's face when he threw up. Now, with the open air and breeze the smell wasn't nearly as strong, but it was still there and it sparked a memory.

For a brief moment, as he walked across the yard, William's mind flashed back to a day when his father and uncle had joined several other men for a hunt. He recalled at least eight or ten horses in that group as well. They were excited and stamped at the ground in anticipation of the chase. The dogs were whining and straining at their leads, and, although the sun had risen, a dense fog still clung to the hills and dales of Dorchester. "Not yet, William," his father answered when he had asked if he could go with them. He remembered being hurt and even a little angry to be left behind. He had stomped off and hadn't even stayed to see them go. As he drew closer to the horses, it hit him that the next day his father left with his uncle and traveled north to fight the Scots. He never saw him again.

Tears fell down his cheeks as he passed by the first horse. The smell of their sweat, along with the dampness in the night air, had triggered the memory, which he had buried that day. His chest felt like it was caving in on itself and he couldn't catch his breath. He found himself leaning against the nearest horse, clutching at its tack, sobbing. He didn't care if anyone would hear him. He had been so angry with his father for not taking him on the hunt and then leaving him the next day, and yet, he had forgotten both of these thoughts until just now. The emotions were overwhelming and he nearly fell to his knees.

As he leaned over, trying to catch his breath, and at the same time not caring if he did, he realized he could curl up in a ball and cry until he had no more tears and keep on until he ran out of breath. The anger he had felt for his father had suddenly been replaced by such a strong remorse; and yet more than just remorse. What kind of a son was he to blame his father for leaving and then dying? How could he even think such a thing? He must be the worst son there ever had been or ever would be.

Sobs shook his body and he stumbled forward, blindly pushing past several more horses. The tears had ended but the anguish he felt didn't. Dry sobs followed the wet and he thought he was going to be sick. He pushed past a horse and still staggering forward he ran into another, which didn't move. "Get… out of the way," he stammered as he pushed on its rump. In response, the horse stamped, blew out a deep breath and then whinnied. "Are you daft? I said to…" He stopped in mid-sentence. William had turned and found himself face to face with Sir John Brent's black stallion.

"It cannot be… How did you get here?" He couldn't help smiling when the courser stamped at the ground in front of him and then shook his head and mane. William caught his bridle, realizing it was the same tack he wore when they discovered him in the New Forest; and found himself staring eye to eye, just as he had when they were in the horse market outside the walls of Southampton. That evening he had seen fear in the stallion's eyes, now it was something different. It was almost as if the horse could tell how upset he was and was trying to reassure him. Despite being tied to a post, the courser turned his head as far back as he could and rested it on William's shoulder. Warm, moist air blew across his neck. He closed his eyes, wrapping his arms around the stallion's neck and resting his head on his cheek. Within seconds he could feel the tension, anger and anguish slip away from him.

They stood there for a long moment, until the stallion quickly pulled his head back and stamped at the ground one more time. William sniffled loudly and wiped his face on his sleeve and nodded. "All right, all right. We should get out of here…"

"You should have while you had the chance," a familiar voice spoke just behind him. William turned around and found himself face to face with Lord Thomas. The last thing he saw was a brilliant, white smile, and then William heard a dull crunch, even as he felt something hard and heavy hit him on the back of the head. Dazzling lights were replaced by swirling darkness and he felt as though he was falling down a steep slope.

•••

He awoke face down on a smooth stone surface. The rock was cool, which helped pull him back alert. His hands were bound behind him with braided leather straps, which were probably wet earlier, but now had dried and shrunk in the process. They cut into the skin of his wrists. He felt like his head was going to split open and, for a moment, wished he hadn't woken. Slowly, sluggishly, his memories returned, until, like a flash, it all played back in a heartbeat.

Somehow Lord Thomas had found the beach house. From there he had followed them down the Somme. It is possible Lord de Clinton had told him who William was while they were still in Hale Purlieu. It wouldn't take much to put the two together and guess the relation between the Simpson's of Dorchester and the de Simpson's of Eaucourt sur Somme. However he managed it, Lord Thomas had tracked them there. A sudden concern crossed his mind. What if they had found his tutor and Helen? Were they here as well? And where exactly was 'here'?

Robert had lectured William on studying his surroundings in order to learn things and tried to put it to use. Although the room at first seemed pitch black, that wasn't completely true. As if a fog was lifting from his vision, William was able to blink away the haze, which cleared his sight and showed a very dim outline of a door in front of him. There was no other light in the room. He took a deep breath and smelled the faint aroma of onions, garlic and dill. There was also the slight taste of dirt in the air, which was cool and dry.

So, what did this all mean? He was in a pantry or root cellar, but probably not below ground. More than likely it was a room off of a kitchen somewhere. As the drumming of his heartbeat slowed and its echo in his ears died down, he was able to hear noises on the other side of the door. What he heard confirmed what he had guessed; the clanging of pots and pans and muffled voices.

As he lay there on the cool, hard cobblestones, he began to piece the events together, which all lead to a question: why would Lord Thomas knock him out, take him somewhere and then dump him in a pantry of a kitchen? Is it possible he was still in Eaucourt? He tried picturing the kitchen they had passed through after coming up out of the servants' tunnel. It had been a single, albeit large room. He was sure there had been no doors, other than the one leading outside and the other to the tunnel.

So, he had been taken somewhere. But, again, why dump him in the pantry? If it had been him, and he had taken someone for questioning, he was pretty sure he wouldn't leave him in the kitchen. Unless something had happened and he had to hurriedly hide what he had done. No one of importance would ever set foot in the kitchen. Even as he thought of this, William was overcome with a strong urge to stand up and move away from the door. As if by reflex, he worked his knees up under him and slowly sat up. Tiny sparks of light danced in front of his eyes and his head thrummed but he was able to steady himself with a couple deep breaths. In through the nose and out through the mouth was what his teacher had taught him when dealing with pain.

The next step was a little trickier. He pulled one knee farther forward until he was flat footed and then, slowly, stood up, continuing his breathing technique the whole time. He tottered and wobbled, but remained standing. Several more deep breaths and William was sure he wouldn't fall over.

As he stood in the dark room, tottering slightly, waiting for his head to clear and the lights to stop dancing in front of his eyes, he heard elevated voices on the other side of the door. He cautiously took several steps backwards and to his right until he bumped into what felt like a table. His hands were bound, but his fingers were free and he felt along the front face and realized it was a large, thick block for cutting and carving. As he moved his hands along the edge he stopped suddenly when he felt cold metal. A quick, careful assessment revealed it to be a heavy cleaver, wedged securely in the surface of the block.

The immediate pounding of his heart drowned out the voices on the other side of the door. The cleaver had been driven deep enough into the surface of the wood to ensure it wasn't going anywhere. William couldn't believe his luck, and then checked himself. This wasn't luck, this was favor. It wasn't God's plan to have him knocked out and dragged away, but He could make it work for good. He silently thanked God for His help as he carefully began cutting the leather straps with the edge of the blade.

A long minute passed as he felt individual braids snap. Finally the last one was severed and his hands were free. His fingers tingled as the blood in them found itself no longer restricted. He was so relieved to be able to remove the last of the binding, he began rubbing them vigorously, paying particular attention to the very tender nature of his right. The voices outside the door rose again, dragging William back to his present situation. His hands were free but he was still in a dark pantry of a kitchen in a house or manor whose location was a mystery.

He quickly explored the remainder of the room. It was roughly square with the chopping block in one corner. Several wooden bins were placed along the walls. He opened one and was nearly overwhelmed with the aroma of onions. Another may have held apples at some time but was now empty. The floor was solidly laid cobblestone. Other than the door in the middle of one wall, the rest were lined with shelves.

Standing in the middle of the room he shook his head. Any second the voices on the other side of the door would open it and his chance for freedom would be lost. There had to be another way out. At that moment he caught a glimpse of a gleam off the blade of the cleaver and stared. The light was reflecting off the side opposite the doorway. Somewhere in the room was another source of light.

He frantically began his search all over again, but the room simply was not that large. It didn't come from the floor or the walls, and yet the tiniest glint of light was there on the blade. Where else could it be coming from? As if answering his own question, he looked up. There, in the middle of the room, was the faintest outline of a square frame. How could he have missed that all along? Desperately he reached as high as he could, only to realize he was at least an arm's length short.

Quickly he moved over to the block and tried to budge it. There was no use. It was nearly as thick as the length of his forearm and easily weighed several hundredweight. There had to be something else he could use to stand on. And then he saw it, the empty apple bin.

As quietly as possible he shifted the large wooden box to the middle of the room and then climbed on top. The framed cut out of the ceiling moved easily but as he did so, bright light streamed into the darkened pantry. After having been in the dark for so long, his eyes had adjusted to the best of their ability. Now, the light streaming in from above dazzled them, and even squinting didn't help.

As he stood on the box, getting ready to pull himself up through the opening in the ceiling, the voices outside the door suddenly stopped. The next thing he heard was an iron bolt screeching in its channel as it was pulled back. He froze, unable to make up his mind. He still couldn't see in the bright light overhead. If he pulled himself up, he would have no idea where he was or which way to go. He was sure to get caught again. He couldn't stay in the room though; there simply was no place to hide.

Even as the bolt finished scraping and the iron ring was turned from the other side of the door, William had a flash of inspiration. It flew in the face of common sense, but he had such a strong feeling, along with the idea, he chose not to question it.

Seconds later, the door opened and several people entered the room with a bright lantern. Anyone who had been locked in that room for as long as William had, would not have been able to see their faces because the bright light would have been shining in their eyes. They had obviously expected to find their prisoner still unconscious because they stood just inside the doorway without speaking. Finally one of them broke the silence, his distinctive high voice barely hiding his anger and frustration, "follow him… and when you find him…" He paused a second and then added, beneath his breath, "One Simpson is enough; I do not care if he is still alive."

Someone followed William's idea and scrambled up onto the apple crate, pulling himself up through the opening in the ceiling. A moment later Lord Thomas sent another back out through the kitchen. "Go outside and watch the roof line. If he makes his way out of the attic, you should see him easy enough." Heavy footsteps left the pantry.

"And if we catch him?" Someone else asked. This voice was deep and distinct. This didn't sound like a common foot soldier or even a lowborn man at arms. At the same time the voice didn't necessarily sound educated, but it remained confident and wary. Perhaps, William thought, it had been one of the raised voices he had recently heard outside the door.

"What? Did I not make myself clear enough just now?" Lord Thomas wasn't screaming but his voice nearly cracked it was so strained. "The Simpson's of Dorchester are no longer a use to me. The uncle is taken and will be kept safely out of the way. If needs be, he can be removed permanently. The nephew is nothing. He has slipped past the men I sent to rid me of him, and now he has managed to free himself from this room. I hope your men are up to the task, Copeland."

"The young Simpson has shown himself courageous and resourceful… for, as you say, just a boy. His actions do his father credit."

"Do you admire him? Lord Thomas squeaked. "He is a fool, a lucky fool. There is nothing more to him than that. His father, however, was an unlucky fool as his uncle should have been as well. But, eventually even his luck ran out…"

"Now you go too far my lord," William could hear a tone of anger rise in the voice. "If not for his father and uncle, Neville's Cross may have ended quite differently. I may not have had my own opportunity, had it not been for their bravery… and sacrifice."

"Yes, they did their duty, just as you will do yours or I will see your banner clipped." A long pause followed and William wondered if this knight bannerette, for he surely must have been one from the comment Lord Thomas just made, would explode over the threat. Only the king could create a knight of his own banner and to make that threat would suggest the king himself would side with Lord Thomas. William heard someone take a very deep breath and slowly let it out.

"His decision to come to France was unexpected, my lord," the knight bannerette continued, at first unevenly, then steadily more under control. "Even you thought he would cower at home until you made your offer. I do not believe in luck but rather being prepared when an opportunity presents itself." There was brief pause and then the other voice continued, "I wondered what my own son would have decided to do in the same situation. Would he leave all behind and come for me?"

A pause followed the comment and William wished he could see what was happening. Finally, Lord Thomas spoke. When he did his voice was like icy rain falling on an uncovered head. It sent a shiver down

William's back. "That letter from Coucy should have forced him to consider selling Crandor in order to pay the debt. If he had done the wise thing, it would be mine even as we speak. Instead he chose this path. He made the choice to come to France and cross paths with me. I did not choose this but I will see it through to the end. Crandor, and therefore all of Dorchester, will be mine. This path he chose is longer but the destination will be the same. Once I have the girl, and my Lincolnshire promise is fulfilled, there will be little to stop me."

"And if he is, as you say, lucky, again and is somehow able to find his uncle and return to England, what then? The Simpson's are still a strong family with favor at court, my lord."

Someone cleared their throat outside the pantry. "Tell me you found him or I will not suffer this interruption," Lord Thomas began then stopped abruptly.

"It is an urgent message for you m' lord. It only just now arrived." The voice cracked and it sounded nervous if not outright fearful. William could hear paper tearing and the rustling of pages.

"Fortune favors the bold, Copeland. I will have all three here in Amiens this day. Send me Godefroy." Footsteps hastily retreated from outside the pantry door. "They are a family which will no longer have anyone to send to court," Lord Thomas continued, as if the message, cryptic remark, and summons never happened. "Remove the child, remove the only heir. The Earl will die rotting in the tower of Chateau de Coucy, the Count has assured me of this; and this boy will never leave Amiens. With the uncle gone I have been assured of the de Simpson land and titles." There was a brief pause, and then he added, "Bring me what is left of the boy; Godefroy will do his part easily enough if this message is true, and then we can go find that irritating girl." No one answered but footsteps slowly left the pantry.

William had a hard time believing what he had just heard. It sounded as though Lord Thomas had been trying to kill him all along. Had he also somehow plotted to have his uncle taken prisoner? He certainly knew details of his capture and the ransom letter he had received just over a fortnight before. As he crouched in his hiding place, William had a vision of a puppet show he had seen put on by a traveling group of minstrels when he was much younger. It was as if he was the puppet and Lord Thomas was pulling all the strings.

An overwhelming sense of helplessness crashed down upon him. Despite his cramped surroundings he pulled his knees up closer to his chest. Despair flowed over him like waves in the channel and hot tears streamed down his face. Soundless sobs racked his body and his throat and chest felt like they were being crushed under an enormous weight.

How could he possibly go on? How could he find his uncle, rescue him and still make it back to Dorchester? How could he even find Helen and his teacher? It was as if the entire countryside of France lay between them or they were a piece of straw lost in a great pile of brush. He would be better off just letting Lord Thomas find him now, end this pointless chase and be done with it.

That final thought shot through him like a bolt of lightning. It shocked him to the core; and, in an instant, he had a flash of realization. This wasn't just Lord Thomas; the greater enemy was orchestrating all this. He had been planting thoughts and ideas in Lord Thomas for a very long time and William seemed to be the lynch pin to his plans. Thomas Denebaud hadn't been careful to guard his thoughts. William understood why that was so important.

The sobs stopped, he took a deep, rattled breath and a clear, quiet voice spoke to him, "*If you understand how important it is, William, are you guarding your own thoughts now?*" He froze. The voice had been so clear and audible William, at first, thought it had come from inside the pantry. His heart was racing but this time it wasn't from fear. In that brief instant he had gone from feeling condemned to convicted. He had let down the guard on his thoughts and the enemy quietly stepped in. But he had made one suggestion too many. William was not going to turn himself over to Lord Thomas. He was pretty sure he knew what would happen to him if he did.

"God, thank You for this revelation. I need Your help; make my path clear and put those in front of me who will help and blind those who would hinder or harm me." As soon as he finished saying his prayer, just barely over a whisper, he felt someone push him. It felt so real it startled him and nearly caused him to shout. "*Go, now,*" a quiet voice urged.

Without second-guessing, William opened the lid of the apple crate and climbed out. The pantry was empty and the door was standing wide open. "A righteous man is as bold as a lion," he reminded himself as he crossed to the door, stepping out into a large kitchen.

Chapter Twenty Five

Those few minutes Robert and Helen spent moving in the shadows down to the riverbank seemed to last hours. Both of their breaths were coming in short, ragged gasps as they bent, nearly doubled over and moved, hand in hand down to the boat. As they approached the water, Robert was relieved to find no sign their pursuers had made it to the river. Once they reached the shore and took their first steps on the loose gravel they froze in their tracks. The sound of the crushed rock shifting beneath them seemed to echo across the water and down the bank. Both their heartbeats hammered in their ears and they were sure they would hear the sound of men or horses any second.

They stood silently for a long moment, but no sound followed except the soft lapping of the water on the rocks and sand before them. The next dozen or so steps were taken slowly and carefully. Finally they reached the boat. Without hesitation, Robert signaled Helen to climb aboard. She took a position at the stern with the rudder, and Robert shoved the craft clear of bank. He took a couple more steps out into the river, to make sure it was free and then climbed in.

Signaling Helen to crouch down lower, he set the oars and began steady strokes to move them away from the shore and further upstream.

Several moments passed and they still spoke nothing to each other. Robert was focused on putting distance between them and Eaucourt and Helen was focused on praying for William.

She was sitting in the hull with her head bowed, nearly touching her knees. Her hands were clasped in her lap and she stared at them as she calmed her breathing. "*God, bless William indeed. Keep him safe. Watch over and protect him, let no harm come to him. Your word says there is no weapon formed against him, which will prosper. You will set a table for him before his enemies. What is being meant for harm, You will turn around for good. Amen.*"

"My lady, I feel we should press on as far as we can tonight, but I am afraid I am nearly spent. My strength is not what it used to be..." When Helen looked up she was startled to see his expression. He was straining to keep the same steady stroke. Most of his face was in shadow, which made it appear all the more pained.

"I know this area well and I know what comes before Amiens. We would do best to find a place to shelter overnight and start out again after sunrise," she suggested.

Robert shook his head in disagreement. "I would want to get you farther from Eaucourt before we stop, my lady." He paused to take a few more strokes. "They will be looking for us..."

"They will, but it will not do us good to continue in the darkness. The Somme enters marshes and has many fingers branching from it, along with creeks and rivers emptying into it, between here and Amiens. It would be too easy for us to wander down one of these, only to find ourselves lost and doubling back. I need the light of day to see the channel we must follow." She couldn't see his expression, but she could see him nod a reluctant agreement.

"You know this area well. Is there some place nearby we can find to shelter for the evening?"

Helen stared out into the shadows. The silvery moonlight danced across the gentle ripples of the Somme. They were in a broad portion of the river, with trees lining either side. Some were so close their branches leaned out over the water, like long, slender fingers gently caressing the river. "There is a bend in the main channel, not far from here. Once past, we will find a narrow creek emptying into the river from the west. We took lunch there once, several years ago. The creek is shallow and just wide enough for the boat and its banks are sandy and gentle. We can move a short way up and then find a well concealed spot to rest."

Robert took a deep breath and nodded again. His shoulders were aching and he could feel blisters on both hands that were ruptured and raw. "God, give me the strength to finish strong tonight." He meant to pray it silently and was startled when Helen responded with an "amen." He looked into her eyes, which despite the dark evening, were gleaming in the moonlight, and something long buried stirred inside. He had forgotten the feeling of knowing a woman cared for his well-being. He swallowed heavily and tried to thank her for her concern, which was obvious from her expression. His voice broke and even to his own ears sounded thick and strained. "Thank you, my lady. For both William and myself, thank you."

As he sat in a brief pause in rowing he noticed something else in Helen's expression. She was doing her best to appear strong and confident, but he could see fear, albeit buried deep. "Do you fear for our sakes, my lady?"

Helen bowed her head and nodded. "For ours, but more so for William's," she admitted softly.

"One of the most difficult lessons I have had to teach William is to let go of fear. If you focus on it, you give power to the enemy who planted the thought in your head." He paused a moment. The teacher inside, ever present, waited to make sure he had her attention and to see if she followed his thought. He used the pause in speaking to focus on taking several more strong strokes.

"I would guess this is a difficult lesson to learn, not to teach," she answered as she took in a deep, cleansing breath and slowly let it out. When she sat up, he could see a brighter gleam in her eyes than just a moment before.

"It can be very difficult to learn and master because we are not in a fight against a man. Our battle is on a greater field and yet we have already had tremendous victories to our credit." He began rowing again, a little slower than before, but still long, steady strokes. Teaching Helen and William was very different. With William he could see so much more of what went on inside, through his eyes. With Helen, it was not as easy. She was much better at concealing her thoughts. Either this was a woman's natural strength, or she had more time and practice at it, or both. Robert found the opportunity to teach this young woman exciting. She was going to be a challenge, but worthy of the effort.

"We are a part of a much greater battle but you, my lady, are a victory; William is a victory. The lives you will both live are victories for Christ. There is nothing Lord Thomas can do to either of you." He spoke this with such conviction and certainty it startled her. And for a brief moment the wall she had so carefully constructed around her thoughts, hopes, dreams and fears, crumbled slightly and he had a glimpse inside. It confirmed what he had suspected. There was still a frightened girl living inside.

"My lady, God is a complete God. His miracles are complete miracles. He does not do anything half way. Find a way to turn your fear over to Him, then praise Him. Worship Him. When you put God in His place, your focus will slowly, gradually change from your circumstances to Him.

This is when God will show up and deal with your circumstances. As long as you are willing and do your part, He is sure to do His."

"How can He possibly use me?" She asked, then, quickly, added, "how can I know what is my part?"

"If you do not know, ask Him to show you. He will give you direction."

She turned, slightly and looked out over the still water, to the western shore and spoke so quietly, Robert had a hard time hearing her over the light splash of the oars. "What if I no longer feel like seeking Him?"

"We all have had those moments, my lady. There is no man or woman alive who has not been tested with them. If you recognize them, also know that is when you need to seek Him the most." They had come around through the bend in the river and Helen pointed out the small stream on the western shore. Trees lined both sides and their branches nearly blocked the confluence from sight. Because Helen had described it earlier, Robert was able to look over his shoulder and realized it would be a well-concealed place to spend the remainder of the evening.

A few moments later and they were a hundred or so feet up the narrow stream. Finally, Robert's strength gave out and Helen turned the bow into the shallow bank. The sand yielded before the narrow keel and the boat's momentum carried it a few feet up the bank. Robert slumped forward, his hands, arms and shoulders shaking from the exertion and exhaustion.

"God, when I am weakest is when Your strength is shown through me. Thank You, God, for blessing us. Watch over William. Keep him safe. Place those in front of him who will help him and separate him from evil. You are the God of angel armies and I call on them now, to fight on behalf of my young ward. Amen." He leaned farther forward and gently cried. These were not tears of fear or desperation, but rather, they were of hope, expectation and complete thanks and praise for God and His deliverance.

Helen sat and watched and felt something stir inside her she had not felt in all the years at Abbeville. She wanted to hold William's teacher and comfort him. Slowly she reached forward with her right hand, but drew it back before touching him. Instead she clasped her hands in her lap and prayed her own silent prayer for William and his deliverance.

•••

He walked out into a kitchen only to find it empty of all save one person. A young scullion stood in the far right corner scrubbing several large pots. William paused a moment to gather his bearings. The kitchen was narrower than Crandor's by several paces, yet nearly twice as long. The doorway to the pantry stood almost exactly half way down one of the long walls. The opposite had small windows spaced every several feet near the ceiling. Two of these were open and through them William could hear shouts and the sounds of horses as well as see a small amount of dim light. It was either dusk or just before dawn, by the look of it. In addition to these windows, the room was dimly lit by several open oil lamps, which hung on chains from the ceiling. To his left, on the far wall were two doors. One was closed, the other slightly opened, and through it more of the dim light shone on the floor.

William took a deep breath and then walked to the open door. Despite the fearful voices in his head shouting at him to turn back and see if the kitchen servant had noticed, and the dull pain from where he had been knocked unconscious, he forced himself to walk straight and not turn around. He reminded himself of Lot's salvation from Sodom and the angel's warning not to turn back. His wife didn't listen and when she looked back with longing on all the possessions she had left behind, she was turned to a pillar of salt. "*Trust in the Lord with all your heart,*" he told himself. There was no need to look back.

Once at the door, William paused briefly as he opened it a little further in order to look outside. What he saw challenged his confidence for a moment. Several dozen guardsmen were moving about in an open courtyard. High stonewalls and a large wooden gate suggested they were in a manor house. William suddenly remembered Lord Thomas telling the knight bannerette he would never leave Amiens. Had they brought him to the very city to which Robert, Helen and he were traveling? What the enemy had meant for harm, God would turn around for good. If indeed he was in Amiens, then somewhere in this city Lady Helen's family had a home. But first, he needed to get across the courtyard and out of the gate.

Even as he stood there he heard a shout from outside the walls and a bell, somewhere in the compound sounded three rings. From behind him, he heard a large pot crash, followed by several curses in French. Although he had been studying the language, the colorful use of it by the scullion boy wasn't exactly part of his vocabulary. What little he did understand was something or someone had arrived early. William felt rooted in the spot, not sure whether to retreat to a dark corner of the kitchen or step out into the courtyard. As he paused to consider a young voice behind him stated, "*Viens avec moi.*" The scullion boy pushed past him and started into the courtyard. He hadn't even realized who William was.

The thought hit him like a flash of lightning. None of these men in the courtyard would know what he looked like and they certainly wouldn't notice him walking beside someone they ignored every day. As if pushed from behind, William stepped quickly out of the doorway and, within a few strides, caught up with the boy. Out of the corner of his eye he glanced at his companion and guessed him to be nearly the same age as himself although shorter. He also noticed his rounded shoulders and the slumped, half dogged steps he took. William did his best to imitate them. Within a few strides they looked like they had worked together for years.

Several men at arms pushed past them but none looked at them. They were the invisible, ignorable staff, which most people disregarded and never took much notice. The moon had dropped beneath the horizon, and despite the change in the sky (which he decided was surely just before dawn), the courtyard was still dim. In the half-light, it looked to William like the men moving about were all shades of gray and yet he and his companion were less than that. In front of the very men who were sent to find him, William and his companion walked across the courtyard and then out of the front gate.

In the street just outside the manor was a large cart pulled by a thoroughly depressing looking rouncey. The horse's winter coat still clung to its gaunt frame in clumps and its head hung down, nearly to its knees. The man standing beside the poor beast didn't look much better. His beard was just as patchy and his threadbare clothes hung about him as if they were either made for someone much larger or he was considerably less of man than he had been.

The scullion walked right up to him and began an animated conversation, which William did his best to follow. Apparently this delivery was much earlier than usual and the kitchen lad was upset. William understood the words sleep and impossible, and realized the early arrival of the produce and meat, which sat in the back of the cart, would make the scullion lose what should have been time to rest before beginning his day anew.

While they continued to argue back and forth, William looked around and realized they were the only people in the street and the surrounding buildings cast odd angled shadows across the cobblestones. Without looking back, William turned away from the cart, crossed the street, and disappeared in the shadows of the neighboring building.

The road ran mostly straight for several hundred paces, with an occasional alley or small cross street, until it came to a large, paved intersection. William stopped at the corner. To cross the paved street would mean leaving the security of the shadows. As he stood there, leaning against a timber-framed building, he tried to remember Helen's description of the home her guardian's brought her to in Amiens. Despite the loud drumming of his heartbeat in his ears he managed to recall parts of several conversations where she mentioned her homes.

Somewhere in the distance a dog barked and another picked up on it and began in earnest. William realized, even as he paused briefly at the intersection, the sky was lightening. Dawn was quickly approaching and he was alone, in a city he thought might be Amiens, trying to remember a conversation which took place several days ago, while ignoring the reminder he had recently been knocked over the head. He closed his eyes for a moment and took a deep breath, slowly letting it out. The dull pain ceased for a second and in that moment he recalled Helen's words. The home was on the canal opposite the cathedral.

William rubbed his eyes with the heel of his palms and then looked to his right and left. As he stood on the edge of the intersection, he smiled and then nearly began laughing to himself. Tears of joy fell down his face and he dropped to one knee, thanking God for continuing to watch over him. To his left, down the wide cross street, he saw in the distance a tall, graceful, gray stoned building, standing high above the rest of city. Even as the first of the morning bells rang out from its towers, a deep voice spoke behind him, "stand up slowly and turn so I can see you."

•••

They had been so exhausted that neither Helen nor Robert made it out of the boat before falling asleep. Despite the cacophony of nighttime noises, Helen was able to curl up in the stern of the boat, while Robert slept in the bow. Their space was cramped but neither complained, even when they awoke at nearly the same time as the sky began to lighten with the approaching dawn.

Helen had never slept in more uncomfortable conditions, and yet, despite the multiple bruises and muscle cramps from her wooden berth she awoke feeling refreshed and ready for the new day. Gone was the fear and concern she had felt the night before for William and in its place was a sense of peace. She remembered hearing that God's mercy was renewed every morning. She smiled, knowing it was true.

"Lady Helen," Robert spoke after clearing his throat, "if you wish to relieve and refresh yourself I will see what meal I can create from the food we borrowed last night." She nodded and carefully stood, then walked to the bow and stepped onto the sandy beach. "I ask you not to stray too far, my lady. We are on the French side of the river now and must remain even more vigilant." She smiled and nodded agreement and then walked a little ways upstream so to be just out of sight. The water was cold and spring fed and she soon was spluttering as she splashed and rinsed her face.

She thought it was strange to be warned of the French. She had spent her entire life in France, raised by French servants. They had been in France for several days and it wasn't the French which pursued her.

Lord Thomas' face quickly appeared in her mind's eye. How could such a man get to where he was? Was he ever a good man? Did he ever feel remorse or concern or sympathy or sadness? Or was he simply no longer a man but something baser; something so completely taken over by evil he no longer felt anything? Dark thoughts swirled around and through her as she finished her morning routine.

When she returned to the boat, Robert had sliced the cheese, bread and apples and laid them out on the blanket he had stretched across the bow. She bowed her head and thanked God for the meal, their continued safety, as well as for William, while in the back of her mind the dark thoughts of Lord Thomas continued to play like flashes of lightning. Robert's head remained bowed a little longer.

Helen hadn't realized how hungry she was until she knelt in the soft sand chewing on the bread and cheese. For several moments neither said anything. Finally, she paused between bites and looked up. Through the canopy she could see a bright blue sky emerging with the dawn light and she smiled again. "Have you found the secret to starting your day well, my lady?" Robert asked between bites of dried apple and cheese.

The comment caught her off guard and she stopped, with a piece of bread poised just before her open mouth. Her brows drew down briefly as she considered it. "There have been many mornings, in recent months, when I felt little reason to look forward to the new day. Today, I am torn between joys for the day and worry over our situation… and for Williams'." She added the additional thought at the end when she realized it might have come across wrong.

"Sorrow may last through the night, but joy comes in the morning," Robert answered as he paused between bites. "King David understood pain and frustration, but he also knew that praising God, despite all his misfortune was the best way to remain filled with joy. Even the great apostle Paul said, when he remembered all his sufferings, he counted them all joy. Did you know the first time he was thrown in prison, instead of asking God why and complaining to God about it, he and Silas sat chained to the wall and sang psalms? Even in the prison they sang songs of praise and thanksgiving to God."

"I do not remember what happened to them."

"In the middle of the night, even as they sang, the earth shook so violently the doors of all the prison cells were opened. The guards were overcome by the miracle they witnessed and accepted Jesus Christ as their Lord and Savior."

"So, God used Paul's imprisonment to spread the good news?"

"God can use any situation to do so. What He looks for are those who believe in Him so strongly they can even be joyful in what may appear to be a desperate or impossible situation."

"If God is for us, who can be against?" Helen answered quietly, more to herself than Robert. The swirling dark thoughts of a few moments ago were still there, but had receded to a corner of her mind.

"Exactly. But those are more than just words we teach our children. If you truly believe it, if it moves from words you hear to words you believe in your heart, then you will certainly find joy in all things." As they spoke they finished the simple meal and Robert folded the blanket, storing it in the bow of the boat.

"Do you think God could do the same for William's uncle? Could He open the doors to his cell in Chateau de Coucy?" Helen asked. There was more than just idle curiosity in her voice.

"God does not change, my lady. He is the same yesterday, today and forever. If you are asking me if it is His will, then I will answer the same. He sent His Son to proclaim the good news and to set the captives free.

If you are asking me when and how it would come to pass… only God knows that."

Helen stood and brushed a few crumbs from her lap. The sun had now fully risen and the trees around them were filled with the songs of several dozen birds, including thrushes, warblers and magpies. Even the birds were thankful for the sunrise and bright clear skies. The clouds, which covered much of the night sky, had seemed to move on, leaving behind a brilliant blue canopy, which was reflected in the smooth surface of the Somme. "It is hard to imagine there is so much anger and hate in the world while standing here." With her eyes closed, she took in the sounds, the smells and the warm sun on her face.

"We live in a world stuck in the middle, my lady. We are not in heaven yet, nor have we completely fallen from God's presence. As we are in this middle land, there will always be both great good and terrible evil around us."

"I wish something terrible would happen to Lord Thomas…"

"My lady, do not say such things," Robert quickly countered. When she turned to him, his expression was anxious, even worried. She had never seen William's tutor look this way.

"Why not? After all he has done to me… to us? He deserves it."

Robert closed his eyes and lowered his head. He still sat in the bow of the boat, his hands clasped together at his waist. Helen thought it looked like he was praying. When he answered, it was slowly at first, as if he was measuring each word precisely. "He may very well deserve what you suggest my lady, but this is one of life's most difficult lessons… and one I have struggled to teach William, because I continue to struggle with it myself." He stopped again and took a deep breath, letting it out slowly.

"God has created each and every one of us in His image. We are all creations and children of God. When God created Adam in the garden,

He called him blessed. Every child born since then has carried God's blessing. If God has blessed each one of us, who are we to curse them?"

"But after all he has done? He murdered Sir Geoffrey on the docks of Southampton. He may have done the same to Gilbert, as well as Chrestien. He has hounded my steps since I left Abbeville and now he has probably taken William, or worse…" she nearly shouted this in one breath and paused to take another but was silenced by Roberts raised palm.

"Be at peace, my lady." He continued sitting, watching her very closely. She looked like she was near panic. Her breath was coming in gasps and a wild look crossed her face. Robert sat quietly his hands clasped, once more, in his lap. Now she saw a deep sadness and sympathy along with concern. Doing her best to control her emotions, Helen closed her eyes and took a deep breath. When she let it out, Robert continued.

"Our Lord has commanded us to love those who hate us and to care for those who spitefully use us. When we decide someone deserves punishment and we ask God to do so, we are bringing the curse back on ourselves."

Helen shook her head, "how is that possible?"

"Because God has blessed each and every one of His creations, even those who have chosen to do evil. The more difficult but more righteous action is to ask God to bless them with the understanding of His mercy and grace in their life, so that they may understand how great and good He is. When you say that, and truly mean it, then you are able to see the world as God sees it… as if through His eyes."

"What you suggest is impossible. No one can possibly live that way."

"You are right, my lady. No one, on their own, could go to God and ask Him to bless those who have hurt or injured or persecuted them, but we are not on our own, are we?"

Helen stood there a moment longer, thinking on what William's teacher had just showed her. She had heard those passages in the bible before. She thought she understood them. Now, on the banks of the Somme, a short distance from Eaucourt and a short river journey from Amiens, with Lord Thomas somewhere nearby, it was as if a great lamp was lit for her eyes. She started to see what Jesus had actually taught. For the first time, those words weren't just something said on a Sunday at Mass and then forgotten for a week. Here was a chance to walk it out. She just wasn't sure she could.

"We are not alone in this fight, my lady," Robert repeated again. He was trying to tell her something. Something important.

"I am not alone in this fight," she repeated to herself. She shook her head, still not sure what she was missing. Then a revelation hit her. "Greater is He who is in me than he who is in the world." She blurted it out, like a student at school, hoping it was the right answer, but she was also beginning to truly understand. "My God shall never leave me nor forsake me. Just before Jesus ascended He told his disciples that a helper would come in His place. That is whom I have. I have a helper sent from God."

Robert was smiling and nodding his agreement. "God's Holy Spirit is our help. He is our guide when we are lost, our lamp when all is dark, our comforter when all seem against, our strength when we are weak, our healer when we are sick and our counselor when we seek His wisdom. His Spirit speaks to us through our spirit and through this we can know the counsels of God for our lives."

"I can hear God? Personally?" Helen had never heard this before. She had always been told she needed someone to go before God for her, to speak on her behalf. She never knew she could go directly to God.

"Jesus came to remove our separation from the Father. Ever since

Adam and Eve were driven from the garden there has been a wall of separation between man and God. Through Moses there was created a priesthood who would go before God, once a year, to atone for the sins of the seeds of Abraham, but God had a better, more perfect plan in mind, when the time was right. Just before giving up His life on the cross, Jesus said, 'it is finished.' He completed everything God asked of Him, including removing the need for intercessors. The Bible tells us, when Jesus died, the curtain between the holy place of the Hebrew Temple and the Holy of Holies, where God's presence was said to be, was torn in two. Jesus removed the barrier between us and God, and God's Spirit came to be with us. When we accept Jesus Christ as our Lord and Savior, we can go before His throne of grace and gaze at His loving face and directly access His strength to carry out even the most difficult tasks here on earth."

"Like asking God to bless Lord Thomas?"

"Yes, my lady. Even asking God to bless him. Will you try?"

Helen nodded but realized she didn't feel like it. This man has done so much wrong. Why should she ask God to bless him? He should be struck down. He should be…

"My lady?" Robert's quiet question intruded on her troubled thoughts. She was shocked how quickly she had gone from the peace she had begun to feel, as Robert was speaking, to anger and resentment. She shook her head.

Before she could change her mind she quickly spoke, "God, we are all created in Your image, even Lord Thomas. Bless Him with the understanding of Your love for him. Amen." Robert echoed her amen. "How is it possible…?" Her eyes grew wide and her mouth dropped open.

"My lady?"

"A great weight has been lifted from me. Oh God…" she fell to her knees, her face in her hands and she sobbed, her whole body shaking. It was several moments before she realized Robert had left the boat and was kneeling in front of her, his hands on her shoulders.

"Are you all right, my lady?"

She nodded and sniffled loudly, gladly taking the bit of linen Robert offered to dry her tears. "I said the words, but did not really believe them," Helen explained between wiping tears and blowing her nose. "Even so, as soon as you said amen, I felt a warmth flow over me and I felt such a peace and joy, like I have not felt since I was a small child."

"God blesses those who are a blessing, my lady. Righteousness is right standing with God. You are standing in God's right place." He smiled a broad, warm smile as tears sparkled in his eyes in the early morning light. She smiled back at him, and then bowed her head.

"God, guard and protect William. Keep him safe. Give him the wisdom he needs, when he asks for it, and guide him with Your Spirit to my home in Amiens. Amen," Robert echoed her and then waited. Slowly she stood, took a deep breath and smiled and then climbed back into the boat. Moments later they were back in the Somme, slowly making their way farther inland.

●●●

William did precisely what he was told. He was sure he recognized the voice as the one arguing with Lord Thomas in the pantry. He stood, turning slowly and found himself eye to eye with a man of nearly the same height but perhaps 10 years his senior. An arming sword was belted at his waist, still in its ornate scabbard, but in his hand he held a very sharp looking rondel. His brilliantly blue eyes appeared nearly gray in the pre-dawn light and William could see several scars on his face, as well as his arms.

"Step out of the shadows lad. Let me look at you." His voice was very distinct and carried with it a whistling sound, which sounded to William like it was from one or two missing lower teeth. William took one slow, careful step forward and the knight smiled a gap-toothed smile. It was two incisors.

"Am I right to assume I have the honor of meeting Sir John Copeland?" William asked, after drawing himself up, setting his shoulders and raising his chin just a little higher than any commoner could get away with.

The knight bannerette paused, his mouth slightly open, and then recovered quickly, snapping it shut in the process. "You do, lad, but how you could possibly know that is beyond me. Who are you?" The tip of his blade hadn't moved but was still steadily pointed at William's chest.

"I am William de Simpson, son of Sir Edward Simpson, nephew and heir to Lord Charles de Simpson, Earl of Dorchester, and Knight of the Garter." It was the first time William had ever presented himself with his peerage and titles, and a strange swelling of pride coursed through him. He was proud of what his father had done and the sacrifice he had made, as well as who his uncle was. He was proud of what he had learned and what he was continuing to learn about his family. He understood what pride could lead to but despite how he looked and the way he felt after being clubbed over the head, a new sense of confidence in who he was and where he was going flowed over him. He wondered if, standing here, facing this armed knight, Bernard might have felt something similar while standing guard over the body of Lord Roland at the Roncevaux Pass.

The knight lowered his blade slightly, but still kept it pointing at

William. His expression may have softened just a little, but it was difficult to see in the pre-dawn light. "I have often wondered what I would say if I ever met a Simpson. Now I do, but under circumstances not of my choosing…"

William shook his head. "These are your choosing, Sir John. The one thing you have in your life, which no one can take away or force on you, are your own choices. One should always ask themselves if this or that choice is really the one they want to be making, no matter how difficult or less desirable the outcome. God will honor your decision whether for good or evil." William had a hard time believing what he just said. Standing in an intersection in Amiens, facing an armed knight who had been honored by the King for his actions at Neville's Cross, it felt to William as if he was standing beside himself, looking on as the scene unfolded in his life.

He said this with such conviction it was as if he had swung at the knight, forcing him to take a small step backwards. His expression changed a little and William thought he saw awe and wonder mixed with a little anger as well. The point of his rondel dropped some more. "You know nothing of the choices I have had to make," Sir John muttered, his voice dropping even lower. Even as he spoke, several dogs began barking some distance behind William. They didn't sound like they were simply welcoming the new day. These sounded alarmed as they began howling and baying.

"You are right, Sir John. I do not know the choices you have had to make, but I do know you are an honorable man and the king trusts you and has rewarded you for your service. I also know where you stood at Neville's Cross when my father and uncle and their men rode in on the Scots, saving many Welsh and Northumberland archers and men at arms. Your cousin, Gilbert, who stood beside you in the assault, was one of those men." This last comment completely surprised the knight. He lowered his blade even farther until the tip was pointing at William's knees.

"How could you possibly know…?"

"Because Gilbert told me how he lost his ear to Robert Keith's lance; how he fell before him even as he saw the de Simpson banner ride into the battle and save his life. He told me he would never forget seeing the banner snap in the wind as the horses and men rode up from the reserves; the crane beside a white door on a red field, even though he did not know whose sigil it was."

"My cousin lives? When did you meet him?" Where…?" There was a gleam in the knight's eyes and he took a small step towards William, his blade lowering a little more.

"The last I saw of him he still lived. That was in Southampton over seven days ago. But Lord Thomas was there and none too pleased our ship cast off while Gilbert distracted him. I have prayed for his safety since."

"Why would he have done such a thing? Why would he place himself in the hazard to help you?"

"Because he saw the chance to repay an old debt to my family."

"But to cross Lord Thomas… that was not wise."

"It seems I have been at crossed swords with Lord Thomas since my uncle left England with Henry Lancaster. Your cousin Gilbert found his way into my story and decided to side with the right, even if it meant hurt, harm, or his life. I hope it did not lead to that, but it will be some time before I know for sure." William could see doubt begin to drift into Sir John's eyes. His expression was slowly changing, even as the sky continued to lighten. As he stood there, still hearing the dogs baying some distance away, a small voice spoke inside him and he heeded the prompting.

"Do you remember your oath, Sir John? The one you took when King Edward knighted you, giving you your own banner?"

The question shocked the knight and his expression hardened quickly. "Of course I do…" His voice had lowered and rumbled from his chest as if coming from deep inside him.

"To be without fear in the face of your enemies, no matter how numerous; to be bold and upright in your actions, such that God will see His love shine through you; to speak the truth at all times, even if it leads to your death while safeguarding those who are innocent, who have no one else to stand and defend them while doing them no harm."

As William spoke the words he felt a surge of energy build up inside of him. These weren't just idle words spoken in haste and disregarded; although there had been men who spoke them in the past and would do so in the future and cast them aside soon after. Nevertheless these words were powerful. This was the very commandment Jesus spoke of when asked what was the most important of the old laws. Love God with all your heart, soul and mind and love your fellow man as yourself. "Lord Thomas does not care how many innocents get in his way. He will push, shove or cut them down to get what he wants." William's heart was hammering in his chest and he could hear it drumming in his ears as he spoke. The rest of the world had dropped away and all he could see was the knight's face before him.

Sir John's eyes drifted away from William for a moment. It looked as if he was trying to recall something. His brow furrowed and he chewed on the inside of his cheek. "Lord Thomas told me the people he pursues were able to flee from Southampton just moments before he was able to stop them." A dark look passed over his face and William saw the grip on his rondel grow tighter. "I heard him once mutter about a bloody hunchback getting in his way, but it never occurred to me he might be speaking of my cousin. I thought he died at Neville's Cross."

"He spoke highly of you and your bravery in the battle." There was a gleam in the knight's eyes, which might otherwise have worried William, but he was pretty sure the emotions beneath Sir John's surface were not directed towards him. "He was proud to be related to the man who captured the king of Scotland. I look forward to seeing your cousin again… when I return to Dorchester where he has agreed to take a position in my house."

The barking dogs suddenly stopped in frightened yelps and William paused at the silence which followed. He thought he might have heard the clash of steel and even shouting mixed in with the barking, but it ended just before the dogs. The shrill scream of a woman cut through the silence and then it too was abruptly silenced. Nothing followed and it was as if the city, which had only recently been waking up, now was holding its breath and waiting.

A moment later the sound of perhaps two horses trotting on the cobblestone street behind William grew slowly louder. It felt as though the steel clip-claps on stone, with their distinctive pause between hoof falls, was now the only sound in Amiens. Despite the circumstances, William hadn't been nervous or worried until now. For some reason, the sound of the approaching horses from behind him started his heart beating quick and loud and his hands began sweating. He rubbed them on his tattered cotte.

The horses continued to approach at the same gait and William did his best to keep his eyes on Sir John. It seemed as though the knight was lost in thought, while at the same time waiting for someone or something. In the ever-brightening morning light, his now blue gray eyes shifted slightly from William's face to looking just over his shoulder. "That was a woman's scream," William stated. The knight nodded but kept his focus in the distance.

The thought of Helen flashed through William's mind and his throat tightened. Could it have been her scream? Is it possible Lord Thomas now has both of them? In a few short seconds he had gone from calm confidence to frightened fearfulness. If he had them both, there would be no stopping Lord Thomas' plans, whatever they were. He would control large sections of southwestern England, while holding the allegiance of many local lords as their suzerain. A flash of insight hit William and it nearly physically knocked him over. He reached out to the building he stood beside, to steady himself. Without realizing it, he spoke out loud. "You understand Lord Thomas plots to knock the crown from Edward's head. Will you aid him in this Sir John?"

The knight stared at William, dumbfounded and speechless. His mouth hung open and he dropped the point of his blade to the ground. "That is impossible… he would have to be mad…"

"Is there any doubt? He told you to murder me. 'I have dealt with the uncle and he will never see England again. Remove the heir and my favor at court will get me his lands.' Is that not what he told you?" Sir John stared at him open mouthed. He didn't realize William had been in the pantry and overheard their entire conversation. "He planned the capture of my uncle at St. Omer, plotting with the French in order to make it happen, hoping I would cower in Crandor and sell the estates to pay the debt. I believe he orchestrated the murder of his brother in law, Sir John Brent, with the help of the outlaw Davey Martin. Through his marriage to Sir John's sister he will control all the land in Somerset, once he removes Sir Robert Brent. Through my family he would have all of Dorchester. If he finds the girl he is looking for, through her he could gain access to the land of the Marches and of Wales." He would also gain access to France herself, through Helen's mother, with a claim similar to Edward; William realized this but kept it to himself. Helen's true identity had to be protected.

Sir John was shaking his head in disbelief. "If what you say is true he would command the entire western half of England."

"At that point there would be little to stop him from threatening our King," William added. Once again William had the vision of a puppeteer directing a play with strings, then shook it out of his head. He would not play along, nor would he simply stand still waiting for the next tug of string. "You can take me back to him, or you can kill me now, Sir John, but I will tell you this first," William clenched his fist and bent his knees, tensing like a bow string. "I will fight until my last breath to keep Lord Thomas from harming this girl, taking my family's lands or threatening my king. I do not know what Lord Thomas holds against you or has promised you, but what you must ask yourself, Sir John, is what are you going to do? Will you fight for what is good and right or give in to greed and gold?"

The trotting horses slowed to a walk as they approached the intersection. It took all of William's self-control not to turn around and look. Instead he kept his focus and full attention on Sir John and his expression. What he saw there was a mixture of confusion, anger and worry. What he didn't know for sure was which one, if any of those were directed at him. Finally the horses paused just a few paces behind William.

"Well met, Sir John," a deep basso voice spoke behind him. From where the voice originated, William had to guess it came from someone mounted on one of the horses. "Is that the Simpson brat? If it is, get it over with and let us get back. The morning meal will be ready for us about now." William forced himself to keep his eyes on the knight, even though it sounded like the man behind him would just as soon take his head as eat breakfast.

"Good morning, Godefroy," the knight responded, quickly changing his expression to one of pleasant surprise. "Lord Thomas has you out early this morning. Where are the rest of your companions… and who is that behind you?"

"Each to his own task, Sir John," the mounted soldier cut back. "You know it is best not to ask too many questions of our benefactor or his motives." As close as William stood, he could catch each small change in the knight's expression. He did his best to hide it, but William could see he was near some breaking point. One of the horses neighed loudly and stamped at the cobblestones.

The start of the morning was cool and damp so near to the Somme. William could feel the tingle of dew on his face and hands. It was the kind of morning he remembered seeing horses on the hills of Dorchester tossing their heads while they ran and kicked the air. "Hold still you bloody black beast," Godefroy muttered. An oath and a curse followed. The horse answered defiantly and William saw a flash of amusement cross Sir John's expression, followed quickly by shock because of what he heard next.

"Please…" a weak, soft, older woman's voice spoke from somewhere behind William. Part of him was instantly relieved when he realized it wasn't Helen's.

"I told you to hold your tongue, woman. The next time my hand will fly," Godefroy threatened, in between curses aimed at his mount.

Relief was quickly replaced by anger, followed by resolve. William knew Lord Thomas had sent Godefroy on a task. He had even heard him say something about getting all three in one day; if he was one and Helen the other, who could be the third; this woman behind him, pleading? She sounded like she needed help. Even as these thoughts raced through his mind he continued to face the knight bannerette, keeping his eyes fixed on the warrior's expression. What he saw mirrored his own thoughts. Not realizing he was speaking out loud, William muttered,

"Safeguard the innocent, no matter the cost." Slowly he turned his back on the knight.

•••

A breeze had come out of the north, soon after they made their way back into the main channel and so they raised the small sail. For the moment Helen was in charge and she directed Robert which rope to pull and tie off and which to loosen. In a matter of a few moments the wind filled the square cut cloth and they were able to stow the oars and sit back to enjoy a brief break from rowing.

"How often did you come to Amiens, Lady Helen?" Robert asked, as he adjusted his seat in the bow of the boat. She was seated at the stern, her sure hand on the rudder, while her eyes darted between the sail and shore.

"Quite often when I was younger. We would come for the high holy days, to attend mass at the Notre Dame Cathedral across the channel from our home. I remember attending the market in the center of the city many times. Amiens is more important than Abbeville and sees more travelers so there was always a chance to see something unusual and to hear stories from abroad. And the food they have there…" she paused a moment and shut her eyes, smiling. "*Flamiche aux poireaux* is simply delicious with its leeks and cream and flaky pastry, and then there are these little biscuits made with almond paste. We would come at Christmas and take enough of them back for the entire household to enjoy as a special treat. I must admit I ate more than my share."

"I will not say I can know what it must have been like to grow up without knowing your mother or father, but it does sound like your caretakers loved you."

"I believe they still do," Helen answered, then turned her attention back to the sail and shore. Robert watched her for a moment longer then turned to keep watch of the shores as well. Despite what she had seen at her home in Abbeville, Helen wanted to believe they were still alive. They were the only family she had ever known, and despite learning they were not in fact her aunt and uncle, she still considered them as if they were. Even as she watched the tree-lined eastern shore slip quietly by, she said a silent prayer for their safety.

As they continued upstream from Eaucourt to Amiens, the river split into many channels and tributaries. Robert was grateful Helen was there and had traveled the route enough times to be confident in her choice as they faced the frequent question of either right, left or even sometimes center.

They now passed through a portion of the river with several switch-backs, in which the channel narrowed dramatically and the shores, with their overhanging trees, included thick patches of reeds, which grew on the bank as well as the shallows. After spending so much time in the wide-open channel, both Helen and Robert felt closed in and uncomfortable. The air grew still and warm in the early morning sunshine and they had to return to rowing as the sail dropped limp.

The birds in the branches overhead no longer sang or whistled but cawed or called angrily from above, and the sound echoed and bounced across the narrow width of water. It was an eerie, unsettling noise. As Helen sat at the rudder, watching Robert steadily pull at the oars, she could feel the perspiration build on her hands and brow as her heart beat quicker. "I feel it too," Robert spoke, using hushed tones as his eyes quickly darted from left to right. It took a second for Helen to realize he had switched to French.

"It is as if the forest has eyes and it keeps watch over our progress," her voiced cracked, despite her attempt to keep it steady. She had responded in French and Robert nodded his approval as he smiled reassuringly. "I wish we at least had a breeze." Without thinking she reached up to pull back the hood of her cloak but stopped when Robert urgently hissed at her.

"You must keep your hair covered," he whispered, while leaning forward. "There is movement on the western shore and we are French peasants. If you must speak, deepen your voice to sound like a young lad."

A very English voice broke through the tense silence. "My god, it is hot. Is it always this hot so early in the spring?" A muffled voice answered. "I do not care if the Pope in Rome can hear me, I did not sign on to go thrashing around some swamp looking for a missing girl." Again a hushed voice answered. "Say that again and you will find your throat cut," the first voice growled in response. Robert lengthened his stroke at the oars and did his best to speed up their boat, without making too much more noise. He could have splashed all he wanted, it wouldn't have been heard over the sudden clash of steel and angry shouting.

Now he really put his back into it. Somewhere deep down inside he found a reservoir of energy. The shore began quickly speeding past and the bow nearly lifted up out of the water with each stroke. He could feel his shoulders burning and knew he didn't have much left to give. A sea borne breeze suddenly greeted them as their boat sped out of the confined canopy. The sail filled with the wind just as Robert's arms failed. He leaned forward, gasping for air and had just enough strength to pull the oars out of the water.

As he sat there doubled over, his racing heart beating loudly in his ears, Helen directed the boat through another switchback, deftly using the tiller and boom to navigate the channel. Suddenly the shores pulled back before them and the early morning sun glistened on the water's widened surface. Tears blurred her sight but she rapidly blinked them away when she saw a handful of boats of varying sizes moving on the widened river. As the morning mist shimmered and disappeared before her eyes, the outline of bridges and buildings appeared. Bells rang out, announcing the third hour since sunrise and calling the people to mass. "Amiens… it is Amiens."

•••

William turned his back on the knight bannerette, only to find he was facing the largest man he had ever seen. His hair was jet black, as were his eyes and unkempt beard. A sword, which looked like it could be used as a plowshare, was strapped across his back, his shoulders were as wide as a handcart and he looked like he could easily weigh 20 stones. It seemed appropriate he wore the Denebaud coat of arms, a red bull on a white field.

Behind him stood a gray palfrey with a woman on its back, the horse's reins held by the giant. The woman was leaning doubled over upon the horse's mane, her hands tied beneath its neck, preventing her from doing more than lifting her head and even that only a few inches. Her loose auburn hair, flecked with just a touch of silver, spread across her back and was covering her face, but from William's quick glance at her clothing he could tell she was of some importance. Even from where he stood, looking around the great mountain of a man before him, he could see she wore a pale linen blouse with a coat and skirt of dark green; her boots were hand tooled of fine calfskin or deer. All of these suggested not only importance, but wealth as well. It was no wonder Lord Thomas was interested in her.

"Bloody great beast, I told you to hold still," Godefroy angrily muttered as he struggled to get control of his horse while keeping a vise like grip on the palfrey's reins. William finally turned his attention back to the soldier before him. Despite the Denebaud coat of arms on his chest, his shield, which hung loosely from the side of his saddle, was painted black. He had probably been a free-lance up until Lord Thomas purchased his services. Robert had told William how to spot those men who fought for personal gain or promised rewards, with no thought for king, country or honor; a blank or darkened shield with no sigil or arms to show their allegiance.

Despite his size and the fact he was mounted, William could tell he was not comfortably seated. He sawed at the reins, while his feet and knees were tightly squeezing the horse's chest. The courser had no idea what the huge man wanted to do. The horse neighed loudly and stamped at the ground again, and William tore his attention away from Godefroy and stared in surprise; it was the same stallion they had found in the New Forest.

As soon as their eyes met, the stallion whinnied loudly, tossed his head and took several steps forward, despite Godefroy's attempts to stop him, until he was nearly touching William's face with his muzzle. He dropped his head slightly, his ears straining forward and his lips twitched as if he was trying to talk. William could have sworn he looked happy to see him; he knew he felt the same and reached out to stroke his cheek and scratch him in his chin groove. The stallion blew warm moist air on his hands and shoulder. For a very brief moment he lost himself in the joy of finding the stallion once again.

"You will leave the lady and the horses and find a way out of Amiens and Lord Thomas' service, Godefroy. To do anything else would be unwise." The words shook William back the present situation; Sir John had given voice to his own thoughts. The knight was standing beside him, one hand on the hilt of his long sword and the other still holding his long, dagger-like rondel. Out of the corner of his eye, William could see the man who, moments ago, had been prepared to take him back to Lord Thomas, now come to his defense.

"Have you forgotten your place?" Godefroy rumbled. His thick, dark eyebrows had drawn down, light gleamed in his eyes and his beard seemed to bristle. "Lord Thomas will never forgive nor will he forget."

"No, but one day he will be forgotten, and on my own last day, when that day finally comes and I have to answer for all I have chosen and all I have done, I will not say I picked the easy path on this day, but I did choose the right." As the knight bannerette spoke these words, William could feel the hair on the back of his neck and arms stand on end. A chill ran down his spine and the courser whinnied in response. As he continued to watch him, William could see the anger rising up in Godefroy. The veins and muscles on his neck were bulging, his mouth was clamped shut but he could see his jaw working. His expression made it look like he was chewing on rocks.

"Sir John," Godefroy rumbled, "you leave me no choice." In one quick motion he reached over his shoulder, grasped the hilt of his sword and drew it from its scabbard. It slid easily and made no sound whatsoever, except a slight ringing, as the blade, free of its sheath, vibrated in his plate-sized hand. To do this he had to move the reins to his left hand, dropping those of the palfrey in the process. Although he still had a tight grip on his own, William could tell he was unsure of himself.

In that very instance a memory flashed before him. "Count yourself lucky, lad," Gilbert had told him. "A well trained stallion can bite, kick and rear with little notice. One wrong word or movement and you would have found yourself lying on your back in that alley."

The words still echoed in his ears as he focused on the face of the stallion, its expression and its eyes; he didn't notice Godefroy shifting his weight or the bunching of the mass of muscles of his shoulders as he prepared to strike. He didn't notice Sir John quickly switching the rondel to his left hand while drawing his own long sword. He also didn't notice the gray mare, with the lady still tied tightly to its neck, begin to shy away, backing up from the courser. He missed all of this as he stared into the stallion's dark amber eyes. Revelation came in a flash from his last Latin lesson, just outside the gate of Crandor Castle; it was the final word his tutor had been teaching him when the courier arrived with the ransom letter from France.

William took a large step back, never taking his eyes off the stallion and shouted, "Augmentum!" The stallions nostrils flared, his eyes widened and his ears immediately flattened to the poll. A second later he was staring at the chest and belly of the stallion whose hooves were striking at the air only a few feet in front of him. The stallion continued to stand on his rear legs for several more seconds and then dropped back down to all four, his saddle empty.

Without a second thought, William grabbed the reins of the courser, ducked under the neck, put his right foot in the stirrup and threw his left leg up and over the saddle. All this happened in such a quick, fluid motion it took himself and the stallion by surprise. A quick flick of his wrist and pressure from one knee and the stallion turned in place and he found himself staring down at Sir John, his sword poised above Godefroy, who appeared to be lying unconscious on the cobblestone street.

"Is he dead, Sir John?"

"No… not yet," the knight answered. The tip of his sword was pressing into the red Denebaud bull.

"Then let him lie," William called over his shoulder as he had already kicked his heels in the flank of the stallion, pointing it towards the gray mare which spooked when the stallion reared. Auburn hair and green skirt trailed in the wind.

He didn't have time to wonder if the knight would listen or not. The palfrey was not only skittish, but quick too, and it took a moment of hard riding for him to come up alongside of her and, leaning over the neck of the stallion, grab the reins. Amazingly, the woman was still in the saddle. It was also amazing the mare hadn't turned down any of the narrow side streets. If she had William would have had little chance to come alongside her. Seconds later the palfrey was back under control and he stopped them both in the middle of the street. When William turned back he was surprised to see how far he had come from Sir John. It looked as though the knight still stood where he had left him.

Quickly wrapping the palfrey's reins around the wide, high horn of his saddle, he slid down off the stallion, crossed under his neck and gently took the gray mare by the bridle. Her eyes were wide with fear and she danced around him, but a few soft words and a gentle stroke on her cheek settled her down enough for William to work on the knot which tied the lady's hands.

"Please… help," the soft plea came from somewhere beneath the loose hair.

"Be at peace, my lady," William assured her, as he continued working on the knot. "You are safe now." The rope slipped just a little and he was able to work the ends free and then loosen the slipknots, which had secured her wrists. She inhaled sharply as he freed her hands. Dark red, nearly raw welts were already visible where the tight bonds had done their work.

"Are you able to sit up, my lady?" William asked. He stood, at the ready, in case, as she did so, she lost her balance in the process. Slowly she raised herself in the saddle, pausing twice when she swayed a little. Once completely sitting up, she took in a deep breath and let it out slowly.

"Thank you, sir," she began, then cleared her throat and continued stronger. "I apologize you find me in such a state." She paused once more as her hands went to her hair and began pulling it back from her face. "A lady must never find herself out of doors with her hair down." She spoke as if lecturing and William thought she might be talking to herself.

While she continued to work on her hair, William turned back towards Sir John and remembered they still found themselves in great danger. "My lady, we must not linger long here. The men who assaulted you may return with more strength… and there are only two of us. Can you ride?"

She had finished pulling the hair back, splitting it into three portions and braiding it down her back. William was amazed at how quickly she had accomplished this, especially with her wrists looking as they did. She was still seated on the palfrey, her head slightly bowed, staring at her hands and murmuring something under her breath. William thought he heard the word insolence along with a few curses. Finally she nodded, "I can ride well enough," she answered. Her voice sounded stronger and she sat up straighter, rolled back her shoulders and finally turned to look down at her rescuer.

William inhaled sharply as he looked up at one of the most beautiful faces he had ever seen. Despite her years, a few wrinkles and gray in her hair, she was stunning to look upon. He stood there, the reins still in his hands, his mouth slightly open and his heart hammering in his chest. In the distance church bells were ringing. He could hardly hear them over the thundering in his own ears. Not only was she beautiful, she had a presence about her, which commanded his attention. Finally, he was able to mumble, "My lady," and bowed deeply at the waist. "William of Dorchester, at your service."

She smiled a radiant smile, which sparkled in her clear blue eyes and answered, "Not Sir William, or Lord William?" She hid it well, but William could hear just a hint of concern in her question. Despite the tone of her voice, the look she gave him made William feel as if he would do anything she asked of him.

"Neither title has been… has been earned, or given to me, my lady." He smiled back, slightly stammering his answer and then stood there, reins in hand, in the middle of the street, as if stone. Finally, he realized how foolish he must appear and murmured an apology as he turned the head of the mare and stallion back towards Sir John and the ringing of bells.

For a time he led both horses, deep in his own thoughts, until she asked him, "do you know who those men were, or why they came for me, William? It all happened so quickly…" Her voice broke and she choked back a sob. For a moment William thought she was on the verge of tears, but she inhaled deeply through her nose, sat up straight in the saddle and wiped her eyes. After clearing her throat, she asked again if he knew who had attacked her.

"They work for Lord Thomas Denebaud," William answered flatly and quickly. It was a statement and she picked up on it.

"Lord Thomas?" she exclaimed. "The nerve of the man." She paused a moment, considering the implications, then added, "What could he possibly gain by taking me? He comes from a minor house and married into a minor house. Are there others tugging at his strings?"

"I believe he has his own designs for the throne itself, my lady. I do not believe there are any strings to be tugged, unless he is the one working them."

"Edward's throne? How is that possible?" She paused a moment and then added, as if to herself, "Have I been away so long?" As he walked between the mare and stallion, William quickly told her about Lord

Thomas' plan to control the Brent name, as well as his plot to eliminate the Simpson's of Dorchester. He made sure he didn't mention anything about Helen. "He is shrewder and more calculating than I imagined," she commented, "this may not get him the throne, but it certainly would place him in a position of great power and authority in the realm. How do you know so much about him, William?" It was a simple question, but he could feel the tension and stronger note of concern, which had continued to creep into her voice.

"This courser was Sir John Brent's," he explained. He then related how they found the stallion, their encounter with Lord Thomas, as well as the Lord High Admiral in the New Forest, and how the former had dogged William's steps ever since. He had just finished describing his capture at Eaucourt and escape as they returned to the intersection and the knight, who still stood guard over Godefroy. The great bulk of a man hadn't moved from where he fell from the stallion. A deep, dark part of William's thoughts had wished to find him otherwise.

Embarrassment suddenly overcame William, when he realized he needed to make introductions and didn't know the lady's name. "My lady, may I introduce Sir John Copeland, a knight of renown…" He stopped in mid-sentence as soon as he turned back toward the knight; he had taken one knee and his head was bowed.

"Majesty," the knight murmured. William's eyes widened as he turned back to the mounted lady. He silently mouthed the word, framing it as a question.

"William," Sir John advised, in hushed tones, his head still bowed "this is the Lady Isabella of France… the Queen Mother of Edward, Earl of Chester, Duke of Aquitaine… and King of England."

Chapter Twenty Six

If Helen had been raised any other way, she never would have known how to manage the sail and rigging of their small boat. As it was, she had spent a considerable time on the water with her guardians, and had shown enough interest and natural ability they encouraged and taught her the art of sailing on the Somme. As Robert lay doubled over, gasping for breath, she maneuvered them out into the widened river. Her target was the cathedral, not only because its immense size and height made it the most visible landmark, but also because the home she visited was nearby. Although it had been several years since she last saw it, Helen was confident she could find the house once they entered the central canal.

As luck would have it, they had arrived on Sunday. Most other days the river would have been choked with boats and flat-bottomed barges, fishing the main channel and its estuaries, as well as transporting to and from the coast. As it was they found only a few river men making their way towards the same canal they sought. Even as the mist had risen from the river and the city revealed, the bells of the cathedral had stopped. Helen realized that mass would begin soon, and sure enough, she could just hear, drifting over the water, the faint sound of singing. She recognized the music immediately and mouthed the words of joy at the dawning of a new day. A new day had dawned, she and Robert were alive despite everything they had been through. She smiled a radiant, early morning smile while trimming the sail and adjusting the rudder. The canal was right in front of them.

Her thoughts immediately turned to William. In the midst of her gratitude, she realized she hadn't considered his condition and she closed her eyes, praying for his safety. "Somehow, God, show him the way to Amiens and bring him safely to our home." Robert's response of "amen" startled her. William's tutor was sitting up, and although he was still taking deep breaths, he was no longer panting.

"My arms were spent, my lady and I could not pull another stroke if I had to, but it looks like God's grace and favor are sufficient. You handle the sail quite well." The old teacher smiled and Helen noticed he was no longer beet red or flushed.

"My guardians indulged my interest and ability. It seems natural, as if some part of me understands the wind and the water and what they are speaking to each other as well as myself." She furrowed her brow and shook her head. "I am not sure if I am making much sense."

"Although I have never mastered the sail and rudder, I think I do understand your meaning. Our Lord told us the Holy Spirit would come and speak to our spirit and share with us the thoughts of God. When we hear the Holy Spirit speaking to us, inside of us, it is similar to the sense you have of the shift in the wind."

"I was thinking about what you told me about the Holy Spirit. I was taught it was only for those in the upper room on the day of Pentecost, that it was not a part of our lives now."

Robert shook his head and his expression turned sad. "I have heard many say this and even preach it from the pulpit. Jesus never said such a thing. He told us we would go to the ends of the earth, preaching the good news and baptizing in the name of the Father, the Son and the Holy Spirit. We all have the opportunity to the same baptism of the Spirit, as did the church elders in Jerusalem all those centuries ago."

"How do you become baptized in the Holy Spirit? Have you?" she added as an afterthought.

"I have, my lady, and you can as well." He took one more deep breath and exhaled slowly, then shifted so he was facing Helen. "First you must accept Jesus as your Lord and Savior. This I know you have done, because I was there as witness, just as I was present when you led William's distant uncles to the Lord. The baptism of the Holy Spirit is different all together. Jesus told us we would be filled with power when the Holy Spirit came over us; that gifts were given along with the Holy Spirit."

"What kind of gifts?" Helen asked as she tacked across the main canal. She deftly maneuvered around one more flat-bottomed barge and then cut back across the waterway. They had drawn within the early morning shadows of those buildings on the edge of the city and nearest the entrance of the canal, namely the warehouses and docks for loading and unloading cargo from the river men's boats.

"Paul tells us there are many gifts, but the same Spirit gives them to each of us. Just as it is the same God at work in each of us, the same Spirit manifests itself in each person with different gifts. Some receive the Spirit of wisdom, to others a message of knowledge. To one, the Spirit gives faith, to another gifts of healing. Some receive the power of miracles and still others are given the gift of prophecy and yet it is the same Spirit in all. Some are given the gift of speaking in different tongues while others are given the gift of interpreting those tongues. In all of these it is the same Spirit at work and God distributes them to each person, as He determines."

"What gift has the Holy Spirit given to you?" The question slipped out before Helen had a chance to consider the private nature of such a request. When she apologized and suggested he didn't need to answer, Robert waved it off, smiling.

"Paul tells us that God has placed in His church first apostles, then prophets, next teachers, then miracle workers and healers, then helpers and guides, and finally those who speak in different tongues. Which do you think He has blessed me with?"

"You are William's teacher, but you are also our helper and our guide. William also told me you speak several languages. It seems God has blessed you with several gifts."

"I am blessed indeed, my lady, blessed indeed. But even as Paul said, if I have all knowledge and wisdom and faith, but do not have love, I have nothing. Prophecies will cease, tongues will be stilled, knowledge will pass away, but love will never fail. I have faith, hope and love in my life now, but the greatest of these is love."

"You have these now? Was there a time when you did not?"

"There was a time in my life when I was convinced I would never allow myself to love another."

"You love William, that much is clear." Robert smiled, but didn't answer at first. His eyes drifted over the waters of the Somme, eventually turning north.

"I found it very difficult to allow myself to love again, after my loss. I did not want to let anyone else get too close, so I would not have to worry about getting hurt so deeply." A pained expression passed over him and he slowly shook his head. "And then God revealed to me a truth I had forgotten."

"What was the truth?" Helen asked, when he had paused again. She thought the loss might have been his wife and son, William had mentioned just a few days before.

"That God so loved this world He was willing to even give up His only son for all of us, to forgive our sins and reconcile us to His grace and mercy. Jesus died for me; what was I willing to do for those around me?" He locked eyes with Helen and it was if she could suddenly sense the loss as well as the blessings. Tears filled her eyes and spilled down her cheeks as she realized how often she had been selfish, focusing only on herself and her needs. She had thought hers was the greatest pain anyone could have endured, and yet here was one who had gone through greater tragedy. A sense of remorse seemed to fill and threatened to overwhelm her.

She was startled out of her thoughts by the touch of Robert's hands on her own. He was leaning around the mast, his arms out stretched, concern and sympathy filling his expression. "The Holy Spirit is God's comforter and is available for you, my lady. It can help give you the peace which surpasses all understanding. It was what brought me through my own pain and despair."

"I wish for that more than anything right now."

Robert squeezed her hands gently and spoke in a quiet, yet strong voice. "God, I ask you to bless your daughter, Helen, with the Holy Spirit. Fill her with its power and peace. Speak to her, making her aware of Your presence and wisdom. In Jesus holy name I pray." Helen nodded and echoed Robert's "amen."

If you asked her later what happened there, in that boat, on the Somme, just on the edge of Amiens, she would shake her head, smile a shy smile and try to put into words the combination of joy, peace, ecstasy, warmth and energy which coursed through her. Her words never seemed to do it justice.

She was crying and laughing at the same time. Only later did she recall Robert was as well. The sun seemed brighter, the breeze clearer and the sounds of singing, drifting across the water, sharper in her ears. Unable to contain what she was feeling, she burst out into song, echoing the music she heard coming from the cathedral. She was young and alive, healthy, healed and nearly home. It was the furthest thing from her mind at that moment, but even if she tried she couldn't recall the pain she had recently been going through.

As it continued it was like a beehive in her head. Thoughts and feelings were cascading into each other; she was nearly overwhelmed with gratefulness and joy. At any other time she would have found herself having difficulty navigating the narrowing canal as it entered the city proper, but even the coordinated effort needed to maintain the trim of the sail and the angle of the rudder were effortless. It was as if her body knew what it needed to do while her mind and her spirit were soaring together.

The music from the cathedral grew louder, until they were nearly alongside it. As they had continued up the narrowing canal, making their way further into the heart of the city, they passed under the occasional bridge, and alongside stairs which led down to the water's edge from the streets and houses above. Either by nature or design, this portion of the Somme cut lower than the surrounding landscape, and the city was built right up to the river's edge, such that one could stand upon the cobblestone path, which ran in front of the houses and buildings on either side of the canal, and look down into the waterway.

There was a pause in the singing just as Helen maneuvered the craft to the western bank and pulled alongside a stone landing and its accompanied set of stairs. "We are here," she sighed, still smiling. A moment later and Robert had the boat tied to the stone cleat and helped her safely onto the landing. Even though they had only been on the water for a few days, it still took her a moment of being slightly unsettled before her legs were steady beneath her.

As she stood, waiting for the light headed feeling to pass, she looked out across the canal, to the homes and cathedral beyond. The water was completely calm and, like a mirror, reflected the buildings and the crenellated roofline and bell towers of one of France's largest gothic churches. The city was quiet as nearly everyone was at mass. It was Sunday, but somehow Helen had lost track of the days since boarding the ship to return to France. The silence added to the peaceful feeling which continued to fill her.

"This is a beautiful city, my lady," Robert commented, echoing her own thoughts. She nodded an agreement.

"Although I call Abbeville home, it is here, in Amiens where I spent some of my best days as a child. We had the canal to float on, the market square with its sights and sounds from all of France and beyond, and the flowers. Oh, the flowers." She paused, closing her eyes while smiling a radiant smile. "I can smell them, even now, in my memory."

"I wish we had come at a better time and for different reasons," Robert added. Helen nodded and thanked him for the steady arm, then turned and ascended the stairs to the street just above.

The houses, which lined the canal in the central portion of Amiens, were of all different shapes and sizes. It was this mismatch of colored paint, bare wood, rock and even the rare brick, which allowed Helen to find her home with relative ease. At first it wouldn't have stood out, but as they walked up the cobblestone path lining the narrow space between the homes and the canal, Robert had a sense of which home they were making for. It sat just a little farther back than its neighbors, giving it a small yard which was grass filled and lined with flower beds. Although it was still early in the season, the weather had been warm enough for the last few weeks that the buds were already showing themselves on the rose bushes. Several other bulbs were already pushing their stems out of the rich soil; it would still be some time before they revealed the flower within.

The home itself was timber and framed with large flower boxes outside the windows on both the first and second floor. These were still bare, but would certainly add a dramatic color contrast to the white plaster walls and dark wood framing. Although it appeared a small home from the front, Robert had a feeling it was several times deeper than wide. Smoke lazily curled up out of the chimney on the roof and he hoped the morning meal was still out on the table. His stomach echoed its agreement.

A large wooden door, painted bright blue, stood in the middle of the house, centered between large windows, which were still shuttered. As they left the cobblestones and began walking down the crushed rock path the sound echoed off the walls of the houses on either side. One or more dogs began barking from inside the home and a woman's voice scolded them into reluctant silence. Robert was pretty sure he could hear them whimpering just on the other side of the door they approached. He glanced at Helen and she was smiling a radiant smile.

"I would recognize those hounds anywhere and that voice." She spoke quietly and Robert wondered if she was simply thinking out loud. "They made it here from Abbeville after all." He was pretty sure she wasn't just talking about the dogs.

As Helen approached the door, she suddenly felt a reluctance to knock. She had recognized the voice of her "aunt" as well as Chrestien's two dogs, but there were other voices she now heard inside. There was a woman and man's voice, the latter being a deep rumble and the former, higher and slightly nasal. She paused at the door, her hand just inches from the wood. The woman's voice was obviously agitated and she could hear her guardian responding with soft tones. Robert could see a sudden reluctance in her expression.

Another voice entered the conversation and a gasp caught in her throat. The reluctance of seconds ago quickly disappeared and she disregarded knocking, instead urgently tugged on the knotted rope which hung beside the door. Somewhere inside a bell clanged noisily while all of the voices were just as suddenly silenced. Robert could hear footsteps approaching the door. When he glanced at Helen she showed no signs that she had been concerned just a few seconds before, instead she looked eager and excited.

A bolt was noisily pulled back and someone slowly opened the door just enough to see out. Robert caught the flash of a green eye through the crack and then heard a loud gasp, a barely audible exclamation, which may have been, "*mon Dieu*," and then a loud thud, as if something heavy fell down on the other side of the door. Once again there were raised voices from inside and it sounded like several people speaking all at the same time. One young voice stood out over the others and this time Robert heard it as well.

"William, is that you?" the old teacher called out over the noise.

The door was jerked open to reveal a narrow corridor, running down the middle of the home, jammed with several people and two very excited hounds. The dogs were already leaping up at Helen, their tongues hanging out of the sides of their mouths with smiles in their deep brown eyes and deep throated basso "woofs" echoing down the hallway, out into the garden and across the canal.

Despite the canine cacophony and furry maelstrom of leaping and licking, which had nearly bowled Helen over, Robert stood in the doorway, smiling the largest most grateful smile he could possibly imagine. It was reflected in a similar look from his pupil. He stole a second to glance at the others surrounding William. One elderly man and a well-dressed woman had both dropped to their knees and were doing their best to revive an older, larger woman who had sunk to the floor. Beside William stood a knight. As soon as Robert saw the coat of arms, embroidered on the left chest of his surcoat, he recognized him, despite never having met Sir John Copeland in person. The knight stood "*En Garde*", with his left hand resting on the pommel of his arming sword, while his right hand gripped his rondel. Both remained in their scabbards, but he was at the ready, nonetheless. His eyes quickly moved from Robert, to Helen and the dogs and back again.

Robert nodded to the knight bannerette. "Well met, Sir John. It does me great good to not only find my charge, but to find him in the care of a trusted man of the king." He was about to continue when the woman, who had been kneeling a moment before, stood and turned to him. William saw his tutor's eyes grow large and the color drain from his face. Without hesitation, his teacher dropped to one knee, his head bowed and spoke clearly, in order to be heard over the dogs, "Majesty…"

As soon as Helen heard this she stopped laughing and, signaling the dogs with her hands, they dropped to their haunches, sitting at attention and the entryway grew very quiet. "Majesty…?" she murmured and turned to look at the woman, standing just beyond William and Sir John. Despite the shadows of the hall, Helen caught the flash of brilliant blue in her eyes, an all too familiar slim, aquiline nose, arched, thick eyebrows and auburn hair, lightly streaked with silver and the realization slammed into her.

Tears welled up in her eyes, and her shoulders shook from silent sobs as she dropped into a deep courtesy, her head bowed and her hands covering her face. Quietly, her voice quavering, she voiced the question, "mother?"

Chapter Twenty Seven

William later described the scene as if out of a dream. Isabella of France, the Queen Mother of Edward III of England, slowly stood, smoothing out her dark green skirt and straightened her vest. As if from long years of habit, she rolled back her shoulders slightly while lifting her chin.

With the lightest touch of her hand, Sir John stepped aside, bowing deeply at the waist. William stood open mouthed, forgetting even his earliest teaching on etiquette, as she stepped past him. He thought she looked so deeply sad that tears were threatening to fall from her eyes. He couldn't tell if she noticed, as her complete attention was on the young lady kneeling before her, but tears were already spilling from his own. The only sounds in the hallway were the light whimpering of the hounds, who were barely able to continue restraining their excitement, the nearly silent sobs of Helen and the soft footfalls of Isabella as she walked forward.

Through the blur of tears Helen thought she saw someone move toward her, followed by a gentle, soft hand cupping her cheek, wiping her tears away with a thumb. She allowed the hand to lift her chin and her eyes slowly drifted up until she was gazing upon one of the most beautiful faces she had ever seen. "You have your father's mouth and eyes… and his hair." A smile grew into a great, loving grin and she felt hands helping her stand on her feet.

Helen suddenly found herself eye to eye with the one person she had wanted to see her whole life, while at the same time dreading the meeting because she had no way of controlling the outcome. What she found, when it finally happened, was open arms and a warm, long, loving embrace. It was more than she had ever hoped for.

She rested her face on her mother's shoulder and gave up any pretense of control. Sobs flowed out of her, but they were sobs of joy. Her own arms wrapped around her mother and, for the first time in her memory, she felt the warmth of the woman who gave birth to her, and she wasn't ashamed or angry or any of the other reactions her fears had played upon her mind. She could feel her mother, stroking her hair, speaking gently in her ear, "my dear child, my dear, dear child."

William eventually realized he was staring, slightly open mouthed, at this meeting and promptly shut his mouth and lowered his eyes. Seeing Helen and her mother embrace and comfort each other brought back feelings of his parents, which had been buried for quite some time. The feeling of loss and emptiness burned like a smoldering fire, which eventually rose up into his throat, tightening it, causing him to take ragged breaths.

He was embarrassed to be seen in such a condition so he turned to the side, dropping to one knee and placed his face in his hands. Tears spilled out between his fingers and his nose ran freely. Part of him knew he should be rejoicing for Helen, but he missed his own parents more than he had realized. Unlike Helen, his sobs were silent, as if his own voice was unable to reveal how much he hurt.

A moment later a hand rested on his shoulder and gave it a gentle, but strong squeeze. "I miss them both so much…" he was finally able to stammer, after doing his best to catch his breath.

"You do your father and mother credit, William." It was Sir John who spoke, which startled him. He had assumed it was Robert who came to comfort him. The deep basso continued, "Your father risked all to save me, my cousin, and those around us. His death was more than your mother could accept. Your grief honors them… but now there are more urgent matters to attend. What of Lord Thomas… and your uncle?"

William nodded, sniffling loudly and wiped his face on the sleeve of his tattered and torn cotte. "It is best not to dwell long on the past and forget the present," he reminded himself out loud. Clearing his throat, he stood to his feet and turned to face Helen, her mother and his tutor.

"Majesty, I think it best if we lay aside any more pretense of secrecy or hidden agendas. The same man who attempted to abduct you this morning, has moved several times against Helen, as well as myself. There is counsel we seek and the only way to do so honestly is to lay aside any masks we carry." William paused a moment and turned to his tutor. Robert nodded his agreement.

"It is time all present understand what is at stake, William," his teacher added. Sir John and Helen agreed. Up to that point, William hadn't thought about the implication of Sir John's presence. If his loyalty lay anywhere other than the throne of King Edward, he now had information he could use to his advantage. Without a second guess, William believed in that loyalty and pushed any doubt that may have tried to enter, to the farthest reaches of his thoughts.

Isabella turned to the older couple, "how is Kateline, Basille?"

"She is strong, Majesty. She will recover quickly."

"Is the table still set for us to break our fast?"

"All is as requested and required, Majesty."

Isabella turned back to Helen. "The morning meal has already been set in the parlor. There we can sit and discuss the situation for as long as is necessary."

A moment later Helen found herself seated beside her mother and across from Sir John. Spread before them was a simple yet glorious meal. The table was set with several loaves of bread, butter, honey, bacon, a dried ham for slicing and wine (for both drinking and to dunk the bread in). William's stomach growled and he started to blush in embarrassment when others in the room protested the same.

It was several long minutes before William pushed back from the table, paused briefly, then stood and bowed at the waist to the Queen Mother, "Majesty," he began, his right hand over his left breast, "my name is William de Simpson. I am the nephew and chosen heir of Charles de Simpson, Earl of Dorchester and lord of Crandor Castle. I apologize for not fully revealing my identity when we first met. I have been traveling as a plain journeyman from Dorchester, since leaving Crandor just over a fortnight ago."

Isabella nodded her understanding and he continued. "My uncle was captured last summer, after an ill-fated attack on St. Omer, and is being held by Count Jean Libourne de Coucy at Chateau de Coucy." At this, Robert stood and retrieved the ransom letter from his pack, which he had hung over the back of his chair, and handed it, across the table to the Queen Mother, bowing in the process. "I recently found myself in a position to overhear Lord Thomas describe his duplicity in this event. How he was able to convince others to make the attack, and coerce others to abandon my uncle during the battle, is beyond me.

"Once my uncle was out of the way, Lord Thomas had hoped that ransom letter," William nodded to the folded parchment Isabella had begun examining, "would force me to sell my lands and title in order to free my uncle. At the right moment, he would have found himself in Dorchester and at my aid. I decided, rather quickly and before Lord Thomas made his appearance, to take a very different course of action, and since then have found myself at crossed swords with Lord Denebaud. It has been my intention since leaving Crandor to find a way to secure my uncle's release and his return home… without paying the ransom." William paused at this, in order to make sure the Queen Mother understood the implication.

"We will return to that point, but for now, please continue," Isabella stated.

"I can attest to this majesty," Sir John added, standing up next to William. "Through manipulation and subtle devices, Lord Thomas acquired my services in England and through these forced my hand in France. During several discussions with him, I discovered his designs on the de Simpson lands and title. He also made it quite clear that neither the elder nor the heir mattered to him anymore, despite his repeated attempts to have William killed or captured, as he had found an even better prize which would move him closer and quicker to his goal."

Helen took a deep breath and stood, looking her mother directly in the eyes. "Lord Thomas, somehow, discovered my identity and decided, whether through coercion or force, he would use me to his own ends. I left Abbeville, in an effort to return to my family in the Marches and he has pursued me ever since." At the mention of the border between England and Wales, Isabella jumped slightly, then quickly regained her control.

"Lord Thomas was in Southampton, waiting for me. If not for the bravery of William, I would be in his grasp now. As it was, God provided me a rescuer and guardians, who have seen me safely here, despite several more attempts by Lord Thomas."

"It is also my concern, Majesty," William added, "there may be other forces at work here; those who have also found out Helen's identity, but would rather see her removed than have her find her way into someone else's possession."

Isabella closed her eyes a moment, while shaking her head slightly. When she opened them again, William could see she was on the verge of more tears. "I am so sorry, my dear child." She paused, as she considered the situation, sniffled loudly, then added, "How did Lord Thomas discover your identity, and why did you suddenly feel it was time to reunite with your father's family in the Marches?"

"Uncle and … I mean, Kateline and Basille, both made it very clear there were sudden dangers waiting for me in France and I should leave before they caught up with me. What those dangers were, I cannot say. I had hoped to ask them after returning to Abbeville. When we arrived there three nights ago, they had abandoned the estate. This home was the only other place I could think they may have tried for as we had spent several days in Le Crotoy and travelled directly from one to the other."

"What do you mean, the estate was abandoned?"

Robert took up the narrative, "Majesty, when we arrived the gardens looked as though horses had torn up the turf. The house looked as though it had been sacked… and we found your caretaker, Chrestien, God rest his soul." Tears appeared in Helen's eyes, as she remembered the death of the old man who used to give her rides in his hand cart and taught her the names of the flowers in his garden. William was shocked to see tears in Isabella's eyes as well.

She shook her head quickly, then stood up just as fast and began pacing back and forth. "Edward must be warned," she muttered two or three times, then paused. "After Abbeville, did you come straight here?"

"No, majesty, we did not," William admitted. "It was late in the evening so we stopped in Eaucourt."

"I imagine the Lord's de Simpson were none too happy to see two Englishmen, even with the distant relation," Isabella murmured, more of a thought out loud than a statement. William answered it anyway.

"The death of Lord David's only daughter, as well as Lord Matthew's only son and grandson, had left them with no vision for the future of their family in France. So, you are right, majesty, they were less than pleased to see us…" His voice trailed off and he wondered how much he should reveal now. Helen's face was a blank mask; she was no help.

"Is there more, William?" Isabella asked.

"The Lord's de Simpson and myself believe we have found a way for there to be a future for the family estate, however, it would require a delicate hand…"

"Ask, William. We have set aside our masks, have we not?"

"As you wish, Majesty. The Lord's de Simpson have pledged their fealty to their suzerain for as long as they live. That commitment remains just as strong today. When they go to be with the Lord, without recognized heirs, the estate returns to the Lord of Ponthieu; it was given to you as part of your dowry when you were betrothed to King Edward's father."

"I am well aware of all this, William."

"Your Majesty may not be aware that Helen's guardians had given their approval, allowing her to be betrothed to Geoffrey de Simpson. The Lord's de Simpson are in possession of a letter stating the same." Isabella turned slightly ashen and found her seat quickly.

"Why would they agree to such a union?" she murmured to herself while shaking her head. Finally she took a deep breath and turned to William, "continue."

"When Marie de Simpson married my uncle, her dowry included a portion of the estate in France. The remainder would pass on to

Geoffrey. He fell, along with his father at Crecy and so the estate will be lost, unless there is a change."

Isabella turned in her chair and stared directly at William. "Was this your own idea, or did others put it to you?" It took a moment for him to realize she had already recognized the solution he had come up with. His mouth dropped open for just a second, then he snapped it shut and continued.

"I proposed this to the Lord's de Simpson, as well as Lady Helen. Neither of my cousins felt there was much hope in it, but they were willing to allow us the chance to ask." William paused a moment, then continued, "will you recognize your daughter, Helen de Mortimer and name her to control both portions of the de Simpson estate in France?"

"If I do so, I declare myself an adulteress and face the same fate as my sisters, Blanche and Margaret," she shook her head, suddenly recalling the terror and pain of that period in her life. She shook her head. "It cannot happen that way… it must not happen that way," she turned to Helen and placed her hands over her daughters. Their eyes met and for a moment they said nothing. "I am sorry child. I cannot do this; not only for my own sake, but for yours as well." A question rose in Helen's eyes and her mother answered it quickly. "Lord Thomas knows of your existence and has plotted to control you and therefore, he believes, to control me, through you. That will not happen. If I name you, others will seek to do the same… or worse."

Helen's eyes dropped to the table, "I understand, Majesty."

Isabella reached up and lifted Helen's chin so their eyes met once more. "We are in private, with close confidantes… mother, not Majesty." She smiled and waited until Helen did as well. "I cannot name you, child, but there are still powers I carry, despite my exile from Edward's court." Isabella paused in thought, glanced up, then around the room and a puzzled look crossed her face. "Where are Basille and Kateline?" It took a moment for William to realize she was referring to Helen's guardians.

"I have not seen them since we moved into the parlor, Majesty," Sir John rumbled as he stood and moved out into the hall. His footsteps receded toward the kitchen and then back again. "They appear to be no longer in the house." The knight remained standing in the hall, his hand not straying far from the pommel of his arming sword. "I do not believe this house is safe for us," his deep basso echoed into the parlor even as the dogs began barking in the foyer.

"I have nowhere else to go…" Helen murmured.

"There is a place I know where even Lord Thomas would not dare to move against us," Isabella stated as she stood, pulling Helen up with her. "We must be quick… there is a door off the kitchen, at the back of the house."

Before they were all out of the parlor a loud knocking started at the front door. By the time they were in the kitchen, the knocking became pounding and the dogs' barking seemed to change from an alert to an alarm. William wondered if he would be able to leave anywhere without Lord Thomas on his heels. He had no idea Helen was thinking the exact same thing.

Once they were near the back door, Isabella stopped them and quickly explained where they were going. "I came across the channel as part of a peace delegation from my son to my cousin. Those who traveled with me had other duties to attend, prior to reuniting here in Amiens. We had agreed to meet, this day, after the fourth bell. The house they are using is not far, but we will have to cross the channel."

"I will stay behind and delay any who attempt to come through the house," Sir John offered. William immediately began protesting but the knight bannerette raised his hand to silence him. "There is no time to discuss this William. You brought me hope, to hear of my cousin Gilbert's survival of Neville's Cross. Now let me also repay your father's courage and sacrifice." William blinked away tears, nodding his understanding. He offered his hand to the man who was one of the last to see his father alive.

"If ever you make it out of this Sir John, and find yourself back in England and near Dorchester, you have only to call at Crandor. The hospitality of our home will always be there for you." The smile on the knight's face was wide enough it even showed his missing teeth. He nodded to William's tutor, bowed his head to Helen and then deeply at the waist to the Queen Mother. Without a word he turned and walked out of the kitchen and down the long hall. "God, bless that man. Watch over him and keep him safe. Let Your angels surround and protect him."

"Amen," Helen and Robert echoed. Isabella watched the scene unfold without comment, but William could see a question in her eyes.

"Once out the door and across the small garden, we will turn right and move down several houses. There will be a well-trimmed brick path, which will lead us back to the channel and a footbridge. With luck, we will find ourselves on the bridge while those who mean us harm are… delayed in this house." She didn't have to say that while they were here, Sir John would keep them occupied.

William stepped forward to open the door, but his tutor grabbed him by the shoulder and gently pulled him back. "Stay close to Lady Helen and her Majesty." He didn't have to add what they both knew was their duty. They would safeguard the innocent, no matter the cost. William nodded and stepped aside.

The brick footpath was exactly where Isabella had described it. Once they were out of the back door, they crossed a small garden, which would normally hold vegetables and an assortment of herbs. It was as wide as the house and a crushed rock path led straight to the narrow street beyond. The alley was really nothing more than a well-worn and slightly rutted packed dirt and stone lane, which the houses on either side backed up to. It seemed to run roughly parallel to the canal and was empty of people.

Even as they turned left into the alley they heard two sounds simultaneously. The first was the bells of the cathedral ringing out the fourth hour. The second was shouting and the ringing of steel on steel within the house. Robert quickened his step, while William brought up the rear, keeping Helen and her mother between them.

William did his best to control his breathing, but he could still feel his heart racing, matched beat for beat with a drumming in his ears. Helen and her mother were arm in arm, matching stride for stride with Robert's own hurried pace. William glanced over his shoulder once or twice but there was no one following. The brick path cut between two houses and then they were at the canal. Out in the open, without the closeness of the walls from either house, the breeze came up into their faces and the sound of crashing steel died away. "Straight over the bridge then right after the first home," Isabella instructed. Her breathing was rapid but she seemed to be in control of her emotions.

As Robert continued forward, William glanced to the left. He could see the landing with the small craft they had used to sail and paddle their way up the Somme. Even as he glanced back toward the house, a figure came out from the front garden and stood frozen in his tracks. His eyes grew wide, his face lit up scarlet red and William was sure, if he had been closer, he would have seen the blood vessels in his neck bulging in anger and frustration. "Leave that one, he means nothing… I see them… out here, crossing the canal!" Lord Thomas stood screaming and pointing.

And seconds later half a dozen well-armed men, including Godefroy, came out of the house.

There was only a hundred or so feet separating William and the others from their pursuers. Why didn't he think to take the stallion and mare? They were stabled in the small barn just off the garden, which they had recently passed through. There was no turning back for them now. Robert saw how close their pursuers were and quickened his pace across the bridge. Helen and Isabella were right behind him, with William at the rear when the unimaginable happened. Isabella stumbled, rolling her ankle on a loose stone, nearly falling to her knees and almost pulling Helen down with her. William was sprinting when they fell and he had to jump to the side to avoid running into them. The Queen Mother's painful shout stopped Robert in his tracks.

It only took him a quick second to see the situation and know what he had to do. "William, help the Queen Mother and Helen. Get them to the house as fast as you can. Do not look back and do not stop, no matter what you hear."

Tears welled up in William's eyes and he shook his head. "You cannot… I will not…"

"There is no time, William!" his tutor shouted at him, pushing him towards Isabella and her daughter. "Safeguard the innocent… no matter the cost. Go! Go, now!" He turned his back on his young student, Isabella, and her daughter; wishing he had something more than the baselard he had kept since Southampton. Lord Thomas and his men were soon on the other side of the footbridge when they realized Robert had stopped and was going to try and block their way; all seven smiled as they rushed forward.

It took all of Robert's effort not to turn around and make sure William and the women had begun moving again. He forced himself to focus on the men in the front. The bridge was narrow enough that only two could pass at one time. It also looked as though all the men wore some amount of chain mail. It would slow them down, whereas he was unencumbered; if he only had a shield.

The first two rushed forward the remaining few dozen feet. The others hung back far enough to make sure they were out of the way of any follow-throughs. These men at arms were well trained, but not for street fighting. They bumped shoulders as they ran the last several steps; neither was expecting what happened next.

Once William was at the end of the bridge he glanced over his shoulder. Helen was supporting her mother and the three of them were making the best time they could, considering Isabella winced and inhaled sharply every time she put weight on her right foot. They had crossed the path, which ran alongside the canal and were passing between two very large buildings. They may have been houses, but William didn't risk taking the time to look closely.

When he glanced back, he was shocked to see one of the guards prostrate on the bridge, a baselard sticking out of his chest. The other was locked, arm in arm with his tutor; it looked like they were wrestling. The remaining guards were bunched up behind them, including Lord Thomas who was screaming something which William couldn't understand. The pounding of his heart and his own panting drummed out most other noises.

"This… this is where we turn," Isabella gasped, as they came upon a well-paved lane. William couldn't see her face at the moment, but from her voice, it sounded like she was in agony. As they turned right onto the lane, Isabella took each step slower than the one before. William tried to continue watching where they were going, making sure he didn't trip over the women, while still keeping an eye on the bridge. What he saw, over his shoulder, made him stop dead and he found himself torn between making sure they made it to safety and turning back to help his teacher.

Robert had learned, as a young man, when facing a better armed and armored opponent, to let them take the first swing, then quickly step into them, right upon them, during their follow through. It completely went against his instincts, but his father had made sure he would control the desire to panic and run. He remembered this particular lesson taking much longer than some of the others. As soon as he stepped inside the swing of the guard he began grappling with him. From the look on his face, this was the last thing he expected the older teacher to do. Robert knew he couldn't outwit or outfight all of the guards, but he certainly could delay them long enough for William and the women to escape. He forced any other thoughts he may have had at that moment as far away as he could.

As Robert was wrestling to disarm the soldier in front of him, Godefroy pushed several guards aside, stepping over the fallen man. The fool with the baselard sticking out of his chest had only been in the service of Lord Thomas for a short time and Godefroy had not even taken the time to learn his name. He snorted a scowl at the dead man. To be killed by a thrown baselard from an old man was no way for a soldier to die. Quicker than you would have thought a large man could move, he reached around the other guard, grabbing Robert by the back of the neck. It was a vise-like grip and it sent a painful blast down his spine. In reflex he immediately let go of the guard, his hands trying desperately to pry loose the grip.

While he held Robert with his left hand, Godefroy swung the other into his stomach. One swift blow of the massive mallet-sized fist folded Robert in half, knocking all the wind out of his lungs. His knees buckled under him and he stopped trying to pry the fingers loose, instead clutching his chest, desperately trying to re-inflate his lungs. Godefroy swung one more time, connecting on the teachers' jaw. His gray-haired head snapped back and William watched in horror as the massive man at arms lifted Robert up and tossed his limp body into the river below.

William stood there, lost in time. Part of his mind was screaming at him to go back to the river, jump in, and pull his teacher to safety, while another part was shouting, just as loud, to help Helen and her mother. Despite the late morning sunshine, William's sight grew dim and the ground beneath him seemed to shift on its own, nearly knocking him off his feet. He closed his eyes and shook his head. In that brief moment he missed seeing a figure running out of the alley they had just left, turning left at the bridge, and heading downstream along the canal.

For what seemed several long moments, but was probably no more than a few seconds, William wavered, unable to make the decision. Then, as clear as if he was standing next to him, Robert's voice rang out in his ears. "Safeguard the women, William. That is your only concern now." Time caught back up with itself. He heard Lord Thomas screaming at his men while Isabella was now whimpering each time she put weight on the foot. She and Helen had only made it a few feet down the cobblestone lane.

The urgency of the moment crashed down on him. What if there wasn't anyone at the house? Lord Thomas would have all three of them; he already knew what that would mean for him. William forced himself to shake off those thoughts and followed it up by physically shaking his head. "Focus on what you can do right now, William. Do not focus on the problem." Two quick strides and he was alongside the Queen Mother. Without ceremony or permission he grabbed her right arm, lifted it up and wrapped it around his neck. "Rest your weight on me, Majesty. We will move quicker." Isabella nodded her understanding.

"It is the fifth… on the left," she gasped between strained breaths. "There is a small courtyard off the lane." William saw the house and realized he needed to help more in order to move faster.

"Helen… run ahead and rouse the house. Do whatever you must, but be quick." Without answer, she lifted her skirt in her hands and ran forward, picking her way around the occasional pile of horse manure. As she sprinted ahead, William grabbed Isabella around the waist, lifting her slightly off the ground, while shifting more of her weight onto his shoulders.

Out of the corner of his eye he could see her face now. It was only inches away. Some of her hair had managed to work its way loose and the morning breeze was swirling it about their heads. William risked a longer glance now; although the pain was clear on her expression, and despite the wrinkles around her eyes and mouth, he could see her steeling her countenance. The resolve he saw in her expression made her appear even that much more stunning. Although he didn't know it then, later he would find that in her youth she was thought of as the most beautiful in all of Europe. It would not come as a surprise. What would surprise him was this moment, with him half carrying her with arm around waist was the closest she had allowed a man since Lord de Mortimer.

Shouts behind him broke his chain of thought. William could hear iron shod boots on the cobblestones. Shutters were thrown open, as others became aware of the chase and he could see an occasional head thrust out, staring at the scene before them.

•••

They had just returned from mass at the gothic cathedral in Amiens. It had been several years since he had been in the city and able to attend services but he had not forgotten the feeling of awe and reverence while standing inside a church of such size and grandeur. In his mind, Salisbury Cathedral was a close second, and the only one in England, which could compare. The mass had been very well attended. He felt as if most of the city of Amiens had turned out.

He didn't have to wait long for the morning meal. At this house, on Sunday, the entire staff attended mass, along with the guests. Most of what they would serve had been prepared prior to leaving for the cathedral. As it was, it only took a few extra minutes to set the table and lay out the provisions. While he waited he found himself in the hall admiring several of the tapestries. One fascinated him more than the others. It was a mother and daughter, seemingly caught between a rampant lion and unicorn. Trees, flowers, birds and grass surrounded the two women.

Something of that particular artwork's subject made him think about recent events. He found it interesting that the mother stood while the daughter was seated. Was she there as protection from the ravages of the lion, while the unicorn represented her innocence and purity? Or was it the other way around? Was she there to show her daughter there was a time and place for innocence, but that time had passed, and now it was time to embrace the lion, to summon up her courage, disguise her fair nature, and show the world the face of bravery? He shook his head, realizing there was no way he could answer that. Besides, it was just a tapestry. There were more pressing matters to keep in mind.

A sudden pounding at the door, just a few steps down the hall, jolted him from his thoughts. The pounding quickly turned to hammering, followed closely by screaming; it was a woman's voice. The household responded instantly. He had to step aside, as those he had chosen to accompany him on this trip rushed out of the dining hall and down the dozen or so strides to the door. He followed close behind the men, only then realizing how little he could help, if called upon, since he hadn't taken the time to arm himself that morning. After all, who would dare?

When the door was opened he stood, staring, open mouthed. "How…? Where?" He couldn't even form a complete sentence. Despite the swirl of copper colored hair hiding most of her face, he instantly recognized her and motioned for the closest guard to help her inside.

"No time… no time. Have to help… William and…" she nearly collapsed as she crossed the threshold, her already pale color blanching to white. Her voice was trembling and her hands were shaking but somehow she managed to will her body to respond. "Help William… please, my Lord" she murmured as she fainted in the arms of the guardsman.

Without hesitation he bellowed, as only a man accustomed to giving orders on the open sea is capable, "to arms!" Turning to the guard holding the young woman, he pointed down the hall, "move her to the parlor, Dennis, and then join us out front." With that, he led the men who had accompanied him from London out the door and into the courtyard. There were only three of them, but others within the house would soon answer the call.

Before he and the men were half way across the courtyard a young man and woman came around the corner. They were holding tightly to each other, hip to hip; arm in arm, the woman's face a mask of pain; the young man's one of bound determination. Like a flash, which nearly caused him to stumble, he recognized both of them. "Dear, God! Your Majesty… and William?"

•••

They had made it to the courtyard, despite the pounding of William's heart in his chest and the burning of his shoulders. He wanted to turn and look, to see just how close Lord Thomas and his men were, but he forced himself to keep his eyes on the cobblestones at his feet. Even though their steps were much quicker, William could tell the speed was taking its toll on Isabella. The grimace and the sharp inhalation now came with every step. "Just a few more steps, Majesty," William muttered as they came to the corner.

The clatter of shod feet echoed even louder in his ears and he could have sworn it came from both in front and behind. Finally they turned into the courtyard and William almost stopped dead to the spot. Before him, were three of the King of England's own guards and several more coming out of the house, and with them stood William de Clinton, First Earl of Huntingdon, Lord High Admiral and Warden of the Cinque Ports.

Chapter Twenty Eight

For a second William couldn't believe his eyes, then he heard his name and recognized the voice. Despite the drawn swords of the guardsmen, he forced himself to move forward, as tears of relief and joy welled up in his eyes. Before he had a chance to speak or even greet Lord de Clinton, Isabella did, forcing control into her pain-filled and trembling voice. "We are pursued, Lord de Clinton. We need your aid." They were now several paces inside the courtyard and William watched as more of the King's guard rushed from the house.

Lord de Clinton took no hesitation. His orders were quick and decisive, such that William found the first guard sheath his sword and step up on the other side of Isabella. "Majesty," he nodded, and then took her left arm, and mirroring William, lifted it up and around his neck. The two of them now quickly carried her past Lord de Clinton, through the wall of unsheathed bright steel, which parted briefly to let them pass, and across to the door of the home. William stopped, disengaging himself from Isabella, turned on the threshold and stood, arms akimbo. He had no weapon but his fists, or rather his fist, since his right hand still wouldn't close completely. Despite only the one hand, he still stood ready to defend the innocent he had been charged with.

Seconds later Lord Thomas and his men ran head long into the courtyard. William watched as, like a closing fist, the King's guards surrounded them and forced them to lie down their weapons. All followed except Godefroy. He refused to accept surrender and the consequence of his choices. Lord de Clinton had to step over his body, being careful not to slip on the expanding dark pool, to accept Lord Thomas' sword.

As he stared at Lord Thomas, kneeling before Lord de Clinton, William broke down. All the pent up emotion and control he had shown, even as far back as Salisbury, suddenly welled up and spilled over. His tears were hot and felt as if they would never stop, but his sobs were dry and silent and hurt his throat. The cobblestones bruised his knees when he fell to them, but he hardly noticed as he buried his face in his hands.

He could hear Lord Thomas protesting, but couldn't seem to understand the words. It didn't matter, the women were safe… he had done his duty; as did Sir Geoffrey, Gilbert, The Lord's de Simpson, Sir John and Robert. That last thought caused the tears and sobs to begin again. He gave up any thought of controlling them and let the anger, pain, fear and frustration wash over him. Not even when he was told of his father's death, or finding his mother's body in her bedchamber had caused such a crashing, colliding cascade of emotions. More than ever he felt he needed the comfort and wisdom of his teacher, and yet, now he was gone. His mind replayed the scene over and over, as he was tossed, like some child's doll, from the bridge.

He lost track of time, or rather, keeping track of how long he knelt there didn't matter. Eventually someone knelt down, putting his or her arm around him. Their long hair falling across his face. He opened his eyes and realized it had to be Helen. Seconds later another knelt on his right, mirroring her embrace; it was the Queen Mother. He looked into her face, his eyes red, puffed and large as saucers. William found himself shaking his head and began protesting, when she raised her hand and placed a gentle finger near his lips. "For saving my life… and my daughter's," she whispered.

William bowed his head once more, this time smiling through the tears, which continued to fall and spoke, each word carrying with it more strength and confidence. "Thank You God, for safeguarding us and giving us the courage we needed. Continue to bless and watch over each of us and each of those who chose to come to our aid. Amen." A hush had fallen over the courtyard as he spoke, and William was startled to hear a chorus echo his own prayer. He kept his eyes closed, adding privately another thanksgiving to God for all He had done and all He had helped William to do, even as he prayed to God that his teacher somehow, some way, wasn't actually dead.

As he continued to kneel, still lost in his own prayer and thoughts, he felt Isabella and Helen stand and move away from him. "William," it was Lord de Clinton's voice. As before it commanded his attention. He looked up, blinking his vision clear, to see several of the King's guards, Helen, the Queen Mother and the Lord High Admiral all standing around him. Lord Thomas and his men were no longer in the courtyard. "Do you swear to serve Edward, Earl of Chester, Duke of Aquitaine and King of England, to come when called, to raise up men who will stand with you when the need arises, to protect Dorchester and the lands of your family, to face fear with the calm certainty of faith, to boldly proclaim God's goodness and grace, to speak truthfully, never seeking or dealing with evil, while continuing to protect and keep safe those who are innocent, especially these ladies entrusted to your care?"

"With all my heart and without reservation, I do, my Lord." The Lord High Admiral turned and accepted a sword, handed to him by one of the King's guards. Lowering the blade he rested it on William's shoulder. Suddenly he realized what was happening. His eyes grew large and tears threatened to spill down his cheeks while his smile mirrored all those which surrounded him.

"Then in the presence of these witnesses and by the acts of bravery, loyalty, and self-sacrifice, I dub thee Sir William." The blade was lifted from his right and placed on his left shoulder and then handed back to the guardsman. Lord de Clinton extended his arm, offering William his open hand. He accepted and stood to be embraced by one of the leading peers of the realm and King Edward's most trusted advisors.

Helen offered a deep courtesy, a warm smile, and then a short embrace. "God blessed me with a wonderful protector, William."

When he turned to the Queen Mother, he was overcome with the strongest urge to take a knee. As he followed it, he bowed his head, "*vivo servire*," he stammered, and then cleared his throat. "If ever your Majesty calls, I and my whole house, which follows me, will always come."

"I have no doubt you will, Sir William." She smiled; looking down on the bowed head of the young man who it seemed continued to find himself at the right place and the right time. If he was not named heir of the Lord of Crandor, she would have asked for him to join her personal guard. As it was she would have to consider other ways to keep the young knight close. There was something about him; the way he carried himself and his concern for others. It intrigued her.

"The title I tried to give you early this morning has now been granted you, Sir William. I can think of few others who have worn the spurs and deserved it more, save perhaps my own grandson, the Prince of Wales." She smiled at the thought of these two young men meeting one day.

The comment startled William, and then revealed a thought, which he had pushed to the back of his mind. He bowed to Isabella, and then turned to Lord de Clinton. "My Lord, Sir John Copeland held back Lord

Thomas and his men so we could escape from the house he found us in. I need to go back and see if he is safe or needs our aid." "*God, I hope he is alive,*" he added to himself.

"Dear Lord, William, is there none of the King's own men who you have not encountered since you left Dorchester?" Even as he asked the rhetorical question he was motioning to several of the guardsmen to follow William on his return to the house.

William bowed to both women. The action raised a few eyebrows from the King's men, but if Lord de Clinton thought it unusual, he kept it to himself. "I will return presently my lady… Majesty." With that he turned and crossed the courtyard with two of the King's guard on his heels.

It went much faster without the Queen Mother to carry. As it was, even as he approached the bridge, he slowed to a walk and then stopped near the spot where he imagined Robert had stood. A dark stain of blood was on the cobblestones but there was no sign of the soldier he saw fall. One of the King's guards cleared his throat. "Sir?"

William shook his head and apologized. "A very brave, very wise man stood here and held back Lord Thomas and his guards, giving me the chance to get the Queen Mother and Lady Helen to safety." He crossed over to the edge and looked down at the slow moving water of the Somme.

"If he wore arms, the weight would have pulled him to the bottom," one of the guards muttered and then shuddered. Any death but drowning, he thought to himself, then made the sign of the cross.

"He wore none and carried only a baselard to defend himself. And yet, here I am, and there he fell." William took a deep breath, closed his eyes and said another prayer for his fallen teacher.

One of the guards must have seen the look on his face. "One of the earliest lessons we are taught as men of the King's Guard, Sir William, is the good of the whole is more important than the need or the good of the one. We have all taken a solemn vow, if the decision has to be made, we will stay behind, as this man did, and pay the price to see the others safe."

"There is no higher honor," the other added. As William stood at the edge, looking down at the slow moving river below, he felt as though his tutor was still teaching him one of his most important life lessons. How would Robert have worded this?

"What is the lesson here, William?" That is how he would have begun: always with a question. "No matter the cost is not just a phrase repeated in a ceremony, is it?"

"No, Sir William, it is not," he was startled when the guard responded. He hadn't realized he spoke out loud.

"Some lessons are harder to bear than others, my old friend," William spoke to the river, then turned and headed across the bridge. He didn't notice the strange look exchanged between the two guards. They followed, but several paces behind.

The door to the Queen Mother's home was standing ajar. Dark stains were on the threshold and the door itself looked as though it had been beaten into submission. From outside, the house was as quiet as a tomb. The thought caused William to shudder. He prayed it wasn't Sir John's.

The guards took their position ahead of William and crossed the threshold first. As soon as William stepped inside, he couldn't believe what he saw. Furniture was piled up in the hallway, as if to create a barrier. There was no sign of a struggle, no evidence anyone was injured in a fight, and no Sir John. Despite William repeatedly calling his name, there was also no answer. Only their voices echoed in return. If Sir John had quickly thrown the table and chairs from the parlor into the hall, his work was well done. Why he was no longer in the house though puzzled

William and his escort. After a short search he also realized the horses they had ridden, including the black courser, were missing.

"Is there anywhere he may have gone, Sir William?"

"I know of no other place he would have found safe in Amiens." What William didn't add was just how little he knew Sir John Copeland. He could have gone anywhere. "In Jesus name I pray he found a safe place, out of harm's way… watch over him, God." The two guards echoed amen to his prayer and then turned and left the house.

The return was slow and quiet, despite the quickly filling streets. Most of the glances were ones of surprise, however there were a few which seemed less than enthusiastic to see guards of the King of England in their city. One very old woman sneered and spit on the ground in front of their feet. William made sure he avoided stepping in it. The guards acted as if they didn't notice.

As they made their way through the growing crowds of people, William found himself getting lost in his feelings. The sun had once again broken through the early morning clouds and he could feel the warmth on his face, but his thoughts were dark. How could he go on without Robert? He was more than a guide or a tutor, he was also his closest friend and companion.

"He was your friend," a voice inside his head told him. *"You cannot do this on your own. What makes you think you can? You would have been better off just staying in Dorchester. At least you would both still be safe… and alive."* William nodded in agreement. There was no way he could go on alone. Even before they left England their road had gotten more and more difficult. How could he possibly think of walking across France and demanding his uncle's release from the Count de Coucy?

William found himself slowing his pace and even dragging his feet. Dark thoughts continued to swirl in and out of his mind. There was no way one of France's most powerful lords was simply going to give up his prisoner because a boy from England came and asked him. What had he been thinking? Lord Thomas' offer would have been much easier and safer.

That last thought rocked him so hard he had to stop a second to catch his balance. What had he been thinking? His thoughts had gotten so dark, so fast he could hardly recognize them. *"Guard your thoughts, William, for out of them will come the circumstances you find yourself in."* He could hear the admonition of the Justice of the Peace of Salisbury.

He shook his head and said a quick prayer. "God, I take those thoughts of fear and worry captive, in Jesus name," then added, "and I ask for Your wisdom in the decisions I need to make concerning my uncle and what I should do next." He didn't realize they had returned to the courtyard of the Lord High Admiral's house. The guards had stopped after knocking at the locked door. If they heard William's prayer, their expressions didn't give it away.

•••

The question from the Lord High Admiral completely took William by surprise. He paused, before answering, but shook his head slowly as he considered what he had been asked.

"You have sworn to answer the King when he calls; and to protect Lady Helen and the Queen Mother," Lord de Clinton reminded him. "I can think of none better to escort them safely to London, as witnesses at Lord Thomas' trial. Especially since you will need to be there as well."

This isn't what William had imagined. Somehow he never thought his quest to free his uncle would end in Amiens. He tried his best to put his frustration in words. He had to admit, later, he sounded like a wounded child. "I understand, my Lord, but what of my uncle and the ransom? Am I to leave him there to continue as a prisoner of the Count of Coucy?" As hard as he tried, he didn't do well controlling the frustration in his voice.

"For the time being… yes." The Lord High Admiral's features softened and he smiled a slight, sympathetic smile. "William, you must be prepared to do what is right and what is good now and be willing to set aside your personal goals until later. This, as much as anything, marks a man as a man; and a knight of England as more than just a good soldier."

Helen and her mother were both seated at the same table with William, the Lord High Admiral and a Captain of the King's Guard. Helen sat quietly, her hands folded in her lap, her eyes doing their best not to make contact with William's. The Queen Mother was not sitting quietly. Her arms were folded across her chest and her left foot was rapidly tapping the floor; her right ankle wrapped in linen. Her expression was one of agitation.

Finally she spoke. "For the love of God, William!" Her exclamation took everyone at the table by surprise. "Never in my life have I had to beg or plead or coerce a man to be my escort, and at my age I will not begin. You told me you would come when I called, *vivo servire*, you said. Well then, consider yourself called." She stood, with great effort, and all the men rose with her, including William. She paused, waiting to see if there would be a response from her young protector. There was none. She nodded, to herself, and limped out of the parlor, not waiting to acknowledge the bows and courtesy around the table.

William snapped his open mouth shut, watching as she made her way, slowly down the hall and was surprised when he heard the Captain of the Guard chuckle. "*La louve*," he stated, smiling and shaking his head. William had to agree. Isabella Capet-Plantagenet had been given the title at a younger age, but nothing would suggest "She-wolf" no longer applied.

As he stood there, considering the position in which he found himself, William scratched at his prickly beard and realized how long it had been since he had shaved. "Is there a bath in the house, my Lord? As I am to escort the Queen Mother and Lady Helen back to England, I think it best I bathe first, sleep second, and then find a good meal." He smiled, or at least attempted to. The Lord High Admiral nodded and William found himself following a servant of the house down the long, central hall to a small room near the kitchen. Inside were a low bench and shallow copper tub. A fire had recently been stirred and the glowing embers were snapping at the split logs, which had been tossed on them.

As he sat on the bench, unlacing the leather thongs, which crossed up his calves, he was reminded of that night in Downton, when he and Robert took their baths at the Bear and Boar. The memory rekindled emotions, which still simmered just beneath the surface. He dropped the laces and buried his face in his hands, rocking back and forth on the bench. Even more than his father or his mother, he missed his teacher. The thought of moving forward without his guidance and wisdom was almost too much to bear. "God, if there is any chance he is still alive, please watch over Robert. Place those near him who can come to his aid." He felt a comfort wash over him, almost like someone wrapping him in a warm blanket. He smiled, wiping tears from his cheek and added, "I am sorry I never had the chance to tell him just how much he meant to me."

The door opened and three servants entered; two carrying large buckets with steaming water, the third with a lidded bronze pot. In short order they had the bath full, the red hot stones from the pot added to heat the water quickly, and a wedge of soap laced with rosemary sprigs and lavender, set beside a stack of folded towels on the bench beside William. They left as quickly and quietly as they entered.

It didn't take long for the small room to fill with the hot, moist air and William took in a deep breath, filling his lungs and holding it a moment. Slowly he exhaled, finished undressing and slipped into the hot bath. As he lay there, just soaking in the warmth, he was reminded of the conversation with his tutor, just before their baths in Downton.

Gone was the attempt by Robert to impersonate his father's voice. The memory was so clear; he could have sworn his teacher was sitting on the bench beside the tub. "You must learn to live a life of no regrets, William. Do not let anger and frustration rule your day. Men have wasted their entire lives, losing any joy they may have had along the way, wishing and hoping for what might have been. Be willing to thank God for what you have been given and be humble enough to say to Him, 'Your will be done Lord, nothing more, nothing less, nothing else, at any cost.' It will be the hardest thing to hear, but it is the right thing for you to learn."

William closed his eyes, and tried to remember how his teacher had eventually learned to live with this principle. He knew he had to work on his thoughts first. His emotions would follow those thoughts. What could he do, right now, to begin living a life without regrets, or frustration or even the anger he felt bubbling just beneath the surface?

As he rolled these thoughts around in his head, he picked up the fragrant soap and began scrubbing, focusing on his knees, elbows, fingers and under his arms. He hadn't taken a bath since the shipwreck. As near as he could tell it had been five or six days, some of it hard traveling, including being knocked unconscious, since he had been found on the coast.

His mind wondered, as he soaked and scrubbed, and then an idea came to him. *"Take an inventory of what you have, William."* It was a quiet, gentle thought, almost like a nudge. Tears started to well up in his eyes, and it wasn't from the soap. Smiling and nodding through them, William began to take note of all he had and all he and his teacher had accomplished.

Eventually he had to get out of the bath. His hand and feet were wrinkled and the water had cooled just enough to become less comfortable. As he dried off, he continued to make note of the blessings and accomplishments in his life. When placed on a scale, it was easy for him to see how there was so much more on the good than the bad. *"Set your mind on these things, William. Write them down, as soon as you are able. They are to be memorials for you and all who come after you, so you remember and they may know the goodness of God and his grace and mercy in your life."*

William hadn't noticed it when the servants were in earlier, but they had placed clean, folded clothes on the bench beneath the towel. There was a pair of very fine, soft hose, a linen tunic and a long sleeved cotte with a high collar and copper buttons. Despite the fine material and tailoring it was the embroidery which caught William's attention. If he didn't believe he was to be the Queen Mother's man, the cotte would remind him. Quartered on the left breast were England, France, Navarre and Champagne.

If he had a knife he would have shaved, or at least trimmed his beard. As it was, all he could do in the way of grooming was to wet his hands and run his fingers through his hair. That just made him realize he needed it cut as well. What he wanted now was a quiet place to rest. The long warm bath had been just the comfort his body needed, and the inventory was just what his mind needed. Now he was ready for a good night's sleep; or rather, a good afternoon's.

•••

When asked to escort the Queen Mother and Helen back to London for the trial of Lord Thomas, William assumed they would be using a carriage. Although he had never been in one, his imagination suggested it would be pleasant and comfortable. He was surprised to find out they would be riding horseback, without additional accompaniment, and it would take four days to reach Calais. If the last several days were any indication, anything could happen before they reached the channel.

William awoke in a darkened room and a quiet house. For a brief moment he forgot where he was. His heart thumped a staccato and then he remembered. He was in Marquise, at a roadside inn, The Fowler. He didn't know what it had been called previously, however he was pretty sure when the French controlled the area it would have had a different name. After the battle of Crecy many things changed in northern France, and not just hanging signs.

Isabella's sigil, a combination of England, France and her family's holdings, felt like a giant target embroidered on William's left breast. What he quickly realized though was the deference, if not awe and respect, paid to him, through his influential patron. Most of the people they saw on the road were peasants. They all seemed in a hurry and without exception were heading north. Those who did look up, gazed at the embroidery, eyes widening as they realized who was passing them on horseback.

On the first day, before seeing many others on the road, William suggested the women remain hooded and cloaked, in order to conceal their identity. The Queen Mother would have none of it. "Champagne is my land and these are my people. I will leave France the same way I entered… openly. Beside," she added, her expression softening a little, "Lord Thomas is taken prisoner, William. If there were still a threat, would not Lord de Clinton have sent a larger escort?"

William had to admit he hoped their travel north across the channel and the road to London would pass with little opposition. Unfortunately, deep down he felt it wouldn't be the case. Some conversation or something that happened in the last few days was nagging at him. It was like a thought, on the edge of a memory, and try as he did to grab it, it simply slipped through his fingers. Not for the last time he wished Robert was there to sound out his thoughts.

Helen and the Queen Mother spent most of their time talking, leaving him happily to his own thoughts and out of the conversation. Helen had a young lifetime of questions and stories to catch up. The only subject Isabella struggled with was Helen's father. She found it difficult to tell her daughter what he was like. Each time she tried, she could only remember the last day she saw Roger Mortimer. He was given no trial but convicted, hung, and left on the gallows for two days; her pleas for leniency falling on deaf ears. Try as she might, she couldn't 'see' him in any other context. As much as Helen wanted to know more about him, she realized how painful it was for her mother and stopped pressing those questions.

Lost as they all were, either in thought or conversation, the day passed quickly and they soon found themselves approaching Eaucourt, even as the sun was setting. They could see the tower from quite a distance and as they drew closer they saw several lights, piercing the dusk through its narrow windows.

Having entered the town from the river, William hadn't noticed just how solid the "wall" was. Each home, shop or shed stood so close to the next, they created a faceted exterior face, which, in the dimming light looked nearly impregnable. The only way in was shut and the rest of the village seemed dark and quiet.

William dismounted and walked his horse up to the gate. The quiet felt ominous and the mare was jittery, sidestepping and tossing her head when he knocked. As William waited, he turned and noticed Isabella's expression was completely blank, while Helen's looked worried. A voice called out from inside the village, "*La porte est verrouillée au coucher du soleil. Personne ne peut entrer à Eaucourt jusqu'à l'aube.*"

While William slowly worked through the translation, with his imperfect French, Helen answered, her voice ringing like a silver bell in winter. "*C'est Helen d'Abbeville. Je suis revenue avec William de Simpson et un invité d'honneur. Les Seigneurs de Simpson voudront bien nous recevoir.*" William was close enough to the gate to hear muttering and several feet shifting about. Finally, after a long moment waiting, the bar was lifted, the latch thrown back and the doors swung open.

For a brief moment, he felt as if he was back on the bridge in Downton. A bright lantern was uncovered and shone directly in his face. He squinted and his eyes began watering but he tried his best to face the light. Finally a voice muttered, with obvious awe, "*Mon Dieu, ils sont retournés.*" The light still shined directly in William's face, but he could hear feet moving and low voices speaking to one another.

Eventually, the lantern was redirected around William and onto Helen and her mother. Seconds later the voices in front of him stopped. Glowing globs of light danced in front of his vision, so he wasn't able to see what was going on, but he had a good guess. Someone had recognized Isabella of France.

●●●

The reception at Eaucourt, this time, was much merrier than the last. Even though it took a little longer for the escort to collect themselves and their composure, they eventually regained their senses and led the three in through the gates, which were closed and barred behind them, across the grassy yard and to the doors of the keep. William wasn't surprised to see the large oaken doors hanging from their hinges with signs of hasty repairs to keep them there. Lord Thomas certainly left his mark.

As they approached the threshold the Lord's de Simpson made their way across the antechamber and stood, ready to greet them. Their smiles of joy and surprise were quickly replaced with nearly identical looks of shock and disbelief. Lord Matthew bowed at the waist, as best his elderly frame would allow, and he straightened, with the help of the sergeant William recognized from their previous visit. Lord David attempted a bow but had to stop himself as he leaned heavily on a carved staff. It was then William noticed one of his eyes was swollen shut and he had several dark bruises around his face.

"Majesty," Lord Matthew began, his now familiar, raspy voice sounding less ominous than when they first met. He and his brother stepped back into the antechamber, he with the help of the sergeant, his brother with the aid of his staff. "You honor us with your presence," he continued as they moved next to the now empty table, causing William to wonder where the shield and broken sword were. "If we only knew of your coming…"

Isabella waved off the apology, while stepping forward and taking both Lord's hands in her own. She was standing beside William, so he could see her expression clearly. Her eyes were smiling, as was her entire face. It caught his breath to see her like this. When he finally forced himself to turn back to his elderly cousins, they appeared to be equally enthralled.

"William and Helen have told me of your bravery and willingness to delay Lord Thomas, in order to give them time to flee. I am honored to consider the de Simpson's of Eaucourt as such strong liege lords to my family."

"But we failed in our part, Majesty," Lord David stammered. William could see it was difficult for him to speak. The Queen Mother saw the same. "I saw William's capture myself. When I tried to pull them off…" He didn't have to say more. Suddenly William found it difficult to swallow and tears threatened to spill down his cheeks. He quickly wiped his hand across his face, as if weary.

"Hush, now, Lord David; I will hear none of that self-pity. Despite all his efforts and his best laid schemes, Lord Thomas failed." William thought she looked a little like a scolding, yet understanding mother, and then wondered if that was one of the reasons so many were willing to give so much to aid her. "He was taken captive by the Lord High Admiral and we three travel back to London to be present for his trial at the Tower." She raised her hand to his cheek and rested it there a moment. As William watched, his elderly cousin seemed to melt; his expression softened and tears welled up in his eyes, spilling down both cheeks and onto her hand. In a brief moment, the Queen Mother, Helen and William filled in the elderly brothers on the events of the past days.

Lord Matthew did his best to stand even straighter, his shoulder back and head high. "We were just sitting down to dine in the parlor, Majesty, and we can easily add three more chairs… but we are missing one. Where is Buckley?" That one omission of their tale had been made on purpose. None of the three wished to relate the tale of the bridge.

The mention of Robert's surname brought back some of those feelings of loss and loneliness William had experienced earlier that day on the road. His eyes dropped, as did his voice, which cracked as he answered. "He… fell, my Lord."

"He fell in order to slow down Lord Thomas long enough for us to reach Lord de Clinton, and the rest of the peace delegation," Helen quickly added. Her fervor was a small shock to William. If he wasn't aware of the impact his tutor had on the young woman before, he certainly was now. "If not for his willingness to pay such a price, we would not be standing here."

Helen had remained quiet as she watched the interaction between her mother and the lords of Eaucourt, but the mere mention of Robert triggered something inside. She hadn't realized how much his company, companionship and mentorship had meant to her. In such a short time she had come to rely on his insight and wisdom and suddenly realized how much she missed his wise council and his wit. Tears of her own filled her eyes and she lowered her head as she wiped them with a kerchief.

"Do you miss him, Lady Helen?" Lord David asked, as he slipped his free arm under her own and guided her into the large parlor where they had spent much of their time just three days prior. The bruises and swelling on his face and lips made his words come out slurred and he hobbled slowly with the staff, but he was still gentle and gallant. She nodded while continuing to wipe her eyes. "Our Lord told us of a greater love, one which has no equal. Do you know what He told us?"

Helen shook her head, so Lord David continued. "No greater love there is than this…"

"That one would be willing to lay down his life for his friend," William finished the quote from John's gospel.

"That is right, William. But to most men, it is just words. Just words on parchment, spoken once or twice a year from the pulpit." He paused a moment in thought, considering what he had just said. "Even to my brother and me so it was; that is, until you were here last, and Lady Helen's admonishment and revelation led us to the truth."

"What did she reveal, my Lord's?" Isabella asked curiously. She also wanted to know what truth her daughter had taught the elderly lords, but she kept that question to herself. As she pondered it, she had made her way to the head of the table and stood beside her chair. It took William just a moment to realize she was waiting for him to seat her.

"She revealed the power and truth of our Savior's words and His love. She helped us see how selfish we had become and she helped lead us to a repentance which forced us to act to ensure there will be an Eaucourt sur Somme for whomever follows us." William pulled back the chair for Isabella as Lord Matthew bowed, first to Helen, in recognition, and then to his suzerain. Despite all they had been through at the hands of Lord Thomas, William was amazed to see their eyes clear and their countenance cheerful.

His gaze wandered up to the tapestry and stared a moment at his distant ancestor and the sacrifice he had been willing to make. When he looked to the coat of arms, just above the hearth, he smiled a broad smile and felt a lump form in his throat; the door had been newly painted white. "When my teacher told me the story of the tapestry, I was disappointed to find out the humble beginnings of our family," William stated, starting out quietly, then gaining strength and volume in his voice as he continued. "Now, I am just starting to realize how difficult that decision must have been for my distant forebear, as well as the courage he needed to be willing to sacrifice everything in order to stand against the Vascones."

The mention of the name of those people who still live in the great mountains in the southwest of France startled Isabella, but she recovered quickly, adding her own thoughts to the conversation. "The one thing I have learned in my years is all leadership requires sacrifice. Any time you strive to move up, you must be willing to give something up. There cannot be one without the other."

"Buckley would have understood this, cousin William," Lord David added. "He was a wise man and a good counselor…"

"And his wisdom is sorely missed," Helen added, cutting the old lord off in mid-sentence. The thought spoken out loud startled her a little.

"I did not have the chance to meet the Seneschal of the Earl of Dorchester, nor hear any of the wisdom for which he and his family were well known and respected. What do you think he would advise now, William?" Isabella asked.

"He would have reminded me of the conversation we had, just outside the gates of Crandor, the morning I received the ransom letter from Count de Coucy."

"Which was?" The Queen Mother inquired.

"I told him of my vision of a simple, quiet life in Dorchester and of my hope that, when the time came to raise my own family, my uncle would be as a grandsire to my children as he had become a father to me. Robert told me all dreams are free at first but would come at a price, the cost of which would be more than I expected, and come sooner than I planned. It would require repeated payments and in the end, may even cost more than I was willing or able to pay on my own." William paused, as he recounted the conversation and the teaching and suddenly realized how each and every step had occurred, just as he had been taught that day. The lump formed again in his throat and he dropped his gaze to hide the emotion, which threatened to suddenly overwhelm him.

"Dear Lord," Helen murmured. "All he told you was true, even…"

"He knew this final cost was more than you should have to pay, William, so he paid it himself, even as our Lord Jesus paid the price for every one of us." Lord Matthew added, cutting off Helen, while shaking his head very slowly. "I underestimated your seneschal, cousin. Now I wish I had spent more time in conversation with him that afternoon."

William hadn't considered what Robert had done while he wrestled with the questions of honor, duty and nobility that day on the rooftop of the tower. "He did not mention you had spent time speaking my Lord."

Lord Matthew waved a knuckled, bony hand, "most of it was trivial, or at least it seemed that at the time." He had drawn his white brow down and was staring at his now folded hands in his lap. "I asked him about you and your parents and what we could expect from you as Charles's heir. His answers were direct, concise and remarkably simple, save one."

"Which was that my Lord?" Helen asked before William had a chance. He shot her a glance, but she avoided his eyes.

"I had asked him if he felt you were ready to make the difficult decisions necessary to lead. He spoke of your earnestness, your commitment and abilities, and then he added, very quietly, almost to himself, that, when the time came and the hard price had to be paid, he was willing to pay it himself, if given the chance." Lord Matthew paused and considered, again, the intuition of William's teacher. "I think he knew it would eventually come to a confrontation, like the one on the bridge, and he was readying himself to make the decision."

"He told me once, that to all men will come a day when they must make such a decision," William stated to no one in particular. "When they must decide between what is right and what is easy, what they are commanded or expected to do." William turned to look once more on the tapestry. "And when, at the end of their days, they stand in judgment for all their decisions, they will not be able to say they were told to do such. A Lord or even a King may command, but, in the end, it is the man's own responsibility to care for the wellbeing of his soul."

"I am a sinner, saved by grace," Lord David muttered, his lisp slurring his words. "If not for that recently embraced fact, I would shudder to think what the Day of Judgment may have been like."

"Buckley has surely found his way to our Lord's presence," Lord Matthew added. "When it came time for your tutor to make that decision, it was his and his alone. He chose to stand and in so doing, show you, William, Helen and your Majesty, just how much he truly loved you all. I told him that afternoon, when he and I spoke alone, the de Simpson's of Dorchester had been blessed by the service of his family. He graciously and quietly accepted the compliment."

"He was the last of his family line," William stated, his voice cracking with emotion as he realized the implication. "There will be no more Buckley's of Crandor... to teach and advise the de Simpson's which come after me." He paused again, to consider what he just told the others around the table and to clear his throat. It only helped a little, as the emotions he felt threatened to overwhelm his ability to continue speaking. "He was preparing me for this, even before we left Dorchester."

"How, William?" Helen asked.

"He told me he had taken what he had been taught by his father and what he had learned through his own experiences teaching my father and uncle, and created a series of important lessons. He called them the most important lessons he learned. When I asked him, on our first evening after leaving Crandor, if he would teach me these, he told me he already had started."

"You must write these down, William." Isabella had sat quietly, deep in thought, while half listening to the discussion. Now the idea struck her and she knew it was essential, making the statement with the deepest conviction. "While the thoughts and ideas are still fresh in your mind, you must get them down on parchment with quill and ink."

William stared at her for a brief second and then dropped his eyes in embarrassment. "I can read well enough but..."

"Most fathers of sons who are not meant to inherit do not feel it is necessary to teach them some of the finer or even essential things in life, William," Lord David consoled. There was a conviction in his voice along with a note of a long buried hurt. Despite his age, there was obviously still that part of his childhood he regretted missing.

"Robert had told me there was more about my family I needed to learn, as well as more about the leading peers of England, but it would have to come later. There were urgent lessons I needed now and those less so would come later. Now…" William's voice cracked and he turned to stare into the crackling fire of the large open hearth, fighting to control his emotions. *"God, give me the strength I need to carry on, on my own. I feel lost without my teacher."*

"You are now the heir apparent and future Earl of the demesne of Dorchester, Crandor Castle and all its surrounding lands," Lord Matthew spoke slowly and with great emphasis on his words. There was deep passion in his voice and it shook the morose feelings off of William. "King Edward's closest confidant has knighted you and by the sigil you wear, you proclaim yourself as the Queen Mother's own. You did all this without the ability to write well, without knowing all you need to know of your country and without the traditional upbringing of a first-born son. Is there any doubt you were meant to be exactly where you were placed? If there is, banish it from your thoughts."

That last comment struck a chord in William. He knew he needed to guard his thoughts. Robert had told him with feelings of doubt came fear and frustration. They were bedfellows. Where one existed, the other two were sure to follow. It was another of those crucial messages he was meant to not only remember, but also be willing to live out. Just as he was to control his thoughts, in so doing, he would be controlling those feelings, which seemed to be on the verge of overcoming him.

He took a deep breath, and once more asked God, in Jesus name, to give him the strength and vigilance he needed in the days, weeks and years to come. Even as he continued to pray in silence, the food arrived. For the next several minutes the only sound was the clink of knife on plate, cup on table and the crackle of the fire.

•••

The conversation after dinner filled the Lords of Eaucourt with awe and wonder. They now heard the details of William's escape from Lord Thomas' estate in Amiens, his meeting Sir John Copeland, and the rescue of the Queen Mother. Lady Helen felt her story was one of safety and leisure in comparison.

"I do not know what became of Sir John," William answered. Lord Matthew was curious as to why the knight was not riding with them as well. "When I returned to her Majesty's home looking for him, he was gone, as was the black stallion we had recovered from Davey Martin in the New Forest."

"Perhaps there was something else Lord Thomas had planned," Isabella wondered out loud, "of which Sir John was aware."

The thought hadn't occurred to William, and he rolled it over in his head as he lay on the soft down mattress, with thick blankets piled on top. He was warm, and safe and for the first time in a very long time felt as though he might be able to let his guard down just a little. William tried to think back to the last time he had slept in a soft bed. The mattress felt as though it was stuffed with downy goose feathers. Even the bed he had slept in the night before in Amiens wasn't like this one, or for that matter the bed in *Le Crotoy*. The more he thought of it, the more he realized he might never have slept on a bed like this.

Lord Thomas was no longer a threat; of that he had no doubt.

What he had sown he would soon reap. The thought, which teased at William's memory, was the idea there may have been something else Lord Denebaud had set out to accomplish. He rolled over onto his side, drawing up his knees. For some reason he always felt safer when he did this.

Like a flash he was back in the apple crate, inside the larder of Lord Thomas' estate, lying in the same position, listening to the discussion just a few feet away. *"The Earl will die rotting in the tower, the Count has assured me of this, and this boy will never leave Amiens. With the uncle gone my own patron at court has assured me of the de Simpson land and titles."*

He would never forget the conversation or the situation he had found himself in, but there was something he missed before. Lord Thomas had let it slip to Sir John. He had a patron in Edward's court! William quickly sat up in bed, his head swimming with the idea. Was it possible someone else was actually pulling Lord Thomas' strings? Or perhaps they were pulling strings he was unable to grasp?

Now more than ever he wished his tutor was here. He needed Robert's wisdom and advice, and even more he needed his ears. Tossing back the covers, he pulled on his breeches and boots. The fire in the hearth made the small room warm enough he only wore his linen shirt, but he put on his cotte nonetheless. He had not been in his room very long and hoped either Lord Matthew or David would still be in the parlor. He really needed someone to hear him out.

When he made it down the flight of stairs, from his room to the antechamber, and across to the parlor, he was disappointed to find both his elderly cousins already retired. What surprised him was finding the Queen Mother still sitting in one of the chairs near the hearth. Her attention was focused on the flames and so she didn't hear him until he cleared his throat before entering the room.

"I am sorry, Majesty," he apologized, as he quietly moved toward the chair beside her. "I had hoped to find either of the Lords of Eaucourt here."

"They retired just after you, William," she answered, not looking up from the fire. "I needed some time to think and this felt like the best place." Something in William's voice when he mentioned Lord Matthew and David made her turn her attention away from the fire and look up into William' face. "Is there something troubling you?"

"I do not know, Majesty. I…" he paused a moment to collect his thoughts. "My teacher was always the one I would go to when I needed to sound out my thoughts. I had hoped one of my cousins would fill the roll in his absence. I am sorry…" William turned to leave when the Queen Mother called him back.

"My own thoughts have troubled me," she stated, turning her head back to the flames. "Perhaps we can help each other." He stood a moment beside the same chair he had slept in during his first night in Eaucourt, and then asked for permission to be seated in Isabella's presence.

She waved the question aside. "For the moment, and in the privacy of this house, let us be familiar. You wear my sigil; I have set you apart as a man of my own household. As the heir to your uncle this puts you in a precarious position. I am not sure you fully understand the implications or consequences or what may transpire when we return to England."

William took the chair and turned it so he could be both warmed by the fire and look on the Queen. "My teacher would have reminded me that each day has its own challenges and it is not wise to focus on the concerns of what may or may not happen in the days or weeks to come. Do the best you can to understand the situation, so when the time comes you are prepared. The rest you leave up to God." Isabella was about to respond, when William continued. "I am deeply honored to be chosen to represent your Majesty and I think I do understand most of the consequences, but there is a larger concern on my mind."

"Then let us talk it out, as you say, and, if we still have talk left in us, we can discuss my own troubled thoughts."

William smiled. Knowing what little he did about women, he was pretty sure Isabella would not have any problem continuing the discussion as long as they were able to remain awake. "When Lord Thomas captured me, I was able to overhear a discussion he had with Sir John. Neither was aware of my presence and so I believe something was revealed in that moment which Lord Thomas would not have wanted to share with any other."

"He has a patron at court." Isabella stated it as a fact, the expression on her face unchanged. William sat with his mouth open, shocked by her insight. "I have spent my entire life surrounded by intrigue, much of it created by my own hands, William. Lord Thomas would not consider making the moves he did unless there was someone placed much higher, who promised him favors for his actions." She continued staring at the fire for another long moment, and then took in a deep breath, turning to face him.

"Your insight does you credit, William. For Lord Thomas to boast of it suggests the person carries a high position. This person would have enough influence to sway the Crown's designation of titled lands."

"Lord Thomas also threatened Sir John with the removal of his banner," William added.

Isabella's eyebrows shot up at this revelation, and then nodded slowly. "Only the King himself can do such a thing. To make the threat would suggest his patron indeed has the ear of the king." She slowly tapped a finger on the wooden arm of her chair, while her lips moved wordlessly. As William watched her closely, he realized she was working her way through a long list of names, men of power and placement in King Edward's court. Finally she stopped and sighed heavily. "I cannot see who would be this spider, spinning such an intricate web. Those close enough to Edward would not dare such a thing. Of all his lifelong friends only Montague is gone, dying in a foolish tournament accident four years ago. His advisors have been with him nearly as long."

Isabella slapped the arms of her chair with her palms, a frustrated and angry expression coming over her face. The sudden change in her countenance shocked William. This was a side of the Queen Mother he had yet to see. "It has been eighteen years since I last sat at court. I have my share of visitors, royal and otherwise, at Castle Rising. And through them I have been able to keep current, but nothing I have heard or learned these last few years shines a light on this." She quickly rose from her seat and strode to the fire, taking a split log from the stack beside it and tossing it into the hearth. Sparks shot up the flue and some smoke made its way out into the room as the flames brightened, attacking the fresh fuel.

As William stared into the fire, noting the changes in color from deep red to bright yellow and all shades in between, he asked God for the wisdom he needed to see through this puzzle. The flames found a pocket of sap in the log and there was a loud snap, not unlike the crack of a whip. At that same moment another thought came to him. "Majesty, if you have eliminated everyone at court who may have influence over the king and be willing to put themselves in the hazard with Lord Thomas, then who could be left?"

"It could only come from outside the court. But who would have influence over the king, and not be at court?"

"What if it is someone who challenges the throne itself, hoping to use Helen and threaten you with her exposure in order to force an opening for themselves? It is possible this person is not even English." Robert had mentioned just such a concern several days before, while William was recovering in Le Crotoy.

Now it was Isabella's turn to look startled. "William, what you are suggesting is the very thought which I had been struggling with when you came and joined me here." She sat very still for a moment, her eyes fixed on the flames, then she snorted, or at least as close as a Queen Mother would ever get to snorting, and turned to William, smiling, her face lit by more than just the firelight. "It seems my choice in naming you a man of my own is already well rewarded."

"I thank you again, Majesty, but do not see how this…"

"You already know Helen's secret and you are aware of what Lord Thomas had been willing to do. You know what we find ourselves up against. I can think of none better to help me through this morass." William smiled and blushed at the sincere compliment; the color of the flames masked those of his cheeks.

"My tutor thought there might be two types of men who would threaten Lady Helen. The kind who wanted to use her to their own ends, and the kind who would want to remove her in order to stop the other from reaching their goal. What if there was only one, who saw a chance to do both?"

Isabella shook her head, a confused look on her face. "Be more specific, William. It is late and I had a few glasses of wine with dinner."

"What if the man behind Lord Thomas," William began slowly, as he worked through his thought, "sees a chance on one hand to use Lord Thomas' greed and Helen's secret to disrupt the crown and damage reputations?" He reached forward with his right hand, palm up, as if holding a large apple, "while on the other," now he reached forward with the left, "secretly reaching out to take the throne for himself?"

The Queen Mother's eyes grew wide and her mouth dropped open. She stared at William for a long moment, her piercing eyes eventually making him feel uncomfortable. "Do you know who would even consider such a thing, William?" He answered with a quick shake of his head. "There is only one man I know of who would even consider it… and the very thought angers me, because I see it could be so and I know it could be him."

"Who, Majesty?"

"My cousin, Philip of Valois."

William's head swam with the thought. The very idea he had been crossing swords with, not just Lord Thomas, but the King of France as well, sent a chill up his spine and set the hairs on his neck on end. "Majesty, how can we… I do not know…" William leaned forward taking his head in his hands and shook it slowly back and forth. If he truly found himself in the middle of this, how could he possibly find his way out?

"Philip is not the warrior like my son Edward," Isabella stated. "He has proven this on several occasions. But, what he lacks on the field, he makes up for in cunning and intrigue." She began pacing the floor in front of the hearth, and although she didn't look at her young confidante, she could sense some of what he was going through.

William looked up amidst dark thoughts, which threatened to pull him down into despair. Later, when he reflected on what took place that evening, it seemed as though real hands grasped and tugged at his mind. Darkness closed around him. Then, strong, warm hands grabbed his own and, startled, he looked up into the eyes of the Queen Mother. An intense, earnest gaze stared back at him.

"I see in your eyes, William, the same dark thoughts and doubts threatening my own heart." She knelt before him, keeping his hands in her own, and her gaze unwavering. "I have lived through days in which I felt my whole world was crashing down around me, with no chance for joy or peace ever to be a part of it again." She squeezed hard, "but now is not that time." A fierce fire sparkled in her eyes; despite the fact her back was to the hearth and rest of her face was in shadow. "This time we turn the table on those who have played us the fools."

William was surprised he was able to smile, despite the situation. The Queen Mother had revealed, once more, She-wolf was an appropriate and descriptive title. He was glad they were on the same side of the table. "How do we do this, Majesty?"

"We have already accomplished half. Lord Thomas is taken, his plots revealed, and justice will be done soon enough." Isabella stood, releasing her grasp of William's hands, and turned back to the fire, her dark green skirt swirling about her. "I learned once, long ago, the best way to find a solution is to not focus on the problem."

This thought puzzled William. He had never heard his tutor mention any such idea. "I do not understand, Majesty. How can we discover what we are supposed to do, if we do not take the time to study the difficulty?"

"Because talking about the problem and studying the problem and focusing on the problem, only leads to a well versed knowledge of the problem. It has never and will never reveal the solution. We acknowledge there is someone behind Lord Thomas, pulling those strings he was not able to reach, as well as those he personally grasps. We believe that person may be Philip, the King of France." She paused and turned, staring at her young confidant. "Take a moment to see the problem we face, William. Do you see it?" He nodded.

"Take hold of that thought and banish it from your mind," she spoke this with such authority it made William sit up straight in the chair. "Now, we ask this simple question; what can we do right now to aid ourselves and Helen?"

The next hour was spent in energized and excited conversation. Some of the ideas were simple and perhaps obvious. William suggested they get a good night's sleep. Isabella agreed. Other suggestions met with less enthusiasm or even instant disagreement. There was one, though, which both agreed was ambitious and perhaps a little reckless. If it worked, they would still have time to make the trial of Lord Thomas. William found it difficult to fall asleep, knowing they would return to Amiens the next morning.

•••

They rode much faster on their return and found themselves approaching the city just past mid-day. They had done little talking, except to answer the obvious questions Helen posed. The suggestion that Lord Thomas had a benefactor and it was probably someone outside the court didn't shock Helen. Who that person might be, did. "What will we do when we get to Amiens?" Helen asked, after a long pause.

"We will attend the peace negotiations, as originally planned," Isabella explained. "William will escort me as a man of my household. You will be as a young lady in waiting, attending to me."

"If this spider, as you call him, is really who you believe he is, why would he be at the peace talks? Would he not just send arbitrators, as did King Edward?" Helen asked.

"My son has many counselors; all tried and trusted men from childhood. Not so my dear cousin," Isabella answered. "There will be others to do the negotiations, but he will be there… somewhere."

"So he may be in the city but not at the meeting hall?" William wondered.

"No, William," Isabella corrected. "He will want to watch, hanging back unless the talks go in a direction he simply will not allow. He will be there, but he may not come dressed as the King of France."

"How will we recognize him?" Helen wondered. "Have you met his Majesty?"

Isabella shook her head. "I was not invited to his coronation, since my own son also had a claim to the crown." She paused a moment and William glanced over to see a curious smile spread across her face. "I think my presence will pull him from whatever dark corner in which he may be hiding. He will not want to miss the chance to meet me face to face… and meet William."

"Me, your Majesty?"

"Yes, William. After all, it was you who brought Lord Thomas down and ended Philip's chance at crippling, if not completely tearing down England from within."

William hadn't thought of it that way. The fact he had gone up against Lord Thomas at nearly every turn since leaving Dorchester didn't seem as impressive, as he reflected on the individual instances which had happened. Now though, the idea he had also found himself placed in front of the plans of the King of France made him a little dizzy. The revelation of the previous night had not worn off nor was it likely to any time soon. "Will I be introduced as your escort, Majesty?" William asked, while trying to clear his head and stay on his horse.

"I will make sure you meet every Frenchman in the delegation, William," Isabella looked over, smiling, as they crossed over one of the many bridges of the central canal of the Somme, on the edge of Amiens. The echo of the horse's iron shod hooves on the cobblestones reminded William of entering Southampton. So much had changed since that day. So much good had been done, but so much evil as well.

William wondered if it would ever have an ending. Would he really ever get back to Dorchester, to settle down at Crandor Castle with his uncle, to eventually raise a family of his own? So much still seemed to stand in his way, not the least of which was the revelation regarding Lord Thomas' benefactor. His dark thoughts must have shown, because Helen noticed. "William, are you well? You suddenly look troubled."

Her voice was gentle and there was a note of deep caring, which came across in her words. He closed his eyes just a moment, nodded and then looked over at her, smiling. "There are times when the path before me seems as if it were leading me up a steep mountain." He shook his head. He knew he needed to guard his thoughts, but at that moment he felt, more than any time since he and his teacher had set out, very small and unprepared.

"When we were separated and you were captured by Lord Thomas, I made a similar complaint to your Seneschal," Helen closed her eyes as she pictured the conversation. "He told me, 'One is too small a number to accomplish anything significant.' When I pointed out what I thought was obvious, that I was alone in my struggles, he told me there was always One other, who we can call on at any time. Ask, and it will be given, knock and the door will be opened. You know of whom I speak, William."

He nodded and closed his eyes again for a brief moment, forcing himself to take his focus off himself and his problems and shifting it to Jesus Christ, His crucifixion and resurrection. He had a brief image flash across his vision, of the Lord on the cross, bloodied, bruised and broken. Tears welled up in his eyes and a still, small voice spoke to his spirit. *"Cast your cares on Me, William. I will never leave you nor forsake you."*

"God, I am sorry for my weakness and doubts. I never want to forget everything you sacrificed for me. Thank You for your grace and mercy in my life."

"Amen," Helen responded to his quietly spoken prayer. When he looked up, she was smiling a brilliant smile and he couldn't help himself but smile as well. The day no longer seemed as dark and his thoughts were less worried, but a seed of doubt had been planted. The question he would eventually need to answer was whether or not he would give it food and water.

"This is the meeting place." The Queen Mother's comment broke William's train of thought. They had approached a large timber and frame two-story building. The shutters on the first floor were closed. In the cool spring air they could see the faint wisp of smoke drifting from all three stone chimneys. "This is the Hall of the *Corps de Métiers* of Amiens," she continued. "Their guild brothers in London helped in the arrangements."

Once again William wished he had more formal education. He knew this was a guildhall, just from the Queen Mother's comment. Unfortunately, that was all he knew. "Is there only one guild, which meets here?"

"No, William," Isabella explained. "Unlike in England, the guilds of France have a loose association with each other and are willing to work close enough together to even share a common hall."

William thought of Helen's comment. Could one guild be too small a number to make a difference? What if they could work together, to aid each other and to help move forward to common goals? Most of the guilds were interested in better pay and working conditions for their members. He wondered what would happen if they were one day able to speak with one voice?

They tied their horses up along the side of the building opposite the canal and Isabella led them to a small doorway, which had been cleverly detailed to look like a portion of the wall. On closer inspection William noted the recessed hinges and knob. The craftsman who created this was quite good.

"William, Helen, follow and do as I do," the Queen Mother advised. "This is the spider's web and I think the best way to get him to show himself will be to act as though we have no awareness of his duplicity. Are we ready?" She stood up straight, throwing back her shoulders and lifting her chin. A quick smile to both, and then her expression turned stern. "Now let them meet *Le louve.* William, attend to me." He opened the door, bowing at the waist as Isabella, Queen Mother of England and last surviving child of King Philip IV of France swept past him, her lady in waiting hurrying to follow.

Chapter Twenty Nine

The time spent in the company of the Queen Mother and Helen in the guildhall of Amiens would always be a blurry memory for William. He was introduced to some of the most prominent men of both England and France, all the while playing a quiet role on the edge of a circle which seemed to constantly surround Isabella.

She was in her element. William wasn't sure if he had seen her truly happy until now, although you couldn't see it on her face; you had to look in her eyes. Word had already spread through both parties of her attempted capture and daring rescue, as well as the flight from her home to the house of Lord de Clinton. On more than one occasion, as Isabella embellished the story, adding subtle shifts in the drama, several pairs of eyes turned to look closely at the young man who attended her. She was lavish with her praise and William could feel the heat in his cheeks as he smiled and stood quietly nearby.

While Isabella entertained both the English and French, the Lord High Admiral motioned William to join him and one other, just outside the circle. "William, I am surprised to find you here. The last we spoke, you were escorting her Majesty and Lady Helen to London for the trial."

"We spent last night in Eaucourt sur Somme, in the house of my cousins, the Lords de Simpson. The Queen Mother and I found ourselves unable to sleep, as we both wrestled with questions and concerns. During the time we spent discussing each other's thoughts, we came to realize we both had come to same conclusion about Lord Thomas."

The mention of the man, who had orchestrated and inflicted so much pain, surprised the elder statesman. "What is it you both discovered, William?"

Here William lowered his voice and leaned closer, "Lord Thomas was not alone in his choices but was emboldened by someone offering him promises." He quickly repeated the conversation he had overheard between Lord Thomas and Sir John.

Lord William de Clinton's eyes grew large, his hands balling up in fists and his expression looked like he was chewing rocks. The color of his face started to turn a dark purple. "There could be none in our king's court," he sputtered, "who would dare to make such promises…"

"Indeed there is not, my Lord," echoed the middle aged gentleman standing next to him whose expression reflected the Lord High Admiral's. William turned to answer and found himself cut off before he began.

"My pardon sirs, I find myself in an error of etiquette," the Lord de Clinton stated. "My Lord, may I introduce Sir William de Simpson of Dorchester. William, this is the Lord Baron, Sir Walter Manny."

William's eyes grew wide as he realized who stood before him. As the Lord de Clinton and all the others in the room, Sir Walter Manny wore no coat of arms or sigil to identify himself. The Queen Mother's own crest, embroidered on his cotte stood out, and if he thought about it, called attention to himself. The thought was banished though as the name and deeds of the Lord Baron standing before him came back from the distant past.

Sir Walter Manny was one of Edward's most trusted military commanders, both on land and sea. He had originally come to Edward's court as a page in the household of the future Queen of England, Philippa of Hainault. He had fought in the Scottish wars, but not at Neville's Cross. At one point, he captured a pirate who had been plaguing English shipping in the channel, and in turn, used his ships and sea knowledge to fight in the Battle of Sluys where the French fleet was almost completely destroyed. He went on to fight and lead men in some of the most critical battles leading up to Crecy, and eventually found himself in a position to aid in the surrender of Calais. It was his resolve and compassion for the people of that city which had struck a chord in William's memory. Queen Philippa begged King Edward to show mercy and he yielded, but before she did, Lord Sir Walter had begged the same. What Robert had told William of him, when word reached them of the fall of Calais, made him realize here was a man of great character. He placed his right hand over his heart and bowed deeply at the waist. "It is an honor and privilege to meet you, my Lord," he stated. "Sir William de Simpson, at your service."

"And I at yours," Sir Walter answered. His voice was like a baritone in a cathedral choir and he spoke his words carefully, with an accent which, even without knowing his birthplace, suggested Northern France or Flanders. "Pleasantries aside, Sir William, explain yourself. Lord de Clinton has had a moment to explain the events of the last few days, but there appear to be a few key elements he may have inadvertently omitted." He paused to take a moment and stare at the sigil on William's chest. Without realizing it, the young knight straightened his cotte.

"Pardon, my Lord," William began slowly, also carefully choosing his words, "but the Queen Mother and I realized the same." He paused a moment, just to make sure two of King Edward's most trusted advisors and longtime friends were both listening closely. "Since it could not be from inside King Edward's court, then it had to come from without. Someone very powerful, who could make these promises seem real enough to cause Lord Thomas to do what he did." William stopped in order to let both Lords catch up to his train of thought. It didn't take long.

"What you suggest…" Lord Manny paused, realizing where the finger pointed, then quickly added, "You are here to confront Philip?"

William nodded. "Neither her Majesty nor I have met him, but the Queen Mother was convinced he would be here personally. She felt he would not trust these crucial negotiations to anyone, but would not come announced, either."

"What do you hope to gain by the confrontation, William?" Lord de Clinton asked quietly. As he too realized the implications, his complexion slowly returning to normal.

This was a question William wasn't expecting and it caught him by surprise. What did he think might happen? Would the king admit it, when confronted? Could he be made to admit it was all his idea? William shook his head. He didn't know much about kings, but he was certain Philip wouldn't simply crumble under the accusation and admit it all. "I think her majesty wishes to let him know we know, in the hopes it will force him to withdraw any other advances he may try to make against the throne."

The Lord High Admiral chewed on that for a moment, his brow drawn in deep thought. Sir Walter stood stone still, his eyes roaming the room, looking for one particular person. "Do you think King Philip would have asked Lord Thomas to do all he did, or do you think he just made an offer and Lord Thomas took advantage of situations as he saw fit?" Lord de Clinton wondered aloud.

Now it was William's turn to pause and consider. He found himself automatically assuming the same pose he saw his teacher take so many times before; his left arm crossed with his right thumb tapping his teeth. "I do not know this king, or my own, for that matter, but I do not believe he would have given instruction to Lord Thomas to have myself, Lady Helen or the Queen Mother taken prisoner, or worse."

Lord de Clinton nodded his agreement, and then added. "What you must understand William is this; men in power will do all they can to stay there. I have seen it myself," and here he paused, his eyes drifting away for a moment. His expression turned sad and he slowly let out a deep breathe. "It is hard for me to admit, but I have had those same thoughts and feelings. As soon as you begin to love the position and its benefits, more than the reason you were placed there, and ultimately who was responsible for you being there, you will find yourself making decisions you never would have considered before. Even our Lord was crucified, for one reason most of all; he threatened the power of those in charge, both Roman and Jew."

"Is it possible it is our fault King Philip did what he did and through him, Lord Thomas?" William asked, trying to wrap his head around what he had just learned.

Sir Walter shook his head slowly, a sad look crossing his face for a moment. "No, Sir William, we are not at fault. In the end, it is always the individual's own decisions and nothing more."

"My teacher did tell me, each man must be prepared to stand on the Day of Judgment, to defend his decisions and his actions. He will not be able to say he was forced to do this or that by someone else. Every decision we make is our own." William stopped and remembered when his tutor had first told him this. "He wanted me to embrace each day with joy, no matter what we found ourselves facing. Later he wanted to show me how decisions ultimately lead to situations, both good and bad, of our own creation." Lord de Clinton listened closely, nodding thoughtfully, as William continued. Having never met this young knight of Dorchester, or the teacher he quoted, Sir Walter found himself staring with mouth slightly open wondering if he was truly hearing such wisdom from one so young.

"There was something else he told me…" he paused, trying to collect his thoughts. "He said the Norsemen told a story of two wolves, which live inside each man, good and evil, fear and faith. The wolf which controls the man is the one which the man feeds with his thoughts and actions. If he were here, he would probably tell me it is also like planting a field. The more good seed you sow the more good you will reap."

"I never had such a teacher, William," the Lord High Admiral admitted. "Nor I," Sir Walter added. "I know your time together was short, but you should consider yourself most fortunate to have had his wisdom to share." Lord de Clinton stated. As if suddenly remembering why they were together, he looked about the room, realizing nearly everyone was still held in steady rapture by the Queen Mother. "We find ourselves in an even more difficult situation than I originally had believed," he stated, then turned back to face his young companion. "If he was here with you now, what do you think your tutor would have advised?" If Sir Walter objected to the question his expression didn't reveal it.

William started to answer, then stopped, suddenly realizing the position in which he found himself; the King of England's most trusted advisors and close friends were asking him for advice. His palms began sweating and his heart began pounding so loudly in his chest he was certain both Lords would have heard it. He took a deep breath and wiped his hands on his cotte. All the lessons he had received since they left Dorchester seemed to be leading up to this. Somehow they all were interrelated, each one like a block of stone, first in the foundation, then, later, the walls and roof. In his mind's eye he pictured the cathedral in Salisbury, its spire rising to the sky, the purple sunset of their second evening on the road changing the color of the white stone.

Like a flash he came upon a thought, and before he realized it, William had spoken it out loud. "He would remind me that even our Lord failed to condemn the harlot, when she was brought before him to be stoned." He considered what he just said, and then added, "I know I should look to Jesus as my example, but I do not think I am ready to forgive Lord Thomas and forget what he has done." He lowered his eyes, "I believe King Philip did what he did because all he holds dear had been threatened by England. I understand why and do not blame him for doing all he could to end the threat. If I found myself in the same situation, I may have done the very same thing. But for Lord Thomas…" William shook his head.

He felt a heavy hand rest on his shoulder and he looked up into the brilliant blue eyes of William de Clinton, Lord High Admiral and Warden of the Cinque Ports. "At your age I would not have been able to admit that to anyone, let alone myself, William." His serious expression crumbled when a great big, toothsome smile spread across his face. "The day I met you in the New Forest I told myself I needed to find an excuse to come to Dorchester, to see what it was which made you, even in that brief meeting, different. The more I see, the more I believe you will be taking back something very special with you to your home." Lord Sir Walter nodded and made a note to himself to seek out this young knight of Dorchester once he was back in England.

William did his best to return the smile, wiping his eyes in the process. He was about to ask Lord de Clinton a question when he noticed a Frenchman, staring at them both, just a few feet away. He hadn't been there long, and William wondered how much of their conversation he had heard. Both Lords noticed William staring and turned their heads simultaneously.

From the back, William could see the muscles tense up in their shoulders, then he watched as William de Clinton bowed deeply from the waist. As he rose, he muttered, "Majesty." Sir Walter showed less formal greeting and simply nodded, repeating the word. William's eyes grew huge and his mouth dropped open. Standing before him, studying him, was Philip Valois, King of France.

●●●

"I am sorry, I think I misunderstood…"

"No, my lord, you did not," Philip answered, his voice rising above a normal conversation; heads turned. William did his best to remember his tutor's teaching on looking closely at others in order to learn more about them. The King of France was just barely taller than himself. Even though he didn't know his age for sure, he guessed it at 50, mostly because of the amount of gray in his hair. He was thinner than William had expected, and he occasionally used a plain white linen square to wipe his nose, which from its sore redness, was probably a long-standing problem. He spoke with a strong accent, but it wasn't difficult to understand, despite the fact that he spoke like someone was pinching his nostrils shut. It explained the kerchief.

He wore a finely tailored, silver buttoned cotte, with a high, tight collar and short waist. An intricately tooled leather belt held a richly embroidered pouch and an empty sheath for a dagger. His hose appeared to be dark dyed linen and his deerskin shoes were pointed at the tips. If nothing else would impress him on William, it would have been his attire.

"Then… what you are suggesting, Majesty…" Lord de Clinton stammered while shaking his head in disbelief.

"Is the immediate end to all hostilities in France," Philip answered. His voice rose again and William could see he was straining, as if it was hard for him not to shout out his rebuttals.

"And the French terms…" Lord Manny began.

"There will be no terms," his voice rose still once more as he sharply answered, cutting off both English Lords with words which cut like a baselard. He used no title in addressing either, and they did their best to bite back their own retorts. As Philip's voice had continued to elevate during their short conversation, it began to attract the attention of the other delegates, until all were circled around William, the Lords de Clinton and Manny, as well as the king. "France must ask for the cessation of armed conflict. If England accepts, we will make no move against English held lands."

"For how long?" One of Lord de Clinton's companions, who just joined the circle, asked. He had been introduced to William, who suddenly found himself searching his memory for the man's name: de Tuddyr. For some reason his family name touched something in his recent memory, then Philip spoke and the thought fled.

"That I cannot say," the king shrugged. As William watched de Tuddyr closely, he could see he was holding something back. It looked as if he had a bad taste in his mouth and was trying to be polite and not insult the host by spitting it out. His eyes told the same story; anger and frustration were both there and something else.

"You are asking us to tell our king, after several years of victory, to stop pressing his advantage, and to wait, until some unnamed future date, to begin again? You must know what he will say," The Queen Mother stated, shaking her head in disbelief. She had followed the other delegates, when they heard the raised voices and made her way next to William. He bowed and stepped back to let her take his place beside the Lords de Clinton and Manny.

In that moment, Philip turned to face Isabella. From his vantage point, just outside the circle of delegates and advisors, William could see Lord de Clinton, the Queen Mother, several members of the Lord High Admiral's retinue, and the French delegation, all grown quiet, their eyes on the king. Only the Baron de Manny was obstructed by the Queen Mother. Although everyone else's attention was fixed on Philip, William's was on Isabella and Helen, who had now joined him, just on the outside of the circle of delegates.

She reached out and took William's hand, squeezing it earnestly. He was surprised to feel it trembling. From the quick glance he gave her, Helen looked as if she guessed what her mother was going to do, and it worried her. Philip was, after all, the King of France and she was out of favor at Edward's court. Despite the fact that she had been secretly asked to participate in this delegation, most of the other men in the circle, whether English or French, did not wish to see her there. "Do something," Helen whispered, squeezing his hand one more time. "I have seen the same look in my own reflection, William, and I fear for what might come to pass." There was such complete urgency in her voice; he didn't have time to consider what needed to happen.

Later he would try and recall what caused him to do what he did when both the Queen Mother and Lord de Clinton would ask him that very question. He couldn't give them a satisfactory answer other than, "I felt… a pinch and it startled me into action. I needed to do this." Although it sounded like an evasive answer, it was, in fact, the truth. Deep down, he suddenly had a feeling, an urge, to do something which defied sense, and if he had taken the time to analyze the thought, he probably wouldn't have pursued it. That sudden jolt was not unlike being pinched or poked. When it happened, William found himself not hesitating. In less than a hearts beat, he had asked God for His wisdom and received an answer. William accepted it and followed through.

•••

The bed at the Fowler truly was one of the most comfortable he had slept in since leaving Dorchester. He felt as if he were slowly falling into a soft cloud. The aches and pains of the past several weeks seemed carried away, as if on a gentle spring breeze. As William lay there, in that suspended moment between wake and sleep, his mind returned to Amiens. All eyes were on Philip of France, while the Queen Mother, who he had pledged himself to serve, was on the verge of challenging the king. Helen was pleading with him to do something and God had provided the answer.

Looking back on that moment, he wondered, not for the first time nor probably the last, what would have happened had he not spoken? Surely Isabella would have followed through with their original plan. How would the king have responded? He couldn't be certain, but from what little he had seen of Philip of Valois' short temper, he imagined it would not have been pleasant, nor ended well. As it was, he had felt compelled to step out in faith on the prompting, which came to him. "God, help me to always respond to You, especially when it comes at a pinch point," William murmured quietly as he lay in that incredible bed. Slowly the picture of what had unfolded next, returned to his minds' eye.

"Majesty," William had stated, from his position on the outer edge of the circle of delegates. "I must beg for your forgiveness." He began walking forward, his eyes fixed on those of the king, and, as if pre-arranged, the few individuals between them, stepped back. The other's expressions were a mixture of confusion, irritation, wonderment and shock, the latter being that of the Queen Mother's. He did his best to ignore these while continuing to focus on Philip.

"You will have it… if I am able to give it," the king answered cautiously. William could see the questions within his eyes, behind the calm mask. He was trying to remember who this young man was. His eyes drifted down to the coat of arms on William's left breast glanced quickly at the Queen Mother, then back again to his cousin's escort. In that flash of a moment William was certain the king remembered and understood.

Stopping a few paces from Philip of France, William bowed deeply at the waist, his right hand over his heart. "I must beg forgiveness for the slight I would have given you this day." He paused just long enough to know he had everyone's attention. "Without evidence to support it, I was prepared to lay an accusation at the foot of the throne, which would have done nothing to aid in these proceedings, except, perhaps delay or even derail the important decisions, which needs must be met."

"And yet, no accusation was made against myself or the throne, so there is no forgiveness to seek," Philip answered warily.

William shook his head in disagreement. "I must beg pardon, again, and disagree, your Majesty. In my own mind it was already made up, and therefore, the accusation already made, even if not spoken out loud."

The King of France stared at the young Englishman standing before him. He had never met such conviction of character before and it stunned him into silence. Slowly, cautiously, Philip answered, "Perhaps… perhaps you should share with me what this decisions was, so I may know what it is I am forgiving." A cautious smile spread beneath his immaculately groomed mustache.

"As you wish, Majesty," William answered. It took several moments for him to describe, in moderate detail, all the events, beginning in Salisbury and culminating two days previously in Amiens, in which Lord Thomas Denebaud played such a prominent role.

William ended with the capture of Lord Thomas and his return, under guard, to London to stand trial. At this he paused, and did his best to keep his eyes on the king. If he had glanced around, he would have seen wide eyes, open mouths, mixed expressions of anger and dismay, along with glances towards both the Queen Mother and Helen, from the rest of the delegation. Philip's own face was blank. If he understood the implications, he was doing his best not to let on through his features, but his eyes were something different. William could see in them the realization that his own plans within plans had been discovered.

"Lord Denebaud's action are reprehensible, but it still does not explain a need of forgiveness on my part."

William could hear, ever so slightly, a break in the king's voice, and knew the truth was there. Once again, he bowed, "Majesty, your mercy is needed in Lord Thomas let slip by his own tongue, while I was his prisoner. He suggested there were those in power who would reward him for the actions he took." William stood, while shaking his head, sincere apology was written on his face. "With no evidence to support it, majesty, I reasoned the blame had to come from outside of King Edward's court; outside of England entirely. Forgive me majesty, but I had convinced others, without evidence, to lay the blame at the foot of your throne."

Philip of France stood, stony-faced for a long moment. William reminded himself of one of his teacher's earliest and most often repeated lessons. To be honest, even if it means your harm, is always the best choice. The burden of what the Queen Mother had intended to do had been immediately lifted from him as he spoke. Now, his own mind was clear and he could see the king working through his response. No matter what Philip decided to say, or what actions he decided to take, William knew he had done the right thing.

"I speak truthfully when I say that in all my years I have never met anyone who has asked forgiveness for a thought not spoken aloud." Philip paused, continuing to stare at William. "It is rare to find a man who will admit when he is wrong, even when the evidence is clear. Now I find a young man, newly knighted from the tale I just overheard, who admits his error, even before any others know of it." He smiled briefly at William, and then continued. "You have asked for my forgiveness twice now and my mercy at least once, and I grant these both. What is done is done and what has been prevented… will be left undone." The king smiled once more, his eyes briefly straying across several faces in the room, one of which barely concealed deep surprise, mixed, perhaps with anger. William bowed.

When he rose, he found Philip looking on him with a questioning expression. "How would you answer this stalemated negotiation, Sir William?"

Without a second thought, he answered the King of France. "A wise man once told me that to find agreement with someone requires you to do your best to put yourself in their own position; he suggested it was as if standing in the other's shoes. If I may be so bold as to take him at his word, I would then have to realize your Majesty would only suggest this proposal if the need was most dire. There are other concerns, greater concerns, than the open threat of England, which weigh upon your Majesty's mind. What they may be I do not know. But if they are as great as it appears, perhaps England would be best to accept the terms and find it in itself the mettle to leave France to its own, for the time being."

The Lord de Clinton, Queen Mother, and most others around them stared at William, mouths slightly open. It looked as if one or more were ready to respond to William's suggestion, and perhaps even none too kindly, when King Philip answered first, his raised hand silencing any possible retort. "Because you did me the courtesy, just now, I will return the favor." Several sharp breaths were taken, both from the French and English delegates. Philip waved those off, not caring whether they were his men or not.

"France faces a great pestilence, Sir William, the likes of which we have not seen in several lifetimes. It rides like the wind from the south, by way of Lombardy, which now sees itself devastated with nearly one in five men, women and children already dead and the number continues to grow." William could see the truth in his eyes. This was the buried concern and the name of the fear he had noticed just moments before.

"God save us," Lord de Clinton muttered while making the sign of the cross. He realized as well the king was speaking unveiled truth.

Philip nodded his agreement. "God save us all, Lord de Clinton, but if my people are like the Lombard's, it will not be so." He paused a moment, then added, "it is best England should look to its own shores and pray this plague does not find its way across the channel."

The Lord High Admiral chewed on this revelation and the inside of his cheek for a very brief moment. As King Edward's appointed chief negotiator it was his decision, and he took only a brief moment to make up his mind. "England accepts France's proposal without condition." He looked around the room, considering what he just heard and what he had promised, then added, "It may be best we do not take the time to put this in writing, but each find the fastest way to whatever place we call home."

The Lord Admiral extended his hand to Philip, who grasped it firmly. "Godspeed, majesty," William stated. The King of France nodded and turned to address the two women in the room.

"Lady Helen… cousin," he nodded then his gaze briefly passed over

Lord Manny. Finally he turned to William, focusing on the embroidery on his chest. "You wear the sigils of France, Navarre and Champagne, Sir. William." It was not surprising the king omitted England from the list. He paused, considering his comment carefully while wiping his nose once more with his kerchief. "I would have expected nothing less from any French knight who bears such arms, although, I do believe I would have found myself sorely disappointed." William watched as he nodded to himself, and then, leaning forward in order to whisper quietly in his ear, added, "I will send inquiry as to your uncle," with that last comment Philip Valois, King of France, turned and marched out of the guildhall, his retinue quickly following.

Chapter Thirty

It truly was the most wonderful bed he had found himself in, in quite a while. Just the realization of how comfortable he felt, for the first time in a very long time, struck him as somehow odd. Did this particular bed make all that much difference just because the last two days on the road with the Queen Mother had been very uncomfortable? The fact that Lords de Clinton and Manny as well as their men, now traveled with them, made William feel like hot iron between two hammers and an anvil. Even the rise in his hopes of his uncle's release wasn't enough to compensate for the cross examination he had endured.

Despite King Philip's revelation regarding a great pestilence which was making its way north through France, William felt, for the first time in a long while, a sense of opportunity to relax. Lord Thomas was captured and being taken to London for trial. King Philip had all but admitted he had encouraged or at least suggested a means to encourage Lord Thomas' treachery and treason, while also suggesting he would withdraw further attempts against the English crown. And then he offered, without solicitation, his help regarding William's uncle. Despite all the pain, injuries, and loss he and others had suffered in the last few weeks, William felt as though he could see the end of the dark tunnel he had been forced to walk through. The bed was a symbol, a chance to enjoy the simple pleasure of a well-earned restful sleep.

As his mind wandered over the last two days ride from Amiens and the questioning he had received, he suddenly found himself sitting outside the gates of Crandor Castle. The sun was bright and warm on his face, truly a rare gem for early spring in Dorchester. He could see the breeze move across the open fields, dotted as they were with pregnant, newly shorn ewes. He smiled at the familiar smell of stock and meadow. There was only one thing missing.

"You have done well, William." He spun around to see a hooded and cloaked figure sitting on one of the milkmaids' stools. He couldn't see the face, but the voice was his tutor's. His heart leapt in his chest and he could feel his throat tighten with joy. "Better than your father, uncle, or even I could have imagined."

"Without your wisdom and guidance none of this would have been possible," he answered, not trying to hide the emotion in his voice as it cracked and tears welled up in his eyes.

"Thank you, William, but you still have one task at hand, before you can return to the safety and comfort of Dorchester." The figure was leaning forward so the cowl cast its features in shadow. His hands were clasped in his lap, but the thick wool material and the long sleeves, covered them completely.

"Lord Thomas' trial."

"As in Salisbury, William," his teacher responded while nodding beneath the hood. "Tell the truth and justice will be done; he will no longer be a concern of yours."

"As in Salisbury," he echoed his teacher's words. "My short time before the Justice of the Peace of Salisbury was a trial in itself. I can only imagine what it will be like in front of the Justices of the King's Bench."

"Lord Thomas will be given what he deserves, his actions have determined it; after all, he never learned to guard his thoughts."

"This will be the second time a life was taken because of my testimony." The joy of being reunited with his tutor coursed through his imagination; for some reason, it didn't feel strange to be having this conversation with him, despite the fact he had not been seen since Godefroy tossed him from the footbridge in Amiens. He also didn't feel it necessary to ask where he had been.

"The Nazarene's own words warn us that he who lives by the sword will surely die by it. Lord Thomas knew this and should be prepared to face the consequences."

William shook his head slowly, trying to clear the vision of Lord Thomas swinging from a rope. "God knows I wish I was not put in this position."

"No one in a similar situation would, William." He turned to see Helen standing with her back to him, just outside the opened gates, staring at the walled manor house with its central tower. He wondered if she was trying to decide if she liked its appearance. "But we have a duty to perform and we must see it through." As she turned to face him, the bright spring sunshine flashed through her hair, and it looked aflame. She smiled and her eyes sparkled as if holding some hidden promise.

The strongest of feelings surged through him. Was she suggesting what he thought? If the Lord Thomas "problem" went away with his testimony, was she offering what he secretly hoped for, since the moment he helped her off the ground in the alley in Southampton?

"You are a knight and an honored member of my household, William," Isabella stated. He turned from Helen to find himself staring into the azure eyes of the Queen Mother. He thought it remarkable how similar her smile was to her daughter's. "There is a duty you must now perform. Always speak the truth, no matter what it costs you, is that not correct? Did you not speak these words just days ago in Amiens?"

"As God was my witness, I spoke those words and I will hold my oath as a solemn vow, but…"

Isabella reached forward, gripping both arms tightly. She stepped forward until his vision was filled with her eyes and her smile. "To say what needs to be said will end this, William. Lord Thomas will get what he deserves."

"What he deserves," echoed his tutor and Helen.

"What about forgiveness?" William asked, startled by the intensity of the Queen Mother's grip and the brilliance of her eyes. "Did not our Lord and Savior teach us to turn the other cheek?"

"Do you really think you are supposed to stand by while someone does all in his power to molest, maim or murder you?" His teacher asked. "The word tells us about men like Lord Thomas. '*You want what you do not have, so you scheme and kill to get it. You are jealous of what others have, but you cannot get it, so you fight and wage war to take it away from them. You want only what will give you pleasure.*' These men are friends of the world, not yours."

"This is your chance, William," Isabella added. "You must realize you were set here, at this time, to be the one to bring Lord Thomas to his knees. This is your chance to see justice done. All of England will know of your greatness and goodness." He turned slightly from the Queen Mother's gaze to see her daughter smiling, her own eyes sparkling in the spring sunshine. For the second time he was certain her eyes held a promise of a reward at the end of this ordeal.

He imagined what that would be like: to be known and recognized throughout England as the one who saved the crown, and in that same action, winning Helen to his side. He could see and hear the crowds cheering when they traveled together. He could imagine what it would be like to be hers, to share everything. Her eyes held all kinds of promises.

As he stood there in the sunshine outside Crandor Castle, surrounded by three of the people he cared for most deeply, William began to reconsider what the fate of Lord Thomas should be. He deserved to be punished for the terrible things he did, didn't he? Men had been killed… good men. A woman and her daughter were nearly violated, his own uncle still sat a prisoner, held against his will in the middle of France, and his teacher, his mentor and the man he respected most of all was taken from him. A sudden hollowness swept over him and, as if on cue, dark clouds covered the sun. If Lord Thomas deserved it, why would it bother William to stand and speak the truth, condemning an evil man?

He could feel an anger he hadn't noticed before begin to rise inside of him. This man, who didn't deserve to be called a man, had done so many vile things. He had encouraged and condoned even more from those around him. There was seemingly little he wouldn't consider. William clenched his fists, as the dark clouds continued to blot out the sunlight. Shadows began stretching across the pasture. Crandor took on the look of a long deserted ruin. Even the walls suddenly appeared cracked and crumbling in on themselves. The great oak doors were broken and hung from rusted hinges.

William looked up and noticed the changes for the first time. His teacher, Helen, and the Queen Mother were all gone. He stood alone, just in front of the broken, crumbling walls of his home. Despite the darkness around him, a thought pierced through it, bringing with it a light of disturbing revelation. This is what his life would be like, if Lord Thomas had his way: an empty, deserted, collapsing pile of rubble.

As if in response, the tower buckled, bent, then fell in upon itself as the ground shook and a great cloud of choking dust filled the air. William hacked and coughed, trying to cover his mouth while keeping his eyes squinted shut. He couldn't hold back the sobs, which wracked his body. Hot tears streaked his face with muddy tracks. There was no future for him or his family name, if Lord Thomas continued to live and do as he planned. As if to emphasize this revelation, lightning flashed across the sky, thunder quickly following. Sheets of rain began falling, soaking his clothes, causing him to shiver. Even when his mother died he didn't feel this alone and depressed.

Just as suddenly as he had found himself in Dorchester, he awoke in bed at The Fowler, in Marquise. Outside his room on the first floor of the old stone inn, he could hear the rain coming down hard on the cobblestone streets and in the distance the roll of thunder. He rubbed his eyes, his hands coming back wet; he had been crying. The entire sequence and conversations came back to him in a rush and nearly overwhelmed him.

He realized several things at once: He missed the wisdom of his teacher more than ever; he felt more alone than he ever had; and he no longer cared how comfortable the bed was. The rain continued unabated, the clouds so thick he had no idea what time of day it was. He felt as though he had been in bed for a long time and when he rolled over and out, his bare feet touching the cool stone floor, any sleep remaining was startled from him.

A fresh realization of what lay before him brought on a renewed wave of isolation. He felt as though his bed was a skiff, adrift on the open sea; isolated and without land in sight. He rubbed the heels of his palms into his eyes until he saw flashes of light, not coming from the lightning. Why did his teacher have to be taken in such a way? He needed him more now than ever. The thought of what he still had to endure over the next several days, without his tutor's guidance, sprang up like weeds in a garden. Without any need of planting, tending or watering, doubt rapidly grew in William's mind.

Did he really think he could simply walk into London, say his piece and go home? And then, once he was home, how would he take up his life in Crandor? Without the guidance of his uncle or his teacher how could he possibly know what was required of him as Earl of Dorchester? It felt as if a great weight was slowly, inexorably pressing down on him. As he sat on the edge of the bed in The Fowler the magnitude of all the tasks still set before him became almost physical. He could feel himself folding in the middle, his chest slowly sinking to his knees. He wanted to cry out for help, but he felt the overwhelming surety there was no one to turn to.

A knock at the door of his small room startled him more than he felt it should. "Yes?" he asked, his voice carrying an annoyance at being disturbed, "who is it?"

A boy's voice spoke, his own anxiety clearly audible in the nervous cracking of his response. "*La reine mère vous a demandé d'assister à elle comme elle rompt son jeûne.*" He could hear footsteps hastily retreating down the hall.

He was to attend to Isabella. He nodded his head slowly, as the realization sunk in. He was to be a footman to the Queen Mother, until such time as death took him or her Majesty released him. Sir William, the butler. He smiled at the irony. If not for the sacrifice of his father, the untimely death of his mother, and adoption by his uncle, his own disappearance and ransom, William wouldn't have been looked at twice by most of the people he had met since leaving Dorchester. He pulled on his hose and soft leather boots then crossed the few feet to a pitcher of water and a basin, both sitting on a small table at the foot of his bed.

He bent over the basin and poured the water over the back of his head and neck, rubbing it in with his free hand. Pouring more water into the cup of his hands he rubbed his face then dried with a rough spun towel, which sat folded nearby. The memory of the bath in Downton at the Bear and Boar, along with Agnes, rushed back to him. He could tell by the smell he needed a more thorough cleaning, but there was no time. A moment later he was walking down the hall to a secluded section of the common room, while buttoning the top of his embroidered cotte.

The Queen Mother was alone with Helen and they both smiled and nodded to William as he entered the room. He had the feeling he had interrupted an important conversation, as Helen had been leaning forward her arms crossed, with elbows on the table; her mothers' pose, the opposite. Their smiles were hasty additions to their appearance. He also thought, by the dark beneath their eyes, neither had slept very well. The Queen Mother motioned to close the door behind him.

William bowed to Isabella, nodded to Helen and set about doing his best to care for their needs as they ate quietly. His stomach growled several times, the last had to have been loud enough for both ladies to hear, but neither said anything. As he stood near one corner of the room, William ground his teeth in frustration. Not only was he hungry, but also the fact he was here, in this room, refilling cups with water and red wine, while slicing cheese, bread and apples, irritated him.

He was so lost in his own thoughts he didn't realize the Queen Mother had asked him a question. "William?" her voice returned him to the room and his task at hand.

"I am sorry, Majesty. Forgive me. Is there anything else?" He stumbled over an apology he really didn't feel like giving.

Isabella took on a stern appearance and William was sure he had erred terribly. "You certainly have a strange way of attending to a lady's needs, Sir William." His gaze dropped and he began to mumble his continued apology, when he heard a chuckle from Helen, followed by a loud laugh from the Queen Mother. "Oh, William, have no fear; I am not upset. I can only imagine how difficult this must be, to wait upon two ladies during their meal, when you have not eaten yourself." She smiled, that wonderful room brightening smile and he couldn't help but smile and blush.

She waved to one of the open chairs at the table. "Please sit and eat. Afterwards we will discuss a question Helen and myself were debating when you arrived." William sat down, needing no other encouragement. Their meals on the road since leaving Amiens had been filling but simple. The cheese was fragrant and soft enough he was able to spread some on the crusty bread. The two textures were wonderful together. He took a sip of the watered wine and closed his eyes as the layer of flavors washed over his palate. If it was at all possible to find someone to prepare cheese, bread and wine this way in Dorchester, he was sure he would never want to leave again.

The thought of Crandor Castle and its surrounding, rolling hills, reminded him of the dark dream, from which he had so recently awakened. The destruction of his home had seemed so real, the pain and anger of its collapse so intense, it affected the taste of his food. He no longer found delight in the flavors. Setting down a half-eaten piece of bread, he swallowed and turned to the Queen Mother. "How can I help with your discussion, Majesty?"

Isabella shook her head. "Please finish…" William shook his head in refusal and pushed the plate away for added emphasis. She shrugged, "very well then." A moment later, William sat in stunned silence, unsure how to answer the question put before him. "Do you see any other way, Sir William?"

William shook his head, trying to take a moment to gather his thoughts. "Surely this is a matter between mother and child. I…"

"Exactly, mother," Helen, responded quickly, her expression a mixture of frustration, anger, and perhaps fear. William wasn't sure of the last except he thought he saw it in her eyes.

"Never the less, I have asked Sir William, as a member of my household, for his opinion." From her tone, it was obvious she would not be denied on this point.

The memory of the dream returned to him. There had been a promise, an offered benefit to his willingness to speak for Lord Thomas' condemnation. Perhaps this was the other way? Another thought crossed his mind at that moment. "Perhaps this was the way it was always meant to be, Lady Helen," William suggested. He watched her expression darken and hastily added, "You first introduced yourself as Helen Tuddyr. Maybe that was no coincidence."

"That name was suggested to me by my guardians, William. Knowing now who they were answering to, do you really think it merely chance they would have done so?"

William could tell by Isabella's reaction she hadn't been aware of this, nor considered it. "If what you say is true, then Lord de Tuddyr's comment during our meeting with Philip was neither chance nor accident."

"What exactly did he say?" William asked.

"He told me how shocked he was at Lord Thomas' downfall and, as a cousin of Roger Mortimer, he felt it was his duty to share in my own protection, as well as any others I felt warranted such attention." She paused a moment to consider what it might mean. Slowly, she sounded out her thoughts. "If the Tuddyr's were only tied with Lord Thomas, his capture would have ended their involvement. And yet," and here she paused, tapping the perfectly trimmed nail of her index right finger on her incisors while her gaze shifted to the closed door. "He approached me several days after Thomas Denebaud's arrest."

"Perhaps his connection with King Philip was not part of Lord Thomas' plans?" Helen interjected. "Is it possible the King of France had arrangements with more than just Lord Thomas?"

"If he has any wisdom at all, he would not have trusted all his plans to one man," William added quickly, then realized the impact of his comment and fell silent.

"Philip may not be the bravest of men, but he is cunning; I do not believe he would have put all his hopes in Lord Thomas," Isabella finally added. "Even the simple know not to leave all their eggs in the same basket. One mistake and they are all broken…"

"The one hope we have, Majesty, is the King's own comments at the end of the meeting," William suggested. "Lord de Tuddyr was there when King Philip said whatever other plans there may have been were now ended."

Helen gasped, her hand quickly coming to her mouth. "I saw…I saw his reaction, but did not think on it at the moment." Her voice was shaking, as was her head.

"Whose reaction, Lady Helen?" William asked, as he leaned forward across the table.

"Lord de Tuddyr," she explained. "When King Philip promised it was ended, he glanced about the room. You bowed, William, so you missed what happened. For a brief moment I thought I saw anger and surprise cross Lord de Tuddyr's face as his gaze met the King's. Something about that look makes me think he will not stop just because France is no longer his patron."

"If the Lords of the Marches know of your true identity," Isabella began, then her voice cracked and her eyes grew sad. William watched as a deep-seated pain crossed over the Queen Mother's face. She lowered her gaze to the folded hands in her lap as she took a deep breath and slowly exhaled. "You know the position I am in, child. I find myself between the anvil and the hammer," she stated, almost to herself. "I do not like to be so restrained."

"Majesty, Helen, our list of trusted allies grows thin." William pushed back his chair and stood from the table. He fixed his gaze on the bread and cheese, not daring to look up into either woman's eyes for fear he may lose his nerve in this moment. "The answer was already proposed once, before we met, Majesty. But that proposal required a bequest from your own person, and, at the time, seemed hardly possible. Now…"

"Wi… William…" Helen stammered, her face turning ghostly white, while her mouth dropped open, lips quivering and her head shook slightly. Tears threatened to spill over.

"They will never stop threatening you no matter where you run, no matter where you try and hide," William quickly added. His gaze wandered up from the table and locked on her own. Her pale blue eyes were suddenly red rimmed and her faced already streaked. The look on her face was like a hot knife in William's chest. He caught his breath, then continued, quietly, but with strength in his voice, which even surprised himself. "How can you possibly trust anyone who may approach you as a suitor? This way you and your mother will both know you will be kept safe."

"Explain yourself, William," Isabella demanded.

It took him just a moment to remind her of Helen's betrothal to Geoffrey de Simpson, his death at Crecy and the hopes of Lord David and Matthew de Simpson for their lands to remain in the de Simpson family. "I see a way to accomplish all these, without exposing Helen's true identity."

William did his best to now keep his attention focused on the Queen Mother. He could see, out of the corner of his eye, Helen's own unbroken gaze on him. "As a newly named member of your household, and, in your own words, 'savior of your person at the hands of Lord Thomas, you could, as a gracious gesture, deed the lands of Eaucourt sur Somme to me and mine as a wedding gift. The Lords de Simpson would be satisfied, the pledge between a young man and woman would be honored, and no one would suspect it had anything to do with Helen's parentage."

Isabella leaned back in her chair, her hands still folded in her lap. Her expression had changed though. "Is that the only reason, William?" Her question appeared innocent, but her eyes betrayed her.

There was so much he wanted to say but he suddenly found the words stuck in his throat like an old, dry piece of bread. He swallowed thickly as he turned to Helen. He gazed into the red-rimmed, pale blue eyes looking back at him and muttered, "I have cared deeply for you since I first saw you in Southampton." Then quietly, almost too quietly for the ladies at the table to hear, he added, "Whatever may come of this that will never change."

•••

The sudden toss of the ship as it rolled in the choppy waves wrenched William from his thoughts. Despite squinting tightly, the rain and wind mixed with and whipped sea foam into his eyes, stinging them with chilled salt water. A fine spring rain it would have been on the hills of Dorchester, but in the open channel, it added to the spray sent up as their cog reached the trough of each successive wave, eventually soaking through his felted cloak. It would have been wiser to be under cover, but Helen and Isabella were together in the aft cabin.

William's life with these two ladies had changed dramatically since that morning at the Fowler. Helen continued to keep him at arm's length, and the Queen Mother seemed more determined than ever to have him in her presence only as a personal servant. He shivered as he was sprayed once again with a fine mist; the chill he felt had as much to do with how wet he was as the reality of his current situation. He was alone on board the ship with both ladies, and no one to whom he could confide his thoughts. More than ever he missed his tutor.

It seemed ages had passed since he received the letter on that beautiful spring morning, nearly a month before, in Dorchester. So much had happened, so many lives touched… and lost. He wondered, not for the last time, about Gilbert. Did he survive the docks in Southampton? What about Sir John? His thoughts turned to Robert and immediately his emotions bubbled to the surface, tightening his throat, catching his breath. Between the rain and the sea, no one could tell hot tears fell down his cheeks; not that there was anyone on board who would have taken notice. He wiped his face with a corner of his cloak, which had stayed somewhat dryer than the rest and forced his thoughts back to the table and his proposal over breakfast.

Helen had sat in stunned silence, her mouth slightly open. William had a hard time determining if she was angry, shocked, repulsed, intrigued or some combination of all four. Isabella was a different story. She sat stony faced as if carved from marble. Even her eyes didn't betray her thoughts but they also didn't waver, remaining fixed on William's. Very carefully, as if measuring each word before speaking, the Queen Mother replied. "I was never given the opportunity to meet Edward, prior to our betrothal and marriage; I was only twelve. It was not until later did I learn the kind of man he was." She paused and turned to Helen.

"Rarely, if ever, do women of position have the opportunity to meet and learn of the man they are to marry. Too often we are used as pawns to better a claim or end some dispute; I do not wish that upon you child. Although I cannot recognize you publicly, clearly there are those who feel they could use you to get to me, or through me to the king."

"Mother, you cannot ask…"

"Please, hear me to the end," Isabella cut off Helen as she began to protest, her head shaking and brow drawn down. William remained silent, watching as the Queen Mother stood and crossed the table to sit down next to her daughter. She took her hands in her own, looked deep into her eyes and continued. "Who can say what is best for any of us, or for you? It is so easy to miss an opportunity for peace and joy when it is right before you. That is why you need to grab whatever chance you have, no matter where you find it. In my own life I have seen we get no more than one or two such chances in a lifetime, and if we let them go, we will regret it for the rest of our lives." She leaned her head forward until it was gently touching her daughters, "I do not wish you to live a life of regrets."

"Was it this hard for you?" Helen eventually whispered, while using a kerchief to wipe her eyes. William recognized it as one he had given her in Southampton.

"Perhaps not," Isabella admitted. "I was told from a very young age I would marry for the family and my country, so I was prepared to do my duty to both." She reached up, taking the kerchief and wiped a tear-streaked cheek of Helen's. "You were sent away in order to be protected from men like Lord Thomas." Her own eyes filled with tears and her voice broke. "I am sorry, my child. I never intended for you to go through these trials. This is a burden you were never meant to bear." Mother and daughter embraced, their heads resting on each other's shoulders both crying silently. William decided they needed time alone and quietly left the room, shutting the door as noiselessly as possible.

He stood in the hall for a period of time, and not hearing the Queen Mother recall his presence, he wandered down to and through the foyer and out into the village of Marquise. Although he couldn't discuss with anyone what had just taken place, he needed a way to think it out. The Lords de Clinton and Manny had gone on to Calais with several of the King's Guard, in search of ships to carry them all back to England, leaving only a few men to accompany William, Helen, and the Queen Mother. They were not going to be any help.

As he was lost in thought, he didn't pay attention to where he walked. His feet crossed cobblestones, gravel and sand. Before he realized it, he was standing on the shore of the channel. The steady breeze lifted foam from the surf, misting his face, causing William to cross his arms to keep from shivering. He could just make out, on the horizon, the white chalk hills of Dover. If the weather held and the tide was with them, they would be in the England the following evening. He picked up a palm-sized rock, and threw it with all his might. He watched it disappear behind a white-capped wave, never hearing a splash over the sound of the surf.

This was not at all what he had planned. From the moment he received the ransom note he was sure he would be able to travel to France, find his uncle and bring him home. None of what had actually happened was in William's vision, or dream, as Robert had called it.

His teacher told him it would cost more than he could imagine; this was undoubtedly true. He looked at his right hand and the puckered scar. He hadn't thought of his left shoulder in over a week. There certainly was a physical payment he had made. Then he thought about Samuel Thompson and the trial, Davey Martin and the New Forest, and

Sir Geoffrey in Southampton. Many had made even greater physical payments than William's. The greatest and still hardest to bear was his teacher's sacrifice. When he told William there may be too high of a price to pay to see his vision come to pass, he never imagined this would be part of the cost.

Standing on the coast, the surf rolling in, relentless wave after wave, reminded him of the pursuit of Lord Thomas, and others who seemed to be eager to fill his vacant position. Anger began to rise up inside William. He uncrossed his arms and clenched his fists as they shook uncontrollably. He could feel the rage as it continued to build and knew it would need a vent before it overwhelmed him. Raising his fists he shook them at the sky and screamed at no one. William released all control over his emotions and allowed them to wash up and over him. It felt not unlike the moment onboard the ship, when he found himself tossed into the channel. Then, it was cold water and the weight of his cloak and clothes, which nearly pulled him under. Now, his own anger, frustration, loneliness, fear and confusion buffeted him and he fell to his knees, his hands holding his head. Hot tears streaked his cheeks and he gasped to regain his breath.

If Lord Thomas was standing before him he was certain he wouldn't be able to control the rage which coursed through him. The man who was behind so much of the personal cost since leaving Dorchester, would have become the focal point of all the emotions currently boiling through him. William tried to control his breathing, to force his heart to slow but he failed and fell forward, his fists burying themselves in the sand. The sobs were silenced but not ended and his head dropped and mouth hung open while his shoulders shook silently.

He had no recollection as to how long he knelt on all fours. All he knew, for those long moments, was that he felt utterly alone and without hope. He had no one to turn to, no one to ask for advice or help. He punched the beach over and over again until he pounded a deep hole in front of him and had grains of sand stuck in his knuckles. He sat back on his heels and stared at his hands, not realizing at first what he was looking at. His hands were shaking and starting to bleed.

Why did all of this have to happen to him? Wasn't it enough to lose both of his parents? Did he have to lose everyone close to him? Why was it his lot in life to suffer? So many people around him weren't going through the same trials. Why not? How were they able to avoid the same pain? The questions raced around in his brain, with no answer to corral them.

As he knelt there in the sand, he thought he heard someone shouting but it was hard to tell over the noise of the surf. A moment later the sound was closer and it was certainly a voice. He took a deep breath and turned to find one of the King's Guards approaching. He seemed eager to get William's attention. He stood, quickly rubbing the sand from his hands and hose, and met the guard half way. As he walked toward the liveried soldier, gently wrapping his knuckles in his kerchief, he hoped it was good news.

Chapter Thirty One

The news had been good after all; they would sail before noon the following day. The tide was with them and two ships were at their disposal. Being with the Lord High Admiral had its advantages. Just before boarding, William was told they would not be returning to Southampton. Instead, they would sail directly to the tidewater of the Thames and then upriver, past Gravesend, to the docks at the White Tower. Lord de Clinton and most of the King's Guards were traveling aboard a separate cog, along with the prisoners. They would deliver them for the trial, which was to take place as soon as they were in London. There would be no long delay in dealing with treason. Lord Manny was intending to stay in Calais on "King's business." William felt it prudent not to inquire for details.

By the time he returned to his room at the Fowler his knuckles were burning and he did his best to rinse them off in the water basin at the foot of his bed. There was a mostly colorless lump of something that may have been soap on the stand next to the bowl. He couldn't get it too close to his face without it making his eyes water, but when he rubbed it into his hands it created a thick foam and did a decent job of removing the dirt and stains from his hands and fingers, leaving them tingling and almost pink in the process.

He quickly repacked the sack he had with him since he set out from Dorchester and sat at the end of the bed. He couldn't shake the feeling of being so completely alone, with no one to confide in or seek advice from. For some reason he vividly remembered the small twig, caught up in the eddy of the brook near the Roman road in Dorchester and realized this was exactly how he felt. The events, orchestrated by the King of France, Lord Thomas, and others he may not even be aware of, had caught him, like that twig in the swirling water.

For some reason the thought of spinning out of control, neither into the main stream, nor onto the bank, made him think of Helen and his proposal. There had been no courtship, no romance. His offer was one made from a calculation, like the simple mathematics Robert had been teaching him. It made sense, no matter which way he looked at it, but again, he was the twig in the eddy. His offer had been made because of the circumstances they both found themselves in. Had the course of their lives been different, they most likely would never have met. And if they did, would she have even looked twice at him?

He knew his feelings for her were strong and true, but what about her feelings for him? He hadn't considered that when he made the proposal. Other than an occasional glimmer of hope, along with the strange dream the night before, he hadn't spent much time thinking about her feelings. Some part of him realized he had been inwardly focused, his trials and troubles first and foremost in his mind; for some reason, as his thoughts had shifted more inward, he felt "smaller." That wasn't the best word to describe it, and again he wished, not for the last time, that Robert was there to sound out his thought, but his self-focus, instead of making him feel better, somehow made him feel worse.

As he sat on the end of the bed, staring at the small pack he had just reassembled, despite the fact they would not be leaving for another day, he wondered if Helen also felt like the branch stuck in the stream. He wondered how his offer had made her feel. As he sat a long moment on the end of the bed, rolling that over in his mind he realized what he had to do.

It took him little time to find both Helen and the Queen Mother. They were in their adjoining rooms, finishing their packing for the crossing. When he told Isabella he had something to tell them both he noted surprise, followed quickly by her well-concealed mask of indifference. She nodded and the two ladies sat in the small parlor, which connected their rooms, neither looking especially excited.

"So, you do not…?" Helen interrupted, a confused look on her face.

William shook his head. "This is not about what I want or what I think makes the most sense. This is about you, Helen." He paused and turned to face her directly. She looked up, and he stared into her eyes. The room had only one small window and the overcast day lent little natural light, so they seemed veiled and violet rather than their typical bright blue. "You deserve the chance to say where you will go and who you will be with." She guarded her expression almost as well as her mother, but he could see hope in her eyes. If he had looked closer he may have also noticed a slight measure of hurt.

•••

They entered Calais the following morning, just after daybreak. William had a restless night sleep, despite the wonderful bed. Whether it was his decision regarding Helen, or his hands, he wasn't completely sure. Either way he had difficulty falling asleep and even more waking before dawn. The basin at the foot of his bed had been changed some time during the previous day and the cool, fresh water helped, as did the chilled cobblestones beneath his feet. As it was, he found himself escorting Helen and the Queen Mother, along with the few remaining king's guards, to the city before he was fully awake.

Calais had been in the hands of the English for less than a year, and there were still signs of the long siege and short occupation. They met the Lords de Clinton and Manny just outside the gates, which were heavily guarded. Despite being in such high company, William was still questioned as to his purpose in Calais (to leave) and how long he intended to stay (only long enough to leave). His brief attempt at humor fell on deaf ears and the expression returned to him made it very clear it wasn't appropriate or appreciated. Finally, it was the vouch safe given by Sir Walter which allowed Helen and he to enter the city.

Passing through the wall, with its raised portcullis, reminded William of Southampton. But this was the only thing similar, for as soon as they exited the tunnel they found themselves on a narrow stone bridge which connected the city to the mainland and crossed over a wide canal. "These canals are what kept Calais out of our hands for two long years," Lord Manny stated.

William looked over the edge of the narrow bridge and could tell by the swelling tide that, even at its lowest point, there would still be a depth to the water in the canal beneath him to make fording it on foot difficult. As they passed over the swirling water, William also noticed the arrow notches, evenly spaced on the facing wall. "With archers on this inner wall and the towers, even at low tide it was nearly impossible to mount an assault with any chance of success, so we turned to a long siege in the hopes of starving them into submission," He continued.

"What was it that finally made the difference?" William asked, his natural curiosity rising like the tide filling the canals beneath their feet.

Lord Manny pointed to a strange group of stone buildings with a tower and surrounding wall, built just opposite the main canal and only several hundred yards from where they walked. "That is Fort Risban. King Edward built that without challenge. The people of Calais watched and could do nothing to stop it. It was the eventuality of starvation and no sign of reinforcements or relief from their king, which prompted the French surrender."

"No sign of relief and a good deal of work on my Lord Manny's part," William de Clinton interjected.

"Were you here for the entire siege, my Lord?" William asked.

"I was here for the final months. I could not bear to think of what might become of the people of this city if they continued to hold out. So, I took it upon myself to speak with the mayor."

"The mayor and the Burghers of Calais had been ordered by King Philip to keep it at all cost, while at the same time offering them no aid in their defense." The Lord High Admiral interjected. "The arrival of Henry of Lancaster, your uncle, and the other reinforcements sealed their fate."

"What or who, rather, were the Burghers, my Lord?"

"The leading men of Calais. They were advisors to the mayor."

"What were they like?" William's curiosity continued to grow as the story unfolded, even to the point he nearly forgot he was supposed to be escorting the Queen Mother and Lady Helen. Neither seemed to mind, as they had fallen back a few paces, and were in their own deep, huddled, private conversation.

"Proud men. Much like any who find themselves in positions of leadership during difficult times. The siege had already gone on for almost two years. There was no relief from their king and no chance of a ship slipping past the Lord High Admiral's blockade. But even wise men, when facing such a desperate situation, will strike out and bite, like a frightened dog in a corner." William suddenly remembered one of the men who had tried to abduct Helen in Southampton. Even though he had found himself abandoned by the rest of his comrades and with his back literally up against a wall, facing a mounted opponent, he was still willing to attack. He turned and looked at her briefly, but she didn't notice. Her mother had her attention and it was clearly an intense for both of them. He turned to Lord Manny who had continued without noticing his brief distracted attention. "They were reluctant to meet until they discovered who wished to parley."

"Lord Manny grew up not far from here, William," The Lord High Admiral pointed out. "He will not say so but his presence carried great weight."

Sir Walter forced a slight smile and nodded his appreciation for the kind word from another of Edward's trusted advisors. "I saw a chance to save lives, so I took it. Fortunately, it worked to everyone's benefit."

"What did you tell the Burghers, my Lord?" William asked.

"Speak the truth always, yes, William?" He smiled when he was sure the young man following his story understood the reference. "Henry was due to set sail from Southampton with more men of England." He paused a moment, in thought and then added, "I remember seeing the garter on your uncle's arm when he landed." He must have seen William's expression change so he quickly added, "I did not have the pleasure of meeting him though, there were more… pressing matters at hand." William did his best to hide the slight disappointment he suddenly felt. Deep down he had hoped his uncle and this great man of England had met. "And so I reminded them of their obligation to the citizens of

Calais who had put their trust in them." He smiled again for a moment, his eyes wandering farther down the cobblestone street they were walking. "There was one man in particular who caught my attention and it was through him the city was truly spared."

"Who was that my Lord?" William inquired.

"Eustache de Saint Pierre," Lord de Clinton interjected.

Lord Manny nodded his agreement. "As you state, Lord William…a singular man." For a brief moment, as they continued to make their way farther into the city, their feet echoing on the cobblestones, Lord Manny's expression grew somber. "These were and still are proud men; leaders of men. And although the mayor had the final say, he was not in charge."

This comment confused William and he interrupted, "how could the mayor not be the man in charge and yet make the final decision?"

"Because, William," Lord Manny replied, with the Lord High Admiral listening as intently as the young knight of Dorchester, "men will respond and answer to a position but they will respect a man." He must have seen the still confused look on William's face. "Men may reluctantly follow what they fear, William, but they will willingly lay down their life for who and what they respect and care for. Do you understand the difference?"

"I think so," William began hesitantly. He chewed on the inside of his cheek for a brief moment. Sir Walter must have realized he was working it through and silently watched William's expressions. "If you are given a title or position of leadership the men you command will have to follow your word but…" he paused as he continued to wrap words around this train of thought. "When the men you lead know how much you care for them and how much you want them to succeed…" the thought was there but he had to search for it. "Then they will willingly follow you anywhere." William paused again, then asked, "Is that what love is; is that truly the meaning of the knight's oath?"

Lord Manny raised an eyebrow and turned to the Lord High Admiral, whose expression was one of "I told you, did I not?"

"William, if you indeed understand what you just said, you will be able to lead men anywhere and they will follow you willingly." Lord de Clinton nodded his agreement and William's ears were ringing with the praise, such as it was. In that brief moment, before he would forget, William told himself that a true leader is followed because his men's love for him is a reflection of his own for them.

"What became of the Burghers, my Lord?" William asked as they continued on from the bridge to a straight, well laid cobblestone street, which led to the central square. On the far side, they turned down a separate wide avenue, which lead directly to the port, the quays and the channel.

"It was at this point King Edward made his offer to the city," Sir Walter continued. "He would spare the people if six of its leaders would surrender themselves to him. They were told they needed to walk out the very path we entered, while wearing nooses around their necks and carrying the keys to the city and citadel."

"It was here, William, that without the intervention of Lord Manny, twice, on the cities behalf, the outcome and destiny of those men and this city may have been very different," the Lord High Admiral interrupted.

Sir Walter nodded slightly and smiled even more weakly. It was clear to William, standing so close as to notice the subtle change in his expression, that the king's advisor didn't feel worthy of the praise. "In the end, William it came down to Eustache de Saint Pierre. He volunteered first and convinced five others to join him; none of which were the mayor, I might add." He paused just a moment, closing his eyes briefly. "I can still picture them in my mind as they came to the city gates. Their clothes were ragged, their faces gaunt, and their eyes… in them they had the look of men expecting to be executed."

"Did King Edward realize his mistake at *Le Crotoy* and spare them?" William asked.

"I do not believe our King would consider *Le Crotoy* a mistake, William," the Lord High Admiral interjected quickly and with perhaps more force than he intended. The young knight of Dorchester dropped his eyes and stammered an apology. Seconds later he felt a hand on his shoulder. They had stopped in the middle of the wide, busy avenue, not far from the city's central square and William looked up to see Lord de Clinton standing quite close. When he spoke it was in hushed tones that were lost immediately in the surrounding cacophony of voices swirling around them. It was a busy market day in Calais and the streets were teaming with men, women and the occasional child. "Have a care, William. Not all ears are friendly… even if they are English." He nodded his understanding and mouthed the words, "thank you."

"It was the second intervention of my Lord de Manny, although I have no doubt history will state it was Queen Phillippa, who saved their lives," Lord de Clinton continued as if nothing had taken place. "Together they pleaded with the king to show mercy and, unlike elsewhere, he agreed. He yielded and the lives of de Saint Pierre, the other Burghers, as well as the entire city were spared."

"In that very moment, our king showed not only his greatness, but his goodness as well," Lord Manny stated. His eyes wandered off into the distance as he recalled the details of the day. "Unlike today, William, that day was eerily quiet. With the Burghers in front, our king rode with his knights and lords through the open city gate. Those brave enough stood upon the circling wall and watched in silence. I remember thinking how loud the gulls were as they wheeled overhead."

William was trying to imagine how the sights and sounds of the day must have felt. It was difficult simply due to the tremendous diversity in peoples, voices and languages which swirled around him. Robert had told him once, that through Calais English wool and beer went south, east and west, while French wine, fine linen, exotic spices and all manner of curiosities made their way north. Whether controlled by the English or French, Calais was, and would continue to be, a prosperous and influential city.

So deep was William in thought, about the end of the siege of the city and the diversity of voices he heard, he didn't realize the Lord High Admiral, his men and Lord Manny had stopped, until he nearly ran into one of their escort. As he stammered an apology to the guard, he tried to discover the reason.

Standing before them, with by his own men at arms, was an elaborately dressed middle aged man with a thick gold chain and medallion hanging from his large neck. Despite his size and girth, his eyes appeared small and seemed to dart from face to face as he spoke with deep baritone and a strong accent. For a brief moment, his eyes made contact with William, then drifted down to the coat of arms he wore on his chest, and he was sure he saw a split second of recognition, then his face returned to its blank appearance.

"I assure you my Lord de Pavia, it is not our intention to stay in Calais any longer than necessary in order to board our ships for London." The Lord High Admiral's voice was strained. Although William couldn't see his face he could tell by his shoulders that the Lord de Clinton was doing his best to keep a civil tone. He glanced to his side, in an attempt to see Sir Walter's expression but he too was far ahead of William and had turned to face the Governor of Calais.

He felt someone near behind him and a voice whispered in his ear, "quickly, William, introduce me to this man, he is the Governor of Calais." It was the Queen Mother and she was insistent to the extreme.

"But I do not know…"

"Sir Aymery de Pavia. Now do this quickly… for me."

He needed no further encouragement, stepping forward and clearing his throat. "Excuse me my Lord," William projected his voice over the crowds, and the discussion which had continued despite his distraction. When he was sure he had the attention of all those around him, he placed his hand upon his heart and bowed deeply at the waist. "It is my pleasure, Sir Aymery, to introduce my patron the Lady Isabella of France and Queen Mother of Edward, Earl of Chester, Duke of Aquitaine and King of England." William stood and turned to Isabella reaching out a hand, palm down. Gently she rested her own on top of his red, still tender, knuckles and he turned once more to the Governor while doing his best not to flinch from the sting the light pressure inflicted. "Majesty, may I present to you Sir Aymery de Pavia, the Governor of Calais." In a few strides they stood before the opulently dressed "voice of King Edward," in Calais. William was surprised to feel Isabella's hand tremble slightly but a quick glance revealed nothing in her chiseled marble-like expression.

"Your Majesty," de Pavia rumbled his deep baritone, which seemed to issue from somewhere in the middle of his extreme girth. His attempt at a bow was not surprisingly feeble as his size prevent him from much flexibility.

"My Lord," Isabella purred, her smile brightening her face. "I have so greatly desired to meet the man my son felt so highly deserved this position of honor. I only wish, as the Lord de Clinton explained, that we had more time to spend in your fair city to enjoy all the… blessings it could provide." She paused and continued radiating her smile such that even her eyes seemed to dance and sparkle despite the overcast sky.

Such was the power of her presence that Sir Aymery temporarily lost interest in the Lord's de Clinton and Manny. His small eyes blinked rapidly several times and he licked his pursed lips. "It is our desire of the same, Majesty," he eventually was able to rumble.

"But where are my own manners, my Lord?" Isabella stated. The bright dazzling smile was gone so quickly Sir Aymery was left staring, his mouth still slightly open and his faced flushed. The Queen Mother turned to the men surrounding her, waving toward the Lord High Admiral and Sir Walter. "You know your king's most trusted advisors," she nodded to the Lord's beside then turned to those nearest to her. "My lady in waiting, Helen d'Abbeville, and newly named to my household, heir to Sir Charles de Simpson, Earl of Dorchester, and recently knighted for saving my person twice in the same day, Sir William de Simpson."

In the briefest of flashes William was again under the impression the Governor recognized either himself or his name, but it was quickly covered with his bland mask. "Now if you would do us the honor of introducing ourselves to your guests, my Lord?" Isabella gently insisted.

This took William by surprise. He had been so focused on the Governor of Calais and his encounter with the Lords de Clinton and Manny that he had failed to look beyond their circle, to the man who stood just behind Sir Aymery and who it would appear had just been in conversation with him before their chance meeting. It also, at first glance, appeared to William that he had never intended to be noticed. It was as if a flash of fear crossed his features, but then it was gone just as quickly and replaced with a demure smile.

"Not at all Majesty," Sir Aymery stated. To William as he listened, it seemed he stammered slightly, but his size and fleshy face and chin could have easily caused this tremor in his voice. He turned and stepped back while bowing as best he could, "Sir Geoffroi de Charny, I have the pleasure of introducing you to Lady Isabella of France and Queen Mother of England. Lady Isabella, Sir Geoffroi de Charny."

Isabella did the French nobleman a deep courtesy. "I thought I had recognized the arms of your family Lord de Charny, but it is your reputation and works on chivalry which proceed you. My son has often been heard to claim you as a model of a true and perfect knight."

"You do me great honor, majesty, as does your son," Sir Geoffroi stated. His smile was pleasant but William could see hard steel beneath the surface. There was something more to this encounter than random chance, but what that could be was beyond him at the moment.

Isabella's introductions and comments were perfectly timed. The minor confrontation which had begun between the Lords de Clinton, Manny and de Pavia had disappeared with no sign of its return. Moments later as they parted with kind words, William found himself meeting the gaze of Sir Geoffroi. His emerald eyes caught his attention and held him for a brief moment, as if sizing him up. William nodded but kept eye contact, eventually smiling a brief smile before offering his arm, once again, to Isabella. During the entire encounter Helen had remained quiet and even flint like. She stood just far enough behind her mother as her supposed rank would suggest, and yet close enough to be able to hear all that took place.

"You just found yourself measured by one of France's greatest knights, William," the Queen Mother advised. She paused, considering something in the interim. "What I do not understand is why he would be here, in Calais."

"Does our king truly consider him a true and perfect knight?"

"He does, William. Of that I spoke the truth." She paused just a moment, as their group continued making their way to the channel and their ships. The occasional surge in the crowds around them and the accompanying noise made it difficult to keep a steady flow of conversation. "Sir Geoffroi is the bearer of the Oriflamme of France, King Philip's banner. As in England, this is a singular honor. None of which explains his appearance in Calais."

"I cannot say for sure, Majesty, but my first impression of Sir Geoffroi was of one who did not want to be noticed." It was the first thing Helen had spoken aloud since they left the Fowler that morning. Her brow knitted and her expression became serious. "It was more than that…"

"He was afraid of something," William interjected. "I saw it cross his face like a flash when he realized he had been noticed." Helen nodded her agreement.

"When we reach the ships, let us take a moment to mention this to Lord de Clinton and Sir Walter. Perhaps they can shed some light on both your observations."

Something about the French knight's presence continued to bother William. He chewed on the inside of his cheek as they made their way closer to the channel. The scream of the gulls overhead did nothing to help him finish the thoughts tumbling around in his head.

"Majesty, why would Sir Geoffroi come to Calais if he knew his presence would arouse suspicion? He would have had to gain passage from the guards at the gate, just as ourselves…" William ran out of steam, his thought incomplete and stopped in mid-sentence. Helen nodded in agreement. She must have been turning the same thought over as well.

"He is trusted as a man of his word, William." When Isabella could see this assurance didn't assuage the young knight of Dorchester, she continued. "Not long ago, he was taken prisoner in Brittany and held by Lord Talbot at Goodrich Castle. Such was the confidence Sir Richard had in the knight, he wrote a letter giving him safe conduct to France in order to find money for his ransom. He found what he went looking for and sent it back to England."

"I have never heard of such a thing," Helen interjected.

"In all my years, neither have I," Isabella replied and took a moment to think deeper upon what she just admitted. "He could have told the guards he had business with anyone in Calais and they would have let him pass, based on his reputation alone."

"And yet, it seemed his reaction, as well as that of Sir Aymery's would suggest that neither man wanted anyone to notice they had been meeting."

The Queen Mother nodded agreement but remained silent. It looked, to William as though she was rolling this revelation around in her mind while her focus drifted off to the distance. "As I said, we should mention this to the Lord de Clinton."

Moments later, as they stood beside their two ships watching Lord Thomas and his men being escorted onto the Lord High Admiral's ship, Isabella, William, and Helen brought up their concern. "You continue to do your uncle credit, William," Lord de Clinton stated. He smiled but his eyes betrayed the gravity of the situation. "Sir Walter and I had been discussing the same thoughts these last few moments. He has other needs to attend to and will not be travelling with us to England. While he is here, he has agreed to keep an eye on both the Governor of Calais and Sir Geoffroi.

"Sir Geoffroi is not a diplomat," Lord Manny stated, his watchful gaze never leaving the short line of manacled men being led aboard the ship. "But he is a brilliant tactician. Given what King Philip admitted to us in Amiens and the coming pestilence, only a military objective would have him leave the relative safety of his keep." His eyes narrowed and William could imagine seeing the thoughts cascading into each other as he tried to come to grips with what it meant.

"Is there a military reason for him to come to Calais?" William wondered aloud.

"Dear Lord," Isabella muttered, her eyes growing large as saucers. "What if Calais is the very military reason?" When she realized she was surrounded by mostly blank expressions, she went on to explain her thoughts.

"And he came here to meet Sir Aymery to what end?" Lord de Clinton wondered out loud.

"Perhaps he did not trust the negotiation to a courier," William interjected. "He wanted to look the Governor of Calais in the eye when he gave his word. A true knight would then know the agreement was sealed."

The Lord High Admiral and Sir Walter stared at each other for a long moment; neither one speaking. Finally de Manny shook his head. "We must be patient and watchful, my Lord." He took the Lord High Admiral's hand and shook it as only longtime friends and confidantes to the king would presume to do. "Majesty," he turned to Isabella, bowing deeply. "Your reputation does not nearly do you justice." He stood up, smiling and nodded to Lady Helen, "my lady." Finally he turned to William and reached out to tap the coat of arms he wore. "Continue to serve those families William, and King Edward himself will notice." William smiled and nodded his understanding and then Sir Walter was gone, quickly blending into the crowd behind them.

"He may never wear the garter," Lord de Clinton stated quietly and just barely heard over the surf and people, "but there goes one of our king's most valiant knights." Coming from the Lord High Admiral, William considered that truly high praise indeed. He caught William's glance and motioned him to the side. There was another pressing thought he had, which he needed to pass along to the heir of Dorchester.

•••

Both ships set out from Calais at four bells. The weather in the channel was fair and breezy giving some of the larger waves just a hint of white foam on their crest. Near the half channel mark, about three and a half hours after setting out from Calais, scattered clouds raced up from the southwest and with them came mist and light rain. It didn't take long for William to find himself soaked through his heavy, felted wool cloak.

"At least this is not a storm like our previous crossing," Helen had appeared at his elbow and her comment not only broke his chain of thought, but also made him jump in surprise. "How is your hand?" It seemed an innocent enough question, but there was something to her tone, which made him turn to face her.

He didn't meet her eyes at first, but stared at his right palm, the slightly puckered and still pink scar clearly visible. Although he could nearly make a fist it was still difficult to completely extend his fingers. "I do not think I will ever be much use in a fight."

"Not with that hand, perhaps, but you could learn to use your left. Besides, there is more to life and living..." Her voice trailed off and if she said anything else it was lost in the sound of the waves.

"It helps to know who you are fighting," William stated. Again he made the best fist he could, turned back to the sea, thumping it on the railing while doing his best to appear as though it didn't really hurt to do this. He couldn't help wincing a little.

"Part of me has wondered if I will ever be free of those who will try and use or…" In this simple statement, Helen's emotions rang through in her voice; profound sadness. William could feel his throat tighten reflexively. He wanted to offer his hand, to hold her own and comfort her, the best he was able, but decided against it. Instead he told her of his vision of the twig in the stream.

She closed her eyes and nodded her head. "I can see the same,

William. It is just as you describe. This is how I am; it is how I feel. The world continues to spin me in place. I am without direction; I feel as if I will never have control over what becomes of me, nor truly trust anyone who would suggest they wish to be with me…" Her voice trailed off and William could see she was fighting back tears. He had to swallow to relax his throat before answering.

"That is why I withdrew my proposal, my lady," William stated adamantly. He had turned from the rail and the sea to face her and this time meet her, eye to eye. "Life may spin us as much as it can, but in this one thing you will have the chance to choose which direction to turn. You deserve that choice." He spoke with such conviction and sincerity it caught Helen by surprise and even shocked himself. He looked out over her shoulder onto the ever increasing white cliffs and tried his best to appear as though he was studying them and not avoiding her gaze.

She stood for a long moment, staring at William. Finally, she turned back to the aft cabin, but not before quietly stating, "Thank you, William, for my freedom to choose and for explaining the reason." He could barely hear what she said over the sound of the waves and rigging but decided against responding. He thought if he spoke at that moment his voice would crack. Instead, he continued to stare out over the water, hardly noticing when the captain and crew changed course to the northeast, following at a safe distance, but matching speed and course with the Lord High Admiral's own cog. In a few hours they would round the southeastern tip of England and make their way to the Thames estuary.

A remote part of William thought he should be excited to be returning home; each moment brought him closer to England after all. Mostly he felt as though he was leaving behind, in France, the people he cared most about. Besides, what had he really accomplished since he left Crandor Castle? He was no closer to seeing his uncle free, he had lost his closest advisor and friend, lost the use of his right hand and set himself against some of the most powerful men in both England and France. In his mind his list of allies seemed short and his adversities and adversaries ever increasing.

He found his attitude darken, even as the overcast sky. Where was the justice in all this? Why wasn't God looking out for him? Didn't He care how much William had suffered and lost? Didn't He see everything, which had been plotted against himself and Helen? How could He let Lord Thomas do all he had planned? His oath told him he should be bold and upright that God would love him, but what about God? Shouldn't He be upright, or had William done something to cause God to turn His back on him? God's own words said that sin would separate them; had he sinned and not realized it? As much as he thought about it, he simply couldn't find an answer. What he could feel, though, was a sense of frustration building. If he didn't find an outlet for it soon…

It was in the middle of this the Queen Mother interrupted his thoughts. "My… pardon, Majesty," William stammered his apology when she had cleared her throat, catching him by surprise. He smiled weakly, but his eyes betrayed him.

"You looked deep in thought, William," Isabella carefully worded her response, and then turned to leave. "I am sorry to have disturbed you."

"Please, your majesty, do not go." He nearly reached out to grab her elbow, but thought better of it. Despite all he had done for her, she was still the Queen Mother. "I admit my thoughts were dark and had wondered far from here but if there is anything I may do for you, please ask." What he really wanted was to take his questions and concerns to his tutor, but without him, he would settle for the chance at a conversation with Isabella, or even just a task she might have for him.

She paused briefly, and then turned to face him, her usual

well-concealed mask of indifference gone and in its place was a look of such earnest concern; William felt he would do nearly anything to see its attention turned to him. She took a step forward and grasped his arm. "Tell me the truth, William. What is your intention with Helen, with my…?" Even here, on the deck of the ship, in the channel, with the sound of waves and rigging to cover her voice, she had difficulty in saying the word, "daughter," in public.

The question caught William by surprise, as did the way she worded it. Something behind it seemed more than just the concern of a parent. A seemingly random thought crept up on him. What if she was concerned about not having William close to her? What if she wanted him to be more than just a member of her household? Her sapphire eyes sparkled, despite the overcast skies. Was there something there or was it just his imagination?

Almost involuntarily, William reached out and took both her arms. "I will not say I love her, Majesty, as I do not know what love is." The urgency in his voice surprised both of them. "What I do know is I will serve you and your whole family for as long as I am able. If service to Lady Helen means I must keep her close I will do so. If I can serve in a greater or different capacity, I do not see or know it yet." He held her eyes in his gaze, even as he continued to hold onto her arms.

"You say you do not know what love is, William," Isabella murmured, not taking her eyes from his own. "But I would venture to guess you understand it better than most men." She withdrew from him and he let her go, his hands dropping to his sides. He was surprised to find his heart hammering in his chest and his breathing rapid. She took a deep breath of damp salty air and smiled the same he had seen before. The dark clouds of his thoughts receded a little.

"We will be in Gravesend by nightfall and London before dawn tomorrow, William. Lord Thomas' trial will take place the following day. The King's justice will be swiftly appointed, and then…"

"And then you return to Castle Rising and I return to Dorchester with little to show for my folly," Even as the words spilled out, William could feel self-pity grasp at him, threatening to squeeze the hope from him.

"Not folly, William," Isabella countered, shaking her head, her expression one of grave seriousness. "Never folly… If there is one great lesson I have learned it is to live life with no regrets and to know that most of the time the blessings of success are wrapped in the appearance of great failures."

"I must be very successful because this all feels like a failure."

"Then stand up, William," she urged him with such fervor it startled him. "The only way Lord Thomas and my cousin Philip can win in the end is if we decide it is too hard or not worth the effort to keep on fighting. We must stay strong, to the very end, to whatever end that may be."

"How do you continue standing, when all around you seems so dark?" If he was willing to admit it to himself, at that moment, William was asking as to a parent for advice. If Isabella noticed this, she didn't let on. Or perhaps she did understand the meaning behind the question, and her feelings for this young knight from Dorchester prompted her to give the best answer she knew.

"There are three areas of your life you must constantly work on in order to be ready to get back up one more time. And it will be one of the three which will present you your greatest challenge." For the briefest moment, William felt as though he was back with Robert, learning his most important lessons. "First," and just like his teacher, she held up her index finger. "Do something." She must have seen the look on his face because she immediately responded with, "it does not matter what you do. It does not matter if it is great or small and in fact, at that moment, it will probably be something which appears small."

"Then why do it?" he asked.

"Because, William, action always conquers fear. As soon as you feel doubt begin to creep into your thoughts, dispel it with action." She paused and turned to look out over the waves and the ever increasing white cliffs and the large pale sail of the Lord High Admiral's cog. "There have been moments in my own life William, that such fear gripped me…" Her voice broke and he turned to see a tear run down her cheek.

"Majesty…?" She waved him off, sniffled loudly and blinked away any others that might have followed the first.

"Many suns have set since those days, William and as I said, I do not regret the choices I made."

"I have never had difficulty in finding things to do or the willingness to do them," William stated, more to himself while expressing the thoughts going through his head, than to the Queen Mother. She nodded.

"As a de Simpson, I would expect nothing less… *vivo servire*, yes?" He nodded in agreement and she continued the lesson. "The second thing you must constantly work on then is keeping a good attitude.

"I find myself challenged with that even now," William admitted.

"This is a decision you must make, William, no matter what the circumstances. Perhaps this is one of the three you will have the most challenge controlling, but you are in control of your attitude…"

"My teacher told me once that I decide whether or not to be happy. It is a decision I make and I control…" his voice trailed off and a deep realization began to take root. "Dark was that recent dream…"

"William?"

"It was two nights past." He paused, trying to put into words what he saw and felt. It took him a moment but he eventually was able to describe the scene outside Crandor Castle. There were some portions of the dream he felt best left unsaid, but, in the end, when he described the collapse of the walls and tower, it was as if all he had hoped for had come crashing down.

"And that very thing, William is the third area you must manage… your dreams."

"You do not mean those quickly forgotten thoughts which come in the night, do you Majesty?" he asked, with just the slightest grin.

"No, William, you are right, I do not mean those. I mean the vision of where you see yourself and your life in the weeks, months and years to come."

"All dreams, at first are free," William murmured. He could see his tutor so clearly, standing outside the gates of Crandor, on that spring morning.

"They are William, they are," Isabella agreed, not realizing the implication of his comment. "But quite often the cost will be more than you think and come in ways you do not expect while…"

"The cost will often come sooner than you think," William's own thought finished her sentence for her. Isabella turned her head and stared quietly at the young knight she had taken into her service. "He told me this as well, on the very day I received the letter stating my uncle was being held for ransom." William paused a moment, considering all that had happened since leaving the relative safety of Dorchester. "I never would have imagined this, Majesty. It simply is not what I expected of my own hope and vision for my future." He shook his head, his eyes no longer even trying to focus on the cliffs or the cog they followed.

"William," she spoke his name so clearly and with such authority, he had no choice but to turn his attention back to her. "Action, attitude and a dream," she stated clearly, so as to be heard over the noise of the wind in the rigging and the crash of the prow in the waves. "Manage and develop all three; imagine they are buckets you need to keep filled and you will find you can take any challenge which comes your way."

William nodded. He understood. Truly understood. The culmination of Robert's teaching could be summed up with those three. For the first time since he watched him fall into the Somme, William was able to think of his teacher without the sharp, breath-stealing pain of loss or regret. He had done so much to pass on to William all that he could in the short time they had together. Now it was up to him to live his life in a way to honor those lessons and his memory.

He took in a deep breath of the salty sea air and it felt as though, despite the overcast skies, his thoughts cleared and the darkness he had recently felt swirling around him receded a little more. "My dream, Majesty, when I set out from Crandor, was to find my uncle, return with him to our home and start a family. I was hoping he would be to my children as he had become to me." Here he paused to consider what he was going to admit out loud; what he had even up until moments ago, difficulty admitting to himself. "If your Majesty asks me, I will leave the life I had dreamt of in Dorchester and come with her to Castle Rising." He stopped and held his breath while doing the best he could to avoid looking at the Queen Mother as she stared at him.

"If I was twenty years younger, William, I would have already asked you." She paused and laughed a short, good natured laugh. "Oh, William," now she sighed just a little, "your sincerity flatters me and I do not now, nor do I ever believe I will regret having named you to my own household." She paused to take a short breath and then continued, "William?" The intensity of his name in a question made him finally turn and face her. She took a step forward just as their cog rolled over a large breaker and lost her footing. Seconds later she found herself in the safe embrace of her young knight. The wind whipped the loose strands of her hair around their faces, masking them for the briefest of moments. "Thank you, William for your gallant offer."

He was never sure exactly how long they stood there, on the deck of that ship, as it rolled over the waves approaching England. It was probably only a few heartbeats, but, as time passed and he reflected on that day in latter days, it seemed quite a bit longer. "How then may I serve your Majesty?" William asked quietly during that brief, close embrace.

"I want to know that my daughter is taken care of..." She spoke in just above a whisper, and if they hadn't been standing so close to each other, William never would have heard.

As it was he did hear and nodded his understanding, "I wish that too." He could feel Isabella exhale a deep sigh and then she stepped back. She smiled and did him the best courtesy she could, despite the rolling of the deck, and in a flourish of skirt, cloak, and those few loose strands of hair, turned and made her way to the aft cabin.

Chapter Thirty Two

William lost track of time. So deep was he in his thoughts, doing his best to remember all the lessons he had learned since that fateful morning outside Crandor Castle, he didn't even notice the change in tack as they rounded southeastern England. Suddenly, it seemed as though they were surrounded by ships of all shapes and sizes. Some, like William's, were making their way towards the estuary of the Thames and Gravesend and even perhaps London beyond. Others were heading in the opposite direction. Even in Southampton he had not seen such a large and diverse group of vessels. It was fortunate for William that they continued to follow the Lord High Admiral's cog. As soon as Lord de Clinton had stepped aboard his ship, the captain raised the Cinque Ports flag. Not only did it convey a message of who was aboard, it also gave them the assurance of wide berths as they made their way closer to the narrowing of the Thames.

Even as his thoughts had wandered, he realized he couldn't stand still at the railing. He knew they were making very good time and would be in Gravesend near nightfall, but he needed to move about now. First, he started pacing from the aft cabins to the bow and back. Eventually, he began climbing the stairs onto the aft deck, crossing it heading down the opposite stairs, and again to the bow. He must have done this at least a dozen times before the Captain caught his eye and signaled to William to join him at the rudder. One of his earliest lessons involved showing an interest in what other people found interesting, even if he did not. He reminded himself of this he made his as way to the stern where the captain stood, arms akimbo, his keen blue eyes constantly flicking from the rigging to the waves and the ships before and beside his own.

"You have restless legs, my Lord." So he had noticed William's pacing. Not that the ship was all that large, or the crew so numerous, that someone such as William wouldn't stick out.

William nodded agreement. "As restless as my thoughts, Captain." A moment passed as they stood side by side. William tried to follow the clear, grey eyes as they moved about the ship, rigging, and waters around them. "You can never take your eyes off her, can you?"

The old sea veteran snorted what might have been a rebuke, but William saw a shy smile creep in. "Take your eyes off the winds and they will shred your sheets. Take your eyes off the waters and they will swallow you whole. Take your eyes off the crew and they will quit the job half done."

"Take your eyes off your goal and you will sail right by," William thought out loud.

The captain paused his scanning for the briefest moment in order to turn his head slightly to William. "If I may be so bold, my Lord, have you not done the same?"

William nearly snapped a rebuttal, then thought better of it. He remembered Robert teaching him a wise man calls many men his counsellor. "Please explain, Captain." William's voice was calm yet restrained.

"A small ship, such as this, is a difficult place to hide secrets, my Lord." He paused as something on the horizon caught his attention. He shook his head, muttering something unintelligible, then continued. "I have had the honor of escorting the Queen Mother once before. Age has done little to dim the light within. It is a quality she has passed on to all her children." It wasn't panic William felt in that moment, but it certainly could have been. Was it that apparent? Or had the captain spent his entire life training himself to keep such a wary eye that he noticed what most others had failed to? Something in William's expression led him to continue his thought. "I will just say that it is clear you have strong feelings for the lass, and unless my eyes are beginning to deceive me, she thinks the same."

"That is a bold statement, Captain," William answered cautiously. Deep down, if he was willing to admit it to himself, a tiny, smoldering flame of hope was kindled. "Is there advice that comes with this?"

The old, weather-worn face crinkled into a gap-toothed smile. "No advice, my Lord. I may know the way of the sea; God knows I have spent almost my entire life on her, but the ways of a woman… now that is a mystery." He must have noticed William's disappointment because he quickly followed the statement with another thought. "I was taught from the first ship I was a 'prentice that honesty will take you very far in life. Perhaps you should start there."

"But I feel I have been honest to her…"

"Then maybe you should take the time to be honest with yourself." This retort from the captain of the ship cut William to the quick. Before he snapped a response he paused, just long enough for a small voice inside to tell him the captain was right. He chewed on the inside of his cheek as he thought about it. Was there something he wasn't being honest about with himself? He had a sudden flash back to his dream the night before last. The strong feelings he had for Helen and the Queen Mother returned like a flash across his minds' eye, followed quickly by the fear and anger he had felt when he watched Crandor collapse around him. What was hidden in there that he wasn't being honest about? Also, just a moment before, a flicker of hope had kindled in his spirit when the captain shared his observation. Was he honest about that too? It wasn't so much that he thought these things himself, but rather these ideas were suddenly planted in his thoughts. The small voice had spoken again.

He crossed to the starboard railing and watched the waves and foam run alongside and behind the ship, leaving a trail in their wake. Eventually the channel erased any evidence of their passing, but his thoughts were different. He had been dwelling on those thoughts and feelings which had entered his dream, and had disregarded everything he had been taught, and what he had already learned, about controlling them. Instead of speaking to himself words and thoughts of hope and life, he had been easily caught up in listening to those fears and worries. Even in that short time, dwelling on so much negative had quickly taken a toll on his attitude. He was reminded, in that instant, of how the desire to keep the sacks of gold and silver they had found in the New Forest had taken such a strong, fast hold on his thoughts.

William knew, honestly, that he needed to take hold of those random, wandering desires he had, before they took hold of him. He had let them play out in his minds' eye with absolutely no restrictions. If he let them continue unabated, they would eventually dominate all his thoughts. Once that happened, he knew they would control his actions, his habits, and eventually his character and circumstances.

Standing at the railing, watching the wake of their ship spread out behind them, he knew what he needed to do. It seemed simple enough. "Easy to do just as it is easy not to do," Robert would have advised had he been standing there. All William needed was the resolve to carry through with the decision he had just made. "God, give me the strength and courage I need."

In that instant, a memory flashed before him. It was one of his earliest lessons with his tutor. He had told Robert of his fears; that he would never be ready to follow his uncle as Earl of Dorchester. "All men have doubts and fears, William," he had told him. "What separates the great from the could-have-been is one of those two trusted God at his word and started. The other did not." When William had asked him what they trusted God's word to do, his example was simple and direct.

"When Joshua was given the leadership of the Israelites, after the death of Moses, he felt he was not ready. How could he possibly stand in the place of such a great man and lead such a large group of people? In a short period, God told him repeatedly to be bold and very courageous. When I read this, it is as if I can see myself, doubting my ability to the task at hand, and each time I bring up another reason as to why I am not ready or able, God just says to be bold and very courageous. I believe that God readies those He calls; He rarely calls the ready. Paul even said that, when he was weak, God was strong in his life. On this I rely daily."

Standing at the railing, reliving these memories and lessons, William smiled. He was so grateful for the time he had with his teacher and silently thanked God for the lessons he had learned. "Trust God at His word and be honest with yourself, William," he muttered to the sea.

Was there something else he had missed? An idea nagged at the edge of his thoughts. He knew it was there but couldn't seem to grab hold of it. He had been honest with the Queen Mother when he told her he would leave Dorchester and follow her, if she wished it. He honestly missed his tutor and truthfully longed for his companionship and advice. He had taken it for granted that he would be there for him, for as long as he needed him. A lesson newly learned took shape. Eternity is never more than a step away. He had always thought of that as something to think about when he was older. Now, he knew the reality was much different. Tomorrow wasn't a guarantee.

A lesson he had learned on the first day out of Dorchester came back in a flash. "Focus on today, William. Dream big dreams, but never forget to live today. Enjoy today. Breathe in deeply today. Smile today. Laugh today. Love today…" His heart skipped a beat as the cog dropped down into a trough between two large waves. It felt as if he floated for just a brief moment and then the bottom of the trough caught the ship and it sent a shock up his legs. He had to grab the railing to keep his balance.

There it was, the honest truth he had been pushing to the side. No matter what would happen tomorrow, no matter what her own decision, William needed to be true to himself and to Helen. He owed them both that much. Before he had a chance to change his mind or come up with an excuse, he left the railing and headed to the aft cabin.

Chapter Thirty Three

Looking back on that decision, William often thought about the ten seconds of courage he found in himself that day. It was a lesson he would pass along as often as he was able. To be courageous is not to be without fear, but to act despite the fear. He wasn't sure if his teacher had ever told him this, but it was something he learned that day on board the cog as it neared the mouth of the Thames.

His ten seconds of courage came as he forced himself to turn away from the railing and take that first step. If he had glanced to the stern deck, he would have seen the captain smile and nod, knowingly, as if he could tell, just from watching William's actions, what he intended. As it was, his feet felt like stones and his legs, lead. His heart was racing and he reflexively wiped his hands on his tunic. Doubt tried to gnaw its way back into his thoughts. He pushed it aside with a quick prayer.

"God, I need Your help," it was one of the shortest prayers he had ever made. Later, as he reflected on the events that followed, he realized that another lesson had been learned that day. God didn't care how long the prayer was, or how eloquently spoken; it was a matter of heart and belief. He desperately wanted and needed God's help. In that brief flash of a moment, a thought came to him and he didn't have to question the source.

"What you feel, William, is me preparing you for what comes next." He paused at the cloth which had been hung across the aft cabin entrance to give the ladies privacy (there were no doors onboard this ship), taking in a deep breath and thanking God for answered prayers, he took an even deeper breath in order to clear his throat.

"Of course you may enter William," the Queen Mother responded to his request. He paused just long enough to straighten his embroidered cote and the linen shirt beneath it. The passing of the rain shower had allowed him to discard the heavy, water soaked, cloak. For the briefest of moments, he wished he had been able to bathe first, but pushed that seed of doubt out of his head. Dirty or not; parched throat or not; ready or not, he pulled back the curtain and entered his patron and Helen's room.

It was fortunate the sun was already setting and dusk was settling in on their cog, otherwise William might have had to wait for his eyes to adjust from the sunlight of a few hours ago, to the dimness of the windowless cabin. Instead he was able to quickly discern between the two ladies. The Queen Mother stood just inside, while Helen was seated at one of the chairs beside the small round table, which made up the only furniture other than a small bed, that would have been difficult for the two to sleep in together, had they any intention of doing so.

William suddenly found his tongue stuck to the roof of his mouth and his hands trembling. Even as he tried to hide his nervousness by clasping them in front of his waist, he felt that if he tried to speak at that moment his voice was sure to break. It felt as if there was a hand at his throat, slowly squeezing it tighter. He swallowed hard and must have shown his distress because Isabella took a glass of wine from the table and handed it to him. Nervously smiling, William raised it to his lips and took a large gulp, doing his best to keep his hand from shaking. He mostly succeeded. Nodding his thanks, he held onto the glass, and stared for a moment at its contents. He hadn't initially noticed a small piece of the cork floated on the surface. It swirled about, the closeness of his breath propelling it across the ruby liquid.

As quickly as it entered his thoughts, he pushed aside the memory of the stick, stuck in an eddy in the small creek beside the Roman road in Dorchester. "When I left my home, just a few short weeks ago, I thought I knew why I had to leave. I thought I understood what it meant to see a vision of my future and to pursue it. I thought that the one person I started this journey with, was sure to finish it with me. I thought I understood what it meant to be a servant to my family, and I thought I understood what it meant to serve. I even thought I understood what our family motto really meant.

"I realize now just how little I actually did and do understand. It took the sacrifice of the one person I relied on for so much more than I knew, to make me see that the people who start our journey with us rarely finish it. It took that loss for me to realize how much I had, and how good God is. No matter what the enemy intended, it opened my eyes to how big and beautiful and amazing this world is, and my life in it. It also showed me that we are only given one chance at this. There is no way to go back and change any of my yesterdays; just as there is no guarantee there will be a tomorrow. What I have, all we have is here… now." William walked past the Queen mother and set his glass on the small table. If he had been bold enough to glance at her as he passed, he would have seen on her expression a mixture of surprise and perhaps even joy. As it was, he stepped passed her with a slight nod of his head, not taking his eyes off of her daughter.

"I will regret for the rest of my life if I do not, with all earnestness and seriousness, express what I have been holding back." He sat in the second chair at the table and continued. Despite the fear that tried to gnaw its way into his thoughts, he didn't take his eyes off of Helen's. "Ever since my father's death at the hands of the Scots and my mother's own passing soon after, and the pain of loss which nearly overwhelmed me, I decided not to let anyone come so close again. I thought if I kept people far enough away, they would not be able to hurt me." He saw the briefest nod from Helen at that point, and he knew she had come to a similar decision. "What I did not count on, was the love of a servant, expressed every day with his care for my understanding and growth in wisdom. Jesus said that there is no greater love than to lay down one's life for one's friends. Perhaps even more than my own parents, Robert modeled love for me. He never told me so, and I never told him, but I have no doubt of that love.

"His patience and persistence allowed me to slowly lower the walls I had created around my heart. It wasn't until the end, when it was too late to tell him so, did I realize I truly loved him back. I will live with that regret for the rest of my life." William paused now, his eyes taking in the dark azure of Helen's. He wanted to remember this moment; to capture all the details. The rolling of the ship, the crash of the waves, the screech of the rigging, the far off calls of the crew and captain, and Helen, her eyes wide and her expression… difficult to read but perhaps, somewhere in it, a glimmer of hope. Once more, something Robert had taught him some time ago leapt from his memory.

"What you get at little to no cost, William, you will never truly appreciate. It is only that which comes at a dear price which gives something its true value."

"So much cost has been paid to bring me to this point that I cannot help but appreciate it much more dearly, and know that I want to do whatever it takes to see this through." He reached out and took Helen's hands in his own. They were soft, cool and trembling. In the dimness of the cabin, William couldn't be sure but it looked as though tears were threatening to spill down her cheeks. He took a deep breath and a knee. "If you will let me, Lady Helen, I will more than care for you. I will help you. I will not only be fair, I will also be kind. I will do my best to not only forgive, but to forget as well. When the time comes, I will hope to not only teach, but to inspire and to enrich those around me. Because it has been modelled for me, I will serve, and in serving live a life that grows and bears fruit. What I want and hope for and know now for sure, without any hesitation or reservation, is that I want you to be a part of my life, where ever that takes me and whatever it looks like." He was sure there were tears on her cheeks now. "Helen would you do me the honor of accepting my hand in marriage?"

•••

The rest of the trip past Gravesend and up the Thames estuary was a blur of sights, sounds, and emotions for William. As he stood at the stern with the captain, he watched the crew retrieve long oars from the hold and begin the arduous process of rowing against the slight current. "We continue to make good time this evening, my Lord," the captain stated. "We should be at the Tower docks by daybreak."

Before departing Calais, the Lord High Admiral had briefly explained to him what was to take place. They would dock at the White Tower of London, and Lord Thomas and the other prisoners would be taken by the King's men to prison cells, which had only recently been separated from the royal residence. These were now permanently moved to Westminster Palace. The trial would take place in the Royal Courts of

Justice which had been, for many years, meeting in Westminster Hall. "A trial for treason is presided over by the Justices of the King's Bench, William," the Lord High Admiral explained in answer to his question. "There are two justices on the King's Bench: Lords Roger Baukwell and William Basset. I have only ever met the former briefly, and never the latter. Along with them presides the Lord Chief Justice William de Thorpe of Lincolnshire. The great hall will be filled with the defendant, witnesses, court scribes, and of course, King Edward himself."

"The King will be there?" William asked. Lord de Clinton answered with a nod.

"The King's Bench is called at the request of the King, and will only sit when he is present."

"I did not realize I would be testifying before him," William mumbled, his eyes drifting across the sand dunes outside the walls of Calais, the channel and England beyond.

The Lord de Clinton took him by the arm and led him a few yards away from the rest of their group. The Queen Mother raised an eyebrow, but saw something in William's face, and let it be without making a comment. "William, you must understand something…" he paused and considered what he was about to say. It was clearly written in his expression. "I have been a close confidante, and even friend, of our king, since we were younger men. When you become a man of power and authority, you will find that there are some men who only want to be close to you for their own gain. In the end, all men, even I, are more concerned with our own selfish desires than any other cause. The King understands this better than most, and yet, here he will have to face the fact one of his own peers of the realm was willing to do what he did to steal the throne. Can you begin to see how this might affect our King's thoughts?"

"I would imagine it will be very difficult to trust anyone." William paused a moment to consider what that might mean. "Then everyone at the trial, even my own testimony, will be judged by the King as to its trust worthiness."

"Exactly, William. King Edward will not want to blindly accept any testimony, just as he will not blindly accept Lord Thomas did all he has been accused of doing." Lord de Clinton paused and glanced back at the small knot of people travelling with them to London and the trial. "Add to that the involvement of his mother and…"

"My Lord…?" William asked when the Lord High Admiral paused in thought and failed to continue.

"There are other complications, William. Despite the evidence she could offer, I do not believe Lady Helen should testify. In fact, it may even be best if she is not at the trial."

Although he knew he should hide his reaction, before he realized it, William responded. "I have begun to wonder the same, my Lord. Lady Helen has set her mind to being there. I think as much to tell her part of the story, as to see Lord Thomas get the justice he deserves." Gulls wheeled overhead, their loud calls drowning out all but any raised voices around them. Lord de Clinton leaned close and whispered in William's ear.

"I know who Lady Helen is, William, and so will many others, as we draw nearer to London." William looked up slightly startled. The Lord High Admiral grabbed his upper arm and gave it a gentle squeeze, as if reassuring him. "The Queen Mother cannot protect her. The closer and longer they stay together, the greater the risk of someone else discovering the same. She is safe, as long as she is with you. She is in your protection, William. Safeguard her innocence, yes?" He didn't need reminding of his oath, but there it was.

"This very day I shared with them both my love and concern for her safety," William answered in hush tones. "While still at the Fowler I withdrew my offer to protect her with my own name." The Lord de Clinton's eyebrows shot up in surprise. William wasn't sure if it was due to the offer or its withdrawal. He felt he needed to explain. "Even as she discovered her parents and circumstance of her birth, she has been pulled in one direction then another, by men who want to use her and to those who wish her harm. I withdrew my offer so she could, perhaps for the first time, make a choice on her own, based on what she wanted."

The Lord High Admiral stared at William for a long moment, and then turned his attention to the tide; it was beginning to shift and they would soon set sail for England. "That was a noble gesture and precious gift, William, and one I think not lost on the Queen Mother. My concern still stands, though; if Lady Helen chooses a path which leads her away from you, I fear for her future safety." He paused again and turned his attention to the tide. "There may come a moment, William, sooner rather than later, when you will want to again offer the protection of your good name. If you will heed my advice, I would seize the opportunity, even if the offer does not come with a guarantee of acceptance."

"Then how do I make my way through this maze, my Lord?" William shook his head and stared out across the dark gray water to the barely visible white cliffs on the horizon. There was no doubt in his mind that his intention was to do all he could to protect Helen. He very clearly made that statement to her and the Queen Mother. "If Lady Helen is not present and will not testify, I will have to guard my words in order to protect her…"

"You have to find a way, William," Lord de Clinton stated with absolute conviction. "Everything I know of our King and his court tells me that to have her present, even if it is to give further evidence as to Lord Thomas' fall, will be a mortal mistake; and not just for her." He considered the options he could see and added, "at least, up until now, no one but us is aware of Lady Helen's part in this affair. Her testimony will not be missed, as it is not looked for."

William thought about that and realized it was true. Even the King's guard, who stood beside and before them in the courtyard, arresting Lord Thomas in the process, only thought they were protecting the Queen Mother. Perhaps there was no need to include Helen in the trial. "You truly fear for her life?" The Lord High Admiral nodded. "Then I understand what I have to do… it is just finding the way to do it." His tutor's advice came to mind regarding the price to pay for dreams. The cost would be more than expected and come sooner than you think. "What would you suggest I do?" William didn't realize he spoke out loud until Lord de Clinton answered him.

"Testify before the King, as a knight… as you are. Your uncle he knows. The king gave him the garter with his own hands. But you are not your uncle… at least not until you prove yourself to the crown."

"I take it you do not mean by feats of arms or strength?" William tried to smile but mostly failed. Instead, he must have looked like he swallowed a piece of bad fruit. The Lord de Clinton slapped him on the back and smiled a large, toothsome smile.

"Take heart, William. Since our chance encounter in the New Forest, I know when the time comes, you will handle yourself in such a way none present will doubt you or your testimony." Two conflicting thoughts crashed about William's head as they walked back to the group, following the signal from their respective ship's captains. First there was a strong, deep sense of pride he felt from the confidence of one of England's great men. The other thought, gnawing at the sides of this new found assurance, was desperately trying to tell him he was destined to fail.

"Which wolf will you feed, William?" it was as if Robert was standing beside him, the voice was so clear. As startled as he found himself, he also understood the reference. He smiled and a tear threatened to spill over. He blinked rapidly in an effort to force it back, smiled and looked up into the bright blue sky. "Thank you for the reminder." He took in a deep breath and walked back to the group as they made their way out across the beach towards their ships.

•••

Even as William recalled this conversation on the beach outside Calais, the smells of London brought him back to the present. At Gravesend the river was wide and back-filled with water from the channel. Each rising tide brought salt water a sizeable distance upstream. Here the fresh sea water mixed with the river, which passing through London caught and carried with it the cities refuse, unleashing a foul brackish odor that now began to insult his nose. The closer they got, the stronger it became, even as the river went through several switchbacks, hiding the city from view; although they couldn't see it yet, their other senses told them it was getting close.

The Queen Mother and Lady Helen were on the bow of their ship, as it continued following the Lord High Admiral's cog through one last turn. Despite how far upstream they were, and the size of the vessels which had carried them safely across the channel, the river was still wide enough to allow several similar ships to pass side by side. William considered this, as he watched another cog pass alongside, heading downstream to Gravesend. Several people on board the opposite ship were pointing, and he realized they had recognized the Queen Mother. Word spread through the other ship, and passenger and crew alike took a knee, as the vessel quietly glided past them.

William once again recalled the conversation on the beach with Lord de Clinton and his recommendation, and made his way quickly to the bow, convinced he was doing the right thing for the right reason.

•••

A complex of buildings, towers, a large white keep, and its surrounding walls made up the Tower of London, the original royal residence, and the mint where the coins of England were created. William was amazed at its sprawling nature, along with its turreted towers on the corners facing the river. Wisps of smoke drifted up from these and points farther back from the stream, blocked from view by the high, forbidding walls. Just beyond, sat the great white hall, with its four cornered, peaked towers and white stone face. William imagined a courtyard stood between the walls before him and the tower he knew stood inside. He only wished it had been full daylight when he first glimpsed it. Stories of the tower were legendary.

For decades, the royal residences had been in the Tower complex, surrounded by stone walls originally built by King William II. The size and surroundings of the Tower had been added onto over the years, with each successive king adding something of his own mark to the structure. At one point, the walls were built down to the bank of the Thames, and there stood an open water gate. Because the soon to rise sun was still below the horizon, all William could see beyond the gate were dark, shifting shadows. The portcullis was raised and water still dripped from its iron tips.

One quay jutted out into the river, just upstream from the gate, and this is what the cog was rowed towards. As William stood on the bow, he watched as the sailors responded with quiet precision to their captain's commands, as he kept a wary eye on the ever growing presence of the dark gate, the Tower, great white hall, and the grounds beyond. Within moments, their ship was secured to the quay with stout lines tied to its cleats, and a wooden plank was lowered upon the cogs' deck by men who had come out of a small door set on the riverside of the Tower wall, which was connected to the quay by a narrow stone causeway. Two men could walk abreast and approach the Tower walls from the river, but if they meant harm, they wouldn't get far. William could see dozens of arrow slits throughout the face of the corner towers and the walls themselves. This was more than just a royal residence, and it reminded William of just how difficult his namesake originally found ruling this hard fought for kingdom.

William stood patiently as the Queen Mother came from her cabin, accompanied by Helen. The latter wore her hooded cloak and kept her face well hidden. The former walked with her chin high and a gleam of anticipation in her eye, her own hood set back to reveal her deep auburn hair, streaked with silvery gray, flashing in the pre-dawn light. For Isabella, this was a bittersweet homecoming. Nevertheless, it was one she would treasure, for the last time she set eyes on the Tower had been long ago indeed.

The riverside of the quay was designed higher than the side facing the Tower complex, so that ships which docked, like their own cog, could unload passengers or cargo without need of ropes, pulleys, or stairs. As it was, the Queen Mother and Helen simply stepped onto the wide plank, and walked from the ship to the quay, following William, who had crossed first. As Isabella got to the end of the plank, he offered his hand and bowed at the waist. Upon rising, he turned, still gently holding her hand and nodded to the men of the Tower, who had helped secure the ship to the quay. Two of the men appeared to be guards, and one, more finely dressed and wearing the arms of Edward upon his left breast, held a large ring filled with equally hefty iron keys. "I have the privilege to present the Lady Isabella of France, Queen Mother of Edward, Earl of Chester, Duke of Aquitaine and King of England." It seemed eerie for William to hear his own words echo those of Sir John when he first was introduced to Isabella.

The guards of the Tower didn't bow, but only nodded then turned and walked back the way they had come; the keeper of the keys, however, bowed at the waist, quietly adding, "Majesty," then turned and followed the guards down the causeway. Out of the corner of his eye, William could see Isabella's expression darken just slightly, then it returned to the mask he had come to expect. "I am sorry if the guards offended you, Majesty. I will have words…"

"Save your breath, William," Isabella hissed through clenched teeth. "I have been out of favor from court since before the time of your birth. I did not expect a warm reception, and perhaps I should be relieved they did not come armed. My stay here will be brief and certainly lacking in extended graciousness, so I will cherish the memory of better days spent inside these walls."

As they slowly walked down the causeway to the door at the base of the wall, William thought he saw more than bitterness in her eyes. She was trying to hide it as best she could, but there was hurt there, which seemed, perhaps more exaggerated by the flickering lights of the recently lit lanterns which were spaced evenly across the quay, causeway, and the approaching walls. He was about to ask her if he could help in any other way, when she began speaking. At first, he wasn't sure who she was speaking to, but then, eventually, he realized she was talking mostly to herself; giving a voice to her long buried thoughts and feelings.

"Being raised at my father's court is much different than the ladies raised here in London. My father, brothers, and now my cousin have absolute power; theirs is the ultimate authority, an authority given to them by the hand of God. There is no great charter of rights made between the kings of France, the nobility, and the people. He had many counsellors, but when the time came, it was my father's decision which was absolute and final. My husband was not the same kind of man, nor England the same country." She paused as they entered the doorway, which, to William's surprise, led them through the outer wall and into a broad avenue running between it and a much higher, wider, and more strongly fortified inner wall. The thought occurred to him that there may come a time when king after king would add layer upon layer of change and expansion that even he might not recognize where he now walked.

In the avenue between outer and inner walls, their escort turned right, and then quickened his pace in order to take his place at the head of the procession. More and larger lanterns on both inner and outer walls lit the avenue and showed William they were being led towards a large central gate. Dozens of people (stone cutters, masons, merchants and court attendees) filled the space before them. Despite the cool reception of their escort, it only took a moment for these people to see the arms embroidered on William's chest. Dozens of pairs of eyes stared, wide with wonder, and were just as quickly followed by bows, courtesies and murmurs of "Majesty." There were also a few looks of disdain and even open animosity. That shocked him and he would have said something, but Isabella simply lifted her chin and set her gaze before her. The occasional nod was the only indication she acknowledged either recognition or rebuff. William wondered how long it would take for all of London to know the Queen Mother had returned to the Tower. In that moment he was so grateful for the advice of the Lord High Admiral.

"Edward's father was weak-willed and ill-favored, by both commoner and most of the peers of the realm," she continued, realizing William was listening, and confident Helen was as well. "He had little personal authority, and even less ability to instill confidence in those around him. When it came down to it, I felt there was no other decision I could make. For the good of England, and to preserve something for my children and theirs after them, I had to seize power before others did first."

"So you fled to France with Lord Mortimer…"

"Yes, William. Edward was still king, and there were men loyal to the throne, if not to the man who sat upon it. In order to secure a place for my son, I needed an army. And there we raised one, returned to England and challenged my husband. He had little chance of winning, but he did meet us in battle."

"Now I understand what my tutor meant when he said, it was then my family stood by the crown. It was the only time he did not mention the king by name," William stated. He also remembered Roberts' tale, given to the pilgrims on the road to Salisbury, and wondered why he had left their loyalty out of the telling. The de Simpsons had only once ever ignored the call of their king, but it was not that time.

"The loyalty of your family to the throne has never been in question, William," Isabella stated. "That fact has not been lost on my son since he claimed it. Although they defended their king, it was their character in doing so which continued to earn the admiration of their peers and my son. Others of my late husband's supporters were not as fortunate. My one concern is my choice to name you to my own household may taint the loyalty of your family in his eyes, and I may have put you in a difficult position during the trial."

"God's will, Majesty; nothing more, nothing less, nothing else… at any cost." William responded.

"Yes, William but to know His will can often be difficult."

A wall crossed their path, connecting the inner and outer fortifications and they followed their guide through the open archway and into the space beyond. They were in the outer bailey, a large open courtyard between the water gate and river to their right, and a round tower and gatehouse to their left. Another wall, with a closed and guarded gate, stood opposite them, and the only other people besides their escort were several more guards watching the water gate as a small skiff entered from the river. Everything he had seen so far made him feel that this was probably the safest place in England. No wonder the royal family had lived here.

As they passed through the inner walls' gatehouse, a long tunnel followed and then opened on the inner bailey. Now, for the first time, William was able to see without obstruction, the four-turreted white Tower of London; once more he wished it had been during the full brightness of day. Despite seeing it for the first time in dawns early light, his response must have been echoed by Helen, who had, up to this point, remained quietly behind her mother and William. Isabella turned to both with a soft smile on her face. "I remember the first time I saw the tower. Edward had silver trumpets made for the occasion. Flags snapped in the early morning breeze and the bright sharp fanfare of the horns, along with the sunrise on the stones, took my breath away." She smiled at the memory, and then added, "I am sure the look on my face was the same as yours." She allowed herself the briefest of tender smiles towards Helen and then turned back, squaring her shoulders in the process.

It seemed to William she wanted to say more, to share with them both, or at least with Helen, what it had been like as a young girl to find herself betrothed to the future king of England, and entering this place all those years ago. But if she wanted to add more, she kept it to herself. They had been allowed a very brief glimpse into her feelings at the moment and that was all they would get for now.

To William, it felt like a hard way to live; to constantly find yourself building a wall to keep yourself apart from those around you. How would they ever truly know what you wanted, or how you felt, or what made you laugh, sing, or even cry? Even as he thought these things, he realized he had been building his own wall for some time. Since the death of his parents he realized, as he crossed the inner bailey and approached the iron-banded large oak doors of the tower, he had slowly, steadily built stone upon stone, reason upon excuse, to ensure no one would ever again get close enough to hurt him. It came as an instant flash of insight, and he nearly stumbled on the cobblestones as they approached the threshold to the tower. How much of himself had he truly revealed to Helen? He had made his offer and asked for her to make a decision, and yet he hadn't taken the time to knock down the wall and let her see inside.

What if he did and she didn't like what she saw? What if it changed her decision? What if it turned her stomach? Like rapid fire these thoughts buffeted him, but he was ready for them. "Then I will go forward, knowing the decision was made with full knowledge of all the facts," he told himself. He wasn't going to let those thoughts get a foothold. The proverb he told the Queen Mother just moments before immediately came back to mind. If he was ever going to truly trust God, in all things and in all circumstances in his life, he had to be willing to give it over to Him. He had to be willing to admit he was not in charge and God was; to admit he wasn't god or the master of his fate.

Like a flash of revelation, all the incidents, accidents, encounters, and hardships he had faced since leaving Dorchester, and even before the day the letter arrived, were suddenly and jarringly replayed across his mind's eyes. These weren't stories in a book, covered with dust that was brought out once a year and read to family members as a reminder, these had actually happened to him. As he relived those moments he felt, once again, the sharp pain in his shoulder, the memory of the shard of wood which had passed through the palm of his hand, the smell of apples and the confines of the crate, his teacher's sacrifice on the bridge in Amiens, and the pain of the cobblestones on his knees when he knelt and was knighted. Through it all, he could see God's Hand at work. He nearly stumbled again as the honest revelation, the knowledge, with no doubt associated to it, struck him like lightning. This was all God's will. It all had a purpose, and he freely, gladly, admitted it, and willingly accepted it. The good and the bad each had a reason and a lesson which came with them. And this was the lesson which tied them all together. When it is God's will, and you are willing to turn it all over to God, nothing else matters, and no other reason will stand in its way.

Tears clouded his vision, making him stumble for a third time on the cobblestone courtyard. Suddenly there was an arm under his, steadying him, helping to regain his sure footing and keep up with the Queen Mother and their guide as they approached the tower. William turned, doing his best to blink the tears from his eyes, but failed miserably and instead smiled the best he could, as they spilled down his cheeks.

Helen was beside him, her own arm crossed through his, offering and helping keep his balance. Through the slight fog created by the tears, William could see she had been crying as well. He reached up with his free, deeply scarred hand and wiped one of her cheeks. "If it is God's will and you will let me, I will care for you, protect you as I would my own body, shielding you, even if it means hurt and harm is done to me, and love you, even though I am not sure I know what that truly means."

They stood arm in arm, just outside the great tower. For William's part, the whole world seemed to collapse around him until it included only the brilliant blue eyes before him. There was a light breeze, which he felt on his neck, but other than that, every sense was focused on that one moment.

Tears had left streaks on Helen's face. Strands of her auburn hair were gently lifted by the breeze. Her cheeks were flush, her breathing flared her narrow nose, and if William stood close enough he may have noticed her heart was hammering nearly as fast as his own.

"I heard the priest at church, when I was much younger, talk about love, William," Helen began. Her voice was weak at first and he thought it might break, but it grew in strength as she continued. "He said that God showed us how much He loved us by sending His only Son into our world to save us. This was real love; not that we loved God, but that despite all we have done and all we would do, He was still willing to give up His Son for us." She paused to collect her thoughts. For William, at that moment, there was nothing else so important in the entire world than Helen, her gaze, her words, and the thoughts behind them.

"That example of love gives us hope, our priest told us. It gives us hope and it takes away all fear, because the Spirit of God in us is greater than any spirit in this world. Robert told me the same thing, or he tried to tell me, the morning after we left you in Eaucourt. He was trying to explain why you had done what you did for us. It was the same reason he did what he did on the bridge. It is what you have done, and how you have lived, since we first met in that alley in Southampton." She reached up with a slightly trembling hand and rested her hand and his cheek. "You say you do not know what it means to love, but I disagree. For the first time in my life, I know I am truly and honestly loved."

Isabella had entered the great double doors of the white tower before glancing back over her shoulder, just in time to see the embrace. It caught her breath, for she could tell, in that instant, her daughter had made her decision. Through her own tears, she realized Helen had been given the choice she never had, by a young man both worthy of her and who truly did love her.

•••

William had no idea how far it was from the Tower to Westminster Hall. He had expected to walk or perhaps even ride in a carriage. What he wasn't prepared for was the barge waiting for them at the docks, three bells after sunrise.

To say he had a restless sleep would have been a great understatement. The knock on his chamber door, followed by the announcement he was called to give testimony by Edward, Earl of Chester, Duke of Aquitaine and King of England in the case of treason against Lord Thomas Denebaud, came just as he felt he had finally fallen asleep; the first bell of the day had just rung in a nearby church tower. The cool water of the wash basin at the foot of his bed helped rinse the sleep from his eyes, but did little to actually awaken him. Finally he gave in and leaned forward enough to submerge his entire head. He came up sputtering and spraying water and decidedly more awake.

The bedroom he slept in, or rather spent the night in, was small, but well appointed. A fire had been stirred up already that morning in the small grate across from his bed, and he wondered at what time the staff rose and began their day. He was told the day before that his traveling clothes would not be appropriate attire for the occasion. And after wondering out loud as to what they would suggest, the royal tailors assured him they would make do with what they had on hand. There, folded neatly on a cushioned chair near the fireplace, were linen hose, leather boots, shirt, and long cotte. For a very brief moment he panicked when he realized the cotte given to him by Isabella, with her coat of arms embroidered on it, was missing. And then he remembered he had been told all of the clothes he had worn would be cleaned and mended.

After dressing himself, he sat at the end of his bed, still in a state of near disbelief as to where he was, and in whose presence he would soon find himself. Just a few years before, his cousin still lived, as did his parents. He was the only son of a second son, with no title, land or prospects, other than those he made on his own. He didn't regret his position, or lack of one. As he sat there, reflecting on his past, he realized he had never done this before. He had never taken the time to truly sit and assess where he had been, what he had gone through, and where he found himself now.

Robert had told him once that experience is a good teacher and a wise man would even be able to learn from the experience of others. William remembered the conversation so clearly he could even see his tutor holding up a slightly crooked index finger as he paused in mid-thought. Once he was sure he had his student's undivided attention, he added, "but the best of all is experience you have taken time to reflect upon."

He must have seen the confused expression on William's face because he broke out in laughter. It was a deep in the chest kind of laugh, which William could still hear, even as he closed his eyes, sitting on the end of the bed in the white tower of London. Robert wiped a tear of joy from his eyes and cleared his throat. "Sometimes, William, it only takes a look from you to bring me such joy." After another brief pause, he explained. "If you do not take the time to stop, and think about what you have experienced, and what you have learned from those experiences, you will find yourself repeating trials and struggles over and over. I would rather live 75 different years, than the same year 75 times." He crossed his arms, dropped his chin slightly and looked up over his thin nose at William. His expression was clear; did his student understand what he had just revealed?

Looking back on that moment, William realized he had told his teacher he understood, even though he really didn't completely understand. However, just now, sitting on the end of the bed, waiting for the call to meet with the others to break their fast, the advice given had finally, completely sunk in. If he didn't take the time to reflect on all he had learned since that fateful spring day, he could find himself repeating some of the same challenges over again. Closing his eyes, he quieted his thoughts and silenced the voices challenging for his attention. Moments later he still sat at the end of the bed, and by all appearances looked to be exactly the same. What his outward appearance didn't show was the inner confidence he had gained in those few short minutes of reflection. He decided he needed to do this more often. A knock at the door and the call for him to join the others found him in a different frame of mind.

One floor down, were chambers which would have served other purposes when the royal family still lived in the tower. The room where they found a simple morning meal set for them had actually been used as a receiving lounge. Isabella told them of the dignitaries to the court of Edward, her late husband, who she had met in the very chamber. "Who was the most interesting?" William wondered aloud.

Isabella crunched on a piece of toast and then carefully wiped her mouth before answering. "I would have to say it was and still is Dauid de Brus, King of Scots."

It took a brief moment for William to realize to whom the Queen Mother was referring. "You met King David of Scotland?" he asked incredulously.

"You forget, William, he is married to my daughter, Joan." As soon as she mentioned this, her expression changed dramatically and it appeared to William she had remembered something very sorrowful. If he had seen Helen at the same moment, he would have seen a similar expression cross her face, but for a very different reason. "She was only seven when she married the boy, three years her junior. Their life together has been difficult and filled with strife, separation, and exile; in a way, much the same as my own. Even with all of his challenges he has remained one of the most interesting and introspective people I have had the privilege to know."

A sudden thought crossed William's mind. "Is he here, in the tower? I know he was captured by Sir John at Neville's Cross." The chance to meet the last of the Bruce line far outweighed the old pain associated with the death of his father on the battlefield.

Isabella shook her head. "I do not believe so, William. He was here for a time, but when our king returned from France, David and his family were removed to Windsor Castle."

"Begging your pardon, Majesty, but that is not entirely correct." It was the porter who had escorted them from the docks and summoned them to their meal that cleared his throat from his position just inside the door; he seemed eager to fill in some details. "Most of his personal staff and family, including the Queen Consort, have taken up residence in Windsor Castle. King David, for the time being, remains a guest of the Tower."

"Do you think he would care to join us?" Isabella asked, without thinking and then corrected herself. "I am sorry, William. If that is too much to ask, considering…" her voice trailed off and she didn't have to complete her thought.

"For the longest time I wondered what I would say, given the chance to meet him. Now… now, I would consider it a great honor and a chance perhaps to learn from someone who has gone through so many challenges. Even a king may be moved by other men, and I do not believe this king set out to invade England on his own; there were other reasons he had. Also, since your Majesty has mentioned how he ranks in terms of men of interest who you have received here in the Tower, I feel I should meet him face to face, and not miss the opportunity." At a nod from Isabella, William could hear the retreating footsteps of the porter.

"William, are you sure?" Helen asked in a hushed tone. He could see the concern on her face and smiled the best he could to reassure her. It didn't seem to help. She had remained quiet throughout the meal and conversation which followed. Now, she leaned forward, her hand resting on William's forearm. Despite the light touch he could tell she was trembling.

"What is it?" he asked. There was something about her expression; this was more than just concern for William, after what his family had been through at the hands of the King of the Scots.

"I do not know exactly," she closed her eyes for a brief moment to collect her thoughts, and then did her best to put them to words. "I have the strongest feeling his connection to the King of France is more than just the Auld Alliance."

"It is true, he timed his invasion after Philip's request," Isabella replied. "Despite my cousin's urgent call, David still waited for his own time to strike. To force England into a war on two fronts was always the goal when the summons of the Alliance was used; and the king and my daughter spent the better part of their youth living in France, so they have many personal ties to the people and places…" Isabella paused as she realized the implication of what she just said. "I never considered it until this very moment, but it is possible cousin Philip had more than one reason to ask for King David's' help."

"And what would that be, mother?" William turned in his chair to face the voice, with its French influenced highland lilt, coming from the open doorway. Standing before him, impeccably dressed, bathed and groomed stood David Bruce, King of the Scots.

William's first impression was the young age of the King of Scotland; the second was the odd, purple colored cloth wrapped around his head. He was just a few years older than William, but the lines on his face and the gray in his hair, just visible beneath the odd wrappings, suggested a life of constant, intense struggle. Finding himself in the King's presence, William nearly forgot decorum. Fortunately, Helen did not and stood, her hand moving from William's arm to his shoulder, which she gently squeezed, dropping it in order to give the king her courtesy. It was a light touch, but it was near enough to the spot where Davey Martin's knife had cut him, that it accentuated its effect. If that hadn't caught him by surprise, William would have noticed the tremor to Helen's touch. As it was, his full attention was on the Queen Mother's words and King David's expression.

"Majesty, may I present my lady in waiting, Helen d'Abbeville," Isabella stated, as she stood up from her own place at the head of the table. As she spoke, she moved to the door. William slid his chair back, its legs gently grating across the timber floor, and placing his hands on either side of his plate, pushed himself up and out of his seat. For some reason, it took greater effort than he thought it should. "And I have the privilege to present, the protector of my own person and member of my household, Sir William de Simpson of Dorchester." William stood and bowed deeply at the waist keeping his eyes on the man standing before him. Even with the buzzing in his ears and the thrumming of his heart in his chest, William was able to notice a change in the king's expression as soon as Isabella mentioned his name.

William did his best to choose the words he spoke with great care, despite a loud voice in his head telling him, in no uncertain terms, now was his chance to get back at the man who was responsible for the death of his father, and through that act, the passing of his mother as well. Isabella must have sensed this slight hesitation, and stepped in with concern in her voice. "Majesty, I had heard you were wounded before you were captured, does it still pain you?" She reached out, as only a mother, or in this case mother in law, could, with words and action; her hand hovering just inches from King David's cheek, where he took it in his own.

"Thank you for your concern." He raised his hand and gently touched the purple turban near his right temple. "The surgeon was unable to remove one of the arrowheads; it remains, like a constant reminder of the folly of so much I have tried in life." He paused and glanced briefly at William, then back to Isabella. "The headaches are infrequent but often disabling." The Queen Mother murmured some gentle thoughts, which no one besides the King could hear, then stepped back so he could enter the room and join their morning meal.

The food was simple, yet hardy; oats, cheese, a dense bread with a thick crust, and the last of the previous fall's harvest of apples. These were smaller than any William was familiar with, and intensely sharp, but the combination with the cheese and bread made each individual flavor stand out and at the same time harmonize with the others. Everyone at the table seemed lost in their own thoughts and for several minutes no one spoke; the only sound was the occasional knife on plate.

"Majesty, did you receive your injuries at Neville's Cross?" William asked, doing his best to keep command of his voice.

King David nodded, paused, then added as much to himself as anyone else at the table, "the English long bow is a terrifying weapon, especially in the hands of men who know how to use it," After a moment he set down the bread and cheese he had in hand and pushed his plate back. "One would think, after having been in exile for many years of my young life, and now a 'guest' of this court, I would have grown accustomed to eating in the presence of… enemies." He spoke the last word as if he had to force it out, despite the obvious bad taste it left behind.

"I do not consider us enemies, Majesty," William stated, before either Isabella or Helen could respond. "A wise man once told me a man, or even a king, may ask another to move and to act, but in the end it is the man himself who must answer for his actions. In the end, our life is only made up of a sum of our decisions and the counsellors we surround ourselves with."

"And yet, the decisions I have made…"

William cut off the king in mid-sentence, much to the surprise of everyone in the room, not the least of which was King David himself. Clearly he was not accustomed to being treated this way. He swallowed his own retort and allowed William to continue. "They were made in the best interest of your people, Majesty. There was no way you could know the end result, my Lord. Just as my father could not know what fate had for him that day."

For a long moment, no one spoke. Finally, King David broke the silence. "That is not entirely true. It was not fate alone which doomed your father that day."

"You speak of Philip of France's request to seek out the argent crane beside a gules door on field sable?"

King David was clearly shocked. "How could you possibly know…?"

"I did not Majesty, until just now, but I did suspect. After speaking with the Queen Mother on the subject, and meeting King Philip, it became more and more obvious there were plans within plans within plans. He has been playing a very long game indeed."

The Scottish king sat silently for a moment, staring deeply and intently into the wine glass the porter had set before him. "Then how is it you can sit at this table with me, knowing what I had been asked to do, and if given the chance, would have completed all, and not just half of the task?"

William raised his own wine glass and held it out to the King. "Majesty, if I knew this glass was poisoned and wanted nothing more than to see you dead, would it make any sense for me to drain the cup?" To add emphasis to his question, William did just as he spoke. Tipping the cup up and back he took the remainder of its contents and finished it in one swallow.

"You would be a fool if you thought to do me harm with poison you just drank yourself," King David answered flatly. He did his best to hide his emotions, but even Isabella could see there was something happening beneath the surface; she couldn't be certain if it was turmoil or revelation.

"One of the earliest lessons I was given by my teacher, after the death of my parents, used this same example and question. Unforgiveness, Majesty, anger, jealousy, rage, these are all like poisons we drink ourselves in the hopes they will sicken another. If you cannot and will not forgive, then those thoughts will do nothing more than continue to darken your life and poison your joy. I did not understand what he meant, when he first spoke of this, until this very moment."

William pushed back his chair and stood up. Isabella inhaled sharply and would have spoken but for the glance from him. Sitting in the chair next to him, Helen smiled a nervous smile and William answered with a gentle touch to her shoulder. It seemed as though a loud, shrill voice was screaming in William's head and he was shocked no one else in the room noticed. It was calling him a reckless fool, throwing away his chance at revenge. He waved the thought aside; this was the right thing to do and for the right reasons.

With his right hand over his heart, William spoke, first hesitantly, then with stronger conviction. "My Lord, King David, as sole heir to the house de Simpson of Dorchester and Eaucourt sur Somme, I want to state before these witnesses, I forgive you with no reservations or regret. You did your duty as best you saw fit for your people, and for that I can find no fault and no reason to hold onto any ill-will." As he finished, William felt as if a great weight was lifted from him. In that very moment, as he bowed deeply before the King of Scotland, tears welled up in his eyes and spilled down his cheeks. He made no attempt to stop them, and when he stood up straight again, all eyes in the room were upon him, even the porter at the door couldn't help but stare.

King David's voice broke as he asked, "How can you do this?" Then added quietly, "can you truly mean it?"

"By myself, I cannot do this, Majesty, but with God, all things are possible if you just believe and trust Him." William paused just long enough to wipe the tears with the back of his injured right hand and then added, through a toothsome smile, "Besides, I know, even at my young age, I have already made some regrettable mistakes and poor choices. I would want to be forgiven of those. In order to reap that forgiveness I know I must sow grace and mercy."

King David shook his head, not sure if he was hearing properly what William just spoke. So he did his best to frame the statement in his own words. "You suggest our thoughts are like seeds and the kind we sow, we will reap a harvest of the same?" The look on his face was mixture of incredulous disbelief and extreme hope.

"There is no doubt in my mind what I sow, I will reap, Majesty; you have heard this, yes?" William paused just long enough to make sure the king understood and agreed to what he said. "If this is true in our garden and our fields why would it not also be true in our thoughts? After all, it was God who created each of us, as well as the land, and it is His principle we see playing out each springtime and harvest."

King David stroked his beard with his right hand while his gaze shifted from William back to the glass of watered down wine sitting before him. "What you suggest… every thought?"

"Majesty, now that you know how important it is to guard your thoughts, would it not be wise to ask God to help you control how you think and what you think about?" Without looking up, the Scottish king nodded, his eyes still staring into the depths of the garnet filled glass. "In the Bible, the apostle Paul tells us to take every thought captive. I think this is what he meant and why he meant it; he understood sowing and reaping. Sometimes those thoughts are our own, and sometimes they are 'planted' in us by the enemy, who hopes we will take them as our own, even though they will lead to our own suffering in the end."

"How is it possible someone as young as yourself would have such insight into the thoughts and actions of men?" He asked, looking up from his glass of wine. William could see a change in his expression. The king was so close to a revelation that William silently asked God for the wisdom he needed to say what was necessary.

"When my uncle took me in to raise me as his heir, he provided the Seneschal of his house as my teacher. He showed me the path to wisdom and insight and began teaching me, in his own words, life's most valuable lessons… and his counsels and friendship are sorely missed." William could feel a lump form in his throat, even as he spoke. Would he ever be able to remember his teacher without the pain of his departure being present?

"You speak as though he is no longer your teacher. Did he return to Dorchester?"

"No Majesty," it was Helen who answered first and with such strength in her voice, it surprised William. "He fell," and here her voice cracked with emotion. She cleared her throat, then continued, "He fell in Amiens, defending William, myself and the Queen Mother from Lord Thomas. He delayed him and his men just long enough for us to reach the safety of Lord de Clinton and the rest of the peace delegation."

"He was willing to sacrifice himself to save us," Isabella added. "If not for his courage we would not be here today."

"As I said, Majesty, he showed me the path I needed to take to gain wisdom, and he did his best to teach and show me by example life's most important lessons; the last one was paid with the ultimate price."

Even as William spoke, the bells of London rang out twice. The porter, who had stood quietly at the door, all the while listening intently and with great interest, cleared his throat. "Sir William, Lady Helen, Majesty, it is time to return to the docks. There is a barge there, which will take you to Westminster." He turned to King David and nodded, adding, "Majesty, I hope you will forgive me not escorting you back to your rooms." He waved off the apology, his gaze returning to the wine glass before him as he clearly continued to roll William's revelation through his thoughts.

William bowed, Helen gave him her courtesy and Isabella took his hand for a brief moment. The king looked up just before they left the room, "if at all possible, Sir William, I would like the opportunity to continue this conversation… at a later date."

"It would be my honor and pleasure, Majesty," William stated as he bowed once more. "Perhaps later today, at the evening meal…"

"You go before the King's Bench, Sir William, for a crime of perhaps both petty and high treason," King David stated with just a hint of superiority in his voice. "I doubt it will end so quickly." He paused for just a moment, then shook his head and sighed. "Then again…" he shrugged his shoulders and lifted his hand, palms up. According to the King of Scotland there was no way to say how long the trial would last.

•••

"Majesty?" William asked, as they followed the porter down several flights of stone stairs, out of the tower, across the inner and outer baileys, and through the surrounding wall to the docks. "King David said this may be a case of petty and high treason. What is the difference?"

Isabella's ankle began to bother her again, which slowed her down and annoyed her, but she bit back her initial sharp response and composed herself before answering. "Petty treason, William, is against your lord whom you have sworn fealty, whereas high treason is against the king or his immediate family. Lord Thomas violated the trust of his suzerain, while at the same time, sought to bring down our family and dethrone the king."

"Would not his high treason take precedence?"

"You would think it would, William, but now we find ourselves within a battle between Edward and his lords; and not just our king but English kings for generations. The crown has long wanted to expand what encompasses high treason while the lords have fought to restrict it."

"Why would it matter to either of them," Helen asked. She had remained quiet for most of their return to the quay but found this point of difference an interesting question.

"It comes down to who will retain the land if a conviction is made," explained Isabella. "If this is tried as petty treason, then Lord Thomas' land would revert to his suzerain. If this is tried as high treason, his lands revert to King Edward."

"Then both want a conviction, but they also do not want the other to gain the upper hand through that conviction?" Helen asked, still slightly confused.

"Lord Thomas alone was a minor member of the House of Lords. However, through marriage and the death of his brother in law, he was in line to potentially inherit a larger portion of land than most realize." Isabella continued. "The sum of that inheritance would have made him very powerful and, if tried and convicted of petty treason, would greatly increase the influence of his suzerain."

"If it was always possible Lord Thomas would fail, could it also be possible the person who would benefit from the failure may have also been one of his supporters and encouragers?" Helen asked. The question nearly caused the Queen Mother and William to stop in their tracks.

"Do you think there were other plans within plans we still have yet to uncover?" William asked and Isabella nodded her agreement.

"Philip has played the game even better and with more forethought than I would have imagined," she responded. They were approaching the dock and the barge was waiting. The men at the oars sat at ease on their benches. They seemed to care little about who was about to board. They were across the gangplank before one of the men looked up and muttered a half veiled curse under his breath. Seconds later all of the oar-men were standing and bowing before the Queen Mother. Isabella smiled and waited until they were at the stern and she and Helen were comfortably seated on the low bench with its cushions, before she continued her thought.

"Philip of France has plotted with my son in law, Lord Thomas, possibly Lord Warwick during the attack on St. Omer, and now, it seems likely he covered all possible outcomes by making sure at least one more person would aid him in his cause, if Lord Thomas failed." She shook her head in disbelief. The amount of planning to pull together so many moving parts was even daunting to her.

"To whom would Lord Thomas have knelt and swore fealty?" Helen asked.

"He would not have sworn because he is the third son. The oldest would bend the knee," Isabella stated. The barge was pushed off of the quay and allowed to drift down stream just long enough to clear the wooden structure. The oar-men then set to their task and the barge turned in mid-channel and soon began the slow, steady upstream trip from the Tower of London to Westminster Hall.

•••

William didn't like sitting idle for long. Soon he was up and walking the length of the barge, watching the timing of the oar strokes and near perfect manner in which each man paced himself with each of the others. The barge made good speed, even against the current of the Thames. If not for the amount of ship and other barge traffic on the river that morning, he was certain they could have made even better time. As it was, they slowly approached a bend in the river that double-backed on itself. The city on one side and woods on the other, would soon block out the white tower from view.

Eventually, he made his way to the stern near the helmsman. "The men are nearly perfectly timed. It is almost magical to watch," William stated, smiling to the small, well-muscled, dark haired man. "Have they worked together long?"

It took a moment for an answer to come. At first William thought he had said something wrong, then when he looked closer he realized, from the helmsman's expression, he was uncomfortable answering; he may have never had any of his passengers speak to him before that moment.

"Aye, sir, they are well-timed," he finally admitted. "But a critical eye can still see young Roger there is just a breath behind the rest." He nodded to a red-haired, ruddy complexioned lad just a few seats in front of William. Try as he might, he couldn't see it himself and admitted it to the older bargeman.

"None the less, it is there."

"Do you only work between the Tower and Westminster?" William asked.

"No, my Lord…"

"Just William, not Lord." He stuck out his hand and the sailor stared at it, not knowing what was meant by it. "William de Simpson, at your service." He withdrew his hand and bowed his head slightly.

The helmsman's eyes grew wide as saucers. Clearly, not only had no one ever taken notice of he or his men, they had also never felt it necessary to introduce themselves properly. He cleared his throat and stood up straighter, "David Pemberton, at yours and your family's." Despite keeping hold of the rudder and his sea legs, he managed a respectable bow.

"Pemberton, you say?" William questioned. Something in the back of his memory tugged at him as soon as he heard the name. "Where does your family call home?"

"Lincolnshire… William." He looked sideways, and even over his shoulder, just to make sure no one was present who would take offense at such familiarity. "Our family's ties to that land go back to before the first Norman king."

The Norman King. Just the way he chose his words told William his family had Saxon blood, or perhaps even older. He wondered, briefly, if

David's, like Robert's, had been an important family prior to the invasion. Despite this thought, there was still something else tugging at his memory; something about his family name or where they were from? He must have gotten lost in his thoughts for a moment because when he looked back to the helmsman he was staring back at him with a questioning expression. "Forgive me, David," William apologized, "but there is something on the edge of my memory that teases me, and I think it has to either do with your family or where they call home." William tapped at his temple as if he was trying to loosen the thought that was stuck there.

"I daresay it is our home, seeing as you are part of this trial of Lord Thomas Denebaud."

"We are witnesses in the same." William paused, shaking his head. Something wasn't adding up. "What does Lord Thomas have to do with Lincolnshire, David?"

"He married the Lady de Brent, William, and it is her inheritance and estates I have heard that moved him to propose, but before this Lord Thomas was the third son of a minor house." David paused, then added as an aside, "When you have worked the Thames as long as I have you make many friends, even counting among them dispatch riders of the king."

William's eyes grew wide and David smiled a gap-toothed smile, then continued. "One such rider came aboard late last fall, with messages both of victory and defeat in France. We spent much time talking of the victory and then he spoke of the defeat. It was a small out of the way village; St. Omer."

William could hardly believe what he was hearing; it was as if great thunderclaps echoed in his ears and he could feel his heart pounding in his chest. "What did the dispatcher tell you about St. Omer?" he asked in hushed tones, his voice shaking slightly, while he did his best to keep it from breaking apart. He steadied himself with the nearby railing.

"Only that several knights of renown were captured at the ill-advised battle, and two brothers were killed; both the Lords Denebaud."

"Good God," William muttered and David made the sign of the cross. "My uncle and his brothers, in the same battle?" If David understood the comment he hid it well. William was beginning to understand how this simple barge helmsman could acquire a nearly infinite amount of information and knowledge, if he choose to seek it out.

"With both of his brothers dead, Lord Thomas became sole heir to his father's estate… in Lincolnshire.

Like a bolt of lightning, William was struck with the memory of a single comment made by Lord Thomas while he had been hiding in the apple crate. He had mentioned a Lincolnshire promise. Once again, William was confronted with the realization that there was yet another layer of plans he was only now discovering. At the same time, he felt as if he was finally pulling at their frayed edges and one good tug would bring them all to light.

David broke his chain of thoughts. "It is clear to me there is more at hand than just this trial, or I am a fool." He paused and then continued, when William remained silent. "Do you think there is a tie between Lincolnshire and Lord Thomas' treason?" David asked. William could hear sincere concern in his voice. "My family has called that land home as long as we have kept a memory of it."

Saxon or even older. Roman? Celtic? With the last name of Pemberton, William guessed his family had Saxon ties. "I do David, though I have no evidence to suggest it, other than a comment Lord Denebaud made in my presence, while unawares I could hear it."

"I know all about that, William," David admitted. "To labor around the great men and women of London is to be invisible. Often there are remarks and trysts made in plain sight for us, yet out of sight for the public, and they assume it goes unnoticed." As the helmsman spoke, William was reminded of Robert's admonition to him to show interest in others, no matter the rank.

"I would imagine you see many things most people consider well hidden. Can you think of any involving Lord Thomas, David?" William tried his best to hide the eagerness in his voice.

"Other than the comment of the dispatch rider, I have not heard the name Denebaud again, that is, until last night…" He paused when he saw William's reaction, noted it, and then checked the channel once more to make sure they were making good time while keeping clear of the familiar traffic of the Thames.

"Last night I took a hooded figure to the Tower, waited for a time, and then returned him to the quays just beyond Westminster." He could see William's protest and ended it short with a raised well-calloused hand. "I may be invisible and simple in the eyes of greater men, William, but I am neither blind nor deaf. 'Lord Thomas is a grasping idiot' this person said to himself as he returned. Despite the waning moon last night, there was much cloud cover later, but just as he stepped off the gangplank, the moon broke through and I saw his profile and recognized him at once." David paused, like any well versed story teller. If William had been sitting he would have been on the very edge, if not forfeiting his seat all together.

"Even as he made that comment, the moonlight revealed my secretive traveler; the Lord William de Thorpe." David must have noticed the searching expression on William's face and added, "He is the Chief Justice of the King's Bench and will preside at the trial today; he is also a wealthy landowner in Lincolnshire." David shifted his gaze long enough to make a slight correction to the rudder, leaving William to stare at the bargeman's profile.

"That seems rather bold for the Chief Justice, to have a meeting with Lord Thomas the night before his trial. If he was caught…" William's voice trailed off, and not for the last time, he wished Robert was there to sound his thoughts out loud. Now more than ever he missed their conversations. Finally he shook his head and heaved a deep sigh. "I do not understand what he would gain from this meeting. To risk exposure when clearly he wished to remain hidden, for nothing more than a conversation does not make sense. There had to be something else at play." William gazed back over the Thames in the direction they had come and watched as the Tower was slowly cut off from view as the barge followed the bend in the river. He was missing something but just couldn't put his finger on it.

"There is a rub in the nubbin' as I have heard say, William; it is there, you just have to find out what it is. As for myself, curiosity got the better of me last night…"

"You followed him?" William asked in awe and excitement.

"It was not difficult. He wished to be unseen by men of station, but he did not care that his hooded cloak was easy enough to pick out despite the concealed moonlight." He checked their progress once more, then continued. "The blessing of my station in life is that there are far more of me than there are of Lord de Thorpe; I can blend in, where he cannot."

"And I doubt he was concerned that anyone followed him," William suggested. David nodded agreement, then continued.

"I sent the lads on the barge back out and down the river and asked them to return within the hour. It was clear to me my Lord de Thorpe no longer was concerned with discovery, as he went straight to Harrow House, the London lodgings for the King's Justices. His pace was quick and path straight forward; despite my distance I could even catch the occasional glimpse beneath the cowl; he was having a right good talk with himself; at times it may even have been an argument. I dared not get closer, but that was the impression."

"There is no doubt as to Lord Thomas' guilt, David. He was caught in Amiens, pursuing, with his own men at arms, myself, Lady Helen, and the Queen Mother. His intention was clearly not honorable." William paused and smiled briefly at his mild attempt at humor. "The Lord de Thorpe will know this now beyond any doubt after meeting with Lord Denebaud…" William paused again, trying his best to sort out his thoughts.

"As his vassal, Lord Thomas does have a right to call on the Lord Chief Justice. It would be the duty of his suzerain to respond to his request for audience."

"David, the message you were told about, the one with the failure at St. Omer and the death of Lord Thomas' brothers, do you think anyone besides Lord Denebaud would have received it?"

"There is no way to know or tell, William. Why do you ask?"

"Because this trial will not hinge upon Lord Thomas' guilt, but upon whether or not this is considered petty or high treason. Do you see the difference?" David shook his head. "If no one, besides Lord Thomas and the Lord Chief Justice, knows that the Denebaud brothers are both dead, then no one will know that it is in fact Lord Thomas who now bends a knee to Lord de Thorpe. And if he bends the knee…"

"Then my Lord de Thorpe will receive all the land held by Lord Thomas when he is found guilty. The Denebaud lands are minor, but through marriage, Lord Thomas is also the inheritor of greater lands controlled by the de Brent's."

"I first crossed paths with Lord Thomas in the New Forest, where I was accused of killing his brother in law, Lord John de Brent. Fortunately cooler heads prevailed, but my steps have been dogged ever since."

"I had not heard of the death of the older brother de Brent," David admitted while scratching the back of his neck. "There is little doubt in my mind the Lord Chief Justice and Lord Thomas are the only two to know of the Denebaud brothers' deaths."

"Why would you think so, David?" William wondered.

"Because, just a day ago, I overhead conversation on my barge that Sir Robert de Brent was recently killed in a hunting accident in the New Forest."

William stared in stunned silence. The thoughts and ideas and plans and questions and assumptions swirled around in his head, one crashing into the other. He tried to shake them into some sort of order. Finally, he decided to work it out by speaking them out. "Lord Thomas married the only de Brent sister, who died shortly afterwards. He then plotted the murder of his brother in law, Lord John, and by accident or further planning, Sir Robert de Brent is killed in a hunting accident. At the same time, Lord Thomas convinced the Earl of Warwick to take a select, small group of knights and men at arms to attack the village of St. Omer in France, where his only brothers are killed and my own uncle was…" William's voice broke and he couldn't continue for a moment. Finally he was able to complete his thought. "Lord Thomas now finds himself heir to the Denebaud lands, and heir apparent to Cossington, Hale Purlieu, and the rest of the de Brent holdings." And, if he had his way, to the better part of Dorchester, William thought to himself.

David whistled between his teeth while shaking his head. "To think he planned all of this… but none of these, as you say, would warrant high treason, William."

"They would not, David," William admitted, and then explained Lord Thomas' coercion of Sir John Copeland and the attempted abduction of the Queen Mother. "It was obvious from the conversation I overheard between Lord Thomas and Sir John, he hoped to put pressure on the king, either for his own benefit or for an outside benefactor." William paused as he realized something. "Without Sir John's testimony it will only be my word against Lord Thomas'." A sudden sense of futility swirled around his thoughts. How could he, an untested, unproven knight, convince the other judges just on his own testimony? "We have not seen or heard from Sir John since Amiens when he delayed Lord Thomas' men long enough for us to reach the safety of the king's men."

"But he is here, in London, William," David interjected.

"How could you possibly… have you seen him?"

"I took him to Westminster Hall earlier this morning. In fact he and several travelling companions were on this very barge just before you." David paused in thought and then wondered out loud. "Why do you think he has done all he did and tried to do?"

It was clear he meant Lord Thomas and it was a question William had wrestled with himself. "He was born with a title, earned his spurs, and had a marriage which placed him into a well-respected family; most people would find it an enviable position." David nodded as his eyes kept a close watch on some of the nearby boats, barges and skiffs; the closer they approached Westminster, the more heavily trafficked they would find the Thames. "There are probably several reasons, but the one I think controlled all the others was Lord Thomas was not enough in his own eyes. He was not good enough, wealthy enough, powerful enough, and important enough, and he thought the only way to fix that was to take those things from other people and try to make them his own."

David nodded agreement. "It seems that is always the case with men such as Lord Denebaud."

William agreed. "He forgot that God created all of us for greatness. We are already smart enough, courageous enough, regarded enough, wise enough, clever enough, and even likeable enough, because each one of us is created in God's image. He does not make mistakes and he did not create us to try and be something or someone we are not. We can be a very poor imitation of someone else if we try very hard, but we are the only one who can be ourselves. He gives each one of us abilities, and the opportunities for us to use them, to glorify Him; our gift is life itself, our gift back to God is what we do with it. Lord Thomas thought gaining those things by force would make him greater than he was, but, since he was not enough without them, there was no way he could ever be any more than less than enough with them."

"Do you think it is possible to forgive someone like that, with all he has done?"

"If you had asked me a few days ago I would have struggled to keep a civil tongue; now I see something different."

"What changed, William?"

"God gave me a vision as I crossed the beach in Calais to board our ship back across the channel. There were footprints in the sand that were being washed away by the incoming tide. In that moment I felt, or maybe even heard, a voice tell me that, just like those footprints, that was what forgiveness looks like. There would be no evidence they were ever there, once the tide was done with them. All of my own sins have been washed away with such completeness. If God so willingly did that for me, how can I hold anything against another?"

"But the sins of Lord Thomas are surely graver than anything you may have done, William."

"Perhaps in the eyes of men, but not in God's eyes. In His eyes, sin is sin, and any sin blocks us from His presence. If we could live our life without ever sinning once, we would not have need of a Savior; but no matter how good we are, we cannot be that perfect. So any sin, no matter how small, separates us from God. Which means any sin, no matter how insignificant in our own eyes or the eyes of other men, is really the same in His."

David pursed his lips and stared into the distance even as he negotiated the barge around several slower moving vessels. It was obvious to William they had both given each other a lot to think about. William stood a moment in deep thought, then thanked David for his confidence and took his leave. A moment later he finished repeating David's story to Isabella and Helen. "Lord de Thorpe? Are you certain, William?" The Queen Mother asked, and then saw the answer in his face. "Very well then; why do we think the Lord Chief Justice of the King's Bench visited Lord Thomas last night?"

"Lord Thomas, with the death of his two brothers, now finds himself sole heir of the, albeit small, Denebaud lands and title. He must bend the knee to his suzerain, the Lord de Thorpe." Helen made the statement in an effort to sum up the information William just shared. "If Lord de Thorpe wishes to keep those lands himself, he will want to make sure Lord Thomas' testimony and actions keep this as petty treason." Again Helen paused in thought and both William and Isabella let her process through what she had started. "Maybe he found out last night exactly what Lord Thomas attempted. Perhaps Lord Thomas overstepped himself when he took you captive; maybe the capture of the Queen Mother was not part of the original plan?"

Once more Lord de Clinton's advice rang through William's memory. He sat down beside Helen on the cushions, taking her hands in his own. Despite the slightly overcast skies that morning, the bright blue of her eyes nearly overwhelmed him. William took a deep breath and attempted as best he could to collect his thoughts. "If Lord Thomas revealed all he did, and all he tried to do, to the Lord Chief justice, he may also have revealed why." He paused to make sure he had her full attention. "It is entirely possible the Lord de Thorpe has learned of you and understands who you are." The only sound for a long moment was that of the oars as they splashed into and out of the river.

"I agree with William," Isabella stated. Her voice was quiet, yet strong and full of conviction. "To ignore one warning may be considered brave, but to ignore two..?"

Helen's eyes fell to the deck at her feet. Finally she nodded. "What do you think is best I do?"

"There is enough evidence against Lord Thomas to convict him of both petty and high treason," Isabella continued. "His family lands will revert to the crown since his actions clearly involve a threat to the king. With Sir John present to give his own testimony, there will be little doubt to that outcome. The only reason you would need to be present is for your own personal satisfaction in seeing him pay for all he has done." The Queen Mother paused, and to William it looked as though she was calling to mind some memory of her own past. It clearly wasn't pleasant, or at least not all of it, and it seemed to him, as he watched her closely, it was a mixture of anger, frustration and maybe even a small portion of joy. Eventually their eyes met and, as soon as she realized what she had allowed to pass beyond her mask, Isabella immediately replaced it. As if to answer what William would have liked to ask, she continued.

"There have been times in my own past when, for no other reason than to see the expression of the one who had hurt me receive what I felt they deserved, I have stayed to watch." She shifted closer to her daughter and gently put her arm around her and pulled her closer until Helen gently rested her head on her mother's shoulder. "Every time this has happened, child," she whispered just barely loud enough for William to hear, even as close as he was, "I have regretted it. If I did not have to say my own piece in this trial, I would gladly retire to Castle Rising and, once and for all, give life at court over to more… interested people."

William shifted his gaze so as not to stare at this tender moment between mother and daughter, and found himself looking into the penetrating slate grey eyes of David. He could see the thoughts working themselves out in the mind of the helmsman and knew that, despite his station in life, his connections and prior observations would certainly lead him to the truthful realization.

He stood and re-crossed the distance to the stern. "What you have seen, and I believe what you are in the processes of realizing, is something only a handful of people know, David. I would consider it a personal matter of honor if you would keep this to yourself; two lives and many reputations are counting on your confidence."

"You speak of honor… my family and name are not titled nor landed, William; what honor can we keep?"

"If you go back far enough, you will find every family, including my own, came from humble beginnings. Honor and nobility are in a person's thoughts, words and deeds, David, not in titles or land. As a great teacher once told me; a title does not make one noble, nor does the lack of one prevent noble actions." William paused to make sure he had the helmsman's full attention. His expression and nodding in agreement would suggest he did. "I believe you are such a man and I believe, deep inside you," William tapped him on the chest in emphasis with his words, 'that man wants the world to know the truth about his own nobility."

"How can you know this?" David questioned.

"Because most people only see what is immediately obvious to their eyes. They see you as your profession. They do not see the man, or the ideas, or the knowledge, or wisdom. For most people, you are only one more laborer serving them and they have little thought, let alone care, for you or your feelings." William paused, realizing what he was revealing, not only about David, but about himself as well. "I may not be perfect, and I have seen myself with those same thoughts, but I also know I will do my best to live every day recognizing the efforts of all those around me. After all, the least shall one day be the greatest, yes?"

Now it was David who offered his hand to William, who took it gladly. The expression on the bargeman's face spoke a thousand words, which he summed up with his voice cracking in emotion, his eyes glistening with appreciation. "Thank you, William. Your trust will not be misguided; you can count on my discretion." The helmsman paused, then drew William closer with his strong grip, until their faces were just hands' width apart. "You have done me a great honor, and it is one I will not soon forget. When the time is right, and a favor is needed, look no further than David Pemberton." He gave William's hand one final squeeze, then let him loose and returned to watching the traffic and pace of the barge with a critical and slightly moistened eye. On his face was simple smile that seemed to make him glow. A moment later William returned to the Queen Mother and Lady Helen with a plan.

•••

Even as he finished describing his idea, they found themselves at the Westminster quays. David immediately agreed to the plan and William found himself escorting Isabella down the short, wide plank where they then found themselves being escorted by two of the King's guard. Helen stood quietly, watching as her mother and William were lost among the crowds gathered to witness the lords and ladies attending the trial. The helmsman said something and for a moment she didn't realize his comment was directed at her. "I am sorry… my thoughts were elsewhere. What was it you said?"

"No apology needed my lady," David answered as he directed the men to prepare to head back into the channel. "I was simply pointing out that there appear to be some men in the crowd who are trying to get your attention."

Helen's gaze followed David's arm to see two cloaked and hooded men approaching the barge. One had his hand raised and she could just make out, over the noise of the crowd, her own name being called out by one of the concealed figures. "Lady Helen… my lady de Abbeville!" She did not recognize the voice and told David the same.

"Just give the word my lady and we will cast off before they have a chance to get any closer." Helen glanced aside for a brief moment to see the helmsman standing with arm akimbo, legs apart and a stern, strong gaze on his face. In the briefest of moments it seemed, William had spoken with the stranger and he now felt responsible to keep her safe. What had he said to garner such respect, and even devotion to duty, so quickly? Whatever it was, she was grateful for it.

Reaching out, she touched his sleeve lightly, "we will let them approach, but be prepared none the less." She watched very closely as the two men made their way through the crowd until they were just feet from the end of the quay. The plank had been taken up, but if they jumped far enough they could probably make it onto the barge; but then they would have found themselves face to face with the helmsman and his crew.

The hooded figure who had called out her name, spoke again. His voice did not have much strength to it and, as she looked closer, she realized he leaned upon the arm of the man next to him, but both faces remained in the shadow of their cowls. "Lady Helen," the voice wheezed, as if just walking had caused him to get out of breath, "we have spent several days trying to catch up with you and your escort."

"We, sir?" Helen's mind was racing and couldn't think of anything else to say at the moment. Were there still others, like Lord Thomas, who were free to pursue her? The speed of her heart matched those of her thoughts; would she never be rid of the villains which pursued her?

"We…" the other figure stated, as he reached up and pulled back his hood. Helen's eyes grew huge and her shaking hands covered her mouth as she gasped in shock. If not for the steady hands of David Pemberton, she would have found herself collapsed on the deck of the barge.

Chapter Thirty Four

Westminster Hall had been built by William Rufus, son of William I of Normandy. The heir of the conqueror had bragged, when an admiring subject told him the size and design of the hall was the most magnificent in Europe, that it would be like a bedroom compared to what he wanted still to accomplish. Although he didn't follow through with that bold statement, the assessment of the hall was correct. The great stone building sat parallel to the Thames. As William and Isabella were escorted from the quays, they followed a well laid flagstone avenue across a short expanse of manicured lawn and into the northern entrance.

Great oaken double doors were thrust open until they nearly folded back on themselves and the gaping, arched entry revealed an immense hall whose first glance stole William's breath. The Queen Mother turned and smiled, remembering her first time seeing the hall; it had been her coronation day. As they approached the entrance, she held out her arm; William saw the gesture and offered his own; together, arm on arm, escorted by the king's men, they entered Westminster Hall and the trial of Lord Thomas Denebaud.

The chamber was packed with lords and ladies alike; outside the doors were the teaming masses of everyone else. More than the crowds, what had captured William's attention was the sheer size and open space. There was no long double row of columns designed to support the massive roof. Through a genius of design, he could see massive oak rafters spanning across the width of the hall. Each beam had to come from its own immense tree as it arched across the open space, anchoring in the opposite wall near the roofline and was supported by equally impressive vertical wooden buttresses. To William the strengthening of the roof looked to have the same design as the outer walls of the cathedral in Salisbury.

An alcove balcony with a repeating arch pattern was built three quarters of the way up both east and west walls and it extended down the entire length of the hall. Behind these arches were windows, which let light stream into the expansive space. Despite the cloud covered skies, the hall was brightly lit by these windows making the massive lanterns anchored along the walls, unnecessary. To finish the interior, large tapestries were hanging from both balconies.

Visually, William found himself overwhelmed, but it was the noise inside which led to a near ringing in his ears. Their escort led them down the center of the hall, where a clear path had been left open, despite the large numbers of people packed in the space. By the time they reached the half way point, William noticed something strange. The overwhelming mix of hundreds of voices, which startled him no less than the building itself, had begun to subside, and the further they walked toward the southern end of the hall and the great table set up there, the more hushed it became. Eventually they reached the end of the hall and were escorted to a small table to the right where there was only one chair. Even as he pulled it back for the Queen Mother to take her seat, the voices fell silent and the hall took on an almost eerie stillness.

Isabella turned to look up at William and he could read the expression easily enough. She had never seen this happen before. For that brief moment, the two of them were the only ones present, and it seemed everyone else in the hall was straining to get a better look or catch the slightest exchange between them. Isabella smiled a slightly strained smile then straightened her shoulders, lifted her chin, and turned to face the empty table set before them. Years of separation from the court had taught her many things, including how to appear perfectly patient; even if inside she felt nothing of the sort.

To their immediate left sat a large, high backed armchair and to the left of that was a table and chair similar to their own. Behind the long table directly in front of them were three darkly stained chairs; these were more ornate than any of the others in the hall. Despite all the tapestries, and furniture, and people, and even the roof itself, the one thing which drew William's attention above all the rest was a modest chair sitting behind and to the right of the long table; it sat directly opposite of the Queen Mother. It was placed on a two-step dais, a gold trimmed, purple cushion on the seat. At the end of each arm was carved the face of a lion, and the only other adornment was the coat of arms, carved in relief on the back of the chair; it was quartered with opposite corners containing the three gold lions on a red field of England, and the other two sections with the gold fleurs-de-lis of France on a blue background. He recognized the sigil at once, having seen it embroidered on Sir Geoffrey's cotte; this was the chair of Edward, Earl of Chester, Duke of Aquitaine and King of England.

William's hands began to sweat and he nervously wiped them on his hose. Until that moment he had not completely allowed the impact of these proceedings to sink in. It was one thing to meet the King of France almost by accident, not truly knowing if he would actually be at the meeting in Amiens. Now, standing behind the Queen Mother's chair, his hands clasped in front of him to keep them from shaking, William realized at any moment he would be surrounded by some of the most important men of England, including his King.

What was he doing there? How could he, an unknown to the great men of England, think he had any place in this hall? There wasn't anything he could possibly add to this proceeding; he should leave now and return to Dorchester. It was peaceful there and he understood his role in that place. He would guard what remained of his families' household until the return of his uncle; if he ever returned. Crandor needed him; he had been away too long. After all, it was his responsibility to the crown to keep safe and prosperous that part of England. He began looking for a way to slip through the crowds undetected. If he left now, there was a better chance he wouldn't be missed.

Isabella must have sensed something, because at that moment, even as those thoughts began cascading and colliding in his mind and his eyes searched for an exit, she turned in her chair and looked up at the young man of her household. "William," she began with a calm, soft voice; he didn't respond. The thoughts, which raced through his mind, were quickly turning his emotions to panic as his heart raced in time with them. "Attend to me!" She demanded. Her voice took on a commanding tone, and although it wasn't loudly spoken, the force behind it got not only his attention, but most of the nearby lords and ladies.

"We are both here to speak our peace, and we have a right and obligation to do so." As she continued, her voice smoothed and softened and a smile crept into her eyes and lips. "You are also here because you are a member of my household, and if for no other reason, because I request you to be here. Remember your oath, William."

He closed his eyes and repeated the knights' oath to himself, "I will be without fear, even in the face of my enemies; I will be bold and upright that God may love me; I will speak the truth, no matter the personal cost and I will safeguard the innocent, even if it means sacrificing my own life for theirs." Twice, then three times he repeated it, finally taking a deep breath, letting it out slowly as he stated it one last time. "God, give me the strength and courage I need today. Amen." Isabella echoed it with her own response.

Despite being turned in her seat, she reached up and grabbed his hand, and, giving it a gentle squeeze, she smiled. It was the same radiant smile he had seen before and his heart skipped a beat, even as it had the first time she bestowed it on him. The worries and even panic of a moment ago, passed away as quickly as they had come. He would do the right thing for the right reasons. He would stand in the presence of great men, because God had placed him here. That last thought caught him by surprise and he reflected on it for a moment. Finally, he whispered aloud, "God if there is a way to glorify You today, please show me how."

Deep inside it was almost as if a voice spoke to him; a still soft voice counseled him and it was as if his old teacher was there beside him, leading him to one more, significant revelation. "Bless your enemies, William. Love them, even in the midst of offenses."

"How can I do that?" he asked the voice.

"Even a sinful man can love someone who loves them back, but it takes a true follower of Christ to love someone who spitefully uses them." The voice paused, giving William a moment to reflect on what he had been reminded, then continued with another statement, "You find yourself in a spiritual battle, William and you need to decide if you will look to the circumstances and doubt or will you continue to trust God and forgive Lord Thomas?"

"To forgive him… what you ask is such a sacrifice."

"There is always sacrifice with forgiveness, William; a payment has to be made and it is never easy and never will be easy to forgive. It is even painful, which is why it is a sacrifice. And yet, God does not want or need our sacrifice, He already took care of that, with His own Son.

"If it is not our works or our efforts or our own sacrifice He wants, what is it that God wants from us?"

"He wants our unconditional love and He shows this by carving His grace on our hearts. When He created each one of us, He made a hole inside our hearts which is shaped just like Him. Trust Him, William; believe in Him and He will fill that hole like nothing else you could imagine trying to put in its place."

William closed his eyes as the words spoken to him continued to echo in his thoughts. Even as he took a moment to pause and reflect, he realized his heart beat once again at its normal pace and his breathing was slow and deep; even his hand no longer sweated. God was the answer; He always was and He always would be. He smiled to himself and for the first time could see how he would respond in the trial. The revelation comforted him and when he opened his eyes, Isabella was still closely watching; her expression one of concern and care. His smile widened when he saw her feelings so openly expressed and he gently squeezed her hand that had still remained in his own. "I am ready majesty." Even as he spoke a door opened nearby; he could hear it on its hinges. A moment later, a King's Guard entered from behind one of the tapestries which hung just beyond the table. He gathered a corner and held it back, as if a curtain, allowing the men behind him to enter Westminster Hall.

The next several minutes William watched as Isabella quietly narrated the name and rank of each of the "great men" who were assembled for the trial. A few he recognized, including the Lord High Admiral, William de Clinton and of course Lord Thomas, who seemed pale and nervous as he was led to the table and chair to William's left. The rest included justices Roger Baukwell, who Isabella knew of but had never met, and William Basset. The latter of the two the Queen Mother was more familiar with; Justice Basset was able to trace his family back to a cadet branch of the offspring of William of Normandy and was, in fact, distantly related to the de Simpsons of Eaucourt and therefore to William himself; he could see a little of his elderly French cousins in the justice's eyes.

Finally, a silver haired, tall, slender man entered and before Isabella could say who he was, William already knew; the Lord Chief Justice Sir William de Thorpe. He wore the same dark robes as his two fellow justices but his was trimmed with gold and a large, heavy gold chain hung around his neck. He smiled and nodded to his fellow judges and, for just a brief glance, William imagined he looked to Lord Thomas before scanning the rest of the hall. When his eyes fell on William and Isabella, he saw instant recognition and something else. Just for a fraction of a second his expression turned dark, then his smile returned. William doubted if anyone else noticed, for at that same moment, all eyes turned to the guard at the tapestry.

There was no fanfare or pomp upon Edward's entry to Westminster Hall. This trial was in the hands of the justices and Chief Justice of the King's Bench, where they were called to serve, just as the King was required to be present, in order for the trial to be heard. Upon his entry, any who were seated, stood and remained standing until he took his seat. Lord de Thorpe then made some opening comments, addressing both the witnesses, Lord Thomas, and gallery. William didn't hear anything he said, as his eyes were fixed on the King.

He sat calmly on the raised dais, his eyes slowly scanning the great hall. Occasionally they would pause on some person or face; there was even the rare nod and smile, but for the most part he sat with his back straight, arms on the rests, and hands on the lion's heads. He seemed almost to find the proceedings an indifference, as he mostly ignored the comments of the Chief Justice. At one point he stopped to clean something from beneath one of his fingernails. Despite this nonchalance, William was drawn to the King's face and eyes.

His hair may have been brown or even black as a youth; now it was lightly streaked with silver, as was his long, well-groomed beard and mustache. Despite the overcast lighting in the hall, William could see Edward's eyes were slate grey and his nose, although long and thin, had been broken at least once and poorly set. William had expected to see an ornate crown of gems and jewels on his head but instead there was a simple, thick ring of gold.

Although he wore expensive robes, dyed in deep blues and burgundy's, William found himself now staring at the king's hands. These were the hands which led the battle at Crecy, laid siege to the city of Calais, passed mercy on the Burghers of the same, and bestowed the garter upon his uncle. These were also the hands which allowed the sacking of Le Crotoy by his men, and pulled Roger Mortimer, his mother's lover, down from the throne, and put himself in his rightful place, at the age of only seventeen. Both his eyes and hands had seen and done many great and terrible things, even at a young age. He was instantly reminded of something Robert had told him on one of his very first lessons. It seemed now, as if it had been years ago.

"Always remember William," he stated, standing there with his arms crossed and the serious expression on his face that he would come to expect any time he was being taught a most important life lesson. "It is not your abilities which make you great, it is what you do with those abilities God gave you, which will determine if you will be remembered as a great man or not."

"What if I am not good enough?" he remembered asking his tutor.

"Just do your best, in your time, William." He smiled then and his hands went to his student's shoulders and his gaze bore right through him. William could picture his teacher's soft brown eyes with the smile wrinkles around them. "You will only ever be as good as your own private standards so make sure to set them high. In the end, you alone govern your actions." As those words echoed in his thoughts he was pulled back to the present and the task at hand, even as Justice Basset stood and began to present the case for the prosecution of Lord Thomas Denebaud.

A moment later, William realized this Justice saw the trial for what it was; high treason. How he had acquired his facts, William never did find out, but they were simply and forcibly present in such a way he was sure everyone in the hall had to be convinced and in agreement. As he summed up the crown's position there was murmuring throughout the assembly. It was obvious the Lords and Ladies gathered to witness this trial had no idea as to the scope and the depth Lord Thomas had gone to secure his position. Even though he knew most of the facts himself, to hear them stated by another, in the company of the peers of the realm, was something entirely different.

As Justice Basset continued, he began to include some of William's own story into the case. It was at this point he paused, and turning to face him, called William to the witness chair. He could feel all the eyes in the hall turn to him while he did his best to keep focused on the Justices. He did take a quick glance to the King, which nearly unnerved him. Edward was staring at him intently. After stating his name, for the record, he was asked to sit down, at which point the hall became eerily quiet.

At the Chief Justice's request, William began with the Battle of Neville's Cross, and the capture of King David of Scotland, including his admission that very morning. This was followed by the death of his mother, his naming as heir to his uncle's estates in Dorchester and the de Simpson title of Earl of Crandor. The garter ceremony for his uncle was followed by the call to France, the fall of Calais, and his uncle's capture at St. Omer. As he picked up the tale at the fateful day when he received the ransom note, he realized his personal effects had been removed from the Tower and brought to Westminster Hall and were sitting on the table before the Justices; these included the final letter he received from his uncle as well as the ransom letter. From that sunny spring day he described the attack in Salisbury and subsequent trial of Samuel Thompson, the attempted abduction in Downton, the attack on innocents they stopped in the New Forest, the encounter with the Lord High Admiral, and the first time he met Lord Thomas.

Then it was Southampton, Gilbert, the street fight, and their meeting with Sir Geoffrey. Following the death of the king's messenger on the quays of Southampton, which resulted in waves of gasps and murmurs from the otherwise hushed crowd, he continued with their escape aboard ship, and their second encounter with Lord William de Clinton. What followed was the shipwreck, his rescue after making it to shore, their trip up the Somme, and the hospitality of his de Simpson cousins of Eaucourt sur Somme. After describing his capture, William took more time to detail the conversation he overheard between Lord Thomas and Sir John Copeland. When he described the threat Lord Thomas made to strip the banner from Sir John, he noticed out of the corner of his eye, King Edward shift in his chair. From the white of his knuckles, William could tell his nonchalance was a well concealed mask.

After his escape came the rescue of the Queen Mother, their flight from Lord Thomas and his men, the sacrifice of Robert on the bridge, (where his voice broke with emotion and he had to pause for a moment) and their eventual sanctuary found with the Lord High Admiral, and his own knighting on the cobblestone courtyard in Amiens. The tale then led from Amiens to Eaucourt and back again, eventually taking them to the peace negotiations and the encounter with Philip Valois of France. A loud gasp came from the crowds behind him when he finished that portion of his testimony, which included the King's admission of pulling so many strings to undermine the English throne, and still another came when he described meeting Sir Walter Manny, Sir Aymery de Pavia in Calais, his impression of both men, and finally King David that very morning at the Tower of London.

William finished and he found himself spent. He had talked without interruption for nearly two hours. Having never been in any trial, other than Samuel Thompson's he had no idea how unusual that was. There had been no cross examination; no question of clarification. What followed though was a long moment filled only with the hushed voices of the Lords and Ladies behind him. Finally, the Lord Chief Justice spoke.

"I believe I speak for my other Lord Justices when I say that what you have accomplished in such a short time is little more than miraculous, Sir William." He paused and looked as though he was collecting his thoughts. William wondered if he was secretly still trying to figure out how to turn the trial to one of petty treason, despite his own detailed testimony. "Lord de Clinton, will you corroborate what has been detailed by this witness?" Out of the corner of his eye, William saw the Lord High Admiral and Warden of the Cinque Ports step forward and come to stand beside and to the right of William's chair; since he had not been dismissed William remained seated.

"For my part and my presence, I agree with the statement made by Sir William. I would also add, although it was by my own hand he was knighted, I have not regretted that decision and would do so again without reservation."

"And you, Salisbury?" Justice Baukwell asked.

William sat up straighter in the chair when he realized the Justice of the Peace of Salisbury had been called to London. He too walked forward and stood beside William. "Although he chose not to identify himself as the de Simpson heir in the trial, I agree with his statement and also will attest to his character and integrity." He couldn't be sure, but when he glanced up he thought he saw Salisbury give him a quick smile and a nod.

"What say you, Copeland?" the Justice Basset asked. It took all his concentration and focus not to turn in his seat in order to see Sir John. Although David Pemberton had told him he had just had the knight bannerette on his barge, William had no idea he was inside Westminster Hall. Apparently neither did most of those present; he could hear the excited tone drifting through the chamber until they were silenced by the raised hand of the Lord Chief Justice.

Steady footsteps echoed in the hall and stopped just behind William's left shoulder. "I would attest to the de Simpson name, if for no other reason than it was their sacrificial charge of the lines at Neville's Cross that I am even standing here before you my Lords." William remembered Gilbert describing the same event and those same tears which overwhelmed him in Southampton threatened to spill down his cheeks, while a tightness gripped his throat making swallowing difficult. He did his best to blink the tears away while fighting to control the rest of his emotions.

"Beyond that," Sir John continued, "I would say, without reservation, if William de Simpson called, I would answer; if he led, I would follow; if he stood, I would stand beside him even as I do now," and here he placed his hand on William's shoulder. "And if he fell I would mourn. Do not look to his age and lack of experience and allow that to cloud your judgement of the truth; he deserves the spurs more than many who have worn them decades longer, and he lives by the truth of the words he spoke in Amiens when the Lord High Admiral bid him take the knee." The hall became hushed; not a sound was heard among the vast crowd. William's heartbeat thundered in his ears and he gave up trying to control the crashing waves of emotions which surged through him. His breath came in ragged gasps and what little control remained was everything he needed to stay seated and not break down sobbing.

"As to the conversation with Lord Thomas in Amiens and my actions there," he continued, "I make no apology and ask for no leniency. Through manipulation and coercion, I was convinced I had no choice but to agree, and the words related by Sir William are accurate. The argument between myself and Lord Thomas happened as described, and yet neither of us knew he was only feet away. Although Sir William did not mention it, it was through his strength of convictions which led me to reconsider my decision, to accept my circumstances as of my own making, and to eventually stand up against Lord Thomas and his men. If not for this young knight I myself may also be on trial today, and for that I owe him my name… and reputation." He gave William's shoulder a reassuring squeeze and then let his hand fall at his side.

Even as the words of these men continued to echo in William's ears, Justice Basset spoke up. "And what say you to these statements, Majesty?" Out of the corner of his eye, William watched as Isabella, mother of Edward, King of England, slowly stood and walked towards him. What happened next shocked everyone in the hall, not the least of which was her own son. She came in front of William's chair and started a courtesy to the Justices but it didn't end there. She settled down on the ground, kneeling before the King's Bench with her back to William and the men surrounding him.

"The truth is often twisted, my Lord's," she began softly, her head bowed, but as she spoke, her voice grew in volume, as its tone did in conviction. "The truth is often twisted in order to make the speaker appear better or stronger or greater than they really are. I tell you now, in the presence of all these witnesses, I have not found a greater or truer heart in all of England and France; nor has a braver or more honorable knight been found, who was willing to lay down his own to defend my innocence and very life. Without regret I offered him a position in my household and never will I repent of that decision. If there is a greater example of chivalry, outside of my own children and grandchildren, I can name no other. His word and testimony are true as I have personally been a witness to much of what he shared."

William stared at the back of Isabella's bowed head, hardly believing what he had heard and what he was witnessing. He could feel his heart as it continued pounding in his chest and thundered in his ears. More than anything, he wished Robert had been here to see and hear what had been spoken about him. He bowed his head and in that moment of exaltation he silently thanked God for all he had learned and continued to learn and for the amazing life he found himself living. In response it was as if he found himself in a great cathedral with the choir singing praises of glory and thankfulness. He had no other way to describe it later than to say, often and with conviction, "my spirit soared."

Nearly every eye in Westminster Hall stared in wide wonder and for a few, disbelief. Finally, not knowing what else he should do, and not wanting to see the Queen Mother on her knees any longer, William stood and stepping around Isabella, came between her and the King's Bench and, bowing at the waist, offered his hand. He was surprised to feel her own tremble as she accepted his offer. He smiled through the threat of tears, and he was shocked to see, when she raised her eyes to him, streaks on her flushed cheeks. She stood, and with still trembling hand, she reached up and wiped away a line of tears from his cheek. Her smile softened and she tilted her head slightly to one side while her hand lingered on his cheek. "Thank you, William," she whispered so that none save the two of them heard, then turned and allowed herself to be escorted back to her seat.

Even as he returned to his own, the Lord Chief Justice cleared his throat to speak, and then suddenly stopped. William didn't know what was happening as gasps and murmurs travelled through the multitude assembled in the great hall. Finally a movement caught his eye and he realized King Edward had stepped down from the dais, walking around the high table of the Justices. "Majesty, you should not…" Lord Chief Justice de Thorpe stopped in mid-sentence. One glance from his king and a simple gesture of his hand forced him to swallow whatever admonition may have been planned. William then found himself face to face with the King of England.

●●●

If you asked anyone who was present in Westminster Hall that day, they would all agree on many things, not the least of which was the impact the next brief moment had on each of them. Edward had left his seat, something a king had never done during a trial of the King's Bench, and approached the key witness in order to speak with him. "There is no doubt as to the feelings these Lords, this knight, and the Queen Mother have towards you, Sir William." Edward paused as if considering his words carefully while looking at each of those who stood by this young man of Dorchester. "If I knew little else of you, that alone would be enough. And yet you also willingly faced men of greater position, challenging them and their actions, despite the fear I could hear in your voice, and you would give all that you are in order to shield the innocent, to safeguard their lives, even if it cost you your own. If those are not knightly qualities, then I do not know what are." As he spoke to William, it was as if the two of them were alone together, and not in the great hall of England, surrounded by lord and ladies, justices and counsellors. Edward placed his hand on William's shoulder and spoke with such deliberate gravity it nearly took his breath away, "allow me to make official what was conferred in Amiens… take a knee."

William's eyes grew huge and tears threatened to spill again. He was afraid if he knelt, he might not ever stand up again and the king must have sensed this, "my Lords, Sir John… mother, attend him." William saw Isabella rise and come to stand beside him even as Lord de Clinton, the Justice of Salisbury and Sir John Copeland came forward. Suddenly there were multiple pairs of hand hands aiding him as he knelt before the king.

"Do you swear before these witnesses to serve the crown of England, no matter whose head it may sit upon, to come when called, to raise up men and arms who will stand with you when the need arises, to protect the lands and the people and the property of your family, to stand in faith in the face of fear, to boldly proclaim our Lord's greatness and goodness both in word and deed, to continue to speak the truth, avoiding any dealings with evil, while continuing to protect and keep safe the innocents entrusted to your care?"

"I am your Majesty's servant. When you call, I will come; where you send me, I will go; with my arms and those with me we will safeguard and defend all those entrusted in our care. *Vivo servire*, Majesty. Command me, I am yours." As he spoke these words the beat of his heart thundered in his ears like the roaring and crashing of the waves along the coast of Dover. King Edward turned and accepted a sword, handed to him by a guard who had stood silently beside the King's chair. Lowering the blade he rested it on William's shoulder. Even though William knew what was happening, it still threatened to overwhelm him. Once again hands reached out to help steady him.

"Then in the presence of all of these witnesses, and by the acts of bravery, loyalty and self-sacrifice, I dub thee Sir Knight and I name thee *Mango Animo*; great heart. Arise Sir William, knight of the realm and King's man." Through the haze of tears, William could see a hand extended to him and he took and stood on shaky legs before realizing it was offered by the king. They shared that brief moment, face to face while the entire hall was silent. "There is little doubt as to Lord Thomas' guilt in this matter, Sir William and his actions will undoubtedly lead to a conviction of high treason despite the desires of other interested parties. How would you lay sentence on him?"

William was suddenly aware of the stares and the hush which fell on those who had just seconds before congratulated him. The magnitude of this request was both immediately impactful and yet didn't completely sink in until much later. The King of England was asking him for his advice and counsel. He closed his eyes and quickly asked God for the wisdom to answer as best he could. "Majesty, you humble me with your request and I feel I am not worthy of such a responsibility." His eyes fell to the ground before him but in his ears he heard, ever so clearly the words of his teacher, 'when your time comes, and you will know when it is, be ready to make a difference; live out your character and give your best. It is for just such a time I am teaching you these most important lessons.'

William nodded understanding and took a deep breath before continuing. "But in this I will serve as best I may." He paused just long enough to glance about him. All eyes, including Lord Thomas' were upon him; the latter's expression was mixture of shock, anger and perhaps even envy. "One could argue," He began slowly, choosing his words carefully as he turned to face the king, "that, if not for the actions of Lord Thomas, your majesty may never have known the full extent of the conspiracy against your throne. In my own life I have regrets and have done and said things I wish I could take back. Although that is not possible, God is merciful just as His word says. It also says because we have been granted mercy, because God has not given us what we deserve based on our own transgressions, we should ourselves be merciful to others. It is easy to say these things but much more difficult to walk them out and yet I feel I have no choice but to ask, even to beg your Majesty, for mercy for Lord Thomas from the King's Court."

Silence once again flooded the great hall. Despite the large crowd, his words were carried by the design of the building to the farthest corners and it was clear no one expected them, not least of all King Edward, his justices, or Lord Thomas. "What you suggest, Sir William… despite all he has done to you and your family, and my own?" Edward shook his head slowly, his eyes wide in disbelief.

"I was told once, not long ago, Majesty, no matter what the results may be, if you are committed to something you should live it out. I swore to uphold that commitment; I swore, that even if my life hung in the balance, I would still speak the truth. I know that what I am committed to is what I really believe; and I am committed to living out my beliefs, including my trust in God and His goodness." If William paused he may have reconsidered what he was saying based on who he was speaking to, but the conviction came from such a deep place within him it would have taken all his effort not to speak those words. "It is His grace alone which has sustained me and His wisdom has guided me. What kind of a man would I be if I turned my back on Him now just because the answer everyone expects is not the one He speaks to my heart?"

For a brief moment, they stood there in the hall, surrounded by many of the great houses of England and yet to William it was as if it were just the two of them; one man of conviction speaking to another of influence. "Speak the truth, at all times, no matter the cost, right, Sir William?" the King asked with just a hint of a smile around his eyes while emphasizing the title. "There are many who claim the rank you so recently earned and yet have not the courage, or even the desire, to live out those principles." He paused to consider what he just admitted, then continued. "Your uncle will be very proud of his decision to name you his heir." He grabbed William's upper arm and, while squeezing it, gave him a broad toothsome smile. "Very proud." That expression quickly faded and he returned to his seat behind the justice's bench. When he turned back to face the audience, which had gathered to witness this trial of treason, he wore the expressionless mask William had seen on his arrival. The King nodded to the Lord Chief Justice to continue.

Knowing what he was told by King David, William watched Lord de Thorpe's' expression closely. He did his best to hide his thoughts, but there they were. For the briefest of flashes William could see frustration, irritation and even anger cross his face, and then he too carried a mask of indifference. He wondered if this is what it meant to be a member of the king's court; did everyone hide their true feelings and intentions behind blank masks. He couldn't be sure, having met only a few members himself, but they all had this ability; it was a trait he didn't want to become proficient at and decided, in that moment, he would be happy to return to his family estate in Dorchester and there do his best to serve his king and country. If there would ever rise up inside him an aspiration to come to court he would remind himself of what he had seen.

"You are released Sir William." A wave of the Lord Chief Justice's hand dismissed him but as he returned to his position behind Isabella he noticed a strange expression on her face. Her brows were furrowed and she shook her head slightly. It took a moment for him to realize she was telling him to leave. His face must have registered the surprise, which she acknowledged with a nod and an offer of her hand. He bowed at the waist and gently taking her hand, brushed it to his lips.

"If you call, I will answer, Majesty."

"I know, William," she took her hand and placed it gently on his cheek; he could feel her fingers tremble slightly. "But for now, you must leave here; do not look back. Return to Dorchester and your home. Trust there are those working even now to see your family reunited."

He swallowed heavily, nodding and took one last look at one of the most beautiful faces in Europe, knowing in his heart he may never see her again, then stood and bowed to the Kings' Bench and the King. William turned and began the long walk down the central aisle of Westminster Hall, even as the Lord Chief Justice continued, "Are there any present who will speak in defense of Lord Thomas Denebaud?"

Chapter Thirty Five

A light misty rain had begun falling since William entered the Hall and as he stepped outside he paused a moment and lifted his face, letting the cool, fresh water collect into larger droplets, which ran down his neck and through his hair. "You did well in there today, William." The voice caught him by surprise. It was the Justice of the Peace of Salisbury.

"Thank you, my Lord… and thank you for your confidence." Any further discussion was cut short by a wave of the Justice's hand. "If your plan is to return to Dorchester, I travel in the same direction." It was an open, generous gesture and one which William appreciated and nearly jumped at the opportunity; then he remembered the barge and the passenger waiting for him.

"I thank you, my Lord, however there is still one duty I have to discharge and it may, or it may not, keep me from my home for a period of time."

"Very well, will you at least walk with me to the quays? I will need to catch one of the ferries across the Thames." William chewed on the inside of his cheek, debating briefly then decided in favor of the company. As they walked down from Westminster, making their way through and around the groups of people who seemed to have gathered there since they came the same way just a few hours ago, the Justice of Salisbury continued. "Listening to your testimony William showed me one important thing."

"What is that, my Lord?"

"That you are better at listening and obeying God than I am." He smiled to himself, nodded and then continued. "This led me to another thought; the only way I can truly revere God is to get rid of the idols in my life."

This shocked William and he nearly stopped in mid-step and had to apologize to an elderly woman who bumped into him in the process. "You have idols in your life, my Lord?" It was clear that William wanted to ask more, but felt restrained in his questioning; this was the Justice of the Peace of Salisbury after all.

"I believe all men have idols. The way to tell what it or they may be in each of our lives is to look at what causes panic or worry. When all else around you is at peace and you are not, that is probably an idol."

William thought on this for a moment and silently asked God to show him what might be an idol in his own life and came to a sudden realization. "Is it possible that control could be an idol, my Lord?"

"Ah, William," the Justice of the Peace said, smiling broadly, while clapping him on the back, just hard enough to nearly rattle his teeth. "That is the one idol most men have in their lives; even myself." He paused just long enough to allow that admission to sink in, then continued. "If you truly believe God is in control, and give up the false vision that somehow it is you and you alone who determine the outcome and actions around you, then you can live an unshakeable life."

"Are you suggesting that we should not try, or strive or do, my Lord?"

"Not in the least, William. Faith without action is a dead kind of faith, yes?" William nodded his agreement and understanding of what

James wrote in his letter. "What I am saying is giving up the idol, the false belief that God is not in control, and completely trusting Him while living your life, in the way you have. What blessed me William about what you have gone through, is seeing the Hand of God on all of it. Each time there was evil or pain directed at you, God was able to turn it around for good. Your words have encouraged and empowered me to confront that idol of control I have. I am grateful for that."

This was a revelation to William. Up to that moment, he had not considered all he had gone through in the last few weeks could have an impact on those who knew him and those he may meet. He knew he had to take the time to write down those most important life lessons his teacher had shared with him, but here, after so much had taken place and so much had been taught, he found a new reason set it down in writing; even his story and his adventure, if it could be called that, could impact the lives of others.

As if he read William's thoughts, the Lord Salisbury added, "Perhaps you could have a scribe write it down so it could be shared?" William smiled and nodded; it was the only confirmation he needed.

They spent the next few moments in silence, but not surrounded by it. Crowds had begun to fill in the empty space between Westminster and the Thames; what should have taken a moment was stretching out much longer as they moved through the throng of people they found before them. At one point William caught the eye of Salisbury and his expression must have been a reflection of his own. Even as they struggled to make it to the quays, a question had begun simmering in William's thoughts and he gave it voice. "How have you been able to give control over to God, my Lord Justice?"

"That, William, has been one of the greatest lessons I have learned," he responded. A smile crossed his lips and his expression and manners became more animate. "It is so simple, people simply overlook it." He paused for effect; it worked. "Just thank God for being in control of everything that is happening and thank Him for whatever the outcome may be. I imagine God telling me each morning that He is God and that He is in control of any problems I may face that day and He does not need my help taking care of them."

William chewed on the inside of his cheek for a moment. "My Lord, if I may, I am no closer now than I was when I left Dorchester, in the rescuing of my uncle. It seems as though, each day, since I set out, has been filled with one challenge after another. Now I find myself free to go and finish what I started but I am reluctant to proceed. Something calls me back to Crandor and I do not know what it is. It is not fear," he added when he glanced to the side and saw the expression on the Justice of the Peace' face. "And yet it is there. Do you think, if I thank God for all that I have been through and ask Him, He will show me the right path forward?"

"Without a doubt in my mind, William. Do just as you said and God will provide the guidance… even if it is not in the way you expect. If you reflect on the testimony you just gave, you will realize He has spoken and guided you in many ways and situations since you left your home in Dorchester."

It didn't take long for William to agree and realize he was having a moment of disbelief. His prayer was short but powerful and sincere. As he finished, they found themselves on the quays, with David's barge just before them. For a moment, he forgot about the Justice of the Peace, when Helen turned and caught his eye. Her smile was radiant and the sunlight, which had just broken through the clouds, flashed in her blue eyes and shimmered in her bright copper hair; the vision took his breath away, and in that moment, he knew everything he had gone through was worth it, just to see that smile and the joy on her face. She waved and then turned her head as if answering someone else on the barge behind her.

"You continue to be full of surprises, Sir William," the Justice of the Peace stated. "I would hazard to guess that she is the duty you still must discharge?"

William nodded, "I will make the introductions my Lord, but know this; she has been under my protection since fleeing Southampton and, for reasons of her own, of which I and the Lord High Admiral were in agreement, I made no mention of her during my testimony. Whether I return to Dorchester sooner rather than later rests on her." William made this last statement as he turned to face the Justice of the Peace of Salisbury. He watched the others eyes grow large and round as the realization of what he was just told sank in. A second later he was clasping William's hand in a strong grip and smiling from ear to ear.

"Then make your introduction and it is my sincere hope that I may be one of the first to congratulate you." The two of them turned and stepped aboard David Pemberton's barge.

•••

It seemed strange to William that the barge master did not greet him or his guest as they stepped aboard, but then Helen was there and introductions were made and the thought fled. Despite everything he had just been through, including the recounting in detail each incident in which Lord Thomas' had a hand in his life, those thoughts and concerns and past frustrations melted away as he stood with the Justice of the Peace of Salisbury and Isabella's daughter. Something had changed since he left for Westminster and he didn't think it was himself. There was a radiance about Helen that was deeper than just her smile, the flash of brilliant blue eyes, and the sunshine igniting the flame of her hair. It was almost as if something was bubbling up within her; something she was nearly unable to contain.

Helen questioned the Lord Justice about the trial and William did his best to pay attention to his answer, but there was such a strong feeling of barely hidden excitement coming from her it was difficult for him to consider anything else. He was so distracted he didn't even realize Sir John Copeland had also stepped aboard the barge; that is until he added his own comments to Salisbury's. Sir John greeted him with a hand shake and a clap on his shoulder. "Well done and well met, Sir William," emphasizing the title recently re-confirmed. He too, seemed barely able to contain an excitement which was more than just seeing each other for the first time since Amiens.

William was about to press the point, when Helen turned to him, "my apologies, my Lord… Sir John, but there is an introduction I need to make to William." At that comment two hooded figures emerged from behind the screens and canopy which shaded the back of the barge. William hadn't even noticed they were there until Helen called for them.

Their cowls were both pulled down far enough to shade their entire face; William couldn't even see their lips move as they spoke. The felting of the hood muffled the voice of the one who stepped forward and yet there was something familiar in it; he knew this person, somehow, but there was a weakness and huskiness in the voice which further confused William. "Lady Helen has filled us in on what has happened to you since Lord Thomas' capture in Amiens. How did you respond before the King's Bench?"

William answered without hesitation. "I have forgiven Lord Thomas and am ready to pursue a life without the burden of hate or revenge towards him; I asked the Lord Justices to do the same and answered King Edward the same when he came forward to address me face to face. Just as God has shown me mercy, I asked the court for mercy for Lord Denebaud but I did not stay to hear their judgement."

For a moment, the only sound was of the water splashing against the sides of the barge and the crowds on the quays. William began to wonder if the hooded figure had taken offense at what he said, and then he saw the shoulders of the stranger begin to shake and he broke into a raspy laugh. He paused in his mirth to catch his breath, "oh William, you are so much the wiser man than I was at your age."

"He does listen better and learn quicker," the other figure stated. William couldn't believe his ears. He instantly recognized the second voice and looked to Helen for confirmation, who continued with her radiant smile, her hands clasped beneath her chin, watching the exchange with sheer joy.

"Perhaps it is his teacher who has grown wiser over the years," the first voice spoke again, while reaching up to lower his hood. The other mirrored his actions. William's heart skipped several beats while it thundered in his ears. Tears welled up in his eyes and freely overflowed and down his cheeks. He could feel his throat tighten and wasn't sure if he could speak. He didn't need to. His uncle reached forward, a great smile on his face, and drew him close into an embrace; Robert stood behind him, tears of joy on his own cheeks, as William broke down sobbing, wrapping his arms around one person he wasn't sure he would ever see again, while staring through tears at the other. It was the most joyful moment he had experienced up to that point in his life.

●●●

Sir John travelled with them as far as Salisbury, before turning north to return to his duties as Sherriff of Northumberland and keeper of Roxburgh Castle. During that portion of their return home, William was able to discover what had happened to the knight, his teacher, and uncle. Robert remembered little after his fight on the bridge. The blow from Godefroy not only knocked the wind out of him it rendered him unconscious. He awoke the next day to find himself in the company of Sir John, at a small inn in Amiens, with no idea where William was.

"I am not a young man any longer, William," Robert explained. "It took me a few days to fully recover before I was able to travel." By then, William realized they had gone to Eaucourt and returned again to Amiens for the peace negotiations. As if seeing the calculations of the days, Robert added, "we just missed you at the guild hall, but we did not miss King Philip."

Everyone was stunned to hear of their encounter with the French king and even more shocked that he offered to send them with a letter, written in his own hand, to take to Chateau de Coucy. "Count Libourne de Coucy will find this letter particularly unpleasant, which is all the more reason for me to send it with you, King Philip told us," Robert stated.

"When I was younger, I was taught much about the great families of France" Helen interjected. "The de Coucy's consider themselves greater than the Valois and even the Capet's; it is no wonder to me that King Philip would find enjoyment in writing the letter to the man. He would even consider it a personal triumph to force the Count's hand in the matter."

"It was just as you describe, Lady Helen," Robert continued. "Travelling by horseback took us only one full day of riding to make the castle and find the Count much indisposed and I would even say angered over the tone of the letter; but in the end, he could not deny the authenticity and therefore was unable to prevent the release of your uncle."

"I had been treated well, William," his uncle stated, "but my injuries in the battle of St. Omer were a long time in healing and have left me weak since." He could see the concern on William's face and quickly assured him of his vastly improving health since leaving Chateau de Coucy. "My strength and stamina increases each day, William, and yet travelling was slow, even on horseback. But, as God willed it, we found ourselves in London on the morning of Lord Thomas' trial, which was fortunate, considering Sir John had been called as a witness."

•••

At Salisbury, the Justice of the Peace invited them to a parting of the company meal at his home on the western edge of the city, just on the banks of the Avon. Sitting in that fine manor house that evening, a light fog drifted in over the river and William reflexively rubbed his left shoulder, where he had been struck by a lucky blow from a knife, thrown in the dark fog and he remembered the trial of Samuel Thompson. "Are you well, William?" Helen asked, her blue eyes a darker azure in the lamp and lantern lit dining hall.

He nodded, stopped rubbing and smiled, "just remembering my only other visit to Salisbury." Seeing the concern still on her face, he added, "but this time I am in much better company." It was hard for him to tell in the flickering light, but he was pretty sure she was blushing.

The next morning they parted ways with Sir John and the Justice of the Peace and the remaining four continued on to Dorchester. At Sir John's insistence, William was given the black stallion, which they had been forced to leave in Amiens, and which Sir John had taken with him across northern France, the Channel, and now back full circle. As he watched the knight bannerette mount his own mare and turn north he stroked the neck of the charger and said a silent prayer for Sir John's wellbeing.

It would take them just over a day to reach Crandor Castle and yet, for William, he felt as if he was being torn in two. The closer they came to Dorchester, the quieter and more somber Helen became. This worried him because he knew she still had a decision to confirm and he did his best to avoid a conversation which might lead to the subject. At the same time though, he could feel the anticipation begin to boil up inside of him as each step of their horses brought them closer to home.

They camped that night near the same whortleberry bushes and rowan trees William and Robert had spent the night under, to avoid the spring rain all those weeks before. It seemed as though it was a lifetime ago, and yet the creek of fresh water still flowed nearby. As William refreshed himself in it, he watched as a small twig swirled around in the eddies near the bank. William smiled and realized he had changed his mind about the twig and his own life. He wasn't being spun around, out of control, or under the control of others; God was in control. He reminded himself by saying it out loud. "Thank You, God that You are in control. Whatever happens I thank You and praise You and give You all the glory." He didn't realize anyone had joined him by the creek until he heard his uncle's voice echo, in its still slightly raspy tone, an 'amen' of his own. He wrapped one arm around William's shoulders and they walked back to their camp and their waiting companions.

The dawn had come bright and clear and it was late spring in Dorchester. The grass had turned a deeper emerald green since they had left and the sheep, which began to increase in numbers the closer they drew to Crandor, were decidedly no longer pregnant. The bleating of young lambs increased in chorus with each mile. Even the stallion sensed the anticipation of the swelling spring season and tossed his head while stamping his front hooves prior to their departure for the last leg of their journey home.

"Does the air always smell this sweet?" Helen asked to no one in particular. It was one of the few things she had said since they left Salisbury and William wasn't sure if she was just thinking out loud or was actually looking for an answer. It was his uncle who answered.

"After what I have seen and what I have done, I can think of no greater sight nor pleasant smell than those of our home." He stood up in his stirrups and inhaled deeply, holding it a moment, then slowly exhaling while sitting back down. "The fresh air of Dorchester does me well," he stated to no one in particular.

The old Roman road continued on straight west and so they left it, crossing the dike on the southern side, in order to strike out for Crandor. It was mid-morning and the dew, all that remained of a light mist and fog the night before, was already quickly drying. Not far off the crushed rock lane they found themselves in rolling hills of green grass and such as it was, Helen didn't see Crandor until they crested a steep sided knoll. She leaned forward, urging her chestnut mare, who took to the task with excitement; she was the first to the crest.

"Oh, William," she said, slightly out of breath, "it is beautiful." Before her, as far as she could see, were the green downs of Dorchester and standing atop a particularly large flat hill, just as it had for generations, since William of Normandy set its original cornerstone, was Crandor Castle. Despite its name, Helen recognized it as a walled manor house, instead of a strategically placed, fortified position, but even that simple description did not do it justice. It was more than she had imagined and she could understand why a family would want to stay in that home for as long as William's had.

"What is happening at my home?" The Earl wondered out loud. He pointed and drew everyone's attention to the gate of the wall surrounding the manor. William had not noticed it before but a crowd was gathered just outside the open gates; between them and Crandor Castle stood several men carrying the banner of King Edward.

Without any prompting, William squeezed his knees and the black stallion leapt forward covering the several hundred paces in a matter of a couple dozen heart beats. He knew the others were behind him but the swiftness of his mount outpaced them. As he drew closer to the gates, the faces turned to him and he recognized all of them. Someone had turned out the entire household.

He didn't stop until he was almost on top of them and he was nearly unnerved by the high pitched squeal of at least two young girls' voices as they screamed in alarm. "What is the meaning of this? Why are you all outside? What has happened?" William asked each question without pausing for the opportunity to answer.

"We stand here in the name of your King, Edward," a sergeant of the guardsmen responded. "We were sent to collect the back taxes owed to the crown by the de Simpson's of Crandor but we found none of the family here."

"Well you have found them now," William's uncle responded as he trotted up with Robert and Helen. William turned his stallion around and walked him back a few paces to allow his uncle to move forward, which he did, nodding appreciation to his nephew and heir. Taking up a place next to Robert, he tried his best to reassure all of the men and women who were looking to them for help.

"Will you identify yourself, my Lord?" The sergeant asked.

"I am Charles de Simpson, Earl of Dorchester, master of Crandor Castle, member of the Order of the Garter and newly returned from France. What is this tax you speak of?"

"I can best answer that, my Lord de Simpson," responded a slim, slightly built man who had, up to that point, remained hidden behind the guards. Now he stepped forward and William could see he carried a large, leather bound book. "The lands and title of Earl of Dorchester," he began as he leafed through the pages to find the correct entry, "owe three years of tax to the crown for a total of £1,000 sterling."

William sat frozen in his saddle. It was the exact amount of his uncle's ransom. Even as they sat on their horses outside their home, a small voice spoke up from the household crowd. "Look mother, it is the men from the woods who gave us our horse." William didn't recognize the voice but what she said caught his attention. He nudged the stallion forward and men and women he had known for most of his life stepped back, clearing a path for him until he came face to face with a woman, surrounded by and clutching close three girls. It was obviously the youngest who had spoken because she clapped her hands and shouted, "It is them; it is!"

He still didn't recognize the girl, or her slightly older sister and it wasn't until the mother spoke that he suddenly understood who he was facing. "The wealth of a sinner will eventually find its way into the hands of the righteous for whom it was set aside," the mother stated.

"Amen," Robert answered. He had followed William forward and they now sat, side by side, looking down at the mother and daughters who they had rescued in the New Forest.

"We kept it secret and kept it hidden," the mother stated cryptically. It took William a moment to understand what she meant and Robert even less.

"Is it here?" his tutor asked. She nodded. "Take me to it," and offered her a hand in order to help her up. Once she was safely seated behind him, Robert turned to face the Earl of Dorchester. "My Lord, I will return in a moment and we will settle the account with the Crown in full." With that he urged his horse forward and with the mother's guidance disappeared around the southern wall.

Several long moments passed and they returned with a large, dirt covered sack, followed closely behind by two chestnuts mares, being led by their halters. William's heart leapt in his chest and he heard Helen's exclamation when she too realized who was leading the horses; Gilbert! There were so many questions he wanted answered but they were cut off when Robert dropped the sack at the feet of the keeper of the ledger and it split open, spilling its contents of gold and silver, rings, coins and jewelry, onto the grass. The precious metals and gems glimmered and glowed in the morning sunlight, capturing everyone's attention. "That should more than cover the debt."

"No doubt," mumbled the book keeper, as he stared in disbelief.

It took a relatively short time for the account to be settled. The contents indeed contained much more than enough, and as it was counted, William explained to Helen and his uncle the origin of the contents. As the King's Guard left, Lord Charles turned to his nephew who, along with Helen was standing nearby, "is there any doubt now, William, God can turn to great good what was meant for even greater evil?

The knight and heir to the Earl of Dorchester reached out and took Helen's hand. She smiled, nodding, and gladly offered it, her eyes sparkling in the mid-morning sun. They turned to their hunchbacked friend and savior from Southampton, motioning for him in order to make their introduction. His expression was a combination of pure joy in seeing the three people he wasn't sure were still alive, and humble gratitude in realizing who he was about to meet in person. He did his best to quickly dust himself and run his crippled fingers through his hair. "No doubt in my mind at all, uncle." William smiled his own day-brightening smile and as he looked to Helen, Robert and his uncle, somewhere in the distance church bells began ringing.

CPSIA information can be obtained
at www.ICGtesting.com
Printed in the USA
LVHW082027161118
597446LV00007B/13/P

9 781595 557353